THE DEMONS

A NOVEL

HEIMITO VON DODERER

INTRODUCTION BY MARTIN MOSEBACH

VOLUME ONE

Printed in the United States of America

Set in Baskerville Typesetting

Cover Design:

Translated from the German by Richard and Clara Winston.

Edited by J.A. Gray

Paperback ISBN-13: 978-1-951319-84-7

Wiseblood Books

THE
DEMONS

CONTENTS

PART TWO

The Art of Archery and the Novel:
The "Commentarii" of Heimito von Doderer

MARTIN MOSEBACH

"Habseligkeiten"—this word counts as one of those untranslatable terms in the German language. Grimm's dictionary informs us that *Habseligkeit* can be seen as equivalent to *opulentia*, to be sure, but our ears hear the word more in its trivial sense, referring to measly odds and ends belonging to people who had no more than a couple of paltry *Habseligkeiten* to leave behind. I would like to describe one particular aspect, for it strikes me as meaningful, of the work of writer and poet Heimito von Doderer, and I will begin, strangely enough, with *Habseligkeiten*—his, I mean. I saw them twice, laid out in display cases containing—aside from his immense literary estate—what he left behind in the world: a hodgepodge of articles for daily use, most of them personal to himself. All the items a chain smoker needs occupied a prominent place among them: metal cigarette cases, pipe tampers he whittled himself, ugly ashtrays. The colored pencils he used to mark different passages—"poikilographically," as he put it—in addition to a whole array of crudely painted things and handcrafted objects made by friends. The prisoner-of-war camps in which Doderer was interred during the First and Second World Wars—in Russia on the Manchurian border and later in Norway and Denmark—brought such objects into being; there were always skillful handi-crafters who could patch and glue together all kinds of rubbish.

Heimito von Doderer came from a well-to-do family, a

dynasty of architects from Swabia, who in the decades before the First World War were active in the gigantic construction projects of Austria-Hungary, the Danube monarchy undergoing explosive modernization; this was a time when railroad routes were being laid throughout the Balkan region and the mountains, when large rivers were being channeled and regulated, when whole new cities were being built. The First World War wiped out the family fortune, but as is often the case when rich people are said to have "lost everything," there was enough left that parents and children alike were able to maintain their accustomed lifestyle. The only one who never managed that was Heimito von Doderer himself in all of his seventy-year lifetime; he continued to live in attic apartments with makeshift possessions. The outright suspicion arises, in fact, that not everything was evenly divided among the brothers and sisters, so great is the difference between the living conditions of the Bohemian brother and the well-heeled existence of his closest relatives.

The bric-a-brac in those glass cases makes a meaningful statement. The impressive libraries, the collections of autographs, the Tanagra figurines on the desk, the country houses the public is accustomed to when it comes to Thomas Mann and Gerhart Hauptmann, Stefan Zweig and Sigmund Freud—none of these can be found in Doderer's instance, partly because of the stark poverty that attended this writer's life for long years—but perhaps as well because of an unspoken refusal by one who had been raised very strictly and harshly ever to abandon the posture of the rebellious son, one who knew perfectly well how the adults lived and what they considered necessary but who himself remained aloft in his airy attic room, steadfastly improvising, free of all needs and soaring above all the ungainly, clanking machinery encumbering

ii

the adults. Considering the long time during which he led a life of hardship or even of mortification, considering the years of starvation during which his first great novel, *The Strudlhof Steps*, was written—I'm thinking here of a photograph of Doderer taken in 1947 and showing a man emaciated and with an expression of bitter intentness filled with fear—such a view may appear thoughtless or frivolous, but when looking at the possessions, those remnants of Doderer's life on display in the dusty glass cases in the local museum of the Alsergrund district in Vienna, the viewer will think not only of the prisoner-of-war camps but of the items in a boy's pants pockets. All the more in that among the pocket knives and metal containers there lie Indian arrows with frayed and plucked quills alongside bows painted in an artsy "barbarian" style, the colors now dried out and faded—the whole museum is fast asleep in the depth of oblivion, by the way, and is purportedly going to be closed at some time in the near future, at which point Doderer's bows and arrows will find their way into cardboard boxes. It would be hard to exaggerate the off-putting effect, even the embarrassment, of looking at these artifacts, which is exactly the reason why it is important to note at once that it was none other than this archery equipment—a second set is preserved in Landshut by the relatives of Doderer's second wife—that opened a pathway for me into Doderer's late diaries, the *Commentarii*, and in doing so gave me an understanding of his two great novels as well as the literary perspective and life experiences underlying them.

The bows, arrows, and quivers were not just decorative objects, even though in the many and various attic rooms Doderer occupied throughout his life and that he liked to designate euphemistically as "*ateliers*"—probably because they were almost always on the top floor of whatever building he lived in—visitors again and again described seeing arrangements of these items on the slanted walls. But the items were also put to actual use.

What I know about Doderer's use of bow and arrow I have taken from one of the most toxic works of biographical literature, Wolfgang Fleischer's *Das verleugnete Leben*, from which I am loath to quote but unfortunately cannot avoid, because one of the many unfortunate aspects of Doderer's reception is that no balanced biography by his contemporaries and those familiar with his life circumstances is as yet forthcoming. As a young man, Fleischer was secretary to the aging Doderer, who was no longer able to cope on his own with the floods of mail his late fame brought in. Fleischer had nothing but good experiences during the short years of his work with the writer, but all the same he apparently developed such an antipathy toward his employer that it demands to be spoken of as downright hatred.

Having to read five hundred pages about a man whom the author detests is not very pleasant as it is, and all the less so when the subject is a brilliant writer every line of whose work disproves the deceitfulness and malevolence imputed to him. In his diaries, Heimito von Doderer sat in judgment on himself with exceptional severity, so mercilessly, in fact, that the reader is tempted to surmise a tendency to self-flagellation from which a biographer with proper distance would have been called on to shield him—in view of what this erstwhile secretary person knew and understood, referring to "a life renounced" when it comes to Doderer is nothing less than defamatory. Even so— and this is yet another of those many unfortunate situations in Doderer's life—this biography is the only really thorough one, so anyone wishing to gain more detailed knowledge about Doderer will be forced to have recourse to this oddity of literary history. And so it is now, when the topic is archery—please forgive me, then, for this extensive parenthetical comment meant to explain my reluctance to quote from this polluted source. In the accompanying book of photographs, likewise published by Fleischer, there are pictures of Doderer practicing his archery in the nineteen-thirties. He is wearing knickerbockers and looking very fierce while drawing back the bow, and there is nothing playful or ironic about his features. He is totally engrossed in this man's work of his, and, as if to propel this athletic transport into a virtually Riefenstahl-like realm, there are also pictures of him in brief bathing trunks in the garden of his parents' country house, the Riegelhof, situated near Semmering in the Austrian Alps.

Taking a close look at these pictures could not but bring to mind thoughts of a scene in Goethe's garden, as described by Eckermann, a scene that must certainly have been familiar to Doderer. Eckermann was also a practiced archer, and Goethe gave him his bow one day to try out.

"Now let me," Goethe said. I was glad he too wanted to shoot an arrow . . . Goethe placed the notch into the bowstring, and he held the bow with the correct grip as well, but it took a little time until he had everything just right. Then he raised his arm to take aim and drew back the string. There he stood like Apollo, everlastingly young inside though his body was old. The arrow flew only a modest distance and then fell to the ground . . . "Again!" said Goethe . . . Goethe's shooting with bow and arrow made me happy beyond all measure. I thought of his verse: *Läßt mich das Alter im Stich? / Bin ich wieder ein Kind?*" ["Is old age now letting me down? / Am I a child once more?" – trans. VK].

Doderer stood there like Apollo as well, and his accomplishment in archery may have been similarly comparable to that of the prince of poets, although not in the sense of relaxing through play but of being marked by that seriousness which only children bring to bear when carrying out their secret rituals. The way in which he came to possess bow and arrow can indeed be referred to as a secret childhood ritual, for that matter: just as Tamino in *The Magic Flute* is presented with his wondrous instrument by the three boys, so a very young Amazon presented these implements to him at a critical hour in his development as a writer; they were adorned with weighty mottoes, pointblank exhortations about his life as a writer. The boyishly slender student Gaby Murad, who was never Doderer's lover, though probably the best friend he ever had in his life and also crucially significant in his turn toward the Catholic Church, gave him for his thirty-eighth birthday a forty-five-pound English bow with arrows, for which she handmade a painted leather quiver. "*HNSP—hic et nunc semper paratus*—always prepared here and now" was what she painted onto the quiver. What all this preparedness entails will accompany our thoughts about Doderer's narrative works. For the time being, though, we can take leave of Doderer as archer by imagining how he made his way through the streets of Döbling and Dachau, outfitted Indian-style with bow, arrows, and quiver, to reach the gardens and parks in which he pursued the sport.

To begin by attempting a portrayal of Doderer's narrative method through the procedures of archery may seem as peculiar as archery itself. However, the figure of Heimito von Doderer ranks still today among the great unknowns—that's what writers are called in literary circles who are familiar to the many through hearsay but whose books are nonetheless read by only the few. The "great unknown" remains forever a kind of secret, the idol of a dedicated small coterie—which, by the way, can then continue to guarantee that the writer's fame will not spread, because coteries like this do not look exactly attractive from the outside. And isn't it in fact somewhat humiliating for authors when the withholding of their due renown is being ceaselessly bewailed with self-satisfied moaning and groaning by their admirers, as if every writer on earth had an inalienable right to be read?

Of course there exists that *res publica* of genuine readers who undertake on a constant basis the effort to sketch out criteria from the individual work as it stands on its own, to fit the single work in its artistic individuality into the structure of literature, a structure never finished and undergoing continuous change. This work is a collective endeavor carried out with no great noise and not even noticeable to non-readers, content to be diverted by the everyday doings of literary publicity. Thus it was possible for the publishing house of Beck, Doderer's literary home for many years, right down to the present day, to bring out recently two extensive histories of more modern literature in which Doderer's name is mentioned only in passing or not at all and at the same time for a certain very deficient treatment of canonical novels —written by a literary propagandist active year in and year out, who never in his life published a single line about Doderer— only now finally to include *The Strudlhof Steps* after all, and that solely because, as they say most aptly about such mysterious processes, it simply could no longer be avoided.

The purely quantitative passage of time plays a significant role when appraising such developments. Doderer has been dead for forty years, but his case is not yet settled. There are authors in the canon just mentioned for whom that span of forty years after their death is not yet over but who will no longer be included in any canon, however dubious, after the fateful forty years have elapsed.

Many reasons can be advanced to explain why true success has eluded Doderer for the time being, and by success it does not do in this context to think of considerably sizable print runs, favorable critiques, and state prizes, but of advancement into the forefront, of inclusion among the acclaimed group of those considered representative of their respective literary eras. Doderer was born in the same year as Ernst Jünger, but during the time between the wars, so very important for the genesis of literary renown, he remained totally unknown. He published his major novels after his sixtieth birthday within a cultural landscape featuring on one hand the great writers before the Second World War and on the other the post-war *Gruppe 47*; he was neither a pre-war writer nor a post-war writer, and so between Brecht and Thomas Mann all the seats were taken. Politically he was "tainted," as they so ominously say, even though his membership as a non-German in the NSDAP, the National Socialist party—outlawed in Austria as of when he joined in 1933—was a matter of utterly featherweight unreality. Doderer never wrote a single line in any way indebted to Nazism, was never at any time or in any place politically active, never delivered any speeches or published any articles with Nazi tendencies, never derived even the slightest advantage from his party membership, and in 1939 was received into the Catholic Church by a priest who had founded and was heading a large organization to protect persecuted Jews. Even so, his admission to party membership, the reasons for which have never really been fully clarified, would later prove enough to bar him from winning the Nobel Prize.

No, it wasn't archery that made acceptance of this author

so difficult, but it certainly belongs among the array of qualities that had made him appear so eccentric and odd. In the 1920s, when famous authors were falling over one another, Doderer somehow managed to forge no connection with anyone in those influential, effusive circles so good at promoting reputations. Doderer lived among a large circle of friends, most of them vividly memorialized in his novels, but he didn't—as snobs would say—know "anybody who was anybody." The priest-like painter and writer Albert Kiehtreiber, who called himself Paris von Gütersloh and who influenced the "Fantastic Realism" of the Vienna School after the Second World War, became his guru. Doderer all but forced upon the older man his role as a disciple and with a stubbornness amounting to denial failed to recognize how extremely disagreeable his mentor was. Gütersloh would then later persecute with open hatred the man who had proclaimed himself the older writer's follower. The word "hatred," strong though it is, now appears for the second time, and not without due consideration. Doderer's personality seems constantly to have triggered off vehement attacks, especially the kinds of antipathies that could not be balanced out by the good will others showed him. One enemy can do more harm than ten friends' good. This summary point about Doderer's life also illuminates the difference between him and Thomas Mann, not necessarily a pleasant man either, but highly diplomatic, whose work was invariably greeted with wide acceptance.

Thomas Mann may also lead us to an understanding of perhaps the greatest difficulty Doderer's novels had to surmount. One need only call to mind the contents of Mann's novels: a family history modeled on the theory of decadence; a scenario suffused with intellectual history that portrays pre-1914 Europe between bourgeois liberalism and budding totalitarianism, a

Europe symbolized by the unnerving stagnation of a sanatorium for seriously ill patients; genius and madness as a theory to account for National Socialism in Germany; religious history, myth, and demythologizing. On the basis of these novels a large reading public became familiar with and was able to discuss historical problems, all the more because Mann's themes are encountered in the literature of far distant spheres as well. Mann treated "the burning questions of his time," as it is so well expressed, especially those from his youth, shaped above all by his reading Nietzsche and Schopenhauer and by the philosophy of the Wagner operas. With *The Magic Mountain* and *Doctor Faustus*, Thomas Mann then succeeded in creating books whose very titles alone encompass entire historical-aesthetic epochs in powerfully compressed form; readers of these works come to believe that they have been able to locate themselves completely inside the epochs depicted and navigate them thoroughly enough to be capable of evaluating them historically and reaching conclusive judgments.

What, on the other hand, can readers eager for enlightenment, education, and instruction expect when they turn to Doderer's two huge novels, *The Strudlhof Steps*, already referred to as brought into the canon by the Suhrkamp Press, and *The Demons*, that even more voluminous novel, Doderer's true masterpiece, which he is either working toward or working away from in all of his other writing? The two novels can be understood as a unified artifact, incidentally, less in the sense of a diptych than as sharing a commonality along the lines of Balzac's method in his *Comédie humaine*. In both of Doderer's works, very different as they are, many of the same characters appear, for example; the fate of one of the protagonists (one hesitates to say "main characters"), Mary K., who meets with a catastrophic accident at the end of *The Strudlhof Steps*—a streetcar cuts off one of her legs—takes a happy turn at the end of *The Demons*. The decision to have the same people appear in the same place, the city of Vienna, in changing configurations and in a variety of aesthetic surroundings, is also Balzac-like. *The Demons*, in so many respects the more radical work, compositionally more open, more musical in the alignment of its inner connections, will be closer to the forefront here, also because, as will be seen later, the way in which it came into being is reflected and expanded on in the diary in an exceptionally unusual manner.

What is *The Demons* about, then? How would one go about characterizing the content of *The Demons* if one wanted to place it opposite Mann's work and attempt to find in it, too, a working formula such as we tried with Mann? Doderer's own characterization appears in this case, at least initially, to be as provocative as it is inadequate: a work can be termed a novel when the reader can't say what happens in it. Anyone who reads synopses in the field of literary history would long since have become aware, however, that the content of *The Demons* makes it the "Great Austrian Political Novel," in which is depicted the burning of the Palace of Justice in Vienna in 1927, the greatest disaster of domestic affairs that took place in the years between the wars, before the annexation by Germany; the event was the "Cannae of Austrian freedom," as the novel itself calls it, the act provoking the civil war that was then later merely stifled by Dollfuss's dictatorship and that ended with the absorption of Austria into the German state. The title of the novel seems intended to lend a particular coloration to the portrayal of these urgently historical occurrences, since there already exists a political novel whose subject is the prelude to a civil war and a dictatorship, a work of notably prophetic vision, Dostoyevsky's *Demons*, which has no longer been appearing under that title for some years now, because *Besy* does not mean "demons" but refers instead to people possessed by them. Doderer, who made it a habit never to speak of Dostoyevsky except as "Saint Fyodor Michailovich," unmistakably composed his novel on the clear model of his predecessor's work. That becomes obvious above all in allusions and quotations reaching deep into the details of the history—if a history is what it's supposed to be. Like Dostoyevsky's novel, Doderer's presents itself in part as a chronicle by one of the characters involved, retired Sectional Counselor Geyrenhoff, who is also referred to by the abbreviation "G-ff," so that the parallel to Dostoyevsky's retired Cavalry Captain Gaganoff will be fully clear. As in the Russian novel, Doderer calls the group of intellectuals among whom large parts of the novel take place "our crowd." The burning of the Spigulin factory matches the burning of the Palace of Justice; as in Dostoyevsky, there is a political murder, the killing of little Krächzi; there is a festive gathering in *The Demons*, the table-tennis party, equivalent to the reception at the home of the German-Russian governor, and in both novels there is an interpolated confessional account of a crime with sexual and ritual background. Whoever searches even a little further will certainly find more. With evidence like this in hand, one could call Doderer's *Demons* an outright remake of the Dostoyevsky material, as they say in Hollywood when filming a new version of an older movie.

Is it that simple? To anticipate the answer—not only is it not so simple, but the relation of Doderer's novel to the similarities with Dostoyevsky's, which Doderer himself emphasized so strongly, is instead so complicated that one is forced to speak of what may be perhaps one of the insoluble riddles of Doderer's work. The similarities just described, heavily underlined and waved under the reader's nose as they are, before mentioning additional parallels between the two novels, could bring about the impression that we are dealing here with kindred or at least similar stories being told, as if Doderer were using his references to Dostoyevsky to lay a trail that would make it easier for the reader to understand and interpret his own book—except that no such thing is even remotely the case.

Let's attempt now to portray what Doderer is narrating to us in *The Demons*, well aware as we are that plot summaries of this kind are fundamentally and completely pointless to passionate and knowledgeable readers. To make this tedious labor of retelling a little more palatable, it is better to sum up the contents as they remain in memory— not, that is, as they stand in Kindler's *Literary Lexicon*. The scholars who draw up those kinds of synopses are keen to impart meaning; at exactly those points at which there appears to be little connection, these writers feel obligated to go on seeking out perceptible connections however they can. We confess that we read *The Demons* with the eyes of love. And love can often be blind, as is well known, but it can also make for sharper vision, even clairvoyance. What elements, then, constitute the mighty cosmos of *The Demons*?

Let's consider first the group known as "our crowd," not because it is any more important than other motifs, but because we have already mentioned it. These are youthful intellectuals, men and women more or less connected with the university, more or less pursuing education, for the most part improvising their living arrangements by renting furnished "digs," caught up in all the attractions and repulsions that so many and varied love stories entail. Politically, the members of "our crowd" appear uninvolved and uninterested. Then there is the circle of "Fat Females," denizens of bakery shops and devotees of their pastries, some of them unsuccessful in sexual matters, others successfully enmeshed in fantasies and intrigues. Then there is the newspaper world, the editorship of the "Alliance" conglomerate, meticulously and brilliantly portrayed but without playing any special role beyond that. There is a young working man who starts learning Latin on his own, becomes the secretary to a book-loving prince, and wins the love of the one-legged Jewish woman mentioned before—these two are the leading lights of the novel. There is a murderer of prostitutes who meets his death in exactly the same way as does Harry Lime, portrayed by Orson Welles in the film *The Third Man*—the scene is replicated in detail from the film. There is a young industrialist who inherits a castle and in its library happens upon a very long report, composed throughout in Late-Medieval German and reproduced in its entirety in the novel, about the ritual rape of a mayor's wife, detained under the pretext of being a witch: reading it, the young man becomes clear about his own sexual predilections. There is an enigmatic dreamer and visionary, a semi-mystic, who is given space in one chapter of the novel to include her dream book.

And yes, there is the burning of the Palace of Justice in Vienna and the extensive depiction of agitated crowds in turmoil, but it is hard to say what threads connect it to all the other motifs or what motifs anticipate it. What appears genuinely important to the narrator is a minor criminal intrigue that extends throughout the whole book: a villain with the unusual title of *Kammerrat*, or Chamber Councilor, has suppressed a will favoring two siblings (though they aren't siblings at all, which no one knows). This whole plot line is so intricately spun out that the solution ends up having to be hastily tacked on; surely there can be few readers and admirers of *The Demons* who have grasped and could recount these machinations about a will and an inheritance. Is there still more? There is a great deal to enumerate and to praise, such as the exhaustive portrayal of the Café Kaunitz—and yet, whatever actual function this Café Kaunitz is supposed to fulfill within the total structure is so far from apparent that I have forgotten what it is. *The Demons* has a characteristic quality: when seeking to locate a favorite passage, it doesn't help to ask at what point in the story it might have appeared or where it most logically belongs in keeping with the structure. Passages one thought were near the end are found at the beginning, and what one thought belonged to the exposition turns up somewhere in the middle. From time to time the author launches an effort to take all the parts we called to mind—while lacking the ability to put them in proper order or to place them into any logical or even illogical arrangement—and to tie them together through improbabilities that border on the outlandish; and it is just then that we can really register the disconnection among the countless motifs in the sense of a story composed along conventional lines.

Why is the book called *The Demons*? The Heimitists, as the passionate aficionados of Doderer's work are known, have an answer. It does not arise from the book itself, for it is not possible, even with the best will and the most bizarre contortions, to derive the title *The Demons* from what is treated in the work itself—very much in contrast to Dostoyevsky's work, in which the protagonists indeed appear beset by all the forces of hell. The most convincing explanation might be as follows: when Doderer began work on *The Demons* at the beginning of the 1930s he gave the emerging novel the working title *Fat Females*. Corpulent women peopled his erotic fantasies as it was, hovering at this time and for many years afterward over his totally obscure literary design like Venus-of-Willendorf-shaped air balloons or tutelary goddesses. In his diary, which complemented the progress and the crises of his work, the Fat Females are abbreviated as *DD*. Abbreviations feature prominently in the diaries and do not make reading them exactly easy. It is not apparent at what precise point *DD* no longer stood for *Dicke Damen* but *Die Dämonen* instead, though it is a safe assumption that *Die Dämonen* was chosen as a title mainly because of the *DD*—a disguise which both jettisons yet still contains the actual title, so precious to the author but in his mind probably beyond the pale as the title of a novel, enabling him to keep it hidden from the eyes of non-readers.

As we know, Doderer was the son of an architect and inherited his father's drawing board. It stood in his small study next to a tiny desk with a surface barely larger than two A4 sheets of paper; on it he sketched his intricate plot developments with colored pencils. Sheets of paper once tacked to the drawing board have been preserved. With those colored pencils and in tiny handwriting these notations are spread out over the large surface and joined by arrows, wavy lines, and arcs into a bewildering network of cross-references and bold connections. Anyone looking at these sheets from the drawing board would be forced to believe that the novel draws on an ingenious system of relations, as in a work by Nabokov. Doderer encouraged this impression. Among the Heimitists a virtual legend came into being about the drawing board. During Doderer's youth, his father hovered over him as a menacing figure; in his fits of rage, as the author describes it in one of his early novels, his father would turn "black as ebony." Perhaps by using his father's working implement the author really did mean surreptitiously to prove to the family tyrant, deceased but still keeping an eye on his son from the beyond, that the building up of a novel was every bit as serious an undertaking, demanding every bit as much expertise, as the construction of a railroad bridge.

To use Doderer's own words, many of which his readers have taken into their thesaurus of quotations, conjectures like this are "basically nothing but spiteful remarks." But one point remains no less firm a certainty among these readers after they have accounted to themselves for the structural content of *The Demons* and of *The Strudlhof Steps* as well: all this busy work at the drawing board, these arrows and squiggly lines, assuredly do not guide us toward the secret of these books. They distract from it, in fact. Let's say it bluntly: whatever design can be discerned in these books appears so utterly far-fetched, so wildly capricious, so unbelievable that we have to picture some assistant engineer having gone insane while still plodding away at the notorious drawing board, his sole concern now being the daft effort to link everything to everything else, by hook or by crook, and to lay it all out in the most meticulous way possible without regard to probability or inner logic. One would have to be a brother in spirit of said engineer, of course, to take offense at this design, and it counts as one of the marvels in Doderer's life—a life rich in marvels as well as bad breaks—that such engineers among literary critics (and they certainly do exist) have not taken up the cudgels against him to any extent worth mentioning.

It even seems to me as if the design monstrosities of the novels have never been properly discerned. That is not surprising. When readers enter a Doderer novel, as travelers might walk out of the train station into a city, they are immediately so flooded with impressions that they just drift along without consulting the map. One could compare these books with grand festivals in which the guests push their way through the crowds; meet up with people only to lose them but then happen onto them once more, though now in new configurations; then find themselves alone or with just one other person on a terrace, which then is suddenly filled with people who want to watch the fireworks; drift along in every mood imaginable until pale daylight breaks and the first birds begin to chirp; and finally leave half drunk, half pensive. Such a feast is united in its dramatic effect in that a great deal happens and at the same time nothing whatever happens; that the whole is more than the sum of its parts; that the guests are tinged and pervaded by the prevailing mood, thus appearing in some indefinite way more distinct, larger, and more complete—this is the sense in which a great epic novel is a festival—with not even a plot, perhaps, but with a setting that holds everything together, a palace with many rooms, perhaps, in which the music from the great ballroom can only be heard very faintly now. An aura of the inexpressible or indescribable reigns where these effects are deployed, which is not to say, however, that Doderer did not go to some lengths attempting to define them anyway, or rather to capture and hold fast the circumstances under which they came about.

Preparatory work as well as follow-up comments surround these two great works by Doderer; this observation was made earlier in reference to the novels and stories that preceded and followed *The Strudlhof Steps* and *The Demons*. The real preparatory work took place in the diaries, however, and these can be divided into three sets. The *Diaries 1920 to 1939* most readily bear comparison to what is familiar from other writers' diaries: notations about the day's experiences and thoughts, though the energizing and fortifying influence of his master Gütersloh is apparent even this early; observations about everyday life apprehended under psychological categories devised in a most individualistic way or by the "mechanism of the spirit," as it is characteristically referred to. All of it in extremely compressed form, so that memories of events noted and their restructuring in the novel are often inextricably condensed. Short essays are a hallmark of these diaries. His work on the novel presents itself as an exercise in self-scrutiny conducted under a system constantly undergoing wider development. It is clear even in these early diaries that Doderer was never at any point in his life as a writer concerned with telling stories, neither in the conventional nor in some ingeniously intricate sense. Thoughts about story-telling, plots, suspense, or any other device of narrative technique never once appear in these diaries, which center exclusively on the work that goes into writing. Only contrast these diaries with those of Henry James, an assemblage of experiences and people out of which a story or a novel could be generated.

It might not dawn on readers of Doderer's diaries for long stretches that they are in fact dealing with a writer's journal as such, but that work is in progress instead on an extensive narration. As in something like an anatomical theater from the Baroque era, this work is being performed on a single body lying spread out in the pages of the diary and being dissected down to the last filament while still alive; to heighten the eeriness of the process even more, imagine a body like that of Prometheus, whose liver, hacked out of his side by vengeful Zeus's eagle, constantly grows back—this is just how the organs in Doderer are restored at once after being removed and are then ready for another removal. What is invisible to the individual, his own personality, is reassembled anew, detective-style, as it were, from sexual activities, from euphoria and despondency, from liking or disliking toward others, from the never-surmounted circumstances of parentage and childhood, and from involuntary memories covering every imaginable aspect of the more recent and more remote past.

There then follow, from 1940 to 1950, the dairies entitled *Tangents*, carrying the Dostoyevsky subtitle *Diary of a Writer*. Everything experienced up to this point appears to be a preparation for these years, in which actual production begins. Doderer was called up for military service in 1940 and spent the war years in administrative and training posts in France, Russia, and Norway. What appears to have been a comparatively easy life made it possible for him to continue working on the *Fat Females / The Demons* (*DD*); *The Strudlhof Steps* was at the same time emerging out of the rib of the *Fat Females*, as it were. The manuscript seems to have gone lost in Norway when Doderer, released from captivity, was permitted to return to Austria. He had come to accept this irretrievable loss as a "penance" specially devised for him when the whole bundle of papers, delayed by a year, turned back up after all.

At this point a parenthetical comment about Doderer's moral constitution may perhaps be permitted, one that will make abundantly clear the contrast between the slanderous comments to which the author is still subjected today and the reality: between 1945 and 1950, the lean years during which he was starving—years during which, because of his manifestly perfunctory membership in the National Socialist party he was penalized by being barred from publishing, whereas his "master" Gütersloh, who had been an out-and-out Nazi, had for quite some time been restored to status and prestige as president of the Academy—at a time in which his manuscript appeared lost, during his struggles about a book that might possibly never see publication, at a time of extreme material deprivation, there is to be found in the *forum internum* of his diary not a single word of rancor or complaint; this grand master practicing daily examination of conscience refuses to make any agency except his own self responsible for any of his life's discordances, no matter how closely to hand blame from outside himself may lie.

A special feature of the *Tangents* is found in monologues the author conducts about the characters of his novel, two of whom in particular are self-portraits: the writer Kajetan von Schlaggenberg, chronicler of the fat females, and René (Heimito-Renatus) von Stangeler—it is important to know that according to Grimm's dictionary a "Doderer," the word for a stutterer in the area around Swabia, can be called a "Stangeler" in Alemannic dialect. And none other than Stangeler is subjected to quizzical speculation like a stranger, the tone cordial but distanced as if discussing a deceased acquaintance about whom one is airing conjectures years later. On the whole, however, Doderer expresses a criticism about the *Tangents* from which he would later draw a strong conclusion about the diaries to follow.

> "13 May 1945 (Sunday). Criticism of the diary (*Diary of a Writer*). A diary will have all the more limited literary quality the more it expands into protraction or moves along the light beam of consciously ordering thought, or: the less it presents epigrammatic prose but instead goes to the trouble of pursuing—or better yet to scurrying after—the *exoteron* in the descriptive mode, even though it means including marginal notes about said external facts: personal journalism. What is being written in that case is proceeding from a stage of not being ready to write, and there can exist no doubt about that. Strange to consider that until they are ripe for being depicted in writing, until they return as freely arising recollections along some surprising curve of the

memory, what are called facts require a longer period of lying fallow than do thoughts, if they for the present lack unity of form and content, in which case they weren't thoughts in the first place. Many of them will rise up from the bath of unconscious thinking, complete and still wet from being born. In the descriptive part of the diary, the writer must accordingly deal with matter that lies far back, depending on how the free arising came about. And that's indeed what he does. Except that you can't call it a diary any more."

An expression has been brought into play here that occupied a major role in Doderer's imagination and that establishes an important connection to the last of his diaries, the *Commentarii*, written between 1951 and 1966. These are the diaries written during the time Doderer was bringing *The Demons* to completion, and they will once more bring us closer to his use of bow and arrows, mentioned at the beginning. Thanks to a work of history that opens out an entire world, Brigitte Hamann's *Hitler's Vienna*, the intellectual atmosphere of the imperial city before the First World War has again come to the forefront of general awareness. The Vienna of these days would have to be called a huge soup kitchen of ideas with many pots in which brilliant and half-brilliant dilettantes concocted idiosyncratic explanations of the world, a goodly number of structures thought up and thought through all by themselves. If we gather together all the world systems hatched by the self-propelled thinkers and fanciful autodidacts of those years, even Sigmund Freud himself would appear to be firmly entrenched as merely one among many in a milieu of intellectuals who shrank from nothing in designing their theories.

Hermann Swoboda, an instructor of psychology who never reached the rank of full professor, taught a course at the University of Vienna in which the young returning veteran Doderer enrolled; it left an impression that lasted his whole life. Swoboda constituted a heretical offshoot of the Freud school. He saw the soul as being subject to objective forces biological and physical in nature, an idea he had developed at the same time as Freud's friend Wilhelm Fliess. In his work *The Cycles of the Human Organism in Their Biological and Psychological Significance* he argued his conviction that every mental and physical process in life recurs in a periodic rhythm, twenty-three days for women and twenty-eight for men; associations above all, controlled by the unconscious dominance of the mind, conform to these rhythms, according to Swoboda; for all people, events emerge into consciousness in that they "freely arise," as he formulated it, which is to say altogether independently of the momentary state of mind, because twenty-three or twenty-eight hours or some multiple of those time units have elapsed since they first occurred or were last remembered.

Whatever value this proposition may have in regard to the natural sciences is insignificant for our present context; it brought Swoboda only a small measure of success as it was, since appointment to the chair was forever denied him. But his concept of "freely arising memories" imprinted itself deeply on his student Heimito von Doderer. *Meaningful Stimulation through a Single Word* is the title of a short piece by Goethe, and it is in this way that the notion of "freely arising memory" became in Doderer's understanding a key concept about the role played by memory as it pertains to the novel.

Scientific theories may well prove untenable and can be rejected by the experts, yet they can still be applied and can yield fruit as patterns governing the imagination of a novelist, for if art consists essentially of bringing order of some kind into amorphous or chaotic subject matter, then any model of order, no matter what, can serve the purpose. And the concept of "freely arising memory" would by its nature be especially congenial to a novelist occupied with the reconfiguring and revitalizing of his own past.

"Freely arising"—those words alone are enough to evoke a rising up of images, less inside the mind and more as in a theater, objective, external visions taking place virtually before our eyes, as Banquo, though dead, arises with his bleeding wounds before Macbeth—freely, to be sure, but by no means welcome. In "freely arising memory" the past becomes visible in the form of pictures—deeply enigmatic but vivid and at the same time charged with meaning—released from their chains of events. In freely arising memory the past becomes a thread running through present time into the future; it weaves itself into the present; during the banal course of workaday life in the present it comes (to use once again a theatrical comparison) as an unexpected guest like the marble statue of the Commendatore in *Don Giovanni*. In its arising the past reveals its true face. That maxim by Schiller is incorrect: "Only that which never has occurred / Is truly never able to grow old." On the contrary: only that which took place once, was then completely forgotten, and now rises up from the grave of this oblivion is what cannot grow old but, in fact, only now awakens to its fullest life. That is the eternally renewed material of the novel, remaining forever young as it skips generations.

The similarity to and even the undeniable kinship with Marcel Proust's concepts cannot be overlooked. Doderer's probably not having even been aware of Proust's work before the end of the Second World War—there is absolutely no trace of his reading Proust any earlier—offers another occasion to marvel at the mystery of how a particular idea will come into its own, as it were, the same thought emerging simultaneously within a given time frame in different places and in the minds of different people who have no connection with one another. This phenomenon makes history suddenly become visible.

It was necessary to turn our attention to "freely arising memories" before any fuller consideration could be given to the *Commentarii*, those diaries from the last decades of Doderer's life. They differ sharply from all the earlier ones, having abundant recourse to individual terms *à la* "freely arising memories." There is no longer any recounting whatever of anecdotal material; "remnants of the day" such as Freud speaks about in his *Interpretation of Dreams* are excluded. The sole subject is his work on the novel, but along lines that have no correspondence to either his own previous diaries or to the working diaries of other novelists. Before we turn to the *Commentarii* for samples, we would do well to have a look at a few more of the terms that recur in them with regularity; the definitions of words and expressions, that is the translations of these concepts into "human language," as Kant referred to attempts to decipher the terminology of Hamann, will yield important insights into the character of these entries. Doderer himself was constantly at pains to redefine his terms anew, hammering and squeezing them into himself with sheer force, spreading them out and holding them before his eyes in ceaseless admonishment. Since what is being aimed at here, however, is to bring Doderer's terms—or rather the method they are meant to help formulate—to the awareness of a larger readership, a more "secular" one, as it were, it would be better not to draw on his own formulations as such but to attempt making them our own in our own words.

The central concept is that of the "writer," to whom

the "anti-writer" is placed in opposition. One can sense that it's not a matter of the writer's professionalism or command of the writer's craft or anything of the kind. The idea of *Menschwerdung*, of becoming human, plays a major role for the heroes of Doderer's novels, so *Schriftsteller-Werden*, or becoming a writer, is in fact nothing more than the extension of and the more specific channel for this becoming human. "Writer" and "anti-writer" are anthropological categories but, beyond that, moral ones as well, and they are measures of spiritual and intellectual development. As Doderer uses the term, it would be possible to picture a "writer" who has not written a single book, whereas "anti-writers" are very productive and are incessantly producing. Through their origins, their political convictions, their aesthetic judgments, their tastes, and their principles, "anti-writers" are rigidly defined personalities hermetically sealed inside the armor of their own opinions, which are ever seeking to fix themselves in the same unchangeable form using their template or schematic of reality. The "anti-writer" already knows what he will see before he has begun to observe; he has taken sides, possibly including through his language, a language marked by his determination to make some point or other. That's just it: the "anti-writer" knows who he is and what he wants.

The "writer," on the other hand, tries, and tries anew every day, to lay aside said armor—often it is no more than a whalebone corset or even a truss—and to risk taking that step into his own lack of definition and form. To draw on expressions from Thomistic philosophy, held by Doderer in such high esteem, the "writer" attempts to separate his own characteristics from the core of his being and to comprehend them as accidents that can be discarded. He attempts to cease thinking those things all of us say about ourselves every day: "Well, that's how I am;

that's not how I do things; I'm a person who . . . " That there can hardly remain any question, given this approach to literature, of "expressing oneself" arises from the simple consideration that the "writer" whose makeup is of this kind will no longer have the faintest idea who he is and thus who the "self" is that he's meant to be expressing. The "writer" finds his culmination in the "non-writer," for whom all intentional stylistic and formal activity has dissolved without a trace. Gómez Dávila may be referring to something like this when he says, "One day the words land near the patient writer like swarms of pigeons." In the work of the "non-writer," the text is translucent and deeply dark like the water of a clear river flowing slowly. By having "precipitated into crystalline form through grammar"—another of Doderer's favorite concepts—the reality being depicted has forfeited virtually nothing, because its shimmering flow can be sensed even in its crystalline state.

What forms both the "writer" and the "non-writer" is "apperception," an expression from Kantian philosophy and for Doderer a key concept denoting an attitude of mind and soul that has seized complete possession of everything about the person of a writer. "Apperception" is the readiness to receive the signals and impressions of the material world and the images rising from the memory. To the extent that one would wish to associate this receptivity with womanhood, the apperceiving writer is feminine in bringing forth nothing that has not passed through him. Grids, patterns, schematics that could insert themselves between the soul and the world, thus hampering "apperception" or labeling experience too hastily in an effort to categorize it: all this the master apperceiver has deactivated. In "apperception" the amorphous communication from the world must come pouring in entirely unformed. This disorder, this chaos is a valuable stage. Doderer calls it the "decay of the situation." Here is where the difference between the political thinker and the writer of Doderer's mold grows especially clear. Whereas the imperative stated by Carl Schmitt—"Recognize the situation!"—applies to the political writer, the situation for the writer needs to grow silent, expressionless, and ambiguous all at the same time. Only in this "decay of the situation" does the splendor of the objective reveal itself in all its unfathomable otherness. In the apperceiving glance into the "decay of the situation," the writer, though here on earth, can feel "air from another planet," as Stefan George puts it in a poem; in it the most distant planet becomes the everyday environment.

Overarching the "decaying situation" is the "pregrammatical space," with which term we have to let our study of Doderer's idiosyncratic German conclude, much as it would be possible to extend such a study quite a bit further. It is essential for the writer to remain in this "pregrammatical space" for as long as possible. Best of all would be for him never to leave it. In doing so, he would have to take leave of his readership, to be sure, but he would no longer miss that readership very much. Wonderfully silent, wonderfully rich reality is "chilled to perfection" in grammar, as it were, which is what we call it when a champagne bottle fetched from the cellar is plunged into an ice bucket. Everything that was dancing in figures and weaving together is divided as subject and object and fixed in place through grammatical classification.

It appears surprising that although language can be a key for a writer, it is one that can just as easily bar access to the world as open it—that barring or even barricading of the gateway to the world by language emerges for the Doderer of the *Commentarii* as the greatest threat by far. In "pregrammatical space" everything is no more than aroma and aura; hence the cult Doderer pursued regarding odors of all different kinds. Just as for the ancient Jews the odor of incense pervading the Holy of Holies in the Temple represented the *shekinah*, the physical presence of the Godhead, and made it possible to experience that presence, so do odors—predominantly of varnish, of lavender, of camphor in apartments protected by mothballs in the summer—establish a space fully filled with reality, charged, saturated existence compressed into a ball, to capture which by means of language is the great masterstroke. It may occasionally succeed early on, but it usually requires an entire lifetime as preparation. The novelist would need to be sixty, and sixty is what Doderer was when he finally brought *The Demons* to completion.

We're getting closer to archery, although we're not quite there yet, even though these observations about Doderer's special vocabulary, sketchy as they are, may have allowed some surmise about what it has to do with archery. After all these many preliminaries, let us now finally open the diaries, altogether at random and not trying to look for arresting passages, since the special character of this extensive body of comments will reveal itself quickly.

"21 August 1952. There is wafting toward me now that area where Trix pursues her activity: the staircase by the river. It is a well-nigh tender feeling. The charm of the surroundings is very modest here, hemmed in by factory buildings and yet so touchingly delicate, like the patches of grass and stalks here and there among the factories. The blue from the other bank, which we can look over to and into, appears heightened and more attractive, framed as it is like this, than it ever could in the spinach-green sublimity of 'nature' surging freely onward."

"Genuine straightforwardness—which is practically my sole concern these days—begins right at the point of apperceiving the immediate surroundings, which causes their outlines to sharpen."

"Döbling, Scheibengasse, where I once lived and where I wrote 'The Case of Gütersloh' . . . It was a new thing for me to be living near all the greenery, among hills and gardens; my walks were delightful: I discovered things. I was still writing for newspapers in those days. That's totally foreign to me today . . . It makes no sense in itself to pursue besides literature activities engaged in by official experts—in medicine, in jurisprudence, and so on; intellectual action and production are only worth discussing, are only possible, as far as I'm concerned, as autobiographical heurisms."

"Sunday, 24 August. Here and now: one of innumerable situations. One need not simply descend into the depth of the moment; one can relativize the moment too. At an air base near Wiesbaden I even sat one time and wrote in an officers' lounge occupied by morons.

"Edge of the woods near Ober-Sievering, a deer; how did that come about? What I mean is: the years, life: admittedly for the most part with nonsense. I will never understand how I was able to produce extensive, complicated, and successful works; the broken vessel I am makes the full-blown plant incomprehensible."

"Sunday, 7 September. Today the lower sky remains enmeshed near the ground everywhere, the greenery shrouded in cotton fog. We have to proceed along even bleak stretches with a strong heart; it would go against nature and in the long run be downright horrible if life consisted of nothing but gardens and sugar-sweet arbors. A man's loneliness is part of his dignity, after all—whether he likes it or not, it keeps him together. Later on he'll freely choose it, take a step back, gain some distance, whereupon he can recognize the beauty of a world that up to then had been for the most part merely the saloon for his binges."

"Wednesday, 17 September, Berlin. Flowers of all colors, my sister's face, behind it all the shallow bowl of green nature: the forest. The silence around Leonhard. The secret of these moments here, in my hotel room on the 'Ku'damm,' as the Berliners say, is none other than this. They are Leonhard's moments of silence in the forest."

"Wednesday, 1 October. Up to a point, it's possible to make one's previous life transparent such that it rests underneath one like a lymphatic fluid containing no solid object: instead, everything appears dissolved, completely diaphanous . . ."

"Wednesday, 8 October. *A Writer's Interim Measures.* The interim nature of a writer's life in every area corresponds to his way of treating language, which avoids any establishment of a position in advance of its verification through the grammar that is added on and makes its appearance. And so he does not create order such that as it comes along it can all the more easily create a space for itself; and so he does not light the way toward any goal for Eros, who demands a free and open trajectory for his arrow, which goes whizzing whenever the god may please. Faced with grammar, then uncertain at the very least, if not mute (grammar as a new source of skepticism!); faced with order, then elastic, if not altogether chaotic; faced with the emergence of love, however, then at least neutral, if not quite impotent.

"The opposite of all this could be called 'The Premature Crystals'; but that's not what they are after all; they only grind in the gears of life but soon turn to mush, because inside they are as soft as filled bonbons—filled with the pseudo-logical, to be specific. To remain provisional or interim in anything and everything, however, means to preserve one's conductivity: for grammar, for eros, for order."

"Tuesday, 28 October. Today it appears to me as if I had never touched my actual and essential past—my very own *locus intactus*—and what I know and have awareness of, nothing but meaningless light gravel. Yet this deeper and more solid aspect is there for me; I can have it; I can excavate it and gain it for my own."

"Wednesday, 29 October. I really ought to thread my way through a new kind of diary—in purple!—designed to create a keel and counterweight for these notes, as it were: in it, what is misshapen could roll along in shape-giving fashion the same way cloud masses roll against each other, blending and separating; the least and the lowest we have and are—just now the area around the Votive Church in Vienna flashed out and blinded us briefly—the belly of life, the abyss of uncertainty above which we are hovering: purged of any order, entirely alien to it and in that very way pointing toward the true connections and tie lines—thus revealing genuine and effective order.

"To keep such a journal would mean starting a new life.

"To keep such a journal would itself *be* a new life. It sends up clouds, like incense, animating and starting everything anew."

"Sunday, 30 November. If we look into our interior, it's like a pond roiled by stones of word-thinking that are constantly being thrown into it . . . One has to wait for a long time, looking for a long time past the surface, now at last placid, toward the bottom, until something finally moves once more and comes swimming our way in the purified water—little silver fish, I salute you!—but my eye is already catching sight of some deeper movement, all the way at the bottom: yes, it is a crab creeping slowly along; and who knows, who knows what all there still is in store for you to see . . . We caused a disturbance. Now we will not move any more: . . . Coldness and matter-of-factness, stand ever by our side! Let us keep our sights on the matter-of-fact chaos and not be dazzled by the reflections of the trembling surface, where our words and phrases were dancing like inebriated corks . . ."

"All of this means . . . being jostled by stimuli, faces, images, most of it against a smoky-dark, twilit backdrop akin to those pages that saw the origin of the *Steps* in the *'cahier rouge'* (Mont de Marsan). A layer still close to the surface, still quite turbulent. School desks come through. Educational pictures on the wall . . . And there the nursery is too. Children's sexuality. The warm, expansively aromatic realm of mama's boudoir, the fireplace . . . Everyone has this and other things like it: it needs to be relativized and yet considered important: but having this is a basic fact; it determines our reactions. A considerable part of what we believe to be our own life is only imagined, however."

I now follow these longer passages with a few excerpted sentences that are characteristic of the whole:

"Clean, paper-like smell in the middle small drawing room, Stammgasse. Deeper into it now, and everything can dissolve."

"Only a totally chaotisized way of seeing can function as the antidote against a deperceptive order as the mask of chaos."

"My uncertainty has increased shockingly. I will as a result grow more capable of experiencing things."

"Disintegration and inundation: whoever avoids these no longer has a chance for unpredetermined apperceptions as a means of reaching his full powers."

"In art, it actually comes down to so little: finding hollow spaces too dimly lit, unknown halls and rooms in the midst of the laborious picking and shoveling of life's mine shafts."

" . . . go at it haphazardly; apperceptivity can never be anything but *not* prearranged; otherwise we don't get hold of it! Overall, then—we can only ever grasp it under chaotic circumstances: this alone is genuine, is firm."

We have heard enough to understand by now—insofar as one can understand such exercises in self-examination simply by gaining familiarity with certain concepts from their full surroundings. What's true of asceticism in any form is that those best understand it who practice its discipline. These exercises, this unrelenting scrutiny of one's own self, this recording of progress, this constant setting of new goals—all extending over a thousand pages of the two-volume *Commentarii*. Practice means repetition, and so the notations in the *Commentarii* are accordingly full of repetitions, modified only by the particular situation of the given day. And these exercises are the humus, the loose, porous earth, filled with nutrients, in which the novel has its roots.

The English playwright Michael Frayn wrote an exceptionally brilliant comedy that takes place in a theater. In the first act we see the stage set of a drawing-room comedy in which this very drawing-room comedy is being rehearsed. In the last act, during the premiere of the play, we see the reverse side of the stage set onto which the actors make their entrances and from which they exit. The *Commentarii* are connected to *The Demons* in a similar way, divided by the thin wall of a stage set into the actual stage and the dark stage house, while the characters and objects—and these are by no means lifeless in Doderer's work—oscillate back and forth through this cell wall. It is almost as if the novels were merely exemplifications of the state arrived at through the exercises—not as far as the degree of their perfection is concerned, but in consideration of the significance accorded to the diaries.

What exact term should one give to this discipline, however, which aims—remaining with his own terminology—to make the writer Doderer into a "non-writer"? Now at long last we have arrived at the bow and arrows, those children's playthings for reenacting Winnetou and Homer in his summers at the Riegelhof. But on the bow Gaby Murad (Licea from *The Demons*) gave him as a gift there stood the motto, this *"hic et nunc semper paratus,"* which reminds one, to begin with, of the "Be Prepared" motto of the Boy Scouts—all the more on a bow, at that—but which can also point in a different direction from Boy Scouts and Latin culture, toward the Far East, that is. It is established for certain that Doderer, at least as of the 1950s, had studied the Japanese work *Zen in the Art of Archery*, as a popular booklet by the Japanologist Eugen Herrigel is titled. In his case, literature about Zen fell onto unusually well prepared ground. Without knowing it, he had long been on the road to Zen mastery; here, even more than in the case of his spiritual kinship with Marcel Proust, we can assume an intuitive resonance and empathetic identification with a temper of those times that brought initial concepts of Zen philosophy, primarily to Europe and North America, through Daisetz Suzuki. Doderer was a Zen disciple *qua* temperament and *qua* artistic experience before becoming one according to the rules of this inexhaustible art, even though archery as such never had for him more than the status of a posture.

This is not the place for even the most vaguely adequate portrayal of Zen philosophy. Different from the scholasticism of Indian Buddhism and its immense cosmological philosophy, Zen seeks reciprocity between appearance and emptiness in the paradoxical nature of reality and the shimmering fullness of existence. Zen is above all a practice: of how to attain to a purely intuitive, non-logical understanding of the world through highly rigorous and patient exercise; of how to achieve an intuitive grasp of the nature of the world through extinction of the ego, to reach the point, put in Platonic terms, of hearing the music of the spheres as they rub against one another and at the same time having agency in producing it. Concepts place themselves between an object and the perception of it like a folding screen; the emptiness of soul being striven for makes it possible in turn to approach the matter at hand with no concepts. Wilhelm Gundert, who in Doderer's lifetime published his acclaimed translation of *Master Yüan-wu's Transcript of the Emerald Rock Face*, that founding text of Japanese and Chinese Zen, speaks of the "stringent severity with which the Zen movement always vigilantly holds its own speech in check, wary of exactly the loftiest and most sacred words and constantly concerned that only the thing itself find the human spirit free of and uncomplicated by words and concepts."

"To be at home in the cabin of empty stillness"—this Zen maxim could also be found word for word in the *Commentarii* and is indeed frequently found in similar but varied formulations there. Emptiness is not the goal for Zen, as it is in certain schools of Indian Buddhism; instead, it is the vacuum into which the world with its unending phenomena can come "streaming in"—"enabling that streaming in" is also among Doderer's favorite terms. Zen philosophy, not being doctrinaire, is not disconnected from our own cultural heritage by anything like an insuperable barrier: when John the Baptist says, "He must increase, but I must decrease," he proves himself a prime Zen master *avant la lettre*, and Jesus's words about the grain of wheat that must die so as to bear fruit and about how he who loves his life must lose it for that very reason would have been hailed by the Chinese masters of the Tang Dynasty with all the ceremonially prescribed gestures of agreement.

Anyone who reads Herrigel's *Zen in the Art of Archery*, a short work we are certain Doderer knew, sees his exercises in the *Commentarii* finding their place effortlessly, almost as if drifting there on their own, in the center of this spiritual discipline. Shooting without taking aim because of confidence that the arrow and the target seek one another out; the intentness with no purpose from out of which the shot drops away from the archer like ripe fruit; the idea of "mastery of artless art," the highest ideal of the master, who himself evolves into artless art and thus into being a "non-master": these randomly chosen concepts easily blend into Doderer's individual terminology and in fact inspired it to a degree, as in the case of the "non-writer," already cited, which is the formulation relevant to Doderer of the "non-mastery" just mentioned. One thing more than any other is confirmed in the *Commentarii*: Doderer understood that Zen is a practice and not a theory, not something to be grasped by concepts if one has not animated these concepts with the experience of one's own unflagging discipline. Hence the *Commentarii* are less a writer's diary than they are comparable to diaries of a religious practitioner, a mystic, and an ascetic; they are a document about exercising control over one's spirit.

Thus it now becomes understandable, too, why the abundance of blatant narrative gaffes in the novels and the unreasonable demands posed by their structures carry relatively little weight even for disinclined readers, who for that matter often never become really aware of them. We sense that the novel "has narrated itself," that the bowstring, to use the language of Herrigel's Zen masters, has not been consciously released but has cut through the archer's thumb with no involvement of his own will. In the great passages of *The Demons* we in fact encounter at one point, and again in the words of the Zen master, "that the id dances between the arrow and the target," as in the scene in which a homemaker—described in great detail, though she never makes another appearance in the novel—puts out a fire that started when she was canning preserves. In other places as well, ones that do not reach such narrative peaks, it remains evident that the author is allowing his material and its language to stream through him and that he is bearing with missed shots—only provided rigidity of the will was not the cause—so that the reader will bear with these missed shots too, for they do not testify to faulty treatment.

No picture of Doderer would be complete if it did not mention his fondness for the grotesque, which can be ascertained in Zen as well, surprisingly enough. In his novel *The Merovingians*, a satyr play that follows *The Demons*, certain excesses of violence, which up to then had been more or less tucked away in the narrow confines of short stories, reach a high point: it is therapeutic violence, to be sure, celebrated here with ribald glee. The *"Plauz"* or whack, that surprising blow with the flat hand on a bald scalp, tugging at beards, and every kind of oafish kick or slap are meant to explode self-importance, "old-age rage," high-handedness, and conceit. It's impossible not to think in this context of the painful punishments Zen masters would mete out with sudden, hard blows from a stick or a yak's tail to self-absorbed, ambitious, or know-it-all pupils so that the shock might derail them from the beaten track of the lives they were pursuing.

In the deepest part of himself, Doderer must have been enchanted by the intersection of utmost spiritual refinement and hard physical engagement. It would not do to forget that the man who was submitting to these disciplines of negating the will was one of the most original eccentrics of his time and was fairly bursting with aggressive intellectualism—had that not been so, there would of course have been no point to the exercises mentioned. It's also understandable, however, that the uniqueness of an art at the center of which this kind of purposeless quietness dwells will not be able to gain such quick recognition. Only when the political, philosophical, and aesthetic discussions of the nineteenth century, which have so vigorously shaped the literature of the twentieth century, are forgotten and have sunk into the dust of the archives will a body of work that had no part of them become fully visible.

LIST OF CHARACTERS

(Principal characters are starred)

Abheiter, *director of Pomberger & Graff, publishers and printers*

*Edouard Altschul, *a bank director*

*Rosi Altschul, *his wife*

Anita ("Piggy"), *a prostitute*

Professor Bullogg, *medievalist at Harvard University, son-in-law of Mme Libesny*

Peggy Bullogg, *his wife*

Lilly Catona, *schoolmate of Fella Storch*

*Countess Claire Charagiel, *daughter of Baron von Neudegg*

Cobler, *editor-in-chief at Alliance*

*Prince Alfons Croix

Mathias Csmarits, *disabled war veteran with one eye, brother of Frau Kapsreiter*

*Anna Diwald ("Didi"), *barmaid, underworld character*

Beppo Draxler, *a "troupiste"*

*Emma Drobil, *a beautiful stenographer*

Dulnik, *manager of a paper factory, suitor to Angelika Trapp*

Ederl, *painting contractor, gambler*

*Captain von Eulenfeld, *leader of "the Düsseldorfers," former hussar*

Fiedler, *a bookseller and classical scholar*

Malva Fiedler, *his daughter, friend of Leonhard Kakabsa*

Lea Fraunholzer, née Küffer, *daughter of Herr Küffer*

Freud, *owner of a brandy shop*

von Frigori, *a haughty baron*

Bill Frühwald, *pianist and "troupiste"*

Alois Gach, *commissioner of markets, former sergeant in Ruthmayr's regiment*

Garrique, *former wine dealer from Bordeaux, brother-in-law of Professor Bullogg*

Mme Daisy Garrique, *sister of Professor Bullogg*

Gaston Garrique, *the Garriques' son*

Lilian Garrique, *the Garriques' daughter*

Agnes Gebaur, *Jan Herzka's new secretary*

Geiduschck, *student at the Gymnasium, one of Mary K.'s admirers*

*Georg von Geyrenhoff, *the narrator, a retired civil servant*

Minna Glaser, *Irma Siebenschein's sister*

Glenzler ("Father"), *member of the editorial staff of Alliance*

Hedwig Glöckner, *head of a gymnastics school*

*Anny Gräven, *prostitute, friend of Leonhard Kakabsa*

Etelka Grauermann, *René Stangeler's deceased sister*

Pista Grauermann, *Etelka's ex-husband*

Frau Greilinger, *Dwight Williams's landlady*

Josef Grössing ("Pepi," "Croaky"), *a boy, Frau Kapsreiter's nephew*

Magdalena Güllich, *Jan Herzka's former girlfriend*

Gürtler, *a Viennese lawyer*

Anatol von Gürtzner-Gontard, *the Hofrat's son*

Doktor Franz von Gürtzner-Gontard, *the Hofrat's son*

*Hofrat von Gürtzner-Gontard, *Geyrenhoff's former superior*

Melanie von Gürtzner-Gontard, *the Hofrat's wife*

Pris von Gürtzner-Gontard, *wife of Franz*

Renata von Gürtzner-Gontard, *the Hofrat's daughter*

Imre von Gyurkicz, *newspaper cartoonist and painter, friend of Charlotte von Schlaggenberg ("Quapp")*

Jan Herzka, *head of Rolletschek's webbing company, heir to Neudegg Castle*

Hirschkron, *a bookbinder*

Holder, *editor at Alliance*

Robert Höpfner, *advertising executive*

Jirasek, *a tailor*

*Beatrix K. ("Trix"), *daughter of Mary K.*

Hubert K., *son of Mary K.*

*Mary K., *a widow who has lost a leg in a streetcar accident*

Anna Kakabsa, *Leonhard's sister, servant of Mme Libesny (in London)*

*Leonhard Kakabsa, *a young factory worker who educates himself*

Ludmilla Kakabsa ("Mila"), *Leonhard's sister, Friederike Ruthmayr's servant*

*Frau Anna Kapsreiter, *widowed sister of Mathias Csmarits, keeper of a dream-book*

Franziska Kienbauer, *secretary at Alliance, mistress of Editor-in-Chief Cobler*

Laura Konterhonz, *a mistress of Kajetan von Schlaggenberg*

Herr Köppel, *head bookkeeper for Jan Herzka*

Doktor Kurt Körger, *Geyrenhoff's nephew*

Doktor Philemon Krautwurst, *lawyer for Baron von Neudegg*

Krawouschtschek, *a carpenter*

Egon Kries, *Clarisse Markbreiter's son-in-law*

Lily Kries, *Clarisse Markbreiter's daughter*

Herr Küffer, *wealthy general manager of a Viennese brewery, a friend of the younger set*

Corporal Anton Lach, *bugler in Captain Ruthmayr's squadron*

Count Mucki Langingen, *hunter of antiques, friend of Prince Croix*

*Cornel Lasch, *brother-in-law of Grete Siebenschein, associate of Levielle*

Frau Titi Lasch, *sister of Grete Siebenschein*

Oskar Leucht ("Oki"), *a "troupiste"*

*Financial Counselor Levielle, *the villain*

Mme Libesny, *Professor Bullogg's mother-in-law, Dwight William's landlady in London*

Lilly Likarz, *an artist and a friend of Mary K.*

Doktor Mährischl, *a lawyer*

Frau Martha Mährischl, *his wife*

Rosi Malik, *poetess and popular playwright*

Clarisse Markbreiter, *sister of Irma Siebenschein*

Siegfried Markbreiter ("Purzel"), *her husband*

Frau Mayrinker, *later occupant of Frau Kapsreiter's apartment in the Blue Unicorn*

Herr Josef Mayrinker, *a banker and a student of dragon lore*

*Meisgeier ("the Claw"), *a murderer*

Mörbischer, *caretaker of Neudegg Castle*

*Hans Neuberg, *a student of history*

Baron Achaz von Neudegg, *father of Claire Charagiel*

Achaz Neudegker, *ancestor of Baron Achaz von Neudegg*

Oplatek, *a member of the Alliance directorate*

*Géza von Orkay (the "bird Turul"), *a Hungarian diplomat, cousin of Geyrenhoff*

*Alois Pinter ("Pinta"), *son-in-law of Franz Zdarsa, a pro-Hungarian conspirator*

Hertha Plankl, *a prostitute, friend of Anny Gräven*

Thomas Preschitz, *a socialist leader*

Ensign Preyda, *René Stangeler's wartime friend, killed in action in 1916*

Sylvia Priglinger, *a friend of Renata von Gürtzner-Gontard*

Protopapadakis ("Prokop"), *a gambler, Anny Gräven's friend Frau Thea Rosen, a fat female*

Pop Rottauscher, *a pickpocket*

Rucktäschl, *a typesetter*

Miss Rugley, *formerly Kajetan and Quapp's governess, now housekeeper for Kajetan's mother*

*Frau Friederike Ruthmayr ("Fritzi," "Friedl"), *an immensely wealthy widow*

Captain Georg Ruthmayr, *her late husband, killed in action in 1914*

Dr. Schedik, *Kajetan von Schlaggenberg's father-in-law*

Scheindler, *author of Leonhard's Latin grammar*

*Frau Camilla von Schlaggenberg ("Camy"), née Schedik, *Kajetan's estranged wife*

*Charlotte von Schlaggenberg ("Quapp," "Quappchen," "Lo," "Lotte"), *Kajetan's sister, an aspiring violinist*

*Kajetan von Schlaggenberg, *novelist*

Frau Schoschi, *owner of the Café Kaunitz*

Kyrill Scolander, *Kajetan's teacher*

Doktor Ferry Siebenschein, *a lawyer, Grete's father*

*Grete Siebenschein, *René Stangeler's girlfriend*

Irma Siebenschein, *Grete's mother*

Alexander Alexandrovich Slobedeff ("Sasha"), *a composer*

*René von Stangeler ("the Ensign"), *a brilliant young historian*

Frau Selma Steuermann, *Kajetan's ideal of womanhood*

Dolly Storch, *Professor Storch's daughter*

Felicitas Storch ("Fella"), *Trix's friend*

Käthe Storch, *Professor Storch's wife*

Professor Oskar Storch, *professor of anatomy*

Captain Szefcsik, *a pro-fascist Hungarian*

Raymond Szilagi, *driver of the Hungarian embassy car*

Szindrowitz, *director of Pomberger & Graff, publishers and printers*

Hofrat Tlopatsch ("Uncle Fritz"), *the "pope" of music in Vienna*

Angelika Trapp ("Angi"), *Neuberg's fiancée*

Doktor Trapp, *Angelika's father*

Doktor Trembloner, *a financial manager at Alliance*

Frau Tugendhat, *an employee at Alliance*

Ruodlieb von der Vläntsch, *author of a late medieval manuscript*

Waschler, *superintendent and doorman of Gürtzner-Gontard's apartment house*

Herr Weilguny, *an artist, competitor of Imre von Gyurkicz*

Frau Risa Weinmann, *former owner of the Café Kaunitz*

Fräulein Wiesinger, *Quapp's accompanist*

*Dwight Williams, *an American lepidopterist*

Frau Lea Wolf, *a fat female*

Xidakis ("Kaki"), *a gambler, Protopapadakis's friend*

Elly Zdarsa, *Pinter's sister-in-law*

Franz Zdarsa ("Old Goatbeard"), *a vineyard owner*

Nikolaus Zdarsa ("Niki"), *a friend of Leonhard Kakabsa*

Sergeant Karl Zeitler, *a policeman and local historian*

Karl Zilcher, *a friend of Leonhard Kakabsa*

Zurek, *Pop Rottauscher's helper*

OVERTURE

FOR A GOOD long while now I have been living in what used to be Schlaggenberg's room.

It is a garret room, but it would be wrong to think of it as a miserable little place. Oddly enough, during the latter part of the period he spent in Vienna and took to living out in our garden suburb, Schlaggenberg formed the habit of setting himself up in studios and proved to have a real knack for finding charming flats of this sort. The first time, as I recall, was when he came back here and started looking for suitable quarters for his teacher, Kyrill Scolander, who was shortly to arrive from southern France. The result was the first and perhaps the finest of "Schlaggenberg's studios," as we later called them. The studios represented, incidentally, Schlaggenberg's sole connection with painting, for as far as I could see, he never seemed to have any great understanding for that art, and concerned himself with it no more than he did with the theater. For Scolander, on the other hand—who had come to Vienna because he had been offered a professorship—the studio actually served the purpose for which it was intended, although as a painter he also had a workroom provided by the government. Yet if you read Schlaggenberg's biography of his teacher, which had just been published around that time, you were apt to form the false impression that Scolander was only incidentally a painter. For Schlaggenberg had devoted so much detailed consideration to Scolander's writings that the man's accomplishments in painting seemed by contrast to have been treated rather superficially. This, then, is the last of "Schlaggenberg's studios," the last one he occupied, so that I have more or less inherited it from him.

1

The room is smaller than the one which had been found for Scolander, but by way of compensation it seems to me that this smaller room has a more gracious and comfortable air.

Through the slanting windows you can see far out into the country. The double-glazed skylight admits a plunging cataract of brightness. In this room you are seated high up as though you were at an artillery observer's post, or in a lighthouse. You are seated high above the city and directly opposite the hills of the surrounding countryside, which bound your horizon in gentle waves. Below and to the right, everything is blurred and indefinite; behind nested cubicles of buildings, with here and there one picked out by a brilliant ray of sunlight, lies a motley and misty abyss where the plain stretches on toward Hungary. On the left the mountains end, drop off steeply, looking from their height out over the land.

Below me lies our garden suburb: roofs flat or gabled, now scattering and thinning out over the green countryside, now again clustering around the solidity of a Romanesque church whose broad towers frame the cumulous expanse of sky like two great gateposts.

Here, then, in these new streets stretched below my watching eye, with century-old ones right beside them, there befell a good part of those events of which I was often the witness and whose chronicler I have become—often taking the latter role almost coevally with the events. For I very soon resolved to set down my occasional sketches with greater exactitude, and to work up the notes I have been taking. I had already reached this point by the spring of the year 1927 (since I never like to leave the concrete details of a narrative hanging in the air, I am setting down the date right here and now).

Not long afterwards I had a chance encounter of an odd sort down there in town. I shall speak more of this encounter later.

These two events—the commencement of my work here and that unexpected meeting with Financial Counselor Levielle on the Graben—came so close together in time that, when I think of one of these events, the other invariably comes to mind as well.

I applied myself then to keeping my chronicle. It cannot be said that I lacked for time. I had recently taken my leave of the civil service, in which I had risen to the rank of Section Councilor. Since the obvious question is going to be raised— why did I abandon my career while still fairly young, contenting myself with a relatively low step of the ladder when I had every prospect of climbing higher?—I shall explain frankly by saying that in the Republic that emerged from the war the life and work of a civil servant seemed to me to have lost much of its *raison d'etre*, whereas in the old Empire, an Austrian government official was in many cases performing a real function. Moreover, during the year 1926 my financial situation had changed fundamentally. This change was connected with the release of the securities and bank accounts of Austrian citizens which during the war had been confiscated—or as it was called, "sequestrated"—in England. I had had shares in certain Pennsylvania steel companies deposited in England. By the Act of Sequestration of 1914 these shares were converted into British war bonds. These shares had been part of my inheritance from my father, and had not amounted to a very significant part of the whole. But now that they were restored to me, after a drawn-out and complicated process and with large exchange losses due to the way it had all been handled, this fragment of my inheritance proved to be very important indeed. For all the rest had vanished with the disintegration of the old currencies.

As things were, I preferred not to stay on in a post which offered little in the way of meaningful work and contribution to society, and merely provided a dull livelihood, for I was beginning to feel in an increasingly oppressive fashion that this livelihood was won at the expense of my toiling fellow-citizens. I would rather have had no part in the privileges enjoyed by a class of people who throughout the worst years had received small but on the whole unvarying and secure salaries, and had thus come through the miseries of those years better than people far more capable than themselves. I would be retiring on a modest pension.

Accordingly, I no longer lacked for time, and I was, moreover, free of what are usually termed "cares." In addition I was a bachelor. For want of cares I created some for myself, as do all people. Only these new cares were of a lighter, I might almost say of a trifling sort, at least in the beginning.

My occupation was nothing more nor less than to keep a diary for a whole group of persons, principally those whom I shall later refer to as "our crowd." It was, however, not only the diary of a collective entity—as a ship's log might be, or the account of an expedition among savage tribes. Rather, I conscientiously performed my task for each individual of the group and kept my eye on him constantly. For that reason many of my reports were written up immediately after the events, and even thus early Schlaggenberg was in the habit of twitting me—for he soon found out about my scribblings—by adding the adjective "novelistic" to the word "reports": "Your novelistic reports, Herr Geyrenhoff." But pretty soon I enlisted him as a collaborator. I did the same with René von Stangeler, whom we called "the Ensign" (during the war he had held that rank in the Dragoons). These two were, after all, writing professionally at the time. I commissioned whole sections of the work from them, and even paid them in the beginning— later Schlaggenberg did it gratis, simply out of pleasure in the thing itself. Not content with that, I would discuss my plans and show my work to, for example, a woman like Frau Selma Steuermann, who was amused by the business and who likewise aided me by giving me accurate descriptions of incidents I could never have witnessed in person. These, too, I was able to put into my record. The good Selma actually spied for me, especially in those circles of hers to which I could not have gained entry, certainly not on any familiar footing. Then, too, there were some persons who collaborated unwittingly in that I sounded them out—for example, Fräulein Grete Siebenschein. But that, of course, is nothing special, being one of the well-known practices of even professional writers.

I had still other collaborators—Frau Friederike Ruthmayr and Herr von Eulenfeld must not be forgotten—but I shall not extend the list of my acknowledgments. Indeed, Schlaggenberg once had the temerity to ask me whether I was not intending to engage Herr Levielle while I was about it! In spite of this diligent research—Schlaggenberg called it "gossip-mongering"—and the innumerable stories people told me upon learning of what I was doing—I remained partially or completely ignorant of many matters as events proceeded, sometimes of crucial matters. So that now—after it is all over and I am sitting here in Schlaggenberg's "last studio" preparing to summarize and revise the whole story—I would feel fraudulent were I to attempt to represent myself as less stupid and ignorant than I actually was, at least in those segments which I relate as an eye-witness and in which, therefore, I myself appear. For we are all of us stupid and ignorant in the face of life as it unrolls before us; we have no way of recognizing the prolongation or line of flight of any given set of circumstances. Although I myself was never actually involved in the events (that would have been the last straw), I was still obliged to depict myself in a corner here or there, so to speak, as many an old master used to do, since the chronicler is inescapably part of the whole. His facial expression, however, must not be painted as more knowing than it was at the time in question.

Today, of course, "Knowing the whole story," I have all the proverbial benefits of hindsight.

And yet—in fact you need only draw a single thread at any point you choose out of the fabric of life and the run will make a pathway across the whole, and down that wider pathway each of the other threads will become successively visible, one by one. For the whole is contained in the smallest segment of anyone's life-story; indeed, we may even say that it is contained in every single moment; start up your dredging machine and you take it all up, no matter whether ecstasy, despair, boredom, or triumph happens to fill the moving buckets on their endless chain of ticking seconds.

I had another example of this recently, up in town, after I had left my spacious, quiet room here. Before leaving I cast one more look through my slanting garret windows, a look of utter astonishment at the white-hot reflection of the sunset, though on clear days it is caught every evening by the glassed-in verandas of the hotel up on the Kahlenberg and lingers long there—it looks like a conflagration, especially later when the glow has turned crimson. Three quarters of an hour later I was walking down the crowded Graben, and as I turned the well-known corner opposite the so-called "Stock im Eisen," where the tower of St. Stephan's seems to advance suddenly toward you in a single giant step, my memory was jolted back twenty-eight years, to the very time I had really begun writing up this chronicle.

At this very spot Financial Counselor Levielle had run into me. That was in the early spring of 1927.

As though it were only yesterday: the evening tinged the sky behind the tower with a greenish glow and the first bright spheres from street lamps and store fronts bloomed forth into the failing daylight. A hat was doffed and waved in a wide slow arc and I stopped, not because I had already recognized the white head, the little white brush of mustache, but because the fact of his greeting had broken my train of thought. As a consequence, both of us lost the impetus of motion which ordinarily carried us past each other with a formal exchange of salutations, and we found ourselves standing side by side. However, after a moment I did not mind, saw the opportunity for a conversation, and even accompanied the old fellow back across the Graben, past the imposing Plague Memorial and even farther.

"As you know, retired men develop a taste for long walks," I said after we had completed the usual polite mutual inquiries as to our health. It turned out, however, that he already knew I was no longer in government service. And the manner in which he now commented on my premature retirement, from two different points of view, as we shall see in a moment—this manner led me to think that Herr Levielle could not possibly possess the remarkable gifts for dissimulation sometimes attributed to him. Either that, or else he did not think it worthwhile exercising them on me. "Why, Herr Geyrenhoff," he said. "You were certainly well on your way to the rank of Ministerial Councilor, weren't you?" His tone, however, was not one of regret for me, not concern for my own sake; rather, it seemed to me that Levielle was actually annoyed, as though by bidding good-bye to a career in government I had put him in an awkward position or in some way deprived him of a possible advantage.

"Recently I had occasion to call at your Ministry in my professional capacity—a matter of an import license—and heard an authoritative higher source express the most emphatic

7

regret concerning the step you have taken; in fact the source in question did not hesitate to declare that you were one of the most promising officials in your category—one of those with the highest prospects, he said."

Levielle might equally well have added: "What kind of conduct do you call this? Where would it end if everyone I knew in government service went ahead and retired on a pension? You really might have borne up until they made you a Ministerial Councilor, my dear sir." For everything he actually said aloud was spoken so entirely without reference to his audience that it sounded almost like a disgruntled monologue with himself. His tone became even a bit contemptuous, but that did not last long either, for now the second point of view emerged. "*Du reste—c'est étonnant,*" Levielle said (for he was Parisian, after all, or at least half-Parisian), "*mais passons.* The funds you regained about a year ago are still a considerable sum, under present conditions (he mentioned the exact figure), and might have been a good deal more if it were not for the stupid way in which the Austrian Board of Trade has been handling these cases, or to put it in other terms, if it were not for the extraordinarily high deductions for exchange. For every single pound you lost . . . and thus . . ." (here again he gave exact figures).

"You are amazingly well informed, Herr Levielle," I said, though without any trace of annoyance.

"Well, you see, since I hold an honorary post in the Board of Trade itself—although I would not have you think that I owe the title which is generally prefixed to my name to this petty little office, but rather to the somewhat more important position I occupy in Paris—since, as I was saying, I am more or less at home in the Board of Trade, as we all tend to be in the places to which we are called or chosen, my acquaintance with your case should not surprise you. But what does surprise me, for my part, is how you could have accepted such a loss without making an attempt to defend yourself while there was still time."

"I did not know that any defense was possible," I said.

"It almost always is in such cases."

"What could I have done?" I asked.

"You should have applied to me," he said. "While there was still time, of course. I had occasion to arrange a very similar affair, except that enormously greater sums were involved. In the nature of things we had to take some losses also, but they were virtually insignificant compared to yours. Well, at any rate, you now have considerable means at your disposal, and it is up to you to do something with them, all the more so since you no longer have to waste your time sitting around the office. Have you already made plans?"

I was beginning to grow angry at this insolence, and brought out the words: "I am sorry I did not apply to you for assistance in time, Herr Levielle," with some effort. As for his last question, I simply made no reply to it. Moreover, I knew precisely what "enormously greater sums" he was referring to.

As we spoke, I suddenly turned my head, in a movement almost alarmed, toward a young woman who had just passed us.

"Someone you know?" Levielle asked.

"No," I said. "Though just for a moment it seemed so . . . It's odd, too."

"What is odd, Herr von Geyrenhoff?"

"I beg your pardon," I said (continuing on the candid note which he had set), "you were speaking a moment ago of a large fortune that had been confiscated in England and was recently released, and were saying that you succeeded in arranging the affair favorably . . ."

"Yes, and?"

"Well, it is easy enough to guess whose fortune it was since as far back as 1914 you were appointed executor of Captain Ruthmayr's will. He had a tremendous sum in securities over in England. The poor fellow told me so himself one day shortly before the outbreak of the war. So it was Ruthmayr you were referring to, was it not?"

"Very well, I was speaking of Ruthmayr—although I have managed and am still managing other affairs of this type. But what has that to do with the lady who just passed and whom you thought you recognized?"

"Oh, for a moment I thought it was Charlotte von Schlaggenberg, the sister of my old friend Kajetan von Schlaggenberg . . ."

"What? What's that you say?"

He actually screamed at me. For a moment his face came close to mine; it was deeply flushed, and ever since that moment it has been clear to me that Levielle came of extremely low birth. In point of fact he had a very common look—as soon as the careful folds of his "à la English lord" countenance became disarranged.

"But what has that little creature. Quack or Quapp or whatever she is called, to do with all this?" he demanded almost harshly.

"You see, Herr Levielle," I said, "it is well known that there are strange resemblances between persons who are far apart in life. In fact, such persons need not even live in the same epoch and yet we feel as though their faces are, so to speak, formed on the same model, or taken by the Creator out of the same box, if I may use such a metaphor. Or as though in such faces the same fundamental idea were being expressed—a fundamental physiognomical idea, so to speak. For me one such pair is represented by Fräulein von Schlaggenberg and the late Cavalry

Captain Ruthmayr, who never knew each other. A few weeks ago this resemblance came to me, quite by chance, one Sunday morning while I was still almost half asleep. People often think of the strangest things between sleep and waking, and sometimes such thoughts strike at an essential truth. Since then I have been aware of this strange resemblance. Incidentally, the resemblance is not always there; it fluctuates. At times Fräulein von Schlaggenberg looks more like the late captain, at times less, and sometimes not at all."

"Upon my word, I have never noticed the slightest resemblance," Levielle said. He was now walking along beside me, puffed up like an irate turkey. It was plain that I must have annoyed him, highly annoyed him, but the reason escaped me.

"Incidentally, we will soon be running into her, our friend Quapp," I said. "For I have often observed this: we see a person on the street who resembles an acquaintance; then after a while someone comes along whom we really might take for the person in question, at least at a distance of a few steps—and then, sure enough, two streets farther on the person himself comes walking along, so that we are strongly tempted to greet him with: "Well, so there you are at last; I have been expecting you for some time . . . There she is!"

Levielle started in alarm; there was no mistaking it. "No, it isn't she after all," I said.

He was obviously nervous and affronted, but he said jocularly: "Well now, you certainly have taken on some strange fancies, now that you're a retired man. Incidentally, since when has the little girl been back in Vienna?"

"She came shortly after the New Year."

"And is sharing a room with her brother again?"

"No," I said somewhat touchily.

"Oh well, time was when. *Mais laissons cela.*"

We had meanwhile, since we had been walking all this time, arrived at the quarter where the monumental buildings of the banks are situated. I had accompanied Levielle a good way. Darkness had already settled, and the streets were aglitter with lights. The pavement glistened damply. At the side entrance to a large building Levielle stopped.

"Business so late?" I said.

A hat doffed and waved in a wide slow arc, the white head beneath it, the little white brush of the mustache—through the glass pane I saw a gold-braided doorkeeper approach across the dusky expanse of the deserted bank and open the two wings of a glass door that closed a stairwell in which all the main lights seemed already to have been switched off; for the bank's regular working day had long since ended.

There is no doubt about it, you have only to draw a single thread at any point you choose out of the fabric of life and the run makes a pathway across the whole; the past masses like clouds to the right and left of your head, as it were, and the sharp and sweet tooth of memory sinks to the heart's core. Out of that past there floats toward you, as though composed of mists, all that combines to form the truth; things we were scarcely aware of now join themselves together, one related image to another. They form a bridge across time, although in life they may never have touched, may have existed in different years, at different places, so that between them no really traversable pathway of circumstances is visible. So it is that I now know that the girl with dull gold hair who came sweeping down toward us on skis in the snow-blanketed woods under the Kahlenberg, the girl who cut across our track, was the same girl who later lived for several strange days in the Blue Unicorn;

for she herself described to me with great precision her stay there; and once more there arises, though only for a moment, the image of that wretched Didi who was barmaid in Freud's taproom (in this case not far in spatial terms from the Blue Unicorn) and thought it such a great joke when the gentlemen of the Alliance newspaper house came to the place "to study the criminal world" (for a *reportage*, as it is commonly called).

But to return to what I was saying about golden-haired Renata, there are dreams which are valid in life also, which are really no longer dreams but rather insights; insights which appear, timidly and yet with a curiously compelling power, with a pallid and simultaneously vital presence, behind the well-ordered facts and brightly shining certainties; insights which swim to and fro like the iris under the closed eyelid; insights which seem only an ineluctable riddle—but we always understand what is intended, even against our wish. Similarly, when we stand in an attractive sweets shop and suddenly see a child's face with the little nose pressed flat against the windowpane outside—then the appeal to our deepest, our innermost knowledge cannot come any closer, cannot speak more plainly.

In cases such as these no verification is required. We do not ask, we make no inquiries. I have never asked Renata, with whom I became acquainted much, much later, whether she was the same person we had seen in the spring of 1927 on the ridge of the hill where "our crowd" was about to start on an outing. She had been right beside Schlaggenberg, so that each of us as we trudged up the slope thought she belonged to him, that he had brought her along (Kajetan was expecting us up there at the top). But that was only chance and an illusion of distance; she was on the point of passing him, and was not actually standing beside Schlaggenberg but a good two paces behind him. And now she went on down along the path our company was climbing, and shot right between us, splitting us into two groups, as it were . . .

The future was to prove the justness of Renata's (for to me the girl on skis was and always will be Renata) dividing us in this way on our outing, cleaving for passing moments a random collection of people who in truth did not belong together and who nevertheless had been thrown together by the imperious will of life.

But now and then I imagine that I can still see her; I think I recognize Renata again in many a floating and shifting shape that settles briefly upon the wall of glass which separates us from the past and permits the illusion of sheer presentness; only with the passage of time the forms are pressed somewhat flat against the wall, like the child's nose I spoke of a while back.

Here, however, we must pause over a point which disproves the chronicler's statement that he himself was never really involved in the events. For in one of them he certainly was, clandestinely though that may have been. And the sharp and sweet tooth of memory now nips the sore spot.

That sore spot became apparent the evening of the grand reception at the Palais Ruthmayr, when Schlaggenberg and I mounted the broad staircase that led from the vestibule with its blazing chandelier up to the landing where Frau Ruthmayr was receiving her guests (Henry Levielle stood to her left, slightly behind her). Kajetan later said that as soon as he caught sight of Frau Ruthmayr he felt the desire to sink down onto the carpet before her and—this was how he put it—to lay all of his previous life in her lap, and confide it to her. As he kissed her hand he held it somewhat longer than is customary, so that I, who was next in line, felt as though I had been waiting a considerable time. While I waited I did not look in Levielle's direction. That certain thread which, I am always saying, need only be drawn out of the fabric of life for the whole pathway to become clear—the pathway was already only too visible, and was, alas, starting to resemble a run in a stocking.

I have just caught myself up and realize why at this point I should happen to think of a stocking.

During Schlaggenberg's somewhat prolonged *Handkuss* I looked down at Frau Ruthmayr's feet, instead of glancing at Levielle; at two small, firm, infinitely charming feet with exquisite insteps and exquisitely turned ankles, below the shaft of a strong leg that seemed rather more suitable to Friederike's statuesque appearance than these innocent extremities left over from girlhood.

And in the final analysis real life stands upon very frail feet, and its ultimate supports—if we sweep away all the alleged and accumulated rubble that has floated up around—its taproots which it sinks deeply into the soil of a reality incomprehensible to us in its details, would bear odd and almost absurdly simple names, if we wanted to and could honestly specify what they are—certain names by no means high-toned or solemn: the afterimage of a color in the dark inner eyelid; the smell of a freshly varnished play table in our old nursery; the run in a stocking stretched over the delicate shaping of an ankle.

But at this point another picture presses against the invisible glass wall which separates us from the past and behind which the pictures appear, many of them overlapping, mingling, and interpenetrating one another. Thus, back of the dazzling vestibule of the Palais Ruthmayr, now quivering with a wavelike motion, another scene begins to coalesce, and it is as though the taut bow of the years were quivering as well, as though today were about to collapse in a heap upon yesterday. Thus,

15

a red light appears behind the shifting waves of guests in Frau Friederike's lovely home, a light glowing dim and red and solitary far beyond the house but gradually filtering through the bright rooms and the variegated company. The glass wall fogs over with a cold and smoky mist, and I recognize the gigantic concourse of the railroad station and know that this light belongs to a signal mast, that it hangs outside, low against the nocturnal sky, where the tracks begin their long march, and that it is shining through the high gray arch, pointing out into the distance. Beside it others appear, farther away and feebler, but near also, white and blue, a long file of silent configurations. But the concourse is full of noise, full of mounds of lethargic suitcases which must reluctantly share the haste of hurrying people, are willy-nilly pushed forward on the carts with shouts of "Watch out," so that you jump aside, for the suitcases must go along with travelers; it is time; the hands of the big clock jerk forward. And once again only a small and insignificant link is needed to connect me vividly with that winter evening at the railroad station. The link is just a strand of blond hair on the temple of Frau Camy von Schlaggenberg, Kajetan's wife, and the way in which her little traveling hat presses into her forehead, with her eyes peering out from under the brim, a little haughtily and yet somehow not altogether in psychological equilibrium.

She stands on the step of the car, small and slender, and holds out a well-gloved hand to me, which strangely enough figures in my recollection as something exceedingly dry.

Such are the trivialities that everyone carries about with him, and yet they alone—I avow it!—contain all the grandeur of life, though still in a formless and nameless state. Such are the possessions of many a solitary man, and when he has extricated himself from the city down there and comes back to his still,

16

empty room which, left so long alone, seems to have stretched itself, enlarged itself—then his property comes closer to him, but in a manner no different from that of the child outside the glass pane. Often, after switching on the light, a man will stand for moments at the window—"lost in thought," as we are in the habit of saying (but in reality he is thinking about nothing at all). Whether the view is sweeping or confined, the lights that appear at the window every evening are always the same, making silent configurations, dim or sharp, or in glowing file. It is everyone's earthly firmament, filled with the sick stars of this world which blink and twitch just like the stars in the sky, different for thousands of lonely pairs of eyes peering from thousands of windows, and certainly perfectly congruent to each of these beholders. Anyone who steps up to his window steps under his own particular constellation; and surely these distant glimmering oracles from the darkness could be interpreted, if only we knew how. There I have the lights of the highway which winds between the hills: they are the "Constellation of the Staff." Outshining this are several closer stars of the first magnitude. Beyond, to the right, almost below the horizon, is a dense stellar cluster. Right opposite, where by day a large building with a tower may be seen, is my "Cassiopeia," with her "W" formation of lights.

Terrible things took place in my native land and in this, my native city, at a time long after the grave and lighthearted stories I wish to relate here had come to an end. And one thing that lay curled amorphous and germinal within the events that I must recount, emerged dripping blood, took on a name, became visible to the eye which had been almost blinded by the vortex of events, shot forth, and was, even in its beginnings, recognizable—gruesomely inconspicuous and yet distinctly recognizable for what it was.

For, yes, by night or by day you can see far out through the slanting windows of this attic room. You are seated high up, as if you were at an artillery observer's post, or in a lighthouse. You are seated high above the city.

But for me there rises, beyond the horizon of a narrow life too fettered to the ever-recurrent same things, troubles, questions—for me there rises beyond the foreground of this mass of trash and secondhand goods and beyond the immediate view of roofs and gardens, a great way beyond the massive towers of the Romanesque church which already lay claim upon the empty sky, seizing it for themselves as their appropriate background—far, far away, over a landscape already iridescent and blurred by distance, beyond even the cathedral with its "finger pointing toward the sky"—no, rather against the farthest blue fringe of the heavens, I discern a gigantic hand. It is a human hand, immensely far away and yet sharply and distinctly delineated, its every curve revealed, its every vein plainly visible—a human hand the size of towers or hills against the blue, above the dwarfed towers of the church and the toy building-blocks of houses and gardens. And this hand points for me beyond the ridiculous boundaries of an individual life, and above all these husks and boundaries, points like the outstretched hand of a gigantic clock whose extension in space is like a shot and rolls like the boom of a cannon through all my chambers.

PART ONE

CHAPTER 1

On the Outskirts of the City

THE BROAD brook tumbles and leaps; curtains of water spill over the water-polished rocks. Mr. Williams and Fräulein Drobil sat right in the middle of the stream, but in perfect dryness, for they were on a kind of island formed of several great blocks of stone (you could lean back against these bolsters of rock as comfortably as against the back of an armchair) and enlarged by the washed sand which had been caught by the rocks. Williams had been residing in Vienna somewhat longer than Emma, who had arrived only six weeks before; but the city was still strange to them, although strange in a friendly manner; they reached out their hands for it as though it were an unknown dish that nevertheless aroused confidence and stimulated the appetite. The situation here was a good one for him, who had wandered here from Buffalo, U.S.A., and for her, who had come from Prague. Now these two distant cities met at one and the same point, at the brook in the so-called Halter Valley in the suburb of Vienna known as Hütteldorf. The water tumbled and purled endlessly toward them on a wide front, as though it were the incessantly passing and diminishing time of their life in which now, however, they were paradoxically resting. From here they could look far up the straight bed of the brook to where it made a turn at last and vanished amid the green vegetation.

Like a bar of cool metal, sharing the warmth of the day, the outstretched bed of the brook lay at the bottom of its gorge,

21

lay in profoundest peace for all its spirited movement. What Williams and Emma were talking about may be omitted here, for it was wholly without importance. Nevertheless, the lightest of small talk penetrates deeply enough into the person who is speaking it—if only because of the resonance in his own oral cavity—so that the words press down upon his actual state of being, compress the very ideas essential to that state underneath the speech itself, as it were—like a pillow which is being stuffed.

In reality the two biographies were present in leaping images underneath everything that was said.

As a boy in his parental home in Buffalo, U.S.A., Dwight had liked the cellar best. Along one wall, there were arrangements for storing wine bottles—cells in the concrete itself, like the cells of a beehive, for the individual bottles. These could be taken by the neck and drawn out slightly, examined, and replaced again within their nooks. When Dwight began attending the university, he invented a name for the wine cellar, calling it the "Assyrian library," for he liked to imagine that books written on cylinders of clay might have been stored in similar fashion. The various chambers of the cellar formed a well-arranged, well-ventilated, and well-illuminated system; there was even a kind of air-filtering device in one of them. In the root cellar were neat bins and barrels, from which rich odors of earth and apples rose. The preserves, for their part, stood on their shelves in colorful, jewel-bright rows. Dwight used to visit the cellars with his mother, armed with two baskets, for taking upstairs the things she had chosen. It was a duty he liked very much, and his mother came to depend upon his assistance. She would whistle across the garden, and Dwight would leave whatever game he might be at to go for his baskets.

That was the cellar. The whole house should have been just

like it. Something of the sort was attempted, but the orderliness and logic of the cellar could not be duplicated above stairs. The cellar was a collection. The acquisitions for and disappearances from the "Assyrian library" were always noted. When Dwight began to distinguish himself by a neat handwriting—it was the boy's first notable achievement—his father entrusted him with the task of keeping the cellar records.

The butterflies were another matter. It was not until he was at the university that Dwight discovered them, and not until he had been immersed in his subject, zoology, for two years. He could not trace his interest in them either to any special episode or to knowledge acquired in childhood. Back in those days, in fact, butterflies had on the whole been the very opposite of the cellar for him. He had barely noticed them as they flitted about the shrubs and flower beds of the garden in thoroughly disorganized fashion.

But there were butterfly books nevertheless, just as there had once been a book for registering the contents of a cellar. A man who studies a science is like a man in search of a bride. The whole of medicine or the whole of zoology or the whole of archaeology is rife with many and diverse objects of love, but the choice of field is not made until by and by out of the almost inscrutable roots of biography an emergent Eros fastens itself upon one such topic: carcinomas, lepidoptera, or brachiata. It is part of the thrill that ordinary people cannot even know what the whole topic is. Dwight himself could not say exactly when his own special Eros leaped to life inside him. He could only reason that it must have been either while he was leafing through an old book—Scudder's *The Butterflies of the Eastern United States* (three volumes)—or while he was looking at showcases of butterfly collections. At any rate, it became apparent to him that these fragile, flighty things out in the garden could also be put in order in just as fundamental a manner as the cellar. Three years later Dwight took his doctorate with a thesis on seasonal dimorphism. For us poor laymen, this refers to the rather amazing fact that a good many butterflies in spring, after they have crawled from the chrysalis, present quite another appearance from what they will have in summer, so much so that at one time they were thought to be different species.

The young entomologist found his way to Brazil in pursuit of his subject, and even to a certain high plateau in the jungle which was later made famous by a novel of Sir Arthur Conan Doyle's. But his life did not assume any personal shape until his prolonged stay in London, where he occupied rooms in the house of a certain Mme Libesny—not an Englishwoman, as we may conclude from her name. As it happened, Mme Libesny came from Vienna.

The brook runs unceasingly toward them on its broad front. Here and there the water drums in a low bass, with purling and plashing trebles above it. The woods stretch to the right and left, with their hosts of trees hanging over the brook; but the brook itself is so wide that it holds the woods apart and keeps open above itself a strip of sky which paints a primer coat of blue over the treetops, over the lower branches, over every last leaf. The brook has flowed through this forested valley for many hundreds, perhaps thousands of years. Valley and brook are old; the trees comparatively young. The earth's hair falls out and grows again. Above, on the right bank, runs the road. From time to time a kind of rushing pours down it when an automobile goes by.

Emma Drobil's father had been an editor in the Czechoslovak news agency. Formerly, in the days of the Austro-Hungarian Empire, he had worked for several years on the *Prager Tagblatt*. The biography of Emma, known among her friends as "La Drobile," was still somewhat scanty at this point when we take up with her—by the brook in the Halter Valley in the summer of 1926. For her preposterous age was only a little past twenty. Since she was competent to take stenography in English, Czech, and German with equal facility, could manage commercial correspondence, and moreover was an intelligent and even cultivated person (for example, her Latin was quite passable!), she had only to present her highly attractive person at a well-known shipping firm to be offered a good position—for I may as well say that in addition to all her other graces Fräulein Drobil was tall and straight-spined and bore her high bosom before her like a herald in the van of a procession. Her mama in Prague reconciled herself to her competent child's setting off for independence and foreign parts, for Emma had always had clearly in mind that someday she would be leaving for Vienna. Now she was living in Hadik Gasse in Hietzing; she had found quite a nice flat, tasteful and bright. Between mother and daughter many an affectionate letter was exchanged.

By the brook nothing had changed—not, as we have mentioned, for a very long time; there is scarcely anything more that can be said about it. Williams, however, was now thinking about Mme Libesny. While everything in his life hitherto had proceeded on a level plane—in a "cellar-like" manner, we might say—his biography was now taking on a new and third dimension, was developing from the realm of planimetry to that of stereometry—although still strictly according to Euclid. But for a person like Dwight Williams the matter had become complicated enough. For there are not only cellar books and butterfly books but psychology books as well. And Williams was now actually trying to make use of them. So far they had led to nothing, to no exit or escape from complications.

Mme Libesny lived in Battersea, not far from Albert Bridge

by the park, upon which the windows of her apartment looked. Dwight's room, too, looked out on the park. His room was well located, somewhat isolated from the rest of the flat. Mme Libesny occupied this flat alone; she was widowed or divorced, or something of the sort; she seemed a lady of some means and did not go to work. Once she mentioned her grown son. Here and there about the flat there were pictures of him: a handsome, dark-haired young man. Mme Libesny also had two married daughters in America, and still maintained a large number of connections with acquaintances in Vienna. Among these was a certain Frau Mary ("my friend Mary"). Dwight saw her picture. She struck him as very beautiful. His landlady mentioned that the lady had lost her right leg in a street accident about a month before. A frightful misfortune. This information caused Williams a brief, stabbing pain.

He was staying in London because of butterflies. Not that he wanted to catch butterflies there. Rather, Dwight had returned after a good many years to his first special paper on his subject, and to an English entomologist who owned private collections relevant to it. Dwight was working with him. The two had joined forces for an article that had been commissioned from them. The professor lived in Chelsea, on the other side of the Thames from Battersea. Dwight was fond of going there. He loved that part of the city with its small narrow houses and neat entrance stoops.

Now and then Mr. Williams took tea with Mme Libesny in her living room. Here too, as in all her rooms, the atmosphere seemed compounded of green and white and a certain glistening satiny pallor, although it would have been impossible to establish that this was so in every detail. Thus, for example, she had several dark Empire and Biedermeier pieces among her furniture. The maid who brought the tea was named Anna and also came from Vienna. Dwight did not know her surname; moreover, he could scarcely have pronounced it. Anna Kakabsa likewise maintained a correspondence and connections with her native city, where her mother still lived and where her sister Ludmilla was a servant in a distinguished home. She did not, however, correspond with her brother Leonhard, a workman in a webbing factory in Vienna. Her only news of him came from Ludmilla, who now and then wrote that he was well.

The greenish-white light in the flat might also have been accounted for by the expanse of sky above the tops of the trees in the park opposite. Against this background, a type of dimorphism revealed itself to Dwight's acute eyes; a dimorphism which, however, did not extend over whole seasons but could be experienced within the span of a day, even of a few hours (horadimorphism). It revealed itself: that was how Dwight thought of it, although as a scientist he was inclined at first to regard the phenomenon as entirely subjective—that is, as existing only in his own imagination; it seemed too singular to be accepted as a concrete fact of nature.

But whatever it was, it had power over him. When Mme Libesny addressed some words to her maid Anna, she looked entirely different from the woman who, a moment later, settled back again in the pale green upholstered armchair. Mme Libesny spoke with her maid in German, but it was a German that Dwight did not understand easily; it had an intonation and word order new to him. This was likewise true when Anna replied to her mistress. She did so in lengthy sentences and with numerous repetitions; but nevertheless Dwight could not follow her. When the girl was in the room, Mme Libesny's countenance narrowed and seemed to slope like a roof over the bridge of the nose and the middle axis of the face. Once the girl had left and Mme Libesny settled back in her chair, she momentarily resembled the picture of her friend Mary who had recently lost a leg. The photograph of Frau Mary had been taken in three-quarter profile; the face was soft, like a fruit that has been broken open, but it had nevertheless a fine, intelligent keenness running through it. The picture, incidentally, in its polished wood frame, stood on a small table next to a large bookcase filled with books. Every time Dwight paused by the bookcase and looked at the picture of Frau Mary, he had a recurrence of that same stabbing pain he had felt when he had first heard about the lady's accident . . .

But now what had just come up—even as he was talking with Emma Drobil—what had shot up like an old log which, trapped at the bottom of a pond, suddenly breaks free, so that it leaps a little above the surface in its upward rush? Something had broken free, had leapt to the surface, and in that moment the brook's confused babble of voices split, and suddenly Dwight heard nothing but a low, drumming bass and a single shrill, ringing treble above it.

In the arms of Mme Libesny he had sought Mary: the yielding was Mary, the broken-open fruit, the thrown-back head, the dark hair on the pillow. But even the keen sharpness came from Mary's photograph; its tooth bit sweetly; and many a time it had a dry, hot vehemence of which Mme Libesny was obviously aware. That and, moreover, an intensely responsive body—with, at the same time, full comprehension; she was a woman full of knowing subordination to her own state. Or something of the sort. Dwight could not have expressed it exactly. But while he and Emma Drobil spoke about light opera, his ear ceased to hear any but the shrillest trebles from the water. All the basses had stopped completely.

To be sure, Fräulein Drobil noticed nothing of this. And yet she had not been born yesterday; this, too, we must say.

She had already performed the obligatory ritual, shortly after her graduation from high school. And no wonder, when a woman goes to sea behind the galleon's figurehead of a bust like Emma's. Then there are bound to be such incidents. But Emma Drobil held to her course. She made very definite, highly specific demands upon men. Thus, for example, if she was going to have a husband—and she was well aware of the reasons for having a husband—she wanted to be secure and not have to worry about anything any longer. But to be married and be faced with an even greater need to earn her daily bread seemed to her preposterous, and she would not even consider it. She was a most sensible girl.

They had left the brook now. Its roar, once they had crossed the highway, vanished into the trees and the dense underbrush that lined its gorge as though a door had been slammed shut. Mr. Williams and Fräulein Drobil now climbed the slope on the other side of the road, their object being to reach that ridge which is called "the Cordon." The side-hill was steep. On top, however, the terrain became an almost level plateau. Here were woods, deciduous woods, real open, rolling, untamed woods—and this barely fifty minutes by subway from the center of the metropolis.

What these two really wanted of each other, with each other, for each other, was for the moment still obscure, vague, and pale, scarcely discernible. They were merely walking together; that was all. But there is no such thing as a "mere" walk when it is being taken by two young persons of opposite sex. Still, Dwight gave no thought to this principle. His mind had wandered to his room on Albert Road in London. In the corner had been an old wardrobe with inlay work representing scenes out of English history: upon one door was King Henry VIII, surrounded by his various wives, each in a small medallion.

The entire cavalcade seemed like a poor joke, especially the representation of the king. Dwight did not like the wardrobe. It seemed to him like a knot in his own interior entanglement.

Dwight had met Emma Drobil in the simplest way imaginable—her firm had transported his crates of books from London to Vienna. So here they were walking together. At the top of the hill there is a terrace with an observation tower and a café.

The Vienna Woods offer a special kind of scenery which is not altogether as simple as it looks. True, everything is leafy and verdant and fragrantly evanescent. But in the background there lurks a certain morbidity, the vapor of melancholia, which is dangerous even to sound healthy people—is more dangerous, in fact, to them than to others. For the Vienna Woods are really a farewell to mountains and hills, to villa-strewn inclines which flow gently into wooded dales; they are a farewell to the pleasant, cozy western individuality and smaller land-masses; in a way they are a farewell to the compactness of Greece, standing as they do close by the portals to the East, to immoderate expanses. Not far from here there begin the great plains which retreat and recede toward Hungary. There everything is on a larger scale, less detailed, less individual; and as the scale of land grows, so also does the scale of time. There, toward the East, not every life has its own special, if invisible, garden plot. Time was when only nomad peoples passed this way. Even today, in Russia, say, we still see people constantly on the move: carrying bundles by hand, pulling wooden satchels behind them on little wagons or sleds. They roam—are compelled to roam. They are driven. Individual life does not rebel; there is too little of it for rebellion. One soul mingles with another like smoke. For that reason, too, people in those parts are fraternal. Here, as far as the West extends, as far as Rome and Greece reach (to put it concisely), a man stands alone between the tended flower beds and the little porticoes of a house from which no one, by law and equity, is entitled to expel him. He stands alone, by himself; the soft blue air is around him; he is unencumbered on all sides, like a statue. This is the only way he knows how to be; only in this way can he be big or little, crooked or straight, good or bad. But not if he is meekly acquiescent, lets himself be ranked and filed into some nomadic herd, swallows bitter pill upon bitter pill, suffers indignity upon indignity, and imagines that this is the way things must be.

Dwight and Emma Drobil might have known all these things, and perhaps in a sense knew them implicitly, as part of their education. But they were not conscious of the background against which they lived and acted. Their relationship to it all was a far more pragmatic one; for the matters we have suggested were what made possible their private existence, their particular form of life as vacillating needles pointing now here and now there, often jerking instead of pointing, often whirling instead of giving direction, but in the final analysis fully accountable for the chosen route. For it lay within their destiny to be figures who could be walked around on all sides, around whom all potentialities remained open, all the possible directions of life, so that ultimately their conflicts and contradictions, their tuggings one way and another, could come to resolution in free competition within the inner core of their being.

Without free dialectic there is no Greece.

But all this is just by the by. What is most significant about every situation is the aspect of it that is taken for granted. At the same time, that aspect is the hardest to discover. Aboriginals in distant lands and on savage islands often show ethnologists their most curious folkways; but the customs and views these peoples take for granted are never so much as touched upon.

31

And yet these very things, the heart of the nation and what differentiates it from others, would surely interest the professors most. But they always have to extract information about these matters gradually, by roundabout means and cautious questioning.

We would have found ourselves in a similar difficulty had we approached Dwight Williams and Emma Drobil. They had meanwhile sat down at a café table to have a glass of beer; Emma hailed from Bohemia, after all, and Americans, too, appreciate a glass of good beer. Of course our Emma would have found a genuine Pilsner even more welcome, but that could be had only in town; and the draught beer here really was not too bad. Both of them were somewhat hot from the climb to the ridge. The sky now arched cloudlessly above them. Beside the observation tower, a young lamb frisked about in a small enclosure. It wore a blue ribbon around its neck, with a little bell attached which tinkled softly now and then. A child appeared at one window of the café and called out: "Chapei, Chapei!" Apparently that was the lamb's name. It answered, what was more, saying: "Baah!"

Dwight was staying in Vienna because of butterflies. Not that he expected to catch butterflies there; but he was interested in assisting in the rearrangement of the Museum of Natural History's lepidopterological collections because this would give him the opportunity to thoroughly examine certain specimens pertinent to his studies. He had therefore contrived to have himself sent, or rather invited, to Vienna. The museum, however, was only one of his reasons for being in Vienna, only one force, though a fixed and ponderous one, he acknowledged, as he looked out the high arched window of his study at the Museum of Art History, a building outwardly the exact counterpart of the one in which he sat—a mirror image standing on the other side of a green park. Above, an expanse of sky. Below, the elevated statue of the seated Empress Maria Theresa surrounded by the mounted figures of her paladins. It marked a point of reference; it concentrated everything that could be seen around here into one point.

Frau Mary was the other force.

She, however, could not be localized; for that reason she was present almost everywhere in a diffuse fashion.

By the time he left Albert Road it had become simply impossible to ask Mme Libesny for Frau Mary's family name and her address in Vienna. Whenever Dwight paused for any length of time beside the bookcase and looked at the picture, dimorphism ensued.

And yet Mme Libesny had two very well-shaped legs.

Frau Mary K. was not living in Vienna in the summer of 1926. She stayed in Munich, month after month, and finally for more than half a year. At that time Munich boasted a famous orthopedist, Professor Habermann. To him came patients of iron resolution who refused to be defeated by the circumstance that at some time or other they had fallen into the machinery of life. Indeed, their characters may first have shown their mettle after a personal tragedy such as befell Frau Mary K. Professor Habermann brilliantly stimulated such mobilizations of the militant ego by psychological as well as the newest orthopedic techniques.

Frau Mary stayed in a well-known Munich hotel near the railroad station and was well looked after. Her spacious room was situated on a corner and consequently had windows on two sides, looking out over two different streets. Here, for many months, she performed her assigned task with self-conquering determination. If peg legs and crutches were to be dispensed with, the patient must practice walking with the new prosthesis every day; Dr. Habermann insisted that the patient not give up, that he clench his teeth and practice as if his life depended on it (and it did depend on it). True, such practice caused soreness and sensitivity at pressure points here and there—Mary's stump, which was only the upper part of her thigh, was placed in a kind of shell or pouch. But the patient must never treat this as an excuse to leave off practicing. Every detail of the practice sessions was regulated in advance and the succession of stages strictly prescribed. Walking with the prosthesis was apt to produce small new wounds or cause healed parts to open here and there. Such sores had to be treated, but if at all possible they were not permitted to interrupt the practicing. The whole process might be compared—although on a far more trivial and milder scale—to a person's teaching himself to wear a denture. At first the denture is by no means a blessing; it irritates the gums and does not help chewing. In the case of an artificial limb—which looks deceptively like a real one and wears ordinary stockings and shoes—it, too, is not a blessing at first.

Here, then, in this corner room of the Hotel Feldhütter in Munich, Mary fought her *aristeia,* as Homer calls the grandest and most glorious struggles of his heroes. For after she had attended Professor Habermann's clinic for a while and had been initiated into the technique of using the prosthesis, the doctor ordered her also to practice daily alone, at home, and continue unremittingly her attempts to walk. And so Mary took up her task and hoisted the weight of her body which had grown so clumsy. With mouth slightly twisted, leaning upon an ebony cane, she made her way from one window wall to the other, diagonally across the room. She felt a dull pressure. Once more she felt the stabbing pain of earlier stages of her recovery. The prosthesis dangled from her body as lifeless as it was in reality. And yet it was supposed to be drawn within the body's frame of reference, to become attached to it as a natural member.

Mary paused in her hobbling and looked up.

She must have been very beautiful at such moments. The light, though the sun was not shining, fell through the high wide window directly upon her. A balanced, truly well-constructed woman; the thoroughbred features of ancient good family calling forth instinctive respect; the coppery sheen of the hair around the temples; the skin shimmering like mother-of-pearl—and all this fineness to be so hard hit in the midst of her climb to the womanly heights of the forties and fifties. She felt as though the accident had not only snatched away one leg above the knee, but both, and her arms as well, leaving behind an insensible, immobile lump.

Her small white teeth dug into her lower lip. The network of delicate lines which a long spell of suffering had thrown across this face—in which a certain fine incisiveness had always been present—the network of lines drew closer together. She bent her head low. The shadows about her eyes deepened, and the lids closed and the repressed tears fell to the floor, one, and then another.

And yet, while she briefly loitered at a low point that seemed extremely close to despair, she felt obscurely certain that the hardest part of this already lay behind her. The hardest part not in reference to her present task with Professor Habermann, and here in this room, but rather the hardest part of all, the terrible necessity that had descended upon her while she had still lain in the hospital in Vienna. That was: to spread this disaster over time; to make of an event that had taken seconds an institution which would go on for years; not to stray back to the time before the accident, to those last unsuspecting hours just shortly before the debacle; not to ask herself: "How was it possible?" but to say to herself that this was the way it was now. It was necessary for her to stretch the horror out over duration, to consume it in small portions, to assimilate it, and finally to transform it into practical life—as she was doing here and now.

But how long it had taken for her to reach that point!

Back home was the wheel chair which had been obtained for her so that she might be taken out for walks—and what a fuss there always was in the elevator. Her two grown children and the doorman would be there each time to help loyal Marie. And then, gliding by the window of a shoe shop one day she had seen, as it were, her own two sound feet multiplied behind the plate glass. Multiplied many times. Yes, that had been too much for her. About-face and back home.

That evening the crisis had come. She had sent Marie out and sat, in her nightgown, on the edge of the bed. She lifted the gown and saw the stump now, scarred, a discolored brown. At that moment she seemed to herself to have become a lumpy, stumpy block, a tuberous shape, a gnome.

Her eyes remained dry. Her misery vanished. She suddenly grasped the grandeur of her situation, and so her hour came; so she became capable of receiving its command. Her eyes flashed.

"Mary!" she said aloud, addressing herself. The maid came in, thinking she had been called. But her mistress had only transported herself momentarily, in advance, to Munich and Professor Habermann.

Several times in those early days Marie had been found by her mistress—who moved about on crutches and so could be heard coming through the rooms from far off—with eyes red from crying. The two children also had no easy time of it—the brilliant boy, who was just entering the upper classes of Gymnasium; and his older sister, auburn-haired and milky-complexioned, slender, with a little turned-up nose. The girl slept beside her mother in the other twin bed—a custom that had been introduced by the daughter quietly, as a matter of course and with the intention of consoling her mother, ever since the death of Herr Oskar K. in February 1924. By this the girl had hoped her mother would be sheltered from the yawning void of a lifeless connubial bedroom; and now her presence offered protection against the night's loneliness and against her mother's new clumsiness; for especially during the early days Mary needed a helping hand in many small and ordinary things.

Even during this early period the thought had occurred to Mary that it was almost a happy dispensation that she was a widow. For she could visualize what a host of highly delicate situations might have arisen had her husband still been with her. That, to be sure, did not lighten the blow of the accident, but it was a kind of assuagement nonetheless.

Mary's daughter—called Trix because her name was Beatrix—kept close by her mother all the time now, with an undeviating helpfulness. The girl, though barely sixteen, was thoroughly womanly and long since quite grown up. People might have thought her almost emotionless. Her personality seemed to be sheathed in an outer skin of faintly aloof serenity—even now. For Mary this quality in her daughter was of enormous value; indeed, during the early days after the accident it formed one of her essential supports.

But her dark eyes—with such a wealth of auburn hair and a complexion like milk glass!—were the most striking feature of the girl's face. Those dark eyes disclosed the deeper strata of her psyche, and one could see that it was susceptible to violent commotions. Almost always when her mother addressed her from the adjacent bed, perhaps asking for one thing or another, her daughter's quiet sure movements as she fulfilled the request were accompanied by a passionate darkening of gaze which hinted at a maelstrom of tenderness, and of sympathy held in careful concealment. In the past, the relationship between mother and daughter had resembled that between close girl friends; it now became a communion of the greatest imaginable intimacy. For in many respects the mother had become a helpless child.

Marie had not been permitted to go along to Munich. A nurse was hired for the trip. Thus the household in Vienna remained in good hands. In addition, friends of the family—the Küffers in Döbling, owners of the brewery of the same name—had assumed a kind of protectorship over Mary's home while she was away. Mary's children spent a good deal of time with the younger generation of Küffers.

By the time she was ready to leave Vienna, Mary had learned to prevent herself from thinking about the accident itself, as well as the last hours before it—the last hale and hearty, the last complete hours of her life on the afternoon of September 21, 1925—it had been a Monday. In Munich, however, she could abate somewhat this timid mental discipline. In Munich, Mary felt more secure in all respects, as though her toilsome and painful daily activity were a firm banister to hold on to.

She had practiced well today. Already she could feel in her limbs a physical premonition of what it would someday be like, must be like, to go about with this prosthesis of hers. She pulled a pad and pen over to her and began, in her vigorous hand, to write a report on the state of affairs to her friend Grete Siebenschein, the elder daughter of the lawyer Doktor Ferry

Siebenschein, who lived in the same building as she, one floor below. And she preceded her account with sincere thanks to Grete for the moral assistance she had given her during the first months after the accident, an assistance no less important than that of her own daughter. It was kind and good of Grete, she wrote, to be keeping an eye on the two children during these trying days. But now the first hard period was over, and soon she, Mary, would be "standing on her own feet again," and would no longer be afraid of shoe shops.

Dwight and Emma had left the café by the observation tower and were again tramping across the ridge. The woods were bright and open for a long distance; among the trunks of the beeches the thriving green of wild garlic covered the ground with already thickening wisps. Here and there the farther reaches of the view let down a curtain, such as, for example, the gray-green canvas of a dropping mountain slope, the clarity of whose outline against the blue sky was somewhat smudged by clouds and by the domes of the countless treetops.

It is still impossible to say whether the two wanted anything of each other, with each other, for each other. They found each other not disagreeable; that is probably all that can be said at present. They waded no deeper into the pool of this joint outing; and perhaps there was no greater depth to it, although such a statement seems an almost outright lie, for there are always depths. But here the water did not even reach to the ankles. You might draw your foot back and say you had merely gone for a walk—with Mr. Williams, with Fräulein Drobil.

Emma Drobil, however, was not thinking about any of these matters. In the whole business between the sexes the men are always the ones who lose their ingenuousness first, because this business is not first but second nature to them. It is thus a matter from which they stand at an unfortunate distance—they are too far away to become one with it, but at the same time near enough to feel sympathetic vibrations. To put this otherwise: Mr. Williams was the first to stumble into the ambiguities of the situation, and remained quite alone amid them. For Emma Drobil still seemed completely unperturbed.

Her unrest would begin later on. But now that they had had their outing, and were having tea together in Emma's room on Hadik Gasse in Hietzing, she remained completely at her ease. It was the most natural thing in the world for them to be having tea together: since at the moment she felt no desire for solitude. And he likewise.

It was in this neighborhood that Camy Schlaggenberg, daughter of Dr. Schedik, had spent her girlhood, and the vicinity was as appropriate to her as her first name, Camilla. (It was not the perfect setting for Emma Drobil at all, but then she was only camped here like a nomad.) The deep, wide, and well-walled bed of the Wien River—which flowed below the windows and looked like a brook, except in spring—separates two quarters of the city which are quite different in character. However, "new" Hietzing on the right bank, with its villas and gardens, has infused some of its select nature into Penzing, the older quarter on the opposite bank, although the houses there are built one against another and not held apart at a respectful distance by gardens, as is the case with the richer homes of Hietzing. Still and all, the houses have managed to have front gardens, though these are little more than strips creating a decent separation between house and sidewalk.

Now this wide, walled riverbed runs straight on, splitting the entire landscape of the city for a considerable distance. The upper stories of the houses on Hadik Casse enjoy wonderful light. Here Dr. Schedik used to keep his aquaria, three or four of them; and the plants with which he experimented. That is to say, he made them "exercise their joints" by turning them away from the sunlight, in fact shielding them from it, so that they had to demonstrate again and again their amazing ability to turn toward the light, even to grow around two or three corners in order to reach it.

It was a very clean neighborhood; from the windows you looked into the green gardens of the villas. Here Camilla had lived with her father (he was a widower and she his only child). It was a very clean neighborhood, and a clean peaceable girlhood she had spent; later in life Camilla looked at everything else through its pure clear outlines as though peering through a gunsight, so that everything slightly crooked appeared to be extremely distorted indeed.

Kajetan, for example.

Years later the stony gray of the riverbed below, which could be seen for a great distance upriver and downriver, stayed with Camy; she would remember the blue-gray veils of mist it wore in the spring and especially in the autumn. She thought of it frequently, even after she had long been living with her father in the heart of town; thought of it especially mornings, just before getting up. Of course the doctor had been compelled to settle down closer to the heart of the city, and to live in style; his practice was steadily expanding. Though what a set of patients he had! The doctor himself maintained that nothing was wrong with them. They only wanted to be treated. Moreover, he almost invariably succeeded in curing them. Early in 1927 even Frau Irma Siebenschein, Grete's mother, appeared as a patient; she had the reputation of having several hundred illnesses annually. Her husband, Ferry Siebenschein, took it all with a viscous equanimity. Frau Siebenschein, too, recovered from all her illnesses, without diet or medication, solely through the application of psychological methods. The medicines that were administered to her were of the mildest nature. Dr. Schedik was an extraordinary physician, and a philosopher and philanthropist as well.

Dwight stared into the deep golden brown of the tea in the half-filled cup and dug out of his pocket a pack of English cigarettes, of which he still had a small supply left over from his stay in London. Emma Drobil did not care for them, but to Dwight they were full of memories of Albert Road, of the green and white drawing room, of the photograph beside the bookcase.

He looked up. There was a narrow balcony which ran outside the windows, and the door to it was open. The sky was pure as lacquer, the silence extraordinary. But in spite of all the purity and clarity outdoors, in the evening sky, and here in this big light room, there was a fog separating him from it all, and from this pretty and intelligent girl as well.

"Is there anything on your mind?" Emma Drobil asked in English as he remained arrested, teacup in one hand and pack of cigarettes in the other.

"I had better tell you," he said, still in the same awkward posture, "about some difficulties I had in London, real serious ones."

"And are they all over now?" she asked.

"No," Dwight said, and fell silent.

They did, to be sure, return to the subject again. But Williams felt toward it a strange kind of glaciality which thawed only after he had been talking a great deal on all kinds of miscellaneous topics. And so he recounted endless anecdotes from altogether other realms of life—he was in general quite good at telling a story and enjoyed the role of spinner of yarns. Thus he told Emma about the jungles of Brazil, which he had come to know in the course of certain butterfly-hunting expeditions. Very nasty places they sounded, too, as he described them.

One day, moreover, he brought Emma Drobil a glass case containing an enormous butterfly that he had caught and mounted. Each of its wings was as large as a man's palm, and of a scintillating electric blue with the gleam of metal. "Morpho Menelaus" was the name of the creature; this Latin, or rather Greek name, together with the date and place of the find, was written on a small label pasted on the bottom of the case. "Morpho" was in a fine state of preservation, and Emma was delighted with the gift, which made a striking wall decoration for her room: a crescendo of blue, a flash of lightning, a scintillation whenever your eye turned in that direction. Dwight took occasion to remark that to his mind not only this indescribably luxurious creature but all of creation in general was pure *art pour l'art* (a fact which lent it such nobility), at which statement Emma Drobil, a sensible hardheaded girl, looked at him with some amazement. Yet she realized she was drawn to him. Williams also told stories of less exotic locales—of Bavaria, for example (so he had been there too!), where several racy tavern brawls seemed to have afforded him a great deal of amusement—though surely he had only looked on at these. Or had he? Likewise a Pantagruelian scene of glutting and swilling—one of the customs of the country (but had he taken part in such a feast?). From this Williams went on to tell a story about an odd little man whom he had once seen at Murnau, who had revealed a quite staggering capacity for food and drink. The little man had been a foreigner in those parts, not a Bavarian but an Austrian, and from here, moreover, from Vienna. In the tavern at Murnau on Sunday—Williams sketched in the scene, even to the forest of white feathers on the natives' hats— in the tavern something had come up, an argument or rumpus of some sort—and Dwight's attention had been caught by the little fellow from Vienna. Apparently he had aroused the ire of several strapping Bavarian peasant lads. The little fellow had an altogether preposterous appearance, rather like a bald eagle with a gigantic hooked nose which seemed to be growing to meet an equally hooked chin; it was an uncommonly hideous and, in some obscure way, a fearsome face. His fingers, too, were like an eagle's talons, and Dwight heard someone refer to him jokingly as "the Claw."

Suddenly they came to blows. The four or five huge, rather good-natured peasants with whom the little fellow had tangled possibly did not take the matter seriously enough, and there-fore did not exert themselves at the beginning; they merely took "the Claw" by the arms to propel him out of the room. Then something almost incredible happened. The whole action seeming to be compressed into a single second: Two young fel-lows were already lying on the floor, one of them moaning, and a third had blood streaming from his mouth and nose; while almost in the same motion the uncanny little monstrosi-ty had leaped through the open window and vanished. And he stayed vanished, although all the boys at once set out in pur-suit of him and hunted for him round about the village until the late afternoon. Not a trace of "the Claw" was found. At the time, Williams remarked, he had first realized the difference between rustic muscle power and that "nervous strength"—as Guy de Maupassant has called it—which is at home in large cities, combined with a fighting skill which can be instantly drawn upon, and which is not hampered by the inhibitions that grow out of the peasant's natural good humor.

Emma Drobil liked listening to Dwight Williams. She enjoyed his way of telling a story. He never lost himself completely in his subject; his speech never became overearnest—a virtue that, it must be added, is characteristic of English, which lends itself to limber colloquial use better than any other language. Emma not only followed his yarns with pleasure, but she also enjoyed his appearance while he talked. When telling a story Williams was in the habit of leaning back comfortably, hands in his pockets and legs outstretched in front of him. In addition, she clearly felt that he was trying neither to persuade her of anything nor to strike any pose, but wished merely to amuse her. Often he would break off in the middle of a tale, and would have to be reminded to finish it. Any interjection she might make he would readily take up.

It is possible that the growing attraction these two healthy young people exerted toward each other was rooted, in a general way, in their national qualities, and thus in their oppositeness. Our Emma was attracted by the Anglo-Saxon element in Dwight, that casual loose-limbed charm of an entirely unconstrained but thoroughly clean-cut manner of living, the freely chosen discipline of a highly virile personality. Emma Drobil, on the other hand, we know to be a young person of the staunchest character, not to speak of her extremely pretty face and other noteworthy physical characteristics. For the American this ravishing dark-haired girl represented the quintessence of his present Austrian environment; and because he saw women and girls of her type and stature fairly often in the streets of Vienna, he regarded her as an ideal representative of this city and this country. Possibly this identification was a little awry ethnographically, but in essence it was accurate.

Both of them were, all the same, living in Vienna as foreigners, living on the surface of the city, and imbued besides with the surface tension of their intensive and at times strenuous work. Dwight Williams's morning walk down Ring Strasse from the Stadt Park, near which he lived—he always went on foot—to the Museum of Natural History, this leisurely stroll to the accompaniment of the bustle of moderate traffic and the tinkling of streetcar bells, gradually stirred in him a kind of astonishment. After a while this emotion became an integral part of his walk, starting up at the corner of Weinburg Gasse and not subsiding until the tall monument of Empress Maria Theresa hove into view. It was above all astonishment at Frau Mary's city, at the place where she lived and then again did not live. It was as though he alone had brought her here from Albert Road in Battersea, like an import, something new that had not existed in Vienna before he came.

And so they entered the autumn of the year 1926. Dwight went on many another walk in the company of lovely Emma. Here and there in the woods the leaves were already beginning to fall; the smells were sweet and somehow suggestive of vast spaces; and this sensation of spaciousness was intensified when, as often happened at this season, standing in the midst of the woods one could look through thinned treetops into an actual distance where stood a mountain peak that faced wholly the other way and belonged beneath a different sky. When the street lamps were turned on in the evenings, which was done earlier and earlier each day now, the rumble of the traffic sounded louder. (In London, on, say, King's Road, Dwight had never had that impression; he had not felt anything of the sort when he walked from Chelsea toward Sloane Square. But then, the total volume of noise had been so much greater in London that such nuances would not have been detectable.)

46

There could be no doubt, however, that the city enlarged itself in the autumn. From certain vantage points one could see straight through the long vistas of the public gardens and parks. Everyone who went walking, perhaps already wearing a heavy overcoat, was walking into the winter, heading toward winter, all alone and by himself rather than in company with everyone else. Changes of season are not collective experiences—as is commonly thought. Rather, they exist for each of us alone and constitute each time for each of us a new and differently shaped building-block in our individual biographies.

CHAPTER 2

The Origins of a Colony (I)

IN 1926, long before the weather started getting cold, I had moved out to my garden suburb. I was, I should explain, by no means ready to regard the Nineteenth District—Döbling—as a land of Pensionopolis. I continued without a specific program and made no attempt to inaugurate a new period of my life; even my resignation from the active civil service had not borne that meaning for me. Nevertheless, people who are quite adult secretly cling to the superstition that an outward alteration in their lives, say moving from one flat to another, or a change of locale, may very well affect the whole of their personality. Possibly we even feel that it should do so, although in fact the story is the other way around; that is to say, sooner or later the inner transformation brings an outer one in its train. The changes that modern folk make in their circumstances are almost without exception dictated by necessity. Once such a change is accomplished, a slight depression may well ensue when, between freshly painted walls and newly varnished floors, surrounded by a host of hitherto unknown practical comforts, our good friends find the same old donkey who would, if he were a cow, stand before all the new splendor bellowing with unhappiness, as that animal stands moodily before the barn door when it is first let out in the spring. But as it is a donkey, it only wags its long ears slightly.

I was spared such emotions this time. I was not expecting any new life to dawn for me. After all, I had already reached mature years. "Maturity consists in no longer being taken in by oneself." As a mature person I had conducted myself accordingly. The epigram I have just quoted had been a casual remark of Kajetan von Schlaggenberg's.

I saw him again after a very long interval on November 20, 1926, though only for six or seven seconds. The incident will be related in due course. I did little more than catch a glimpse of him.

My first apartment out in the suburbs was on Scheiben Gasse, in a house belonging to one Frau Trabert. She was an old lady whom I seldom saw; her deceased husband had been director of the Meteorological Institute, which is situated nearby. I had two rooms, one of which was very large. The flat was on the second floor; it was easy to talk from the window with anyone who stood at the sidewalk below, by the gate to the tiny front garden. I liked it here. The service, moreover, was excellent—it consisted of a very young and droll Czech maidservant who had been well trained by Frau Trabert. For the most part I spoke Czech with Maruschka; but if I addressed her in German she would answer in German, and that was even more delightful. My friends and acquaintances adored Maruschka's German; it was an extra bonus of enjoyment when they paid me a visit. They also loved to hear her on the telephone. In fact, they somewhat spoiled her with their tips. She was a good child.

During the second half of November that year it turned quite cold. The Dutch stoves were already going in my rooms.

I had occasion one day to go into town to meet René Stangeler near the University.

I was going to have to be back by six o'clock. A former colleague of mine from the Ministry was still struggling with a case I had bequeathed to him; he needed my advice, or at least

50

wanted to discuss the matter with me. Since he also lived on the outskirts of town, he had gladly accepted my suggestion that he call on me after working hours, on his way home from the office. I therefore had to be back home by six. I could not very well make him wait.

It is curious, incidentally, that I later made use of this affair, long after it was all over, as an excuse not to have to go to a party—or rather, to arrive only toward the end of the party—which took place the following year, on May 14, 1927, at the home of Frau Irma Siebenschein. When, on that occasion, I served up the story of an erstwhile colleague in the Ministry whom I had to help, it was an outright lie. I intended to have lunch in the city and meet René afterwards.

Now, in retrospect (after nearly twenty-eight years), I realize that the business with my colleague of the Ministry—the genuine meeting with him in November 1926, not the fictitious one—was symptomatic, proving as it did that I still had many contacts with my previous associates. Only a few months later that was no longer so. But toward the end of 1926 I was still associating with the same persons who used to make up my circle when I lived on Daponte Gasse in District III. I continued to call on friends who lived in the vicinity of the Hohe Warte, which was quite close to my new neighborhood, and in winter attended gatherings in one or another of the lovely villas of that quarter. At the close of the evening I would always be agreeably surprised at how short my way home was, now that I lived in Döbling.

From the very start, however, I never considered young Herr von Stangeler—he was already thirty, but I thought of him perpetually as "young von Stangeler"—as being in any way connected with my "former circle," although in actuality he fell within its sphere. Even before the First World War I

51

used to be in and out of René's parents' home, and often visited the Stangeler villa near Mount Rax during the summers. Thus my acquaintance with René could be dated far back to the time when he was a boy in Gymnasium; by now he had long since been a doctor of philosophy and graduate of the Institute for Austrian Historical Studies. He continued to work at the Institute—a young historian whose career had been postponed by historical events and four years as a Russian prisoner of war . . . As I was saying, I did not consider René part of my "former world." He did not fit in there at all. In my mind he had always stood aside from it, aside also from his own family, who for me had become entirely a part of that past, almost an embodiment of it. I had lost touch with them. I no longer called on them at all. But I had resumed contact with René some time around the autumn of 1925. I had read a piece of his (on Gilles de Rais) in the magazine section of a newspaper, and shortly afterwards we happened to run into each other at a little party in honor of someone's taking his doctorate. Naturally I thought of reviving my old association with his parents and the younger members of his family; in fact I promptly asked after them. But he behaved rather oddly; he told me no news, seemed to have nothing to say about them. Some time later I happened to run into his favorite sister, Frau Haupt, the architect's wife—and discovered that he had not passed on any of my regards. Frau Asta Haupt seemed surprised to learn that I was seeing René— altogether astonished, in fact. More than that, it was almost as though she felt that he was no proper associate for me. Or . . . was it that I was no proper associate for him? She seemed to think us extremely ill-suited to each other, and in this she was undoubtedly right. Nothing came of that meeting, and I did not again see any members of the Stangeler family. Today I know that René actually went to some trouble to prevent such contacts.

He belonged, then, not to the circle which I was on the point of leaving when I moved out to Döbling, but to an altogether different circle which I was soon to enter. And here at any rate he had a place, he was not merely a detached and dismal outsider, as he seemed to be in his parents' home and in the class to which he belonged by birth. I might put it that he had proved himself incompetent in that milieu.

This is not to say that he showed himself singularly competent in the Siebenschein family. René had fallen into this altogether different milieu a year after his repatriation, and was quickly saddled with a role which he could not seriously justify either here or at his parental home: that of prospective son-in-law.

But enough of this. We had met in a café near the University, and we did not speak of these things until the end of our talk. We spoke too long about them, until twenty minutes to six. I had to take a cab in order to be back home in time for my caller.

Darkness had long since settled in; the streets were brilliant with lights; the traffic was heavy, as is custom in the city at this hour. We traveled fairly swiftly; I had luckily hit on a relatively new cab and a young driver. Even under the traffic conditions of those days—so quiet by comparison with today—there had frequently been jams at the Wahring Intersection: seven streetcar lines, a bus line, and the ordinary auto traffic converged here . . . I saw a youngish man who suddenly swayed and at the same time made a curious and almost ludicrous gesture with both hands, groping about the waist of his overcoat as though he were losing something and trying to hold on to it. It seemed almost as if his suspenders or his belt had torn and he were afraid of losing his trousers. Swaying somewhat, he stepped forward off the traffic island. The nearest automobile managed to avoid him by only a few inches. It was the cab in which I sat. Then we were past. The man was Schlaggenberg; I had recognized him beyond the shadow of a doubt. I did not have the driver stop, but went my way; today I find it necessary to mention this expressly.

During the previous six months I had not seen him at all, nor did I know where he was then living; and yet I knew all, even understood what his staggering signified. In passing I had, as it were, cast a glance at the clock-face of his life.

I was perfectly sure that his wretched state was connected with the final collapse of his marriage. Moreover, I had visited his wife only the week before. For I had remained in touch with her.

At any rate, I drove past and reached home ten minutes before my colleague from the Ministry turned up.

Actually, the new segment of my life, my secession, I might put it, was already beginning. Thus my more frequent association with René these days by no means pointed back toward the past. It was, rather, an anticipation of the future. Even at the time I already had a premonition of the permanence of my relationship with him, no matter whether I was annoyed with him or learned things from him or raised severe reproaches against him, or even blamed him for everything imaginable. In May of 1927 I was to deal mercilessly with the poor fellow (who has long since ceased to be a poor fellow in my mind). I cherished a virtual formula which amounted to: "Stangeler is to blame for everything." And in fact he was constantly upsetting me—by his incomprehensibility in general; by what I called the crack in his nature, and should have quickly seen as a profound gulf; by what seemed to be his imperiousness, so that no matter how you tried to jolt him he would always go on

54

talking a blue streak, producing the same worthless drivel; by his unsteadiness, his being all twisted into knots, denuded of his real abilities. And yet almost every moment you spent with him, and even when he showed himself at his very worst, you felt that he was struggling. You knew that his personality had been shattered, his life cut into two separate halves, and that at times he wanted to get out of one and into another, while just as often, with a kind of blind mole's passion, he did not want to at all, or at any price.

But today I know far more about it all. I know that René not only kept me away from his family but also that it was he (I once said angrily of him that he lived "as if torn to shreds") who kept me, after I had come into my inheritance and resigned from the civil service, from growing into a careful, dignified old gentleman. For I have him to thank that I did not. He took to teasing me immediately after my move to Döbling. "Now you can become a typical Döbling autocrat of breakfast culture. A pity that you did not move into Sternwarte Strasse or Anastasius Grim Strasse without delay. Such nice, cultivated, and intellectual people live there, with beautiful libraries. The amazing thing is how those people manage to keep intelligence at bay. As soon as they smell it, they're against it." For he could be very biting. His bitterness was not so much against persons or things as against the idea of entrenched respectability. He hated its very shadow. Hence his gravitation toward the Siebenscheins.

I had just parted from him at the café, and my mind still dwelt on our conversation throughout the ride from the Ring to Wahring Intersection—thenceforth my thoughts were occupied with Schlaggenberg. Still, until then, René was present with me, in my nostrils. I must apologize for this incongruous phrase—I shall explain it at once. Once upon a time—in the summer of 1911—I had had a talk with René, then still a schoolboy, out at his parents' villa. The boy had suddenly exclaimed: "You smell good," and since I found this charming and perfectly natural, I had sent him a bottle of the after-shave lotion which I used. He thanked me in a neatly indited note, which he concluded with some phrase or other about regarding this "as the beginning of something new." I confess that I did not entirely understand what he meant by this. Everything has to be lived to be understood, to be grasped through living; and one must live long enough to grasp it. The time would come when I too would understand the allusion and how each phase of life has its new scent.

At any rate, René went on using that lavender water—a large perfumery on the Graben puts it up—and uses it to the present day. Thus, since 1911 we both stood in the same odor, literally speaking, and so we had remained in the same odor to this day. This was something which had forcibly impressed itself upon my senses during our meeting, so much so that it was somehow expressive of the firmness and tenacity of our relationship. Whenever I was annoyed with René, either then or in the subsequent period, sixteen years later, I seriously considered changing my toilet water. That is how human relations are.

What follows now is a strange matter, and even lies outside the scope of the nose—for all that it is our most sibylline organ. It was shortly after the day I had seen Schlaggenberg on the traffic island and my cab had nearly knocked him down—possibly the very next day. At any rate it was morning, and sunny. My room had already had its morning cleaning and lay about me, bright, warm, and spacious. I was busy arranging some sheaves of notes on various subjects. I had them in regular file folders (though not from the Ministry). I was sitting at my desk. Today I can appoint that sunny morning as the actual start of my chronicling (and to what that has led me!—*primum scribere deinde vivere*—yes, yes!). Among my notes was a sizable paper which René Stangeler had drawn up for me: a Hungarian story of the late Middle Ages.

I was sifting through these notes when I suddenly sensed some unpleasant ray touching my spirit, if not my actual body, although but a moment before I had been in a state of perfect well-being. And while still inwardly crying out to myself: "Nonsense—what can be the matter?" (this is how we always suppress what we do not want to face; we force it down, compress it, and thereby intensify it), I found I could no longer stay in my chair. I bounded up from the desk, walked to the middle of the room, and as though quite by chance raised my eyes, lifted my gaze above the things around me and the room as such into the upper emptiness of space where we are surely not in the habit of looking. I peered at the spot where ceiling and wall met, for the sensation came from up there. That was the seat of it. The wall was quite bare, but it was just as if the portrait of a woman hung there, a most beautiful woman with dark braids, whose face looked down into my room, into my life and doings, into my notes, my associates, the whole animated hollowness of my existence at that time, with scorn, with contempt, and a boundless, stupid arrogance, so that everything—Döbling, Scheiben Gasse, René, Camy von Schlaggenberg, and Kajetan himself—turned as pallid as bleached bone and literally perished in utter ludicrousness. Everything, not to speak of my first feeble efforts at keeping a chronicle.

It was gone in a trice. No name had come to my mind, no person, but only someone's essence, as it were (in somewhat the fashion that a painter engaged on a still life completely forgets the concrete purposes of the objects lying before him, seeing in them only the dynamics of color, curvature, and planes, no longer knowing that the pipe on the table can be used for smoking—such a process lies behind those paintings so disagreeable to the autocrats of culture). The link to consciousness was not forged at this time. It was not until after my above-mentioned walk with Herr Levielle down the Graben on March 24, 1927—Annunciation Day—that something made me think of the Baroness Claire Neudegg, later Countess Charagiel; not until then did I realize that she had already been present in my mind that November day, and thus that my thoughts had traveled far back into my youth, to my sixteenth year.

Well, we shall hear enough of the bothersome countess in due course. For the time being I forgot her who had only reached out an anonymous antenna.

Winter had not yet descended. I went walking a great deal, thoroughly enjoying these strolls by which I was conquering my new neighborhood. Scheiben Gasse led toward the hill and in those days ran along a large, as yet vacant meadow. All dips and hummocks, its grass withered to a color scarcely to be called green, the meadow stretched on like the one opposite my windows. The street soon led to the crest. On top of the hill it ran level for a while, and if I turned a corner into a side street and passed by several villas, a few steps further uphill took me out to a surprising, absolutely open view.

Like a banner against the sky the dun-colored mass of the Kahlenberg stretched to the left in shallow billows; in the foreground the flank of the Nussberg slanted off to the right. The woods, already wintry and leafless, were grayish blue, like down or hair, and below these the empty vineyards were the color of earth. The whole composed itself into a picture beneath the overcast heavens, a picture which, despite the softness of the horizon, was not without a certain austerity.

Before me a footpath dropped straight to the highway that led to Grinzing. I turned back and took another path farther to the right, a somewhat winding way that clung to the slope and ran among the vineyards of the Haubenbigl, as it is locally called.

During the early period of my liberated life and my living out in the suburb here, I was particularly fond of this walk. Just at the point where the path begins, there was a sizable house standing quite by itself. From its balconies one would have a truly tremendous view into the farther distances, a view such as I did not enjoy from my place on Scheiben Gasse.

With such a view, I thought, one would really possess the whole enigmatic charm of this edge of the city.

But in the now: when I look out upon the big Romanesque church, I must lower my gaze; and if I wish to look out beyond it, I need not raise it. But it has taken twenty-eight years to reach this point; and the reader (if I may conceive of one) will have gathered, perhaps not only from the dates I have given, that today I am an old man.

I really do not know how what followed came out here to the suburbs, so that it dogged me when I strolled about discovering my new quarter of the city—which was in fact an entirely new city. Suddenly as I stood looking out over distant prospects— say, from the height of Hartacker Park down into Krottenbach Valley and toward Neustift am Walde—there would leap to my mind a café on Franz-Josephs-Kai, an enormous place that occupied an entire block along the Danube Canal, and a good portion of the side-street façades. Moreover, the café was three stories high. Inside, all was plushy and reeked of old-fashioned luxury: the seats were wide, deep, velvet-upholstered divans; there were the usual racks of newspapers, and hordes of waiters running about with trays loaded with spires of whipped cream. The ladies who patronized this establishment extended the little fingers of their right hands when they spooned up the white froth, for they were ever so refined. But in spite of the gentility of this gesture they were all constantly growing fatter from the whipped cream.

In the rear were rooms for cards and other games.

Today—when, incidentally, not a stone of the place remains standing—I am aware that this whole world (for it was a world in itself, and a most self-contained one at that) belonged neither to my former sphere nor to the new one into which I was now imperceptibly entering. Nor did the card room represent any connection between the two. It connected nothing at all, led nowhere; it was simply there, it existed in all solidity, in almost obtrusive solidity. What it had to do with Döbling, I do not know. True, I once ran into one of the ladies of the bridge club in a street in Döbling—Frau Wolf, the chic and quick-witted wife of a physician. But that means nothing, for such an encounter does not establish a relationship. On that occasion, incidentally, Lea Wolf asked precisely the same question I was much later asked—on June 23 at Friederike Ruthmayr's big reception—by Bank Director Edouard Altschul's wife: why did I never come to the café or to their bridge games any more? I found myself unable to answer Frau Wolf, just as later on I could think of no reason to give Frau Rosi Altschul—although with her it was scarcely essential to have an answer, since Frau Rosi was in the habit of scattering questions right and left while ranging over a number of quite disparate topics of conversation.

In the pattern of our past there repeatedly turns up one incomprehensible strand. Our true past lies in it, wherever we meet it, wherever it happens to crop up. We will never find that strand entwined in the midst of relationships which were once important to us, which make up the obviously significant portions of our life-stories. The true past is always peripheral, I might almost say "marginal" in nature. It is found at the margins of experience. It manifests itself—like another existence which is really ours—through persons whom we have seen for only brief spans of time now and then, or even only once in our lives, at places and in neighborhoods where we never set foot again. At times it almost seems as if we possess a second and as it were retroactive biography.

Of course a few oddments can be dug up out of the lumber room of the past, but in the very act of rummaging for them we discover what a vast and spacious warehouse the past is.

About a year before my removal to Döbling I had been introduced to that café and the bridge club by Ferry Siebenschein, the lawyer (and father of Stangeler's sweetheart), although he was not one to frequent such a café either for its refreshments or its games. In fact, the place was not his kind at all. He was only chopping by to pick up his wife, who had been having a good gossip there with a group of other ladies. Incidentally, Frau Irma Siebenschein was also by no means a regular patron of this café; she turned up there infrequently, with long intervals between appearances.

Among that group of ladies, most of them of mature years, I found a kind of charm and humorous intelligence quite new to me, and highly attractive. Some of the women were pretty, all of them extremely *soignee*. Frau Selma Steuermann was distinctly beautiful. As she later informed me, before the spring of 1927 she withdrew completely from the café and from the bridge club because it came to seem "too silly" to her—how and why we shall eventually learn. This withdrawal was fraught with consequences, though not for me.

Ferry Siebenschein—one of the most honest persons I have ever known—had handled all the legal complications of my inheritance shortly after my father's death. He had also helped me with those funds which had been sequestered in England, not only giving me advice (which Herr Levielle, as we have seen, deemed poor) but speeding things up when they seemed to come to a standstill. For such matters went through the Austrian Clearing House, situated in the Board of Trade building on the Stubenring, which institution appeared at times to need a little jogging.

Thus I had known Herr Siebenschein a good while, on a business basis; I had only a casual acquaintance with his wife, from our meeting in that café, and did not know his daughter at all. At the time I spoke with Stangeler on November 20 about his relationship with Grete Siebenschein, I had as yet never seen her. Not until Christmas was I introduced into the family circle. As it happened, I was brought there by Camy von Schlaggenberg, Kajetan's estranged wife.

Thus Stangeler had nothing to do with my meeting the Siebenscheins. Frau Irma was a tough morsel; you had to know how to swallow her, and even then she would not go down easily. This alert intelligent little woman was in the first place a virtuoso pianist. Her reading taste ran primarily to memoirs and letters. But she also had a special predilection for the nineteenth-century novelist Fritz Reuter, and read him in the difficult Low German original. Chaotic juxtapositions exist, especially in contemporary life, where nothing is really fixed and settled, where everything rather inclines to be a hodgepodge. Tirus, for example, Frau Irma Siebenschein knew whole passages of Reuter's *Dorchlauchting* by heart. But after all, there are factory chimneys in Alpine villages, and lovers will meet in the dead of winter at a bathhouse that has an open door, if there is no other place to go, and perhaps because they will be safest there. I knew a man who conducted his amours in the faculty room of a junior high school—he had an affair with the daughter of the school's janitor.

For my part, I went on walking about in Döbling, conquering my new neighborhood. I was permeated by its qualitatively different light; I steeped myself in that sky which overhangs no other part of Vienna. I gazed out into the surge of its hills, turned back toward the diffuse edge of the city, or surveyed a vineyard whose endless rows of leafless vines—each wound around its staff like a crippled serpent of Aesculapius—stabbed at the edge of the sky behind me and marched off into the distance. And as I looked, I thought of a card room. One is constantly receiving from oneself sharp lessons in the practice of *nil admirari.* I might add that, since I was also acquainted with other European cities, I had this insight at the time: that there were few cities where moving to another quarter would mean so profound a change. In many cities the "districts" are merely postal-zone numbers. That is largely true in Germany, even in Munich. In Paris the principle applies partly abstractly and partly concretely, I might say. Nevertheless the VIIth Arrondissement of Paris is not really entirely individual, as Döbling is, or Wieden, Chelsea, or Battersea; in London you need only cross the Albert Bridge and you find yourself in a neighborhood which in no way resembles Cheyne Walk.

It was about this time that Schlaggenberg unexpectedly ran into me out here in my suburb, while I was taking a walk among the leafless vineyards. I had not seen him—aside from those few moments on November 20—for nearly nine months. During the last and sorriest period of his collapsing marriage Kajetan had not turned up at any of those points where our various circles of acquaintances intersected. He seemed almost to have gone into hiding. Now I learned that the week before he had unobtrusively become my neighbor. He was living a short distance from me, on the other side of a hill whose road, at this point no longer lined with houses, made a serpentine curve as it climbed to an open prospect. Now, standing beside me on the footpath between the marching rows of bare vines, he stretched out his arm to point to the spot. It lay amid the checkered jumble below us, where the last true streets ended and there began the area of scattered villas and farmsteads, cottages, barns and bungalows, fences and shacks—the whole of the dissolving edge of the city advancing in irregular columns and with a jagged front line against the first vineyards, mowings, and tilled fields, repelled here and there, thrust back and split open by a deep salient of untamed ground. Farther away the jagged, staggered outlines of the houses were stacked up one behind another, closer and closer together, their whole expanse enveloped in that haze of bluish-gray whose density increased with the density of the city.

It was a cold, dry, wintry day, still in the old year, in which as yet no snow had fallen.

Although we had not seen each other for so long, we were not cast into that state of embarrassment which, under similar circumstances, is apt to afflict persons who fundamentally have never had anything in common but have not cut the nominal bridges between them: then we are attempting to bring up to date a person who is essentially a stranger; we are using a language that is certainly foreign to him and trying to sketch a picture that he can never possibly see. Of course at the start

64

Schlaggenberg, too, found that the very number of things he had to say obstructed one another at his lips; but he knew that they could all be said to me, and without much difficulty. Moreover, he was already beyond being too anxious about the figure he cut or the picture he might be presenting of himself; and although he had his normal share of vanity, he let others think whatever they pleased about him. Indeed, as life moves on, a kind of weariness at last overcomes even our vanity; we then can spare ourselves a good deal of effort . . . As far as I was concerned, order reigned in myself and in my affairs—order and, I may as well admit it, a certain emptiness.

"You are—alone?" I asked, for I already knew that much about him.

"Yes, alone!" he replied, as though he were telling me of a triumphal achievement, and with a gratified nod surveyed the tiers of the landscape spread out before us. I had long since made it a practice not to take at face value any statements by my fellow-men concerning matters of the heart, no matter how resolutely such statements were made. Moreover—how often Kajetan and Camy had been separated before!

A quiver of broad rays burst from the clouds in the west, and a good half of the sun's orb, already sinking so early in the afternoon, appeared within a fiery gateway. We descended the hill. I asked Schlaggenberg whether he cared to have tea with me, and took him to my place.

I wrote down the conversation we had that evening—I needed thirty-three pages and nearly a week to do it. I have the text, and others have seen it. It formed the beginning of my chronicle, although it is almost worthless as documentation of what followed—worthless in the same way that photographs of that period would be. Even at the time I might have arrived at a theory about personal journals. I had always kept a journal. Now, however, it expanded. On the whole I wrote it immediately after the events. To distinguish essentials from inessentials is impossible without perspective. For such total chronicling I would have needed—had I been consistent—a scale as large as the segment of life that came under my purview. But since I was not consistent, I did not think of this, did not promptly carry my task *ad absurdum*. Not until some time later did my craft smash upon the reefs of reality.

I understood, of course, that Schlaggenberg had to give some kind of form to the pack he now had to carry—namely the separation from his wife, which had all the earmarks of being final; that he had to sum it up, bundle it together, and make it decently portable. He seemed, moreover, to have succeeded in finding a kind of formula for his present situation ("Yes, alone!" and "a new life!"—these were some of the phrases he bandied). By dint of this formula, he was evidently able to derive a certain pleasure from the situation, to put it to fruitful use. He was looking spruce and well (quite a change from November 20!), and his various endeavors were progressing, he told me.

However, certain details—I shall come to these in a moment—soon made me realize that he had tinkered with various arguments until he had put together a weird, crooked structure of self-deception. At this point I decided not to go on coddling his fine equanimity, and his spurious formula, but to drive him back to the wall, to force him to face the truth. That would be more worthy of him. To my mind he could well stand it without the least damage to his health—this great lubber who had never been ill in his life.

While I was engaged in this, he acted in a highly curious

fashion. He "ebbed"—for so I termed this mode of behavior in him. He listened, without interrupting. When I finished and fell silent, he waited, and though I really had nothing further to add, he suggested: "Do go on talking, do go on"—looking at me with expectant, in fact with challenging expression, as though he were paying me for speaking (as later I was to pay him for writing). "Do go on; what you say is important, very important . . ."

"You, perhaps, may find it so," I said, suddenly quite out of humor. For all at once I realized that Kajetan had been more and more taking refuge in these ebb tides of his. There had been a time when he had been a master of the flood tide, but now he seemed to find the opposite extreme more to his liking.

But he would not let me retreat.

"Well, since I am the subject under discussion . . ." he began, broke off, and then went on: "You really do me good. You are—so settled. You know how to listen." (I had not been listening at all; I had been doing most of the talking.) "You don't five for yourself, so to speak. Things ought to be arranged so that there are regular, official posts for people like you . . ."

In those words he really formulated my role in the simplest possible terms. And then, that phrase: "official posts"! (His sister Charlotte, whom we all called Quapp, later expressed the same idea even more cleverly in the epigram: "Every man his own department head.") But perhaps this clever phrase also originated with Kajetan.

"What the devil were you doing that day on the traffic island? You looked as though you were about to lose your trousers," I said—perhaps with a touch of vengefulness.

"Not my trousers," he replied. "But the bottom of every thing had just dropped out on me, so to speak. Twenty minutes before, I had seen Camy for the last time."

His whole marital predicament had actually been as simple as a slap in the face—he alone made it seem complicated. Kajetan had never been able to afford a wife. All along, Camy had been living with her father, the doctor (for whom Kajetan had the highest respect—quite understandably, for the old man was a magnificent person). Camy wanted to marry; her affair with Kajetan had been going on for rather a long while, to put it mildly. Kajetan, however, should never have allowed himself to be persuaded. He had no right whatsoever to enter upon marriage. He had no certain means of livelihood, and in addition was, in my opinion, totally unfit psychologically for the married state. Call it incapacity for attachment, if you will. You might also say that his personality stood in no need of complement.

Oddly enough, he seemed to have felt that his situation was far more awkward with regard to the old gentleman than with regard to Camy. That was something he could not shut his eyes to and in the end it was more as though he took his father-in-law in marriage than Camy herself. Of course she had the usual arguments and reassurances ready to hand: being married would not change anything, would merely make things "more convenient" for them and would avert embarrassments, and since in any case he had "other aims"—by which she meant his literary ambitions—and therefore had "so much on his mind," she would be the one to "deal with practical things," and so on and so forth. But now, sitting with me over tea, when he started to complain of the demands she after all ended by making—and to pretend, moreover, that he had been the victim of "trickery"—I met him head-on. I told him I would not listen to such absurdities, that he should have had the sense to evaluate the talk of a woman who was bent on marriage. I was amused to hear how he expressed himself in regard to the "other aims" and "so much on his mind." "You see, Herr Geyrenhoff" he said, "her language used to be so much more polite. Later on she used to talk about my utter inability to manage life. Utter inability was what she called it."

Inability to, say, pay a doctor's bill—a detail which struck me as in some way suspect.

Yet this was the very point on which the marriage foundered. It is necessary to know that a little less than a year earlier Kajetan's father, Herr Eustach von Schlaggenberg, had died on his estate in southern Styria. The condition of his affairs was not very satisfactory. The estate, consisting primarily of woodland, carried a heavy burden of debt. Aside from the widow, Schlaggenberg's mother, the heirs were of course Kajetan and his sister Charlotte. Herr Eustach, however, had appointed them only residuary legatees; the estate remained undivided for the time being, and Frau von Schlaggenberg retained the rights of disposition and usufruct. Charlotte received an allowance from her mother, and Kajetan, unfortunately, also continued to be supported by her, at least in part.

The provisions of the will had been on the whole wise; the securities could continue to be held intact, and the dividends could be used to defray the interest on the mortgages. Thus it was possible to hold on to the forest lands. The widowed Frau von Schlaggenberg did not administer the property herself. A capable and honest Viennese lawyer, an old friend of the family, arranged a highly favorable tenancy lease. It began to seem that the estate could cover all its own expenses. Moreover, not only was there the regular income from the tenant, but in the early summer of 1927 a number of stocks of which Frau von Schlaggenberg held a sizable block took an enormous upswing. Thus the precariously balanced situation tipped at last toward the positive side. In other respects as well, as it happened, the financial situation of Frau von Schlaggenberg and her children took a distinct turn for the better at this time, and for quite different reasons.

Only after cross-examining Kajetan had I extracted from him all these details in regard to the financial difficulties that ensued from his father's death. It was very difficult to make him stick to this subject. Exact, and even hairsplitting, as he usually was, in these serious matters he often displayed a lack of thorough knowledge, and would give me only the most offhand answers. To anticipate, I may say at once that the calamitous situation Herr Eustach had left at his death had been brought about by his association with the Austrian Lumber Industry Bank.

Camy could have known all this—although undoubtedly Kajetan had been just as offhand and vague in his explanations to her as he was to me. She might have listened and understood, or not. The fact that the daughter of a physician should have had difficulty settling a doctor's bill in itself suggests that something was up. Here was a prime example of Kajetan's "utter inability." Camy now rallied her father to her aid, sent him as an emissary, so to speak, to have a good talk with Kajetan. "The question here is simply and solely one of money," she briefed him, "of purely practical matters. Not a word must be said about any personal difficulties that may exist between Kajetan and me."

The whole business was stupid and clumsy; it was simply a matter of Camy's going off the deep end in her despair over "Kajetan's utter inability to manage things—his lack of desire to make a go of things." (These were her very words to me.) Her father would have wanted to show his beloved daughter that he was ready to help her in any way he could. And of course he would have volunteered right off to pay the outstanding fee but for Camy's insisting that this must be her husband's responsibility. Still, for all his affection for her, the old man had to give himself an enormous push, and take a running start, as it were—for he hated the very thought of the whole affair and of the kind of scene he was being asked to act out. But the thing went off in all seriousness; the playlet was staged. "This time Papa was really marvelous and didn't retreat, as he always does with everybody because he's so sweet. He wouldn't put up with Kajetan's digressions and stuck right to the one subject." The old fellow had actually committed the grave mistake (I would call it such) of rigidly excluding all the more important matters from his conversation with Schlaggenberg and hammering away on one theme—in accordance with his instructions: "But the question here is the money, nothing but the money." Thus Schlaggenberg was attacked on his weakest and most helpless side. The specialist who had been treating Camy had already filed suit. When I first heard this from Camy, and now again heard of it from Kajetan, I wondered about it. Kajetan spoke of some injection cure for a rheumatic complaint; for obvious reasons I never did succeed in learning the rights of this matter.

At any rate, the suit had been filed when Schlaggenberg ceased to meet the installment payments he had agreed on with the doctor. Now came the last straw. In order to be let alone, his only recourse was to take what is called a pauper's oath. This he could easily have done: he owned nothing, had no resources. But quite naturally he was disinclined to do this. I should not like to assert that the affair had been arranged from the beginning by Camy to bring matters to a head. Still, it remains curious that she absolutely would not hear of her father's stepping in and settling the bill. In the course of the big scene, the theatrical fireworks, she finally said: "Since you are so dead set against taking the pauper's oath, I can only assume that you have some funds you wish to conceal from me." Of course

71

she had no need to say more. Kajetan immediately began to storm, despite the presence of Camy's father ("I became totally desperate and raging mad, and finally extremely abusive"); he threw up everything, demanded an immediate separation and a divorce, and finally ran out of the apartment and out of the house, slamming every door violently behind him. Shortly afterwards—that was on November 20 at fifteen minutes before six o'clock at the Wahring Intersection—"the bottom dropped out." That was when I had caught that glimpse of him. Now he said to me: "Do you know, it was not until some hours later, when I was sitting alone back home, that I realized the abominable viciousness of what Camy had said, grasped it in its full 'extent,' I might say."

Poor Camy! Undoubtedly the worst of it for her was that her father, too, strongly condemned her for that remark; given her character, he could not help doing so.

So there Kajetan sat "back home." He had never lived with his wife; there had not been time for them to establish a home.

Poor Camy! She was quite unable to look behind what Scolander called her cultivated "garden plot of a horizon," which consisted in a kind of rational idyl, or her wish for such an idyl. All breadth of spirit was eliminated from it. Moreover, she was weak; that is to say, she lacked robustness and her position was also weak. Camy was endangered. A person in danger has the right to defend himself, and will use whatever means he has to hand. On the whole there was something about her exceedingly—dry would be the word. It may have been just this which had attracted Kajetan, who had perhaps an excess of the sap of life. It may have been an attempt on the part of his nature to penetrate an alien element. He had tried to make his way into a sound, self-contained, harmonious character. The elastic rebound of such a character after every deep disturbance can be inhumanly cruel, or sheerly and simply inhuman. And perhaps Camy actually wanted to be inhuman, wanted nothing else. Perhaps she was seeking a real cause for separation. There was no doubt in my mind about her intention. She wanted to get rid of him—as he, fundamentally, wanted to be rid of her. Only she was able to bring it off sooner, by virtue of her very lack of imagination. I believe that by December she no longer remembered what Kajetan looked like. He took it much harder.

I gave up on him, although at the start I had set out to demolish the whole Maypole beribboned with self-deceptions which he had planted upon the now-established structure of his "new life." Let him have it as he liked, the "deadly insult" ("abominable viciousness," as he had put it) and the "trickery" too, for all I cared. He badly needed this—or, to use a somewhat technical metaphor, he needed such an explosive charge in order to escape at all from Camy's sphere of attraction. At the moment everything depended on his escape velocity.

The sharp points to which we grind things in our lives now and then may be, at the time, really essential. Once the sharp points have blunted again, they seem incomprehensible and even ludicrous.

And so I let him luxuriate in his consciousness of deadly insult (which he did rather noisily), and said only: "Do you know what I think, Kajetan? That all of this is only occurring to you now, in hindsight. As it occurred to you only later that evening when you were by yourself."

"Does that in any way invalidate it?" he retorted promptly. He then began to speak of his wife's Jewish birth. This, too, I recognized as mere pretext. Her totally alien cast of mind indeed! I did not say so—but if this were the case, then logic ruled out any deadly insult. Moreover, it would be difficult to find a greater alienation than that which exists between the sexes; all the rest can be only a mere additive. This, too, I forbore to express. Now he went on to tell me that in company, whenever he had taken the floor in some dispute and was advancing his own point of view, Camy had always attacked him violently—under the protection of the others, so to speak—or at least emphatically sided with the opinion of his opponent. In general, he said, he virtually had to hide his face from her, so ready was she to vent her hostility against him.

I had an idea of my own in regard to this first point: namely, that women quickly turn impertinent when a given situation forces a man to abide by the rules of gallantry—which otherwise men, for their part, are only too lax about.

But for the rest I did feel—at last!—a certain sympathy for Schlaggenberg. All at once the whole affair appeared to me rather as if a whole cyclone of organic life had been unleashed around some small, hard, chance pebble; the cyclone whirled madly around it, whose central position, whose stoniness, endowed it with the qualities of a hereafter in the here but whose unfathomable mystery lay simply in its sterility.

But now here was the very thing I at first could make nothing of, his last vehicle of escape, which had only now come into view: his allusion to his wife's racial stock. Here the ground dropped away from under my feet; I lacked all knowledge, all experience in this realm. In order to follow him, to know whether his remarks had any basis, I should have needed some personal contact with the matter. I rummaged through my mind. Stangeler? On that very critical twentieth of November I had in fact talked a great deal with Stangeler about his relationship with Grete Siebenschein, and discussed the possibilities of his future with her; but we had not approached the side of the question now touched upon by Schlaggenberg. Finally my silly card room came to mind. In order to make some contribution to the subject I told Kajetan about the ladies there, described beautiful Frau Steuermann, Director Altschul's wife, and Frau Clarisse Markbreiter—mentioning how incredibly, not to say absurdly, the latter differed from her sister Irma Siebenschein . . . (But what in the world did any of this have to do with Camy Schlaggenberg?)

The effect of my little tale upon Kajetan was such that for a second I seriously thought he had lost his mind—after all, better men than Herr Kajetan have gone to pieces over an unhappy affair of the heart.

While I talked on, he had relaxed, and sat sprawled in his armchair, toying with a long cigarette holder. But now his hands suddenly froze, he looked obliquely past me into a corner of the room, and his face seemed to narrow, as it had done earlier, betokening that Kajetan was once more becoming obsessed with some lone detail. This time, however, his face did not seem overcast, but only—there is no better word—slightly imbecilic. The change of expression was so clear and so surprising that I involuntarily broke off in the midst of my account. There was a lengthy silence.

"Are these females stout?" he said at last, still staring into the corner.

"What's that?"

"I mean," he added, without the slightest change of expression, without the trace of a smile, speaking in a flat tone and staring all the while into his corner, "I mean corpulent, obese, portly." And as though he had now explained all to my perfect satisfaction, he fell silent.

"As it happens they are," I replied, losing the thread of my discourse completely, as the result of this unexpected caprice. "Especially Frau Steuermann. . ."

"Really!" he exclaimed. He looked up, keenly interested.

"Tell me, is she fat? Really—well stuffed?"

"Yes," I cried, "fat! Really well stuffed! Corpulent! Obese! Portly! But what the devil is this all about? Why should you care?"

Schlaggenberg had subsided again, was once more sprawling in his chair staring into the corner, toying with the holder. I looked perplexedly at him, and after a pause he condescended to offer the following clarification.

"Then there's a possibility there," he said casually, talking to himself as though he were only thinking aloud, speaking with many pauses, with carelessly tossed-off words and phrases. "I see some light there, so to speak. Assuming real corpulence, of course. Somewhere between a hundred and eighty and two hundred pounds . . . Well, yes . . . You see, I was at the opera recently, well, up in the third gallery, oh well. Felt hungry afterwards and dropped into a beer cellar nearby. Next door to it is a fancy restaurant. You know the one. The Opernkeller. Always a line of automobiles in front of it. Passing by, I glanced into the vestibule where the patrons were removing their coats. . . And just for a moment . . . in passing, as I said . . . and it wasn't till later, some time later, that it came back to my mind several times . . . I'd seen a woman in there—a lady in a brown evening dress, very plump, broad in the beam . . . it was a brown silk dress, or something like that. Yes, a brown silk dress. Yes, yes. But I beg your pardon, do go on—I'm afraid I interrupted you . . ."

"I should say you have," I replied, and went on, resolutely ignoring his confused utterances, which made not the slightest sense to me.

He left around eight o'clock. We must always be prepared to apply to other persons the lessons in *nil admirari* we

76

have received from ourselves. I reminded myself of that then. Maruschka knocked, entered, bobbed a curtsy, removed the tea wagon, threw open the window—we had been smoking heavily—shook down the stove, inquired: "Can I make the bed?" and disappeared into the adjoining room.

I did not at all feel like spending the rest of the evening at home, having dinner in my room, and turning to some task or other. With Schlaggenberg out of the way I was inclined to view the wretched debacle more in the light of the general masculine dislike for marriage. Perhaps, I thought, this incapacity for marriage reached a special degree of intensity in my friend Kajetan, making any permanent intimacy with another person impossible. And had he not, in fact, been maneuvered into the marriage? Probably Stangeler's situation was similar, although he might be somewhat better adapted for the marital state than Schlaggenberg. At the moment this whole masculine fanaticism about freedom seemed to me nothing but a desire to lay claim potentially to all women not yet possessed, and an urge to escape the one example at hand at any given time—from whom, alas, the man might have to learn his lesson. It was an instance, then, of escaping into a multitude of examples, which obscured the real issue. *Variatio et per spem delectans,* Captain von Eulenfeld would have said, for he was given to these Latin tags. Another of his favorite phrases was, though not in Latin: "An old hussar is not a dog."

At any rate, I had a glimmering that none of this applied to me. There were, somehow, other reasons for my having remained a bachelor for so long. Later on I was to discover what they were.

I went out. First I dropped into a bistro, what we Viennese call a *Beisl,* for something to eat, although I do not usually patronize these little restaurants. There was one by the rail cut

77

of the subway line, where the main street of Döbling bridges the tracks; from there on down the area is called the Hohe Warte. What does one order in a *Beisl?* Goulash and beer—it's best to be on the safe side, and goulash is at its best in these little restaurants. The proprietor knew me—Maruschka always came here for soda water for me. As I passed the bar he snapped to attention for the briefest of moments; he had been a corporal in the uhlans during the war and knew that I had been a reserve officer in the cavalry. He was a well-set-up figure of a man but had only one leg. Nevertheless, he was afraid of nothing and no one. I was present once when he flatly refused to hand out playing cards to three drunken rowdies—as rare a phenomenon in this part of Döbling as crawfish in the ornamental pools of a park. Whereupon the three misplaced ruffians took themselves off. But then anything can happen anywhere, though perhaps only once. On Daponte Gasse I once actually found a little scorpion in the bathroom, in good condition and very much alive. I hailed it as an emissary from the south, from the lands of the classics, cajoled it into a box with air holes, and set it free at a lonely spot in the Prater meadows. Incidentally, specimens of the praying mantis (*Mantis religiosa* L.), a preposterously large insect of southern Europe, are also found in, of all places, the vicinity of Frankfurt am Main . . .

You see the kind of diffuse plankton that drifts through one's brain when one sits alone in a bistro, eating goulash and drinking beer. But the thread-pulling of association (the *ultima ratio* of all adepts of psychologism) tapered off somewhat; the associations ranged themselves to one side and formed a kind of frame around a certain utterance of Schlaggenberg's: "There was one particular time when Camy made me feel my spirit confronted with an utterly alien spiritual principle. It was only in a few words she said, but the effect upon me was overwhelming and unforgettable. It was in summer and we were taking a stroll in a small resort near Vienna. I no longer remember by what route we came to it, but we began to describe, first I, then she, what we considered to be our deepest and most intimate feeling about life. Our relations were such that that sort of thing would come up between us at any time. We had chafed against each other to that extent by then. I put forth the idea, which I imagine you and I both take for granted, that I felt my own psyche or my own inner life to be like a well-shaft of unlimited depth, or at any rate like a room which cannot be pictured as closed on any given side, there always being a side from which something still unknown, something I have never before experienced, might come rushing in. Camy came to a halt, obviously quite astonished; she looked down at the ground, thought for a while, and then said to me in her precise, sensible way that that sort of thing was incomprehensible to her, for she felt her own nature to be a familiar space enclosed on all sides, so that it would be quite impossible for anything she could not understand—that is, anything actually new—to come at her from it. Now what do you say to that?"

I had not answered. But now it seemed as clear as day—if what Camy had described was true—that she had chosen the better, more rational, and probably easier way of living. No doubt about it, one ought to make every effort to become like this. If one were like this, one would be spared those waves of coldness and depression rolling down from the upper emptiness of a room, where wall and ceiling meet and where we ordinarily seldom look. One might also be spared these intense feelings of displeasure which, every now and then, make staying home intolerable. "Of course everyone feels that way occasionally," I now thought and at that lost the imaginary or the real thread of my associations. I became disgusted with myself, paid, and left. But not for home. I had no slightest inkling, however, that I would soon be running into a person who was likewise almost disgusted with herself . . . I crossed the bridge and walked along the subway cut for a while as though I were moving through a cool and unfamiliar lateral valley of my life.

On the corner of Billroth Strasse and Chimani Gasse stood (and still stands) the Café Döblingerhof. It was a considerable distance from my flat; I had walked far.

Now I entered this place, likewise somewhat plushy from all the soft chairs with which it was furnished. The decor was in black and green; in summer these colors would harmonize well with the trees and gardens along Chimani Gasse, the strong sunlight and the deep sharp shadows, all of which would be visible through the ample windows of the front. So I thought as I walked slowly through the café, which was two-thirds empty. Well, now it was winter. Although one did not feel the winter too acutely here, except that the place was somewhat overheated.

In the midst of such idle thoughts (the plankton had certainly been thick tonight!) I saw, three or four tables farther along, a strikingly beautiful woman. Moreover, she looked gracious and kindly and even threw me a smile. Why, it was none other than Frau Steuermann! It was as though I were being compensated both for my patience and for the malaise I had suffered all evening. I could sit down at her table—and in fact she seemed pleased and quite cheered when I did so.

She did not ask me why I no longer came to the bridge games (that had been Frau Lea Wolf's first question); and this, it seemed to me, showed a noteworthy difference between the two women. In fact it was I who brought the conversation around to that subject; I asked her whether she still went to the café by the Danube Canal, or whether she now preferred this place. I myself, I said, had never been in the Döblingerhof before. At this point in our conversation I noticed that she had not sat down in one of the velvet-covered chairs but on a black-lacquered wooden chair, for there were also some of these in the café. It was not hard to guess why. The soft chairs were small and relatively low; this lady might have had some difficulty getting up from one. On the marble table top in front of Frau Selma stood a half-filled glass of eggnog. I had meanwhile ordered the same beverage for myself.

"Oh yes," she replied to my question, "I still go there. But I don't really enjoy it any more. One of these days I'll just stay away entirely, I imagine. It rather disgusts me. You know, Herr von Geyrenhoff, what all these ladies go there for, aside from playing cards? Each one eyes the other to see whether, God forbid, she's had any luck reducing and maybe has lost another pound. And it's all a joke, you know. Do you think any one of us—at our age, I mean—is ever going to get herself down to a modern figure? And what else are they interested in? Whether any of them is wearing something new and where she bought it, and what it cost. That's how it goes. They are all mean as hornets about one another. And they call that a nice, friendly get-together. I sometimes come here to play a little bridge. But it isn't so very different. The girls are still at it in the game room, playing away, one rubber after another. I'm sick of it. I thought I'd take a look at the magazines, but that gets pretty dull too. Anyway, now I have some nice company to make up for it." She laughed, looking like a happy baby.

You could not really have said of her that she was an intelligent woman of the type of, say, Mary K. (whom, however, I was not to meet until after all the events described here had taken place). It would not have done to place any great demands

81

upon Frau Selma Steuermann's conscious mind. But she was good-natured and receptive, and wide awake enough to be impressionable. Her heart was not tone-deaf, so to speak. She was therefore by no means foolish. You might think of her as a big, swelling heart moving about on a pair of very small feet; what was more, this heart had two somewhat shortish arms, small white hands, and a full complement of the other appropriate features, such as a milky complexion and abundant hair shading her pleasant little face like a block of ebony. I was strongly taken with her mildness and her engaging manner; for both these qualities one might possibly have to thank her deceased husband, who had been director of a large silk mill in Meidling. Here was a lady who had never known a moment's indignity—and what better bequest can a husband leave to his widow? All in all, sitting there as she was, she was a perfect treasure.

I accompanied Frau Selma as far as the door of her home on Chimani Gasse. I am aware that even while we were still in the café I was several times on the verge of speaking with her about Schlaggenberg and his whole case. Perhaps I should say that her personality constituted an invitation to tell her about everything and everyone; and yet to really do so would have been almost an abuse of her innocence. Later on she did hear some of the story after all, largely from me, in fact, though I withheld the names of the people concerned. That second evening spent with Frau Steuermann in the Café Döblingerhof paved the way for her becoming a collaborator in my chronicle. Her opinion of Kajetan and his marital affairs was, on that occasion, somehow quite shattering to me. "Does the whole thing surprise you, Herr von Geyrenhoff?" she said. "Not me, not a bit. They all behaved absolutely wrong. The father too. It couldn't have turned out differently. Believe me, it's wrong to try to ignore these differences."

I walked slowly homeward. It was around ten o'clock. Again I followed the subway cut; again I seemed to be moving through a cool and unfamiliar lateral valley of my life. Far back against the slope, as though looming up against a hill, a possibility glowed into life. It was one of those possibilities which shine upon us only briefly, and for that very reason remain the most delightful we have ever experienced.

I did not see Schlaggenberg again until after the New Year—to be precise, on the Saturday after Epiphany, which made the date January 8. Once again I caught only a glimpse of him, at night, for just a few minutes. That Saturday night Baron von Eulenfeld, the cavalry captain, had organized another of his roundups, or mass pub-crawls, for which people were summoned from all over the city and even brought around in automobiles; some, whom the captain insisted on having, were surprised in their homes and shanghaied (as was done to Schlaggenberg); others were fetched out of coffeehouses or even, if they were encountered by chance in the street, taken captive at once (as was done to Stangeler) and pushed into one of the numerous cars that made up a veritable cavalcade. These cars were a regular feature of the parties. In the van rode the captain's red sports car—and by no means slowly. It was a dreadfully riotous procession that wound through the small bars and cafés of the downtown section and on into the suburban taverns, with the whole affair finally, after innumerable changes of scene, after a succession of cafés, bistros, private homes, studios, cabarets, and night clubs of all sorts, ending up in one of those perfect Eulenfeld nebulas which no one ever seemed able to locate again, probably because by that time everyone was "drenched"—as the captain would have said. The participant in one of these parties always wondered how he had got back home in the end, and how the whole thing had happened.

Among the captain's charming idiosyncrasies was the sudden appearance of his monocle whenever, toward the end, things became a bit wild. Along with this, he would intensify the gallantry and formality of his ordinarily involuted etiquette.

The nebula of the eighth, or rather actually of the ninth of January, proved to be—as we shall see later—an astronomical event of unique character. For a nova, or new star, appeared within it.

An old hussar is not a dog. Well, here was one hussar who really proved the proverb. It is a fairly long way from a captain in the Fourteenth Regiment of the Imperial German Hussars—garrisoned in Kassel—to a leading post in the Vienna branch of C. C. Wakefield & Co. Moreover, this way had been somewhat winding. In fact, let us be frank—the way had had a few rather dark turnings . . . Still and all, for having covered such a road, the old hussar deserved all honor; to have survived it without loss of form must have cost what energies remained from a strenuous life. However, from time to time the old storm and stress fizzed and overflowed like an opened bottle of soda pop. These parties, therefore, fulfilled a need of his and had a period like that of comets, after which they returned again.

There is no doubt that Eulenfeld wielded a spell over the entire band. They sailed along behind him like a regular comet's tail, male and female both. Eulenfeld had a kind of superiority *ab ovo*. Such a thing does exist in people of high breeding. It was a combination of charm and self-assurance; the former quality is particularly appreciated in our country: a person with charm can sin to his heart's content and will be forgiven almost everything. It is as though the gods had nodded assent beforehand to everything he might wish to do. No one can be so churlish as to oppose him. There is a mystery about such gifts; they are present almost before the infant has opened his eyes; but the most casual of his glances subdues everyone in the vicinity, makes everyone complaisant. . . Eulenfeld's superiority was by no means based upon his patent of nobility. For example, the train of his nebula included persons of far higher and older nobility (though I did not see Count Langingen on that January 8, nor did Frau Titi Lasch appear this time—luckily for Stangeler, since she was his Grete's sister; the captain's circles overlapped many others!). "The captain wishes it." "Since he is the captain." People actually talked that way. They sometimes referred to him by the American phrase "Big Chief," or called themselves "the Düsseldorfers"—the title stemming from a tale of Eulenfeld's to the effect that it was no easy matter for a hussar to travel by rail from the Rhineland to Berlin cold sober, because from Düsseldorf to Berlin the way was "totally plagued" by members of a regiment of uhlans going on furlough; you were inevitably shanghaied into some compartment where . . . And so on and so forth. The gang also called themselves by the French word for herd: *troupeau*.

Kajetan used to circulate the story that the captain had once put all his debts into the hands of a Berlin usurer named A. Mandhus; when at last the moneylender decided to present the notes to old Baron von Eulenfeld and was on his way to see him, there had been a railroad accident and dear A. Mandhus had been burned to death, along with all the dangerous papers. Thus the elements of legend were already gathering around the captain; no matter what his fix, the stories indicated, a sort of Providence looked after him.

It was rather late in the evening when I arrived at Eulenfeld's apartment. He was not home, had been out and around since about six o'clock, hunting up victims, so to speak. I was informed that some five levies were planned, two of them in Döbling, as well as raids upon several cafés regularly patronized by Eulenfeld's friends. The roundup appeared to me to be on a grander scale than usual—in the end this would make for impressive results. Some fifteen persons were already assembled in the captain's apartment and had settled down comfortably around the available beverages. But no one was the least tipsy as yet. I noticed Dolly Storch, the daughter of a professor of anatomy at the University; she was a very pretty girl, though a bit on the plump side; and beside her a brawny, clumsy fellow with Negroid lips whose name, I was told, was Oskar Leucht, Oki for short. Bill Frühwald, the son of a well-known Viennese architect, I had met before; he was famous for his talent at improvising light pieces on the piano—a perfect bar pianist, in fact; but there was no instrument for him here. Someone had brought along a phonograph. In the adjoining room people were dancing very soberly.

There was not much noise, but the volume swelled sharply when the motorcade drove up and Eulenfeld appeared, with only a few new companions; among them was Schlaggenberg, whom the captain had promptly taken into his red sports car; the second seat of the car had in fact been reserved for Kajetan beforehand. The majority of the crowd stayed in the cars; Stangeler, too, was already among them, but I did not see him; he was sitting in a sedan, having been quickly stuffed in with others who could hold him, once he had been caught. His capture had taken place near that large café where I once used to play bridge with Frau Markbreiter and Frau Wolf. I heard that he had been found "absolutely lost in dreams on the sidewalk" (Eulenfeld). Not until some time later did I learn what he had been doing there. This was the first time René had ever joined the *troupeau;* he was anything but a boon companion of Eulenfeld's, but they had known each other a long time, from the war.

The confusion mounted; more and more *"troupistes"* had been clambering out of their cars and coming up the stairs; the quacking of women's voices could be heard; the stairwell rang with conversations flung up and down from different levels. I saw the cartoonist Imre von Gyurkicz, who was well known at the time, and Holder, the theater critic, a modest and quiet man (unlike Gyurkicz); somehow the whole circle was connected with literature or journalism, among other things; but in a vague and indefinite fashion. In Eulenfeld's back room couples were still dancing soberly. Now, however, the company was whipped into action, urged to hurry; the next destination was being discussed.

Later Kajetan described to me how he himself had been "levied." The circumstances must have been similar to what I was now witnessing in Eulenfeld's rooms, except that Kajetan had been alone at home when the swarm had come pouring in upon the dense silence of his study out there in Döbling, on the other side of a hill on whose slope the road, at this point no longer lined with houses, made a serpentine curve as it climbed to an open prospect. . .

He had joined Eulenfeld in the little two-seater, and the captain had started the motor at once. But then a tremendous outcry had arisen. No one agreed with anyone else on what their destination should be. Yet some of them were already roaring off, shouted to and shouting back, with those in open cars waving their arms wildly to those behind them.

Then the noise faded away, and windows closed in houses

where people had been looking out to see what the racket was all about. Kajetan had turned to look back. The street once more lay deserted behind the cavalcade of cars. Darkness had already descended, but it was somewhat brightened by the snowlight. At the end of this street, which consisted only of scattered single houses, telegraph poles could be seen marching out into open country; they reared up against a sky restless and inflamed from the reddish glow of the city.

So now we too were sailing along, though at a more reasonable pace; for out in the suburbs they had (according to Schlaggenberg's account) roared like a conquering army down Grinzinger Allee. They kept up the pace only as far as Sievering Intersection—for police were stationed there.

One remembers little of such nights, virtually nothing. Today I recall a huge studio of some painter, along the rear of which there was a series of booths formed of Venetian blinds. The middle of the expanse of floor was filled with dancing couples moving very quietly in slow fox-trot and tango steps. For a moment I thought a small band must be playing, a sort of mandolin and banjo orchestra; but the complicated music was being produced by a single young man manipulating a huge double guitar with stupendous virtuosity; what was more, he occasionally sang Spanish and English songs along with his strumming. Behind the dancers and the spectators the enormous glass skylight slanted darkly and obliquely down to the floor; its tremendous curtains looked like sails puffed out by the wind; they had been shifted aside to right and left. I did not know where we were, nor at whose place, nor even in what part of the city, for finally I had driven along with the rest in a closed car. Glass in hand—everyone was drinking brandy and soda here—I circled around the dancers, whose numbers were steadily increasing, and went up to the window. To my surprise, I found myself gazing miles down and out into the darkness; the great distance could be measured by the numerous lights of the city which hung, darted, and blinked in a glowing extension of silent configurations out to the horizon. This might be Salmannsdorf or Ober-St. Veit, scarcely Döbling. I could find no landmark by which to orient myself, and did not want to ask; I had lost sight of the few familiar faces about me, and there was no one around whom I knew. A while back Schlaggenberg and René Stangeler had still been in view, standing at the edge of the dance floor talking to each other; Kajetan had placed his arm around René's shoulders. Later Schlaggenberg brushed by me and said: "Do you know him?"

"Yes," I said.

"I've told this fellow Stangeler he must call me up, and I've given him my number. I hope he does." Whereupon he vanished into the maelstrom. The captain too—already wearing his monocle!—had likewise become invisible. None of us met again until the last eruption—in the heart of the nebula, so to speak; it was amazing that the wind should have blown us all back together again right there.

Unimportant as all this seemed, it nevertheless formed a divide in time; and afterwards a new constellation suddenly emerged, one which had lain in wait inside me, I felt, and now took outward form. As the spring drew nearer, moreover, the writing of my chronicle proceeded at a smarter pace. Was I inducing life? *Primum scribere cleinde vivere.*

As for such binges, they are seldom writ in water, are seldom a mere churning without consequence after which the still pool of our lives returns to its original smoothness. Usually some new element has been introduced into our life, of which we become aware just as soon as our hangover has ebbed away— for at first we are under its physiological delusion. Sometimes we are spared the hangover and the new impulse is born while the waves are still surging high (so was it with Stangeler on this occasion); waves that rinse their prey clean and cast him fresh and new upon the smooth sand of the following day. But even if someone goes too far and is caught by the storm, as it were, when the whipped foam and the waves abruptly freeze in place, in a surprising, unpredictable, and undesired form, like pillars of salt or ice—even then something new has been brought to light. After a binge we feel lonelier, Charles Baudelaire once said. Is that a law? It is, and a valuable one, I should say.

Two days after our carousing, Kajetan's sister Charlotte arrived in Vienna. Not long afterwards, on February 1, she moved out to Döbling. In the course of the month the captain followed us (had he become fed up with his *troupeau*?). Then came Gyurkicz; he too moved out to the suburb. Furthermore, two usable relations of mine turned up in the city. Usable—in other words, a standard of usefulness was already being applied by this "Döbling Montmartre" (Grete Siebenschein)! Stangeler was already hanging out constantly with us. "With us," I said. With "our crowd." René had already become a kind of habit of mine; a bad habit, I firmly believed at the time.

Frau Mary K., in whose house, too, a "crowd" had formed, though one composed of far more youthful elements (this was during the time she was off in Munich heroically learning to walk again), once remarked, in connection with some complications that had arisen, that we must not weigh such things in the balance, since they are simply inevitable in every group; young people in a group often crawl all over one another like

90

kittens in a basket. Truer words were never said. They enable me in hindsight to take a good many things more lightly; they dispel some of the gravity of things, reduce certain things to their proper dimensions. The magic of language consists precisely in this, that the turn of a phrase can make the yoke of life rest more lightly on our shoulders, gently shaped to our constitution. We feel this with every *bon mot*, even with every accurate metaphor.

CHAPTER 3

Cheese Pastry

THE TELEPHONE, as was the custom every morning, had been noiselessly carried into the room by the maid and plugged into a socket beside the bed. When it rang, Frau Clarisse Markbreiter reached straight out of sleep for the receiver.

"Yes, here I am, sweetheart, this is your mama . . . What's that? . . . Cheesecake? With a yeast dough? . . . Oh, I suppose so, if it rises well . . . How can I explain it to you? . . . Oh, about as firm as a bosom . . . Mine? Hahaha, no, my girl, rather like yours. Is Egon at the office already? What are you two doing? I mean—is everything all right? Yes? Well, well, congratulations . . . Oh, just remember what I once told you, that's how men are. Well, if he's a good fellow, that's fine, then I like him too— Here's a kiss for you, sweetheart. Will you call me or should I call you? . . . After four in the coffeehouse . . . I'll call you again."

She hung up. The bed beside hers, now empty, was rumpled. Her husband had slept badly last night. She pensively regarded the blurred imprint of his body. While she lay looking at it, she seemed ten years older, fifty-five rather than forty-five. Her chin, pressed against her chest, made rolls of fat. She reached over and briefly patted the hollow in the pillow in place of the head which was already busy at the office, working for the family. Did he have worries? Business was not so good these days; the good big years seemed to be over. Nevertheless, Clarisse never heard about such matters from him. "Don't

93

think about it, my girl, don't you have a worry in the world. Go into town today and buy yourself something nice. Business is my business." That was how he always spoke. For twenty-six years Markbreiter had slept in the twin bed beside hers every night. What did she really know about the small, dark, rotund man? That he was good and capable, and the best father and husband a man could possibly be. Now she was looking younger, more like her actual age. The telephone rang.

"*Gruss Gott,* Irma! Grete? What now? When? . . . At four in the morning? Good Lord, what is the girl up to? . . . Who? . . . Him! . . . Yes, I've caught a glimpse of him two or three times in your vestibule . . . Really? . . . No? . . . She wants to leave home? Girls are all crazy today. Come, don't cry. Wait, we'll meet today. Does Ferry know . . . ?"

After she had hung up, it was her turn to make a call.

"Hello, yes, this is Clarisse, Minna, now what do you say about that little goose of a Grete . . . ?"

For some time past the gentle gurgling of a filling bathtub could be heard. Now the maid appeared.

"One moment. I have to call my husband."

In answer to her rapid flow of words, a sonorous voice replied from the telephone receiver, a voice which gave the impression that nothing in the world, not the most fearful elemental catastrophe, not even the sensational news about a wife's niece, could disturb the equilibrium of its owner.

"But my dearest, you take these things much too much to heart. Just send for the girl and give her a good talking to. She always listens to you. It's because she likes you, because you're good to her. I don't think Irma knows how to handle the child. You know all those things are different nowadays. What do you say he is? . . . Where? . . . At the Institute? For what? . . . For Historical Studies? So, there are all kinds of ways to

94

earn a living! Well you see, that's nonsense of course. But calm down, my dearest. We'll work it out. Just send for the child."

"Your bath, madam," the maid said again.

"Yes, Cilli. While I'm having it, will you call the milliner and tell her I'm coming this morning. One moment, I must just call my husband once more."

Again the sonorous, wise, reassuring voice answered. In the course of the last twenty years Clarisse had come to depend upon this voice to sweep away all the evils of the world for her; at least that was how she felt when she heard Markbreiter speak.

"Oh God, I'm so relieved," she cried into the telephone. ". . . Yes, my good clever Purzel, come to the café after you're through at the office, if you can. Oh, darling, Lily is coming too; I was just talking with her; she'll be so glad to see you, but I won't say anything to her about it. Imagine, this morning she called me about a recipe, a cake—I couldn't think right off how to tell her quickly—oh, I'll explain that to you later—they're so cute, the two of them, with their housekeeping . . . Yes—I'll be good, Purzel."

She threw off the blanket and climbed out of bed. If the reader could see her now, he would be surprised. In bed she looked enormous; huge arms and massive bosom under the thin nightgown, throat upholstered with fat, face round. But standing by the bed, she was small. Not a single curve in the nightgown suggested any bulkiness at the waist. Rather, to the back and sides the long gown fell straight and smooth; only in the higher reaches of the front was there a great promontory. After a glance at the upper stories of this personage, one would have expected corresponding proportions in the lower parts. But nothing of the sort. The whole woman was shaped like an inverted pear; the rich swell was up above. As she got out of bed, the nightgown slid aside to reveal a tiny foot and an exceedingly slender and shapely leg which would have been the pride of any young girl.

The Markbreiters' bathroom was the height of modernity. Along with the living room, it formed the crown of an otherwise modestly furnished apartment.

Frau Clarisse Markbreiter slipped out of her nightgown, stepped into the tiled tub, and slowly settled down in it. Cautiously letting herself lie back, she felt the water level rising along her skin until at last her whole body lay underneath the warm surface. She regarded her body in that absent fashion people have when lying comfortably in the tub. She was wondering why her husband was not already bored with her. She often wondered about that. After all, they would be reaching the twenty-sixth year of their marriage soon. Yet the opposite seemed obviously to be the case. With a certain self-contempt she reflected that she would never have married if she had been born a man. A man! Did a man need such a creature as herself? Ha, she would have shown women what for!

The reader may think that this woman has a great deal of time at her disposal, leads a languorous life, and that by now it is ten o'clock or later. But this would be a grave mistake. When Frau Markbreiter stepped out of the tub and disappeared inside a large yellow bathrobe, it was only half-past eight. Her husband had left the house at half-past seven; at eight she had got out of bed, after the round of telephone calls which were the usual thing in her circle. To be sure, Markbreiter would have liked his wife to sleep longer; he was always quiet as a mouse when he rose. But now Frau Clarisse needed nearly fifteen minutes to button herself in. First the abdomen. It had to be flattened, no matter what became of the stomach. The apparatus for this purpose was a kind of tube, fairly long, covered with pink silk, and with some thirty buttons running up the side. It was a struggle from button to button. When Frau Clarisse straightened up and took a cautious breath, she not only had relatively narrow hips but in the mirror gave the impression of being actually slender. At this point she picked up a kind of diminutive double hammock and rang for her maid.

For here self-esteem ended and desire for convenience began; she would permit the maid to fasten her brassiere at the back, although if need be she could have managed it herself—with the greatest difficulty, to be sure, because of her short arms. But after all, what was the girl for? (As it was, Frau Clarisse washed her back herself, with a long-handled brush.) There were nine buttons on the brassiere.

While the girl was buttoning her, Frau Markbreiter considered the day which lay ahead of her and found it a good and pleasant one, in spite of the botheration over Grete. For today, in accordance with her weekly schedule, she had to face neither the masseuse nor the gymnastics nor the steam bath, all of which consumed such a dreadful amount of time. But most of all today—Saturday, January 8—was not a weighing day. There stood the platform scale in the corner of the bathroom, its long, white-enameled pole looking like a gaunt governess; and every night before Clarisse went to sleep it threw her a glittering metallic look that struck deep into her guilty conscience, especially when that conscience was burdened with cups of hot chocolate topped with whipped cream and a dish of good sweet pastries. On Mondays those looks held the least danger, but as the week advanced they became fiercer and more penetrating. For Friday was weighing day. This was a law that Clarisse had imposed upon herself, and she had never yet broken it, not once in many, many years—a fact that can be considered characteristic of her. Well, today there was no weighing to be dreaded. After lunch she had only to go to the hairdresser. Of course lunch was going to be a boring, almost a dreary affair. For Purzel would not be there; he was going to be busy this noon.

She finished dressing for the street, in the meantime breakfasting on a cup of unsweetened tea and a piece of zwieback. Then she reviewed the household. The cook suggested something, and she said: "Yes." The menu for the evening meal had already been decided yesterday. In the course of many years they had succeeded gradually in finding out what Markbreiter, for all his modesty, really liked to eat—although he never expressed an opinion on such matters and praised everything that was served.

While she talked to the servants another remarkable change in her face might have been noted, one as radical as that earlier when she had studied Markbreiter's bed and looked ten years older. Her face appeared to lose its womanly, maternal breadth and converted itself into a profile emphasized by the nose; it lost flesh and seemed possessed by a disturbing and impetuous vivacity. This was how she looked as she listened to the maids' little reports on domestic work done or to be done; she interrupted with many quick insistent questions. Both the girls seemed to find this daily conversation a considerable strain, accustomed though they were to it; they appeared to be a little troubled and surprised, even when their consciences were quite at ease about the performance of their duties. They expressed themselves as plainly as possible, as though fearful of being misunderstood. Both Frau Markbreiter's maids, incidentally, were excellent in the sense that they were neither lazy nor slatternly; they were at least halfway competent and well mannered. For these qualifications they were well paid and received generous gifts at Christmas and for the New Year.

Now Frau Clarisse donned her big black fur coat—she had put on her hat during the conversation with the maids—and left. However, she returned to the vestibule once more to make two telephone calls.

Then she went at last, and was gone until half-past one; during the forenoon she testified to her existence only by three telephone calls to the maids; in the course of these she issued a number of instructions that had belatedly occurred to her.

At four o'clock Clarisse was sitting in the café with her sister Minna, who was so very different from herself, waiting for poor Irma as well as for Lily and ultimately Herr Siegfried Markbreiter. This was the large coffeehouse which occupied an entire block of a broad square on the Danube Canal and consisted, moreover, of three stories. The instant you entered this café you obtained a true picture of the real nature of social intercourse among people of the day, a picture of visionary clarity precisely because of its exaggeration. For so deafening was the clamor that you could only leap to the conclusion: everyone is talking and no one listening. Yet it was even more astounding to observe later that this was almost literally the case; for sure enough all the mouths and hands within your range of vision were incessantly engaged in the movements of talk.

Four-fifths of the patrons were women at this hour, since offices had not yet closed for the day. If their menfolk came at all, they did not appear until nearly six o'clock. These hundreds of women who filled the air with their shrill voices represented every imaginable age and condition of their sex, from young girls who flitted down the aisles of the café like so many wands crowned by little wigs, to personages of amplitude such as Clarisse Markbreiter (but only when she sat at a table), or even Frau Selma Steuermann—who incidentally would provide us with another pretty surprise if we could see her getting out of bed, a surprise quite the reverse of that offered by Frau Markbreiter.

The observer who had come beyond the first torrent of impressions—which included waiters rushing past, holding high in the air trays on which stood lofty architectonic creations of whipped cream—would soon become aware of a certain organizing principle in the mass of women. In general their position in the room seemed to follow their weight. Thus, the biggest, fattest, and bulkiest ones occupied the wide velvet seats of the booths built along the walls, including that by the window. Here they held their conventicles. These seats seemed also assigned to the few old ladies of the congregation. But most of the women who displaced sizable segments of space were around forty-five, or slightly beyond; and the majority of them were quite presentable, some in fact very pretty. (Clarisse, too, sat at one such table.) Toward the center of the café, however, where plain, narrow, straight-backed chairs stood around the marble tables, the average weight of the population dropped in a steep curve, vanishing to almost nothing in a few young girls of modern outlook who moved about from table to table, from Aunt Ilse to Aunt Ria, paying their little coffeehouse visits.

It will be noted that not every woman is talking. This somewhat sweeping impression, though correct in essence, is modified fairly quickly. Some of the ladies have reading matter before them. Some, however, make no headway with their reading because a woman beside them is chattering on at such a rate that no one can hear herself think. Here, for example, sits a group of five, four of whom appear to feel squeezed under the lid of a pot which they attempt to lift each time the speaker pauses for breath. But bang!—down it comes again, for she goes on talking. And the four are not listening at all, although they stare at the speaker as if spellbound. They must stare at her in order to pounce upon the faintest pause. For then they may have a chance to put in a word. They lie in ambush. We can observe something similar among groups of men when jokes are being told, and especially when war experiences are being exchanged.

Some, then, are busy reading. All available newspapers. All available magazines. Mounds of paper, printing, pictures. I observed one—a kindly, harmless creature in the light-heavy-weight class, who interrupted herself after every four or five lines, looked around, then went back to her reading and continued this same alternation for five hours. Not that she was expecting anyone. She did this every afternoon. For though she read, she also liked to know what was going on, whether Frau Thea Rosen, say, was wearing another new dress, or whether that curious young man who always looked at Frau Rosen in that way had arrived yet. Aside from such questions, she just wanted to know, in general. And if nothing were happening, she wanted to go on reading. But in the meantime something might be happening. This woman might have been conceived as an infernal torment for a damned writer who would be condemned to watch her to all eternity reading his most difficult and complicated piece of work. Murder, of course, being strictly forbidden.

In proportion to the number of patrons, the café really should have had five to seven hundred telephone booths. For in their dependence on this utility, all the ladies were much like Frau Markbreiter. One circumstance, however, preserved the owner of the café from ruin. It was after all a bit of trouble to edge out of a booth, squeeze by a table set so close to the bench, and wind through the many tables on the floor. Here you were properly entrenched in a good seat, established in all solidity and dignity. That was a strong deterrent. The vehement urge to affect the outside world, the irresistible craving to do something, to query, to speak, to find out, to undertake—this urge was simply discharged in conversation. Thus conversation itself was heightened by the impossibility of reaching for the telephone at any given moment. Take the lady who now read, now looked up, in an unvarying pulse. It is a safe hypothesis that if a telephone had been installed within her reach she would have called some relative or acquaintance (to find out whether anything was going on) at every third or fourth interruption of her reading. But as things were in the café, with the crowding, with the tables, booths, and chairs blocking the way, the eight existing telephone booths were not stormed by a clamoring mob. In the main they were besieged only by flocks of wand-like girls who had paid their little coffeehouse visit to Aunt Ria or Lia and were now telephoning their Bobbies or Teddies. After six o'clock, however, sonorous and deliberate male voices would begin to resound from these booths.

The billows of prattle which greeted us on our entry were characteristic of those three or four coffeehouses of the midtown area to which women of Clarisse's social class repaired every afternoon from about four o'clock until the approach of evening. Our conventicle sat here too, in the midst of the racket. It consisted first of all of Minna Glaser, Frau Markbreiter's younger sister; secondly of a remarkably well-preserved, rosy-complexioned, appetizing, neat and pretty woman who was the wife of a highly placed bank official—her name was Rosi Altschul; she had auburn hair and a small but much-indented figure. Frau Selma Steuermann had meanwhile also put in her appearance. And finally Frau Markbreiter, presiding over the table. So they awaited Irma, Frau Markbreiter's elder sister.

While they waited, the ladies were enjoying themselves. They owed their entertainment to Frau Glaser, the only one of the ladies at the table who was a career woman. She thus came to the café only once in a long while. She was the head—"the directress," she called herself—of the office of one of the most elegant of Vienna's hotels, one with an international clientele. One can readily imagine what this occupation offered in the way of colorful anecdotes and stories. Moreover, it was pleasant to discuss and to hear discussed people who were well-to-do, in fact reliably rich, and who might even be celebrities besides.

The ladies at this table were therefore really listening, and with the utmost zest. One story in particular aroused amusement, sympathy, and gentle outrage—the story of an old American woman. Frau Glaser was now in the midst of this tale, frequently interrupted by her own laughter. The lady in question was eighty-five if she was a day, and could not have been a beauty even as a girl. A very young scoundrel of very good family had, it seemed, decided to shear this overseas sheep by marrying her. The couple were now staying at the hotel. As you might imagine, the young man had by no means given up his former way of life—on the contrary, he quartered one of his mistresses right in the hotel, one floor down. The chief difference from the past lay in the fact that he could throw around the money his aged wife had brought to the marriage, which he did with great effect. The waiters and chambermaids were one and all on the young husband's side; they regarded him as at any rate the more acceptable half of the couple. Whatever their opinion of him otherwise, they kept it to themselves and his juicy tips in their pockets. His wife, however, lived in total ignorance, whether real or pretended, of what was going on. When her husband complained of being very tired in the evening, she solicitously put him to bed in his room, returned through the intervening sitting room to her own bedroom, and dozed off an hour later. One more hour and her husband's room was empty. Perhaps there was some connection between the frequency and intensity of his spells of tiredness and the fact that his wife saw fit to lose her gold-rimmed glasses . . .

Frau Glaser told her story with a lively insistency, with a kind of exclusive concentration upon the tale she had to tell. Her eyes were wide apart. Ordinarily this gives a restful quality to a face. In her case, however, the contrary was true. These eyes seemed constantly to be wandering, and indeed while she spoke Frau Glaser kept turning her head and jerking little glances to one side and then the other about the café. This lent her something of the manner of a horse which shies readily.

Well, then, the American woman lost her gold-rimmed glasses and made a tremendous fuss about it with the management: they must have been stolen; the police would have to be called, and so forth. She raised a tremendous hullabaloo; before long everyone in the hotel had heard of the matter. Down in the lobby people were talking of nothing but the glasses and this ridiculous couple.

Finally Frau Glaser herself had to go up to their suite and arrived just in time to see the glasses found, in the presence of the entire staff of the floor—found in the young husband's bed.

"Which must have pleased the old hen no end," said Rosi Altschul, who had quite a reputation for the lightning swiftness of her thinking.

All the others laughed. "What do you mean, 'pleased'!" Frau Glaser said. "She'd arranged the whole thing, of course . . . Just a minute!" she abruptly interrupted herself. She left the table and hastened through the café toward the telephone booths. She could afford to—she was tall, slender, and much younger than any of the others. They watched her as she wound among the tables. When she returned she said: "Just a minute!" caught the passing waiter, paid, and quickly and amiably bade the others good-by.

From morning on, of course, she had had an inkling of the impending business of this conclave. Sure enough, shortly afterwards Frau Irma Siebenschein put in her appearance. Frau Siebenschein looked no older than Frau Markbreiter, and was in fact barely two years her sister's senior. She dropped onto the upholstered bench while the chorus, under the leadership of Frau Markbreiter, eloquently expressed sympathy, indignation, and concern.

Frau Irma promptly ordered a cup of hot chocolate with whipped cream, did so without a single twinge; weight was no problem with her.

The chorus quieted down. The first member to fall silent was the one who had least roused herself. This was Frau Steuermann, who now settled back heavily into her foundations. Finally tranquillity came even to Frau Rosi Altschul, who like a child was apt to immerse herself completely in every new impression, taking in outside reality with swimming eyes and a madly inquisitive nose. Frau Steuermann was now gazing into space once more, with as much melancholy as before Minna Glaser had told her spicy stories. Indeed, even during these recitals, merriment had only rippled in little waves against the surface of her imposing frame. The fact was, it did Frau Steuermann's morale not a whit of good to leaf through these illustrated supplements, and especially through these magazines. She became wearied, annoyed, low-spirited, and in the end embittered. For there she saw repeated again and again, in a thousand guises and variants, the unchanging ideal of the period, the slim athletic girl: at the beach, on skis, doing gymnastics, or in whatever environment or occupation. And these hussies always had the same face and the same smile; really, it was all stale, not to say insipid. Yet, on the other hand, what right did she have to pass such judgment? Wasn't it simply envy? Here she was forty-four years old and widowed for twelve years, and really not bad-looking at all; she knew that perfectly well.

But six or seven years before, suddenly, it had all been over; the thing had come upon her shortly after the war, and just overnight, so to speak, she had been dubbed an elderly fat woman . . . Wasn't that a true description? Ah yes, it was. Suddenly there had been a tangible vacuum all around her. Men her age, and even older men, had run off to these revues and had started raving about those empty-headed chorus girls with no meat on their bones. Why, lots of the men had ironed the rheumatism out of their joints and started learning to ski and God knows what else (not to speak of the younger fellows), and now they were off every weekend carrying on with all this modern youth. It was sickening, always the same thing and the same talk, and all of them wild about the same thing, some film star or dancer or ice-skating champion.

And every single one of those females was thin as a rail.

And here she herself sat in the coffeehouse with these other women!

While Frau Steuermann's thoughts had turned inward, just the opposite had happened to Frau Rosi Altschul. This was in keeping with her disposition. We have already remarked that Frau Thea Rosen was the object of considerable interest on the part of other members of her sex. For there was something definitely provoking about her. Like Frau Steuermann she was a widow, but she exaggerated the matter; she made a profession of her widowhood and often repeated that since the decease of her dear departed husband men no longer existed for her. Ah no, she intended to remain alone—"give up everything and remain alone, as I once vowed"—these were the very words Frau Rosen had rashly uttered. Yet she was only thirty-five. So she was under constant observation.

In private Frau Altschul had nicknamed Frau Rosen "the Madonna." Her small face really had a madonna look. True, there was nothing ethereal about the rest of her. The young man who persistently stared at Frau Rosen, as we have noted, had so far behaved with perfect propriety. Perhaps the notion that he stared was only born of imagination, an imagination overstimulated by much (though intermittent) reading. If the truth were known, Frau Altschul had never caught him in the act of looking. Rather the opposite. Then how had she linked this young man with Frau Rosen? After all, the young man sat rather far away from that lady. Nevertheless, Frau Altschul firmly believed that such a link existed. She could not have given any evidence for her belief. But in such matters she possessed intuition. Genius cannot be held accountable. It produces its discoveries abruptly, in pure creativity. Frau Altschul, too, cannot be held accountable. She really could not have assigned any reasons for her theory. She had no reasons. And yet there had gradually matured in her a decision to pursue this matter further someday. Perhaps today would be the day for it.

Meanwhile the case of Fräulein Grete Siebenschein had been brought before the committee, presided over by her mother, who had finished her hot chocolate. The case had been analyzed and discussed at length. Frau Selma Steuermann was greatly in favor of a forbearing view of the affair. "Let them enjoy themselves while they're young," she said. "What have we got later on, I'd like to know!" Rosi Altschul could not afford any such position; her contribution had to be more emphatic, more sympathetic, more concerned, or had at least to seem so, precisely because in reality she was not concerned at all; her thoughts were entirely concentrated upon Frau Rosen. Luckily the useful little word "shocking" occurred to her. She resorted to it each time the phrase "at four o'clock in the morning" dropped from Frau Irma's lips: "Shocking—and a girl from such a fine family!" Frau Clarisse was thinking privately that the whole affair was quite absurd. "She'll be twenty-two soon," Frau Siebenschein said, moist-eyed. "Where will it end?"

"Don't take it so hard," her sister observed, and perhaps the slightest note of impatience had entered her voice, for suddenly Frau Irma became deeply offended.

"It's easy for you to talk," she said with some asperity. "Yours isn't twenty-three yet and you've got her disposed of already."

"Why, Irma, what a tiring to say," Clarisse replied quietly, with a touch of resignation. "It's been a real blow to Ferry and me to lose the child so soon; we miss her every minute of the day. You don't know what that's like."

"Come on now, a blow! Say it's a weight off your mind, that's more like it."

The somewhat sharp tone of the discussion drew Frau Altschul's attention back to her tablemates; that childlike, absorbed look came over her face, while her nose thrust forward inquisitively.

"But now look here, Frau Siebenschein," she said placatingly, "tell me, isn't there a prospect at all?—I mean, you yourself said before that he comes from a real good family . . ."

"Family, family, don't give me any of that, you don't see or hear anything of his family. The way it is with that kind of people, none of them bothers about the others. You can rest assured they're all against it. And anyway, I ask you, a man without a decent occupation!"

108

This disagreeable topic was abandoned upon the arrival, or rather the fluttering approach, of Frau Lily Kries, the young married woman of not yet twenty-three, who was welcomed with a tornado of greetings. Before these had subsided, Herr Markbreiter and Herr Altschul appeared (it was six o'clock by then); the two had met in the draperied entry. "Everybody's coming at once," Frau Rosi observed with childlike delight, for now her beloved husband was there; she was tremendously fond and proud of him. Undoubtedly he was the handsomest and most distinguished-looking of all among the husbands of her friends, and moreover better educated than any of them. Altschul came from Frankfurt and still maintained ties with his venerable native city. He was in fact very good-looking, not only in his wife's eyes; a tall man with a sensible intelligent face, extremely well groomed and urbane.

The Markbreiters, too, greeted each other tenderly; anyone who had observed the meeting of father and daughter would have been genuinely touched. The modest gentleman looked at the smartly dressed young lady as if she were a small idol and he blessed for being its devoted servant and priest. Then husband and wife sat down side by side, their child opposite them, holding hands under the table.

The new audience brought forth a second unreeling of the case of Grete Siebenschein. The problem had to be put before the menfolk. And what was Frau Irma's annoyance when she found the matter viewed in the mildest light. The men did not say much at all. Markbreiter delivered the opinion that nothing should be done that would in any way push the girl too hard. The business of her moving away from home was not to be taken too seriously. But, he declared, a good deal of foolishness in this world was done not for its own sake but out of defiance.

Lily Kries felt greatly elated that this whole matter should be discussed openly before her in the family council—something that would have been entirely out of the question six months before, when she was still a girl. What privileges attended the married state! She was actually asked to give her opinion. Although she did not venture to express it, two words came to her mind which both summed up her opinion and expressed the whole of her present happiness. Those two words, which she thought slowly and deliberately, were: "Poor creature!" Meanwhile the waiter had bent toward Altschul and said: "Director Altschul, you are wanted on the telephone. The bank is calling."

When Altschul returned to the table, it was evident that he was annoyed. "I must run up to the office again, Rosi," he said.

"Now really!" Markbreiter said. "So much to do? Still, if business goes well, we don't mind the work involved, do we, Herr Altschul?"

"Rosi," Altschul said, "please call me at the office in half an hour; perhaps we'll be through by then. It would be nice if you'd come to meet me. All right?"

"All right," she said with a smiling nod and a look of infatuated pride. He went out with a preoccupied air.

Frau Siebenschein was still prey to her maternal worries. Her whole body emanated uneasiness and irritability. Moreover, for the past half hour she had been vainly awaiting her daughter Grete, whom she had arranged to meet here, perhaps hoping that one of her friends would say a sensible word to the girl. But the others had left the subject behind. Frau Steuermann was dreaming, her big dark eyes gazing into space. The Markbreiters were beginning to behave like unruly children, whispering to each other and communicating across the table with Lily by signs. And look at Frau Altschul!

Rosi Altschul had just had a little shock. The young man

had vanished. How long had he been gone? And now, of all things, Frau Rosen was summoning the waiter to pay her check. Deep in her heart Rosi Altschul came to a decision; she too beckoned the waiter. It would soon be time to leave to meet her husband anyhow. But she had first to telephone him. If only that Rosen woman did not escape her this time! Today must be the day; she was determined to find out something definite at last. To be sure, Thea was moving very slowly and casually, as though she were in no hurry whatsoever. But this very behavior seemed suspect. When Rosi bustled back from her telephone call, Thea was already sliding out of the booth in which she had been sitting.

Frau Altschul bade the others good-by, saying that she had to meet her husband in a few minutes.

When she emerged from the revolving door onto the sidewalk, she feared for a moment that her prey had escaped her. Partly it was the darkness outside, partly it was the dazzle of all the street lights. In any case, she saw no sign of Frau Rosen. Perhaps she had already been swallowed up in the stream of traffic. But no—there she was! Walking alone across a big open square. Now she turned into a street. Rosi strained her eyesight to the utmost—lo and behold there was already somebody at Thea's side. With an access of boldness, Rosi trailed the couple for a little way and established beyond the shadow of a doubt that Thea's companion was the same young man who came to the coffeehouse. Heart pounding, she stood still at a corner, and then almost ran straight into a person whom she had not noticed who was standing motionless on the sidewalk staring blankly.

Bound for the bank, she related the story of Frau Rosen and her admirer at least five times to her husband before she had even reached him. Why, it was simply shocking. Of course she had a perfect right—but *such* hypocrisy!

At last, immediately after Frau Altschul's departure, Fräulein Grete Siebenschein arrived at the café. At this moment, at least, Irma Siebenschein would have liked to have seen expressions of gravity and composure imprinted on the faces of her companions. Especially on the faces of the Markbreiters, who had after all come more or less to act as her allies in this matter. But it turned out differently.

The "poor creature" was an exceedingly chic and distinguished-looking young lady. She bore scarcely any resemblance to her mother, since she belonged to a quite different facial type. To the type of Clarisse Markbreiter, as a matter of fact—Clarisse when she was speaking to her servants. That is to say, the face was emphatically profile, with a very straight, finely shaped nose; a face with a good deal of incisiveness, but no womanly, maternal breadth. Perhaps she looked this way only now and then, as did her aunt. But this particular expression seemed more deeply stamped into her face, less exceptional upon it. Moreover, she had just had a violent quarrel with her lover, and perhaps the traces of it still remained upon her countenance. This lover (René Stangeler) was standing outside, near the coffeehouse. He was waiting there since Grete had promised to escape alone if possible and return shortly. René was the person Rosi Altschul had nearly collided with.

Grete Siebenschein went up to the table. At first something resembling a cloud of feminine solidarity rolled toward her; Frau Steuermann in particular seemed to be emanating something of the sort. The outside observer could easily have been confused by this, for Fräulein Grete was certainly quite a different sort from, say, Lily Kries. You would be inclined to say that she was far "superior."

Her mother was of a mind to unreel the whole affair for

the third time, and so she did, although not quite in the manner she desired. Grete's acute distaste for this family conference was only too plain.

"Look, my child," Herr Siegfried Markbreiter now took the floor, signaling to Irma with a sage and kindly flickering of his eyelids that he wished her to be silent for a few seconds, "none of us has anything against Herr Stangeler, we have absolutely nothing against him. From all I hear, he is a very fine young man. But after all, we are concerned about you, you know, you and your happiness, your future. Believe me, Grete, your relatives are your best friends. If this young man really loves you—fine, then he's a friend of ours too. But he has to prove it by action. You've told us that he absolutely refuses to enter into any—how shall I put it?—any binding ties . . ."

At this point Grete's face showed that impatience restrained by politeness which younger people feel when an older person is beating about the bush. At this moment, perhaps, she was really Stangeler's beloved, perhaps entirely so.

"You've told us," Markbreiter continued with patient kindliness, "that he flies off the handle if you so much as mention it, as if it were some kind of insult."

"When it comes down to it, he's right," Frau Steuermann suddenly proclaimed. The others gasped. But she said nothing more and returned to her daydreaming.

"No, that's something none of you could understand . . ." Grete wanted to reply, but she held her tongue and looked in perplexity at Selma, who, however, continued to pay no attention to the further course of the conversation.

"Well, then," Markbreiter continued, "let us drop this point. There are different opinions about that."

"Not at all!" Irma exclaimed. "What do you mean, different opinions? There are no two ways about it!"

Modestly but masterfully, Siegfried Markbreiter's eyelids pleaded for silence. "There is something else I wanted to discuss with Grete." There was really something extremely ingratiating in his manner. "I was saying that the young man ought to prove in some way that he really loves you. If not in one way, then in another. For example, a man must have some occupation, a real occupation that supports him, that enables him to earn his livelihood and eventually a livelihood for a family. Along with that it's perfectly possible to have all sorts of interests in intellectual matters. There have been famous men who have been recognized for really great achievements in the intellectual line and at the same time have worked at a practical profession . . ."

Grete's features betrayed signs of her earlier polite impatience. But this expression was a little softer and less emphatic now.

"Look, Grete," Markbreiter continued persuasively, "I want to make a practical proposal to you, which I hope will help the two of you to be happy. I should like very much to have a talk with Herr Stangeler sometime. And I should very much like to do something for him. As it happens, I would be in a position to do so now. It's a lucky chance. A real fine position where someone just like him is needed, a man from a good family, former officer, and so on. It's a position of trust for a respectable young man. At the same time it would leave him time for his studies if he's serious about them. It wouldn't be bad at all; he'd have his evenings free. At the beginning it might be a bit hard, but later on—at any rate, he'd see something ahead of him. And we would be relieved of our anxiety about you two. Whereas now—I'm only saying that he ought to give us some proof that he loves you. And is it anything so enormous that we're asking? We're not demanding the impossible. Just accept what he's offered—that's all he needs to do. Incidentally, I cannot imagine that he would refuse. But if he did—why then I myself would really have to begin to doubt . . ."

Perhaps—we cannot of course know this with any degree of certainty—perhaps Grete Siebenschein might gradually have been won over by her uncle's persuasive gentleness, at least to the point of giving ear to him. Until now she had not seriously listened to him—above all because she knew Stangeler better than he. Now, however, her mother burst in and ruined the whole thing.

"You'd begin doubting all right, I can guarantee that. My doubts are over already, I can tell you, I haven't any doubts about it. I'm beginning to give up. Are you going to offer his lordship a cabinet post on a silver platter maybe? Do you know what he would say to you? Something no one in his right senses would understand—and off he'd take himself. He's crazy, I tell you. A fanatic, a neurotic, there's something absolutely morbid about him that doesn't go with a fellow his age. How in the world should I know what he's got in his mind? Crazy, I'll bet."

At this the Markbreiters rightly retreated. Siegfried had done his level best to arbitrate the matter. But once Irma got on her high horse you couldn't talk with her—especially these days. They therefore pulled out of the thing and resumed their earlier whispering and sign language across the table to their daughter. Or to put it as Irma saw it: they went back to their nonsense again.

Irma continued to hold forth, though the only persons really listening to her were her already wearied and affronted daughter and Frau Steuermann. But the latter suddenly came to life and delivered the following utterly fantastic speech, into which no one could get a word edgewise. And if there had been the slightest chance that the gentle reasonable urgings of Grete Siebenschein's uncle might have taken root in the girl's mind, and the girl had begun, however vaguely, to conceive the kind of future Markbreiter projected—if any such chance had existed, it was ruined now. She was carried off in an entirely different direction by Frau Steuermann's harangue.

"I really don't know, but it may be that you're all mistaken. Who says any of us are perfect? What does the girl get out of her youth if she always has to keep after the boy with marrying and jobs and all that? In the end she'll lose him because of all that even if she's married to him ten times over. And then—maybe there really is something in the fellow. How can we tell? And maybe the right thing for her to do is let him alone and let him go his own way. If he does something in the world, he'll be endlessly grateful to her that it was that way all along, without this kind of thing coming up every so often. A man feels he's being hounded. You know, not everyone is a scoundrel. I think if she doesn't make any demands at all now, that's the very thing that will bind him to her better than anything else. Otherwise he's sure to throw her over. That's my idea. Now please, it's only my own private opinion. When I was a girl I would have been so happy to find someone who—who was somehow different, special, not like everyone else. They just are a different type of people—how can I put it?—people who count. A man like this needs a companion, a friend, an understanding woman—not just another girl who keeps after him about marriage and earning a living. If you ask me, she's lucky to have met such a fellow. Nowadays when all the young men are so silly and care about nothing but all kinds of nonsense . . ."

But by this time Irma had at last recovered her breath, and she broke in violently and vigorously. It was a veritable explosion.

"I absolutely don't understand how you can talk like that, Frau Steuermann, and I may mention that you chose quite another type of man." (Frau Steuermann's face swiftly sagged into profound resignation.) "It seems to me that you've read too many novels. How can you say such a thing to a girl! What's the use anyway—I come here to you grownup people" (she would have liked to have said: "you old cows") "and what happens, you talk like a bunch of children. . . What's the matter!" she interrupted herself, angered by some disturbance. "Grete, what are you looking at . . . ?"

The Markbreiters had for some time been struggling to suppress their steadily mounting laughter and giggling. Clarisse was whispering some story into her husband's ear, and Lily, opposite, was evidently begging to be told what it was all about. Now Clarisse tore off a corner of a newspaper and wrote something on it with her little silver pencil. Just at this juncture in Irma's speech, this scrap of paper was pushed across the table from mother to daughter. But it never reached her.

"A lot of use it is talking to you!" Irma cried out violently. She reached out, snatched the note, crushed it, and tossed it back onto the table top. "A lot of good it does coming to you with any problem! Your silly jokes are a thousand times more important to you. Of course!"

And then there was one of those embarrassing, disgruntled, hasty leave-takings and departures on the part of Frau Irma Siebenschein, a typical Irma departure such as her family had experienced time and again, for every imaginable cause. She literally dragged her daughter away with her.

"What ever has got into her?" Frau Steuermann said with unruffled composure. "I just don't understand her."

Siegfried Markbreiter only smiled. He picked up the crumpled little note and unfolded it. On it were written only two words, indicating the subject he and his wife had been discussing with such hilarity: "cheesecake."

CHAPTER 4

Friederike Ruthmayr

THIS TIME she was not wearing a brown silk dress nipped
in at the waist. Her entire toilette was different this evening,
and she sat at the railing of her box at the opera. The crowded
orchestra pit below her respired darkly, charged with restrained
movement, while the rising curtain admitted that familiar cool
dusty odor of the stage into the auditorium, where it mingled
with the respectable atmosphere of the boxes and the rows of
orchestra seats, an atmosphere compounded of fifty years of velvet and lingering perfume. It frightened Friederike Ruthmayr
a little. The low cut of her dress at the back produced a solemn
chill, and there behind her on the bench sat Herr Levielle, who
was, she knew, at the moment discreetly regarding her shoulders. With strange and complicated tonal hues the instruments
of the orchestra underpainted the voices of the singers. At first
these voices sounded isolated, ringing out in a sheer vacuum; it
would be a while before they effectuated anything and sent the
warmth of dramatic action out in spreading concentric rings
beyond the stage into the audience. Friederike Ruthmayr felt
frightened by the odor of dead perfume in the withered velvet.
All winter long she had been aware of similar anxieties every
time she visited her box at the opera. Nothing of this kind had
ever used to trouble her. She came to the realization of this
about halfway through the first act. She knew, moreover, that
Levielle had not been staring steadily at her back, but that he
had also not been listening, merely sitting patiently behind her

with mild pleasure in her listening and with intense respect for "the artistic taste and the breadth of intellectual interests" of one for whom, he averred, he felt always "the deepest admiration." He had even sat through *Parsifal* in this fashion, both here and in Bayreuth. That anyone could so successfully hinder another person from listening, while remaining absolutely still, no longer annoyed Frau Ruthmayr but had become a subject for sheer wonderment. Tonight, too, he succeeded in doing this. She asked herself, among other things, what his name might have been in the past. He employed what seemed a rather old-fashioned bonhomie and gallantry as a curtain to cover some obscure past, the way a well-groomed beard might hide an unknown mouth and chin. Not that Herr Levielle himself concealed either mouth or chin. He wore only a neat white English mustache upon his upper lip.

After Easter this year—who would be waiting for her at the station in Paris? He. Solicitously. So solicitously. Who would kiss merely her finger tips, so delicately? He. On journeys, who was it who forever and a day always asked at first meeting in the lobby of the hotel: "Have you rested well, my *dear* friend?" Herr Levielle. Who would escort her to Merano in the autumn and to St. Moritz in the winter? He. Who was a strange and inscrutable hybrid of a grain dealer invested with some diplomatic mission and a diplomat with incidental interests in cereals? Who occupied some median line among three nationalities: Austrian, Parisian, and some unknown X? Who never referred to Georg Ruthmayr, erstwhile cavalry captain in the reserve who had been killed at the beginning of the war in a cavalry charge in Galicia, by any other phrase than "our dear deceased friend"? And who had brought Ruthmayr's tremendous fortune virtually unharmed through collapse and inflation? Who had saved it all for the widow of his deceased friend, and was continuing to administer it with infinite wisdom? To whom was she in duty bound to be grateful in innumerable ways? Whose quiet but tenacious adoration was in itself a form of wooing that never ventured so far as to disturb seriously this entire delicate equilibrium?

Always and again Herr Levielle.

All these reflections meant no more than that this evening brought Friederike Ruthmayr one of those revelations which came to her periodically at long intervals. On the occasion of such revelations she recognized more clearly than ever that life without this insistent but discreet, this reticent quiet friend, was scarcely conceivable to her any longer. Yet as far as the present evening at the opera was concerned, she suddenly realized that undoubtedly the most unpleasant feature of the whole situation was the visit customarily paid her in the box during the intermission by her friend's two sons—for Levielle was likewise widowed. And after the performance the four would go to dine, as they did every Saturday while in Vienna. The character of these sons reminded her of the odor of velvet here, or of that cool and vacuous atmosphere that came from the stage when the curtain rose. Both sons were blond. Both had good positions on the Foreign Exchange Board. Both were excellent young men. Both addressed Friederike with deepest respect.

The trumpets in the orchestra blew a sharp fanfare. Frau Ruthmayr sighed, the silk rustling and crackling softly around her well-developed bosom. The curtain fell, the lights went on. And sure enough, soon after she and Levielle had removed to the back of the box, there was a polite knock and the red door opened outward.

This time, however, an unknown young man presented himself. "Herr Doktor Neuberg," Levielle introduced him; he had obviously been expecting the young man, but at the same time greeted him with a touch of pleased surprise which aptly conveyed that he had in the meanwhile quite forgotten this pre-arranged but unimportant visit, was just recalling it, but was of course delighted. "My sons are terribly disappointed," he explained, "but they were unable to come to the opera. This is the night for Baron Frigori's ball. But I should be delighted if you would nevertheless—may I assume that Herr Neuberg and my humble self may dine with you after the performance, *gnädige Frau*?"

Frau Ruthmayr felt the disappointment as a very pleasant one.

"A promising young scholar!" Levielle explained. "How is your teacher, Councilor von Rottenbach?"

"You are a historian, then?" Frau Ruthmayr asked; she knew von Rottenbach by reputation.

"An extraordinarily perspicacious scholar, and a remarkable personality, is he not, Herr Neuberg?" Levielle observed.

Young people often make the mistake of ruffling the smooth, oiled surface of conventional phrases because they consider it more important to assert themselves than to see to it that social life runs smoothly, that the psyche remains untroubled, which is of course the prime thing. This was the case with Herr Neuberg. He thought highly of his teacher as a pedagogue and scholar of the first rank in his field. But he had never noticed any signs of an all-round, creative personality in his esteemed professor. It would have been proper for Herr Neuberg to say simply: "He is the finest teacher I can imagine." Nor would this have been a white lie. Indeed, he did say something of the sort. But he spoke not in the tone of one adding a note of additional eulogy to Levielle's praise but rather in the manner of one making a sensible emendation which reduced the nebulous phrases to their core. Levielle, who had been showing off his interest in intellectual matters before Friederike, was checked and upset. Now, however, he revealed his displeasure only by rapidly changing the subject. "How did you like the performance this evening?" he asked.

Friederike Ruthmayr's attention was caught by this little break in the conversation, and she now took a closer look at Herr Neuberg. The young man was tall, heavy-set, somewhat rotund, and straw-blond, with broad, slightly flattened features—a face whose structure bespoke candor, except for a slightly turned-up nose that suggested a certain sly impudence. He looked highly intelligent. Women are well known to have far more of a capacity than men to feel their way intuitively behind the façades of strangers. Friederike did not like Neuberg at all; it might almost be said that in a vague fashion he appeared repulsive to her. But she sensed in him a certain hold on things, and a real freedom, a more direct contact with life such as she always longed for after such evenings as this one. For everything was presented to her in a smoothed and prearranged fashion, and at a suitable distance, like the events on the stage down below there. The result was that she lived amid the lingering perfumes of the past clinging to all the folds which no fresh breeze ever parted. Even now, this unknown young man paid his due respects chiefly by donning evening dress and brushing his hair properly; no doubt he felt that no more was necessary. Of course such people really had other things to worry about; everybody had quite other things to worry about nowadays. A middle-aged woman with a well-developed figure could not ask more of young men.

The bell announced the end of the intermission. Something that would have been considered impossible on the plane of everyday life was quite socially acceptable on the boards. The opera was Strauss's *Rosenkavalier*.

"I am leaving tomorrow," Levielle replied to Frau Ruthmayr's question as he helped her into her flowing evening cloak. The last act was over. From two sides the patrons of the boxes edged slowly down the grand central staircase, while outside at the entrance of the opera house motors were already starting up. The brilliants in Frau Ruthmayr's raven hair shot sparks of colored fire. Descending was like plunging into a bath of noise and motion. The din of the streets poured through the swinging doors into the lobby. A feeling of submissiveness softened Friederike's mood. She stepped forward into the surf, which was yet only a last lapping tongue of the larger sea, the whole nocturnal city. But she had only a narrow prescribed path before her; only a few steps separated her from her big, smooth, silent car, which would roll forward in a moment, enclose her, and shut her off from everything.

When they were halfway to the car, Neuberg in hat and coat came forward.

They drove off as they did every Saturday after the opera, whenever Frau Ruthmayr was in Vienna. They went to the same restaurant—it was scarcely any drive—where the table in the same small room was always reserved for Friederike and Herr Levielle. These arrangements no longer required discussion. Even the reception by the staff was such that young Neuberg felt like a guest entering an orderly household in which established habits prevail and everything moves like clockwork. Levielle ordered a substantial dinner for all three, and contrived to let fall the paternal phrase: "My dear young friend, permit me to consider you my guest," at the very moment when the historian was beginning to feel a pinch in the region of his pocketbook. Here the older man definitely had the upper hand. But such a gesture makes only the most fleeting of impressions upon a well-bred young man. Moreover, Frau Ruthmayr now turned to him very graciously.

She was not his cup of tea, far from it; it would be a great mistake to think so. But although this was his first encounter with her, he knew quite well who and what she was. Herr Neuberg had that profound contempt for society people which is characteristic of many learned professionals, and very young men of this type sometimes tend unjustly to extend their contempt to women also. Nevertheless, Herr Neuberg did not respond with some negligent commonplace when Frau Ruthmayr asked him a question. He replied precisely.

No, he said, he had never had the desire to live "in another age," in classical antiquity, say, or in the so-called Renaissance. All serious and proper study of history must necessarily aim "at the bull's-eye of the present (as a greater mind than mine has said)"; one's sights must never deviate from the present. Indeed, this was the only purpose of historical studies: to confer a still higher reality upon the present.

"I only meant," Frau Ruthmayr said, "that when a person knows remote times so very well, as you do, Herr Neuberg, you might now and then feel a kind of nostalgia for them. . ."

"I believe Madame is thinking largely in artistic terms," Levielle explained respectfully. "Her intense feeling for art prompts her to wish, let us say, that she might have lived in the time of Raphael."

"No, no, I understand what Herr Neuberg is saying," Frau Ruthmayr observed, more or less pushing Levielle aside—for without stepping into the actual context of the conversation, he had utilized his courteous comment to interpose himself between her and the young man. "My objection was based purely on feeling, and perhaps is romantic. But I should almost think that according to you, Herr Neuberg, we must regard history as we do our own pasts, in the same light, and then it all derives its meaning only from the present."

"Quite so," Neuberg said, pleased and surprised. His eyes had begun to shine, and a touch of color appeared on his cheeks. (In general his face had changed greatly since his appearance in the box, and Frau Ruthmayr now became aware of this.) "That is precisely the way you must regard history, like an extension of your own past. Some parts of your past are closer to you, some more remote, according to how you feel about them, and certainly things that are most recent need not necessarily be the closer ones. I mean, when you look back upon your own life, there are certainly periods which today seem quite alien and of no consequence to you, whereas some other period, which may lie much further back in the past, kindles your interest to a high degree. A year ago you may have seen it quite differently, and a year hence you may feel a greater bond with some other portion of your own past, whereas still other periods will seem remote to you again. There are certainly times when we feel very close to our own childhoods, or to some other bygone segment of our lives, times whose inner attitudes we come very close to assuming again, whose phrases, images, smells, and other impressions constantly come flocking back to us. There are moments, in fact, when it seems to us that only a very thin partition separates us from what has been, a partition we could break through with ease. And we feel rather as though 'time' and 'past' are only a kind of illusion to which we yield. . . It is the same, on the whole, with mankind. Every age has its preferences from among preceding periods, and we call these preferences the Renaissance or Romanticism or Classicism or what have you. Whole nations and cultural groups at times live close to some such segment in the past, far closer than they do to recent events. Gestures and modes of feeling and thinking return, and even ways of looking at the landscape will be revivals of past attitudes. Yet each time

126

this resurrected vision seems entirely new and fresh—and is felt as such. For real repetitions do not exist. Each time the entire past must be rearranged and sifted anew, since each time the center of gravity, which, governs the direction of the whole, has been displaced to some other point—has been displaced, that is, to a different present, and simultaneously means a different, deeply related, and extremely contemporary part of the past. That is why all true historiography (as a great thinker has said) is the history of the present, whether it happens to deal with Roman times or the High Middle Ages or any other particular period. No, the past is nothing fixed; we are always creating it anew. The tremendous masses of its facts are nothing, our conception of them everything. That is why every age must write history anew, and in doing so each age will always reawaken and infuse with life the dead facts of those very periods whose motifs touch consonant chords within it. And now I must beg your forgiveness for this long speech, my dear Frau Ruthmayr," Neuberg concluded in a warm vibrant voice, "but I wanted very much to answer your question precisely and completely."

"Thank you," Frau Ruthmayr said, impulsively extending her hand across the table to Neuberg, who kissed it.

Levielle seemed to think it time to change the subject. "How is your fiancée?" he asked.

"You are engaged?" Frau Ruthmayr said with faint astonishment.

"Why yes," Neuberg replied cheerfully. Normally he liked to be asked about Angelika, but this time the question, coming from Levielle, rubbed him the wrong way. "She is very well," he said. "Monday evening I am having dinner with her parents."

Ludmilla Kakabsa, the chambermaid, closed the garden gate and front door behind her mistress. Outside, the big car could be heard purring softly as it started off again. Friederike Ruthmayr passed through the vestibule of her home. She told Ludmilla she might go to bed.

She stopped in her husband's study, which had been left completely unchanged, just as it had been during his lifetime. The room was kept heated; it remained her favorite place in the house. Not that she came here to dwell on memories of past happiness. In the first place, that happiness had not been anything so extraordinary. In the second place, it was not in Frau Ruthmayr's nature to bury herself in the past. She liked the fact that her husband's aura dominated this room, and she was glad to be reminded of Ruthmayr by the pictures of the estate where they had spent so much of their time—there were several water colors of the place on the walls—by the photographs of his favorite horses; and by the horseshoes saved as mementos of this or that fine steed; by a whole collection of riding crops; by another whole collection of English novelists, the best represented being Dickens and Hardy; by the numerous small objects a man of Ruthmayr's class would naturally have accumulated, from cigarette cases and tobacco pouches down to the heavy ash trays and a row of English pipes; and by the whole masculine atmosphere of the room, a rich harmonious chord in which the smell of the leather armchair predominated. All this made Friederike feel good. But not so much for the sake of personal recollections.

Rather, and curiously enough, the atmosphere gave her a kind of support. Here in this room she was able to feel herself a free and independent individual, a feeling which otherwise was barred to her. Whereas from this masculine room it seemed to her possible to step in any direction she chose, even if it should mean stepping over all her relatives, and even over Herr Levielle himself. Here in this room such thoughts could be entertained. But not away from it (on the staircase of the opera house, say) where innumerable glances were directed at her and she had to uphold the amplitude of her unmistakable femininity before all those eyes. With all those eyes upon her, she was a woman without a doubt, a woman to the nth degree, but invested with that strange rank of "lady," a rank whose actual conditions no one could precisely define. At any rate, she was girded round with all the blunt and sharply cutting weapons of strictest etiquette.

There it was—and oddly enough, in her feminine bedchamber she often felt equally cribbed, though the room was spacious and fragrant, all pastel colors, with scarcely a single austere line or sharp edge in it. This bedroom, she felt when she came home in the evening, was her place of banishment after her hand had been kissed at the garden gate and her escorts had stridden off down the street with echoing masculine tread—where to? Here she was supposed to remain to preserve the proper order of nature, here among these beruffled muslin curtains and drawers filled with scented lingerie, here among fragile, delicately shaped objects of glass, silver, and porcelain. Into this room she was thrust aside, pushed back from the world; to this prison she was sent with all due respect; this boudoir was regarded as the proper place for her.

And that is why she sat down by preference in the masculine room of the deceased captain.

To be sure, here she was also visited by certain recollections of him, and his voice frequently spoke to her, saying something like: "Fritzi, try though I will, I cannot understand how you go on drifting through the years. Certainly you never learned that sort of thing from me." And now he would laugh like a schoolboy: "I never would have dreamed it."

Or: "But he's just a silly old idiot. I'd look for a different type of company if I were you. Gratitude is all very well. But I assure you he himself has lost nothing by it, certainly not; you don't know him if you think anything of the sort."

This was the kind of remark hearty Captain Ruthmayr might well have made; during his lifetime he had never been one to deprive himself of anything. But Friederike did not conduct her life at all in her husband's spirit. She had become timid; her timidity had woven a net around her (or had Levielle woven the net out of the thread of this timidity?), and now she felt caught in the meshes of this net.

The strangest part of it was that she was very well aware of this, and that this knowledge from time to time infuriated her to the point of self-contempt.

CHAPTER 5

The Great Nebula
or
Passing by Friederike Ruthmayr

EVENING SPLASHES the wall with a deep red-gold. From the high vantage point of my apartment the magnificence of the view, hazy here and excessively transparent there, is as astonishing as ever. The slanting rafters and the big sloping window admit the sky even while they shelter me from it. And outside, receding beneath me, interspersed amid the green bells of the trees, are the roofs of houses and cottages, roseate in the evening sun or still gleaming a chalky white, continuing as far as the sweep of hills and the margin of the sky, where the horizon sends forth thick vapors—for summer has already come. A stormy gray citadel of clouds looms beyond the towers of the Romanesque church.

I am reading over these notes. There are always, as Herr Neuberg effectively explained at that dinner with Levielle and Friederike Ruthmayr, portions of our personal pasts which at any given time are closer to or remoter from us; and the most recent years need not necessarily be the closest. They are so only in a relatively crude and superficial sense. Memories of much more distant times often hover over us. Sometimes the memory will be no more than the face of someone we once knew.

During the period before the First World War, I had known a certain Baroness Neudegg. A good deal was seen of her around 1900 or so, here and there, and then she suddenly vanished. Later I happened to hear that she had married a Count Charagiel and was living in Morgins, which is in Switzerland. Ever since my encounter with Herr Levielle on the Graben on Annunciation Day 1927, Countess Charagiel, née Baroness Neudegg, had been very much present in my mind. After some time I discovered why. At that time, around 1900, I was still a very young man indeed, scarcely more than a boy, I had met the baroness for the first time in my mother's home, had been ordered to accompany her downstairs and open the garden gate for her. Her carriage was waiting on the street outside. While I was escorting her downstairs, she seemed to me incredibly beautiful. She smelled wonderful, too; her perfume trailed behind her. At the carriage she turned and extended her hand. As she did so, she assumed an expression of utterly inimitable arrogance and inordinately stupid impertinence. Yet there was not the slightest pretext or reason for her to act this way toward a humble high-school boy—whom was she trying to impress? The senseless outrageousness of this conduct shocked me so thoroughly that for days afterwards I had a kind of aftertaste of it, as though there were some spoiled food lying in my stomach. Exactly this sort of lingering feeling remained after my walk with Levielle on the Graben, although I had at first viewed our talk as just a pleasant chat and had even accompanied Levielle part of the way back, as far as the bank, as the reader may recall. But afterwards I became fully aware of his quite mysterious arrogance, although I had sensed something of it right at the beginning of the conversation. How did these people get that way? I asked myself; and as a schoolboy I had actually asked myself precisely the same question during those days after the incident with Baroness Neudegg. To this day I have never found any answer to this question.

Later, after the war, I met Claire Neudegg, now Countess Charagiel, somewhere again. But where that was I cannot recall. My mind fastens on the Hotel de l'Europe in Salzburg as the most likely place; I think first of the corridor and then of the dining room. At the time I did not notice any gentleman accompanying her; perhaps the count was already no more. Something of the sort had been bruited about. I gave her the appropriate greetings. She thanked me in exactly the manner in which she had once thanked the high-school boy. Time seemed to have left no mark upon her in any sense. She was a beautiful woman. But I was no longer a lowly, adoring high-school boy. Nevertheless, she thrust me back to my sixteenth year; she could do that. And so it seemed as though time had left no mark upon me either.

Enough of this. The tale I am about to tell will possibly be branded a fantastic one. But is not chance what chances to come a man's way? Moreover, it must be recalled that I am presenting here—a chronicle. "But a novelized one," a certain person will object. That may be. Nevertheless, what follows is not only true in a "higher" sense, "or however you say it," to use Stangeler's expression. It is true word for word, in each and every detail. This is exactly the way it happened:

Frau Friederike Ruthmayr had spent several hours in the master's room. She would have liked to have gone on talking with Neuberg. Indeed, she felt something of a craving to do so. But as things were, she read Benedetto Croce. She had found a book of his (as she told me later, it had been "an essay on the essence of writing history") in the small library of her deceased husband.

As I say, she had been reading this book.

Schlaggenberg, Stangeler, Eulenfeld, and Gyurkicz were by now thoroughly drunk, I may as well say unspeakably drunk.

The details of what happened afterwards—after, that is, they had left the studio and the fandango or tango tunes—can no longer be determined. There were rooms, unknown rooms, unknown women, a bar, another bar, a coffeehouse—and then they had come to a garden gate and seen a light on the upper floor.

They clambered over the gate. Schlaggenberg and the captain could no longer keep up. The gymnastics at the gate finished them off. They stayed where they were, leaning against the gate. But Gyurkicz made it, and so did the tango player, along with his guitar. (His name, incidentally, was Beppo Draxler.)

Ah, how beautifully he played.

Now two altogether improbable things happened.

Frau Ruthmayr came to the window, the one that opened on the terrace. That is the first improbability. And she was not particularly frightened. That is the second. But as if that were not enough improbability, a half-empty bottle of brandy was held out to her with a flourish.

And she drank from it.

She drank from it!!! (Or at least made believe to drink.) We cannot set down too many exclamation marks. Schlaggenberg was unfortunately not on the spot, due to a lack of talent for that sort of thing, or on account of "fate" ("or however you say it"), on account of drunkenness. Stangeler likewise. They were leaning against the gate—Captain Eulenfeld also. No doubt the principal reason was that they were too drunk. But Gyurkicz! Well, we have said he was there.

Suddenly they were all gone. Friederike heard an automobile start up. It swooped up the last scattered stragglers of Eulenfeld's *troupeau*.

In truth, she thought she had dreamed the whole episode.

134

And probably the others did likewise.

Frau Friederike Ruthmayr's maid, Ludmilla Kakabsa, had a sister and a brother: Anna, who was in Mme Libesny's service in London; and Leonhard, who worked in a Vienna webbing factory.

Mila, as she was called, exchanged frequent and on the whole foolish letters with Anna. For what was the burden of these letters but that their ladies were very fine ladies and the households the height of fashion. Mila had a slight edge on her sister in this regard, since her house was obviously richer. Her sister's lady could not provide an automobile, chauffeur, and butler. On the other hand, Anna once wrote from London: "We now have a world-famous professor of zoology staying with us. He occupies a big room in the wing [*sic!* The houses right beyond Albert Bridge and the wall of the factory yard, on your right coming from Chelsea, are if anything small!] facing the park. His name is Williams and he has been all over the world, in Brazil too." In return Mila wrote in her next letter: "Yesterday our administrator, Financial Counselor Levielle of Paris, came driving up and called on my lady." Her letters usually concluded: "Leonhard is well and satisfied. I'm sorry to say I don't see him very often."

This Leonhard, who will subsequently engage our attention in the pleasantest fashion, differed in essential respects from his two silly sisters. Leonhard lived alone. His father, a foreman in the steel mill of Wahlberg & Company, had been killed in the First World War just about the time Leonhard became an apprentice in the webbing factory. His mother, a very pretty, dark-complexioned, buxom, and jolly woman, had later married again, and had had several more children. And although Ludmilla and Anna were already out in service, and Leonhard was on good terms with his stepfather—a letter-carrier—he soon felt that he had to break out of this domestic stall. It had become impossible to stay at home without being made to look after two or three fairly unmanageable boys and girls.

Now he occupied a clean little room on Treu Strasse, close to the Danube Canal.

In a certain sense our Leonhard's biography might be everyone's. For with the preconceptions that we have acquired from our early experiences, we proceed to hurl our original selves into whatever sets of circumstances the outside world happens to offer. It ought to surprise no one that we then find ourselves stuck somewhere where we do not belong. And in difficult situations these choices can scarcely be rescinded.

No such difficult situations obtained in our Leonhard's case. For one thing he was still young, and in youth life offers room, within certain time-limits, for acts of recklessness and folly, even for mistakes and delusions, without pinning us down finally to any one track. This was one reason. But the principal reason was that Leonhard had an unusual and inveterate peculiarity: a tendency to avoid all entanglements, all involvements which would be likely to lead him into any particular rut, no matter where it might be situated. He seemed, in fact, to be almost a little cracked in this respect. One result had been, for example, that at the age of twenty-four he still had no permanent relationship with a woman, had found neither mistress nor fiancée. Furthermore, he was a very lukewarm Social Democrat; for there seemed some obstacle in the way of his attaching himself to a political party and its principles, and perhaps his class-consciousness was not all it should have been. His leaving home, clearing out of the letter carrier's household, also appears to have been prompted somewhat by a need to keep his distance from people. He felt a disinclination bordering on repugnance toward complicated conditions such as inevitably arise out of marriage and raising children and all the fuss and fuming, all the cares and affairs of family living. Yet even Leonhard's manner of setting up house for himself was marked by the same fear of entanglement. For as a young man of clean habits he would have been a desirable tenant for many a substantial widow or still vigorous woman with a good pension and a pleasing appearance. But Leonhard promptly ruled out any such possibility and moved into his quarters on Treu Strasse, a furnished room in the apartment of a female past seventy, the widow of a warehouse attendant of the Danube Steamship Company.

He had heard of this room via various connections belonging to the days when during a spell of unemployment in his trade he had been a sailor on a Danube scow.

For a reason of which we shall in due course tell, he did not like to cast his mind back to this period. Nevertheless, although he had now lived once again amid the clatter of looms for some time, this period made itself felt within the here and now like a stuffing of a chair or the stone of a fruit, with an obstinate and profound presentness which could not be banished or forgotten.

That particular quarter of the city is in the main close to the river, though not all the avenues and streets reach to it. Nevertheless, it seems as though everything in the quarter is more or less conditioned by the river, and by its quality of cutting through the landscape. It is all the more effective as a dividing line at this point because it flows between level banks; Kahlenberg and Bisamberg up above the city are the last elevations which seem to thrust gently against the course of the Danube, the one approaching the water's edge, the other curving away as if in retreat toward the receding sky. From here on, however, the level East begins. The smokestacks of the

137

paddle-wheel steamers move slowly; they can be seen a great distance off, and the low grinding noise of their engines can be heard as they toil upstream. When the wind lifts the skirts of the willows, the silvery undersides of the leaves appear. On the horizon hang steamy clouds; these preside over the region known as Marchfeld. Hungary is not far away.

This quarter of the city lies on a large island which is shaped roughly like a gigantic ship, like a ship that once sailed up a greater stream than the Danube now is and let down anchor there. The waters have diminished, and it can no longer sail on. Fore, the Brigittenau has spread itself, amidships Leopoldstadt with the Prater attached, and far aft is the race track in the Freudenau.

Leonhard felt the river. He felt it in his room evenings when he lay on his back on the smooth leather-covered divan.

The river smelled. The river was tainted. This fact formed the core of that fruit stone or stuffing which extended from his past on the water to his present life. Not that the river's waters smelled, for it flowed swiftly, in its main bed at any rate. But life on the scows, up from Budapest, past the high promontory at Gran, past Komorn, that slow life on the scows had always been accompanied by odors which were carried in these broad-bottomed boats through the meadows that lined the rivers, offending them and tainting them: odors of kitchens and bedrooms, of women and children, who were often to be found on such vessels. Outwardly the boats looked trim and clean, big as lake ships, tarred black. It was not the tar that offended Leonhard's nose; he liked the smell of tar. Nor was he much bothered by the smoke from the stacks of the steam tug up ahead, which the wind sometimes pressed down upon the train of scows. He did not mind that particularly, although it was a popular subject for complaint on board. Rather, the musty

138

staleness and uncleanliness that the scows carried up the river stirred in him a profound uneasiness.

Troublesome smells have a certain kinship with a troubled conscience. A person of more than average sensitivity may almost feel the former as equivalent to the latter; his conscience will suffer because he is living in evil-smelling surroundings, in "bad odor."

The fabrication of webbing, on the other hand, is clean work. A single skilled worker tends two mechanical looms at a time, going to and fro between them on a kind of running board. His hands are not kept busy all the time, but he has to intervene quickly and intelligently when some hitch occurs.

The factory where Leonhard worked was emphatically bright. This was not solely because its buildings consisted mostly of up-to-date recent additions. Rather, the raw material itself was of a bright nature; its smell was clean and bitter, like the materials in a harness-maker's or rope-maker's shop. Emerging from the looms the finished product ran in dry reptilian coils into clean wooden boxes: Venetian-blind tapes, slings for the moving of heavy objects, drag-belts, yard upon yard, with blue or red threads running through the sandy colors of jute, hemp, or flax. There were no clattering shuttles. It was far quieter than a textile factory; the attendants at the looms could hear one another speak without difficulty. The big rooms were filled with a regular low humming and clicking; row upon row the tappets swung eccentrically, the drums of wood or aluminum rested like round shields on their looms.

This atmosphere was altogether pleasant to Leonhard. It had for him, we might almost say, the odor of an untroubled conscience. And it was set apart in his mind, not only from the period he had spent aboard the Danube scows, but also from another world of odors: that of the school he had attended.

A layer of sawdust had invariably covered the floor at the entrance to the school, and some disinfectant with a dismal and poverty-stricken smell had been used there. In the classrooms the floors had been oiled. This oil had the laudable effect of keeping down dust; but on the other hand it filled all his years of schooling with a sense of dejection, with the conviction that whenever he entered the building he was completely separated from whatever abilities and talents, whatever courage and animation he possessed; that he was dependent solely on what he learned by study. And sometimes he had not learned too thoroughly, although Kakabsa *père* had himself had a good basic education and tutored his children with a great deal of patience and loving tenderness—Mila and Anna as well as Leonhard wrote a good hand. Inside the school building, however, even during the recesses, he was prey to that strange sense of having all his native faculties switched off. The building frequently smelled of the janitor's pipe. This man, good-natured and something of a tippler, smoked a regular peasant weed—what is called "country tobacco" in Austria. This smell mingled with that of the disinfectant, as well as with the vapors of whitewash. At the very back of the corridor the smell of the *pissoir* could also be detected; its door was constantly flying open and shut during the recesses, occasionally banging against the wall, for which reason a door stop had been installed.

Later on in life Leonhard encountered the smell of the school now and again. He tested it against his present life and was satisfied to find that it had virtually no power over him. But it never became entirely innocuous, whether he met it at the community hall or in a union beer hall. It seemed also to occur in heavy concentration in certain pamphlets which occasionally came his way. And although Leonhard did not exactly concern himself consciously with this nonsensical stuff, yet its

140

essence occupied a large place in his mind.

He lay on the leather divan with his head tilted upward. From far off, from Komorn or the big island of silt, the Danube reached to him, into him. He had sailed upriver this far, and had landed here in this room. It was very still. Smells paid brief calls on him. Suddenly one of them, that of the sleeping cabin on the scow, was present more vividly than it had any right to be. He swung his feet to the floor, sat on the edge of the sofa, and said aloud: "What the devil was I born for—to smell things?"

What followed his question was strange. He looked at the somewhat rickety brass bed in his room, which the landlady regarded as an object of luxury and to which she sometimes referred by way of justifying the price of the room. Above the brass bed—it was no longer possible to shine it to its one-time brightness; it had a kind of dark gleam—above the brass bed, right in the center over the wine-red spread, hovered the unequivocal answer: "Yes."

Smelling would have to clarify everything for him. Smelling was a power in the world. It came before all else. Its veracity was beyond question.

Here, as everywhere else, there was an immediate environment whose dangers (as seen in the light of his disposition) Leonhard soon recognized. From these dangers he had temporarily taken refuge on the leather divan. Moreover, still another factor closed to him the joys of conviviality: Leonhard did not like beer or wine. He was disagreeably affected by a certain slight acidity emanating from these beverages, especially when they were spilled or dregs stood in glasses. A chance incident in the small taproom diagonally opposite his house had engendered a disgust which by now had settled rather deeply in Leonhard's consciousness. He would have drunk hard liquor. But it was simply not the thing in his circles. A decent young man did not go to the "brandy shop." Hardly any of his friends or fellow-workmen did so. Leonhard was far from being an abstainer; it was simply that drinking meant nothing at all to him. Sometimes he would buy a bottle, but these occasions were rare. During the early days of his life on Treu Strasse he was equally indifferent to coffee and cigarettes. He smoked only now and then.

But all his surroundings soon showed him their teeth—though he took care not to stick his fingers between the jaws. These teeth consisted in unassailable sameness, in those aspects of any given surroundings which simply withstood the slightest disturbance.

The folks in this neighborhood lived the way they had been living ever since the new times began, especially since 1918.

On the sidewalks the employees of the municipal gasworks came swinging along in rows of four and five, dressed in their blue uniforms, with tool boxes slung from their shoulders: cashiers and meter readers and repairmen. They blocked the whole sidewalk, made way for no one, and also paraded sizable paunches before them; it was obvious that the age had reached its peak in them, and had done so only in order for them to enjoy their prosperity. Dr. Catona, a neighborhood doctor, once refused to give up the sidewalk to them, stood his ground, and let one of the paunches ram right into him, thereby arousing a surge of indignation. Most people, however, timidly retreated before the phalanx of "the gashouse gang," as they were called.

Anyone whose face betrayed signs of intelligence was sure to be on the receiving end of contemptuous and challenging looks from them. For it was intelligence itself that aroused their antagonism, not at all superior economic position, which at this time was no longer bound up with intelligence—quite the contrary. For intelligence had failed—here lay the real core, the true and bitter root of their antagonism. Intelligence had not been able to prevent the World War and its unfortunate conclusion. Intellectuals, with their gift for language, had done the talking for the inarticulate people. And they had spoken evilly, had preached madness. Afterwards a general hatred for every kind of authority erupted. It manifested itself not only as rebellion but as a kind of ostentatious rowdiness. A highly class-conscious hospital patient with little knowledge of socialism expressed this attitude bluntly to a famous surgeon. A medical man had no right to higher pay than the furnace-man in the hospital, he said. Both were workers and both equally important to the running of the hospital. "Enough of this, my friend," the surgeon replied, laughing, "or else I'll let the furnace-man operate on you tomorrow."

Everyone in the district shared in this challenging and self-assured spirit. In the taprooms each man spoke of nothing but himself. "I don't go in for that." "I won't stand for that kind of thing, that's the way I am." "I've never taken nothing from no one." "I've never made no bones about where I stand." "The gashouse gang" were the heaviest drinkers.

In the taproom Leonhard once ventured to remark that he was satisfied. That was one thing he should never have said. He was immediately driven on the defensive. "Easy for you to talk. No wife, no children. What do you want anyway? Satisfied!" They came down hard on him with their wives and children.

"We sure love them satisfied!" a voice at the adjoining table boomed.

The atmosphere was charged. Leonhard felt an unwonted

inner need to be fair and frank with them. For a moment there appeared before his mind's eye something resembling a geometric figure. Perhaps it was only a straight line against a brighter background.

"You are right there," he said. "But a person can also be dissatisfied at the same time—with himself, for example."

The challenging looks froze into smirks. The others shrugged their shoulders.

"The devil only knows what you would be dissatisfied with yourself for. It's none of our business."

The deliberate misunderstanding was quickly barricading him in. But then an elderly man in a blue blouse spoke up in a quiet, almost benevolent voice: "Don't be unfair to the young man, boys. If I understand him rightly he means that he still wants to learn, that he'd like to get on and not be stuck right where he is now. Young people oughtn't to be satisfied with themselves, or they'll never amount to anything."

He drank to Leonhard. The barricade of misunderstanding remained, only constructed now of less refractory material. The smirks faded here and there; some of the men continued to shrug, but in the end they had a round of drinks, inviting Leonhard to join them. But Leonhard saw clearly—in the same way that shortly before the geometric fine had appeared before his mind's eye—that the others had not been reconciled to him, that not a step had been taken in that direction, that everything remained as it had been—on the level of a dull complacency, into which he, too, in the end dropped back. He smelled the sourness of the wine. Some of it had spilled on the table top.

It was wiped away, but the smell lingered. That was the way everything ended eventually. Something was spilled and then it was wiped away, the memory was wiped away, but something lingered.

At times Leonhard felt that he was entirely surrounded by a world of enemies. In this he was completely mistaken. All those others, including the young fellows his own age, were merely utterly indifferent to him, for he did not appear to them as a rival in any way, nor as one seeking their friendship. When we are indifferent to someone, we are not going to allow him to ruffle our complacency, and we shall certainly feel not the slightest inclination to sacrifice it to him. It would have taken a good deal more than a Leonhard Kakabsa to rouse them—and even then the issue would have been in doubt.

In addition to the various bistros and the cafés large and small—whose clientele overlapped only to a degree—there was also a very curious place named the Café Kaunitz, after the famous statesman of Maria Theresa's reign. It was situated across the river, that is to say, not in the working-class quarter of Brigittenau proper.

The Café Kaunitz had a special schedule, if we may call it such. By day it was a place of quiet and meditation, like a proper Viennese café; each guest took his seat as far apart as possible from all the others, resisting the pull of collective living (they were here, after all, as patrons of the same café) and forming instead a small island. At the same time, however, all the islands were constantly molesting one another on account of the newspapers and magazines; to this end they wandered about with an obstinate restiveness, and every now and then sent probing glances in every direction. The more superfluous nonsense is printed, the more has to be read (we all agree on that, don't we?). In the Café Kaunitz, however, there was less reading than cramming; for no apparent reason it had become a students' café, although it was situated at some distance from any of the institutes of higher learning. To be sure, there was a large student dormitory fairly near the Café Kaunitz, and students from all the faculties seemed to find their way from this dormitory to it. Those who lived in private rooms also came in winter, probably to save on fuel for their stoves; once the habit was formed, they continued to come in summer and autumn. Many found studying easier in the café, where the example of many others equally diligent warmed their zeal, even as the large stove warmed their bodies.

In those days the only expense was a few groschen for a cup of reasonably good coffee. That, in the humane manner of the Viennese coffeehouse, permitted one a stay of unlimited length.

All this, however, does not even touch upon the really remarkable aspects of the Café Kaunitz.

Among these was, first of all, the proprietor or "coffee brewer," as the Viennese say—even the owner of a large and elegant restaurant will be referred to in this offhand fashion. In the Café Kaunitz the owner was a woman.

The Café Kaunitz was large, but only someone from the provinces would ever have thought to call it elegant. Nevertheless, the physical dimensions of the place were considerable. It took up the whole of two sides of a corner building, and in the two perpendicular wings a swarm of marble tables and chairs extended along the upholstered booths to the left and right. The entrance was at the corner, opposite it the traditional cashier's seat, and to the right of this an upright piano. A word to the wise is sufficient; to the initiate this signified that the Café Kaunitz was not really a substantial coffeehouse. Pianos are not tolerated in the better Viennese cafés. An air of the night club hung about this piano, even though it remained tightly shut during the day—if only not to disturb the students at their study.

The cashier's cubicle was constructed of glass and metal, but it was empty. There was no cashier perched on the seat provided. Nor did the proprietress take her seat behind the raised, polished semicircle of marble counter with its pyramidal pastry stands to the right and left and its mirror-doored cupboards on the rear wall. Her predecessor, however, used to sit enthroned there, a considerable adornment to the place, for she was a handsome woman named Risa Weinmann. Now and then she still dropped in as a patron, and she would always sit at the owner's table.

Both women, the present and the former owners of the Café Kaunitz, seemed cut out of the same cloth, and yet again at some point difficult to determine there existed an acute difference, a point at which their patterns seemed precisely in reverse. Perhaps in reality the difference was only a matter of a line, a dot, and yet that line or dot was critical.

Frau Weinmann looked like a Snow White who had somehow been dropped into the Arabian Nights, and hence into Oriental lushness: she was all peaches and cream, a piece of Turkish delight, a mass of curves and billows, and at the same time easily fifty if not more. She was always alert; it seemed quite incredible that she ever went to sleep. Sleep lulls, sleep settles. No such dimwitted state seemed possible for Frau Risa Weinmann.

When she awoke in the morning (for she did sleep after all), when she apprehended her surroundings again, and her ideas and thoughts leaped up anew, seized upon one another, bickered or wrestled with one another, the first clear outcome of it all, which she soon gripped tightly and held as with tongs, was the point at which profit could be made. That is what everyone is after, it may be objected. But in Frau Weinmann's case her concentration upon it amounted to genius.

Her second thought was for anyone who might dare to contest her right to such profit, and who might want to stop her from making it. There were always such people. If in a given case she did not know right off who it might be, she assumed this enemy's existence and went looking for him. Moreover, she always found him. Her mind was like her teeth: pearly white and sharp. By origin she was a Balkanese, as we say in Vienna. Pyorrhea and dental caries have made the smallest inroads among the Balkan peoples. How their teeth flash!

So it was with Frau Weinmann. She could show her teeth and the whites of her eyes like a Central African warrior. Yet talents such as these did not really come into play in the Café Kaunitz, and that was why she had traded her café for a smaller place, pocketing the considerable difference in cash. As she had foreseen, moreover, the smaller institution was soon netting under her supervision far larger profits than the Kaunitz, whose patrons and customs were not to the taste of Frau Risa. (Here was one great difference between her and her successor.) She would, for example, have liked to throw the students out altogether. Now she ran a café far out in the suburbs, a place with only three windows on the street. Punctually at the police curfew hour the shutters were lowered, everything closed up tight, and everyone stayed put inside. Along with Mephistopheles, Frau Risa could say that she knew perfectly how to get on with the police, as well as with the rest of life's authorities—the concierge, for example. Once the shutters were down, the concierge admitted certain persons whom Frau Weinmann had previously certified. The practice proved doubly advantageous to him, for he was rewarded first by the late patron and secondly by the proprietress; when it suited her, she knew how to tip well.

She passed her first tests out there in the suburb with flying colors. At the right time she drove her fist into the right man's face—big and strong though he was. The right time was, of course, when the shutters were down and a sufficient number of reliable guests were present. The right man stood there like a sluggish bull, black pouches under his eyes, swallowing his fury, his hands thrust into his trousers' pockets and clutching the cloth so that they would not leap out and strike back. For the woman knew too much. And he knew that she knew. And she knew that he knew that she knew. Without a word, he left. And he left behind a Frau Weinmann encircled by an aureole of general respect. Another man, early one evening, merely sat in the café, nothing more. He waited, and Frau Weinmann knew whom he was waiting for; she knew other people's enemies as well as her own. This man was not being sought by the police at the moment; Risa was always fully informed on such matters. In fact, if the police had been looking for him he would scarcely have been sitting there. She assumed, however, that the blade of his switch knife was somewhat longer than is permitted by Austrian law. And so she went out the back door and took measures to have her café raided and her guests "shaken down." As it turned out, she had been right about the knife. That was all there was to the affair; nobody was arrested. While the police were busy, the expected guest materialized and at once went his way again. Risa saw him and said nothing. But since she could guess that he, too, carried a switchblade knife several inches longer than the legal limit, there was no doubt that the café had been spared a rather ticklish stabbing incident.

The lady who had taken over the Café Kaunitz would never have been able to handle such matters. Risa could handle them with her left hand.

Outside of business hours she occasionally appeared with a husband, a little runt who gave the impression that he was a kind of parasite upon her massive corporeality. This husband was a clerk in the lower middle ranks of the civil service. During the period after the First World War, Frau Weinmann had risen swiftly in the world by black-market trading—in this respect her life-story exactly paralleled that of her colleague who now owned the Café Kaunitz. The little parasite of a husband had been useful to her for delivering goods and collecting bills, always behaving with perfect propriety within the sphere of his improprieties.

But when the black market in foodstuffs subsided and Frau Weinmann opened her small café in Ottakring, the differences between the two women became fully apparent.

The new owner of the Kaunitz was the kind of woman whom everyone, at first glance, would have taken for the madam of a house of ill-fame; but in point of fact she was the widow of a respectable physician from Troppau. She was the same age as Frau Weinmann, and just as pretty and soft of complexion, with a round gentle face, a neat stub of a nose. She had a way of raising her eyelashes very gracefully; her gray eyes had a kindly look. However, if you forced your own glance straight into that soft look, if you penetrated deeper into those pretty eyes, the effect was like stepping on the smooth gray surface of a frozen puddle: the feeble coating gives way and the icy water comes pouring into your shoe. The eyes of Frau Schoschi, as she was called, were like that. But you really need not have troubled to make this little experiment; you could have guessed the whole thing. For there was a distinct breach in the prettiness of her face. Her upper lip was frequently raised, revealing only moderately good teeth patched here and there by the art of the dentist. It must be granted, however, that the little flashes of gold became her blonde doll's head. But that drawn-back lip gave her face a somewhat rodent-like quality, and it was probably this that invested the pretty face with the madam's look, this and the icy puddle below the surface of the eyes. Frau Schoschi raised her upper lip frequently—and sometimes her nose moved along with it. You had the impression that something was bothering her, that something was biting or paining her nose.

Perhaps—it is impossible to state this with any certainty—this nasal discomfort was connected with a crisis in Frau Schoschi's life. This crisis was marked by the cessation of the large profits she had made on the black market during and after the First World War, profits which had first enabled Frau Schoschi, like Risa Weinmann, to rise to the ownership of property. Risa Weinmann had abandoned the marts of trade altogether, out in her café in Ottakring. But Frau Schoschi went on with commerce, although she dealt mainly in another type of wares—in which formerly she had only dabbled. The article in question is a white powder which is at once extremely good and extremely bad for the human constitution. It is said, according to writers whose opinions must be reckoned with, to affect eventually the septum of the nose. This powder is sniffed. (Frau Weinmann, on the other hand, would have tossed any narcotics dealer out of her café, though she would never have called in the police; she kept such matters to herself.)

Now all this is supposition, and it may be objected that we have carried our suppositions too far. For the rodent-like, madam's look might have been something that Frau Schoschi had not acquired but was simply hers from the very beginning. Certain facts, however, are established. Among these is the information that a prostitute named Anny Gräven obtained her "junk" at the Café Kaunitz; whether she got it from Frau Schoschi or from someone else has not been settled. This Anny Gräven had been the wife of a dental technician until her thirty-fourth year.

Her husband had become an addict. He had had no trouble obtaining the stuff, perhaps from dentists for whom he worked. Naturally he led his wife into addiction also, and into mounting degradation. Gräven did not survive his third or fourth withdrawal cure. Anny, however, did. She no longer felt capable of any work, and went on the streets, properly registered. Strangely enough—indeed it is almost incomprehensible—she did not become addicted again. We will encounter her later in connection with Leonhard Kakabsa, in whose youth she played a modest but significant and salutary role.

Played, played—yes, now we have the association: Frau Schoschi never played cards. This was one vice she denied herself. Otherwise she probably would have gambled away her Café Kaunitz very quickly. She was capable of standing for hours, passionately watching a game of "sixty-six" among her guests. This is by no means a game of pure chance; it calls for concentration, wider vision, and a sharp eye for the profitable point; for like every real card game it is an image of bourgeois life, both play and hazard. No wonder that cards are the favorite pleasure of the average member of the bourgeoisie. For in cards the guiding element in his life (a stoic philosopher, for example the Emperor Marcus Aurelius, who lived in Vienna, would perhaps have said: his *hegemonikon*) was kept flowing outside of business hours also. For if it ever stopped flowing, what would become of it?

Ederl, the painting contractor, was an absolute whiz at sixty-six. His talents as a house-painter were far inferior to his skill at cards.

But let us return to our comparison of Frau Weinmann and Frau Schoschi. Frau Weinmann was a powerful draft-animal of the underworld, whereas Frau Schoschi was a kind of sewage snail, but one not likely to be crushed underfoot, because ever since the turning point in her life—the disappearance of the black market—she had crawled only upon soft ground, in the finest mud. She had the cunning of the sick, the subtlest kind of craftiness in existence.

Both women were acquainted with Gyurkicz and with Captain von Eulenfeld, although neither these gentlemen nor any members of the captain's *troupeau* were numbered among her patrons, at least not among her regular patrons. The acquaintance was due to a certain Oki Leucht, the lover of a professor's daughter named Dolly Storch; the Storch family lived in the same building and on the same floor as the Siebenscheins. Leucht turned up now and then in Frau Weinmann's café in Ottakring. He had the build for such a place, for he was a hulking fellow of six feet two. He used to sit at the regular table of the Atlas Weight-lifters' Club—a little association of strong-men. They met here once every two weeks. Leucht himself was not a member and not a weightlifter, but he had friends in the club.

Back to our timetable and the clientele of the Café Kaunitz.

The students usually stuck to their books until late in the evening. Between ten and half-past ten, they drifted out, while here and there a pair of lovers drifted in. Spindly girls, a small coffee, a young white-collar man: they were like sparse bouquets of flowers scattered here and there among the booths, for naturally they preferred booths. Perhaps, if it had been dark, the couples would have glowed modestly, like fireflies. But full illumination remained on in both wings of the café; the swarm of marble tables stretched out into space, gleaming dimly. Gradually an almost perfect silence spread over the place. The café's two wide frontages on the deserted streets shone bright and empty, surrounded by midnight darkness like a haunted house. But the café was not closed. It remained open

153

to everyone, though scarcely a person passed by in the streets outside. The clock ticked away, fifteen after twelve, half-past twelve.

By seven o'clock in the evening the proprietress had already gone to bed. The waiter left every night at eleven. Henceforth supervision and service were in the charge of a very ordinary and stupid-looking female, blonde and unprepossessing. No one would have suspected her of being Frau Schoschi's younger sister. She was even more than that. It was Frau Schoschi herself, plucked out of the accidental surrounding flesh like a sallow root out of its trench. A midnight turnip, a mandrake root, the naked truth by night.

Shortly after one o'clock the street in front of the Café Kaunitz came to life in a matter of minutes. New arrivals poured into the café from all directions. These were the discharge from bistros, taprooms and taverns, and from those cafés which closed at one. This was the hour for all those who had fallen into a rut in the course of the evening—or who had started the evening in one—and could no longer hoist themselves out of it and make their way home. So they went to the Kaunitz. For about twenty minutes its revolving door whirled incessantly like a turbine propelled by the current. Around half-past one the café was jammed; Frau Schoschi's sister raced about with bottles of wine and broad serving trays on which glasses of schnapps stood in rows. Now, too, the upright piano opened its jaws and showed its white teeth; a musician sat down in front of it, and beside him stood a more than skinny, a deathly emaciated female with intense black hair and dark rings under her eyes. The man struck the keys, the woman sang. A regular patron with a talent for malice had once called her the "singing lungworm." She was likewise a relative of Frau Schoschi, who evidently liked to do things for members of her family.

Soon the guests were singing too.

At last the owner herself reappeared, refreshed, eyes shining, as though she had just emerged from the bath. Moreover, she was dressed quite tastefully. Usually she wore black; black looks well on blondes, and in her case was further dramatized by the gold caps on her teeth. Within a few minutes the owner's table was fully occupied and besieged by favored guests, enlivened by cold bottles beaded with condensation and yellow-gummed glasses of eggnog.

The fauna which put in at this hour of the night necessarily represented a mixture of districts and origins. Like liverwurst bursting from its gut casing, they poured out of those public places which shut down at one o'clock, marched separate ways to the Café Kaunitz, and once united there produced more noise than at any earlier part of the night. Soon the oily laughter of businessmen from Alsergrund and Wahringen mingled with the lower-pitched rumble of workingmen who here as everywhere else were exploited by imperialistic monopoly capitalism—embodied in this case by Frau Schoschi. And along with the wheezing notes of the singing lungworm there sounded, amid this cacophony, the broad and self-assured trumpetings of some members of "the gashouse gang," who sat in the back part of the café, now and then pounding on the marble tables, and saying *in toto* little more than that they wouldn't put up with that sort of thing, the hell they would, and they'd tell anyone to his face that they wouldn't. The noise of other segments of the crowd was likewise considerable, though not laid on quite so thick as that of the gas men. We must also count in the tootlings of numerous women, which formed a tonal foundation for the wheezing lungworm, while the gas men made up the percussion section of the orchestra.

Painting contractor Ederl sat at a marble table set in a

window embrasure. He sat alone. He was half asleep. His big round face was softened by drink. Ordinarily he had a rather brisk look. But he had played cards in three different taverns since five that afternoon, and had won a few hundred—he played for high stakes—not to speak of the bottles of wine which the losers had had to stand him. Ederl was rarely among the losers. He had a faculty for keeping a close watch on the game even when he had been drinking heavily. Yet he had never invited anyone to join in a card game; rather, he was literally pursued by his partners. Everyone knew that he played honestly. That made the others all the more eager to try their skill against his. To win a hundred or so schillings from Ederl, or a few bottles of wine, would have been a real triumph, one that even the gas men would have had to sit up and notice. But it never turned out that way. Again and again the losers insisted on their "return match" with the already exhausted master. He granted it and won. His partners trailed him from one café to the next. He exerted some magnetic attraction upon them. He had only to take a seat somewhere and they swarmed around him. Moreover, when he had cleared out their pockets, they would go home for more cash and come back again. If in the course of an evening Ederl had taken three or four men for a loss, these losers would sooner or later turn up in the Café Kaunitz to demand their "revenge." They would find Ederl already sitting there, a spider weaving its web reluctantly and catching flies it no longer desired: another bottle of wine, another hundred or so schillings. Ederl won both: he was a spider gorged with alcohol. He actually had to be shaken awake for this last game. The owner came over from her table; her companions would have to make mirth without her. Once cards were dealt, there was no more fun to be had with her. She was lost to anything but the game. Now she stood beside Ederl, kibitzing in utter

156

silence, without letting fall a syllable. The icy puddle quivered in her eyes.

Meanwhile the clock had struck two. About this hour the noise in the café attained its second level. Often three or four persons sitting side by side talked simultaneously and incessantly. From the percussion section in the background came a low steady rumble of thunder.

Hirschkron the bookbinder, a man in his mid-forties, had now appeared. A silent figure whom the winds had carried in at this ungodly time of night. He stood, wineglass in hand, behind Ederl's partner. Hirschkron seldom sat down. He circulated around the tables like a specter among graves. In the winter he always kept his overcoat on, its collar turned up. He could watch a card game for hours without ever taking a hand in it. He belonged to no table, and belonged to all. Everyone had long grown accustomed to his habits; he troubled no one.

Probably without being aware of it, Hirschkron constituted a distinct higher class among the variegated mixed fauna of the Café Kaunitz. Consequently his wanderings among the tables expressed an inherent truth. He really did not belong to any of these tables but always to the space in between where people stand when they have left a table. Hirschkron stood where others sat; he was no joiner. His benign face undoubtedly showed a potentiality for higher things; it was not an unimportant face; it inclined toward ambivalence, even toward dislocation—and a readiness to embrace new, different, unheard-of, and perhaps greater tilings. But novelty would have meant going off at a tangent from the circle in which Hirschkron moved. And although his face showed the tangential impulse—sometimes strongly—his circle was an infinite curved space, and in the end the tangents proved to be curved lines also; they led inexorably back to the curved infiniteness of that space, and back to the endlessness of the games of sixty-six that were played within it.

Everyone liked Hirschkron. It was apparent that he was liked for the same reason that Leonhard was disliked; for intellectual gifts are not hated in themselves. But roving tangents—as in Leonhard Kakabsa's case—are regarded as monstrosities; they arouse antagonism; they are assertions of contrary principles. And everyone has principles; people even do a good deal of boasting about their principles and their character. That is only natural. Having principles leads a man into the society of his fellows—but does not necessarily make others like him. Intellectual gifts must emerge from such a total lack of principle as characterized Hirschkron. Kakabsa, for example, dreaded and shunned every entanglement. Hirschkron, on the other hand, had long before become entirely entangled; the liana jungle of life had become tightly wound around his every limb. At home he had a wife whom he had married out of common decency, because he had made her pregnant, and who was now repulsive to him because of her growing slatternliness. His children took entirely after their mother. He no longer had a home. He moved about among the tables, half-filled wineglass in his hand; it was always half-full and it was always the same wine, long since grown tepid. In the end he put it down; he was a *pro forma* drinker. When he kibitzed and there happened to be an unoccupied table behind him, he set the glass on it; in this way he got rid of it. He ought to have drunk a little; it would have been better for him and would not have undermined his capacity for work. But for some reason he could not stand drink; it did not go with his constitution. In his trade as bookbinder Hirschkron was extremely competent, although one of his fingers had been slightly maimed by a stray bullet during the war. He managed nevertheless, in spite of this handicap.

Ederl, the painting contractor, was on the other hand adept

not only at cards and house-painting but also at wine-trading. Among the tavern keepers of the neighborhood there was one who lacked that dash of rustic temperament which is essential to an innkeeper in a wine-growing country. For in order to be a good wine-buyer the innkeeper must know how to talk with the vintners in Lower Austria or Burgenland, to say the right words in the right tone, to join in innumerable tastings: with the consequent risk of a heavy head, to have a strong stomach, and at the same time to cling to every advantage through thick and thin. Now the innkeeper in question was a city man through and through, bespectacled, and apt to shilly-shally. Ederl bought his wines for him, and that massive round face of his was right up to the peasant standard. Just as he played cards brilliantly while drunk, so he could handle a business deal in the same state. Thus, while he drank immoderately on these trips out to the wine country, he came back with topnotch contracts. Of course he did not do it for nothing.

We might devote a whole chapter of Ederl's biography to the business he had done with various foreign military missions after the First World War, when they came to set up their offices and apartments. New offices and apartments have to be furbished; they have to be decorated; and a good many such jobs came Ederl's way. Such clients paid their bills in the solid currencies of the victor countries, and could be charged stiff prices besides. What was more, foreign agencies did not bother to inform Austrian tax bureaus of their payments to Austrian citizens. All in all, Ederl the drinker gradually became a rich man, and Hirschkron remained soberly poor—so that we are tempted to paraphrase the title of that famous novel by the Marquis de Sade and write: *"Ederl, ou la prospérité du vice."*

Toward three o'clock the café began to reach its third level of noise. The table abandoned by the proprietress had been extended by the process of pushing several small marble tables together, and the row of bottles had similarly stretched out. A dozen persons were talking simultaneously and without the slightest pause. Here and there the wine remained untouched while trayfuls of reviving black coffee were hastily provided; this was done by the owner's charming sister, while the night waiter, who had appeared at one o'clock, took care of other orders. He frequently communicated across the room with the patrons in a roar, partly on account of the music—the lung-worm was still favoring the company with vocal selections—and partly because of the occasional detonations from the percussion section.

As Noise Phase III approached, Jirasek the tailor usually began to sing. He came to this café only at intervals of a month, but once there he could be counted on to appear on several successive days. This rotation, as he would always candidly explain to whoever happened to be his neighbor at the owner's table, was connected with Frau Jirasek's biological rhythms. Toward three o'clock, then, he would begin to sing in a melancholy basso. There was a predictable point at which Jirasek would begin to sing, for he would have reached the degree of intoxication at which he fancied himself a medical man. Then he would assure all and sundry again and again, in the most casual and supercilious of tones, that it would cost him only a telephone call to have everybody here taken to the "police presunk" (!) and "psychiatrized" on the spot. The whole kit and caboodle of them were crazy as loons anyhow, he maintained. This he reiterated until he suddenly broke into song. It may be added that Jirasek, after the Café Kaunitz closed at four o'clock, habitually took a number of complete strangers, men and women both, back to his flat with him. What Frau Jirasek thought about this is unknown—perhaps she even enjoyed these surprise visits—for, God be thanked, events at the tailor's home are not within our purview. It may be mentioned, finally, that Jirasek was at this time sixty years old, and when intoxicated, perspired at the temples from weakness. When Noise Phase III reached its climax you could easily believe you were already "in the other place," as Johann Peter Hebei so chillingly puts it in his "Curious Ghost Story." Several couples were dancing quite respectably among the tables, there being no real dance floor in the café. But suddenly two unknowns slipped agilely onto the bench to either side of the pianist and began pounding on the keys with both hands in a pure orgy of noise-making. Immediately the dancers shouted and swore at the disturbers, the loud drinkers protested the din, and the would-be virtuosi were dragged by the collar away from the piano and back to their seats. The pianist played again. By now the lungworm had quavered out her last note. But the card game was over, Ederl had won another couple of hundred, and now the proprietress herself sang. She was acclaimed on all sides. Jirasek, however, could not be silenced; he had passed the "police presunk" stage before three o'clock and was now babbling away with the nerve-racking obstinacy of the totally drunk. Several men took hold of him and dragged him out to the men's room, amusing themselves by giving him a good drubbing while they were about it. The owner's singing was swallowed up in the general din with remarkable rapidity; it vanished without a trace; no one gave it an ear. By about half-past three the café was indisputably a sheer hell; there could no longer be any doubt about its being "in the other place." But already several of the patrons were reeling from the premises, for they knew that the owner, aided by her sister, the pianist, the night waiter, and the concierge (who was hired especially for this work), would ruthlessly, brutally clear everyone out at the stroke of four. Just as the influx had kept the revolving door in constant motion at one o'clock, so now the outflow whirled it faster and faster, although in a convulsive rather than steady manner. The café vomited its contents. For a short while the vomit left dark stains here and there upon the dark street.

It is difficult to define precisely the line at which a human being's personal environment ceases and the atmosphere of his age begins. Yet a person need only avoid his tavern, out of disgust with what he knows too well, and go a short way down the street to another one—and he has undoubtedly crossed that line.

But crossing the line is also possible while he lies on a leather sofa. The evening Leonhard realized that he had been born to use his nose (and this was an insight he clung fast to; henceforth he would not have it gainsaid)—that evening he left his leather sofa to go out. He stepped into the vestibule, entering it at the same time as his landlady, the aged widow of the warehouse attendant.

"Goin' to church tomorrow, Herr Kakabsa?"

"Why should I? You know I never go to church."

"Oh, I didn't mean nothing. Well, no matter, I'll do your prayin' for you."

This Saturday-evening exchange was repeated verbatim at intervals of three or four weeks. Sometimes it also took place on Sunday morning. Leonhard did not even shake his head as he descended the stairs. He was accustomed to the little dialogue by now.

At the corner of Treu Strasse he turned to the right, away from the Danube Canal, and headed down broad Wallenstein Strasse.

It was just beginning to grow dark. The street had a Saturday liveliness. The air was mild; the warmth of incipient spring had suddenly descended. Along the street ran a ribbon of light from still-open shops; others were already closed. A bluish-gray mist hung over the pavement of the roadway, in spite of the rumbling, rolling traffic. Leonhard observed that a wispy fog was rising from the river.

At Fiedler's bookshop the big glass door of the show window stood ajar across the sidewalk, supported by a small iron stand that looked something like an automobile jack. One of the shop attendants was on guard to see that no one walked into the glass. Evidently the window display was being redone this Saturday evening. A girl was kneeling inside. Now she stood up, stepped out onto the sidewalk, several books under her arm, and inspected the display. It struck Leonhard as slightly incongruous that she should have a cigarette dangling from the corner of her mouth. Ribbons of smoke rose obliquely past her face. Kakabsa noticed the smoke at the very moment that the books she was holding slipped from her grasp and started tumbling to the sidewalk, which was coated with a film of moisture. The boy at the window seemed unaware of what was happening. Leonhard reached out and caught the books before they fell. For several seconds the two of them, Leonhard and the girl, stood close together, both supporting the books which were wedged between them. A grateful look from two green eyes in a feline face struck Leonhard. But this was only an extra dividend, for during those seconds Leonhard felt the girl's body with an almost unbelievable palpability; he stood pressed close against her, after all. He felt distinctly her soft compactness, the very curve of her abdomen.

Together, they placed the books safely in the show window. Now, however, the boy came over to assist them.

"That's what comes of smoking at work," Malva Fiedler

163

said gently. "Smoke got into my eyes. Thank you, mister." She looked at him as she had done before: feline face, feline eyes, soft compactness. He would not have been a man had he failed to notice, so early in their acquaintance, her wide hips and pert breasts.

Leonhard immediately gave her good day and made off; he strode on and on without pausing. Oddly enough, the thought came to him that he was being an utter idiot to run away like this, without the slightest attempt to strike up an acquaintanceship. But then again a girl working in a bookshop could be found again; she would not vanish forever like some stranger in the street who had attracted his notice but who could not be held, could not be grasped, and would be gone in a moment—chance encounters of this sort had always disturbed Leonhard. The reaction in him occurred precisely in front of the former Northwest Railroad Station, which was no longer in use for passenger traffic and stood big, gray, and lifeless like a now opaque window into the outer world.

The reaction was: that he was caught. Or that something had caught on him, like a burr. The bookshop on Wallenstein Strasse had not vanished into nothingness but could easily be found again . . . He looked down at his body as though expecting to find protruding from him some missile that had struck him.

It had hit home. It had taken him all this while, all this walk, to realize that. Up to this point he had been privileged to keep some perspective on what had just happened to him, on the missile that had impinged upon him. Now it was already well in his body, partaking of his own warmth; now it was part of him. It was as if the thing had only just happened.

And now, here in front of the station, the last bit of the train of events pulled in, like the report of a shot heard long after

164

the flash of it has been seen in the distance. And the last bit was essential to complete the whole of it, for it was: an odor. While he was close to the girl he had not been conscious of it. Now, afterwards, he felt it as a kind of certainty: this was the way she must smell, just like this, not one whit different. There was something like honey penetrating through the sharpness of the fragrance in his nostrils. Like a dark comb of honey into which one has pressed the thorn of a rose . . . Leonhard was not in the least alarmed by the confusion in his mind. He did not attempt to dismiss the whole matter with a contemptuous, violent wave of his arm; such brash adolescent defiance was no longer for him. After his recent insight he had had to abate his conceit, and his illusion of absolute independence. He had been enlightened. Not in breadth, to be sure, not in the spirit of progress. But surely in depth. He had admitted that he was born to use his nose, and now he clung to this. He had gained in wisdom. Though wisdom is not to be equated with power, as knowledge was so equated in the exuberant early stages of mankind's enlightenment.

Walking on from the Northwest Station he became aware, after a while, that he was on his way to see Anny Gräven, who lived on Franzensbrücken Strasse, which is near the Prater. She would certainly be in one of the cafés of the neighborhood.

Right now she seemed to him trustworthy, benign, and reassuring by comparison with the bookshop girl, although Anny's background—her culture medium, her mycelium, the pot in which she grew—was not exactly of the kind to engender confidence. But the Gräven girl was guileless because she was essentially truthful, despite the lies that she might prattle. Her aloofness from all morality was plain as day; like a treeless

165

mountain-top open to the sky, Anny Gräven was in the clear all around; all the superstructures and substructures which men force upon women, which are often erected upon their altogether alien foundation in such a way as to hide it completely, had been cleared away. Of course, in all women that foundation remains, lying hidden from view. But Anny Gräven was like an open-pit mine that could be exploited directly. To be sure, she never gave anyone the opportunity to do so. She never complicated her life with intermediaries. The reason may have been that she had come to her profession when she was already of mature years.

Leonhard, as he walked, summoned up the details of her appearance; her thin face, like a friendly shrew's; her body, which in contrast to her small face was soft and rounded, though slender, rather reminding him of a small child's body. And her jovial, arch expression when she drank! She drank too much. Someone who has escaped from drugs retains at least this susceptibility to alcohol, as a kind of feeble substitute. Anny also gambled. The great game of the time was a special kind of dominos, "bookie dominos," which was played in many cafés. It was very easy to lose money at, and Anny Gräven lost a great deal. (She could not play a decent game of cards; the only games she liked were those of arrant chance. "I only have an eighth of a brain," Anny was in the habit of saying.)

Leonhard had met her in a taproom. Ever since, he had been going to see her now and again. She could usually be reached afternoons by telephone at one of the cafés on Prater Strasse. He would call her up and make an appointment. She asked nothing of him, but took gratefully whatever he gave her.

The house in which Anny Gräven lived was ancient and rambling, with winding staircases and long narrow corridors. Part of the building belonged to a hotel that had been occupying it for nearly a hundred years. The other wing, facing on Franzensbrücken Strasse, was separate and used as a boarding house with largely permanent residents. Anny's room could also be reached through the hotel. However, Leonhard would never have found his way to her door unguided. The corridors were scarcely illuminated. He usually met Anny at a small bar and she would take him home with her. The old building's walls were thick; you plunged deep inside them, as though you were leaving the world, putting a dense stone barrier between yourself and the outside. Anny's room was not bad; it was well furnished. Her earnings were high. Leonhard would lecture her about stopping gambling and putting some money aside. She would only laugh, having just lost two or three hundred at dominos.

As he walked along now, his thoughts dwelt pleasantly on her. But when he arrived at the beginning of Prater Strasse, he turned on his heel and started back toward home. Before he reached his neighborhood again he dropped into an unfamiliar tavern for a beer.

In general a workingman does not see a bookshop open; this is a fact worth remembering. When he passes such a shop in the morning, its shutters are down, and so they are again in the evening when his day's work is done.

The power of things (*"la puissance des choses,"* as old Metternich put it) therefore somewhat reduced again that swelling, that small tumor, which contact with Malva Fiedler's midriff had formed in Leonhard's imagination.

The day after it had taken shape was a Sunday. Toward three o'clock Leonhard was sitting with his sister Mila in the upstairs kitchen of the Palais Ruthmayr—the tea or breakfast kitchen, as it was called, because it was located on the same floor as the bedrooms and was used only for preparing soft-boiled eggs, oatmeal, and the other items proper to a breakfast tray.

From the kitchen window you looked down into the garden—into the rear garden, not the one on the street whose gate would be vaulted one day (to be exact, not quite a full year later) by Eulenfeld's *troupeau,* to the accompaniment of singing and guitar-playing.

The garden in the rear of the mansion virtually deserved the name of park. On a cloudy day in, say, early spring, the light made everything look frozen in silence, in a stillness that did not underlie things like a soft thick cushion, but wrapped them round like a coil of glass. That was the look of the naked treetops and of an arbor whose wooden framework still stood bare, not yet entwined and shaded by vines. The kitchen smelled strongly of coffee. Mila poured a cup for her brother. When they did not talk (and they were not talking at the moment), this kitchen was a place of almost perfect silence; it bothered Leonhard that he had to scar this silence by rattling the coffee spoon. She was a pretty girl, his sister Mila. Peaches and cream. A little too white, though—too deep a pallor. A lovely child. Their father would have been happy to see her. She resembled him. Didn't she want to go out on her Sunday afternoon off? A girl like her, looking so sweet and neat, must have admirers.

Mila almost always asked Leonhard on one of his rare visits to fix some article, usually something which her mistress, Frau Ruthmayr, prized, which needed delicate attention and yet was such a triviality that a regular workman scorned to give it sufficient care. Leonhard was always willing to do such little jobs, for although he liked Mila, he found her extremely boring;

168

on the other hand he would have thought it impolite to leave too soon after the coffee. Mila, for her part, took a childish—perhaps childlike would be closer to it—delight in surprising her mistress by fulfilling some little wish she had observed or guessed. This was why she requisitioned Leonhard. Whatever needed to be done was then done in all secrecy. Leonhard was very handy at such household tasks.

This time, too, Mila had something in mind. The arbor in the garden had become rotten and rickety here and there; at one spot it had almost collapsed. Mila had repeatedly asked the butler-handyman to take care of it. But the fat fellow showed little inclination for such jobs, and the carpenter he sent for had not yet shown up. Now the foliage would be out on the vines before long. Mila had therefore obtained scantlings, assembled tools, screws and nails, and then sent Leonhard a postcard inviting him for coffee on Sunday.

They went downstairs.

Crossing the landing, their footsteps muted by the yellow carpets in front of Frau Friederike's bedroom, they tripped rapidly down a winding staircase which led into the garden. Even while Leonhard still smelled the still, pure, faintly fragrant air of the stair-landing, they were outside on the gravel, under the arbor. The windowless rear walls of several rather distant houses stood like pale peaks against the cloudy sky. Mila tripped over to a small tool shed to fetch the materials. Leonhard looked over the arbor, to see what needed to be done. He shook it slightly here and there, took in the nature of the structure and the simple repairs that were needed. The low posts in the ground, which supported the framework, were still firmly set and sound; only a single lengthwise piece and two cross-braces needed replacing. Mila returned. Her brother removed the rotten pieces, pulled out the nails, and took his measurements.

Mila helped him, holding the wood while he sawed the new braces. In an hour or less the arbor stood firm and straight once more; it would no longer sway in the wind. Leonhard had used no nails; he had fastened everything with screws which he had carefully countersunk so that you could run your hand over the wood without being caught on the screw-heads. When he was finished, he went down the whole arbor, shaking it gently all the way, and then replaced two more braces. Now the job was done.

"You must paint the new braces green, like the rest," Leonhard remarked.

"Let's do that right now. I'll bring the paint," Mila said enthusiastically.

She brought the can and two paintbrushes from the tool room.

While Leonhard was carefully opening the can, an automobile could be heard stopping on the street at the front of the house. Mila gave it no heed. She was expecting the car to return empty. After the midday meal, Frau Friederike had driven out to see a friend and probably intended to stay the afternoon. She did not like making her chauffeur wait a long time, and preferred sending him home with the car and having him return for her later.

Leonhard stirred the paint with a fragment of wood.

Friederike Ruthmayr appeared on the small terrace which overlooked the garden outside the vestibule. She was followed by Herr Levielle. They descended the steps to the garden. Mila hurried forward to meet her mistress.

"Why, Miluschka," Friederike exclaimed, "I thought you were going out."

"Leonhard is here," Mila said radiantly, kissing Friederike's hand. "He's fixed the arbor. We were just going to paint it."

Friederike walked on, under the bare trellises. Levielle had stopped; the light rear wall of the house formed a background for his figure. Leonhard put down the paint can and glanced at his hands. There were no paint stains on them. He walked forward to meet Frau Ruthmayr and bowed.

"How do you do, Leonhard," Friederike said, extending her hand. "Thank you very much for going to so much trouble on a Sunday. But you don't come to see your sister very often. She has complained about it."

Hitherto Leonhard had only seen Friederike for a few moments now and then. Once, more than a year before, when he had come to take Mila for a walk, she had presented him to her mistress, who happened to come by. Now he stood facing Frau Ruthmayr in the muted and yet bright light of this early spring day, and she produced a wholly extraordinary effect upon him. He was able to regard her quietly, without constraint. But this was not due to any quality of his; rather, it emanated from her. Before her countenance everything seemed to acquire depth, a depth which did away with all nervous tension, all awkwardness, all nervousness, as it is generously called. Even now the manner of her approach still reverberated within Leonhard, the way she had come toward him down the leafless arbor, with a floating motion, like a pretty ornamental fish swimming up to the glass wall of an aquarium. No doubt about it, there was something fishlike about her. Her very large dark eyes were just the least bit slanted, perhaps. They had a mute and lonely look. An absurd pity took hold of Leonhard, and a longing to join her somehow in her unknown suffering. He felt this emotion lifting him above all the usual things that filled his life, even above the recollections of the Danube scow, the girl at the bookshop, and Anny Gräven—far above all these. Far above the Danube Canal, even. For the duration of a breath he stood in his thoughts on the square in front of the Franz Joseph Railroad Station, his back to the old-fashioned terminal, looking across at the houses, and at one especially, on the corner . . . What was the meaning of this, why was he thinking such thoughts? For seconds Leonhard was overcome by incomprehensibilities, face to face with this incomprehensible woman in the garden here, a stranger's garden with a stranger in the background, who stood motionless, keeping his distance, wearing a gray suit and white spats. Why white spats? Leonhard was totally bewildered now, but still not in the least embarrassed.

He said: "Yes, ma'am, I guess Mila is right. Some of my associates at the plant are married, and I often have to help them out with various things . . ."

"So you should. But come to see Mila more often. Thank you very, very much again."

She looked at him unfathomably, like a lonesome fish looking out the wall of its aquarium; then she turned and walked through the arbor toward the gentleman in the white spats.

"May I serve the tea for you and Herr Levielle before I leave, ma'am?" Mila asked in a low murmur as Friederike passed her.

"Don't let me be keeping you, Miluschka," Friederike said. "Johann will take care of that—today *is* your day off." But the girl ran swiftly, light of foot, to the door leading to the winding staircase which she and Leonhard had used to enter the garden. Leonhard followed her with his eyes. She had a pretty way of running. Her slender legs flew. A sweet child. Their father would have been happy with her. Why had he just made up that story about the married men at the plant? That was the last straw, added to all the other incomprehensibilities. True enough, Karl Zilcher was married, but had he, Leonhard, ever devoted any time to Karl's affairs or Karl's family? The Zilchers, incidentally, were in something of a spot at the moment. They had had to pay some debt all of a sudden, and had spent too much money beforehand, so that the previous Saturday there had not been enough in the house for groceries.

Leonhard saw Friederike and her escort mounting the steps to the terrace. They disappeared into the vestibule.

Now he was alone in the garden.

He took up the can of paint and a brush, but then considered for a moment and went first to the tool shed. Sure enough, he found what he was looking for: a large piece of burlap, part of a one-time potato sack, perhaps. Leonhard took off his good jacket, rolled up his shirt-sleeves, and tied the burlap around his waist with his belt to protect the trousers of his Sunday suit. Then he painted the new slats and touched up the old paint here and there. Once again the stillness poured glass around everything. The crackle of his brush-strokes seemed almost too loud to him.

Toward the farther reaches of the garden there were trees, a whole little wood of them. A round coping of stone could also be seen, perhaps surrounding a pond.

Mila returned.

Now the work was done. Together they put away the tools. They went back upstairs for Leonhard's hat and coat. It was almost too warm for the coat. The stranger in the garden had not been wearing a coat; possibly he had left it in the car, or removed it in the vestibule. "Financial Counselor Levielle, our administrator," Mila said in response to Leonhard's question. She was dressed differently for going out, had discarded her apron. Leonhard had washed his hands in the kitchen. Mila gave him a pack of cigarettes. "From the mistress," she said. Leonhard rarely smoked. He thanked her and put the box into the pocket of his jacket. Mila had put on make-up; that meant

173

she must be meeting some young man. "Otherwise she might ask why I am leaving already," Leonhard thought. Brother and sister kissed each other good-by.

He left the quiet house, passed by Johann, who greeted him benevolently through the window in the vestibule. . . What a garden! If he could have his way, he would return to it once more. There was more garden outside the fence. Leonhard walked along it, but then he had to turn into another street.

He walked on alone on this overcast Sunday afternoon. There was little life in the streets. His topcoat was too warm. Leonhard took it off, although that meant carrying it on his arm. He did not take the shortest route, but only walked approximately toward the district where he lived. He was thinking again about the "married associates" at the plant. So you could say something that you had never remotely thought, something that had never occurred to you. (In days to come Leonhard also realized how affected the phrase "associates" was for men who did manual labor side by side—but his realization of this was connected with Malva Fiedler and need not be discussed here.) The urbanite is never lost within his native city and can easily find his way through unknown streets and districts. Leonhard went along with an instinctive certainty. He came to a small triangular plaza with a vacant parterre in the center and a few benches. Leonhard sat down on a bench, draping the coat around his shoulders. He felt the cigarettes in the pocket of his jacket and took them out. They were a foreign brand, the wrapping handsomely lettered in gold and adorned with a crescent moon. He would have liked a cigarette at the moment, but not being a habitual smoker, had no matches. The package was not sealed; it had been opened at the side. Perhaps it was no longer full. But no, it was. Under the tinfoil, folded over the cigarettes, lay a sizable banknote. Evidently the pack had been opened for this purpose.

So there it was—Leonhard made a remarkable discovery here in the barren little parterre: under certain circumstances you could give reality to a senseless remark that had slipped from you for no reason at all. He set out at once for Karl Zilcher's house—that meant taking a streetcar. During the ride it struck him for the first time that of late he had been managing better and better on his earnings. He had been saving. A capitalist. Ever since that strategic withdrawal to the leather sofa.

Several persons were present in Zilcher's kitchen. In addition to Karl and his wife there was a fat old woman accompanied by a small gray-haired man. (This kindly soul had evidently brought coffee, for the cups were standing around.) Frau Zilcher instantly bristled when she caught sight of the young man, for she took it for granted that he wanted to inveigle her husband off on a drinking spree—and under their present circumstances that was certainly not indicated! Nevertheless, she poured coffee for Leonhard. Two children scrambled back and forth between the kitchen and the two other rooms. Kakabsa did not want any coffee, and moreover felt out of place here, rather stranded; he could sense Frau Zilcher's attitude. A small, squat, rather knobby woman, she became visibly grimmer. Leonhard decided that he had made a serious mistake in coming here. He could just as well have given Karl the money on Monday, at the plant. The worst of it was that now he had to pry him loose from these others for a moment. But he could not. Karl protested. So he had to drink the coffee. In one respect the coffee was an advantage. Not because of its taste, but because the odor of it filled the kitchen, smothering all the other possible and in fact highly probable smells that would otherwise have

175

prevailed there. Oddly enough, Leonhard was perfectly conscious of this.

At last he was able to break away. He plucked Karl's sleeve surreptitiously, indicating by a look that he would like to step out into the hall with him; but he was aware that Frau Zilcher had also caught this interplay. Everything was going wrong. He should not have come at all. In the dimly illuminated corridor he handed Karl the banknote and a handful of cigarettes from the box. For a moment Zilcher was completely stunned. "But . . . but when do you want it back, Leonhard?"

"I don't care, in a year, or whenever you can . . . I have no need of it."

"Anna!" Zilcher called into the kitchen; but she was already there. She had come to quash the whispering in the hall. "Look, this is what Leonhard has brought us," Karl said, handing her the money.

But his wife could no longer find her way out of the anger and aggressiveness that had taken possession of her. Her face remained fixed in these emotions and drew the woman herself along behind it, so to speak; she was too clumsy to fling herself instantly into the new situation. "How come?" she snapped at Leonhard in coarse anger.

"Thank you," Karl said, shifting the cigarettes to his left hand and extending his right to Leonhard. By the time Leonhard started off, Frau Zilcher had recovered to the point of calling "Thanks" after him, but it still sounded curt and harsh and unfriendly. Karl Zilcher disregarded his wife. He stood looking down the staircase long after Kakabsa had vanished and not even his footsteps could be heard.

It had grown dark meanwhile. Leonhard reached the

corner of Hanover Gasse (the street on which the Zilchers lived), crossed Wallenstein Strasse, turned toward the Danube Canal, and went home. As he opened the door he could hear from the widow's part of the flat the murmuring voices of several old crones. There was the leather sofa now.

He had evidently made several mistakes today.

First there had been the one about his "married associates." Then had come the erroneous correction of this mistake: his visit to the Zilchers had been wholly unnecessary. He had been forced to sit there for almost three quarters of an hour. That horrid woman. The noisy children. What was the use of it all? His afternoon was wasted. Of course the smells might have been even nastier, without the coffee.

He lay on the leather sofa, head tilted back. From far off, Komorn or the big island of silt, the Danube reached to him, into him. He had sailed upriver this far and had been stranded at the Zilchers'. How still it was here. On the scows, too, the smell of coffee or tobacco had cut through evil odors like a razor blade. Now the day presented its real and fully ripened fruit to him as upon a tray: Leonhard felt with absolute clarity, and probably for the first time in his life in just this way, that he was alone, completely and absolutely alone. Even though last Sunday he had visited his mother and stepfather, and this afternoon had seen Mila—not to mention Zilcher. He was alone; there was no help for it, no kicking against the pricks. Far better to lie perfectly still upon the leather sofa.

Lie and let in the smells.

Slowly, with grinding machinery, the past came up the river, the tug in the van, the long streamer of smoke trailing over the scows, dissipating above the silvery-gray spume of woods along the banks.

Not long after this Sunday afternoon there was a change

177

in Leonhard's working hours. The current business boom had produced a backlog of orders, so that the plant instituted a night shift. The foremen asked the men already working at the plant whether they wanted to change to this shift, to have the days free for a while. The married men did not care much for the idea, but Leonhard was willing; the time seemed ripe to him for some kind of change. And change certainly came; that is putting it mildly. A workman found a bookshop open as he passed it.

Those who sleep by day sleep fewer hours, though this sleep is sometimes deeper than that by night. Leonhard now left the plant every morning at half-past five. The warehouse attendant's widow ("I'll do your prayin' for you") fixed his meal along with her own, since he now no longer took his midday dinner in the canteen at the plant. By one o'clock Leonhard was already wide awake and ready to eat, alone in his room, of course.

So it happened that he passed the open bookshop once (Malva Fiedler stood near the door, in plain sight), a second time (there was no sign of her), and a third time (she was half concealed by the counter). A wheel was beginning to revolve more and more swiftly.

The third time, Leonhard stopped in front of the show window.

He stared into it for a long time. New as well as secondhand books were on display.

He read a good many of the titles, though rather absently. But tin's kind of distraction is precisely the state of mind in which life's projectiles thrust deepest and stick most effectively. Still and all, it is remarkable that Leonhard, much later, was able to recall having seen in the display a novel by Kajetan Schlaggenberg.

There was also a Latin grammar, marked at a very low

price. It was Scheindler's, which is the best grammar to be had, though Leonhard did not know this. Probably some liberated student had cast it behind him along with all the rest of his academic paraphernalia.

Now something took place which belonged in the same category as the phrase about "married associates" which Leonhard had played off against Frau Ruthmayr like a card of which he had been unaware but which nevertheless had actually been in his hand.

He entered the bookshop.

Entering a store is like stepping into a vehicle. Whatever has been pending starts moving. So it was here.

Leonhard asked for the Latin grammar. He did not address Malva, who stood off to the right, but a small bespectacled gentleman behind the counter (who was Malva's father). Malva went to take the book from the window. She stooped to reach it; Leonhard saw this, although he did not look; rather, he imagined it more than observed it. Now she came forward with the volume. "Let me see," the bookseller said. "Yes, this edition is still being used in the schools. What class is the pupil in?"

"The book is for myself," Leonhard explained, taking out his wallet. Now he looked up, full into Malva's face. It seemed to him that he could see it better today, when it was unobscured by any cloud of cigarette smoke. Now, standing at her ease, she was much prettier than she had been then, scrambling to catch the sliding books. Her green eyes were oblique, her mouth large, her breasts like the hint of an explosion.

At the same time Leonhard was conscious continually of the clean and sterile odor of the many books in the room.

The situation tautened like a drumhead, like something caught between tangible contradictions.

"Why, we know each other," Malva said. "Father, this is the

179

gentleman who saved the books from falling the other day—remember, I told you about it."

"Why, then, I must add my thanks to my daughter's," Fiedler said, laughing. "That comes of the girl's always having to smoke at the most inappropriate times, in the shop and everywhere. Naturally the smoke makes her eyes water." But although he made his criticism in a tone of mild complaint, he placed his hand tenderly on his daughter's arm. It was perfectly plain that his happiness was wrapped up in this girl, that perhaps she was the whole content of his life. Leonhard had the distinct feeling that this was so. He and Malva shook hands, and Leonhard bowed slightly.

"You are studying Latin?" the bookseller asked.

"I have not been. But I would like to."

"For professional advancement?"

The question opened a chasm of perplexity before Leonhard. He did not even attempt to answer it.

Luckily, Herr Fiedler immediately went on: "Unfortunately, I sold the Latin exercise book that goes with it just yesterday. Secondhand, too, and at the same low price. You ought to have that as well. At the moment I have no other copy, not even a new one. Perhaps you'll drop by again in a few days?"

"Certainly," Leonhard said. For the second time he looked squarely at Malva. He had felt her eyes resting on him all the while. Now, for seconds, a bridge of looks stretched between them, as strong as iron. It could hardly be broken—but at last it snapped.

Leonhard shook hands with Herr Fiedler and again with Malva, and made off with his Latin grammar.

Leonhard could not grasp the actual situation, for he was

not an experienced ladies' man eternally well supplied with self-assurance. But to give truth its due: he had literally fascinated Malva. Women are not dilettantes in matters of love, and so Malva bluntly asked herself: "Why?" She told herself: "He's a perfectly ordinary boy." She was trying to classify him with a borrowed phrase. But in truth he was precisely Malva Fiedler's ideal of a man.

When she left the shop that evening, the sight of the sidewalk and the show window brought back her first encounter with Leonhard, that encounter in the most literal sense, body touching body, with the books between. At the time she had felt Leonhard. Or had she only imagined feeling him? She actually pursued this question in bed that night, as she lay with closed eyes waiting for sleep.

The bookseller's living quarters were not in the same building as the bookshop. His apartment was across the Danube Canal, though close enough to it for the windows to look out on the canal itself.

Malva's mother had died young. Malva (who was always being told that she resembled her mother more and more) preserved a kind of phantom recollection of her, a memory out of a biography that unreeled backwards, and which scarcely belonged to her any longer. Amid all that she had been told about her mother there existed a few scattered bright pinpoints of real memories. But of all this she never really thought consciously.

She was everything to her father, as she well knew. She herself felt affection, but no more, for the aging little man. She looked after him; she respected his hobbies, which included classical languages and an unaccountable fondness for the arms and armor of Greco-Roman antiquity, although little Herr Fiedler would scarcely have been able to wield a sword or draw a bow or throw a lance. In accord with his plans for his daughter, Malva had attended Gymnasium and had served a regular apprenticeship in another bookseller's shop before entering her father's business. She was twenty-seven years old. She was a virgin.

We mention the last circumstance in order to throw some light on Malva Fiedler's character. It was basically cold, though often shaken by storms which died as swiftly as they had arisen. As long as these storms lasted, they stirred up enough dust to block the sunlight, creating total night. The events of her inner life resembled the probable climatic phenomena of the moon. The green of her eyes reflected that uncertain boundary between ice and water. Thus some of the lining of Malva Fiedler's character peeped through the bodily lid.

The night after Leonhard's visit to the bookshop she was alone at home, her father having had some business to attend to after supper. For a moment or two Malva's room must have shrunk back in alarm from her. A whole band of cats glared out of her eyes. Her back arched, her breasts strained through the fabric of her dress, as though to tear free.

Leonhard, this would-be Latin student, had entered a powder magazine with a deferential candle in his hand.

A wind rose up outside. Malva saw lights across the Danube Canal.

Abruptly she changed her position. The tension eased, drew off from her like a banner that has pressed its living folds flat against its post but now is once more caught by the wind, bellies out, rises, and flies calmly. She went into the living room, sat down at the big bare table, and finished drawing up a list of copies to be returned to publishers.

The exercise book took its time turning up. In all

probability, old Fiedler wanted to obtain another secondhand copy for his customer, to save him the price of a new one. In this way Leonhard paid two or three visits to the bookshop, each of which involved something of a chat. Once more cigarette smoke wafted across Malva's face—as it had at their first encounter. "You can start on the grammar meanwhile," said Fiedler, the lover of classical languages. "How did you happen to hit upon Latin anyway?" he asked with interest. Leonhard could scarcely have replied: "On account of my married associates"—although this would by rights have been his answer, for he had already arrived at a fairly clear recognition of the connection. First you invented "married associates," or else, standing in front of a window, you invented a desire for an inexpensive book; then it was a question of doing justice to the impulse, of following it, of accepting the consequences. Around this time Leonhard was struck by the outlandish thought that he himself had not come into the world intentionally, that it had happened quite by chance, in the same way that the "married associates" or the desire for the Latin grammar had leaped into being. But this fact altered nothing; you had to lie in the bed even though you had not made it. In any case his task now was to learn grammar. He had to, despite the fact that he could not have answered old Fiedler's question; or perhaps he had to the more just because he could not.

"Latin grammar," Fiedler had gone on to say, "is not only the foundation of the grammar of all other European languages, but the foundation of everything that goes by the name of culture. In learning Latin grammar, we take in mouthfuls of logic, prosody, and rhetoric just by the by." Leonhard did not know what prosody was. So he asked. (That question was the first of innumerable questions. It was like the beginning of a new childhood. Intellectual development may well, at the start, be marked by an increase of ignorance.)

Fiedler was quite willing to explain. "The word comes from the Greek and means literally the art of singing aloud, of recitation," he said. "The person who knows something must also know how to say it. Never believe people who claim they cannot find the right word because their thought is so profound." In short, the bookseller was a Roman, though puny of physique. Leonhard did not grasp the range of consequence implicit in Fiedler's last statement.

Just as, at the Zilchers', he had stubbornly carried out his intention in spite of all obstacles, he now attacked the grammar as if it were a new type of loom which he had to learn to operate. And within some eight weeks he could rattle off the declensions and conjugations with respectable fluency. This was the result of hard work every afternoon. As the weather grew warmer, he took his book out to the embankment along the Danube Canal. It became a kind of mania. For two weeks he did not go near the bookshop. But after this interval they had a secondhand exercise book for him. He bought it but put it aside for the time being (the consequences of this were to develop later) and continued working away at the new machine. It began to function more and more smoothly although, as is plain, the whole operation was not entirely systematic.

It may be that old Fiedler took a liking to Leonhard. Perhaps he also observed his daughter with a keener eye than he might be credited with (for love sharpens insight). At any rate, the young man was invited for coffee on a Saturday afternoon, for educational purposes. Fiedler promised to show Leonhard various things bearing on actual life in Greco-Roman antiquity.

Leonhard arrived punctually and with a dual passion at the small apartment on the Danube Canal. We shall not attempt to decide which passion was the stronger at the moment; each

184

complemented the other, and exerted a reciprocal influence.

But as he walked along the canal, on his way to Fiedler's, Leonhard had a definite feeling that all this meant something. That what was happening to him was nothing casual, nothing incidental. The ammunition was live, so to speak. He was stepping into something, entering some place; this was an involvement. And yet it was his nature to shrink from involvements. But when the moment comes, even such a disposition will consent to give the thing a try, will subdue and silence its deeper warnings. After all, what was there to worry about? He was on his way to look at books, and was really looking forward to the evening. Of course he did like the girl very much, granted . . .

The spirit is weak, but it is also free, if you will. The body, however, is more fettered to truth. Leonhard's steps slowed. He paused on the shore road and looked out over the river.

The neighborhood maintained a haughty silence, as is the way of neighborhoods. It gave no reply to the questions which were tossed at it like a ball against the wall.

The ball rebounded. Leonhard walked on, reached the house, climbed the stairs.

The place was small, with a box-like comfortable air, the living room full of books. Here the rites of a Viennese *Jause* were performed—coffee, *Guglhupf*, and all the fixings. Leonhard needed patience—that is to say, he was thoroughly impatient. At last they moved to Fiedler's study. Here was a room that had power over Leonhard, that closed compellingly around him, that enclosed him and swallowed him. Seated at the broad desk you could look out over the river. The chair in front of the desk was odd, simple in construction: a leather seat stretched over the frame and visibly fastened to it with zigzag straps. The back and armrests were short and smoothly polished. There were old folio volumes in the room also, their scuffed calfskin shining softly like certain velvety golden forest mosses.

A classicistic engraving on the wall (probably late eighteenth century) showed a young couple in the costume of antiquity, the woman with thrusting, almost bared breasts, the man with idealized strong arms. The man stood with his right hand on the woman's two hands, with a gesture of taking possession, and his eyes were fixed upon her face. At the bottom of the picture sat a tortoise, and alongside it the sentence: *Sortes cadunt.*

"The tortoise is the symbol of fertility," the bookseller said, smiling. (That he should smile as he said this sent a flash of terror through Leonhard.)

"And *sortes cadunt*?"

"'The lots fall.' The man who begets takes part in a lottery. He may bring a genius into the world, a good average man, a criminal, or a cretin."

Leonhard felt as if he were standing on cotton or on clouds. He became aware of vast empty spaces.

Moreover, Malva had come into the room.

They disposed themselves about the bookseller's desk. Fiedler sketched, after his own fashion, an outline of the ancient world, a skeletal framework or stand which would do for Leonhard to hang his still scanty wardrobe of knowledge on without his falling victim to the mistaken view that so-called world-history consists of a succession of revue-like costume changes. Moreover, Fiedler made the point that what was called "world-history" was, of course, only the history of Europe. But a person had to do his looking from the window at which he stood. If not, you fell into the vagueness of abstractions. Looking through Chinese eyes was quite a different matter. And first of all you had to learn to use your own eyesight. Every intellectual act must have a substantial, material locus.

Fiedler proceeded to tell Leonhard that the Battle of Marathon had been the dividing line between ancient eastern forms of social organization and what we call our own; soon afterwards Europe arose on that small peninsula which lay to the southeast of the large peninsula; arose in concentrated form, to be sure, but even then quite complete.

Leonhard wondered how, in view of the disproportion in power which Fiedler had described, it had been possible for the Greeks to win the Battle of Marathon.

"It was due to the superior physical training of the Hellenes. They were able to cover a relatively long distance at the double, in full bronze armor, without losing their breath or battle order. The physically softer Asiatics did not believe it possible. But then the enemy was in their midst and slashing away. And surely Athena Parthenos—the sponsoring goddess of orderly combat—appeared in all her divine might behind the Greek ranks, shouting, urging them on. For what we call Europe was at stake. Of course only the goddess knew that at the time; the soldiers did not know. Incidentally, the Greek losses at the Battle of Marathon were low. There is a special term in Greek for the method of attack they chose at that battle. . . I can't think of the term at the moment. . . "

"*Dromo,* or as the case may be, *dromon tein,*" Malva said.

Leonhard was so surprised that he was almost unhinged. Moreover, the bookseller seemed to believe that these ancient gods had actually existed, or at least that they had acted. But if they had acted, they had been actual. Leonhard was not aware that he was riding to the gates of thought upon words—that through those gates there was no other way to pass.

But he did realize one thing while the bookseller continued to discourse on all these matters in a casual, chatty tone. Here sat Malva, who even knew Greek; she thrust out her breasts, studied him with her cat-eyes; she even let some of the lining peep out through her eyes. Leonhard suddenly felt, with a deep certainty, that here was a planet prone to swift and icy storms.

His skin prickled.

Nevertheless, he felt more self-assured now. No matter if he were dealing with live ammunition.

During the following weeks Leonhard dropped in at the bookshop only two or three times. Herr Fiedler had put a book aside for him: a handbook of Greek and Roman antiquities, used to supplement instruction in the Gymnasium. He let Leonhard have it for a few groschen—for nothing, really.

Malva was present on these occasions, of course. She now seemed to Leonhard to have taken on a great physical substantiality. She stood solidly before him; she no longer beat about him like a violent wind coming from all sides, as had been the case at first.

Shortly afterwards Leonhard ran into the bookseller while he was taking a stroll along the Danube Canal. Fiedler was doing the same, but alone. Where was Malva? What was she up to? Her absence upset Leonhard. He had grown accustomed to seeing her with her father all the time; it seemed to him new and unreasonable that she should be free to go about anywhere by herself.

Everything was green. While Leonhard had been living an inward-turned existence (already more walled in than he imagined), the season had rapidly reached its height and fullness, and here and there white horse-chestnut blossoms were already beginning to fall, those festive signs of spring's climax and terminus snowing down and vanishing. Softly, summer's heat was forcing its way in, summer's earnestness, summer's harassment and solitude.

As Leonhard and the bookseller walked on the embankment, they fell into one of those conversations in which Leonhard could find no answers. He was already familiar with this state.

"I dare say you intend to change your occupation sooner or later, Herr Kakabsa?"

— — —

"I make that assumption because you are more or less preparing yourself for more schooling."

— — —

"Of course education is always a benefit in itself."

— — —

"You might then find opportunities in the Municipal Cultural Office, say. Are you a member of the Social Democratic party?"

"I am."

"Well, then. Or take my own profession. Of course a formal apprenticeship is necessary, but that is something you could probably manage."

Leonhard had already suspected that sooner or later live ammunition would be used. (This was a thoroughly subjective interpretation, a touch of paranoia with regard to entanglement and being tied down. A tic.)

"I am completely satisfied with my occupation; it is good work and essential."

"Essential, yes," the bookseller dutifully replied.

"I mean for me. It is essential for me. I'm happy in what I am doing. I like making webbing. It remains to be proved that

. . . (Gymnastic exercises in the art of rhetoric; no, he had not quite the muscle for it.) It must be proved that a worker is not an unfortunate, hopeless person who can only wait until conditions in the world improve, until which time there's nothing for him but his family, the movies, and the saloon . . . It remains to be proved that right now, right this minute, at this time, everything is open to a worker, without class struggle and all the rest of it. It remains to be proved that he needs his work not only to maintain himself, not only to earn his livelihood, but actually as a counterweight to the rest, to make sure that the rest is genuine, not fake. That remains to be proved." (In the end he had pretty well managed that bit of gymnastics.)

Again and again that urgent phrase "It remains to be proved" had fallen from his lips . . . Now he felt utterly exhausted. Here and there intonations of lower-class dialect had sounded in his speech. But he had made a speech for the first time in his life—though without being conscious that this marked a milestone in his biography.

"You have already proved it," the bookseller said. He had been listening with great attentiveness, peering rather sharply through his glasses. Perhaps he was a tenacious and patient man. Perhaps also he had more than a modicum of kindliness. At any rate, he liked Leonhard Kakabsa very much.

Toward the middle of the summer of 1926 Leonhard's working hours were changed again. The night shifts ceased. Once more he passed by a closed bookshop mornings and evenings. After a week he noticed a neat sign on the shutters. It read: "Closed for vacation until September 1." Meanwhile August had come along.

At this time Leonhard, too, took his vacation. The factory

190

maintained a vacation place for its employees. It was situated in the mountains two hours from Vienna.

At first the surroundings acted upon Leonhard as a stimulus to curiosity. He looked around. He did not look around at people, or at his unmarried female "associates." These stretched out in steamer chairs on a terrace and displayed their legs. The rest home was situated in a large neglected park. The fountain was still, the pond dried out. It had once been a big private estate.

Leonhard looked around in this park. The farther end of it, the part more remote from the village street, rose sharply toward the wooded mountains. There was a gate that led out into the woods. The day Leonhard went through the gate he did not have his Latin book with him; usually he sat with it in the park, pursuing his studies.

He stepped out through the gate and entered the woods. It was not so much an exit into the stillness of the woods—for the park, too, was quiet—but rather an entry into an essentially different order of entanglement. He soon came to a path that cut at a level across the steep slope. Uphill, to his left, despite the day's strong sunshine, the woods became lost in darkness. But a bird's song sounded, repeating the same motif again and again at equal intervals. To his right and ahead along the path was an area of brightness where the woods ended, thinning into shrubs and tall scattered trees. In the distance hung a haze over some rocky cliff, and among the dark angularities of evergreens were the rounded tops of deciduous trees. The fragrance of all the green things was immense, spice upon spice. The bird behind him fell silent. Now it was perfectly still.

CHAPTER 6

A Winter with Quapp

IN THE late forenoon after that night which had so bizarre an ending in the garden of the Palais Ruthmayr, Schlaggenberg awakened in tolerably good spirits. He felt inwardly ventilated and refreshed. Since he had drunk mostly brandy, which scarcely ever upset his stomach, he had no severe hangover. On the bedside table lay a telegram. So the maid must have been in the room already. Probably she had tried in vain to wake him. Schlaggenberg tore it open and read it.

With one leap he sprang from the bed to the middle of the room and stood there, staring wide-eyed out into the snow-covered street. The telegram read: "Arriving Monday four o'clock. Quapp."

During the very first moments that his sister entered his imagination—and at the same time this sunlit room, though only in prospect—two very different and in fact opposite images of her face and personality floated through Kajetan's mind, gradually approaching each other like the two wings of a slowly closing French door. Finally one image moved in front of the other, but the first still showed through, as when a pair of photographic negatives are held one over the other.

Not until the images fused did he really see Charlotte von Schlaggenberg, known as "Quapp."

Kajetan had long been familiar with this juxtaposition of images; the same disturbing phenomenon occurred each time he saw Charlotte again after a longish separation, or even when he received news from her.

She was a good deal younger than he. Brother and sister had become acquainted with each other only a few years before, since in 1918, when Schlaggenberg returned from the war, he had found his sister still half a child—for she was that, in spite of her seventeen years—and had paid little attention to her. Nevertheless, that relatively short stay of a few months in southern Styria, on his parents' estate, had given rise to the double image which Quapp had since presented to him whenever he laid eyes on her or whenever his thoughts turned to his sister. Yet he could never seize upon its precise point of origin, much as he tried and important as it seemed to him to do so. There was undoubtedly a connection between these two aspects of Quapp's face and an old English governess who had remained in the household after the children grew up, and who still lived on the estate with Schlaggenberg's widowed mother, as companion and housekeeper. Shortly after the war there had been some conflict between Quapp and Miss Rugley, who was then approaching fifty. (Where had it taken place? Perhaps in the big garden room with the huge green punch bowl on the buffet and the innumerable glasses which belonged to Miss Rugley and had her shape, as though they were her offspring.) At that time, at any rate, Quapp had adopted a certain expression, a way of rebuffing and dismissing old Rugley, as if she were pouring cold water over the Englishwoman. A sudden, wholly senseless arrogance seemed to lift Quapp's face out of its known and familiar foundations . . .

The effect was repeated after he read the telegram . . .

Thereafter Kajetan remained away from home for years. And then one day a young person, female to judge by her apparel, had turned up in his room here in Vienna and addressed him as "Brother." Soon he was using the same word to address her, for that is how he felt toward her. Later the nickname Quapp became the rule. It had originally been an abbreviation of *Kaulquappe* (tadpole), partly because to Schlaggenberg's eyes there was something of a tadpole's look about Charlotte's wide face (others protested against such a nickname for so pretty a girl), and partly because the name suggested an incomplete and developing creature.

That she certainly was; indeed, she was incomplete and developing quite consciously and intensely. Her meeting with her brother gave great impetus to this process, and she ran about the big city which had become the world to her in a state of exalted wonderment. Overnight, reality seemed to have acquired tremendous depth and significance for her. During the years before Kajetan's short-lived marriage, he and she had sometimes shared an apartment, and for one brief spell a shortage of funds actually compelled the strange pair of "brothers" to lodge in a single room. For their parental estate in Styria had suffered a severe economic setback, especially after the decline and collapse of the Austrian Lumber Industry Bank during the years 1924 and 1925. Herr Eustach von Schlaggenberg had become involved with this bank through Levielle. These same reverses had resulted in a large part of his forests' sliding down the lumber chutes. Yet Kajetan remained dependent on his parents' support for many years after receiving his doctorate at the University. For he had chosen to make literature his profession. And now when Quapp too insisted on going to the city and entering the University, their parents had been compelled to make severe sacrifices. In their love for her, they had done their best. Nevertheless, it was often not possible for them to send financial assistance to her with any degree of regularity. Quapp, on the other hand, could scarcely bring herself to ask for money in her letters, no matter how dire the emergency. She

loved and respected her parents, and was aware of their difficulties. Moreover, she hated to reveal how pinched things were,
for fear of making all too incontrovertibly clear that she could
not really continue to live here in the city without a means of
livelihood. For that would have meant burying herself on the
isolated estate once again. Charlotte could not even conceive of
this solution, for all that circumstances urged and often literally
compelled it.

The result was that she had to remain in a kind of permanent trance, for only in such a state was it possible for her to
bridge the gaping abysses of reality, and on her good days even
overlook them, simply ignore them. In periods of weakness,
however, an advocate of practicality sprang to life inside her
mind, and introduced still greater strain into her life.

That, however, happened fairly seldom. Usually she had
her goals in mind—they were still primarily interior goals. This
was so even during periods dominated by her monumental
laziness and its mirror-image, a guilty and indeed a tormented
conscience. This business of interior goals, however, is a frail
and delicate matter, a fire that warms only when it is burning
very brightly, and must keep roaring away in order to spread
a strengthening glow over the wasteland of a desolate outward
pattern of living. The business of living by these goals was far
more difficult than the practical and manual tasks of her musical studies, the success of which ultimately depended, after all,
upon her state of mind and the development of her personality.
In short, she suffered periodically from extreme depressions.
Logical enough in the circumstances. Moreover, human beings
consist of more than a stomach and consciousness of a task.
There is also the matter of so-called emotional life, which at
times can even degenerate into love. In young women, especially, it likes to manifest that particular form. Fräulein von

Schlaggenberg naturally had to undergo that form of experience in the city, and even to repeat it more than once. She had had such feelings with great intensity, had repudiated them with equal vehemence, had railed contemptuously against them. For from the start it had seemed to her that she had no right to indulge such emotions, that the perplexities they brought her robbed her of time which should be devoted to a better cause, that indeed they stole from the slender resources of her parents. Curiously enough, moreover, precisely on such occasions the true state of her poverty became more painfully evident than ever, and this contributed in turn to an intensification of her scruples. In short, there were many sources for unhappiness and occasional melancholia.

Shortly after the death of her father, old Eustach von Schlaggenberg, she had gone back to the parental estate just as hot weather settled upon the city. She was to spend the summer months there, as she did every year. This time, however, she arrived with the resolve to crush a principal source of torment and indolence. One farewell had been taken; now she felt it necessary to take a second, inward farewell to match the first. This came harder, especially in the rural solitude of the estate and in the company of her grief-stricken mother, in whom she felt unable to confide. For the first time, however, she found herself shrinking from the autumnal return to the site of her struggles and defeats, and she decided not to go back until the wound in her heart had properly healed. Moreover, she hoped that country living would restore her strained nerves and body. This young woman's body—she was now twenty-five, and her maidenhood had been left by the wayside some while before— this body now began assailing her resolution on its own account. And as a plowed field exhales its vapors, overpowering yearnings rose from body to brain, which despairingly endeavored to retain its clarity and superiority. It was a horrible summer for her. And when the oats had been cut down and only stubble remained, she had come no further along her way than she had been at the time when the cornflowers bloomed. The snow came. Kajetan, in Vienna, knew precisely what her continued absence signified.

But he did not dare to ascribe an equally unequivocal meaning to her imminent arrival. Had she "come through"? The correspondence between Quapp and himself had dried up shortly after her departure—the fault was his. For then he had run into the miseries of that particular summer, and she for her part had been caught in similar straits. But Quapp had sent an S O S note once in the autumn and once during the early part of the winter, without ever receiving a reply from Kajetan, although she pleaded for an answer. Quapp, who loved her brother fanatically and cherished an exaggerated respect for him, in the end took his silence as a kind of pedagogic measure. Obviously he must want her to go her hard way alone all the way to the end, without aid or encouragement. Arriving at this explanation of her brother's conduct, she concluded without reservation that he must be right.

Kajetan, however, had had a guilty conscience. And now, as he stood still with the telegram in his hand and looked out into the snowy street, his conscience pricked him as soon as his initial joy subsided. This guilt alone would suggest that the theory of pedagogic measures did not hold water. Moreover, we know what Kajetan's state of mind had been up to only a few months before. It seems likely that he did not wish to expose himself to his sister in his utter weakness, even if only by letter. In other words, his silence was a form of vanity. But a kernel of vanity can be found, if we want to look for it, in almost all human actions and omissions. It may be that he was also motivated by a certain sense of responsibility toward his sister. For even when she lived in the city he always carefully avoided contact with her when he had reason to be dissatisfied with himself. On such occasions he practiced evasion with a singular cunning, and on the spur of the moment invented the most ingenious excuses for not seeing her. He had few difficulties, since Quapp respected everything and anything that came from Kajetan. He, for his part, knew by experience (to which his fleetingly brief marriage and its long prehistory had contributed a good deal) what dire effects his own bad traits had on others if he did not keep himself in hand . . .

Next day he went to the station. Twilight was already falling; the traffic surged noisily through the gray streets, and the first lights gathered the oncoming darkness around themselves. The railroad platform was almost deserted. A cool sooty atmosphere prevailed under the vaulted roof where distance itself, pouring in along the tracks, seemed to pile up in dense layers. Down there along the tracks, signals changed, red and green. From down there along the tracks, Quapp was coming.

As always happens in such cases, the train glided belatedly into the station just as Schlaggenberg, relaxing from the prolonged tension of waiting, had grown inattentive for a few minutes. The passengers poured out onto the platform, and there suddenly was her face, with reality's magic power utterly expunging the images that had hovered before his mind's eye. He had already overcome, by anticipation, the uneasiness described above.

They embraced. He felt her narrow shoulders. Her face seemed to him small as a clenched fist, it was so worn. Her eyes, far apart and almond-shaped, seemed excessively large, giving her head a curiously insect-like quality. But they were shining now with relief and joy.

Only a person with unusual powers of observation would have taken them for brother and sister. For their resemblance was scarcely physical, nor a matter of detail; to examine their separate features would be to discover only divergent traits. Significantly, the two bore not the slightest resemblance to each other in photographs. But when they talked, something like a "relationship" appeared, though this was partly in their manner of expression. Of course people also said that Quapp imitated her brother.

Now Quapp replied to a half-spoken question with a reassuring nod. "Yes," she said. Then she qualified cautiously: "At least I think so. It's probably over. . . And what about you?" she asked suddenly, opening her eyes wide as though the really important matter had just come to her mind.

"Likewise," he answered, and looked out through the tall bare windows of the station at the lights of the city extending into the distance, the bright and strident lights from advertising signs, and smaller, dimmer, ordinary lights. At that moment he sensed out there, lying at the outermost edge of his range of vision, as it were, one isolated pang like a red lamp glimmering in the distance. Perhaps his lips twisted slightly. Quapp laid a hand on his arm. Meanwhile a hollow inside him closed, though with painful demur. He started in fright. Yes, it was unmistakably fear he felt. Quickly, he changed the subject, spoke of the night before last with Eulenfeld (whom Quapp knew well) and the others. "Total strangers. I doubt that I've ever seen a quarter of those people before. It was indescribable. I could not believe my eyes when I saw them really clambering over the wall and onto the terrace. There was a light upstairs (he was describing the prank in the garden of the Palais Ruthmayr). Incidentally, you must meet that Hungarian . . . " Schlaggenberg trailed off; he seemed to be pursuing some thought.

Quapp had been laughing immoderately, her wide mouth agape from one ear to the other. "Marvelous, marvelous!" she guffawed. But now she stopped abruptly and looked at Schlaggenberg. "What are you thinking about, brother?" she asked.

"Oh, nothing," he said, and began laughing again. "You know, it was marvelous the way he handled it. They said that the lady at the window actually took a swig straight from the brandy bottle. . . Oh well, that may be, that may be. At any rate—this is the funniest thing of all—the boys claim they can't remember where we were. Maybe they're only joking. But as far as I'm concerned, I really haven't any idea. I remember that when we got into the car someone told the chauffeur to drive anywhere, it didn't matter where so long as he drove fast. We were bundled into that huge dark sedan—the captain was there too; oddly enough his own roadster had vanished some-where during the night, but at the time neither he nor anyone else thought that strange. Someone there had simply driven brazenly off with the car and didn't bring it back to him until Sunday afternoon . . ."

Quapp shrieked with amusement and gasped for breath.

"I've moved." Schlaggenberg made a breach in his story, with a certain emphasis. "I'm now living . . ."

Her face suddenly became small and wrinkled as a new-born baby's, frozen in the pattern of laughter. "What!" she exclaimed. "Oh no! I went to so much trouble to get my old room back. I wrote three letters to the landlady, and made a deposit. I have to live near you!"

"I had to move," he said. "Times have changed . . ."

"Of course I understand, brother," Quapp put in at once. "Forgive me my mutiny. Of course you had to move. I'm glad to know you're out there. Besides, I could move out there too, couldn't I?"

"Of course, splendid!" Schlaggenberg said. "That will be great. There are no end of furnished rooms available out in Döbling. I'll start looking tomorrow, and you can give notice now that you'll be leaving your place the first of February."

Quapp looked pensive, and tiny furrows formed on her small brow. "I don't know, though," she said at last, "whether I really—have a right to move out there. It would just be imitating you, of course—but only outwardly. Have I really come as far as you have yet . . . ?"

He waved that aside, while that momentary twist of harassment appeared on his face again. "I haven't come anywhere," he said. "But I must . . . Anyway, a change of environment would only do you good."

"Really? Do you think so?" she exclaimed in childish pleasure at his countermanding her scruples and giving her a pretext for doing what she wanted to do. And then after a pause: "You're right. What is the sense of shutting myself up again inside those same four walls where I went through such horrors . . . ?"

"Yes," he said. Then they fell silent, standing in front of the station, waiting for the next free cab.

Quapp's room was pleasant. It contained a white-enameled metal bed that looked like a child's crib, next to which stood a music stand. Schlaggenberg had often been there. He stood in the middle of the room, still in his overcoat, turning slowly around to savor all the memories. Meanwhile Quapp unpacked a little, carried brushes and soap to the bathroom, and examined with great care her violin, whose case was protected by an outer cloth case. Many a pang was connected with this violin— an old Italian instrument. It represented the greatest financial sacrifice her parents had ever made for their daughter.

The Dutch stove crackled. As so often in the past, in joy

and in sorrow, as they had done more than a year before and were now doing again, this strange pair finally sat down to tea. In their tumultuous lives these two young people had passed through virtually all the states possible to average young people; but no matter what befell them, one thing was sure, that they would end by having tea together.

"Do you hear anything at all of Camy?" Quapp asked without preamble.

"No," he said.

"Where do you stand on the divorce?" she pushed on. "I know no more than the remarks Mother occasionally drops."

"Quapp," Kajetan said forcefully, "I must ask you to forgive me! I haven't written to you at all. Will you forgive me if you can?"

"Why, brother," she cried, "I knew perfectly well that you must have had good reasons . . ."

"No," he interposed, "I had no reasons at all, or at any rate not good ones. I was wretched, desperate, half insane, a selfish monster wrapped up in my own problems. That's all. But I haven't had a word from Camy. Neither she nor I have taken any legal steps. I haven't stirred, and there isn't a sign of any stirring on her part. That's all."

They fell silent.

"But wouldn't it be better to take care of the formalities?" she said after a while. "Then you would really have your freedom back entirely . . ."

"I don't know, Quapp," he said slowly. "The essential thing is that I feel quite good as things stand now, and I've been doing a halfway decent amount of work."

"Ah," Quapp moaned. "So I come here and find you in top form—after all you've been through. While I . . ."

"If you had come in the autumn, the picture would have

203

been altogether different," he said. "Anyway, our recoveries always take place in silence and obscurity, and it's only long afterwards that we pull ourselves together and go about in something like 'top form'; the essential features of our recoveries, I mean."

"But how do we tell? I mean, what these essential features are."

For a while Schlaggenberg did not reply. He sat quite still. His sister looked at him mystified, and wondered whether he had not fallen asleep, for his eyes were closed. But suddenly he answered: "We must look to the red lights."

It was almost as if he were talking in his sleep.

"What? What's that?" Quapp exclaimed.

"Yes," he said, "it's like the railroad signals."

Her mouth stayed slightly open. Kajetan stood up, laughing.

"Some other time, Quapp," he said, taking her by the shoulders. "Listen, now: it is of the utmost importance that you start regular, disciplined work tomorrow morning. Tomorrow morning, understand! Have your supper soon and get a good night's sleep. I'm doing the same." He shook her hand, and left.

Quapp obeyed him like a soldier. Next morning she woke of her own accord, unusually early, and taking this circumstance as a good sign, sprang out of bed.

An hour later, when she stepped up to the music stand, violin tucked under her chin, she did not feel quite the same degree of misery that had afflicted her all the previous summer. But she did feel instantly such coldness and indifference that merely raising the bow seemed in itself beyond her strength. From the street she heard a bicyclist's bell. In the vestibule the landlady was gossiping with some woman. Quapp was on the verge of dropping into a chair and drifting off into reverie. But in that case it would probably be better to go out, into the street, into the fresh air, insofar as there was any fresh air in the city and a walk in such a district, with its endless, completely built-up gray streets, offered any allure. In these few minutes a small volcano of despair erupted inside Quapp, during which interior catastrophe she began playing finger exercises, dully and without concentration. It was miserable. She could not remotely imagine why she was staying here and playing finger exercises. Such was her terror that for a moment she actually thought of telephoning her brother and appealing for help as though something had happened to her. But she recognized immediately that this project was only a means of getting away from the violin, if only long enough to go into the vestibule where the telephone was. And so she went on playing, if such a term can be applied to what she was doing.

Gradually she grew calmer, as if she were recovering from a fright. Her blood returned. While she played, she heard through the walls a slowly rising and falling hum, perhaps the sound of an electric motor being used in some workshop on the ground floor of the building. Quapp suddenly had a vague image of such workshops, and the next moment she was frightfully glad she had not collapsed into a chair and begun brooding over the senselessness of her presence here in this city—senseless because she could not manage to work. As she looked back upon the recent crisis which she had endured and vanquished, its meaning was not merely that she would have given up before she had really tried; nor was it merely that she would have sat, for a spell, upon that alluring chair. As she looked back, it seemed to her that had she given way just now, she would have committed a terrible and irreparable mistake (and must we not concur that in so evaluating the matter she had truly hit upon the crux of it?).

Quapp, then, listened to the humming of the electric motor and rejoiced (though with a somewhat tempered pleasure) that at least she had her place in this world of work. She had managed to get up early enough so that now, at nine o'clock in the morning, she could assume responsibility for some kind of mechanical and regular activity—although she was convinced that whatever those men were doing with their electric motor downstairs was far more purposeful and meaningful than the kind of violin practicing she was doing here.

After a while she left off the finger exercises in order to attack a more important assignment, that is, to exercise her right hand and improve her bowing technique. For a moment she gazed out the window at the façade of the building opposite (this morning the façade looked plain and shabby; not, as last night in the glaring arc light, like a white termitarium full of holes). As she looked, there sprang to mind her room in her parents' country house, this image being instantly followed by that of the hallway down which she had to pass to reach this room. The picture was dim and flickering. But amid the mistiness something emerged and defined itself, something like a small piece of metal; oddly enough she saw it first in the dim hallway and then again in her room. Suddenly she understood that there must be something extremely important about this memory. And then she uttered a little cry. That was it!

The piece of metal was the small, nickel-plated octagonal screw at the frog of her bow. She had thought about this bow with great intensity while hastening down the dim hallway to her room (that had been sometime in August; she was sure of it). She had hurried upstairs from the garden, for amid the stupor of her life during the summer (it could scarcely be called life, with its writhing, smothered animal longings) there had been brief moments of clarity now and then. And one of these moments had beckoned her with the promise of recovery: some remarks of her teacher on bowing technique had occurred to her, and suddenly it had seemed to her that for the first time she correctly understood what he had said. Fired, she had rushed to her instrument to test this insight. And a few moments later her room had been filled to its farthest corners with a tone such as she had scarcely ever before been able to produce (and never again since; by the time dinner was over it had all vanished again, leaving only the crippling torment in her heart—torment that had established a kind of permanent residence for itself below her left breast, in the form of downright physical pain).

That tone she had achieved filled her ears now, but did not animate her hand. If only she could have it again. Beside such happiness, everything else would be ludicrous.

She closed her eyes and lashed furiously at her memory, trying to reanimate that lost moment. But all that remained in her mind was the knowledge that it had happened. Nothing of it was left in her hand; that was lifeless. At the time the power had poured in a single tide of blood down into her finger tips, But the tide had swiftly ebbed. And now . . .

Cautiously, Quapp turned back to the music stand. She went up to it softly, as though there were someone asleep in the room, and began, just as mechanically as she had exercised her left hand, to work away at the right. Basically the result was exactly the same, though perhaps slightly less dismal. Once again she heard the electric motor humming. For about twenty minutes Quapp dutifully went through the prescribed exercises.

But suddenly the corners of her mouth drew back, her front teeth descended sharply upon her lower lip, and her wide-spaced almond eyes narrowed to slits.

A tone filled the room which would have made any string player prick up his ears. The Italian violin, touched at last at the right spot, at the inner core of its being, cried jubilantly and poured out its mysterious life in abundance.

Quapp went through the various bowings and positions. She continued all morning, for some three hours, with only slight interruptions. Her face was rather frowning all the while, her small brow sharply creased above the bridge of her nose.

About one o'clock in the afternoon Quapp stopped working.

For a while she sat dully in an armchair. The maid brought in her lunch. She was not hungry. But after she had eaten a few spoonfuls of soup, she felt a prickling animation coursing through her whole body and proceeded to eat every last morsel, with quite a vigorous appetite for a young lady. By the time the coffee arrived, she was striding about the room, feeling enormous strength, pleasure, and an urge to turn outward. Above all, she wanted to communicate her discovery. She started toward the telephone to call Kajetan and tell him . . .

It was odd that in such situations she always felt, as she did now, a change in her face, as though it were growing a mask. It was as though her physiognomy were suddenly becoming rigid and lifeless, her features immobile, as though caught under the hardening mass of some substance like paraffin. She knew the feel of the stuff from waxing her skis.

Already it had taken form: a sluggish, lame, cardboard face.

Suddenly her hands fell slack. A sense of terror gripped her, as though the air were thinning and everything becoming once more empty and dead. Such "breakthroughs" as she had experienced this morning ought really to form the normal course of her working day. Yet how often, in her rapture over a few such wonderful hours, she had forthwith run off the track, allowed herself too easy a conscience, rewarded herself with a free afternoon or some diversion—only to come home and find that the grace which had been partly accorded her had been withdrawn. The following morning would inevitably be torture; she would do all sorts of senseless things, pursue all kinds of follies, under the pretext that they were essential, but in reality solely in order to keep away from her violin. In that fretful irritability which came from guilt she would be ready to yield to any misunderstanding, to plunge into any quarrel.

Her hands fell slack and her chin dropped to her chest; her face was frowning again, but an expression of wakefulness and alertness had come over it. She was experiencing a moment of decision similar to and perhaps just as crucial as the moment that morning when she had been tempted to drop into the chair to daydream and brood. Standing in the vestibule in front of the telephone, she heard the electric motor on the ground floor start humming again. A minute later she was taking up her violin once again. The instrument felt strangely heavy, and she was frightened by a cool sensation in her arms.

Just as that morning, there was a bad quarter of an hour. But when it was over, the true Italian voice came from the instrument's hollow belly (came imperceptibly, from what point on she did not know; it was simply there). On Quapp's face appeared an expression of deepest secret understanding. She cast a grateful look out the window at the gray urban sky.

Two hours later, with conscious deliberation, Quapp stopped work for the day. This time she had literally to tear herself away from the instrument. But she recognized that she had done enough. After her first exhaustion had passed, the exuberant urge to communicate stirred once more. Again she wanted to telephone Kajetan. But she remained sitting, actually quivering with strain and anxiety, sitting over her cup of tea.

209

Five minutes later, Schlaggenberg entered the room.

They spent the evening together. Sitting opposite her brother, Quapp told him something of her inner life over the previous months. Regarding this life in retrospect, she felt a curious pang. For in hindsight her accomplishment on this day seemed to her the natural and obvious matter it should long since have become. She realized too that her present state represented merely an ordinary minimum, a prerequisite and starting point for any self-mastery. Moreover, it now seemed to her that it had not been so difficult, after all, to achieve this. What had it amounted to but two little jerks, twice pulling herself up sharply! You simply had to be prepared to do this at the right moment—and she knew that she should always have been able to do it—all this past summer, for example. Why, she could have done it any time! (Quapp had no awareness that she had already entered the danger zone of self-deception.) Now she was furious with herself for not having several months of such work behind her, and came close to regarding the reason for this failure as nothing more than a tiny, practically superficial omission—that she had not performed that little act of will to which, she thought, she owed all of today's success.

But who knows, perhaps that was actually the case. At any rate she surprised her brother by suddenly remarking: "Brother, I understand what you mean by the 'red lights.'"

"Do you?" he asked, laughing.

"The same thing as: there are times when you must be able to get up out of a chair at the right moment."

"That may well be," Kajetan said.

During the following days Quapp settled into these new and wholesome habits without actually succumbing to cockiness or forgetting that she had reached no more than the level of mere prerequisites. For her working day was barely long enough to comply with minimum requirements for all so-called "artistic" work. There were days when she did not even fulfill this quota. But in the weeks to come Quapp remained aware that she was living in a transitional period. In some respects she was terribly childish, and so she made a crude calendar for herself, on which she joyfully canceled out each day when evening came. She had given herself permission to move out to the garden suburb on the first of the month. A room had already been secured in the immediate vicinity of Kajetan's apartment—though this had been no easy matter, for house-hunting was fraught with problems for Quapp. The landlady who can endure all-day violin-playing without having fits has not yet been discovered. Therefore, she had to find a landlady who was either away from home all day—who went off to work, say—or was deaf (and the latter characteristic had its own disadvantages). Moreover, Quapp needed a room well separated from the quarters of others, in fact fairly isolated. As the description of her practicing must by now have made plain, she tended to be extremely sensitive to disturbances of all kinds.

On the first of February, then, the time came. Quapp left the scene of her struggles and defeats which in the end had become the scene of a miniature triumph.

CHAPTER 7

Bickerings

FOR SOME time past Stangeler had been visiting the Siebenschein home more frequently. He was received there, was
constantly going in and out. Strangely enough, this new state
of affairs had become established subsequent to that January
8, 1927, when Grete Siebenschein had been called before the
council of her kinsfolk and when René Stangeler had been
caught up in the whirlwind of Eulenfeld's *troupeau.*

There is such obscurity about the whole affair that it is
difficult to list the motives which led the girl to institute this
arrangement. Perhaps her sweetheart's presence in her parents' home gave her the illusion of a legalized relationship, of a
kind of engagement; for at heart, of course, she had a deep and
understandable craving for some such definition. Stangeler's
insistence that she must never think of this—and not only
because of his financial situation—would have struck any girl
as pure foolishness, and certainly a girl like Grete Siebenschein.
Since, however, this fixed and foolish standard was repeatedly
thrust under her nose, she found herself in the middle of cross-
fire between her lover and her family (with whom she inwardly
agreed). She therefore hit upon a number of little devices for
reassuring both Stangeler and her folks, and making each
acceptable to the other. She could reassure her family by pointing to her undoubted chances of marrying him sooner or later.
She could reassure her lover by declaring that she had long
before ceased to be concerned about anything like marriage.

Hers was a thoroughly feminine kind of conduct; instead of riding herd on a whole complex of contradictions and driving them toward a decision, she endeavored in each instance to use prudence and conciliation—for the purpose of preventing these contradictions from coming out into the open, appearing in the light of day. Therefore she always listened with a serious mien to whatever Stangeler said. Therefore she was consummately skillful at avoiding any conversation with her mother.

Probably there were other, specific reasons for Grete's encouraging her "death's head" (for such was the Siebenscheins' nickname for Stangeler, because of his deep-set eyes) to visit her at her parents' home. There were also reasons for Irma Siebenschein's tolerating, even approving such visits. For example, she thought it desirable to be able to keep her eye on "the children" (as she privately called the two of them). We know, of course, that Irma could not possibly have entertained the illusion that the relations between Grete and René had remained within the bounds of "decency." Nevertheless, the affair seemed more respectable this way, not only as far as others were concerned, but for Frau Irma Siebenschein herself. René's frequent presence in the house gave him the air of a proper "suitor." In this matter, however, we do not wish to overestimate the similarities between mother and daughter. Yet it is well to know that such similarities did exist, here and there in various corners of their natures.

As a result of the new arrangement, Grete was now home far more often; for hitherto her meetings with her lover had taken place in cafés, public parks (while it was still warm), and similar places suitable for rendezvous; often enough they had resorted to more or less unspeakable rented rooms.

Grete Siebenschein kept an eye on René to see what impression he would make upon her family. She knew very well that he could present an excellent face to the world if he wanted to. It pained her deeply that he did not always—to some extent because her plans with regard to her family were thus frustrated. For Stangeler's manner at this period was strange indeed. He seemed to be distorting himself by his spasmodic impulsiveness and shyness, by the exaggerated unbalance of his statements, by his facial expressions and gestures. His entire behavior seemed a pose of some sort, for the benefit of himself as well as others. Nevertheless, in spite of all, the young man was at times quite charming—and at such moments Irma would think of the pair as "the children," and would cherish the secret hope that he would "learn common sense after a while." In this house common sense certainly surrounded him on all sides. Grete too (and this was a source of profound unhappiness to her) never quite lost hers, for all that love had wrought great changes in her personality.

"Not a bad-looking boy, really," Frau Irma thought now and then. "When he behaves naturally you might almost take a liking to him."

It must be remembered, of course, that René's birth and background occupied a certain place in the thoughts of the Siebenschein family. On November 2, All Souls' Day, Irma and her husband Ferry had gone to the cemetery to visit a grave. As chance would have it, while strolling down a wide lane between scattered, aristocratic family vaults, they read the name of their "death's head" on one of these marble edifices. They stopped and stood for some time regarding the last resting place of the scions of the von Stangeler family, exchanging speculations on whether that nail in their own future coffin (René), that pigheaded, gloomy, rude young man, might not after all be directly connected with this line. Frau Irma displayed intense interest in this matter; her husband seemed less concerned about it. Herr

215

Ferry Siebenschein, the lawyer, was a stout but pallid man with a large spongy face, who added to the burdens of his profession an almost excessive honesty. He was the recipient of endless reproaches from his "womenfolk"—a term which he applied to his wife and Grete's younger sister Edith, called "Titi" (for there was this other daughter in the family, although she, thank God, was already married). He endured an incessant series of criticisms of his shoes, ties, cigarette-yellowed fingers, and similar matters with the same viscous crossness with which he patiently listened to the symptoms of the two thousand three hundred and eighty-five illnesses from which his wife suffered annually. His only compensation for all this was Grete's love and respect. For his part he was ready to grant without qualification that she was a "superior" girl.

René Stangeler was asked—by Frau Irma, of course—about the vault and the family and the "baron business." He growled affirmation, and suddenly shot out of the room in a fury. For the young man had long before reached that altogether normal stage of development, indispensable to every growing mind, of breaking loose from and renouncing the family; the stage in which the name of a famous father or important ancestor lies like a coffin lid upon the self awakening to consciousness. Whoever dares to speak of the still nebulous and unformed individual in the same breath with the sprawling old clan appears a nasty-minded enemy to the young man concerned. For any such juxtaposition seems a deliberate affront to the temporary goals of the incipient and very temporary personality which is necessarily obsessed with itself. Yet on the part of others, the emphasis on membership in a given family is often fair enough, and only does justice to reality; for a person has to chalk up a pretty good record before where he comes from becomes a matter of indifference, before where he now stands and where he is going can be regarded as more important than his origins. It takes a while before the relationship is turned topsy-turvy and people ask other members of a clan: "You wouldn't happen to be related to so-and-so?"

But that is not the case with young delinquents who face the marital scaffold with empty pockets. When Frau Irma asked her question with such avidity, our delinquent could practically feel the executioner whetting his long blade.

Moreover, the poor devil had his vanity. And here this horrible woman was simply classifying him as someone who bore the name of Stangeler, nothing more. She practically took no notice of him himself.

Had anyone attempted to explain this whole state of affairs to the Siebenscheins, the explanation would in all probability have met with not the faintest gleam of understanding. Our Irma would simply have said: "He's gone absolutely crazy again. Why should he be ashamed of coming from a good family? But since he does you might think he'd behave a little better—and all that sort of thing!"

That sort of thing! For example, he sat beside her bed (she was at the moment suffering from the year's eighteen hundred and seventy-sixth illness), and she was talking about something, and moreover what she was saying concerned him, or at least she fancied that it did. René Stangeler sometimes played the part of an absent-minded deep thinker; but at other times he really was that, and quite unaware of it. Whenever he put on this act, his Grete was thrown into a state of fierce vexation; but when he was genuinely distracted—"concentrating" would be the better word for it—she loved the look of his face with an equal fierceness. We shall shortly have the opportunity to observe the sureness with which she usually could distinguish between his pose of, and his actual, concentrating.

And that sort of thing! "You! Will you have the kindness to listen when I talk to you!" Frau Irma exploded at last. She had been watching first with wonder and then with rising annoyance that "disappearing act" in Stangeler's face which was altogether alien to her nature and therefore doubly provoking to her. This time, however, Stangeler's conscience was at ease. Hence he did not fly into a fury (which was his usual reaction). Rather, he roused himself from his state of absorption to mild surprise, which was accompanied by a polite, almost apologetic smile. Frau Siebenschein had sat up slightly in bed, her intelligent face thrust forward with a look of intense interest. At the moment she looked like a clever little animal, a marten or a rat, say, peering over the brink of a wall into unknown space where traversable ground comes to an end. Here, indeed, Frau Siebenschein had reached the limits of her rather considerable cleverness.

The same cannot be said for her daughter Grete. With regard to her, we must speak more poetically. Perhaps the space was equally empty and equally unknown to her, but she was carried over it on the pinions of love. At this moment, in any case, she displayed a remarkable degree of inspiration. Her eyes flashed with radiant kindliness; she bent protectively over Stangeler, brushed her hand over his hair with a wonderfully tender, womanly gesture, and swiftly bending, kissed him on the forehead.

Frau Irma looked on at first with an expression of irony (she was in any case no pretty sight, sitting up against the pillows in her bed-jacket), then rather mockingly, and finally with but a slightly sour face.

Grete's home life, however, consisted not only of her mother and her mother's partly pathological, partly only too normal reactions. There was a room in the house in which Grete lived as sole mistress, lived, mused, and meditated, we might say. She had some fine old things, a good many knickknacks—all of which, however, bespoke good taste—and a wide embroidered bell-pull on the wall. It was not used to call the maid (there was an electric bell for that, of course), but simply hung there as an antique, a decoration. It is very odd, and by no means purely imagined by the author of these chronicles, that such old things—chubby-cheeked baroque madonnas, too, or Biedermeier grandfather clocks, or among the richer classes "Gothic" pieces—are always to be found in the rooms of "superior" girls like Grete Siebenschein. They have a bent in this direction, and adore visiting antique shops. They also go in for candles. To Stangeler, such tastes were novel. So was much of the jocularity and lightness in Grete's surroundings; and this lightness in particular had its special importance for him. We must not imagine that René always felt depressed and uncomfortable in the Siebenschein home. His own remarks prove the contrary, although at times he spoke with a bitter, partisan animosity against everything connected with the Siebenscheins.

The Siebenschein family's rather spacious apartment was situated in a quarter of the city which long before Stangeler's acquaintance with Grete had possessed a peculiar charm for him. The Siebenscheins lived on the third floor, in apartment No. 14, of a house situated on a wide square opposite one of the major railroad stations. The house itself was one of those frightful, bloated creations of the nineteenth-century real-estate boom, with a fancy entrance gate, candelabra, a stairwell whose banister was adorned with cords and tassels, and a number of entirely useless mirrors; later, an elevator had been installed in the narrow shaft of the stairwell. The apartment itself was exceedingly bright, though not sunny. The light contrasted with the building itself, and with the Siebenschein furnishings.

For the Siebenscheins had crammed it full of neo-Gothic monstrosities, mirrors in huge carved frames which it had taken four men to move, and a sideboard whose removal was practically inconceivable; it was an edifice in itself with various stories and compartments, carved shells and satyrs (and all that sort of thing, to use Frau Irma's phrase). Yet the apartment, as we have remarked, was bright. This circumstance became very important to Stangeler. For at home, in his parents' low, sprawling rooms—the Stangelers lived in a strangely frowning little mansion of their own—it was almost always dark, even in spring and summer. At the Siebenscheins', moreover, someone's more experimental taste had boldly scattered its seed among the pompous dreams of long-dead cabinetmakers. Hanging right in the middle of it all would be a really good modern painting in a smooth plain frame; there was a contemporary armchair shaped like a pure cube and just as uncomfortable as the tight, old-fashioned chairs—a fact you would not know until you had sat down in the thing.

The dining room, too, showed evidences of such breaches in a nonexistent tradition. That room was the center of family life, whereas the adjoining music room (Frau Irma had once been a pianist and was a graduate of the conservatory) rather served for purposes of intellectual uplift. This does not imply, however, that the dining room was a haven of stupidity; quite the contrary, intellects often clashed there with open visors. This candor was the factor that at once stunned and intrigued Stangeler during his first visits. These people talked with one another. Even the children talked with the parents. And how! For we know already that the womenfolk of the family—with the exception of Grete—did not handle Siebenschein *père* with kid gloves.

One winter afternoon, when René Stangeler turned the corner and emerged upon the square in front of the railroad station, the distant hills, the lights by the Danube Canal, and the lowlands of the city, segmented by the line of the canal, lay under a shroud of smoky fog and gathering darkness. Only two days had passed since that riotous night which had ended at the Palais Ruthmayr—we may perhaps remember that Captain von Eulenfeld's revels had taken place on a Saturday night. It was now Monday (Schlaggenberg was meeting his sister at the station). The day before, Stangeler had begged off coming to the Siebenschein home by telephoning some excuse to Grete. His girl had not been exactly overjoyed; she worked part-time at her father's office and naturally liked to spend her only wholly free day of the week with René. But on Sunday, Stangeler had not waked until noon, and then had felt only a single craving— to sleep. Sunday dinner at his parents' home, with various near and distant relations assembled, had been strenuous enough. To top that off with the Siebenscheins would have been all he needed.

Nevertheless the aftereffects of that night had been extremely beneficial. René was feeling buoyant. This was evident from the fact that in spite of his hangover he sat down happily to his books on Sunday evening and attacked his studies and his writing with real pleasure. Hence, when he used the word "work" in his Sunday telephone conversations with Grete Siebenschein, he was not exactly lying. Incidentally, Fräulein Siebenschein called up once again around ten o'clock to inquire in a warm, bell-like voice how he was feeling—and to convince herself that her René was actually at home.

Nevertheless, on Monday he was given a cold greeting when he entered the Siebenschein vestibule in a mood of high-spirited gaiety. He had been looking forward to being with Grete,

221

and felt an irresistible craving to tell her all about it: about the wild night and the fortuitous effect of all these experiences upon him; about the Sunday he had slept through so pleasantly, and the delightful smoothness with which his work had gone in the evening; in short (and this was the main thing), he wanted to tell her that life in this world was glorious, expansive, wide, and free.

He wanted to scurry right off into Grete's room. But she blocked his way and said with what seemed to him an inappropriate sternness: "We must go in there" (she meant the dining room). "There are visitors, Titi, her husband, Uncle Siegfried; we have to join them."

"What's the matter with you?" he said, vexed, his buoyancy sharply deflated. "What have I done now to offend you?"

"It's outrageous!" she said in a choked voice. "What happened on Saturday? I kept after my mother to hurry because I knew you were waiting outside the café. Then you were gone. I called you up. You weren't at home. I was terribly upset all evening, threw up twice in the bathroom, my heart was fluttering so—naturally my parents noticed . . ."

"But on the telephone yesterday . . ." he ventured to protest.

"Of course, you always think you've made everything all right," she said indignantly. "But to think of other people for a change—that never occurs to you Stangelers. . ." A hard, bitter, despairing expression flitted over her face. "All right, come along," she said sulkily. "Wait, your hair's all mussed, come into the bathroom."

She fiddled with him a bit. Then she led him into the dining room.

Stangeler bowed somewhat woodenly. Wooden was the way he felt at the moment; it was as if something had snapped inside him. At the same time a violent rage was rising to the surface, and he was able to control it only by considerable effort and a slight distortion of his face. If he had been asked what was making him seethe, he would undoubtedly have replied somewhat at random: because she (Grete) was always fighting against the good in him; that she always succeeded in quelling his bouts of buoyancy, in depressing him, putting a damper on him. . . And if anyone had reasonably suggested that his Grete was after all right about Saturday and Sunday, Stangeler would have shouted (yes, shouted): "No! That isn't what matters. Suppose she is right! This time she happens to be in the right. But it's absolutely mysterious: no sooner do I come sailing along cheerfully, looking forward to seeing her, and sure enough she comes down on me with something like this. There are always relations around, or she's just had a row with Mama, or Mama is so terribly sick again, or she herself has such a frightful headache and has just been upset on account of Titi and thrown up in the bathroom; or else the seamstress is there and has taken over Grete's room for her sewing-machine, so that we have to go to the dining room and can't get a chance to talk alone; or else the telephone rings every three minutes . . ."

And René would have waved his hand wildly as though heaping more such examples on top of the others.

A lovely couple. Especially with Stangeler feeling as he did at that time. And, it should be added: in those surroundings.

Meanwhile greetings were exchanged. Papa Siebenschein always greeted Stangeler with a special brand of cordiality whose roots were somewhat obscure. There was something of unspoken understanding, as though he viewed Herr René Stangeler as a kind of fellow-sufferer and was tacitly saying to him: "Well, young man, now you're beginning to see what I have gone through half my life with these womenfolk." (By "womenfolk," to be sure, he meant only his wife and his younger daughter, Titi.)

223

Siegfried Markbreiter regarded René attentively; he seemed to be studying the young man. Irma was particularly friendly, which somewhat placated Stangeler, for he thought of the fluttering heart and the bathroom and the fact that her parents had naturally noticed . . .

Titi was thin as a rail; that is to say, according to fashionable ideas she had a wonderful figure. For this was the period when that ideal of feminine beauty had triumphed and was universally subscribed to.

The center of gravity in this company, however, was Titi's husband. As soon as Stangeler caught sight of Herr Cornel Lasch, he realized that he had noticed the large automobile standing in the street below, near the entrance to the apartment house. Herr Lasch only half rose to greet him, and immediately resumed his conversation. He was surrounded by all the Siebenscheins; all the Markbreiters likewise surrounded him with that respect compounded of joyful pride and petty bourgeois restraint (we wouldn't want anyone to think that . . .)—precisely the kind of respect he merited as one of theirs, but at the same time as a hero, a hero whose works they could understand, for his deeds were woven out of the stuff of their wishes.

"Levielle is talented," he was remarking at the moment, letting the words trickle from his lips as though he were chewing a fatty morsel. Then his heavy jaws clicked together again. All fell silent and looked expectantly at him. Especially Papa Siebenschein, who had always found earning money a painful, urgent affair; he seemed altogether intoxicated by the airiness with which this bitterest of themes was being treated. "But Altschul is heavy-footed. Reliable, sure. But that isn't the way to go about it nowadays."

None of those present knew anything about these matters

(not even Markbreiter, for he too was what is generally called a decent man). They remained silent, embarrassed. Lasch's big car stood down below. He had married their daughter. They really liked him. But as for following the flights of his thoughts—much of the time they could not . . .

"You know, Herr von Stangeler, there's a subject you ought to write on sometime. 'The modern *condottiere.*' In olden days men waved their swords around in the air" (Stangeler looked askance at Papa Siebenschein; he abhorred such historical improvisations) "and such people were called heroes. And nowadays a man" (he pointed to his son-in-law) "does it with a single telephone call from Vienna to London. That's what I call making history! Eh? Forgive me, of course I don't know much about history, but when I think that somebody might write that just the way stories about heroes used to be written . . . eh?" The steep, angry furrow which now appeared between Stangeler's eyebrows—his somewhat oblique eyes had narrowed to a crack—was due not to Papa Siebenschein's remarks but to the coaching glance that Grete was casting at him out of the corners of her eyes. Evidently he was now supposed to prove himself, to show how learned and intelligent he was. Evidently he was now supposed to make a good impression again, take up the theme, graciously enter into the other man's conceit, display his wit, give pleasure to Grete's mother and father (and indeed it would not have been difficult for him to do so).

No fear of that: he acted as badly as possible.

"I damn well don't agree at all," he snarled balefully and fell silent. A cloud passed over Grete's face; a bitter, soured, disappointed twist appeared on her features, and finally a spiteful smile. And at the same moment there appeared almost exactly the same smile on Herr Cornel Lasch's broad face. Stangeler recognized the similarity, and this perception seemed to him an inspired insight.

Even in his sullen anger, however, Stangeler could not help being aware of Papa Siebenschein's utter harmlessness. And now he had given such an ill-bred response to the kind old boy's attempt at higher conversation; he knew he had, and his conscience was already gnawing at him; and so he had once again been put in the wrong. He looked toward Grete. But she turned indignantly and haughtily away (how marvelously her straight, blue-black hair curved around her finely shaped forehead!), rose, and went to the sideboard to pour another cup of coffee for Cornel. "Would you care for another too?" she asked René with curt coolness. Of course he answered: "No."

Herr Lasch, as she passed, placed his arm around her waist with amicable self-assurance. She laughed and briefly sat down on his knees.

"It was better," Stangeler thought in furious despair, "it was still better and less disgusting. In spite of the lice and the shrapnel. It was still better and less disgusting."

"Say, Cornel, what did really happen that time?" Uncle Siegfried Markbreiter took up the thread of conversation. "You were still in the ranks, or had they made you a platoon leader? Anyway, you were due to be sent to the front. And then all of a sudden . . . How did you pull it off?" Siegfried Markbreiter displayed as keen an interest in the matter as if war were about to break out any moment and he, old businessman that he was, had to learn quickly the art of shirking.

The point he had touched upon here was important in any case, for it marked the starting point of Cornel Lasch's career. Oddly enough, the old Empire had not always disdained the services of such people. They actually performed a valuable function—until, at any rate, they had entrenched themselves well enough to set about shearing the sheep (that is, the government). Such was the case with Lasch. His particular fortune had been made by the collapse after the war; for the general breakdown saved him from being caught and held to account (which otherwise would surely have happened sooner or later). In addition, and this is of course well known, that historical upheaval had created a condition in public life which proved particularly fertile for Lasch and all his ilk.

The principal thing for him at the start, however, was to escape the main body of the army, where people of his sort counted for nothing and were only bawled out and chivvied. The meshes of military law are fine or coarse, according to the degree of pull enjoyed; a fish had to slip through them in order, with a vigorous stroke, to reach free water; there he quickly grew alarmingly and soon swam off as a regular shark. Such was approximately the course followed by Private Lasch in his rise to a lieutenancy. By the end of the war he occupied a leading post in one of those bureaus of the War Ministry which was responsible for the distribution of raw materials and the awarding of contracts to vital war industries.

We can readily imagine that this work offered all kinds of opportunities to our friend Lasch. Opportunities which he, of course, did not repudiate.

Markbreiter's question, however, related to the turning point in this saga. Cornel Lasch's face glowed; it is always sweet to recall perils successfully breasted.

"Levielle showed me how to go about it," he said, smiling. "Of course the thing had to be arranged through his brother in the surgeon-general's office. He examined me for the thousandth time, looked me over from top to bottom, and found nothing. Thank God my health is still as sound as it was then!" Everyone laughed, and Siebenschein *pere* patted his son-in-law lightly on the shoulder, as testimony to his respect. Only Stangeler did not laugh.

"In the end a disease was found," Lasch continued. "I am probably the first person who ever had it. You see, it had no symptoms and . . ."

"What did they find?" his father-in-law asked amid a burst of fresh laughter.

"Don't interrupt him, Papa!" Grete intervened. She was listening to her brother-in-law with what was clearly an immense interest, leaning forward and gazing up into Lasch's face.

"Wait a moment," Lasch said. "Now I have it—I can even remember the Latin name. 'Endocarditis obsoleta.' It means something like a hidden heart defect. The poor fellow who has it might not even know it—and then one day, some little exertion and he falls over dead."

"For heaven's sake!" Irma cried. "Maybe there really is . . . did you ever talk to another doctor about it?"

Lasch waved her suggestion aside with both hands, and laughed in low gurgling tones. The others joined in, except for Uncle Siegfried, who apparently did not consider the matter laughable, but rather highly instructive and worthy of deep consideration (with which view we are in thorough agreement).

Stangeler, too, saw nothing the least bit laughable in the story. Would that he, too, had given the tale his deep consideration. But not he. He yielded to his mood of rage. He gnashed his teeth. Between himself and Grete stretched a taut bow of tension; the relationship between the two lovers was in a bad way at this moment. But we must not imagine that two opposing camps confronted each other. To put the matter that way would be to oversimplify. It was not that all this lascivious stuff seemed good and admirable to Grete, nor that Stangeler saw the filthy swindle simply for what it was. Rather, he was overwhelmed by a sense of his powerlessness to meet life's demands, while here he saw power wearing a face that turned his stomach. Ordinarily, perhaps, and certainly in the past, his powerlessness had scarcely troubled him, for he had regarded it as a temporary and passing phenomenon. But because of his love he now found himself nailed fast to it; his tie with Grete chained him down so tightly to his helplessness that he could hardly imagine a means of moving forward and escaping.

The only way of escape, it seemed, was to tear himself free from the whole relationship, from "all that sort of thing." And this was the direction in which his thoughts now burrowed and probed. For some time now each of these excruciating incidents had brought him to the verge of such a decision.

The reader will understand that at this point the telephone had to ring.

We shall avail ourselves of the opportunity offered by this interruption to say a word about Dr. Levielle of the surgeon-general's office—yes, it was true that he had held a very high rank during the First World War—and was later chief physician of a private hospital in Vienna. Many persons considered him Financial Counselor Levielle's twin brother. This was altogether wrong, for the doctor was a good five years younger than the financier. Nevertheless, the two men were frequently taken for each other, although their outward resemblance was not great enough to explain the confusion. Rather, it stemmed from the similarity in the manner of the two. There are people who display a senseless hauteur and arrogance wherever and whenever we meet them; and often they are persons whose professional or social position provides only the scantiest justification for such an attitude. In almost all such individuals we find, if we look closer, that such behavior was already manifest in their younger years. If later they amount to something, the arrogance only becomes more obnoxious. But essentially this arrogance of theirs is independent of their importance. It is a trait essential to their spiritual budgets. To others it can be a tormenting enigma. The Levielle brothers were really identical in the vulgar superciliousness which underlay their whole nature, their manner of sauntering along the street, say, with eyebrows lifted, fixing their eyes haughtily upon every phenomenon that had the impudence to violate their isolation—although, to be sure, everything was vouchsafed only the most casual and indignant of glances, was quickly dismissed as patently of not the slightest value . . .

Grete went to the telephone. Her voice sounded clear as a bell and altogether jocund as she answered. She spoke amiably, jestingly. Stangeler was affected unpleasantly by the swift change in her personality; it seemed almost uncanny to him that she could suddenly be so sugary.

"Who was it?" Titi asked after Grete had replaced the receiver.

"Beppo Draxler," she said, and added in explanation to Lasch: "An old friend." Lasch nodded unconcernedly.

Bitter fury was by now raging unchecked in Stangeler. Not that he was in any sense jealous. At bottom he was very well aware that for his Grete nothing but himself existed in the whole world, and that he had not a thing to fear from these "old friends." But these friends provoked him in another way. They were without exception respectable and more or less harmless average young or older persons whom our self-obsessed René regarded as hateful for two reasons. In the first place he was convinced that his sweetheart always got along better and communicated more easily with these friends than with him. In the second place, however, it seemed to him that his Grete derived her yardstick or foot rule, with which she was

230

in the habit of measuring him, precisely from this group, and that those friends confirmed her in her habit of scaling him down. Probably, too, he thought, they were far more danger-ous in this respect than her family.

At any rate, Stangeler precipitately decamped. Here we may note with surprise his resemblance in this respect—and prob-ably only in this respect—to Frau Irma Siebenschein. They shared the habit of making sudden, embarrassing, disturbed, and disturbing departures. This one was exactly like those typ-ical Irma leave-takings which could arise out of any imaginable pretext, and of which the entire family was heartily sick.

Stangeler rose, murmured with considerable effort some such phrase as "I must go now," answered Irma's astonished inquiry as to whether he was not staying to supper with a smile that failed completely to develop beyond a grimace, mut-tered indistinct words like "work" and "Institute"—and finally snatched his hand with a violent movement away from Grete, who could always manage to be kind and conciliatory in such crises. . . He left the room. She followed him out, painfully con-scious of the eyes of everyone in the room on her back. She felt deeply that once again her "death's head" had exposed her to ridicule.

While René, in the vestibule, was thrusting his arms with furious clumsy motions into the sleeves of his overcoat, Grete stood facing him, scarcely two steps from him; and for the first time that evening they looked straight into each other's eyes. Her face displayed a rare harshness, probably the converse of her real feelings of despair.

"Where were you Saturday night?" she burst out.

This was probably the least suitable moment to demand an accounting of Stangeler, and win from him an admission of his misconduct. He was, he thought, absolutely in the right in a deeper sense, and he believed in this rightness of his with savage conviction. He was at the moment as obsessed by this belief as his sweetheart's wounded and offended spirit was possessed by sorrow.

His somewhat oblique eyes narrowed and flashed. He paused in his movements and stood with arms half bent backward, imprisoned by the coat which he had not yet drawn up to his shoulders. He said nothing. His silence did not bespeak any inability to answer, but rather a final extreme concentration and condensation of hatred and resentment, a search for the most cutting phrase, the one that would strike to the heart, the deadliest insult. It was a drawing back of the bowstring to its utmost, to give the released arrow the greatest piercing power.

"Saturday night? At any rate in far better company than I am now." And he indicated with a motion of his head the double door of the dining room, through which the voices of the family, the laughter and medley of speech, could be heard.

Like a fighter already bleeding from so many wounds that one additional injury is scarcely felt, she did not parry the blow.

"Where were you!" she said, and her tone was no longer a question but a determined statement. Now she was attempting to escape from her own anguish, which rose to flood under Stangeler's hate-filled gaze and coagulated into a clot of obstinacy not characteristic of her. Moreover, jealous impulses were now stirring.

"Where were you?" she repeated in a monotone.

He had at last finished putting on his coat. "With Captain Eulenfeld," he replied, and there was actually a lilt in his voice. "I stood forever in front of that café where you and your family . . ." Again he jerked his head scornfully toward the door. "Then he came along in his little car, and a whole flock of people behind him, friends of his. . . They simply swept me up and jammed me into one of the cars. And I was glad, understand! Glad! When you keep me standing forever in front of that stinking café . . ." He put special vehemence into his enunciation of this polite phrase. "I was chilled to the bone. Half an hour before, one of those idiots comes tearing out of your café, some fat female who almost knocked me down. That would have been it. You let me stand there like a stupid fool! Who the devil do you think you are anyway, the whole bunch of you? Who?" These last words had come out in a brutish roar.

Since she did not understand quite what he was talking about (we, however, remember very well that Frau Altschul was pursuing Frau Rosen and found René Stangeler blocking her path)—since she did not know what it was all about, her mind was momentarily turned from her anguish and resentment. Moreover, it occurred to her that there might be some excuse for René's behavior of which she was unaware, so that perhaps she was doing him an injustice.

But this impulse lasted for only a moment. Immediately her features set again. "With Captain Eulenfeld . . . she repeated slowly, striving to express her bitterness with a faintly contemptuous distortion of the mouth and an equally disdainful nod. "So that's your good company. Is that it? Drinking like fish, and women, and—ugh! That old rotter. Of course! The rest of them were probably just that kind. Ugh!" She stamped her foot. "I wouldn't touch them with a ten-foot pole. You're a degenerate!" She ground her teeth. Her face was frozen in icy indignation. Her extremely straight and fine nose—next to her violet-blue eyes perhaps her finest feature—was drained of blood and snow-white, as if in the first stages of frostbite. The narrow bridge—you might almost call it the edge or blade of her nose—stood out, sharply emphasized.

"Don't you dare!" Stangeler snarled. "What do you know,

you with your gang"—he gestured a third time with his head toward the door of the dining room—"what do any of you know about decency and honesty? I suppose your Herr Lasch is a shining example! Those are your standards—yes, *they're* worth an 'ugh' . . ."

"Enough! Go!" she cried.

"No, I'm staying now!" he spat, in uncontrollable fury. "How dare you insult the captain, who was at the front with me, like . . ."

"Oh yes, now trot out the honor of an officer," she said with cold scorn. "Yes, yes, I know the story, comradeship and all that, one rotter won't hear a word against the other . . ."

Had Grete been in a condition to observe her lover at this moment, she would have noted a sudden change in him, a visible effort to collect himself, evidently caused by alarm. Perhaps in that fraction of a second he had become aware of the extreme dangerousness of the ground onto which he had already staggered. He probably felt the demoralization rushing upon him—as it had so often before—so that he found himself, horrorstruck, upon the brink of frenzied brutality. And so he attempted at the last moment to check himself. Perhaps he was stirred by a tender, fleeting recollection of the happy mood in which he had entered this vestibule a little less than two hours before.

"There were other people there, too," he went on, outwardly much calmer. "Among others, Kajetan von Schlaggenberg, the writer. The man is incredible; I'd like very much to know him better. We picked him up somewhere out in the suburbs where he lives . . ."

He paused. Her eyes had suddenly widened, had become fixed and threatening.

"So," she said between her teeth, and now she had actually

234

reached that pitch of rage in which it took all her control merely to be able to speak. "So, Herr Schlaggenberg. You've certainly found the right company for yourself. Do you know that he is a horrid, horrid, disgusting person? The nastiest, the lowest of the low? Do you know what this Herr Schlaggenberg has done to his wife, Camy Schlaggenberg, a wonderful fine girl, a good woman? Do you know that he brutally left her after she had sacrificed nine or more years, the best years of her life, for him? . . . The tenth year he finally condescended to marry her! And in November this year, in the most brutal manner imaginable . . . So such people are your models! But if you think you're going to treat me like that, you're mistaken, you're very much mistaken, let me tell you that . . . By now her voice had risen. "I want a decent man, a man I don't have to be ashamed of, not a selfish, brutal rotter!" She stamped her foot, and at the same time began to cry. "You make yourself ridiculous all the time." Now she, too, gestured with her head toward the dining-room door.

"Everybody laughs at you and your crazy ways . . ."

A literally frightful transformation took place in Stangeler. He himself, his whole personality, seemed to vanish under a terrible contortion. For what remained of his face was nothing but a hard, compact knot with two slanting slits for eyes. A low growl issued from his chest, and his lips drew back from his clenched teeth. He suddenly darted at Grete and began shaking his fists rapidly in front of her face while he jerkily gasped out broken fragments of sentences.

"Stinker! Stinking bastards . . . I make myself ridiculous! . . . Who do you think you are! . . . Siebenschein . . . marvelous! Herr Lasch! They're *your* people! And you have the same miserable filth in your stinking little brain . . . Enemy! You—my enemy. Enemy! . . . Everything rotten—always against me . . ."

235

He uttered a repressed cry of rage, flashed his teeth like a wild animal in front of her face, then abruptly pulled himself back, turned, and rushed out, slamming the door of the apartment behind him.

Suddenly, now, the silence was fearful, in spite of the voices from the dining room and the thump of his feet on the staircase outside. These past few minutes, fortunately, the conversation in the dining room had grown very loud, as it was still; and yet it sounded muted to Grete, as though she had cotton plugs in her ears. She had leaned against the wall. Her blood gushed from her heart in a jet too large for her small body, flooded her brain, and clouded her wildly circling gaze; it found no outlet, carried her stomach along with it; and then the heart paused. Her breath paused with it. But the pounding pressure in her temples remained.

She groped her way into the bathroom and vomited. What she brought up was bilious mucus.

It might be thought that Stangeler, as he stepped out into the street, would likewise have been utterly shaken and shattered, although his emotional condition could not possibly affect his body so violently, simply because he was more robust than Grete. And the fact was that hitherto, after every such clash with Grete, he had inevitably experienced a complete paralysis of all his vital forces, a stunning of his aspirations and motivations.

But this time his reaction was different.

He felt liberated, and rushed off without thinking of what he was leaving behind, or of what might be happening up there in the apartment. The city belonged to him once again, its lights and its long lamplit avenues down which he could look as far as the eye could see. His life belonged to him once more; he had become fully himself again, and had a right to be himself;

236

he was no longer dangling from the hook of an obligation he could not meet in the foreseeable future, and which in any case was hateful to him (how right Frau Steuermann had been!). Up there in the Siebenschein apartment that obligation spoke to him in every kitchen smell that lingered in the vestibule, in every line in the corners of Frau Irma's mouth—when it was not driven home to him far more directly and distinctly.

But now what amounted to a break between him and Grete had occurred. Now he was no longer bound to Grete, or at least had some justification for regarding himself as no longer bound.

Now the horizon lay wide open before him again.

His ego darted madly hither and thither, as though seeking an Archimedean point beneath it in order to lift itself up. In the meantime, however, all impulses of altruism had to be fended off; these were useless to the ego and would only make things more painful for his antagonist as well. René knew that, too; or at any rate the knowledge was there as a kind of dark tumor in his conscience (which often leads us further than the clearest thought). But it is almost inconceivable how much can happen merely incidentally in the course of such a search for a stable point (unfortunately these incidental happenings later prove highly consequential). A single example will suffice. *Exemplum docet, exempla obscurant,*" as Prince Alfons Croix—whom we have yet to meet—once remarked.

René entered a café to calm his nerves and refresh himself by washing his hands and drinking a cup of coffee. And at once his own psychic mechanism tripped him up—aided and abetted by the instantaneous appearance of external life. "Freedom" was being waved under his nose, and René did not observe that it was a highly malignant freedom. For at the moment he craved opposites which would enable him to push

237

off successfully, and forever, from the shore of those menacing "powers" which wanted to devour his "freedom." . . .

The wicked shore in this case was named Siebenschein, and the longed-for coast on the other side was represented here and now by several *troupistes* who were standing around a billiard table toward the rear of the café.

Here was a glorious salutation from the free world! At any rate, it cheered him immensely; for a fragment of a broken bottle on a heap of refuse can flash like white-hot metal in the sun. This shard of an uproarious night had an enormous psychological effect upon René, compared to the usual effects external things had upon him. This coincidence made everything complete. And whereas after previous serious quarrels with Grete it had often taken him days to resume his life, today he had no trouble at all. Barely an hour after that violent episode in the Siebenschein vestibule he was to be seen sitting in the manuscript reading room at the National Library translating a fifteenth-century codex. And as he worked, freedom veritably puffed from his nostrils, like carbonic gas from the nostrils of a person who in his thirst has gulped down a bottle of soda-water too fast.

He had not lingered long in the café. Today, he thought, he would be able to make considerable progress, for the manuscript reading room at the National Library stayed open until nine.

He took the streetcar, and then had a short walk to Josefsplatz. Relief washed beneficently over him because today it would scarcely be worth the trouble to go to the Institute for Austrian Historical Studies, which closed its doors at seven.

The Institute, too, was one of the "powers" that hemmed him in. He anticipated the National Library with a tactile pleasure: the old building itself with its monastic, stone-paved corridors; the pure, austere air of the stacks; the clear light above the reading tables; the low rustle of turning pages. Here the well-ordered and completely cooled layers of the past extended back through the centuries like the succession of rooms in the imperial palace. Here he was released from all pressure—as was essential if he were to do any work at all. Here it was vital that he have a head calm right down to his collar button and two well-washed hands to handle the precious manuscript pages. Nothing else. No entrails. Yes, the National Library was a power, just like the Institute. But the latter always smelled of its oiled floors. That horrid greasiness was far closer to ordinary life, closer too to the surprisingly consistent and yet ultimately incomprehensible human types who frequented the place.

Yes, it too was a power, sufficient unto itself, and a power precisely because it was that. As yet René had not seen that an individual like himself who had, as it were, wandered away from the smell of his own stable, broken through his natural aura, could never acquire another. Henceforth this was true no matter how much he liked some other aura, whether it was the cultivated and bureaucratic air of the National Library, the irresponsible freedom of the *troupeau,* the easygoing atmosphere at the Siebenscheins' (for at times he had breathed that in with pleasure), or the oily reek of the Institute. Any one of these except the one he had left would have suited him, had he only been able to enter into them completely. But the door that had slammed behind him also shut him off from all others. The "powers" weighed heavily upon him, each one of which would be a hereafter in the here in relation to the others, each sufficient unto itself (and each of which, naturally, was unencumbered by any self-criticism, which was precisely what made them all so terribly strong). It made no difference whether they were the "*troupistes,*" or his family group, or those competent thorough-minded individuals from Upper Austria or the Tyrol who labored in an oily atmosphere over documents dealing with the diverse problems of their regional histories, harmonious among themselves, their keen senses instantly scenting anyone who bore traces of a strange stable smell, whose odor was not their own. Nor was it any comfort that René now knew what a few years before he had not even begun to suspect: how little communication exists between the humanities departments of a modern university whose forces of mind and spirit exert pressure upon the whole man. For specialists permit themselves to respond only as far as the collar button, and the classical philologist is as much a technician as the student of modern history. The regional historians could look forward to jobs in the provinces, and most of them had fiancées waiting there for them. Nothing outside their province carried any weight with them, no hereafter in the here, not even springtime in Vienna, though spring descended upon all the streets each evening, its dulcet airs mingling with surprising grace with glaring lights of every size and color.

But what lies beyond while he walks down Augustiner Strasse as if within a lower realm of reality and upon a false bottom, beneath whose panel lies the space which it is incumbent to break through, so that he can at last fall through to his own valid ground—what lies beyond? Why should Ensign Preyda come to mind right here and now, though Ensign Preyda has long been dead, killed in June 1916 in the course of a counterattack? (They had spent four months together in the foremost trench before it happened.)

Abruptly, it was all gone. For seconds René had felt almost as if the pressure on all sides had lifted. But already it was back, and he had to defend himself once again. Against the Siebenscheins. Against their incomprehensibility, surely as

240

great as that of the regional historians. René was always making war on institutions which did not admit him. His parents' home had basically been just such an institution. It was as though he could not stand erect unless he continually made sorties in all directions.

It remains a curious fact that in the manuscript reading room Stangeler worked on late medieval subjects, whereas at the Institute he studied Merovingian matters. There was one element in common between these periods so far apart in time: their evident inchoateness. As he went into the lobby after closing time, he encountered Doktor Neuberg. He had not noticed him in the reading room. Together they walked the many stairs from the manuscript section. As they crossed Josefsplatz, heading in the direction of the Pallavicini Palace, Neuberg said: "I have been guilty of plagiarizing you, Herr Stangeler."

"I can't imagine what of mine you would find to plagiarize."

"Oh yes," Neuberg replied, and began a lively account of Frau Friederike Ruthmayr ("magnificent woman, buried treasure"). Then he told Stangeler what he had said about the nature of the historian's task. "I followed your argument almost word for word. That is, I spoke entirely in terms of the thesis you once held—we were walking back and forth under the arcades at the time. I repeated exactly what you had said about contact with remote portions of our personal pasts."

"Oh yes," Stangeler said. "I think somewhat differently about these matters nowadays. But 'contact' is bad, 'in terms of' is rotten, and 'thesis' is absolutely terrible. Look here, you really mustn't use such gibberish. You probably pick it up in the History Seminar. That stuffy style just drives me crazy—all that sort of thing!" ("Mama Siebenschein is already poisoning me with her style," he thought fiercely.)

They walked on together—Stangeler had nowhere in particular to go—down Schaufler Gasse and along the Lowel Bastei out to the Ring. René asked Neuberg about his plans for the future. He asked purely to keep the conversation going since he had no mind for such plans and no eye for the perspectives of a career. Doktor Neuberg promptly explained with considerable passion that he had not the slightest intention of taking the teacher's examination and becoming a secondary-school teacher ("that would mean surrender!"). He thought of trying for the post of *Dozent,* the first step toward a university teaching career ("at any rate I am keeping my fingers crossed"—this expression, too, seemed to displease René, for his oblique eyes narrowed somewhat).

Where was he headed for now? Stangeler asked, realizing that Neuberg was directing their steps. Doktor Neuberg replied that he was dining with his future in-laws; he had been allowed to work at the National Library until nine o'clock, and was not due for dinner until half-past nine. ("He had been allowed"— here was another who stood well with the "powers" and did not mind at all!) "You'll make a good university professor," René said.

"Perhaps I shall someday—I hope so," Neuberg replied.

"And then you will marry."

"Before that, I should hope," Neuberg exclaimed, laughing.

At this, Stangeler made a bon mot which was quoted much later on: "To be a professor and married strikes me as the height of gruesomeness." Undoubtedly the remark was put in circulation by Neuberg—who found it vastly humorous.

"Rumor has it that you are engaged, too, Herr von Stangeler," he replied.

Stangeler abruptly changed the subject and described the

242

events of Saturday night (Neuberg, incidentally, already knew Captain von Eulenfeld by name, having heard him mentioned by his future in-laws). René spoke of the last invasion by the remnants of the *troupeau,* the nebula, and the "nova" that had appeared inside it.

They stood, as they talked, under the dark trees on Ring Strasse.

"You say she was beautiful?" Neuberg asked.

"Yes, extremely beautiful. The light was falling on the terrace. She actually drank from the bottle."

Why hadn't he also climbed over the fence? Neuberg wondered.

"I was too drunk," René explained.

"And not one of you knew where it happened or who she was?"

"No, I hardly think so. I didn't, certainly."

"If you ask me, you sound like a born bachelor!" Neuberg exclaimed. "What an adventure. Just like you, though . . . I wouldn't mind having a night's fun again for a change!" A quick little frown appeared on his brow, a private reflection lasting only a few seconds; but there was some depth to it.

Then they parted cordially.

René walked back along somewhat the same route they had come, strolling from Ring Strasse into the heart of the city, still without any destination in mind. He paused in front of the still-illuminated window of a bookshop. But there was little there to attract him. Then he suddenly spotted Kajetan von Schlaggenberg's name above the title of a novel.

Once again he felt a sense of repetition and summons such as he had experienced earlier at the café when he blundered into the *"troupistes."* He turned away, raised his head, and looked across the long avenue filled with light, motion, and the sounds of horns, looked up and over to the roof of a distant building where a neon sign glowed dark red and somewhat somberly. Now what he had seen a moment before mingled with the sight before his eyes, and for the tiniest fraction of a second the title of the book with Schlaggenberg's name on it appeared in the distance, as though the red light were above it, illuminating the printed letters.

It was already nearly half-past nine when Neuberg climbed the stairs of the carpeted and pleasantly heated hallway to Angelika's parents' apartment. A manservant opened the door, and behind appeared the maid's friendly smiling face. She informed him that the family were still in the dining room. Neuberg followed the girl through several rooms large and small; preceding him, she switched on a light in each room in turn. Then she opened half of a double door and stepped back.

The Trapps were sitting around the dinner table. The table was or seemed very small, set as it was in the middle of an extraordinarily large square room whose outer reaches were beyond the orbit of the hanging lamp suspended above the white tablecloth. Thus the edges of the room remained in dusk. Neuberg greeted Frau Trapp. Herr Doktor Trapp was leaning back in his armchair; he removed the cigar from his mouth and casually offered his hand to Neuberg. Only then was it Angelika's turn to be greeted. Neuberg had noticed her unwontedly erect posture as he entered and wondered what it meant. The manner of her greeting was also rather cool.

Neuberg had just entered the apartment of a Viennese landlord. For the entire building was the property of Herr Trapp, doctor of jurisprudence, attorney-at-law. It belonged to him, was subject to him. Unlike his quite prosperous but essentially nomadic tenants, Herr Trapp sat squarely upon his own property here, a fact he liked to make evident. Inevitably, such unspoken assertions vexed Neuberg, and perhaps his annoyance was especially keen this evening. In order to overcome these emotions—which usually marked the beginnings of his visits here—he asked with lively interest about the cross-country trip which the family had undertaken the day before, Sunday, in their automobile, starting out very early in the morning. (Neuberg had not been invited.) And while Herr Trapp expatiated upon driving times, road conditions, and different places, Neuberg—who knew nothing about these matters but pretended to be much engrossed—felt his fiancée looking at him and realized that it was time at last to respond to her gaze. But he plunged feverishly into the conversation with his future father-in-law; it was as though an almost physical force kept his face turned toward Herr Trapp. Meanwhile the manservant had begun serving dinner to the young gentleman—the family had long since finished theirs. The servant, who had been in the room all the while, standing in semidarkness at the sideboard behind Neuberg, made the latter distinctly nervous. Neuberg ate faster to be free of the man.

"I went to the opera the day before yesterday," he said abruptly, between bites.

"We too went out Saturday night. Took the car then, too. We were invited out to a place in the suburbs, the Cottage Suburb, as people call it nowadays. My wife and I, that is; Angelika stayed home studying . . ."

"What opera were they giving Saturday, Herr Doktor?" Angelika's mother asked, taking up the subject which her husband had ignored.

"*Rosenkavalier*," Neuberg said.

At precisely this instant his and Angelika's eyes met. She looked firmly at him as if to say that he knew perfectly well, as

245

men always do, what he was guilty of, for all he was determined to play dumb as long as possible.

"*Rosenkavalier* . . ." Frau Trapp repeated. She seemed to be looking with moisture-laden eyes at the images aroused by this word. She was particularly fond of the opera, unaware that above all she was attracted by indecencies legitimized by "art" and which (right in the first act) were presented publicly in a packed theater. Frau Trapp, a large woman with threads of gray in her blonde hair, a weathered face, and a general air of being rather crushed, looked more than ever like a misshapen Edam cheese whenever she was carried away by artistic emotion.

Neuberg, of course, knew exactly what was the matter. After the opera on Saturday he should have telephoned Angelika, who was sitting at home alone with the dreary prospect of being dragged out on an all-day automobile ride by her parents next morning—carried off, moreover (and this was the worst of it), without her Hans, whom she would not see again till Monday. Herr Trapp had decreed it as far more important to invite a new and highly important client for an outing, in order to acquaint the gentleman with his wife, and particularly with his daughter, Angelika. It is easy to understand that on Saturday evening after the opera—whose closing hour Angelika could find listed in the newspaper—she had lingered in some suspense near the telephone. But in vain. The black thing had remained stubbornly silent, produced no electrifying tinkle . . .

A young man ought not to act that way.

Frau Trapp now asked about the cast of *Rosenkavalier,* and Neuberg, who never took any interest in those details, rummaged rather distractedly through his memory with the absent air of a person lost in thought who meanwhile searches through his trousers pockets for matches. However, he mustered together some sort of reply. At the same time he felt enormously annoyed by all the to-do. For actually Angelika was supposed to have gone to the opera with him on Saturday night; but the Trapps had suddenly decided that it would be improper for the (not yet officially) affianced couple to go out in public unchaperoned.

With the overbearing and autocratic bumptiousness characteristic of men of his type, Trapp now interrupted the musical chitchat between his wife and Neuberg. He thrust it all aside and took up his earlier subject: "As we were driving out through the suburbs Saturday night I noticed again how the police completely overlook a certain kind of public disorder. I'm referring to people running wild in automobiles. Nowadays there is a type of automobile rowdy whom I should have convicted as a felon. There I was, at the wheel as usual, the chauffeur sitting beside me, and all of a sudden—we were already pretty far out in the suburbs—a regular horde of whooping redskins comes tearing along. Heading the party was a small roadster, followed by four or five cabs, the whole lot of them bunched together and taking up almost the whole width of the street. It was a regular auto race, and back of that mob were another couple of passenger cars. The whole gang were shouting back and forth at the top of their lungs—and naturally not a single policeman in sight . . ."

Angelika laughed. "That *would* happen to *you*, Papa . . ." (It was well known that Herr Trapp had never driven more than forty miles an hour, and held the chauffeur down to that speed, even on the open road. The ladies of his family found this lagging pace a bore.) Neuberg again looked across at Angelika, but she avoided his eyes.

"If everyone drove the way I do, there would be no accidents," Trapp said emphatically, with a faint note of irritation. This statement could not be disputed . . . yet Herr Doktor

247

Trapp proceeded to develop upon it.

Neuberg did not pay attention. His fiancée was again keeping her eyes averted from his, perhaps with the same obstinacy as he himself had displayed a few moments before, and he was conscious of a keen vexation. Neuberg looked at the dark-green liveried back of the servant who was carrying a tray out of the room. The mild blue lightning of electric sparks from the streetcar line hung in the windows for the span of a second, and he heard the approaching rumble of the cars. Suddenly Neuberg had a mental image of Stangeler; he heard him speaking, vividly recalled his gestures, and was immediately overwhelmed again by astonishment: did he really need all this (for in one swift mental operation he lumped together Herr and Frau Trapp, his fiancée, the manservant, and their whole milieu)? And what was the reason for it? And how had he ever stumbled into it? In these few seconds it seemed to him that only the smallest fraction of his life hitherto had really been his own. "You drift into it," he thought, "and all of a sudden you're caught. And here they are sitting around me. And I have somehow to answer for a telephone call I did not make. Ridiculous. Stangeler is right."

Meanwhile Angelika had begun talking in a light chatty tone: "Director Dulnik would have liked to have driven faster yesterday, but you gave him such a lecture at the start that he didn't dare go a mile over forty. It was funny the way he kept glancing anxiously at the speedometer every so often . . ."

"Listen here," her father said, "when I take someone with me as my guest and trust him with my car, I think I have the right to insist that he abide by the speed limit I set. Incidentally, I know that Dulnik is an excellent driver. But that doesn't mean I'm going to abandon my principles."

Neuberg's attention had been aroused (or he had awakened, if you will), and he was looking across the table with

248

a somewhat inquiring expression. Frau Trapp, fulfilling the requirements of social form, explained amiably: "Herr Dulnik is the gentleman who was with us yesterday. Director Dulnik, one of my husband's clients."

"A very likable person, incidentally," Angelika said to her father. "There is something so calm about him, so reliable . . ."

"Oh, he's terrific!" her father interrupted her. "He not only has good ideas but the money to put them into practice. What's more he's a man who can do a day's work, for all his ideas."

"You say he's something of an inventor? What exactly has he invented?" his daughter asked.

"Oh, this and that. But his last thing . . . well, that isn't fit to mention right here." Trapp began to laugh loudly. His family looked astonished. Trapp waved his hand in dismissal. "I'm not supposed to talk about it anyway . . ." He laughed again and choked slightly over his cigar smoke.

While Herr Trapp was still coughing, his prospective son-in-law's newly awakened vexation had reached such a pitch that the latter completely lost his balance. His understanding of his own situation deserted him; he became wholly involved in a craving for vengeance, and committed the enormous indiscretion—once Trapp *peres* spluttering had subsided—of talking about his supper with Frau Ruthmayr and Financial Counselor Levielle after the opera Saturday night. It may well be that he sang Friederike's praises far more extravagantly than was justified by the feelings she had aroused in him. At any rate, he made it sufficiently plain why he had forgotten to telephone.

But even as he defiantly went on speaking in this manner, he was overcome by a sense of such alarm that he involuntarily tried to qualify his words. For their effect upon Angelika was unexpectedly strong (after all, Neuberg knew her well).

She turned slightly pale, especially near her temples—always a bad sign with her—and then flushed, so that she looked on the point of tears. Neuberg paused, breathless. He seriously feared a scene, a scandalous outburst. For once he was really grateful to old Trapp, who of course took no umbrage at the account of the supper and, equally of course, never noticed the change in his daughter. Trapp immediately snatched at Levielle's name.

"Well, well, him. A fine bird. There's no understanding that woman. You say you were in her box, Neuberg? That's something you oughtn't to do, by the way. I wouldn't want—well, well, it's not important. After all, you don't know anything definite about the man. Who does! Except for a few people, absolutely confidentially. Surely you remember Friedl Ruthmayr?" he said, turning to his wife.

"Why, of course!" Frau Trapp said, nodding slowly. "Why, when we were children . . ."

"Tell me" (Trapp almost always interrupted his wife when she spoke), "what is the whiskery old sourpuss up to these days? Did you hear anything at all . . . ?"

Neuberg had not yet completely adjusted to this sudden turn of events. His acquaintanceship with Levielle was extremely superficial, and his relations with him simple and unequivocal. Levielle was a type who considered himself obligated to make the proper gestures, now that he had crawled out from somewhere in the depths to the sunny surface of life (just where the original depths were is unknown even to the writer of this chronicle). Thus he felt a responsibility toward "culture," whatever the word meant to him. Levielle had made a number of grants for academic scholarships, stipends as they are called. He had been known to underwrite certain scholarly undertakings. Young people recommended by the proper authorities (this counted for everything in his eyes) could apply to him for small grants to be used for study tours, and so on. Highly praiseworthy, no doubt about it. . . Well, this whiskery old sourpuss, as Herr Trapp had disrespectfully called him (I do not know why, for I never saw Levielle other than clean-shaven and wearing a small brush of a mustache), this sourpuss with the imagined whiskers, then, had once paid travel expenses for Neuberg, enabling him to go to Italy for a month. The person who had recommended Neuberg and arranged the whole affair had been that Councilor von Rottenbach who had been mentioned during the conversation in Frau Ruthmayr's box at the opera. In the course of this business the young historian had at one point been introduced to his patron. This was the origin of their acquaintance, and that was all there was to it.

"I hardly know him," Neuberg therefore replied, and reminded the Trapps of his tenuous relationship with Levielle. At the same time this turn in the conversation was providential for him. Angelika had been somewhat startled by her father's remarks, which were necessarily incomprehensible to her since she knew Levielle only by name, her fiancée having mentioned that gentleman from time to time. For a few moments she was therefore diverted from her sulk. Neuberg profited by the opportunity to redeem himself by indicating that Levielle's invitation had resulted from a chance encounter at the opera, and that he could not very well have refused since he was under obligation to the old gentleman. Consequently, he had had no choice but to visit the box (he turned to Herr Trapp as he said this), once he had run into Levielle in the lobby and been asked to come up during intermission . . . In any case, he added, Levielle was important to him, for his career, and might continue to be in the future. Moreover, any discourtesy toward Levielle would have been an offense to his teacher, Herr von Rottenbach . . .

251

We cannot forbear to remark that if old Trapp had so low an opinion of Levielle as he had hinted, or if he was better informed about the man than Neuberg, from sources of his own (and this appears to have been the case), this was the moment for him to rush into the breach. The least that could be expected of a respectable lawyer, property-owner, and future father-in-law might have been something like: "My dear Neuberg, you will no longer need to depend on old Levielle. Leave that to me. Naturally you are right not to wish to offend anyone, but as far as your future studies are concerned, you need not, as my son-in-law, depend on the dubious patronage of this financial counselor."

But far from it! When the discussion showed signs of turning in this direction, Herr Trapp lost interest. "Of course, of course," he said. "You're quite right about that, Neuberg. I did not mean what I just said to be taken in any rigid sense . . . If the man is important to your career, if only because of his connection with your teacher, you have to be on good terms with him. That showed good sense in you, and you were absolutely right. Never push anybody so far away from yourself that you can't bring him back when you need him . . ." And with this fine bit of advice he snatched a newspaper from the table and vanished behind it, henceforth participating in the conversation only by interjecting a remark now and then.

If we were to imagine that the feud between our affianced couple had been cooled, suspended, or even terminated by this interlude, we should be sadly mistaken. Neuberg was now furiously desirous of talking matters out with Angelika. In the Trapp household, however, there were considerable difficulties in the way of such a talk. The couple were never left alone, or at most might sit together in an adjoining room, with the doors open, if they could find some excuse well within the bounds of propriety for doing so. Usually the reason given was that Neuberg had to help his fiancée with some work for her classes at the University. Right now, however, no such subterfuge presented itself. These restrictions were in any case peculiar, for the Trapps could not help but know that the young people frequently met with each other alone, not only at the University but in town and in the country.

Neuberg, then, wanted to lure his Angelika away from the table and out of the room for a few minutes, or at least to the farther reaches of the dining room, where several easy chairs stood clustered. The young man was no longer feeling the least bit quarrelsome or vindictive. He tried to make his conciliatory wishes plain by small signs. His fiancée, however, who had sensed them even before he revealed them, responded with an unyielding passive resistance, and just as he himself had earlier pretended innocence, she now did the same.

This behavior, of course, roused Neuberg's vexation afresh. At this point Frau Trapp asked: "Shall we have a game of patience?" When Angelika rose to fetch the cards, which were kept in the card table at the back of the room, near the easy chairs, Neuberg immediately sprang to his feet as if he intended to anticipate her. They found themselves together at the back of the room. Neuberg was prepared to whisper some words to his Angelika, and tried to protract their stay at the card table by rummaging through several drawers. But Angelika straightway picked the pack of small cards out of the front left-hand corner of the top drawer and returned at once, perhaps somewhat too quickly, to the table. There was nothing for him to do but return too, and sit down again under the lamp.

Herr Trapp rustled his newspaper. Mother and daughter set the cards out in rows. Neuberg, for his part, sat foolishly looking down at the place on the tablecloth where the bread basket lay between two napkin rings. He felt exhausted. A painful mood of emptiness and heaviness settled upon the room.

Finally the paterfamilias yawned.

So it was time to say good night. Neuberg made his farewell to Frau Trapp with a heavy, overdrawn, and altogether reasonless cordiality. Herr Trapp again extended his hand in that lax casual manner of his, while he held his other hand over his mouth, yawning again and even more expansively. Then it was Angelika's turn. With her left hand she carelessly muddled the laid-out cards as though it were no longer worth while to finish the game. When Neuberg had kissed her right hand, she looked into his eyes, gaily and very warmly, and said: "Eleven o'clock tomorrow at the lecture, all right?" She seemed to have forgotten their whole war.

"Yes, of course," he replied, and at the moment he forgot everything, including the fact that he had to have things out with her. The maid, who had entered in answer to the ring, preceded Neuberg through the rooms, switching on the lights. In the spacious polished vestibule the butler was holding Neuberg's coat ready for him to slip into.

Stangeler, the sprites of freedom circling round his head, had meanwhile landed in another café. For the streets were cold; winter set limits to idle strolling. Nevertheless, René was determined not to go home yet.

He began to feel really good. The only negative factor was that he had quarreled with Grete, and that because of the ugly scene he had a guilty conscience. Otherwise, freedom was delicious. If it could have been attained with the full accord of Grete Siebenschein, it would have been perfect. But he did feel a trace of uneasiness, and this feeling was growing. For here was the secret by means of which Grete could have bound her half-savage lover to her: by leaving his freedom, or what he conceived as his freedom, completely untouched during these crucial years. For him such a relationship would have represented the firmest of ties, as firm as any sweetheart could have desired. But Grete seems never to have apprehended this: she could not completely espouse this principle, which had recently been hinted at by Frau Steuermann.

René could have telephoned her from this café and asked her forgiveness. She had once more succeeded in putting him in the wrong; by telephoning he could to some small extent assuage his guilt. But he circled warily about this decision in the course of an hour's leafing through newspapers and magazines. In those days people's opinions of him and the image he presented to others were still very important to René Stangeler. And now he had gone and made that damnably poor show in the Siebenschein dining room.

He would have to set that straight. That was actually how he phrased it to himself. Just setting it straight would have sufficed for him: a superficial reconciliation, something that did not touch him inwardly at all, just an exchange of a few friendly words. That was what he really wanted before the day was out—in his insane childish egotism. But still he could not make up his mind to go to the telephone; meanwhile he was becoming more and more sluggish and sleepy.

At last, and too late, he abruptly made his way between the white marble tables, only a few of which were still occupied, down the whole length of the room to the telephone booth.

The signal sprang into being; in the wires was a distant humming of a thousand other lives; and out of them all emerged, single and distinct, the voice of Frau Irma Siebenschein.

Stangeler was tempted to hang up. A tangible sense of dreariness and weakness overpowered him, almost paralyzed his tongue, robbed him of his otherwise winning persuasiveness, his warmth, his buoyancy. Nevertheless he answered (diving headfirst into the business, as it were), giving Frau Irma his name, though expecting trouble, at least hinted reproaches if not a sharp reprimand. Nothing of the sort came over the wire. When he asked for Grete, Frau Irma, coldness itself, in that almost baritone voice of hers which always affected him disagreeably, asked him to wait a moment. Then he heard her calling loudly: "Grete! Telephone!" And there came the sound of approaching footsteps.

Grete seemed unaware of who was calling; perhaps her mother had not informed her. "Hello?" she cried into the telephone in an ebullient friendly tone which greatly heartened René.

Thus encouraged, he said all sorts of things to her which on the whole came down to a plea for forgiveness. But every word was brittle in his mouth and literally resisted being pronounced; many of the words, especially those he had planned to say, he could not find. She answered him now in a completely altered voice. Whereas her tone at first had been reassuring in its ebullience, quite unlike that of a person in a state of agitation or psychic torment, the pitch now seemed to drop several octaves, so that it sounded shockingly like her mother's.

"No," she said very slowly. "There's no point. I am not coming down." (In his rising agitation he had asked her to come to the front door, at least for five minutes!) "No. Please hang up. I'm going to go to bed." Then she fell silent. He, too, did not speak. Between them the wires hummed, and the tension was unbearable.

"Grete . . ." he said.

"There's no point to it any more," she said quietly. "Good night." There was a click. She had hung up.

CHAPTER 8

The Origins of a Colony (II)

ON THE Tuesday after Captain von Eulenfeld's revels, I ran into Stangeler on the street. He was, it seemed to me, in a wretched state. When I asked him whether he was still suffering from a hangover, I did so only to provoke him. I soon learned of what had taken place at the Siebenscheins' on Monday evening; in fact the story came out in a rush. I recall that a fat woman who was walking down the street paused in her course, turned around, and stared after us for some time; it was only afterwards, when it was too late to greet her, that I realized it had been Clarisse Markbreiter.

Stangeler must have remained unhinged for the next several weeks, and no doubt this was why he did not get in touch with Schlaggenberg throughout this time, although Kajetan had asked him to telephone. When we met on the street I asked Stangeler whether he intended to call on Herr von Schlaggenberg soon, but received no reply.

The snow which had fallen heavily in February lured Quapp and her brother out of doors. The countryside around Vienna, with its rolling hills and soft slopes, is wonderfully suitable for leisurely ski expeditions, and there is a special charm for the dweller on the outskirts of a big city in being able to reach open, snow-covered fields without needing to take a long ride. Only a few hundred yards from your front door you can strap on your skis and slide off toward the sugared hills which surmount every street. From the Kahlenberg ridges you can see parts of the city, divided into segments by the snow-wreathed trees, lying like a dark lake at your feet. On the easy return journey it greets you with the first early sprinkling of light.

René, however, crossed the trail of Quapp and Kajetan on a wooded declivity facing away from the city. They were coming from above, to the left, and he was making a traverse from the right. Kajetan and René immediately recognized each other, which has always seemed to me remarkable in view of the entirely different setting and attire of their first meeting. Each of them slowed up in a stem turn, and the momentum carried them close together. Quapp followed in Kajetan's track. "This is Stangeler," he said to her. "He was with us too that night I've told you about." The two men drew off their mittens and shook hands.

They continued their jaunt together, and ended it with tea at Schlaggenberg's. The angle at which Quapp and Stangeler encountered each other was determined by the circumstances of both as precisely as the angle at which René's and Kajetan's tracks had intersected. From the very beginning Quapp regarded Stangeler as a kind of pioneer on the road of her inner development and her music, which at this time she considered as one and the same. Later on, Stangeler was in a devious manner to deepen this unfortunate misconception of Quapp's.

Above all, however, at this first meeting a kind of socket joint instantly snapped into place; henceforth it served to support and to allow play to Quapp's persistent conviction that René was the right and only pacemaker for her along a track which would inevitably lead her far away from all her entanglements during the past winter in Vienna, and from all such entanglements in general—would lead her away from all this and into the depths of her art. Of course she assumed without more ado that her art lay at the opposite pole from such affairs. This socket joint in the mechanism of the situation was created (as such bits of machinery almost always are) by an altogether trivial happenstance: the fact that his lordship René, who could not afford a ski suit, was wearing an old pair of riding breeches and his erstwhile uniform tunic, a dark blue one such as had been worn by cavalry officers in the old Austrian army. It made, as a matter of fact, a good-looking outfit. The jacket provoked several queries from Kajetan, who asked among other things whether René had chanced to participate in a cavalry attack during the war. Stangeler, who had actually been in one such old-fashioned skirmish—although on the smallest scale—began to tell about it. Halfway through he suddenly broke off his narrative with the words: "But that isn't really how I experienced it."

"I don't quite see what you mean," Schlaggenberg murmured (naturally enough!).

Whereupon Stangeler, instead of finishing his story of the skirmish, began telling what he called the essence of the experience. The essence of it for him, he said, was that the whole of life, in the form of a vast number of vivid images, converged on him with tremendous sharpness while he was galloping with his contingent over a gently sloping meadow past a tiny springhouse, actually no more than a largish box from beneath which a thin gleaming trickle of water emerged, the cool shaded spring felt rather than seen under the wee roof. . . And on either side the snorting horses, the flashing sword blades. "Ever since, when I hear phrases like 'the breadth of life' or 'all of reality' or 'the wide world,' as they say, or anything like that, all such concepts have been comprehensible to me in terms of that experience. For it was then, in the flash of a second, that

I grasped the truly astronomical distance which intervened between my jogging saddle and the quiet silvery gleam of the water."

"As they say"—the phrase gave Kajetan food for thought, as he later told me. Who were these "they"? People who apparently expressed themselves more fluently and skillfully, and probably also more conventionally, than René Stangeler, who for that very reason appeared to dislike them. Because things were easier for them to articulate, or in general?

Now the socket joint snapped into place.

"Yes!" Quapp cried. "That's it! Things always have twisted and grandiloquent names. Cavalry attack, World War. I've had a similar experience, though naturally it hadn't anything like the incisiveness or scope of Stangeler's . . ." (Schlaggenberg observed that René was beginning to writhe inwardly.) "Once, a long time ago, last summer, I realized what playing the violin means, what it demands, and what a true tone is. And the way I recognized it was—by the nickeled screw on the frog of my bow. I ran to my room right away . . . it was back home, at our place, in the country . . ."

Thus it was that those key phrases were born, "spring-house" and "frog," with all their implications, the beginnings of a jargon which was to be resented by the other members of "our crowd." On the whole, this first conversation among the three moved at a lively pace, and toward its latter part they began without preliminaries—almost without the slightest transition, as Kajetan told me—to address one another with the familiar pronoun of the second person.

Just by the way—because the matter has come to mind—I used the *Du* with Captain von Eulenfeld right from the start, though he was not a fellow-countryman. On the other hand, Kajetan and I always employed the formal pronoun. Things of this sort are mostly decided right away, *ab ovo,* and do not change.

So much for that. In retrospect I would say that Quapp's life would not have taken the peculiar turn it did had it not been for her strange relationship to Stangeler. At times she literally used his company like a drug to ward off onsets of weakness, or what she considered to be "weaknesses." For that other province of her life, which had caused her so much torment during the previous winter and well into the summer, had not been swept from the face of the earth, or buried beyond resurgence, by Quapp's new resolution to keep her eyes fixed on the frog of her bow, or something of the sort. . . Thus she was soon to take up with a person who was far removed from René Stangeler and from everything else she considered at the time to possess validity.

For all the sympathy I have always had for Quapp, I felt her double life at this time must have been distinctly barbarous.

Stangeler—grieving over his Grete, who this time would not make up their quarrel—seems to have overlooked Quapp right from the start, even at that first tea. I asked him what he thought of her. "Very talented. Seems to have what it takes to make some kind of splash." When I made my question plainer, he said: "Yes, pretty, I suppose so. A nice, slow-moving sort. Most of the time she sits like a mason after the twelve-o'clock whistle, arms hanging down between her knees."

The Sunday morning after the meeting on skis Schlaggenberg, at my flat, opened a new chapter in his life. Certainly all his actions were unlike himself. I was still in bed. Standing in the doorway with an astonished Maruschka behind him, he took off his coat and tossed it across the width of the room to the sofa. His hat followed. "So you have known this fellow René Stangeler a very long time, as I learned yesterday!" he said, sitting down on my bed without more ado and looking at me like an inquisitor. He nodded his head slowly as though he had caught me in a shabby trick which he had long anticipated. It was almost as if he were saying: "I always thought you a scoundrel—now here's proof of it."

"Would you care for some tea?" I asked.

"Of course I would care for some tea," he said. "What do you think? Kindly spare me such frivolous asides. Then you admit you have known René Stangeler a long time. Do you see him often?"

"No," I lied. "In any case, how do you know about my old acquaintanceship with Stangeler?"

"I heard about it from the captain. I was with him last night, drinking. We were by ourselves and undisturbed, there in his den, and I started telling him . . ."

"So you spent last night helling with the captain. And here you are up and about and dropping in on me by nine o'clock Sunday morning. What went wrong?"

"Look, it's none of your business how much sleep I get. As I was saying, I was talking to the captain . . . Well, I'll have to tell you about it too, and a few other things, to bring you up to date . . ."

Meanwhile my morning tea had arrived. Schlaggenberg fell to without delay. He described the encounter on skis. Breakfast took half an hour, and it took him all that time to render his account. "I can't really blame Eulenfeld on this score," he concluded. "He hadn't seen Stangeler for at least six months before the drinking bout in January. But now it's your turn. Are these all the cigarettes you have? They'll hardly last us . . . Oh, good, here's another box. Should I go out and get some? Oh, well, if you have enough—all right. Now kindly answer my questions. Do you know some people by the name of Siebenschein?"

"Yes. But not through Stangeler."

"Then how? I had the impression you frequented quite other circles. Oh, of course. That's it. Your bridge partners! Stout ladies. Well-stuffed, eh? Frau Starkbreiter, isn't it? I suppose the road to the Siebenscheins leads through those circles. Highly interesting, most important, Frau Starkbreiter . . . !"

I must admit I really came fully awake for the first time at this point in the conversation, as I became conscious of something I might almost call danger, though I could not see its outlines clearly. I distinctly felt that something was in the offing. Of course it really did not concern me, could not possibly matter to me. . . It is odd that I instantly feared Schlaggenberg might provoke some kind of scandal in connection with these people. My consciousness still overshadowed by sleep, I nevertheless had an extremely crucial insight (or at least I know today that it was crucial). Schlaggenberg went on talking without waiting for any response from me, telling me what he had learned from the captain; much of what he related was already familiar to me, though now it was given a peculiar Eulenfeld twist. And as he spoke I suddenly thought of the odd similarity and dissimilarity between Schlaggenberg and his sister. And like an inspiration it occurred to me that Stangeler, in spite of his oblique eyes and his altogether different appearance, had a face that belonged to the same category of faces as those two. While this was revealing itself to me, I realized with the utmost distinctness that the faces of Kajetan and Quapp were absolutely lacking in a single common family trait, whereas . . .

At this point Schlaggenberg's peroration disturbed my train of thought: "You know the way he talks, of course." He was referring to the captain, of whom he now gave an imitation.

"'Seems to have found an anchorage there, the Ensign, I mean. No need of it, no need of it, I should think. Not that I mean to say anything against the girl . . . '"

"How do you know all this?" I asked him, and then he said something about two girls of his *troupeau,* you know the ones, that gang we were with shortly after the New Year. It seems these two girls are acquainted with the family, or rather with the sister of Stangeler's lady-love—Mush or Lush is her name . . ."

"Lasch," I said.

"Lasch, if you like. Eulenfeld happens to know this Lasch woman too, but all he has heard about Stangeler comes, not from her direct, but from the girls. . . And now will you kindly tell me how *you* come to know the Siebenscheins. Through Steuerschul? Altwolf? Starkbreiter?"

"Why murder the names to suit your prejudices?" I remarked and fell silent, not caring to say anything more. For as he talked on I had at last had a clear vision of what had been tantalizing me all along . . . A face appeared before me, one seen many years before and belonging to a person no longer living with whom I had had only the most casual acquaintance. It was Ruthmayr, Frau Friederike Ruthmayr's husband, landowner and cavalry captain in the reserve, killed in Galicia in 1914. Here was a real similarity—that between him and Quapp—a distinct kinship in physiognomy! And suddenly I had to break into laughter. For it burst upon me that I, and I alone, knew where we had landed at the end of that memorable night of carousing—for after all, I knew the Palais Ruthmayr. Subsequently I had not acted upon this knowledge in any way, although the mystery was much discussed among my fellow-revelers. At the beginning it had seemed too fantastic that none of the participants should be capable of finding the place again. When it turned out after all that they had been quite as drunk as they claimed, and really had no conception of where they had been, I became even more firmly resolved to keep my counsel. What were my reasons? Was I acting from a sense of discretion toward Frau Ruthmayr?

"Will you now most kindly deign to inform me how you know this Siebenschein family," Schlaggenberg at last said bitingly, blowing cigarette smoke rudely in my direction.

"Do you absolutely insist on knowing?"

"I do."

By this time I was so irked by his conduct that I said curtly and unsparingly: "Through your wife. She met the Siebenscheins around the middle of December in Kitzbühel, and took me along to see them one day after Christmas. It so happened that I already knew the lawyer, Ferry Siebenschein. Frau Irma Siebenschein, incidentally, is one of your father-in-law's patients."

"If Camy associates with the Siebenscheins, it surprises me that she doesn't know Stangeler."

"That is easy to explain. For more than a month now, your wife has not been in Vienna. That leaves only the time roughly between Christmas and New Year's for her association—if you want to call it that—with the Siebenscheins."

"Where is Camy?" he asked.

"In England," I replied, observing him closely. It was fairly obvious that my information stirred him, but I could not make out whether he felt relief or a sense of depression remotely related to longing.

He must have done some rapid and careful reckoning, for suddenly he exclaimed: "Why, then she left at approximately the same time as that wild party of Eulenfeld's during which I first met up with Stangeler."

"Not only approximately. Exactly the same time, the very same night. She left by an evening train. I myself took her to the station and went on to Eulenfeld's apartment, where part of the *troupeau* was already gathered—I had decided to go along this one time, to please Eulenfeld. You saw me there, though only for a few minutes. Afterwards I stumbled into a car filled with people I did not know at all, and at the first bar I was crowded into one of the booths, so that I didn't catch another glimpse of you until we reached that studio, or whatever it was, where all those people were."

"And you did not think it necessary to . . . ?"

"No, why should I have?"

"All right, all right. But you know," he suddenly blurted out, "it's simply too disgusting! New acquisition—what's her name? Siebenschein. Of course. It all fits together. Against Stangeler too, of course, I can well imagine . . ."

"Listen here, Schlaggenberg," I interrupted this flight of fancy, which was becoming all too characteristic of him, "you seem to be living under the delusion that everybody who has a different nature or a different attitude from Herr Kajetan von Schlaggenberg's has nothing more important to do and spends all his time thinking about establishing a kind of Anti-Schlaggenberg League. A rather egocentric idea, it seems to me."

"But a correct idea," he said firmly, not the least chastised. "If you think it is exaggerated and egocentric, you're right as far as the facts of the case are concerned. But you're not right 'biologically,' if I may put it that way. This idea happens to be one which I ride like a wave; it raises me up high, so that in special circumstances I can perceive what is essential for me and my life sooner and more clearly than when things appear upon the normal horizon at objective sea-level. But from everything you say I gather that the territory which Stangeler has made his own for the present is virtually forbidden ground for me. Quite aside from Camy—incidentally, how long does she intend to remain abroad?"

"How does that concern you?"

"You seem to have taken a lease on my wife."

"Your wife intends to return in the autumn, at the earliest. And I have in no way taken a lease on Camy. Incidentally, you know perfectly well that in this affair I stand entirely on your side, perhaps just because the blame rests squarely upon you and because your behavior was of the kind which might arouse—and does—cheap indignation on the part of almost anyone. Since as it happens I know a little more about it than just anyone—well, enough of that. There is scarcely any question of my sympathizing with Camy."

"Then what prompts you to—associate with her? I mean, to maintain or continue your association?"

"In the first place your own interests, my dear fellow. So that there will not be still more territory forbidden to you. Or to put it another way, so that there will be someone around to look out for your reputation a bit. But in the second place it would have been positively dishonorable to drop Camy like a hot coal after your breakup."

"Right. But—is my reputation really that bad?"

"Rather. Consider the situation. A deeply offended woman. What's more, the opposition party takes a stronger line than even your wife would approve."

"So you too speak of an 'opposition.' Strange. Apparently my idea isn't so insane after all."

"Perhaps there really are two parties, after a fashion," I said at last, speaking in a murmur, as if to myself, "two parties whose members sort of recognize one another at first sight.

Anyway"—I pulled myself together—"it's all nonsense. What makes you think you have to enter the Siebenscheins' territory in order to be close to Stangeler? Damn it all, leave them out of it. Stangeler has plenty of friends and cronies from the war who have never met the Siebenscheins. All nonsense!" I repeated to reinforce my point. "Please . . ."

He laughed in my face. "You seem to think me a halfwit," he said. "Kindly omit your claptrap and tell me straight out whether, as far as you know, my evil reputation has already spread among these Siebenscheins. That is all that interests me at the moment."

To this I replied quietly: "Yes. As far as I know, it already has."

"Have you any substantial evidence?"

"Yes."

"What is it?"

"Fräulein Grete Siebenschein considers you an utterly despicable individual." I really saw no reason to equivocate, or leave Schlaggenberg in doubt. Perhaps the truth would do some good here, or at least avert some evil. "She said so straight to my face," I added.

"And of course you did not say a word in contradiction," he said, laughing.

"Of course not." I entered into his tone.

He stood up and began pacing the room in silence, taking long strides back and forth. I noted again a belligerent expression on his face. Suddenly he waved his arms wildly and began exclaiming loudly: "Steps must be taken! Absolutely! The devil with your nonintervention policies! Maybe they're all right in general. Maybe so. In most cases intervention isn't worth the trouble and leads nowhere. Very well. Besides, intervention distorts our picture of the world. As soon as we begin making demands upon a person, with the idea of changing him and his life, we cease to see him clearly. And yet the time comes when this sort of thing, too, becomes a duty. A duty we must undertake—in spite of native indolence. There's more behind this matter than you think. We'll come back to it again sometime, won't we?" As he spoke these last words he had slipped into his coat. "You will see, you will see . . ." he added, already in the doorway. And with that, he left me. Somewhat tired, with a sense of submission to whatever might come, I sank back onto my pillow.

It was around this time that Eulenfeld, and later Gyurkicz, each independently of the other, moved out to the garden suburb, thus becoming neighbors of ours. Both gave various and widely divergent reasons for taking this step. Thus Eulenfeld alleged that he had moved out in the hope of escaping the insomnia that plagued him throughout the spring and summer. It seemed that this beautiful and quiet neighborhood had been made fashionable by Schlaggenberg's appearance in it. These removals indicated quite plainly that in spite of everything Kajetan still formed a kind of pivotal point in our society.

In the case of Gyurkicz, however, it turned out that he had special reasons of his own for coming out.

No one really knew much about Gyurkicz's past. He had been an army officer and was supposed to have distinguished himself in some way during the war. His father, a Hungarian landowner, had shot himself over some gambling debts when Imre was barely six years old; such, at any rate, was the tale I heard. These same gambling debts accounted for the loss of the father's huge estate in Sexad County. Gyurkicz himself would sometimes elaborate on his participation in the Hungarian civil war which led to the overthrow of Bela Kun's Soviet government. At a relatively early age he seems to have come into the possession of a fortune from various collateral inheritances. According to his own statement, he proceeded to squander this money as fast as he was able. His mother had married a second time, and since Imre had been unable to get along with his stepfather, he had gone out into the world when he was still a young man.

This was about all the substantial information we had concerning Imre von Gyurkicz. (Strictly speaking, to be properly Magyar, his name should have had a different ending.) In recent years Imre had lived with a woman who for a time was very well known to the Viennese public, more because of her eccentricities than anything else. This affair had by now faded out of existence, although at one time it had been reckoned a grand amour. In fact the story went that Gyurkicz had once attempted suicide on account of it. At any rate, that was now long since over and done with. Only sluggishness held him for a while in their common apartment, where he had a kind of studio room of his own; the place was in a somewhat disagreeable quarter of town. His wife (she was generally regarded as that) had meanwhile struck up a new liaison with, so it was said, a member of the high nobility. But she still went on living there with Imre. It was obvious that these conditions had long been due for a radical change. Gyurkicz was ripe for moving, if nothing else. All he needed was the impetus. That was provided by Quapp.

As we may recall, Schlaggenberg had said a few words to her about Gyurkicz on the railroad platform immediately after her arrival. Perhaps he had done so with conscious or unconscious intent. At any rate the picture of the Hungarian he sketched for his sister (and during the following days he returned to him again once or twice) was pithy enough and perhaps calculated

270

to appeal to Quapp . . . "A simple, healthy, masculine fellow. You can't take everything he says seriously, but he's a good sort. Without problems and tragic undertones. Naturally it wouldn't do to set too high standards for a chap like that; the honest straightforward comradeship the two of us have could not be called an intellectual affinity. That sort of thing is out of the question, of course. But he's the man for fresh air, uncomplexity, athletics. I envy the fellow, incidentally. He has a first-rate job as a caricaturist on a big newspaper, and earns his thousand a month with no trouble at all . . ."

At each mention of Gyurkicz, Quapp had, however, asked about Stangeler, whom Kajetan had referred to only once and then very briefly—though apparently in such terms as to arouse a greater interest on her part. But at that time, before they had all met one another out on skis, Schlaggenberg himself knew virtually nothing about René and could give Quapp only some of the impressions he had gathered on that famous crazy night.

The first meeting between Quapp and Gyurkicz, however, came about by sheer chance. It happened in a restaurant where Kajetan and Quapp were dining. It was altogether exceptional that they should have been here, for they almost always took their meals in a small, rather rustic inn in their neighborhood. This time, however, Quapp had called for her brother at noon, and they had ridden into the center of town together.

Gyurkicz did not arrive alone. Accompanied by two other persons, he passed the window embrasure where Quapp and Schlaggenberg were sitting, and Kajetan hailed him. As he turned, the light from the window brought into prominence his large blue eyes, which held a look of unusual good nature and, at the same time, a pining childlike quality. Still and all, one could tell that Gyurkicz was well aware of the effect he could achieve with those eyes in certain circumstances, and that he must often have sought this effect . . . Quapp greeted Gyurkicz with a somewhat reticent openness after Kajetan had made the introductions. Meanwhile Gyurkicz's companions lagged behind for a few moments, in a posture of uncertainty and expectation. After the usual formalities were completed, the whole party joined Kajetan and Quapp at their table.

A man and a woman had come with the Hungarian. The woman's name was Hedwig Glöckner. She was the head of a popular gymnastics school and seemed at first glance cordial and forthright, a young woman who worked hard, perhaps too hard, and had the rather brittle shell and somewhat mildly deformed nature of such persons. The man with her was someone Schlaggenberg already knew. His name was Robert Höpfner; he was immensely tall and strong. His twisted face was reminiscent of a crescent moon, or of that type of crescent-shaped roll which is called *Kipfel* in Austria. His chin was long, sharp, and slightly off-center. There was, indeed, something disconcerting about the crookedness of that facial axis.

Gyurkicz, brash and direct as he was, fixed upon Quapp at once and bombarded her with the usual questions: since when had she been in Vienna, and had she been there before, and what was she doing there, and how did she like it? She replied that she was working toward becoming a real violinist. "But does a person have to work all the time?" he countered and immediately passed on to another subject, a new film he had seen the day before. Then he spoke about dress, declaring that in his capacity as cartoonist and sketcher of fashions he naturally knew something about this subject, and that she absolutely must wear a different kind of hat. With a few deft strokes he outlined the shape he had in mind on a paper napkin. This sort of thing was quite new to Quapp, and while she looked on in sheer amazement he drew a face beneath the hat—moreover, her own face, a passable likeness in the form of a well-meant caricature.

All of this was a glimpse into another world for Quapp, who was simply astounded by aptitudes so completely out of her sphere. Schlaggenberg, who was half at home in his sister's mind, grew anxiously aware of the host of misunderstandings this little incident might plant in her; he saw that she was on the point of according reverence to abilities possessed by every third-rate talent, abilities which come to the surface in such people simply for lack of any better substance underneath.

When they had finished dinner, Gyurkicz asked whether any of them had anything special in mind, for otherwise he would suggest that they all come to his studio, where they could "brew up a pot of coffee" and relax. Schlaggenberg, who through long travail had formed the habit of completing the bulk of his daily stint in the mornings, so that he need undertake nothing but revision or some other less earnest task in the afternoons, could have agreed without a qualm. But he waited, saying neither yes nor no, holding himself fluid, as it were, so that Quapp could take whatever course she preferred uninfluenced by his decision. The conflict of her feelings was mirrored promptly on her small face and her serious forehead. "I really ought to be practicing now," she said, and seemed to be listening to something inside herself; perhaps she was actually hearing a concerto of opposing voices in her own mind. She looked across the table at her brother, but he carefully avoided giving her any directive. "I wouldn't mind," he said with the greatest unconcern, so that she should understand he had not by any means expressed a wish.

The group decided to walk over to Gyurkicz's place; it was in the downtown area and not too far. Hedwig Glöckner led the party, with Kajetan and Robert Höpfner on either side of her. Gyurkicz and Quapp followed behind. In places, the sidewalks in the old heart of Vienna are extremely narrow, and the traffic heavy, so that the party was bound to break up this way.

Quapp felt a sense of strain, and a slight pressure within her head, especially in the region just behind her ears. Gyurkicz was firing a whole barrage of genial, careless questions at her, each of which he had left far behind by the time Quapp began, with considerable difficulty, to formulate her reply. For she actually went into each of his questions in a serious and thorough way; every one of them really set something in motion within her. And yet at the same time they were so framed that, from Quapp's point of view, each had first to be straightened out and reframed . . . "How do you go about it, trying to be a violinist?" he said. "You say you get up early in the morning and practice for hours on end?"

"Yes . . ." she said.

"And isn't that boring?"

"Yes," she said, "it's boring . . ."

"Then why do you do it?" he asked.

"I'm happy when I can do it . . . I can't always."

"Then sometimes you like something else better?"

"No," she said, "there is nothing better."

"I can't figure you out . . . If it's boring . . . ? How do you like these suede jackets?" He had stopped in front of a shop window. Quapp, who in all seriousness had intended to explain to him what it meant to her "to be in form," and that happiness or well-being were simply inconceivable to her without this factor—Quapp stared, wrenched from her train of thought, at the suede jackets. But she was weak enough to enter into Gyurkicz's manner and even to venture an opinion—that, say, the jacket up front, on the left, would probably be the most becoming.

They walked on. Gyurkicz stopped in front of shop

windows five or six times more, usually in the midst of conversation. This conversation must have been difficult enough for Quapp without such side issues. Moreover, the streets were slippery here and there, although the snow had been cleared away, and Quapp was wearing new shoes whose soles were still very smooth. The result was that she felt insecure walking, so that the sense of strain which was in any case all too usual with her became even more pronounced. She made every effort to grasp this new country which was so casually opening up before her. Above all she wanted to learn to respect it, for she assumed at once that it deserved respect, if only because it was new and incomprehensible to her. Respect was her strongest faculty, while that vigorous summary criticism which eliminates so much waste in life, saves strength, and avoids detours, was her weakest.

"Back home we have gypsies who are simply terrific on the violin without ever having studied it like that—I mean, the way you are doing, and people at the conservatory."

"That's something altogether different," Quapp said. She knew with absolute certainty that that kind of fiddling was different in essence from hers. But here occurred one of her gaps in thought and expression, gaps which Kajetan would occasionally help her to fill. She felt incapable of continuing and explaining more precisely what she meant.

Probably she would not have been given the chance to explain in any case. For Gyurkicz said: "I play the violin too. But there's something very mysterious about that: I can play only when I'm drunk."

At this point Quapp was able to pull herself up short with an energetic little jerk, and draw off from him at an inward tangent. At that same moment she found a finished, clear statement on her lips: "That, see, is what makes the difference between a gypsy fiddler and a real musician."

"How's that again?" he said, and out came his usual line, one he was accustomed to adopt with young ladies as soon as the preliminaries of conversation were past and he felt somewhat better acquainted with them. "What do you mean by 'real musician'? Perhaps the others are the real musicians, people with natural genius who don't need to practice all these intellectual things for hours every day. Have you any talent at all, young lady?" he went on, already slipping into impertinence.

She replied with perfect calm: "No."

This one little word, with which she passed right over his taunts in a manner quite beyond his comprehension, with which she returned to her own proper sphere, should have taught Gyurkicz the kind of person he was dealing with—if, that is, there had been the faintest hope that he could learn anything. Instead he said lightly: "I'm going to study music too. I'll knock it off in three years. Want to bet?"

"That is quite possible," she said pensively, with a modesty which no longer had the slightest connection with good manners but was simply a by-product of reflection.

"What shall I study? Piano? Of course, piano. I have to be able to accompany you, after all . . ."

By then they had reached the house in which Gyurkicz lived. All of them went upstairs together. There were many flights of stairs to the studio floor. Gyurkicz unlocked the door of his apartment.

The morning of the next Sunday, two weeks after Schlaggenberg barged in upon me, Eulenfeld paid me a call. I had already finished dressing when he arrived. "Morn'n." he said, and dropped into the armchair by the bookcase. It was a gray day. The snow on the meadows, which I could see from my window, was beginning to melt, for it had warmed up somewhat, but as yet there was not the slightest foretaste of spring in the air.

"Are you in your new digs yet?" I asked, and he scribbled his new address on a sheet of paper. Then we breakfasted together.

"I spent last night with Schlaggenberg," he remarked after a while. "I—hmmm—have come to see you in connection with that. Wanted to ask you about something."

Odd, I thought. Saturday nights they get drunk together, and the problems that come to the top on those occasions are brought to me on Sunday morning. It was beginning to look like a regular institution. I had to laugh.

"Well, what's this?" he asked. I told him that Schlaggenberg had been to see me just two weeks before . . . "I've come more or less on Kajetan's account," he said.

"What is this all about?" I asked, with some foreboding.

"Do you know who a certain Herr Levielle is?"

"I do. That is to say, as far as anyone can know."

"I see. Now listen to this . . ." And then he told me—though of course with his customary wide digressions, marginal comments, aphorisms, and Latin tags—that on the day after his move out to Döbling he had decided to pay an inaugural visit in his new district and to call on Kajetan.

The landlady, an exceedingly friendly woman, had informed him that Herr Schlaggenberg had left to call for his sister, and that they had probably gone into the city. While he stood in the vestibule, Eulenfeld had noticed a visiting card of Levielle's— it lay in solitary splendor in the center of the big green bowl placed there for the purpose. (Incidentally, it soon turned out in the course of Eulenfeld's story that he knew quite well who Levielle was.) Naturally I knew the very green bowl he meant.

While the captain was standing there, reading the card as bold as you please in the landlady's presence, Stangeler appeared; he likewise intended to visit Kajetan. The two frustrated callers went to a quiet nearby café and fell into a rather prolonged conversation (*"non sine libationibus"*—the captain, it seems, drank several glasses of rum). They talked about a good many things, but in particular they together "took the bearings" on the Ensign's situation. At one point Eulenfeld asked René with a degree of sternness whether it was true that on Monday, January 10—that is to say, two days after the great nebula—he had quarreled with Grete Siebenschein in the vestibule of her parents' home, and whether in the course of this quarrel he had struck her. René pleaded guilty to the first charge and utterly denied the second.

"So I thought," the captain responded. "I gave several people what for about this business. The nerve of them."

What sort of people were they?

The very same ones who had, the story went, brought René to such a state of intoxication that he had, the story went, been the worse for drink all day Sunday—in short, people belonging to the damned *troupeau* which he had now, having changed his quarters (*"Rubicone transgresso"*), left behind forever, so he hoped . . .

Among other things Eulenfeld commented that René had been seen on Monday the 10th—it must have been immediately after the above-mentioned quarrel—in a café, obviously in a perfectly balanced state.

"Yes," Stangeler said, "there were some '*troupistes*,' there, as you call them. But I didn't speak to them."

The captain was aware of that too. "Everything noted. Lia, Ria, Mia, they have hundreds of eyes. Like flies. You might make a note of that for your deeper study of the biological sciences.

278

As far as I'm concerned, it's as clear as it's disgusting that regular and well-worn paths—and maybe Frau Titi Lasch is not the only one of them—lead from such creatures straight into your friend Grete's family, and without a doubt to the young lady herself. There's Lasch, that ill-smelling tuber, and right behind him Levielle—well, I'll say nothing about him. So there you are. I moved yesterday. That's part of the story too. I want to clear out of it. Schlaggenberg is right. I wanted to talk with him about it too. Kept after me to tell me the whole story, he did. So we're going to turn over a new leaf. Though it's not so easy. That whole crew from right after the war are still hanging on to me. Some of the boys and girls are nice enough, they'll really go out of their way for you. But inside—good night! And as your friend and fellow-officer I'd like to—hmmm—suggest a similar course for you too, offer it for your consideration anyway. No more than that, of course. Still and all, give you a lead."

However, the captain's roundabout allusions to a link between the highly respectable Siebenscheins and the *troupeau,* in which there were not a few little Lasches (or people who would have liked to be Lasches) as well as numerous species of the genus "Titi"—this whole attempt on Eulenfeld's part to persuade Stangeler also to turn over a new leaf, for which the captain had his private reasons (the same reasons which had prompted him to change his residence)—all this was inevitably lost upon René. For René had only recently come to regard the *troupeau* as a striking contrast to the glum sobrieties of the Siebenscheins, as a symbol of freedom and independence, even, as we have mentioned earlier, as actually "spiritually fructifying" (!) . . . And was Eulenfeld now asserting that the two realms were one and the same?

So his lordship René had apparently not taken hold of the

rope the captain had thrown to him.

In the course of this conversation with Eulenfeld I learned a few things about Stangeler's current life of which I had had no inkling. For example, I learned that during the past year he had not been writing his articles on historical subjects at home. These articles—one of them, on Gilles de Rais, had brought us together again—were composed in his Grete's room when she was not around. It is understandable that such semi-journalistic work, which was destined for publication in the magazine section of newspapers, would not go as well amid the walls of books and the pure scholarly atmosphere of the Historical Institute. Still, René had given a variety of reasons why he was no longer working in his room back home but was doing his writing in the Siebenschein apartment. For one thing, he reported that since the departure of his sister Asta some distant relatives from Bohemia now lived on the second floor of the Stangeler house; they were mother and daughter and had been informed beforehand that René's room was sacrosanct. They were therefore trying to drive him out. The mother, in particular, made her proximity felt as unpleasantly as possible, raising a frightful din in her quarters, which lay next to his, and so on and so on and so forth. (Part of this was true, part of it imagination and a minor attack of paranoia.) When someone asked for René on the telephone, she answered rudely; this was particularly embarrassing to him, he said, when editors called up to ask for a piece. . . He had finally arranged to have people call him at the Siebenschein number in the late afternoon; Grete was very competent and took messages for him when he was not there. The other reason that René shifted "the weaving of his textiles to the home of the Shining Seven," as Eulenfeld punned,[1]

---

1. *Sieben* = seven; *Schein* = sheen; *scheinen* = to seem.

struck me as more significant. "It's better for me that way," René had said. "I feel that more and more. At Grete's there's a certain atmosphere of brightness, lightness. Besides, I much prefer that part of the city; it's really meaningful to me, and always has been. Ever since I was a boy. You know Liechtenstein Strasse in the vicinity, where it narrows down, and there's that building called the Blue Unicorn . . . But the main thing is that my room at home is where I spent my childhood. I looked out the same windows at the same houses, and watched the sparrows in the trees of our garden or in the next-door garden, listened to them chirping away on summer evenings just as they do today, with the sunset rose-red beyond the same chimneys at the same time of evening—funny the way the horrible façade of the apartment house in front of that bit of sky took the color and vulgarized it, changing it to a sugar-candy pink . . . Anyway, it gives me the shivers. Ever since my return from Siberia I've been stuck there. And ever since, I've kept wanting to move right across to the opposite end of the city."

"And so these days he is weaving his textiles where the Seven Stars reign supreme," the captain concluded.

In spite of a residue of hostility, I felt extreme sympathy for Stangeler at this moment. I could well understand him. What he said about brightness and lightness struck me most forcibly. People are entitled to do what they can to fend off the onslaught of depressing factors from their environment or from their past, or from both, since each is contained in the other.

My room was bathed in somewhat sallow light, from the reflection of the outside snow, whose random melting revealed patches of discolored grass. But the sun did not emerge. Eulenfeld stretched out his long legs and drank the cognac which I had produced after breakfast. Now that we were sitting silent for a little, I looked above my head, into the upper emptiness of the room, where wall and ceiling met. The stillness of this Sunday morning was almost absolute. Nothing could be heard, not a streetcar, not an automobile; no one was playing the piano anywhere in the house, or letting water run through the pipes.

At any rate, from all that the captain had said it was evident that all was well again between Grete Siebenschein and Stangeler—though the reconciliation had not yet taken place at the time René encountered Quapp and Kajetan on the slope of the Kahlenberg, in the snow.

The captain rambled on. He had asked Stangeler whether it was possible to work without disturbance at the Siebenscheins'. The working conditions were excellent, Stangeler had said. In Grete's room, he enjoyed complete privacy. Nowadays the maid always led him directly to the room and treated him with the greatest politeness. This maid, incidentally, was the only source of noise in the apartment, inasmuch as she apparently had difficulty communicating with Mama Siebenschein, or vice versa. So that at times he could hear Frau Irma at the other end of the apartment saying something three or four times, with rapid insistence, until the girl at last grasped what she meant. . . There had been only one real disturbance, Stangeler had said, about three or four days before—three or four days before his meeting with the captain, that is. That had been due to some kind of conference in the Siebenschein apartment between the son-in-law, Cornel Lasch, and an old man with a falsetto voice.

At this point Eulenfeld himself had asked: "Levielle?"

"Yes, he was the one," René said. "I didn't see him, by the way, only heard the voice. The two of them were talking incessantly in the adjoining room, just as I was arranging my papers and preparing to start writing. I managed to begin nevertheless, just because the talking was continuous; I quickly accustomed myself to the constant hum. Like the barracks in Siberia. I used to have no trouble doing my writing there. This time, however, that falsetto voice bothered me; it had an unpleasant penetrating quality."

"*Summa summarum,*" the captain concluded, "it seems to me, *mihi videtur,* that what we have here is one sweet muddle. With him up there at the Siebenscheins' writing an article on good old Ulrich von Hutten—that was the one, I've read it—and those two in the next room providing a musical accompaniment by arguing over what I can damn well imagine are other subjects, devil take it all, here we've got ourselves right at the peak of the messiest damned sichuashun, haven't we, one hell of a mess outside and inside. That whole business of Lasch and Levielle, side by side, right next door, that's all we needed, fits like a glove."

But, to keep to his language, things "could be worse," and the very looseness of his speech was proof that the captain's equanimity had not been basically disturbed by the "sichuashun" he had described.

But the mention of Levielle led us back to the visiting card in Schlaggenberg's vestibule.

"Tell me this," the captain asked, "did you ever have the slightest idea that Schlaggenberg and Levielle associated with each other? I thought they were not even acquainted. Certainly I've never heard Kajetan mention Levielle's name."

"Levielle has known Schlaggenberg's family—for years, as far back as I can remember. That much I knew. But I've never heard of his seeing Kajetan. Still, all it may amount to is the renewal of an old acquaintanceship dating from Kajetan's boyhood. You haven't asked him about it?"

"Me? You won't catch me asking!"

I was surprised by his circumspection. The thing must have been on the tip of his tongue a dozen times during the previous night's drinking with Schlaggenberg.

"You musn't think I want to spread any nasty gossip," he said. "Far from it. But to me all this means that—I wouldn't have thought—hmmm!—here I'm moving out to Döbling just to get away from these ghosts of the past. And in Schlaggenberg's vestibule I find the visiting card—hmmm!—of the so-called financial counselor. Don't misunderstand me, Georg. I personally have no bone to pick with the man; I've never had a thing to do with him. But that name is like a symbol to me. Or let's say rather: an omen. And then to find it here in Döbling and in Kajetan's own place."

"Perhaps the fellow looked Schlaggenberg up in order to play the philanthropist—this time in the field of literature. Rich patron calls on young writer. Perhaps he wants to give Schlaggenberg a little grant, so he can go traveling." (Was my wish father to the thought?)

"That may be," Eulenfeld growled. "Incidentally, I'd like to meet Grete Siebenschein," he said after a while. "She's beginning to interest me."

"That should not be difficult for you. You could easily meet her through Titi Lasch," I said cautiously.

"Not so. Don't want to come to her from that side. So far as I know, there's a bit of prejudice in that direction. That is, in spite of family loyalty and all that, Fräulein Grete is supposed not to think very highly of her sister's circles—you know, the *troupeau* and all that crew. Though when he says: 'Grete hasn't anything to do with all that,' there's a mite of exaggeration . . ."

"Who says that?" I asked.

"Stangeler. Anyway, I don't want to arrange it from that side."

Now I knew what he wanted of me. I saw at once that Schlaggenberg was behind all this, Schlaggenberg with his determination to take action . . .

"How did you find Schlaggenberg yesterday?" I asked. "Distracted, or depressed, or in good humor?"

"Somewhat distracted," Eulenfeld said.

I suddenly hit upon what seemed to me the proper parry. "I can't advise you to seek an introduction to the Siebenscheins," I said. "You'll find you don't have a very good reputation there."

"Don't give a damn," he replied, showing not the slightest interest in this aspect of the matter (extremely unlike Schlaggenberg, it struck me). "Don't exactly have a burning desire to impress. But Stangeler, you see, and all that . . . By the way, I know the apartment in question. Was up there once with Titi, when nobody was home."

"I suppose Schlaggenberg wants you going in and out of there because for good reasons he himself cannot," I said bluntly.

"True enough, true enough. Don't mind telling you the truth. He's kept after me about it in the past, and started last night again; I'm supposed to get introduced to the Siebenscheins through you."

"I wouldn't dream of it," I said, and we changed the subject.

About a week later—it was already March—I found them all together, the whole of "our crowd," and a few others besides. Of the others I knew only Neuberg and Hedwig Glöckner with any degree of intimacy; the former had probably been brought by Stangeler, and the latter by Gyurkicz. The face of Holder, the editor, aroused in me only vague recollections of the famous night—I had seen him at Eulenfeld's at the time. There was likewise an American doctor of philosophy—perhaps a zoologist, but I was not sure—named Williams. He was accompanied by a smashingly pretty young girl from Bohemia, Emma Drobil. They must have been introduced to our group by Eulenfeld, who frequented a café in Josefstadt which was also the headquarters for a club of American physicians studying in Vienna. I supposed a zoologist could easily have drifted into such a circle. Later Eulenfeld confirmed my supposition that he had met Williams there. That March evening Williams talked chiefly with Stangeler; for the rest he and Emma Drobil entered into the fun mostly as good-humored, laughing observers.

It was a kind of minor party which was being held at Schlaggenberg's place, in celebration of Eulenfeld's and Gyurkicz's move out to Döbling, which had meanwhile been accomplished. In days to come we would refer to this evening as the "foundation festival"; at the time, however, none of us could have perceived that we were entering a new phase inwardly as well as outwardly.

The vestibule was hung with coats, and below these stood a whole row of overshoes, for we had just had fresh snowstorms; the last stages of the winter were exceeding the winter itself in severity. I was the last to arrive. The maid, dressed in black with a white cap and apron (Schlaggenberg's landlady made a point of doing things well for a gathering like this, but she herself almost always remained out of sight on such occasions), opened the door for me and helped me remove my coat, while I tried to make out from the hubbub of voices behind the white-painted door who was present. In the vestibule I noticed a trivial detail: the green bowl near the mirror—in which not long before the captain had spied Levielle's visiting card—had vanished.

Then I went in.

It smelled good in the room. Schlaggenberg seemed to have sprayed the whole place with a pine scent. Added to that were the fragrances of cigarettes, tea, and rum. The predominantly masculine company—Quapp, Fräulein Drobil, and Hedwig Glöckner were the only ladies—produced an even rumble of voices in an impure bass. On the sideboard stood a huge samovar, steaming lustily. Next to it sat Stangeler, of course, probably because he felt at ease in the vicinity of this symbol of Russia. He looked in excellent spirits, and moreover seemed especially well dressed (probably he'd had his best suit pressed). A lively conversation seemed to be in progress between René and the American, a fair-haired, vigorous-looking, long-limbed man; they did not even look up as I entered. Stangeler was illustrating what he had to say by movements of both hands, as though he were speaking of some winged creature. During our exchange of greetings, the rumble of voices subsided somewhat. The guests had all settled themselves comfortably about the room, sitting or half lying on the sofa, in the easy chairs, even on the bed, which Schlaggenberg had stripped of its bedding so that it looked simply like a very wide and long ottoman.

I avoided the group in which Quapp and Gyurkicz were sitting and found a seat near the samovar. Here, in addition to Stangeler and the American, were Neuberg and Höpfner, who was listening—this struck me at once—with exaggerated interest to the conversation of the other two. I asked Neuberg how Angelika Trapp was, and inquired about her parents. Meanwhile Captain Eulenfeld had appeared from somewhere at the back of the room and asked Neuberg: "Do you know the Trapps?" I replied for the young historian, explaining to Eulenfeld that Neuberg was engaged to old Trapp's daughter. The captain sat down beside us.

"We once sold a car to your father-in-law *in spe*," Eulenfeld

287

said. "I was representing an English company at the time. That was how I met him. I still remember an enormous dining room in his apartment—tremendous room, really; I'd been invited to dinner."

"Yes," Neuberg said, laughing. "And the table stands in the middle, looking very small. I believe I've heard Herr Trapp mention your name, Captain. Incidentally, Herr von Geyrenhoff has told me a good deal about you." He smiled in his engaging, simple-hearted fashion, his face spreading wide.

"I suppose he's handed you quite a yarn, eh?" Eulenfeld said, indicating me. It struck me again, during this interchange, what a horde of people the captain knew. Mention any name at all and there was a good chance that he knew who it was or had even met the person.

"Do you happen to know Director Dulnik?" Eulenfeld asked. I noticed Höpfner raise his head at the mention of this name.

"No," Neuberg replied, "but I have heard the name at the Trapps'."

"There's a very odd affair going on right now, in connection with Dulnik. It's all been very hush-hush up to now—but at last the secret project has had its wraps taken off. Oh well, no harm in telling it, the ladies are out of earshot," he continued, turning slightly. "It seems these geniuses have hit on the magnificent idea of exploiting a hitherto unused surface for advertising purposes—hm, well, to be brief; I suppose you know that Dulnik runs a paper mill." He mentioned the name of a plant situated about two hours' ride from Vienna. Höpfner nodded. "In this plant he also manufactures paper for—let us call it hygienic use. A while ago someone sold him the idea of printing one side of this paper with advertisements, and in verse, no less. Naturally only pure, nontoxic, harmless inks could be used for the printing. Herr Dulnik is looking forward to exercising a significant influence upon the human race by this means. He maintains that this is the only opportunity to bring a message to modern man—when he is in a really collected and receptive state of mind. And a message in an attractive poetic form, moreover."

Everyone laughed except Neuberg, whom I had known at other times to be somewhat immoderately risible. This time he looked preoccupied, even a bit depressed. After a while he turned to the captain and asked: "Just what sort of person is he really, this Herr Dulnik?"

"I don't know him too well," Eulenfeld said. "A handsome man, though. About forty."

Our laughter had aroused the attention of others. The conversation revolved a while longer around the drollery introduced by the captain until one of the ladies—Fräulein Glöckner—joined us. Then the subject was changed. Up to this point my eyes had been roving the room while I listened. There was much coming and going across my field of vision, but at last I was pleased to spot what I had been looking for. The bowl from the vestibule now stood here, pushed off into a far corner of one of the shelves of the bookcase. At first I had not even recognized the thing, for it was capped by a lid that obviously belonged to it but had previously been absent.

In my distraction I next found myself engulfed in the group of which Quapp and Gyurkicz were a part. Schlaggenberg, it seemed, had unobtrusively taken me by the arm and steered me over there. I was annoyed. Of late it had happened that I had seen Quapp and Gyurkicz together two or three times, and each time the sight of them as a couple had been intensely painful to me. They were always talking in that insane manner we have already witnessed, talking past one another, with

Quapp laboring hard to "understand" him and with Gyurkicz apparently chiefly concerned in projecting his masculine dignity and proving his superiority. To make matters worse, Schlaggenberg—upon whom I privately called down a few curses—brought up a difficult, not to say infamous subject. (He seemed to be feeling his oats that evening; of course nowadays I know a good deal more about the whole matter than I did then.)

They were discussing, of all things, the ancient question of the possibility or impossibility of "pure" friendships between man and woman. One could not help suspecting Schlaggenberg of deliberate malice in launching this topic; perhaps he wanted to amuse himself by demonstrating Gyurkicz's inanity. But to whom? Quapp had already had samples enough of that swaggering stupidity—to what avail? At any rate, the discussion soon grew lively, and seemed to arouse the intense interest of one person in particular: Stangeler. With that keenness of hearing characteristic of him in such situations, he quickly realized that over there in the other corner some thick problematical stew was being stirred, and he left his place beside the samovar and came over to us.

In the course of this conversation something came to light: that Stangeler, Quapp, and Schlaggenberg all used the *Du* to one another. This did not surprise me, for I had already heard it from Kajetan. But the fact apparently offended Gyurkicz. The first time Stangeler employed the familiar form in addressing Quapp, Gyurkicz frowned as though he had not heard aright; the second time he displayed ostentatious astonishment; and the third time he committed the folly of asking Stangeler when he had established so fraternal a relationship with "this young lady." The battery of conflicts on the point of boiling over here was so ill-concealed, so glaring, so plainly marked with the brand of utter futility, that dreary boredom overcame me at the thought that all of it would have to come out, be worked out in reality, and played out with all of reality's little deviations.

I would gladly have rejoined Eulenfeld at the other end of the room, where the captain now seemed to be faring splendidly with Höpfner and the excellent Fräulein Glöckner. But at the moment I could not escape. The most harrowing thing about the whole situation was its transparency. To Gyurkicz that instantaneous brotherly relationship between Stangeler and Quapp was something incomprehensible, and would remain so; of that there could be no doubt. For he himself was utterly lacking in the qualities that could permit such a friendship with a girl like Quapp, even if his infatuation had not stood in the way. Without his infatuation, in fact, he would never have given a girl like Quapp a second glance. Schlaggenberg knew that perfectly well, and for this reason I was furious with him. Toward Quapp I felt absolute disgust throughout this episode. She was already up to her ears in Gyurkicz soup, and treating the fellow's inanity like someone who, having found a long hair in his soup, goes right on eating, not wishing to let himself or others take notice of this embarrassing circumstance, while at the same time trying to fend off the foreign body by complicated feints with the spoon.

Schlaggenberg contributed little to the conversation. At one point, however, he said: "In most cases it will be sheer fraud. Either a love-relationship is growing, and the friendship merely serves as a screen because a certain type of woman needs that kind of thing to satisfy her sense of propriety; or else the friendship follows after, as a stage in the atrophying of love. In both cases it does not appear independently, as the sole bond. Of course there are states of suspense that can go on for years with the matter hanging in the balance—such affairs can even last a lifetime. They are mistakenly cited as examples of friendship between man and woman. On the whole all that is sentimental rot."

"But it is possible for there to be friendship and simultaneously love," Gyurkicz observed.

"Yes, but we are not talking about that now."

"Then we ought to."

"Still and all, real friendship may very well exist between brother and sister," I took occasion to interject.

"A special case," Schlaggenberg replied. "Only because the path has been cleared by the blood-relationship. In all these things we must look to see where the center of gravity lies. In any such intimacy between brother and sister, is the bond the friendship they feel for each other? Not at all. Rather, the friendship is tied to the blood-relationship. To my mind, friendship between man and woman is the rarest of phenomena. All other possibilities must actually exist, but the fraternal relationship must have established itself as the most powerful operative force, must be acting independently as a governing principle and, by its own activity, exclude all other possibilities."

"Now look here," Gyurkicz said, with a great show of cogency, "in that case your couple would still be lying to themselves, since you yourself have just said that all such alleged friendships might have been on a different basis . . ."

I noticed how Quapp checked him with an impatient wave of her hand. "You don't understand what Kajetan means," she said. A scowl appeared on Gyurkicz's manly countenance. He was, it was clear, going to take this in bad part. At this point I at last succeeded in escaping from the group. Someone called to me from the other side of the room, and I was only too glad to cross over. Once again I settled down beside the samovar. Since in the meantime Fräulein Glöckner, Höpfner, and Neuberg had begun talking about modern dance, a topic which the captain found most boring, Eulenfeld rose (the act seemed quite involved because of the massiveness of his shoulders), circled the little group, and sat down near me, at the end of Schlaggenberg's bed.

"Have you already noticed it?" he whispered to me. "The bowl of wrath?"

I nodded. We now knew enough—but in reality knew nothing at all.

In the meanwhile a general conversation had been launched, and gradually this united the whole company, drawing all of us into it. Conversation is, perhaps, too fulsome a word for it. Rather, there was a hectic exchange of crisscrossing exclamations, phrases, beginnings, attempts to take the floor—that is, to catch hold of a pause—and efforts to speak simultaneously with others.

Someone, apparently, had remarked that we could sense the dawn of a new era, that the period which had begun immediately after the war was now drawing to its close. Phrases like "sterile revolutionaries" and "utter rigidity of this whole attitude" were bandied about; and in the course of all this the talk grew surprisingly loud. I had had no idea hitherto that so many different opinions prevailed in our circle.

"The most repugnant feature of it all," the captain put in, his quiet manner securing him a hearing more readily than the blatancy of the others, "is the supercilious dismissal of values which, I think, will live longer in men's memories than all this other tripe. The upshot has been that a man who did his duty as a soldier and lost his life in battle has been treated as a ridiculous figure and the whole thing so twisted that it's made to seem that he laid down his life for a swindle. Until recently you did not see the phrase 'a hero's death' except in quotation marks."

"I beg your pardon, Captain," Neuberg made reply. "You are still speaking exclusively on the basis of the old views . . . It's time we realized that those are the very root of the evil, from which wars will come again and again—inciting the people to mass psychosis. So we're perfectly right in regarding some poor devil who died like a dog at the front, not knowing what for, as a victim, if not exactly as the victim of a swindle—that is too crude a judgment, I grant you. But he certainly is the victim of outmoded ideologies . . ."

Eulenfeld did not answer. He sat stooped forward, and I observed to my astonishment that his nostrils were quivering as though he were striving to catch an evanescent scent.

"We can never do enough to oppose war and all that," Fräulein Glöckner exclaimed. "Only recently I was reading a pamphlet, 'Documents from the Western Front.' What indescribable horrors—it must never happen again. Our sole mission must be to prevent war by all means. That should be the foremost thing in everyone's mind. We ought to think of that and nothing else every minute!"

"I can perfectly well understand your taking this view as a woman," Schlaggenberg said. "Still, something so entirely negative as the prevention of war cannot constitute a position, and . . ." The rest could not be made out. Gyurkicz and Holder interrupted simultaneously. I caught Holder, the editor, saying: "But that isn't purely negative, not at all, you take too formal a view . . ."

Gyurkicz produced the following gems: "I liked being in the war. We always got plenty to drink. Once I was a prisoner of war, too; a captive of the Russians, too, incidentally." (He was evidently thinking of Stangeler.) "But their rations were awful, so I gave them the slip. Taken purely as a sporting proposition, war is fine." For the first time I became aware of how vain he was, and sensed that his healthy simplicity was merely a fake, something he put on.

I saw, of course, that Quapp, who had been following the conversation with strained attentiveness (for she always took everything in deadly earnest), looked pained at Gyurkicz's words, though her embarrassment was mingled with contempt for her own suffering. She raised both arms, stretched slightly, and placed her hands lightly at the back of her head, almost touching her ears.

Stangeler made the strangest impression on me. He had been listening with greedy absorption to Eulenfeld, Neuberg, and Hedwig Glöckner; and now Holder, who had been unable to get a hearing from the others, was jabbering away at him. What was going on in Stangeler's mind must have been incredibly muddled and terribly depressing. He sat there like a miserable hunched fetus; even his face gave the impression of crawling back inside itself, as if it were shrinking and would shortly disappear entirely except for the forehead. I could not hear, of course, what Holder was saying to him, but it would scarcely matter, since I doubt that he was listening. Quapp, too, was falling into the conversation like a non-swimmer lurching into the water.

Meanwhile, however, the talk had shifted like a flag in the wind, as so often happens in all kinds of society. They were now off on something entirely different, another favorite subject: "today's youth," also known as "the younger generation." As always, falsetto obbligato voices arose on the surface of the topic. Right off, there was talk of "sports," soon followed by "comradely, frank relationship between the sexes, real friendship between girls and fellows"—though someone growled out "sounds like a mooncalf sort of business to me." (I need not tell you who had made this last remark.)

I was no longer listening. Instead, I studied Quapp, who kept leaping from one to another of these rapidly tossed-off observations, in breathless confused pursuit of what was being said. She had long since had to abandon the solid ground of ideas for which she could find tangible examples. Stangeler still sat in his embryonic posture. Gyurkicz simply looked on with a superior expression, which was probably the best he could do.

It occurred to me by the by that none of those present had any connection with this much-discussed "youth of today." Neuberg, who was the youngest in the room, had passed his twenty-fifth birthday. Quapp and Stangeler were older than that; in fact Stangeler was several years older than Schlaggenberg's sister. Once again I had to remind myself that Stangeler was already past thirty. Had I not been certain of the dates, I would have thought him the youngest of the company. In a sense he was, in spite of all. When I considered the matter, I realized that the people here belonged largely to the war generation, which of course included Schlaggenberg and Eulenfeld. This very fact obliterated the age-difference between them and René.

I, too, had popped out of the same box. It had always seemed to me—though I may have been only hoodwinking myself—that all of us had to continue representing the role of "youth" even after the war—perhaps just because of the war—although we had meanwhile all grown older. History, I felt, had overleaped the generation born too late to take part in the war or by some other fluke spared any direct relationship to those events. The members of that generation had had no personal experience with the turning-point from the old to the new. They seemed to lack all reference to everything except the desire for good living. Whereas we who had first awakened to personal consciousness on the battlefield acquired a tragic disposition from the start. We felt that we were not born for happiness, or that if happiness came our way it would quickly be lost again. And it seemed to me that we had a mandate not to lay down the burdens and the duties of youth (and René thought likewise, as I now know only too well!). We had to go on bearing the load until a new generation had grown up, one which unlike the faceless, overleaped generation would be caught in the gears of history and thus would release us, their wearied predecessors, from our unduly protracted youth. The terminus of the journey for us would be the same sword that had once awakened us to consciousness. Our destiny could not be "maturity." The sword would return us, still young, on the unchanged battlefields to the unchanging earth. For no pitcher goes to that well twice . . . Such was my general view of the situation around 1927.

"For this reason the present generation of girls," I heard Schlaggenberg saying, "is utterly unfit to become companions of anyone with aims going beyond bourgeois security—and that means simply and solely someone upon whom it is incumbent to represent youth—for at the core remaining young is an achievement of the spirit, ladies and gentlemen. These girls are unfit because there isn't one of them who has any grasp of the meaning of our life, of its historical legitimation, if I may put it that way. All they have any grasp of is their natural mission, the one that has come to them without any effort on their part, that is the same nowadays as it always has been: namely, to get themselves a husband and have children. Everything else is ridiculous pretense, or prevarication. In the end you'll notice that each and every one of these girls sooner or later has an attack of honesty. Then the 'intellectual companion' starts demanding a good provider. Enough, enough of this. It's as clear as it can be. Any man whose view is not blocked by accidental circumstances—for example, the unusual and almost paradoxical circumstance that the woman he takes up with happens to have a lot of money, which will make life easier instead of more difficult—and I almost think that such things ought not to be in the cards for anyone who is truly living out a destiny, which of course includes living in accord with the whole situation of his age, which would call, for example, for the lady in question suddenly and dramatically to become impoverished after the joyous nuptials—any man, I say, whose view of the general situation is not blocked, will have to recognize that there is no place at our side for these modern girls. Of course that's a misfortune, an altogether unusual and extreme situation. Incidentally, my own opinion is that we can without a qualm leave reproduction to the type of 'modern youth' who exist only in a zoological sense, so to speak. They will take care of it very well, and they're good for nothing else anyway. It may be that in this way a generation will be born whose brains are cleansed of all the old rubbish, so that they will obtain without effort what we have had to get for ourselves by hard labor." (I glanced casually at Neuberg, who was nodding vigorous assent, and realized how completely he was misinterpreting Schlaggenberg at this moment—fitting Kajetan's ideas in with what he himself had said earlier, of course.) "Well, no matter. The generation now living between two wars began their youth with rifle in hand and will probably end in the same way. It looks as though these representatives of historical continuity in Central Europe will have to hold off from the natural desire of their sweethearts—the desire to become wives and mothers. That has to be, if this cadre of young people is to cherish and pursue a suprapersonal mission. For these are people who in their innermost selves can never bend their lives toward a peaceful autumn. They all have a very special and intimate concern with death. That is

298

why we cannot offer these girls anything, since they can only get angry at us but never understand us. And they for their part can never represent anything to us but obstacles, guilts, misfortunes, and even, if we weaken, total ruin."

Now it was time to steal a glance at René Stangeler. He had passed from the embryonic state to one of openness and pure receptivity. Quapp was listening in the same manner; this, apparently, was stuff which she could understand. The picture presented by these two listeners and the speaker bordered on the ludicrous because of the three-way physiognomical kinship—it could not be called similarity—among them. The faces of all three belonged to the same class.

Schlaggenberg, meanwhile, began to lay it on thick: "However, there is one type of woman who belongs essentially to our between-wars generation and who for that reason is under a mandate, like ourselves, to prolong her youth, or rather to break through to a second youth, to find her second youth—which is ourselves."

No one quite knew what this was all about, except myself, for I already had a premonition of something dreadful. I suddenly recollected that odd, rather imbecilic expression which had come over Kajetan's face during his first visit to my Döbling flat, when he began showering me with those silly questions. Now, however, even those who had been bored—Hedwig Glöckner and Höpfner, for example—came to life.

"For what this generation between two wars needs is not the kind of girl who is waiting impatiently at the doors of life, waiting until the doors open and she catches sight of—the set dinner table. We are not concerned with these eternally demanding women who want to drag us off our path, force us to pursue their everlastingly monotonous ends. Our age has been thrown so entirely out of equilibrium—economically speaking, too—that such ends, which were formerly taken for granted, can no longer be pursued, let alone attained, except at the expense of the whole mission of young intellectuals. Perhaps we are weaker than our fathers. Perhaps people like us, if we are to summon up the energy for vital achievement, must be careful about broadening the basis of our lives; we must beware of all settling down, all anchorages, all ports . . ."

I began to realize that all this was aimed directly at Stangeler. For as far as Kajetan was concerned, these warnings were scarcely applicable. He already had been through this business of anchoring and, if one were to believe him, had come away with nothing worse than a few bruises.

At Schlaggenberg's last words René had fiercely tossed his head.

"What we need, fellows like us, is the mature woman, the maternal woman who is older than we are but has resolved to share our youth, to engage likewise in a prolonged youth, just as we have done—possibly not with such clear awareness of what it means, but in a woman that does not matter. The generation of women who are now approaching forty-five has been confronted with a great task during these past few years—but so far as I know, the ladies have not noticed it. Engaged in the trivialities of their lives, they have failed to grasp their mission. Which is to rescue and preserve us in a time thrown violently out of joint—out of a dusty and ancient joint, I might say. We have barely succeeded in holding our own mission above the waters of accident and pettiness. We have proved unable to resist the lures of the flesh—at least not for very long. It was up to these older ladies to save us until we had found relatively solid ground underfoot. Yet during these precious years we were thrown into company with a vacant-minded generation of girls who vegetate in the given fact, in the here and now, of girls who possess nothing but 'demands upon life,' as they like to call it, who have robbed us of enormous energies, have—I might almost say—drunk our energies like vampires . . ."

Some of us were beginning to realize what he was getting at and were listening with suspense and growing amusement. No one interrupted, although people are generally only too ready to leap upon any pause.

"But the mature woman, the stout woman, who has already been wife and mother, and who is no longer instinctively driven toward these biologic commitments the way a girl is—and our girls, I must say, often want this marriage-and-family business in order to legalize or eradicate a checkered past—the mature woman no longer regards these events with breathless suspense, like a student awaiting his graduation. She is finished with them; her social vanity no longer pants after them. And since she has gotten safely past that danger zone which among girls is characterized by such phrases as 'old maid,' 'spinster,' or 'left on the shelf'—and don't let anyone try to tell me that the 'free and independent' girls of today are any less terrified by that prospect than their great-grandmothers were—since, as I say, the mature woman has long since passed out of that condition and has attained a firm foundation for her life, she can reach out and take up other enjoyments, even some highly dubious ones. If only for that reason she gravitates toward our troubled youth; in fact she becomes, or can easily become, the partisan and supporter of our youth."

Gyurkicz seemed on the point of hectoring. Fortunately he did not have the chance, for Schlaggenberg went right on. Had Gyurkicz actually spoken, I suspect he would have run the risk of being slapped by Quapp, so intent was she on what her brother was saying.

"Now, however, nature comes to our aid . . . It is a well-known fact that many young men incline toward women far older than themselves, that they are especially attracted by this very type of mature, stout woman. Not that this is a universal rule. Nevertheless, many do feel this way, feel, I should say, a boyish attraction to this kind of woman. And when I say 'stout' I do not mean that in any figurative or metaphorical sense." ("Ha, here it comes," I thought.) "Far from it. The kind of woman I have in mind is a maternal, massive type of woman, the most feminine kind of woman, the very opposite of all our young ladies; a strapping, buxom, in short well-stuffed woman, to put it bluntly. And now I must add a strange note, a rather strange idea I have had. Perhaps it really is silly . . . But it occurred to me that all of us who have remained, as I said, young and 'immature' in a certain sense, must still be carrying, buried somewhere deep inside of us, our former inclinations toward such a motherly woman. We must reawaken our love for mature women, for this will be the thing which will lead us out of that area of dangerous entanglements . . . We must implant in ourselves a physical horror of the modern type of girl, of the sharp, denatured, sinewy, muscular character of these creatures, whose resemblance to maleness introduces an almost homosexual element into love . . . Yet all such qualities are by no means to be taken at their face value, for disguise the thing as they may, underneath it all is the old stew of marriage and family . . ."

At this point Gyurkicz took the prize with: "So we'll get ourselves a scale and weigh every woman—only ladies of mature years, of course. And if she's under two hundred pounds—whoosh—away with her!"

The burst of laughter disarmed even Quapp, and she laughed along with the rest of us. For my part, I was also laughing at the highly involved fashion in which Schlaggenberg was striking out at Grete Siebenschein. What a lot of trouble he was going to. If only he had known her. For Stangeler's beloved had little in common with the lean athletic girls he was so viciously making fun of. I doubt that she had any muscles or sinews at all. The fact was, at the time I thought Schlaggenberg was concerned exclusively with Stangeler and Grete. I never dreamed that he was ready to try out his own program.

When the hilarity had subsided, however, it turned out that there was a surprising amount of agreement with Schlaggenberg. Even Neuberg expressed hearty approval, which struck me as rather strange. Höpfner said in his sourish, embarrassed manner: "Something to it, damned if there isn't." Though I could have hit him for that, since I could very well imagine what the sole attraction for him was. Quapp kept nodding her head.

Meanwhile the maid had come in. She went to the samovar and began filling a row of glasses with grog. At her side the captain was fussily opening bottles.

"To sum the whole matter up," Schlaggenberg was now saying, and the way attention swung back to him attested to the power his speech had carried, "to sum it up in a phrase: for the men of tomorrow we want the women of yesterday, not the girls of today!"

The glasses had just been distributed. Eulenfeld picked up his, turned from the sideboard to face us, and cried: "Hurrah for fat ladies!" He raised his glass.

"Hurrah for fat ladies!" everyone shouted, amid bursts of laughter. Hedwig Glöckner laughed harder than anyone, and kept saying again and again: "I'll have to close my gymnastics school." She was a good sort who never spoiled our jokes.

I left toward midnight, together with Eulenfeld. It was cold, and the snow crackled under our feet. My way home led past his house.

"It occurs to me," Eulenfeld said, "that our René damn near met Frau Titi Lasch among my damned *troupeau* the night we had that party. She had been wanting to disport with us again for some time, and could have that night because Lasch was away on business. But I didn't think it would do, with Stangeler along; so we left her out of it. Too bad, though. It would have taught him a salutary lesson about the overlapping of two worlds. Hmmm."

"The portrait of Grete Siebenschein as one of these sinewy, sport-crazy girls amused me," I replied.

"I don't know whether he intended it quite that way. If he did, he was swinging wild. But I doubt it. He was getting at something else. A while back he was going on to me in just the same way, about fat women and all the rest of it. A pretty obsession. Though I must admit there is much to be said for the idea."

I remained silent and pursued my thoughts. At Eulenfeld's door we said good night. The door clicked shut, and I walked on alone over the crunching snow.

I had been living out here for nearly six months, out here in this neighborhood set high above the city where the twilights extend themselves wide and red in the open sky, while down there in the tightly packed rows of many-storied houses people are conscious only of the consequence of evening: that it is necessary to switch on the lights. Out here, the view was wide from almost every window. The eye plunged into a lake of darkness which upon closer study separated out along a gently curving line into night sky and mountains. You saw far across to the other side of the city and the lights of houses ranged one above the other along the slopes. You did not see the endless sameness of rows of street lights between equally endless lines of buildings. Rather, everything was dispersed here, and after nightfall the windows of this suburb awoke to light one by one, almost as in a village.

This spring, then, it would be six months, and yet it seemed to me that my actual stay in this quarter had only just begun. I was, moreover, spending more time out here than I had at the beginning. Unexpectedly, a change within myself had accompanied my change in residence. Imperceptibly, I had almost completely abandoned the old paths of social life in the heart of the city.

Such thoughts accompanied me on my solitary walk. I stood still for a moment. The street made a serpentine curve here and climbed the side of a hill to an open prospect. I looked down and outward. I thought about our circle, which had sprung into being with such rapidity and which already had a definable nature. It was borne upon me how imperceptibly and suddenly life forms such closed configurations—and though normally my whole desire was for detachment, I felt, standing there under the dark night sky in the pallor of the snow, that the suburb and its people were becoming a new, more tightly knit native place to whose fateful movements I was closely bound.

CHAPTER 9

A Delightful Conclave

THE CITY was beginning to wrap itself in greenish-blue twilight. Between the eaves of roofs, a last wedge of sunlight sent its rays down into the still wintry mist, but this almost unnerving testimony to the existence of open sky was visibly growing more and more abbreviated. Vehicles tooted and snarled, their tops and sides coated with the light of the street lamps. Along the façades of buildings crawled a broad continuous ribbon of light as shop windows were lit.

Frau Selma Steuermann had arrived first today, and sat amid the deafening gabble of the café at a big empty marble table in one of the "booths" by the window. The waiter bustled around her, making preparations for a conclave. It was obvious that something special was in the offing today, for from all sides the Parisian and Viennese fashion magazines were being gathered up, recalled on some polite pretext from faintly protesting guests of lesser distinction than the ones who were expected, and brought to Frau Steuermann. She hid them all, piling some on a chair at her side so that her widespread self shielded them from the public eye, placing others on the window sill behind the curtain, standing some in a corner or leaning against the wall. "By the time the other ladies are here, we'll have them all, Frau Steuermann," Max, the waiter, reassured her. He spoke in a tone of complicity based upon a long history of substantial tips.

Still to arrive were Clarisse Markbreiter, Rosi Altschul, Frau

Lea Wolf, and more or less as a guest in this group, Frau Thea Rosen, also called "the Madonna." (Today, too, conclave or no conclave, she would probably be meeting her young man somewhere at a safe distance.) Fortunately, Frau Irma Siebenschein was not expected. By tacit agreement, nothing had been said to her about this rendezvous; consequently, the afternoon promised to be pleasant.

Frau Steuermann added a magazine to the pile. But it was clear from her expression that she was not in good humor during these preparations. The emphatic quality of her gesture suggested that she would have preferred to sit there in peace and quiet, rather than act as a collection agency for magazines for the other members of the parley—who were of course late. Indeed, her mood might well have been expressed by Frau Siebenschein's "and all that sort of thing"—a discreet cover for a host of emotions.

Actually, the difficulty was that Frau Steuermann could well be called a beautiful woman. As a consequence, she was constantly being pushed—inwardly, at any rate—to the forefront of a contest in which she occupied far too wide a sector, according to present-day standards. Ever since that family conference in January, Frau Selma had made up her mind to win moral equality with Clarisse Markbreiter, and the two ladies now talked over the telephone every Friday (which was, we will recall, Clarisse's weighing day). They reported their weight to each other, for Frau Steuermann had undertaken to mount the scales too each Friday. She was now doing so regularly, to her soul's torment. Once a week she stood naked, white, and tender-skinned like a mussel torn from its shell on the ribbed-rubber platform of the scale in her bathroom. But with what result? What was the good of it all? Let us tabulate the results:

308

Frau Clarisse Markbreiter (pounds)	Frau Selma Steuermann (pounds)
167	$192^{1/2}$
167	192
166	191
167	$191^{1/2}$
168	193
167	194
166	195
167	196

Enough! Angrily she crammed the slip of paper with its dismal little table back into her purse. Those silly women were certainly taking their time again today. What did they have to do that was so important?

Frau Selma had nothing to do, no one to worry about. She was a childless widow.

Meanwhile the darkness outside was complete. The innumerable lights cut wide slashes into it. Frau Steuermann loved the look of the street, loved the hurry and bustle of it, and her thoughts as she watched it in her moments of daydreaming (in other words, most of the time) had a certain unitary character, pointed in the same direction, like wisps of cloud driven by the same wind; her thoughts usually drifted toward the same spot on the modest horizon of her desires. For example, every now and then a certain type of woman passed by on the street. To Frau Steuermann's eyes all these women seemed to be thrust, beneath their broad shoulders, into a steel corset. They gave her the impression that they had springs inside their impossibly narrow hips, springs which enabled them to leap like a bouncing rubber ball. That was how it struck her. When she was caught looking, she felt silly. She would at once assume her haughtiest air.

A waiter was going from window to window, closing the curtains by means of a hooked pole. The small metal rings at the top of the curtains jingled; the folds smoothed out. When the man reached Frau Steuermann, he shut off the horizon of her vagrant dreams. Everywhere inside the café great excess of lights had been turned on, some of them in small electric candelabra above the individual seats along the walls, some in huge milk-glass globes depending from the ceiling which lighted the central tables. The powerful hum of voices had swelled; the voices sounded screechy from close by, rumbling from farther off. Frau Steuermann picked up a newspaper, opened it to the fashion page, and read:

GRAVE BUT NOT HOPELESS
Fashion Hints for the Fuller Figure

After we have examined with all due interest the various new collections unveiled at the beginning of every season, and after our first and justified enthusiasm has subsided, one important question remains: Do women with fuller figures still have the right to live? In spite of all comforting promises, the line continues to grow slimmer and straighter. The styles seem intended for no one but the movie star who lives on a daily ration of orange juice and lettuce, and checks her weight every half hour. Yet there are many women who have more important things to do, or whose doctors have forbidden them to follow such starvation diets. They need not necessarily be shapeless, but their measurements are such that the creators of fashion ignore them.

With some thought and skill it is possible, of course, to manage to dress oneself becomingly and even fashionably. Models can be made which, while remaining within the general framework of present-day fashion, deliberately depart in certain small respects from creations based entirely upon the slender line. Naturally, the wearer herself must first determine her own "sore points," for it is a little risky to depend entirely upon the dressmaker. One warning, however: Do not be seduced by the models being shown, even though you are dying to have a dress like the one you see. Everything looks different on a size 10; everything seems idealized, so to speak. And when the mannequins parade by, remember that these walking personifications of glamor don't have to make so many or such complicated motions as we do when we wear a dress for any length of time. Therefore don't go overboard. Know thyself. That is the absolutely essential motto for a woman who weighs over 140 pounds.

"One hundred and forty? Ridiculous!" Frau Steuermann thought.

Colors hold all kinds of perils, and fashion this year unfortunately offers far too many temptations. That noble combination, black and white, is always advisable; brown, blue, and darker shades of green may be worn; but keep away from red. Red makes a figure look terribly full. As far as pattern goes, only small dots should be chosen, and narrow stripes, preferably used vertically. The high waist is particularly unsuitable for women with fuller figures. Rather let the waistline agree with your natural waist and be satisfied with a narrow belt.

All this would certainly have sufficed for Selma. But this season had ushered in something absolutely frightful, on top of all the rest. She suddenly felt a painful constriction at the thought that "the others" would be coming along any moment now. No doubt they would be talking about this new development.

In the face of such unpleasant prospects she fled to one of her long cherished islands of entertainment, which always sent a faint but pleasurable shiver through her. She opened the want-ad section of the newspaper and turned to the heading "Personals."

Yes, this was sheer enjoyment. Remote, mysterious possibilities opened up before her. And her attitude—that she was reading this stuff only for amusement—was like a comfortably upholstered theater seat which would permit her at any moment to lean back with a superior air.

To be sure, there was a certain monotony about these "personals" which at times irritated Frau Steuermann. For example:

Gentleman, 38, *with honorable intentions seeks sweet-tempered, pretty, slender, modern girl for a pal, up to 28 years of age, for week-end sports and amusement. Reply in detail to "Horoscope 3087," care of this newspaper.*

Or else:

Pretty, full-figured young lady, *owning own home, sought for discreet friendship by gentleman, honorable intentions, mid-fifties, tall, smart-looking, still extremely vigorous, frequently in Vienna. Only earnest replies requested. Send picture, which will be returned promptly, to "Serious 3389," care of this newspaper.*

"Earnest—serious," Frau Steuermann thought irritably. "An old goat still chasing young girls. He'd do better to look for someone more his age."

Along came the following bid:

> Smart-looking young man, *blond, slim, likable appearance, seeks honorable acquaintanceship with mature, independent lady. Reply to "Serious 2675"* . . .

"Another serious one!" Frau Selma thought. She read the advertisement through once again, then glanced up, involuntarily seeking a glimpse of the street, but the soft bulk of the curtain was impenetrable. "Hm, it's clear enough what he wants," she thought. She let the newspaper sag toward the table and stared into space.

"What are you reading that's so fascinating, Frau Steuermann?" Rosi Altschul said. She had suddenly appeared beside Selma and was poking her charming little snoot past Selma's widespread self into the newspaper. Frau Steuermann did not commit the error of making some excuse—explaining, say, that she needed a maid and therefore had to read the want-ads; but she came very close to showing how startled she was, though ordinarily she was not a person easily disconcerted. Nevertheless, she slowly and casually laid the newspaper aside, at the same time deftly turning the pages to conceal what it had been opened to.

"Frau Steuermann, permit me to introduce Frau Mährischl," Rosi said, indicating her companion, a rotund, dark, quite small woman with tanned skin. After the ceremonies of greeting were completed, the two new arrivals sat down.

Frau Martha Mährischl had a sweet little face, but there was something not quite pleasant about it. After a little study

313

the disturbing element emerged: her eyes were too small and too active; they reminded one of a mouse's eyes.

"Well, how are you, Frau Altschul?" Selma Steuermann asked in her soft dark voice. Rosi shifted about a bit in her seat. Beside her, Frau Mährischl was spooning up the tower of whipped cream from her cup of hot chocolate, manipulating the spoon with an affected movement and oddly spread fingers. Her hands were tanned, very small, and strikingly thin, whereas her wrist was wrapped in a round cuff of fat. "Is your husband still so busy all the time?" Frau Steuermann pursued.

"Yes, he is," Rosi Altschul said. "That's the trouble. He never gets away before seven in the evening nowadays, and recently, when I went to the office for him, they were still in conference with that Frenchman—the deal got going around the New Year. Naturally, my husband is glad for all the new business, but I say he's overdue for a rest. This summer we'll certainly be going to Gastein. Where are the other ladies? Is Frau Wolf coming? Imagine, just recently I saw Frau Rosen with a smart-looking young fellow. She knows how to have a good time. Oh well, she's pretty and has no children, and her husband's been dead four years now. By the way, she's become a good deal slenderer."

"Have you seen the spring models yet, Frau Steuermann?" Frau Mährischl asked. Her approach was polite and respectful; perhaps she wished to underline the fact that she was the younger of the two. But her voice was cold, high-pitched, and grating. There was also something hard about her; Frau Selma felt that instinctively.

"Oh yes—I've got everything together," she said, laughing good-naturedly. She began heaping her piles of fashion magazines on the table. "But I haven't looked at any of the pictures yet. Is there any sense in it for me? These things are all made for a different kind of figure. How can I tell how they'll look on me?" She tittered again.

"Good," Frau Mährischl said. Each time she spoke she prefaced her words by rocking her head back and forth. "But of course my dressmaker has to find a way. The things have to be adjusted to suit."

"Yes, you see, Frau Mährischl"—Selma Steuermann handed across the table the newspaper she had perused earlier—"here is one article that has some good suggestions."

Frau Mährischl read, eyes flickering rapidly. When she came to the critical passage ("Therefore don't go overboard. Know thyself. That is the absolutely essential motto for a woman who weighs over 140 pounds"), she gave a quick short laugh and said contemptuously: "Terribly exaggerated." Then she added: "I've lost twelve pounds since the New Year. I'm down to 135 now. Incidentally, Frau Steuermann, what do you say to the way skirts are going up? Almost above the knees now."

Now it had come out. The dreaded subject had been broached.

"What do I say to it?" Frau Steuermann countered—but suddenly, in the extremity of her distress, she was seized by a perfect indifference to everything, even to this woman opposite who seemed to be a source of nothing but unpleasantness. And so she continued: "Absolutely out of the question for me."

"Oh well," Frau Mährischl said.

This "oh well," which took Frau Steuermann's heroic self-abasement as the statement of an evident fact that could be brushed over without more ado, tried the generous limits of Frau Steuermann's tolerance. But what could she do? Quick repartee was not one of her gifts. Fortunately, her predicament was eased by the arrival of more of the ladies: Frau Clarisse Markbreiter, accompanied by Frau Lea Wolf; and behind this pair fluttered Clarisse's daughter, that charming young newly-wed Lily Kries. Now the full complement was present, except for Frau Rosen, and the table was soon entirely covered with opened fashion journals. Henceforth at least two ladies were always talking simultaneously (Frau Steuermann excepted), and consequently the conversation is rather difficult to reproduce . . .

". . . silk crepe . . . you see, this one here . . . no, Mama, that's nothing for you . . . maybe if the sash were narrower . . . it simply depends on what kind of legs a person has [Mährischl] . . . why? . . . exposed knees are out of the question . . . the tucking should go here . . . that emphasizes the bosom too much, Mama . . . the things you say! . . . everything depends on the waist . . . now that the big bodice is out of style . . . where can Frau Rosen be? . . . she will have a hard time of it . . . everything has its limits, after all . . . size 60 . . . hahaha . . . size 60, very good! [Rosi Altschul] . . . one moment, there was that model on the other page . . ."

As soon as she could, fundamental principles and essentials having been discussed, Frau Lily Kries evaporated. She had stayed barely half an hour.

Not long afterwards Frau Thea Rosen, "the Madonna," put in her appearance. She looked charming. Well-padded, frail as glass, with a bit of a nose, a little mouth like a small red bowl full of sweets, an aura of extreme grooming and polish. She was excellently dressed, and so it may be rewarding to describe her façade more precisely. First of all a tiny toque for a hat, of the finest brown felt (*solé*), pulled down to the right and trimmed with a small thin aigrette of the same color, a very delicate transparent quill lying close to the hat. Frau Thea had probably taken it into her head to suggest delicately the approach of spring, or to appear as the harbinger of spring this afternoon, and consequently we have no silver foxes to report (though a week before we might have observed such a fur on her, worn over a gray tweed costume). Instead she wore two blue foxes with her brown *tailleur,* of a shade which, in textile circles, would have been described as "fawn." These foxes were, of course, crossed at the back between the shoulder blades. Her blouse was of pink satin crepe; the more precise technical name of this color is "blush pink." The neckline of the blouse was treated as a shawl; in other words, it wrapped itself snugly around the throat, effectively bringing out the madonna-like quality of her face. Of her stockings we need say only that they were absolutely skin-colored, and the tiny, slightly too fat feet—chubby, they might be called, as a baby's hands are chubby—these tiny feet were shod in brown, crocodile-leather shoes—crocodile leather through and through, naturally, with not a trace of any other material, no inserts of any kind. Her suede gloves and outsize pocketbook were, of course, likewise fawn. This pocketbook, however, showed that Frau Rosen not only anticipated coming seasons in every respect, but looked much farther ahead in time, to epochs of fashion still lingering on distant horizons. A large nickel clasp on this pocketbook proved her a prophetess.

She and Frau Lea Wolf (a physician's wife) were undeniably the most attractive women in the whole group, aside from youthful Lily (no longer present), of course—and also excepting Frau Steuermann for the different reason that by the ruling standards of the day she stood absolutely outside the realm of possible evaluation (because of that too wide sector of front she was forced to take in female positional warfare, which inevitably spelled defeat for her). These standards had already been operating long enough to reshape the nature of men's desires. But any man who by some chance had escaped the tyranny of such standards would have regarded Frau Selma as a

317

magnificent woman, which indeed she was. And such a man's unprejudiced eye would have preferred her to all the others. For her head simply belonged to a better category than that of any other female in the place. It looked like a wholly delightful import from the East—after all so close, here in Vienna. And as for the expression of her face, it showed so much kindliness, such appealing warm-hearted geniality, that faces like those of the ladies Markbreiter, Altschul, Rosen, or even Mährischl seemed by comparison vacant, or else marred by questionable features, including a certain harshness. By comparison, there was something ignoble about the faces of all the others.

Frau Wolf, however, constituted a special case.

In her the sharpness took precedence over all other qualities. Her face had an extreme alertness, expressed an intelligence actively and unabashedly engaged in probing everything within her immediate vicinity, an intelligence which constantly stepped right up to the brink of an altogether monstrous impudence. Yet, and this was curious, obtrusive facial marks of such harshness were quite absent; there was no such narrowing of the features as might be observed in Frau Markbreiter when she spoke with her servants, or occasionally in Grete Siebenschein. Those other ladies possessed sharp, or at the very least energetically shaped noses, and in some circumstances they would come forth with a darting, birdlike, forward motion of the head, or a flashing look from deep within the eye-sockets. No such traits were to be noted in Frau Wolf. Indeed, there was a certain concavity about her face; it was turned inward, and her nose formed a highly insignificant part of the whole, being slightly flattened and broadened, as if it had been crushed. At the same time Frau Lea Wolf might well have been called pretty, or at least very attractive. But it was a harsh, a suction-like attraction. She was always in good humor, and had rapidly moving gray eyes. Neither in the movements of her head or her limbs was there ever a trace of aggressiveness. Her large, shapely, well-padded figure was the best among the whole group of women, including Thea Rosen, who was obviously short-legged. Frau Wolf had a dignified carriage. Her dignity was of a dry and self-sufficient character, the dignity of a person who let things go as they would. Expressions of astonishment, let alone shock, would have been inconceivable on that wide flattened countenance. Her face simply lacked the means of expressing such emotions. That was the reason for the look of abysmal impertinence which seemed to lie just beneath the surface of Frau Lea's face.

To an attentive eavesdropper from one of the neighboring upholstered niches, it would have been apparent that the fashion conference, which had gone on for about an hour, was beginning to dissolve. The whole discussion had been a cautious tacking, accompanied by halfhearted sorties, around the matter of shorter skirts—a matter really and truly catastrophic for these ladies. Our attentive eavesdropper would have noted that, after the first hour, other topics were introduced into the agenda, although not always the entire table took up these side issues and although the objective (and all too humanly subjective) question before the conference still held first place for a while.

"I heard him with my own ears making all kinds of complaints against Gretel," Frau Markbreiter said to Rosi Altschul. "And right out in the street, no less. What do you think of that? And how! There he was telling all kinds of things to someone—I would have walked right on past, but I happened to catch the name . . ."

"Who was the person with him?" Rosi asked.

"Ah, if I only knew. Some man. As a matter of fact the man

seemed to be someone I know, though only distantly—I haven't been able to recall the name. I think I've seen him at the bridge club where Siegfried plays sometimes. Anyway, I stopped on purpose and turned around, because I thought: 'Maybe his lordship will recognize me.' But he didn't notice a thing, he was talking such a blue streak. I must admit, though, that I myself haven't seen Herr Stangeler very often—just run into him now and then, up at Irma's—whoosh, and he's gone. Avoids people anyway, he does. I can't say the boy's manners are very good. I've told her often enough, Grete, I mean, she ought to have him around when her relatives are there, so they can get a look at him, but she never does. Though I think Siegfried was there that time they had the row. And then the very next day I saw the fellow. Naturally I told Irma about it, I wanted her to know what kind of young man she has going in and out of her house."

"And did he really slap her?"

"He did. The poor girl was simply—well, she was simply done in, I can tell you."

"And still they made up again?"

"Well, now, that's just it, did you ever hear of such lacka-daisical parents! I myself would put a stop to it, once and for all. It will just lead to misery. But that same evening he called her up again. Begged and pleaded with her to forgive him, he didn't mean it, and all the rest. But Grete was firm for once on the telephone, so Irma told me later. And I certainly gave Irma a talking-to right away, on the Tuesday after the row. After I heard the fellow saying all those things right out on the street, I went there right away . . ."

"Oh well, if he said things after a fight—I mean, after all, it's only natural . . ."

"I beg *your* pardon! Talking that way, and to a stranger. You should have heard his language."

"How awful. Then when did they make it all up again?"

"The whole thing didn't last a full two weeks. That's the way it always is. He kept begging her, called up at least ten times, stood downstairs in the street at night—why doesn't he behave better if he's so crazy about her? There's something wrong with that boy up there, if you ask me." She tapped her forehead. "I told Irma so, too. If you knew the worries they have with the poor girl. And aside from all that, the fellow is unpleasant in other ways. You know Lasch—he's Titi's, the younger girl's, husband—Lasch handles some pretty important business affairs. He really is somebody. So why shouldn't he have a conference with a business friend in his in-laws' apartment? After all, the people he deals with are first-class people. So he invited someone up there, a big wheel, I think, anyway somebody who was important to him. Titi's flat was all topsy-turvy because she's having the bathroom done over; the plumbers were still working there, and so . . . Now imagine this, Cornel was up there at Irma's talking with this gentleman, the two of them right in the middle of their conference—Irma left instructions for tea to be served to them in the music room because it's the best room in the apartment—and now imagine this, right in the middle of their conference they hear somebody rustling papers in Grete's room when they thought she was out of the house. Irma had told Cornel beforehand, I think she even promised him, that there'd be nobody in the apartment. And who should be sitting there large as life at Grete's desk but Herr Stangeler. Acting as though he's right at home, writing something—you know, he writes these crazy things. And after all, I ask you, how should anybody know what? Really—I mean, he could have taken down every word that was said in the next room. That Mizzi, their kitchen maid, the little dumbbell Irma had—and let me tell you, she doesn't know how to pick her

321

servants, or how to handle them either—as I say, Mizzi naturally goes right ahead and humbly lets his lordship in; that was two hours before. He makes himself at home even when Grete isn't there, and dumbbell Mizzi doesn't say a word to Irma about it, though to him it's always: 'Yes sir, Herr Baron'— she falls all over herself showing respect to him, though why she has to respect him so much I'd like to know; the rest of the time she has as much respect for people as a bedbug. That young fellow Stangeler—there's something I don't like about him. Makes me uneasy. He's so—so peculiar. Of course I don't know what Lasch and the other man had to discuss, but still, you know, there's something very odd about it. And how embarrassing for poor Irma . . ."

One by one the fashion journals were laid aside on two empty chairs, and Max, the waiter, restored them gradually to general circulation. Each time he passed the table he took some of them, tucked them under his arm, and carried them here and there, wherever the demand was greatest.

"I always think, we mustn't insist on having everything," Frau Mährischl said, smiling and shaking her head back and forth. "What can come of it in the end? Such affairs lead to nothing but disappointment. I really felt sincere pity for her . . . She spoke of an unfortunate acquaintance of hers who had had an affair with some young man which had finally ended in great unhappiness. The most important aspect of this story was that this acquaintance had just been invented by Frau Mährischl, along with the entire love-affair and its tragic outcome. There was not a word of truth in the tale. Frau Mährischl's fiction was intended to rile Frau Thea Rosen, concerning whose private life she had recently been informed by her newest friend, Frau Rosi Altschul.

Frau Mährischl had just been introduced to the circle of

ladies by Rosi, in the same way that Clarisse Markbreiter had brought Frau Wolf along on this occasion. The true background of the brand-new friendship between Frau Mährischl and Frau Altschul was not to be revealed until much later. At the time everyone had the impression that they were extremely intimate. Yet the psychological basis of the relationship could not remain obscure to any fairly keen person, and Frau Lea Wolf, for example, was such a one. Frau Mährischl undoubtedly had a spiteful disposition, to put it mildly; but at the same time she was quite intelligent. This latter quality was certainly not one of our Rosi's attributes. But Frau Altschul also had an inclination, though a rather childish one, toward spitefulness. Unfortunately she could not very well pursue this tendency (just a little, at any rate, and only for the fun of it) merely by employing her own resources, for these were inadequate for really effective spite. Here her new friend came to the rescue. Moreover, Rosi herself occupied a safe buffer area over which the trajectories of the missiles traveled without descending upon her. From her secure position she had the pleasure of observing each shell burst.

Why this position was so absolutely safe is not apropos here. Sufficient to say, it was noted by fairly keen persons that Frau Mährischl never whetted her sharp tongue on her friend.

For this reason Rosi Altschul had for some time been burning to introduce her friend into this particular group. A spiteful person always has a strong effect upon any circle he enters; for one thing his presence always tests the loyalty of the circle. Frau Rosi enjoyed watching such tests, while she herself took shelter behind the windbreak of Frau Mährischl's intelligence.

"I really felt sincere pity for her," Frau Mährischl continued. "But of course you know the way the whole thing strikes me, it's like many women today who've reached the age when they can't go on dressing like a young girl and still they run around like they'd just come from their dancing class—oh well, this spring we'll see it all over again if skirts really do go up as much as they say, maybe almost above the knees. But a woman who's got piano legs has no business trying to dance on ice. What use has she for a man who's ten years younger than herself? Naturally he'll run out on her sooner or later—I feel awfully sorry for her, but anyone could have foretold it. Now of course . . ."

"But I beg your pardon, Frau Mährischl," Selma Steuermann spoke up. "After all, it's perfectly possible for a young man to have real feeling for a woman considerably older than himself. I mean, you can't just take it for granted that . . ."

"Of course, of course," Frau Mährischl said. "But unfortunately, most of the time the only ones who swallow such a story are the older women themselves. I don't mean to contradict you, Frau Steuermann, anything is possible—oh well, everybody has his own opinion—I mean, it's your affair if you want to believe such a thing."

Frau Mährischl had already reached that frontier across which lay the terrain of undisguised extreme impertinence. Frau Steuermann belonged to that category of persons who think of their most trenchant replies on the staircase, or worse still not until the following morning while brushing their teeth. This time she was thoroughly vexed, for all her good nature. She came close to demanding: "What do you mean by 'your affair'?"

However, she remained silent. But Frau Rosen, well aware that the speeding missile was actually aimed at her, felt so relieved to see it slewing off toward fat Selma that she foolishly began to laugh, and her laughter infected Rosi Altschul. Lucky for her that Rosi laughed too, for otherwise she might have been paid for her laughter with an even crueler shot.

Clarisse Markbreiter took no part in these verbal skirmishes. To her credit it must be said that even during this day's ticklish discussions she had not been conscious of her own charming, slim, and shapely legs in such a way as to make inward capital of them. Certainly she did not do so outwardly. Yet her position here today, in the face of the terrible crisis created by certain vacillations in spring fashions, was actually a superior one. She could easily have allowed herself great latitude. But she did not do so. Lily, moreover, had advised her not to let herself be involved in this business of still shorter skirts. That settled it for her.

After some two hours of discussion, the council adjourned and the session came to an end. The waiters, their faces the very image of cupped palms, hurried over to help the ladies into their furs. While this was going on, the following incident took place.

Frau Rosi Altschul was squeezing out between table and upholstered bench. As she did so, her skirt worked up a handbreadth above the knees, so that a fairly keen person who happened to be standing at the end of the bench slipping into her fur coat could have observed and assessed these knees in all their glory. The knees, as it happened, were more than substantial, were worthy capitals for the columns beneath. Not until she had reached the end of the bench did Frau Rosi discover her plight. At the same time she distinctly felt that someone was looking at her from above. Smoothing down her skirt and raising her eyes could be accomplished in one swift simultaneous motion. Frau Wolf was smiling. She was plainly smiling down at these knees, and at the hands hastily pulling and brushing smooth; and upon Frau Wolf's smiling face Rosi read the words: "too late."

Thus it was that Frau Steuermann was avenged for the day, although the vengeance did not directly strike the dispatcher of bitter distant missiles—Frau Mährischl—but only her protégé and advance guard, Frau Altschul.

As they followed one another through the heavy revolving door, Rosi quickly whispered into her friend's ear: "Did you see what she was reading when we came? Lonely-hearts ads. I'm sure of it."

"You don't have to tell me," Frau Mährischl replied coolly. "What do you think I have my lorgnette for?"

CHAPTER 10

Our Crowd (I)

NOT LONG after our "foundation festival," two kinsfolk of mine arrived virtually simultaneously to stay permanently in Vienna. They were my nephew, Doktor Körger, who had hitherto resided some of the time in Munich and some of the time in the Austrian provinces; and Herr Géza von Orkay of the Budapest Foreign Office, who had been assigned as attache to the Hungarian embassy in Vienna. Orkay, who was a cousin of mine, fully took after his late father, who had married one of my mother's sisters. He was a thoroughly Magyar type, with all the Magyar characteristics strongly marked, in spite of the admixture of blood from our family, who had been natives of Vienna for ever and a day. His heritage, the position his father had once occupied, his handsome estate in Hungary, and finally his family tradition, had combined to draw Géza to a career in diplomacy—in which, later on, splendid prospects were to be opened to him.

I had expected Körger to become quickly part of our circle, which had itself taken shape with such rapidity. In fact it was not long before he moved out to our garden suburb. On the other hand I did not know Géza well at all—neither of the two had what you might call frank, open natures. Nevertheless he, too, frequently came to our gatherings and became an accepted member of our circle.

It seemed to me remarkable that these two relatives of mine, coming from opposite points of the compass, and having different backgrounds and different blood, who became acquainted with each other only after their arrival in Vienna, should within so short a time have formed a fast friendship. Before long they were inseparable. They certainly made an odd-looking pair. Körger was the type who never entirely loses his baby fat. Moreover, this man of twenty-seven no longer had a hair left on his head—a baldness inherited from his father. The thick rosy nakedness of his head looked even more pronounced, when seen from the rear, because his neck was like a bull's.

Kurt Körger had a number of deeper-lying and highly peculiar traits. For example, the bathroom seemed to him a place in which one spent as few minutes as possible, at most just enough to shave in haste, and that with a minimal consumption of water. At night—I was present on one such occasion—he would stand in front of the bed, peel off his shoes, clothes, and undergarments, jump into his pajamas, and crawl into his nest, his exuviae remaining right on the rug where he had dropped them. Was there some connection between this and his extreme reluctance to spend a schilling unless it was absolutely unavoidable? (He often showed amazing talent for inducing other people to take care of even the smallest expenditure for him; it might only be a tip for a chambermaid, but Körger never happened to have any small change!) I do believe that his stinginess and his toilette habits bore some metaphorical relationship to each other. His father was one of the richest men in Austria and had (this is rare) already made his son independent by transferring to him during his lifetime a sizable portion of his fortune. Körger's bank account was large, his wallet stuffed. His only hobby cost him nothing. For it amused him to play the amateur architect, drafting plans for many small houses, dividing them up precisely (and even including bathrooms) into one-family houses, two-family houses, bachelor apartments, and so on. He would work out their exact dimensions, calculate the required materials, and above all determine the costs of construction. Often he sat with his fat naked head bent over the drafting board, his shoulders hunched, the rest of him shaped like a sausage.

Alongside this figure we must imagine our Géza with his narrow, horsy, aristocratic head, heroic aquiline nose, slant eyes, and umber skin, his whole body light and graceful, a vibrant bundle of muscles. Géza's manner was extremely restrained. We thought him almost too smooth. Latent in his face was a kind of gloominess which harkened back to something oriental. I should add that Géza always impressed me as an extremely prudent person. All of us were struck by the attitude he displayed from the very beginning toward his fellow-countryman, our jester, Gyurkicz. I say "displayed," because here for the first time we saw Géza consciously dealing with a situation, rather than relying on his usual smoothness.

I recall the incident most vividly. We were sitting in my apartment—"we" being Quapp, Kajetan, Captain Eulenfeld, Stangeler, and I—when the telephone announced Imre Gyurkicz's imminent arrival. Meanwhile, quite by chance Géza dropped in to visit me. Already acquainted with everyone present, our Magyar turned to Stangeler (toward whom he evidently felt drawn) and involved our ex-ensign of the Dragoons and professional historian in a discussion of early Hungarian history, which gave Stangeler an opportunity to hold forth to such an extent that my head began to swim at the spectacle of such vast and thorough knowledge.

Just at this point Gyurkicz entered, impeccably dressed as always, his exterior proclaiming a conservatism which was in manifest contrast to many other aspects of his person. Below his large, well-shaven, and banally handsome face he offered to the world the sight of a wide solid necktie which descended straight down the middle of his vest. In his choice of collar, too, he had opted for dignity rather than gaiety of form, though of course he remained within the limits of prevailing fashion. In other words, while there was nothing old-fashioned about his dress, it bespoke a certain attitude of restraint toward the very newest developments. His shoes were heavy and solid, of that broad triangular shape whose smartness was to become fully established only much later. Had Gyurkicz still been among the living at this later period, I am sure he would have been seen marching along in far more pointed shoes. His well-pressed trousers fell a shade further down at the front of these shoes than was then customary among young people, and this extra length was no doubt also intended to express an attitude, a certain dignified respectable homage to the styles of yesterday as against the fads of today.

So he appeared in the doorway, in the bright snow-light which flooded my windows, reflected as it was from the white meadows outside and making the big room seem even larger than it was. Gyurkicz approached the bay window in which we were sitting, greeted Quapp—and doing so by kissing her hand, thus proclaiming his more intimate relationship with her before a stranger, since it is not the custom to kiss the hand of young girls, which was the rank Quapp occupied in our society. Then, in proper order he greeted me, as the oldest person present and the host, and finally the others. Toward Stangeler his greeting had a certain casual lightness, as if to suggest that it was always amusing to see René, but nothing more.

Then, speaking in Hungarian, "Imre Gyurkicz of Faddy and Hátfaludy is my name," he introduced himself to Géza, who was still standing while the rest of us had sat down again.

330

"I've heard about you and am delighted to meet a fellow-countryman." (I had said: "Here is my cousin from Hungary.") "Unfortunately, it is long since I have had the good fortune to stand upon Hungarian soil, and so a fellow-countryman is like a salutation from my native land. Aren't you related to the late Szell Elemer, an old friend of mine? He once mentioned your name, if I remember rightly."

"Good evening," Géza said in German. Nothing more, not even his name. He shook hands curtly, stepped back, and sat down again.

Imre did not follow suit. As an experienced Austrian, I knew that among Hungarians to reply in German in such a situation—quite aside from the terseness of the reply—meant nothing less than the setting up of a barrier which henceforth could never again be crossed. Indeed, it was a deliberate insult, and I was rather surprised at how well Gyurkicz managed to keep his composure. He merely sat down slowly and directed some abstracted question to Stangeler. Géza, however, leaning loosely back in his chair, looked around the circle, studying each one of us with close attention. Only then did I realize that the little drama had possibly not been grasped even by Eulenfeld. (In this I was mistaken, as I later learned.) Stangeler seemed to have noticed nothing at all; perhaps he was still in the fifteenth century. Quapp, however, was holding her head bowed, making no attempt to conceal her pensiveness. I was not sure whether she knew what had actually happened. She did not know Hungarian—I was the only one in the company aside from Géza and Imre who did—but intuition had undoubtedly informed her that something highly unpleasant had just taken place.

I have mentioned this little incident because of the revealing light it casts upon the nature of the relationship between

Géza and Imre from the start, as well as to assign Quapp and my cousin their places in regard to each other. Géza very quickly manifested a special respect toward Schlaggenberg's sister. She, for her part, exhibited a searching interest in his character; she seemed constantly to be drawing comparisons, and it was not hard to guess with whom. While we were still sitting together in my bay window that day I distinctly perceived—it needed no special keenness!—that Gyurkicz had about reached the limits of his patience. He put up with "our crowd" only out of necessity in any case—for he could not very well protest Quapp's association with her own brother and the latter's friends.

Here, too, a contradictory element was entering our circle, disturbing its inner unity, which was in any case frail enough, and now and then tentatively coming to the fore.

We obtained a brief furlough from such conflicts one day around the middle of March, a day that has remained vivid in my memory. This day also stands out in my mind as marking the approximate end of that happy period which Kajetan and his sister had enjoyed together during the first weeks after Quapp's return to Vienna.

We had had the last snowfall of the year, as is usual in our climate almost the biggest of them all. A few hundred steps from my front door we buckled on our skis and pushed toward the sugar-coated mountains which surveyed the end of every street in this part of the city. An hour later we were looking down from the top of the Kahlenberg. Between the lanes of trees, freshly decorated with their masses of snow, a steel-blue lake of houses stretched off into the distance far below us. We stood without talking, leaning forward somewhat, supporting ourselves on the leather loops of our ski poles, the mist of our breath puffing out and dissolving between us and this landscape of white-upholstered, windless silence.

We were a regular gang of banditti, and only men. Schlaggenberg was there, and "the Ensign," Körger and Géza, even Höpfner and the captain were part of our company this time. Although it was an ordinary weekday, the latter two had managed to escape from their offices. The meadows, on Sundays dark with sportive humanity, were almost deserted that day, and in the woods through which we glided we encountered not a single trail.

We were entirely by ourselves.

My Hungarian cousin proved to be an excellent skier. He had, as I now learned, only recently spent several months diligently practicing in Switzerland. Deep in the woods we found a steep clearing. We draped our parkas and shirts on the bushes that rimmed it, and climbed and descended the slope stripped to the waist in the brilliant sunlight. The heady intoxication of the snow seized us all, and I found myself obliged to recommend caution to Eulenfeld, for part of his left knee had remained behind at the well-known road intersection near Ypres in 1915, with the result that his kneecap was made of silver. The captain, however, seemed to have forgotten this matter entirely. What was more important, the knee, too, no longer remembered its warlike past.

After about an hour of this, we continued on our way once again, swooping rapidly through the woods. I followed Géza, who always chose precisely the right spot for turns and traverses, which helped me to keep in his track. Suddenly we noticed approaching us, still at some great distance, a skier—the first we had seen that day in this relatively lonely region. He moved swiftly along between the tree-trunks and the white-ribboned grating formed by the wintry branches of the woods, tracing a long straight trail in the powdery new snow, diagonally along the slope at an obtuse angle to our course, braking now and then with small turns. As he reached us, he passed precisely between Orkay and me, and I recognized that it was a fairly tall, strong, dark blonde girl gliding so adroitly and alone through the woods. She had taken off her jacket and was wearing a blue, short-sleeved blouse; the sleeves reached only halfway down her upper arm. I watched her; she held to her course, flying in one great swoop diagonally across the whole side of the hill, and vanished from our sight.

From up front, where Schlaggenberg was in the van, came shouts. Our rough voices resounded like ax blows in the stillness. We changed course and let our momentum carry us a long distance uphill again. Eulenfeld started a bottle of cognac going down the row. Our sport-loving Géza—ordinarily never averse to a round of drinks—strongly disapproved of this, but Schlaggenberg welcomed it heartily. The path became almost level for a considerable distance. We made our way along the ridge of the hill, where we had a clear view to both sides. The snow was tremendously deep here; there were even small suggestions of alpine formations, whimsical miniature snow-bluffs. To our left and right, between scattered trees, flashing sunlit expanses dropped away, on the city side etched over with innumerable sharply checker-boarded details, on the other side blurring into innumerable wooded slopes. Some of the talk that went on as we glided along at a leisurely pace was rather raw and would have been quite impossible in the presence of sensitive ears. Kajetan again seemed to consider it necessary to tell us about his everlasting fat ladies. And Höpfner, who had lagged somewhat behind the rest of us, seemed to sense what sort of prayer-wheels were being set spinning, for he suddenly came to life and hastened to catch up to us with a few strides of his enormously long legs.

"The well-stuffed woman," Körger was holding forth at the moment, "the juicy female, should as such be regarded as the most desirable of all. Undoubtedly she is the true archetype of woman in general. Yes, yes," he added in a slow drawl, after meditation that would have been worthy of a better subject, "yes, yes, when I look into my own soul, I realize that fundamentally this is the kind of woman I find really ravishing." Whereupon there followed his inevitable: "Say what you will."

However, no one heard this last phrase. At the words "look into my own soul" Géza had made a small unmistakable gesture which raised a general guffaw.

The laughter resounded over the ridge and through the woods as though scrap-iron were being unloaded.

Truly, we were among ourselves, in the shallowest sense, but in all probability in a deeper sense too; we were among ourselves and thus freed of all futile contradictions with their accompanying torment of mind. We were free men who had reason to be merry and of good cheer. For out here we had left behind the things that obstructed mutual understanding and that forced people to grope their way, stooped, on separate paths. Out here each of us could be himself in the highest as well as the lowest degree. And so we strode along over the deep snow of the ridge, between the silent trees, overlooking the glittering landscape; noisily and jubilantly we strode along.

And yet one of us was missing, and by her very absence contrived to call to mind that complex of relationships which weighed so little here, so much down there in the city.

It was Quapp whom we missed, whom we old-young fellows missed.

We started down toward the valley, homeward. The sun slanted low, annihilating with its glare whole expanses of white countryside. On a meadow still far out we lingered for a last time, prolonging our outing until complete darkness should fall.

Then we started again, and the faintly luminous snow hissed under our racing skis, field after field; and like a rising of a gigantic Milky Way, seemingly near enough to touch, the illuminated face of the city appeared, a clouded sky, glowing reddishly, full of twinkling darting stars. We could already see, far across the valley, the lights of cottages perched one above another on the slopes, against a swell of darkness which upon closer inspection divided along a gently curving line into night sky and mountain. And once again, stooped forward, with the wind of our rapid passage whistling by my ears, I felt with a strange new astonishment that the place and people down below there were my home, that I was indissolubly linked with their movements.

When Schlaggenberg told me that Levielle had called on him and invited him to become a reader for a new firm of book publishers he was going to establish ("Now what do you say to that?"), I immediately thought: "Schlaggenberg is lying." Not for a moment did I think otherwise. I took it absolutely for granted that he was lying. And it was, after all, an unprompted lie, for he said it to me on the street, while we were talking about quite other things; I had not asked him about it at all, or indicated that I knew of Levielle's call.

The fact that he took the trouble to lie convinced me at once that behind all this an important matter—important to Schlaggenberg, at any rate—must be concealed. For he was plainly establishing an alibi in case any of our crowd should sooner or later learn that he had taken up with Levielle. Apparently, then, he intended to keep on with the man, and was taking the opportunity to erect defenses which he might need in the near future.

Today, when I know from Schlaggenberg's later and off-repeated accounts virtually every word which was spoken between him and Levielle, I possess the key to the whole mystery. Levielle's first visit, the first one at which he found Schlaggenberg at home, came some four weeks after that ominous calling card affair. Later we found it easy to establish the exact date of that first conversation between Levielle and Kajetan. It was the 28th of March, a Monday. On the preceding Friday, Annunciation Day, I had taken that walk along the Graben during which I ran into Levielle, the encounter I have described in detail at the beginning of my chronicle. I mentioned that meeting to Schlaggenberg when he served up the preposterous story about the old fellow's visit to him and the "book-publishing house" offer. It pleased me, moreover, to remark that Levielle had not let fall the slightest hint of anything of the sort in the course of our walk, although Kajetan's name had actually cropped up in our conversation . . .

The financial counselor oozed benevolently into the room, rubbed his hands, and looked around. "Glad to see you, Cajétan." (He made a point of pronouncing Schlaggenberg's first name in the French—his French—manner, whereas he always called Quapp "Charlot"; these were two of his little whims.) "Glad to see you, Cajétan," he said. "It's been a long time. How is your—sister? Charlot, I mean. Are you living with her again?"

"Sit down," Schlaggenberg said measuredly, without answering any of his questions. "To what do I owe the honor of your visit?"

"Oh dear, nothing in particular, my young friend. No special reason . . . I haven't seen you for a very long time and things have happened that have made me think of you frequently of late . . . So I felt I owed it to the memory of your father, if for no other reason, to look in on you for a change and see how things are going . . ."

"What has made you think of me?"

"Oh, your name has been mentioned several times recently among a family with whom I maintain friendly relations."

"Probably not in a very flattering manner."

"Why not? You are highly respected there—at least as a writer . . ."

"Have you actually come to me today as an ambassador of the Siebenschein family?"

"You don't say—hahaha—your humor is too much for me, Cajétan. Incidentally, though, joking aside, I should also like to say a few words to you in that connection."

"Then go ahead and say what you came to say. You mentioned that you 'maintain friendly relations' with the Siebenschein family. I fancy that is not quite exact. Your connection with those people is based mainly on your business ties with a certain Cornel Lasch."

"The things you know, Cajétan . . . Your little spy seems to be very efficient. Who knows what other valuable information he has given you?"

Schlaggenberg could not help laughing. Stangeler as a "spy"—he would have been as useful in such a capacity as a guitar is for a mousetrap or a young hedgehog for a collar button.

"I hardly need a spy to tell me that you and Lasch are mixed up together. I heard about it long ago from another source—although I must say that such information doesn't interest me in the least. There is probably only one other person whose laziness in that respect surpasses mine. Namely, the spy Stangeler."

(Even as he spoke these words, he told me later, a novel idea

338

crept into his mind—it was the exact opposite of what he was saying.)

Levielle smiled subtly, unconvinced and unconvincible, after the manner of his kind, who judge everyone by their own standards—and in general, as we must unfortunately observe, hit the mark in doing so. Behind this subtle smile, however, he now made a strategic withdrawal; for he sensed that he had probably ventured too far in his anger with Stangeler and his nervousness over Schlaggenberg. Both these emotions, moreover, and especially the latter, lacked any tangible basis, at least at that time. Therefore he placated: "As soon as one begins talking with you, Cajétan, one is forced into a dispute."

"Not 'one,' " Schlaggenberg said. "You."

"Very well, very well. You have an argumentative nature. But I did want to talk with you about those two young people. I freely admit that I came here with that intention, or with that subsidiary intention . . . There seems to be no doubt that you exercise a strong influence upon young Stangeler. In itself that influence is undoubtedly for the good, having a positive direction; but whether it is beneficial for him at the present time and in your young friend's present stage of development— whether it can possibly be beneficial—seems to me at any rate questionable. You affect other people without considering the consequences, Cajétan . . . You have been the cause of terrible unhappiness, unhappiness to a good and innocent person whom you do not even know."

"I should be very pleased to make the acquaintance of Fräulein Grete Siebenschein," Schlaggenberg said quickly, with a slight change of expression. Levielle, who had not been expecting any such remark, seemed for a moment quite taken aback.

"That omission might be remedied sometime . . . although

at the present moment . . . in any case, everything depends upon your conduct. A great deal depends upon it, Cajétan. You are not only hurting others, but perhaps yourself as well . . ."

"Aha!"

Aha. Now we see it. This conversation was not taking a very pleasant course. No doubt about it, Kajetan's tone toward the old fellow had been impudent from the start, characterized by a kind of deliberate, forced, insistent cheekiness which could not possibly have been genuine. He admitted as much to me. Since he simply did not understand the reason for Levielle's call, and found himself facing a seamless wall of his own ignorance, while at the same time he distinctly felt that he was playing a role of some kind, for all that he was innocent of its nature, he tried consciously to provoke Levielle in order to get information. But then, losing patience, and simply in order to be rid of this whole enigma which he could not begin to understand, he strove to offend the man until he left in anger. But Levielle, whose vexation did threaten to get the upper hand now and then, each time withdrew from his own annoyance into some unknown hinterland, while Kajetan throughout the scene was hampered by his own uncertainty. Thus the two of them came to within inches of a violent collision, and then shrank back. The curious result was that Kajetan, after trying to make Levielle leave in anger, found that the man was departing too soon.

"Very well, you say: 'Aha.'" (This was one of the points at which Levielle threatened to lose his temper.) "And you feel enormously superior as you say it. You go around parading certain principles . . ."

"It seems to me," Schlaggenberg said, "that you, Herr Levielle, are, like me, far more concerned with Stangeler than with poor Grete Siebenschein. Only I don't happen to understand why. Do you seriously believe that I am having you spied

340

on by this boy who is virtually deaf and blind to ordinary affairs? For that matter, I did not know you were involved in anything worth being spied on. You are literally forcing the idea upon me. Schlaggenberg's detective agency—with René Stangeler as chief agent. Bull in a china shop. God knows, I have other things to worry about."

"Come now, all this is joking and nonsense," Levielle said. "Please do not take it amiss, Cajétan, if I speak quite frankly to you. You have reached an age when other men have been earning their living for a long time. As I have recently learned from your mother, with whom as you know I occasionally correspond, you have not succeeded in that endeavor . . . That is to say, your literary activities are not quite sufficient to provide you fully with the necessities of life, or to do so in any permanent and regular manner. Naturally, in saying this I do not mean to impugn the inherent and lasting value of your work. But I do not think I am far wrong in assuming that you find this state of affairs troublesome—the circumstance, that is to say, that you are still dependent on your good mother for support."

"Certainly," Schlaggenberg said simply.

"I intend to put the matter briefly," Levielle continued, "and tell you a few things for the nonce, Cajétan, without pressing you for any decision. Although, incidentally, I do not think you will find such a decision a matter of great difficulty. Well then, I was recently elected to the board of directors of the Alliance Newspaper Corporation. My vote is decisive there. I and my group hold a majority of the shares. You understand? You know young Holder, don't you? He is now employed as editor of one of the concern's newspapers. I brought him into the firm. Very well. But you are not, properly speaking, a journalist like Holder. Still and all, am I correct in thinking that you would be very glad to become a contributor, a regular contributor? You certainly would not have any objection to a fixed agreement. For literary work alone, of course, with no strings attached. But to achieve such a position a writer must—have someone backing him up. Do you understand? Everything depends on that. And if the person whose career is to be promoted also happens to possess great ability, as you do—why then, the whole affair is child's play."

("Let him think you're for sale, let him think so! What difference does it make? But what the devil is his motive for wanting to buy you? And what is the price? The price?")

"However, I am now coming to the real *pièce de résistance*," Levielle continued, as expansive and benevolent as the rising sun itself. "We plan to establish a large book-publishing house, specializing in belles-lettres, you see. What possibilities are open there! The whole thing is going to have extremely substantial financial backing. In a firm of this sort, you could get somewhere very rapidly, both as an author and as a reader and editor. You could publish your own work and at the same time, as one of the literary heads, exercise a key influence upon the output of the house. In connection with this whole business, incidentally, I have already thought of Stangeler as well . . ."

Levielle took out his watch, displayed ostentatious alarm at the length of time that had passed, suddenly manifested the greatest haste, and gave Kajetan no chance to ask a single question. "My dear young friend, you will hear from me again. Think over carefully everything we have discussed today— everything. As I say, you will be hearing from me. A pleasure to have seen you, Cajétan. My regards to Charlot."

And he was gone. This abrupt termination of the conversation was undoubtedly a tactical maneuver, as Schlaggenberg realized immediately after Levielle's departure. The arrow had struck; now let the wound fester. Levielle must have flattered himself that he had left Schlaggenberg in a state of considerable confusion.

That was actually the case, although in a sense different from what Levielle imagined. What confused Schlaggenberg was not the sudden dawning of all these prospects for earning a living. It was not the offer of rescue from a condition of unfreedom with its more or less constant accompaniment of guilt (for in this regard our Kajetan was altogether bourgeois and felt his inadequate earning power as something shameful). It was not the miracle of having a happy solution of all the problems of his present situation placed virtually within his grasp. Nor, strangely enough, was it the wealth of ambiguity which underlay the offer. Rather, his perplexity stemmed from this: that since this person was coming to him with offers, trying to render him malleable for something, his name must already be enrolled in some unknown books, must be serving a function in some calculations—though what these were he could not imagine. Schlaggenberg described that evening to me very frequently, dwelling especially on his state of mind after Levielle's departure, and he always came back to this point: that at the time he felt himself "threatened and literally attacked" in some sinister fashion.

In other words, he no longer dominated the area of his own life. He was playing parts of which he knew nothing. He was contained within contexts whose nature he could not plumb.

He "no longer dominated the area of his own life"—again and again he was to repeat these words. He had wrenched himself free from Camy, his wife, and into a vacuum which at first must actually have looked like a building site for a new existence. Indeed, it soon became filled with orderly structures—for he had realized at once that from the moment of his flight everything depended upon the single factor of disciplined work. But now, damn it all, there was "a scurrying in the walls." And what threatened him, what oppressed him, was not Levielle or any conspiracy that Levielle may have set afoot. Rather, it was the last dreary dregs of his own life, a silt of unappeased guilts and a thousand inadequacies, which now suddenly and poisonously rose to the surface, stirred up by this matter of the Alliance newspapers.

That evening Camy's face came back to him, really came back for the first time since the parting, and with it the heart-rending proximity of many a happy hour—although still held at bay by a certain rigidity in the remembered images. It all seemed behind glass, but he felt that it might at any moment awake to a new and for him terrible aliveness. Once again the sore spot flamed, low on the horizon, a depressing red. To sit there in his room was unendurable. Springing to his feet, he flung open the window and looked out through the lowering dusk and over the gardens of the suburb.

The moisture of a world but lately salvaged from snow wafted into his face. Droplets of water hung from the telegraph wires that slanted uphill through the air close by him. The bare boughs of trees stood on end like tousled hair. The lights of neighboring houses were already blinking among the fretwork of their twigs.

Should he go to see Quapp? No. She would be no help. Stangeler? No. Suddenly and with deep alarm he felt the lack of that normally ever-present sense of the dire opposition between his own world and that of Camy. The tension between these two poles seemed to have vanished, slacked off completely. The gulf no longer gaped; it had become filled with saccharine.

He made ready to go out—without a goal—and such was his state that in the street he almost ran straight into a little fruit stand offering the first Italian cherries of the season. An acetylene lantern hung over the stand. Under the intense light the fruit gleamed crimson against the damp grayness of the street.

Within this light, which exaggerated colors and flattened the shapes of things, a woman stopped. She spoke a few words to the fruit peddler, paid him, and turned to go. She was wearing a brown fur jacket, a tiny hat with a veil of the same color— and that was actually all that Schlaggenberg could discern of her. When she leaned forward, the fur around her broad hips seemed to tighten somewhat. The fact is that Kajetan followed her instantly—he was chasing after all fat women, in accord with the program he had drawn up for himself—although he had scarcely seen her face. He kept her in sight, although he tried to do so as discreetly as possible and lagged a reasonable distance behind her. The woman headed toward the city, and Kajetan followed.

This pursuit lasted for some time, although at many junctures Schlaggenberg felt that he was being frightfully silly.

The woman stopped in front of a window displaying kitchen utensils. He was able to observe her face. It was anything but pretty, was in fact extremely ordinary and utterly without attraction. While Schlaggenberg stood there in consternation, the woman vanished into the next doorway.

René and Grete had spent the springlike afternoon out in the country, enjoying the amazing echoing emptiness of the still bare woods, the first green shoots, the trickling from the trees, the shrill solitary bird cries, and the early lights of the city rising at the foot of the hill like a red-hot gridiron. They walked hand in hand, and their state of mind came under the heading: "Somehow everything is going to work out between

345

us." The Siebenschein apartment was going to be dependably deserted this evening; Lasch had arranged an automobile trip and had taken the entire grateful family with him. Grete was happy, and once again standing firmly upon the ground, not reeling amid a tangle of griefs.

She turned around, while climbing the stairs, and threw her lover a conspiratorial smile. It was not hard to see why: she was smiling because of this successful evening when they could be alone in the quiet apartment, and because she had managed to avoid going on the outing with her family.

The two scarcely talked. Their small supper was quickly finished. Something like a fanatical seriousness marked both their faces. Grete swiftly cleared the table, and when she returned to her room from the kitchen her eyes were sparkling. She stepped swiftly behind the screen that shielded her wide bed and switched on the night-table lamp. Then she put out the other lights.

Schlaggenberg was just turning away from the hardware shop—his face as empty as a vessel with the bottom knocked out—when someone nodded a greeting to him.

Laura Konterhonz.

He took a step toward her, and she stood still. Where was she bound? Oh, nowhere, really; she only wondered what was playing at the cinema here. Alone? "Yes, quite alone," she said with a mixture of indignation and faint reproach.

Those who did not know her and had only glimpsed her on the street, might not have perceived what a well-equipped female this Laura Konterhonz was. Her figure, of course, was noteworthy: she was slightly over medium size, but strong, not exactly corresponding to the contemporary ideal, rather a model caryatid by academic standards. However, this physical structure was always dressed with such peculiar tastelessness that her advantages were swathed and defeated. Such frumpishness is a rare exception in Vienna. It constituted a great drawback for Fräulein Konterhonz, though it was plainly an attribute of her whole being as much intended by the Creator as, say, her tiny, finely shaped hands and feet, or her extremely modest intelligence.

Her sudden appearance on the scene this particular evening was truly all Schlaggenberg needed. He realized at once that Laura Konterhonz was virtually the inevitable climax of this curious day. There was something "threatening" about her running into him, just as there had been about Levielle's sudden departure. At the same time she did offer him a sanctuary from his thoughts.

Our caryatid, Laura Konterhonz, indubitably formed the darkest chapter—aside from his marriage—in Kajetan's past.

She was the daughter of a high-ranking general staff officer who had died a few years after the war. In 1912 or 1913, when Schlaggenberg was doing his year's military service, he had served in the same unit as her brother, and in this way had come to know Laura.

Even at that time there had been, if I remember rightly, some sort of superficial flirtation between the two. I know for certain, however, that later on—as early as the middle of the war—Laura was considered to be engaged. Her fiancée was a general staff officer whom I also knew. However, nothing came of this engagement, either because her fiancée saw his career ruined by the collapse of 1918, or for some other, private reason. Shortly afterwards Laura's father, the major-general, succeeded in installing his daughter in a government office (this old gentleman was probably the most energetic nepotist I have ever known, and that is saying a good deal, for our fair country provides frequent perfect specimens of the type). Laura received her appointment at the very time the newspapers were hammering away about the urgent necessity of cutting the civil service and reducing the government budget by eliminating all jobs not absolutely essential.

Around this time she also seems to have begun seeing Schlaggenberg more frequently again. His affair with Camy Schedik had been going on for several years, and several of their "separations" had already taken place. I assume that crucial developments between Kajetan and Laura occurred during one such separation. During these intervals Schlaggenberg was capable of, and perhaps driven to, all kinds of diversions.

At any rate, Kajetan laid siege to the girl, who was already past thirty, overripe but still intact. He succeeded in awakening her somewhat sluggish nature and before long had her completely in his toils. He filled her with tinder until she caught fire.

The place he occupied in her existence was completely disproportionate to the place she occupied in his. He formed the content of her days and the stuff of her nocturnal dreams. A number of other circumstances combined to drive her the faster into Schlaggenberg's nets. Both her appearance, which no longer corresponded to the contemporary taste, and the above-mentioned dowdy wrappings in which the package came, left Laura with few other possibilities. Now and then, it was true, she would encounter a few men in her mother's home, or at the office; but none of these could bear comparison with Schlaggenberg. Moreover, she already loved him. Perhaps, indeed, the germ of this emotion had entered her years ago, even before the war. Now, however, in a period which deemed it the height of insanity to miss even the smallest pleasures life offered, she began to suffer from that gravest disease of the left-out woman: she craved "life." And although not a trace of the new virus could be found in her mother's home, the infection was passed to her from the street, or from some woman friend.

Schlaggenberg, however, was basically entirely bound up with Camy Schedik. And here began the base part of the story—if I may be permitted to pass judgment. For it was beyond question that Laura could not compare with Camy in any way. She lacked entirely Camy's clear-headedness, love of truth, and insight. Not to mention the fact that Schlaggenberg's future wife completely surpassed her rival in certain of the finer female attractions, in grace and in taste.

I should not have used the word "rival," for it may give rise to some misunderstanding. Schlaggenberg never remotely considered Laura a rival of Camy. It is an ugly thing to say, but I know for certain that Kajetan always felt dislike for Laura Konterhonz. It was not that deeply buried dislike, quite smothered by admiration, which he sometimes bore toward Camy (and which verged almost on a secret fear). Rather, it was an irritated dislike whose real sources were quite clear to him. I always thought it perfectly understandable. If anyone had called Laura an inflated silly goose, I should have found it hard to contradict him. In peacetime—before 1914, that is—her father had been a regimental commander; and anyone familiar with social conditions in the old Austrian army knows what part the daughter of a regimental commander played, especially if she was pretty (and she was prettier then). Even if she was ugly, she never lacked dancing partners. In such a case as that of Laura Konterhonz, the most attractive ensigns and lieutenants presented themselves on their knees and with broken hearts in endless succession. It would have been a heroic task even for a girl of considerably greater intelligence than Laura to make the shift from perpetual belle of the ball to wallflower. As a matter of fact, in my opinion Laura would never have needed to make so drastic a switch, had she been somewhat less banal and pretentious. She could very well have won a modest place for herself outside of military circles.

But she did not have it up there. There are actually women who so surround the roses of their charms with the thorns of their arrant and arrogant stupidity that no one has the slightest desire to pluck them.

Moreover, she was one of those persons who cannot go about except under the banner of some pompous phrase. First it had been virtue. Then, after Schlaggenberg seduced her, the watchword became eternal and indestructible love. Thus she clung to Kajetan with terrible, unyielding obstinacy in spite of the round of distressing experiences with him that soon followed. The high-sounding epithets she found for her passion for Schlaggenberg were basically false; yet for her these over-emotional linguistic formulas had at least a kind of truth. We might say that she had been addicted to him, succumbed to this addiction again and again, and was still addicted at the time of the events being recounted here. Such was the result of Schlaggenberg's playing with tinder; and in the end he may often have felt like an incendiary who by mistake has shut himself up in the already flaming building and now stands behind a locked door, about to scream for help.

So it went through the years. He took up with her, and let her go again. His sense of responsibility may occasionally have troubled him, but oddly enough, he thought to quiet his conscience by constantly urging Laura, with all the arguments and sophisms of libertarianism, not to impose any restraints upon herself, certainly not to think of being "faithful" to him. It may well be that he really liked knowing that she had relations with other men. At every possible opportunity he emphasized his and her utter freedom. During such speeches she sometimes twitched all over, as though undergoing physical pain.

She knew nothing about Schlaggenberg's love for his wife-to-be, in fact was completely ignorant of the existence of Camy Schedik. I know for certain that this was the case (and why should I have been the one to enlighten her?). Such ignorance—testimony, by the way, to the crudity of Laura's intuition—may at first sight seem incredible. But we must remember that the geography of the society in which Laura moved was entirely different from that of Camy Schedik; there was no land bridge between their two continents. Moreover, Kajetan was often separated from Camy for long periods of time.

What I am saying is that it must have been easy for him to hide her from Laura. Nor had he any reason to do otherwise: for him the relationship with Laura was simply a stopgap affair, which bound him to nothing in the way of explanations.

Certainly Laura never seriously imagined that Schlaggenberg was being faithful to her. He saw to it in the bluntest fashion that no such mistake should arise. Her prudishness and her pretensions of respectability impelled him to tell her the most incredible stories of affairs and pranks he had actually or allegedly engaged in—usually in the earthiest terms. I once witnessed such a scene. "Schlaggenberg," she said, "the kind of language you allow yourself in my presence is really an outrage." Through the shams she always maintained in my presence (calling him by his last name, and so on, as though there had never been anything between the two of them) I realized that she took a certain prurient pleasure in his obscenities.

Of course, when Schlaggenberg suddenly married it may well have been a hard blow for her, the annihilation of her last, secretly held, tenacious hopes. So far as I know, she remained completely out of touch with him during the period of his marriage—which, however, lasted little more than a year. The following winter Kajetan mentioned Laura in conversation several times; he thought she ought to know of his separation. I cannot say whether he ever actually informed her of it. In any case her reappearance that memorable night just after Levielle's visit came as a complete surprise to Schlaggenberg. Of late he had no longer given her a thought, he said.

This time she behaved toward him with far less aloofness than was her habit after each fresh reunion. They went cheerfully to the cinema, sat arm in arm eating candy, and decided to continue the evening together by going to a café after the film.

The hour was far advanced. Grete knew that Lasch and the rest of the family intended to meet another party for supper at a certain country restaurant no earlier than nine o'clock. Nevertheless, she and René would have to bring their enjoyments to a close by eleven o'clock at the latest, to avoid any possibility of an unpleasant surprise.

When she had finished her toilette and restored everything to order, they left the apartment. In the street a warm gentle wind blew directly in their faces, bringing with it a sense of the open country which began not so far away. They walked slowly, arm in arm, leaning toward each other.

When they entered a café, they did so simultaneously with Laura Konterhonz and Schlaggenberg. They encountered one another in the curtained entranceway in front of the revolving door.

Stangeler was overcome with confusion. Grete, however, took a liking to Schlaggenberg at first sight. She was, so to speak, pleasantly surprised, and that was probably the decisive event of the evening. She proved capable of casting aside all her prejudgments, and of recognizing and accepting what she found. The two couples sat down at the same table. Stangeler felt as if he had been caught red-handed. Kajetan scented this at once, and seized upon Grete's friendliness and conciliatory manner toward him to treat her with particular cordiality, intending in this way to reassure his younger friend. The situation on both sides during this first meeting made for something closely approaching harmony. Laura Konterhonz sat there stupidly, not knowing what it was all about, but fortunately so void of intuition that she did not realize she had stumbled onto a crossroads. She merely noted that Kajetan "obviously was an old friend of this gentleman's," and was for the rest quite content to "have a little company." So she thought to herself, and remained unaware of her own isolation, so that she did not even resent Kajetan's gallantries toward Grete. As a prophylactic measure, however, Schlaggenberg patted Laura's chubby hands under the table.

Grete Siebenschein, however, was quite delighted with Laura, and frequently addressed herself to her. Stangeler's beloved was not slow to recognize beauty in other women, and she had a pronounced preference for it. Aside from this, she may well have felt a sympathy that sprang from some deep premonition. Schlaggenberg sensed this. Above all he sensed (and was moved by) the extent of Grete's peaceful intentions, her obvious desire for harmony between them. This desire did not spring from prudence. Rather, it was simply the attitude most appropriate to her nature. Conciliation and concord seemed to be, for Grete, the line of least resistance, the natural course her temperament chose, if it were not driven by force in another direction. How quickly there sprang up in her the sincere hope of healing all conflicts in this good and gracious manner. She wanted to live for her love, nothing more.

That evening Kajetan felt a warm affection for Grete, and probably he knew whom she stood for in his mind. Certainly he tacitly admitted as much to me next day. "She would join our crowd, would want to join it, innocently and honestly, believing in all sincerity that somehow she would be able to conciliate the hostile people who want to part her from her boy, these Eulenfelds and Schlaggenbergs. She would gladly join, with Stangeler."

At the same time Schlaggenberg was irritated with Laura. She seemed to him in no way deserving of so much attention from Grete. "That goose had not the slightest notion whom she was dealing with," he said to me next day, "and utterly lacked any deeper respect, any subtle appreciation, such as a basically tragic figure merits."

Certainly that evening he was conciliatory, and full of thoughts of Camy. The red light rose painfully and alluringly above the horizons of the past. His firm conviction that his marriage to Camy was fundamentally impossible turned vague in this mist, lost its sharp outlines. Schlaggenberg's violently stirring desires—the desires of a prophet looking backward, as it were—took the form of an overwhelming benevolence toward René and Grete, toward them both as a couple, that is, as a unity of two. Certainly Kajetan had never dreamed a few hours earlier—say, during the conversation with Levielle—that he would be having any such emotions that evening.

They left the café together, and all four walked for a while through quieter streets, and through a park whose paths were damp in the warmth of a night on the brink of spring, while the shrubs and trees, still bare to the casual glance, hid themselves in the darkness. But here and there, reaching surprisingly out into the amber light of a gas lantern, would be a branch with rows of buds breaking out into green. Grete was the first to discover one of these shoots. "Why, it's already green," she said, and stooping with maternal tenderness to the shrub, she saw that it was completely covered with tiny emeralds. Laura Konterhonz and Stangeler strolled on, in the van. Apparently René was saying all sorts of amusing things or amiable nonsense to Laura, for she was laughing merrily. It is not difficult to guess that Schlaggenberg's friendly attitude toward Grete—which lifted an enormous burden from René's mind—devolved to the benefit of Laura. For in other circumstances Stangeler might very well have regarded Laura Konterhonz as nothing more than the silly goose she undoubtedly was, and he might very well have behaved insultingly toward her. For he often displayed a lamentable lack of control toward such persons.

Here in the park Kajetan reached the ultimate of all the reverses of that evening. As the girl beside him bent over the budding shrub and spoke with a tenderness well-nigh freighted with tears, as though each of these tiny green buds were a beloved child—as she stooped, it seemed to Kajetan for one terrible moment that the destruction of his marriage (which in the final analysis had been the work of his own stubborn will), that everything he had done in obedience to his convictions, and to what he thought the true commandment of his destiny, had verged on criminal insanity, had been the sheerest idiotic fixation upon the past. And suddenly he also became aware of the fact that month after month lately his strength had been ebbing away, as though from a hidden hemorrhage, or as if more and more of it had been consumed in holding closed the edges of the gaping wound, in suppressing the pain, in smothering it under the stony block of will that he had rolled over the grave of his love. But, damn it all, all this stuff came from the brain (as he now believed), and what right had it to . . . ?

Here his thinking dissolved in confusion, and at the same

time he became aware that Grete was looking attentively at him as they walked on. And oddly enough, she looked at him in almost the same manner, with the same radiant kindness, as she had contemplated the shrub.

"Will you help Stangeler?" she asked softly.

"I will," Schlaggenberg answered promptly. "Levielle came to see me today," he added and at once took alarm at his own candor (or unforgivable stupidity). "Did you know that Levielle intended to call on me? Was his visit by any chance at your request?"

"No," she said in genuine astonishment. "What would I have to do with Levielle? How do you happen to know him?"

"Hasn't he ever mentioned knowing me?"

"No. How does that come about?"

"Through my parents. He arranged—in our family—certain important affairs—but that isn't pertinent—it's all very long ago, anyhow." ("Have I gone completely out of my mind?" he thought even as he spoke.)

"What did he want of you?"

But Schlaggenberg was regaining his self-control. He told her nothing about Levielle's offers, although she tried to probe, for the sudden mention of Levielle in connection with Stangeler (and by her question she had meant chiefly furtherance of his literary plans) had given Grete food for thought.

In our garden suburb, the spring soon grew more pronounced. The first delicately green, still almost gauzelike curtains of leafage were drawn before the yellows or grays of the small houses, and the terraces of the Kahlenberg showed a hint of sprouting winter grain. Water and mud vanished from the fields, and soon from the still bare woods, under the warming sun. At last—after the first walk, say, on paths which you had disdained on your swift skis, and scarcely even noted in the snow—at last you felt that the cold season had been left behind. And where such paths sloped downhill you had to accustom yourself step by step to the sense of being earthbound, for the winter's gliding down the slopes was over now. In clearings and amid undergrowth the earth sent up a strong fragrance, and out of sun-warmed pockets among dry leaves the hepatica glowed. The sky stretched like silk over distant ridges of hills.

At this time several additions were made to our circle. Besides my two kinsfolk, Körger and Orkay, Angelika Trapp had begun to appear frequently with Neuberg, while Schlaggenberg was accompanied by no less substantial a personage than Laura Konterhonz. (I may add, incidentally, that she very soon made a ludicrous impression on the whole crowd.) It seemed, then, that something in the nature of a lasting relationship had developed between her and Kajetan, instead of the fitful one in which Schlaggenberg each time had descended like a disaster upon the pitiable girl, rending her away from the peaceful if wretched refuge of gentle forgetfulness in which she was beginning to settle down.

Of greater significance was the appearance of Grete Siebenschein in our crowd.

I knew, of course, that this could have taken place only with the "approval" or "permission" of Schlaggenberg. And a remark of Eulenfeld's—"might not be the worst method, at that," he said—made me suspect that deliberate intention underlay this "step." Perhaps only after much consideration and consultation was it decided to give "'the Ensign' a *placet*," to speak with Eulenfeld. It did not occur to me at the time that the explanation was much simpler, that Schlaggenberg had simply been won over by the girl—that evening in the café and the park. Since I knew nothing of her effect on him, I thought his obvious breach of consistency was due to some deeper plan.

The special attentiveness he showed Grete struck me as further evidence of such a deliberate plan. She, incidentally, seemed to be especially delighted to find me in the circle she had just entered. Apparently she had not expected anything of the sort. "It's really very nice that you are here, Herr Geyrenhoff. That means at least one sane, objective person without any prejudices . . ." She said this to me when we were standing to one side, out of earshot of the others.

I could think of no reply the least bit quick-witted. What I was instantly conscious of was a great disorder within myself, and at the same time I felt that I had already succumbed to certain influences that emanated principally from Schlaggenberg and Eulenfeld—and lately, with particular force but in a form that might be described as "mute," from none other than my good nephew, Doktor Körger. Actually I was already looking at things through their eyes, or at least beginning to. At the same time I was still trying hard to cling to the idea that all these attitudes were phantasmagorias, and that I had only to "recollect myself" in order to fend off this pressure . . .

But enough of myself and the changes I had personally undergone.

Around the middle of April, shortly before Easter, another outing was arranged. This time all of "our crowd," took part, including the "new acquisitions." There were fifteen of us altogether. Not since that evening at Schlaggenberg's which we later called the "foundation festival" had we been together in full strength this way. For some reason the majority had agreed to assemble in the city (I was among these, though I no longer remember what reason I had for going to town that morning).

In fact, the meeting place had been in a neighborhood

which not too long afterwards achieved a mournful notoriety. On one side of a spacious square stands a public building: the Palace of Justice. It certainly cannot be ranked among the finest buildings of the city, but it is fully in keeping with the taste of the time at which it was built. At any rate, Grete Siebenschein, regarding the façade of this massive structure, exclaimed something like:

"What a monstrosity!" I do not think that my nephew, Doktor Körger, had in mind to defend the taste of the nineties when he replied somewhat sharply: "No—beg your pardon—better than a great many of today's productions. I grant you, it isn't exactly to my taste. But *you* are only following fashion in passing such a judgment upon it." Thus Körger. And from that moment on a kind of uncontrollable irritability overtook our little company. It continued even after we were out in the country, and lasted through almost the entire outing.

First there was a good deal of argument back and forth over the trifling matter which had unleashed my nephew's spleen. We stood there in the warm spring sunlight waiting for two or three of the crowd who had not yet arrived. The intimate blue of the sky, the beds of massed yellow tulips in the gardens, the penetrating sunlight, formed the ground colors for a rather tense conversation whose contents and logic were of no account, but whose hidden antagonisms and alignments were all-important. The square, and the streets which streamed majestically into it from various sides, gave the impression of being extraordinarily neatly swept. I observed that Stangeler, who for once ostentatiously held aloof from the general disputatiousness, was absorbing the picture of our surroundings with a literally passionate intensity. He looked happy. Körger's views were opposed with wordy eloquence by Neuberg and Holder. That good soul Hedwig Glöckner also defended Grete's verdict with some heat. But the leader of the opposition was Gyurkicz. Suddenly I observed an outrageously supercilious grin upon the face of my Hungarian cousin, who said nothing at all. Then he turned away, as though all this chatter were not worth listening to—it had, of course, quickly gone from one thing to another and was in truth smoke without a trace of fire. Orkay stepped up to Stangeler and stood looking into the distance with him. Out of that distance Laura Konterhonz came sailing, waving to us; she came in all her substantiality, accompanied by Höpfner.

Even the streetcar into which we piled soon afterwards was gleaming with clean fresh color. The trolley train consisted of three newly painted cars with all their brass scoured to a high sheen. Everything on this day seemed to aim at a heightened distinctness.

We met Schlaggenberg only after we had reached the country. He was waiting for us by prearrangement on a hill not too far from his flat. From the end of the streetcar tracks the road led between villas and garden fences to a chain of rolling hills whose sides were dotted with more yellow and white houses and cottages. From this vantage point we could already see far out over the wooded ridges and peaks. When I first caught sight of Kajetan after a turn in the road, I thought he had not come alone. For against the light blue, slightly hazy sky stood a second figure beside him, a fairly tall strong girl with dark blonde hair. I was soon able to discern that much detail. But the whole thing was chance and an illusion; she was actually about to pass him, and was not standing beside Schlaggenberg but a good two paces behind him. Only from the distance had she seemed level with him. And now she walked on, down the road which our company was climbing, and passed right among us, splitting us into two groups. As a matter of fact I should have been surprised had Schlaggenberg actually brought someone, since Laura Konterhonz was with us in all her substantiality—chivalrously accompanied by Höpfner, whom she had met on the street when they were both wending their way to our meeting place in front of the Palace of Justice. Of course I thought Schlaggenberg capable of anything, even of such an outright blow against Laura as turning up in the company of a hitherto unknown female. He would have done that kind of thing in spite of the stability which his relations with Laura had attained of late—or perhaps for that very reason, as an act of defiance.

The view from the ridge of the hill was so surprising that all of us stopped with one accord. The green mist overlying the landscape had long since coagulated into the domelike, rounded lines of deciduous woodlands as they appear in summer, and on the rims of the hills the sky no longer peered between the bare branches of the topmost line of trees as if through sparse unkempt hair. The framework of the trees was once more clothed in green life. The strong sun flashed in the windows of the cottages, encouraging the birds to shrill whistles which rang high and clear in the brittle stillness.

We continued on in two groups. Ahead walked Eulenfeld, my two kinsfolk, Schlaggenberg, Stangeler, and Quapp, who walked beside me. None of the other ladies was with us. At some distance the second troupe followed, led by the formidable couple Konterhonz and Höpfner. (Whenever I mention Laura Konterhonz I ought to add "in all her substantiality" as I have done hitherto; henceforth the reader may supply the term. At the same time I should like to say once again that the image she presented as she sailed along "in all her substantiality" was something extremely silly, on the order of such high-flown locutions as: "I recently indulged in a lovely and refreshing stroll in the company of several ladies and gentlemen of my acquaintance, in order to catch a breath of air.")

In the rear group Holder and Neuberg were holding forth. We up front were not doing very much talking. It is time, incidentally, to take note of a matter which even at that early stage of the game could no longer be overlooked. It concerns my two kinsfolk; or rather, it emanated from those two young men. First of all, there seemed to exist some sort of tacit understanding between them. For example, they were apt, when among us, to smile simultaneously at the most varied provocations— and the provocations were indeed most diverse, although they all had a kind of inner similarity too. The two men seemed to grin, like people who have already been through something, or know something, and see someone else groping and struggling toward this knowledge. It was as though they knew the other person would sooner or later come to the same solution they had already found, though at the moment he held an opposing point of view. Once, for example, they gave one of these grins when Schlaggenberg spoke of conditions in the literary market and Grete Siebenschein volunteered the thought that readers must be won over to better literature by education and advertising. Another time they grinned when Quapp spoke with excessive thoughtfulness of high pure values which lie concealed, locked away, and unable to find an outlet, in such hail-fellow-well-met personalities as Gyurkicz. In short, on many occasions they assumed a know-it-all attitude. Körger's temperament inclined him to occasional outbursts—such as the one that had just taken place in front of the Palace of Justice. Géza, so far as I knew, never let himself go in that fashion, this in spite of all the talk one hears about hot Magyar blood. Well, he was after all a diplomat by profession. He held his peace, tanned as he was, lean, slant-eyed, with a sharp vulture's nose, looking like that legendary eagle Turul which had once upon a time shown Arpad, the Hungarian national hero, the way to the land between the Danube and the Theiss River.

If you stopped and turned around now, you saw the city lying down below like a vast puddle, swimming in dark, violet hues, pouring and receding to the farthest horizon, advancing toward the great flatlands.

"We are marching with divided forces today," Stangeler said, for he had turned around. "In two entirely separate groups. Not even the two Hungarians are together."

Orkay gave a short laugh.

"If you take this divided march in a figurative sense, you will have a picture of the true state of affairs," my nephew remarked.

"How's that?" Stangeler asked.

"For my part, let it serve as a model of a better future."

"What does he mean?" Quapp whispered to me.

"Oh well, we might steer a few of those back there over to us. Höpfner or Angelika, I'd suggest," Körger murmured.

"And what would you do with my fat Laura?" Schlaggenberg replied.

"We could do with her too. She can come over."

Just at this point Grete Siebenschein left the group in the rear. She came up front to join her René and entwined her arm in his. Evidently she had heard these last words, for she promptly said to Körger: "Who may come over? Do you mean me?"

"Oh no, not *you*," my nephew replied imperturbably.

"You do not know what we were discussing, Fräulein Siebenschein," Orkay said with a friendly laugh. He could not bear the slightest lapse of courtesy and in all such cases would skillfully intervene and cover up. "We were thinking of organizing a table tennis tournament among the men—ping-pong,

363

as it's called—with two opposing teams playing for five bottles of wine. But my cousin—or whatever he is to me, I'll never really understand it—wants to have all the good players on his side, including the captain. He was just saying that the captain could 'come over'—on his side, that is."

Eulenfeld, who had never in his life held a table-tennis racket in his hand, regarded Orkay with undissembled warmth.

"Wonderful," said Grete Siebenschein. "Oh, I've been wishing so for a chance to play ping-pong again; I've been wanting to for ever so long. René, we'll buy a set and practice in the dining room; there's room enough there, isn't there?" She had been immediately reassured, restored to her innocuous gaiety. Her sharp instinctive premonition which had led her to join us at exactly the right moment, was only too readily lulled into a false sense of security. Immediately, one of her kindly, well-intentioned wishes acquired again the power to father her subsequent thoughts. We, however, by tolerating and even furthering Orkay's lie, were curiously welded into a community which shared certain common knowledge, and from which she was barred as an alien.

Körger went even further. "I don't know about that, Fräulein Siebenschein," he said. "Not every big dining-room table is suitable for table tennis. There are rules regarding the measurements, you see—did you know that? Besides, a table lengthened by leaves naturally has horizontal grooves, even if the leaves fit very closely, and a ball striking one of these grooves takes an unexpected bounce. The best thing would be, I think, for all of us to contribute and have a carpenter make us one or two table tops simply out of straight, planed boards. We could have them painted green and mounted on something like sawhorses. If we all contributed, it would only mean a small sum for everyone."

So he was actually going into detail!

"The tables could then be set up every time we wanted to play, at the home of any of us who happens to have enough room. Perhaps one of them could be kept at your house, if your dining room really is large enough."

I was staggered by this elaboration.

"Yes, wonderful," Grete exclaimed with delight. "We'll organize a table-tennis club. At my house. Of course. There's plenty of room. But then the tournament must not be restricted to the men. That won't do."

"No, of course not. Ladies, too—since you're participating, of course," Schlaggenberg said in his friendliest tone. "That will be ever so much more entertaining anyhow. Say, Quapp, you used to play pretty well, as I recall."

But Quapp, with her straightforward simple nature, could no longer bear this outrageously growing lie. "Ye-es," she murmured vaguely. "But it's all such a long time ago . . ." She had a tormented, sad expression in her eyes. She looked at me and gave a somewhat forced smile. I knew that she felt ashamed for all of us.

As it happened, this feeling did us an injustice. All our attitudes were governed by a constraint which had crept in ever so gently, but which had now become inescapable. And it was Quapp herself who was responsible for some of this constraint. She too lived, like Stangeler, torn asunder; she too was constantly visiting that no man's land where the act of treachery required at any given moment is performed, somehow, in the semidarkness of the soul, until with increasing practice it can be done with a certain agility. Almost every other day she hastened "over the hill" (as we were accustomed to say; but I shall speak about this phrase some other time). It was a real hill, a slope set with houses and vineyards, beyond which lay a lower portion of our garden suburb. For Quapp and Gyurkicz both had emigrated there just recently. She climbed the hill in order, say, to visit her brother, at whose quarters she also frequently encountered Stangeler; or to have a cup of tea with me and the captain, and perhaps talk with my two cousins. And each time she talked too much and the time passed and she would hurry back over the hill again, because Gyurkicz would already be waiting at her flat; and the minutes or even the quarter hours of these waits swelled thickly inside him the way a vein might swell in his temple, for he could well imagine where she probably was. And Quapp hastened down through the park which occupied the "other side of the hill," and on the way she had to violently throw all the interior switches of her being, which in conversation with her friends had pointed in the one direction which constituted her "way"—had to violate and bend or break this whole mechanism, this framework of her life, in order to feel once more genuine and whole while she was with Gyurkicz. For the one thing she could not do with him was prudently act a part.

Everything went awry with her. She was incapable of changing her nature so rapidly as she panted over the hill, past the little shelter by the streetcar stop, which capped the hill, and down into the gloomy park.

Often enough she would engage in hour-long quarrels with Gyurkicz, during which she hated him.

In time all of us became as accustomed as was possible to this whole situation, and tolerant about it, taking our cue from Schlaggenberg, who had formed the habit of accepting his sister's love entanglements uncritically. So in the end we put up with Herr von Gyurkicz, and with what a dashing figure he had cut during the war—although during such recitals the captain would at times clear his throat with excessive loudness.

It sometimes seemed to me that in spite of the occasional warning murmurs of certain facts, we ourselves no longer knew where truth ceased or began. Among the lot of us, only my two kinsfolk were really uninhibited. But even Géza, whose attitude had been perfectly unequivocal when he first met Gyurkicz, fell in the end under the same constraint as the rest of us and accommodated himself to the man, although he did so only for Quapp's sake. Our Herr von Gyurkicz treated the bird Turul with distinct reserve, which was natural enough, given the situation.

Such were my recollections and trains of thought as I walked along beside Quapp up the gently inclined path, the spring sun resting like a warming but weightless topcoat on my shoulders and back. However, Grete Siebenschein soon called my attention to herself.

"To tell the truth, Herr von Schlaggenberg," she was saying, "though of course I didn't know exactly—how could I have?—I thought stepsister or something like that . . ."

"Why, what do you mean, stepsister? First time I've ever heard that. No, Quapp is my real sister. Who ever told you different?"

"No one—I really don't know what gave me that idea . . . Let me see you"—she studied Quapp—"yes, when you look closer you do see a kind of resemblance, a kind of deeper resemblance, sort of—I mean, stupid people wouldn't take you for brother and sister at first glance. I guess I'm one of the stupid ones. After a while you begin to see it. But we were talking about old Levielle." Apparently I had missed this, since I had been lagging behind a few steps with Quapp. "You must really know him much longer than I do. He isn't really connected with our family—rather more with yours—I mean, as an old acquaintance of your parents, as you were telling me the time we first met."

367

Eulenfeld had turned around.

The expression on Quapp's face told me beyond the shadow of a doubt that what she was hearing was nothing new to her, nothing in the least bit surprising.

"Yes, that is true," Schlaggenberg said. He maintained his composure, though with considerable effort, and was coping with the situation created involuntarily by Grete Siebenschein. "He used to be in and out of my parents' house. But at that time I was practically a child. I hardly remember having seen him after my father's death, but while my old man was alive Levielle did turn up fairly often. I think he was a kind of adviser in business or financial affairs, the administration of the property and such stuff—although we didn't have too much property to administer, aside from the farmlands, and Herr Levielle certainly didn't know anything about cows or crops. Well, at any rate, whatever he was up to, he was what you call a"—Schlaggenberg abruptly caught his breath and concluded—"a manager."

"A typical character of the 1880's," Körger threw back over his shoulder to us, with a burst of laughter which struck me as unnecessarily loud.

"Still common in Hungary today," the bird Turul cawed; he did speak occasionally, after all.

"Yes, yes," Eulenfeld cried. Oddly, he sounded inordinately relieved, as though for some reason a tremendous load had been taken off his mind, as the phrase goes. "Yes, we've had dealings with the type, too. My old man had someone like that. Doktor Benno Isserlin. A droll sort of fellow. Sometimes helps my mother out even to this day. Honest as they come, incidentally. Once asked for my sister's hand. I can just imagine how my father reacted to that. As a matter of fact, Isserlin once described that little episode to me. 'Well I'll be damned, what

368

did the old boy say?' I asked Isserlin. 'Nothing, not a thing. He didn't utter a word. You know'—this is how Isserlin told it—'he sat sunk into the lowest easy chair, looking up at me from below, but in the strangest way, his face with that walrus mustache of his lowered so that only his eyes were sort of peering up at me.' 'And how did you act?' I asked him. 'Oh me,' he said. 'Well, I said my piece and then I just stood there, and he didn't say a word and stared at me so strangely, and I waited.' 'And finally?' 'Finally—well, finally I began to feel pretty queer. Queer; I tell you I was scared stiff, and I left the room, but you know, the funny part of it was that I backed out, step by step, facing him all the time. And he just kept staring at me, peering up at me, and I reached behind my back for the doorknob and opened the door softly and was glad to get out of that room. And now you see, Herr von Eulenfeld,' he said, 'how it was I did not, I'm sorry to say, become your brother-in-law.'"

Everyone laughed. "I shouldn't think you regretted it so terribly," Grete Siebenschein said.

"Still and all, I must say," Eulenfeld went on with all deliberation, "those old bags of bones had a damned good technique for keeping things within bounds. We don't have that today."

"That is to say," Körger contributed, "those old bags of bones were liberal to the bone, but their bones weren't quite so liberal, and so the old bags of bones kept liberalism within bounds."

"Frightfully witty," Eulenfeld said. "I can hear the future lawyer's wit and wisdom in every word you say. Over these bones now do I prophesy you'll be an ornament of our courts someday."

I was astonished to observe how skillfully Grete Siebenschein adapted to this sort of banter, without revealing the slightest touchiness. At the same time I fancied that she had raised the subject in order to engage in a bit of surreptitious aggression against Schlaggenberg. But how could this possibly be proved? At any rate, she had not got far with her attack.

My ears were alert again. Kajetan was saying: "For some reason he seems—let's say, disgruntled, toward you. Have you any idea why? What do you think, Fräulein Grete? I had the impression that the estimable financial counselor was somehow antagonistic to our 'Ensign.'"

"Why should he have been?" Grete countered. "It may be that he was irritated once or twice when he heard that René wasn't being nice to me (she actually so described it), but after all, that's another matter. Besides, Levielle never has anything to do with Stangeler. At most, they just happen to run into each other at our place. You haven't seen the old man for weeks, have you, René?"

"No," Stangeler said.

"Of course you all have your prejudices about this too, but I can tell you that your opinion of him is all wrong; he's an extremely intelligent person, an important person, in his way, though I suppose most of you don't believe that a man who is engaged in nothing but business can have any importance. Anyway, as far as higher matters go, Levielle has done things there too, by his generosity. Dr. Neuberg, who's walking right behind us, was able to spend half a year in Rome on a stipend provided by Levielle."

"Fine," Schlaggenberg said, refusing to take up this line of argument, "fine—but I had the impression that Levielle must have been personally annoyed somehow by our 'Ensign.'"

"I wouldn't know what I've ever done to the old geezer. Anyway, as far as I'm concerned, he can—he knows what he can do."

"Very well, he knows what he can do," Kajetan repeated.

"No one is going to object to that. But I wish you would think about it. To tell the truth, I'm very much interested. You say it's weeks since René last met Levielle up at your parents' place, Grete? Didn't anything happen there? Wasn't there some sort of run-in?"

"Oh yes, now I realize," Grete said. "Of course. Just three weeks ago. My brother-in-law Lasch and Levielle were in the music room, having some sort of important conference. They were talking about things that perhaps weren't meant for others to hear, thinking themselves alone, and there was René stretched out on the sofa behind the piano. It was already growing dark and they hadn't switched on the light, so they didn't notice him until later on. René suddenly made a movement—the talking in the room woke him up—and so—I mean, the others were quite put out. René has his 'Russian' habits, you know. He comes to see me, doesn't find me in, and just because my couch happens to have a few hatboxes on it he throws himself down somewhere else and goes to sleep."

"How jolly," Quapp said.

"Call it jolly if you like," Grete replied. "But not everyone thought so. I mean, my brother-in-law said that apparently it wasn't possible any more to meet a business friend in my parents' apartment for a private talk—and so on, you can imagine the rest. Of course it was a little embarrassing for us—after all, it wasn't the first time, because something of the same sort had happened before."

"Now I've had enough! The things that go on behind my back at your house!" Stangeler exclaimed. "Revolting! People talk about me, this Herr Lasch makes a fuss, and of course you"—he turned his head and looked at Grete with what was plainly rising anger—"of course you're right there and don't even think it necessary to say so much as a word to me about it.

371

It all has to come out later . . ."

He was well on the way toward the sort of outburst we have already witnessed. Schlaggenberg, however, took his arm and pressed it lightly, obviously admonishing him to control himself.

"Look, René, sweet, I knew these things would annoy you—that's why I said nothing to you about them—but I've hinted often enough that you—that you oughtn't to let yourself go that way. You know, we aren't, I mean, let's say we aren't in Russia."

Stangeler took a deep breath. I saw Kajetan press his arm again. "Hell and damnation," René began, "why the devil should those two think I have the slightest interest in . . ." (At this point Kajetan made his third admonitory signal, and René actually checked his mounting outrage in mid-flight.) "Oh well, Gretel . . . I understand how you felt—and of course they couldn't know . . . I know it was disturbing for them—I have enough imagination to see that . . . but, but—believe me, I was really asleep and didn't hear a single word!"

"But, sweet, not one of us doubts *that!*" Grete said at once, smiling radiantly at him. She wrapped her arm around his shoulders and with the tenderest expression she looked into his eyes for a few seconds, her face close to his, her lips moving and whispering affectionate intimacies which no one else could hear.

As soon as Stangeler had subsided, Schlaggenberg pursued his interrogation with the same casual air. "Grete, do you think you could remember a little more precisely just when this ridiculous affair with Stangeler, Levielle, and your brother-in-law took place? You were saying it was at least three weeks ago. That must have been around the end of March, then, wouldn't you say?"

"Wait a moment," Grete Siebenschein said. She pondered. "It was—oh, a very short time before that evening you and I first met in the café. Three or four days before, at most. You remember, don't you? You came along with Fräulein Konterhonz, and René and I ran into the two of you in the entrance. That business in the music room had happened shortly before. I'm sure of it."

"And you also mentioned that similar incidents had taken place earlier, didn't you? You know, Stangeler," he went on, turning to René, "I can very well understand that such incidents would upset people. You'll have to be more careful about such matters in the future, for Grete's sake."

"Yes, of course," our "Ensign" replied.

Grete suddenly laughed. "Now I remember something similar happened barely a month before—I no longer remember just what it was all about, but I recall it because my brother-in-law Cornel raised the roof about it then. René was sitting in my room quiet as a mouse, writing something—something very good, by the way, the essay on Ulrich von Hutten which was published shortly after . . ."

"Bravo!" Schlaggenberg exclaimed.

"Well, then, those two high and mighty gentlemen were in the next room having their private discussion. Afterwards Cornel notices that René is sitting at work in my room and he says, in that arrogant way of his that I can't abide: 'A person is never really undisturbed in your house.' I assure you, I pointed out to him that if anyone was disturbed it was René, by all the jabbering in the next room. 'After all, he could just as well do his work at home,' he said, and I snapped back: 'And you could just as well hold your conferences in your own apartment.' Well, anyway, one word led to another, we quarreled about it, and I told him to his face that it was none of his business whom I lent my room to, and so on."

"And you say that happened just a month before the incident

373

in the music room."

"Yes. That was why they were all the more annoyed."

"The boy sure has had a run of bad luck," Schlaggenberg said, laughing. He slapped René on the back and changed the subject.

Strolling all the while, we had long since left the last of the cottages behind us. The echoing, brightly greening open spaces received us. The path began to ascend more steeply. Glancing at Stangeler, who was now walking alongside Quapp and me, I was struck by a strange yielding change which seemed to be in progress beneath the surface of his features. Plainly, he was utterly remote from all of us, and filled with happiness.

To the left of the path the trees receded. Freshly leafing bushes scattered out into a meadow which farther off dipped sharply downward, so that you looked across a new valley toward rounded hills and treetops rushing away. If you turned around now, you no longer saw the city. We came upon a few rickety old benches and decided to sit down, since the other group had loitered far behind us and we had lost sight of them.

Stangeler suddenly began speaking very rapidly. We stood or sat in a semicircle around him, and he moved back somewhat into the meadow. "Now I know," he said, obviously addressing all of us, "now I remember, all of a sudden, what I was dreaming, that time I was asleep in the music room. It's very queer. There was something, round and shiny, an apple, but made of a different kind of material, like a white pearl, but no, it was really more like an apple, round and gleaming . . ."

"Sounds like fresh horse manure," Doktor Körger muttered. But Stangeler did not hear and went on undeterred.

"This apple was—myself. White. All white inside. Unfinished. Part of it was missing. Something sharp and pointed pierced me, ate its way into the roundness of it . . . It was

374

white or brightly illuminated too, but not smooth; fibrous, rather, and—very sour. Sharp. But I knew I had to remain whole and intact, or rather not remain but become whole, 'roll myself into a ball'—I actually thought those words distinctly in the dream, and wanted to go on dreaming, but then I was awakened . . ."

"Stangeler rolled into a ball, floating freely in space, a thinking sphere—just imagine it, Stangeler, *'le globe philosophique'* . . ."

I signaled to my nephew to hold his tongue. This whole incident—René's story, our listening group facing him, the hills and woods in the background—all of it affected me mysteriously and violently, stirred a profound excitement in me. I felt deeply certain that Stangeler was not making this up, that he was striving with all his might to convey to us a vague and still obscured reality, an extremely important truth. But above all he was trying to bring it more clearly into his own consciousness.

"I did not want to wake up," he went on. "I wanted to hold on to this tremendous, unbelievably distinct insight. So much depended on my perfecting this rounding off of myself; or, to put it differently, on my replacing the piece which had been broken off and spoiled by the penetrating sharp point . . ."

I glanced at Schlaggenberg. His feelings seemed to coincide with mine. He was looking conspicuously grave. Quapp—it is easy to imagine with what intensity she was listening to "the Ensign."

Grete Siebenschein seemed totally absorbed in her sweetheart's face. Her eyes, bright and violet-blue, were opened wide; they expressed an extraordinary degree of empathy. A kind of odd wrinkle in the corners of their lids set them sharply off from the rest of her face. At least that was my impression. For the first time I noticed a few faint lines around her mouth.

Unquestionably she looked at this moment very much like her mother, and considerably aged.

Stangeler dropped into a more ordinary tone. "I know enough about psychology," he said, "to understand how such half-dreams arise. What I mean is, something actually happened which was the nucleus of that dream. The sharp pointed thing that was piercing into me proved to be, as I gradually awoke, as I bobbed up again to the surface that forms the boundary between waking and sleeping—proved to be, of course—and it was extraordinary how apparent that was, how I took it for granted—the voice of this Herr Levielle. That was the very tip of the point, the most sharply tapered part of it, the piercing, penetrating end, where it was fibrous and sour . . . You know, there's something falsetto about his voice. And then, farther back, along the broader section of the blade, where it was not so clean and white, but began to be darker—its substance proved to be the oily voice of this fellow Lasch . . ."

He fell silent. Grete Siebenschein's face was absolutely impassive. Every faintest furrow around her mouth could be seen. I particularly noticed that at the time. From the rear, our second group was drawing nearer the benches.

"Yes, Grete!" Stangeler suddenly exclaimed—and she started as he so unexpectedly turned directly to her and spoke so loudly. "Isn't it funny, now I do remember a little of their conversation. I was telling a falsehood a moment ago, though without intending to—the words have just come to me. The words entered into my dream. He kept saying again and again: 'The devil take him' and 'Let him fall.' Or something like: 'Ruin him' and 'worthless now.' It was . . . cold and spiteful and terrible. In the dream these phrases referred to me. I was to be ruined. Or let fall. Into a bottomless pit. Be lost, forever, absolutely and completely . . . In the dream there was a gigantic dark mill wheel carrying me down into the millrace, into the torrential masses of water, and as I fell the revolving, rumbling noises mounted to a wild roar . . . Now it is all clear to me. That is why I made such violent movements as I awoke. And then they were frightened. Of course."

"Spring-house. Metal screw on the frog of the bow," Schlaggenberg said loudly and distinctly.

"Yes!" Quapp and René exclaimed simultaneously. "Exactly!" Everyone looked dumbfounded at the three who had evidently achieved complete communication in such obscure terms.

"You three are already talking a jargon no one else can understand," my nephew remarked irritably.

"There she is again!" I cried in a low voice, pointing up the path.

"It's not the same girl," Gyurkicz said. As an artist he evidently had a keen eye for faces and for all the external details of a person's appearance. And he had understood me at once. That is, he knew whom I meant. "The girl who stood at the top of the hill, next to Schlaggenberg, was wearing a pink silk scarf, I think, and a darker jacket. But otherwise this girl is very like her, at least at first glance."

A tall and strong-looking girl with dark blonde hair passed on the path, and turned around for a moment to look back at us.

What had just happened? Nothing. Virtually nothing. Nothing worth mentioning, nothing that could really be defined. And yet I felt as if a cold and almost sinister breath had touched the back of my neck. As we continued our walk, again in two groups, I lingered behind with the second half of our company. Somehow the atmosphere had become too oppressive for me up front.

Stangeler and his sweetheart also lagged back. Laura Konterhonz, on the other hand, decided it was time to walk alongside Kajetan—whom she continued to address, in our presence, with the utmost formality. Höpfner, on her other side, made it a threesome. From what I have already said about the relationship it should cause no astonishment when I add that Schlaggenberg was pleased rather than displeased with Höpfner's attachment to fat Laura.

In our group Gyurkicz was now holding forth, exuding he-man vitality in all directions, while the "intellectuals"— chiefly Holder and Neuberg—listened and seemed greatly edified by such "dynamism." Grete, on the other hand, seemed distinctly critical of it all, whereas Fräulein Glöckner hung upon Imre's words. The same could not be said of good little Angelika Trapp; but still our hero's stories made some impression upon her.

As usual Gyurkicz was relating the ups and downs of his richly adventurous life. This time, for a change, he was not talking about the war, but about a period several years later when he had merrily run through his first inheritance and struggled through several years of the deepest poverty here in Vienna—until his second inheritance came along, providing him once again with the means to live according to his station, and with the opportunity to send another few thousand acres of good Hungarian land down the drain. (He really must have come from a frightfully rich and illustrious background.) In this connection the name of the Atlas Weight-lifters' Club was mentioned. I pricked up my ears, for this association of strong-men was familiar to me by name and reputation.

In Vienna the sport of weight-lifting (or "heaving," as it is

378

sometimes called) is well established among the populace; there have always been such clubs in the suburbs. So far so good—here was a sport with old and honorable associations. But as for the Atlas Club in particular: originally, no doubt, this club had been simply an ordinary group of sturdy philistine muscle-men, like every other weight-lifters' club. But I happened to know that the Atlas Weight-lifters had taken on another complexion. In the period of postwar upheavals certain interested parties had lit a fire under the association, which had ever since been held at a red-hot temperature, politically speaking. It was odd to find a Herr von Gyurkicz in such company, since according to his own statements he had taken an active part, not long before, in suppressing Bela Kun's red terror in his fatherland. Why, incidentally, had he not returned to his liberated country after the triumph of the counterrevolution?

"Physique, vigor, nature!"—"And to hell with all this intellectual stuff"—"Those are the kind of people I've always felt at home with"—"Simple souls, with a healthy delight in the physical, at the same time decent, wide-awake, wonderful boys"—"I have always lived by my instincts"—"After all, what does all this intellectualism amount to?"—"Coffeehouse!"

It seemed to me that I had listened to this kind of talk endlessly. Perhaps I might once have attributed a certain degree of validity to such phrases (although never, certainly, when they fell from Gyurkicz's lips). But in this context they were nothing but a device for currying favor with people who, as I realized now with particular sharpness, equated "intellectualism" with weakness, aimlessness, alienation from life—who, to put the matter crudely, regarded the intellect as something altogether rotten. All of them seemed agreed upon that: Holder, Neuberg, Fräulein Glöckner, and the rest; for not a single dissenting word was raised against our friend Gyurkicz. They were all ready to bow servilely before any rough lout; even the pretense of roughness and loutishness was enough for them. Acting like a muscular idiot seemed the surest way to impress them. Evidently they had never realized that real intelligence can only be the outward extension of inner strength, not its opposite—and that there is nothing rotten about such intelligence. Since we are dealing with the subject, however, I must candidly confess that during those years, both in our own little circle and in wider spheres, only this utterly corrupt notion of "intellect" prevailed. It had been passed around like an axiom, and at the time, in all probability, people knew nothing else.

Evidently Angelika Trapp did not. The very qualities she missed in Neuberg she found, oddly enough, in Gyurkicz. Before long she was as spellbound by our Hungarian hero as good Fräulein Glöckner.

It was the latter who now gave the conversation a somewhat more titillating turn, sent it off into higher dimensions. She flapped her wings and took off from a generally respected ideological springboard: "And what is the orientation of this group as far as enlightenment about certain things goes? I mean, do you think there is any likelihood that this group could be incited again and seduced by certain slogans, so that, for example, they would go to war again—what I mean is, do such people have enough political education so that, I mean, that would make a second catastrophe of the same kind impossible?"

In some dark corner of his nature Stangeler must have been displeased by all this talk about "intellectuals," for the knot of his slant-eyed face grew even tighter than usual. Now, however, he spoke up: "Since the example of Russia is there for all to see, and the layer of dead lies enclosing people's brains has been broken through at last, in the long run that sort of thing will be out of the question."

In so saying, Stangeler provided an opening for our scion of Arpad to flaunt his opposition: "Beg your pardon—I am no Bolshevik. And what we had in the past, our old army and a decent social order—that was good, I tell you. In my opinion. Please—I don't mean to be spouting ideologies or anything of that sort, but—beg your pardon, but opinions can differ on that score. Why shouldn't people go to war again sometime? War is a good thing. For every real man. I thought it fine. Best time in my life."

René Stangeler was beginning to remind me of a person just learning to ski: each ski tries to shoot off in a different direction.

"You are right, Herr von Gyurkicz," Holder, the editor, now said. "I too felt there was a kind of salvation in it—in that vigor, that lack of problems, I should say—once when I had occasion to hobnob a bit with people like that. Of course, come to think of it, they were a somewhat different type. Not really respectable people—rather, criminal types. We were doing a story on them. Vienna underworld and that sort of thing. I went along as a reporter. Not into the very worst areas, or into the hideouts in the sewers—what we did was have one of the detectives brief us on that. But we did go into one of the local dives—what we in Vienna call a 'brandy-shop.' Of course there were plenty of utterly wretched people in the place—people gone to the dogs, poverty-stricken, weak. Incidentally there was a one-time theologian whom the rest of the gang always called by the nickname 'Padre,' and strangely enough there was also a deacon or sexton, or whatever the fellow had been. When these two were thoroughly pickled, we were told, they sometimes conducted whole masses with the full Latin texts—it must have been quite something. But what I was about to say, we also met some real criminals there, typical thugs—I must say I admired them. Really admired them! If only for the risks those

381

men took—they had to be daring as well as strong. We reporters, being strangers, naturally attracted attention, although we were somewhat disguised as far as clothing went and all that . . ." (Holder dressed up as an apache, without his gold-rimmed glasses—what an image!) "Still and all, we obtained some impressions, and certain insights into the kind of life these people led."

"I know that world well, very well, like the inside of my own pocket," Gyurkicz said. "I can go about among such people without sticking out like a sore thumb. They have their own customs and their own slang. It is hard to win their confidence. But some of them are actually friends of mine."

"I can imagine that would be far easier for you than for me," Holder said, readily acknowledging Imre's superiority in matters of crude strength. "The most interesting personality in the place, though, was a woman. The girl behind the counter. A second Grushenka from *The Brothers Karamazov*—or at least, that's the way I always pictured Grushenka. This girl was called Didi. Fantastic creature. When any of the guests invites her to have a 'shot,' she never refuses. Only what she is drinking is some tinted water. This goes on all evening long. The result is that she can drink anyone under the table—she let us in on this professional secret, since we were strangers and she assumed we hardly would turn up there again. There was a woman for you. She'd been through everything—hunger, cold, homelessness, police lockup. One thing she asserted was that she'd never walked the streets. I believed her without question—why, I really can't say. I simply felt she was telling the truth. She had a brash strong look. For instance, her eyes—shaped like almonds, a kind of green fire in them—eyes full of depravity, but still with a kind of primitive strength and purposiveness in them, like the eyes of a wild animal, one of the big cats perhaps . . . You could see she was afraid of nothing and no one. I mean, even if one of those thugs flashed a knife at her, she wouldn't be fazed. Oddly enough, I had the impression that this woman could be loyal to the point of laying down her own life, if only the right man came along."

"Oddly enough," Grete Siebenschein said, "I have the impression that you, my dear Holder, are a wild romantic."

I happened to notice that at these words Stangeler's face gave a curious twitch. Grete did not see it.

Holder, however, took no offense at this somewhat acid comment.

"Very likely," he said. "To me the word 'romantic' carries no pejorative sense. A whiff of romanticism often perks me up better than a cup of black coffee. To my mind a metropolis is in its essence altogether romantic, a kind of artificial enchanted forest, for all that everything in it is so practical and technological. It is a return of the great forest that once covered all the land; it is the ultimate stage of that forest, a 'metastasis,' as the technical term goes. But to return to the subject of Didi: she had a certain trait which seems to me somehow characteristic of such unsavory types . . . for I don't deny that she was, after all, unsavory. I've had occasion, over the years, to notice this trait in any number of people. Incidentally, I may add that it isn't always associated with criminal characters. You will notice it among certain kinds of persons of low social status, people a little down at the heels; people, let's say, who've been involved with the police once or twice.

Such people often carry all their documents around with them—letters, identification cards, photos, and school report cards, all tucked into some battered old briefcase. And they're only too eager to tell you their whole life-story, right off the bat. Usually it turns out that they have a brother who's gone to the university, or an aunt who's been a concert singer—that sort of thing. They immediately begin talking about themselves to a perfect stranger, which is surely a sign of disequilibrium, and perhaps even of a certain degree of degeneration. Then they start bringing proofs for the whole story out of the briefcase, and you have to look at the stuff, whether you want to or not; even though you'd be only too glad to take every word on faith, you still have to look at those proofs: the letter from some official, and an old newspaper clipping with a picture of the aunt and a favorable notice of her concert, or some membership card with photo. Usually it's expired. Or a letter to the sister's husband addressed: 'To the Honorable . . .' You won't be left in peace until you've read through every item. Such people have what you might call an 'identification compulsion.'"

"Oh, I know them, I know such types!" Neuberg exclaimed with animation. "For instance, if you go into some cheap bistro to eat, one of them is sure to sit down at your table, and out comes the life-story. And sure enough, at the end the 'identification compulsion' begins to operate. An excellent piece of observation, Herr Holder!"

"All in the day's work for us journalists," Holder said modestly. (His modesty was what made him likable, though it could not have been an asset in his professional life; in his editorial capacity this selfsame modesty often caused Holder to overdo what he thought was the point of view of his superiors. Schlaggenberg was soon to find that out.) "You know, newspaper work leads us into all kinds of places," he continued. "As for the 'identification compulsion,' my theory would be that every so often such people want to assure themselves of their own identities, which otherwise begin to fade and become questionable to them . . ."

"Probably," Neuberg said.

"Oh well," Holder commented, "I suppose some of them have no secure place in which to keep all their treasures—possibly no real home at all. And so they carry everything on their persons . . . Though come to think of it Didi did live there, in the brandy-shop keeper's place. Somewhere in one of the back rooms she had a leather briefcase kicking around, stuffed full of letters, testimonials, two old identity cards, photos: Didi in a bathing suit; Didi in a dirndl dress at a shooting competition; Didi surrounded by admirers; and Didi accompanied by a really frightful little man, pure criminal type, who looked like a spiteful plucked vulture . . ."

"Probably a 'bimbo,'" Gyurkicz said.

"What is that?" Neuberg asked.

"Jargon for professional criminal, also for a first-class card sharp," Gyurkicz answered proudly.

During this last conversation we had gradually caught up with the group in front. Our path rose steeply before us to a wooded ridge and an open prospect. While we all climbed this last ascent together, everyone saved his breath. We could hear the birds peeping in the pale green woods, and in one place, where the sun could penetrate through the still delicate foliage, its warmth brought out the scent of wild garlic, already sprouting.

Like pictures upon a swiftly moving belt, a train of recollections of former walks and outings in these environs of our city unrolled before my mind's eye. I recalled returns homeward with girls, arm in arm, the last kisses in some twilit meadow, the looking with ever fresh wonder at the blazing firmament of the city below with its infinitude of bright and dim, twinkling and fading stars . . . Even now, before we had yet reached the top, where our gaze could plummet all the way until it came to a halt upon the dark ribbon of the river far

down between the receding ridges—even now the silent harmonious impingement of our surroundings, of our city's lovely
green environs, eased the tensions of the past hour, and so
assuaged the contradictions within our little group that they
became incomprehensible to me, foreign and easily forgotten.
The others, too, seemed to have the same response. Joking and
laughter cropped up here and there in the group, and when
we reached the top, lighthearted and freely mingling, we all
sauntered contentedly in the sunlight of a broad clearing which
sloped away toward the other side of the wooded ridge and
toward the valley of the Danube. Blithely we strolled over the
pleasant greensward toward the tables and benches of the inn
which had been opened there. We heard a violin tuning up,
and soon, as we headed toward a table, the musicians greeted
us, the newly arriving guests, with one of those genial polished
Ländler to which our great-grandparents had danced. A truly
heartfelt and levelheaded sort of music.

CHAPTER 11

Alliance

THE WEEK after the joint outing of "our crowd," Schlaggenberg went up the broad staircase in the Alliance building. It is clear that since the evening of Levielle's call and Kajetan's first meeting with Grete Siebenschein, he must have discussed details again, perhaps several times more, with Levielle. Afterwards he admitted this to me, in the course of his entertaining and exhaustive description of the Alliance firm.

The very streets in the immediate vicinity of the building provided a foretaste, and at the same time an aftertaste, for Schlaggenberg. For once upon a time he had trudged this same route often, though without much success. That had been years before, when he had kept his head above water by writing articles for the same newspapers which now were under the aegis of Frau Ruthmayr's worthy protector. They had since been enlarged, amalgamated into a company, and revivified by a transfusion of fresh capital. Also—this soon became evident—a new political spirit had invested them. The latter, as well as a considerable part of the money, came from Prague. As was only right and just, the two transfusions were embodied in two forms. One of them was named Oplatek—he was scarcely visible, and occupied a seat on the board of directors. The other was named Wangstein, and he could be plainly seen in one of the editorial offices by any ordinary stray Kajetan or René who happened along. He appeared to be a modest editor like any one of the other thirty-three; in addition he was a sociable, corpulent man with pink rolls of fat at the back of his neck.

At the moment, however, "Cajétan" was looking neither at these rolls of fat nor at other Alliance phenomena, but only at a few empty, smokily dim streets whose pavements were coated with the slipperiness of a misty, rainy evening, so that his own footsteps rang with an unpleasant loudness. Inwardly, however, he was already experiencing the aftertaste. How many times he had climbed those broad stairs; how many of those times had been in vain. Each such visit was heaped one upon another in his memory, layer upon layer, and all the layers were held together with the glue of the particular kind of melancholy that had invariably followed. With a few cleanly typed pages folded in his breast pocket, he had climbed those stairs, had passed the nodding doorkeeper. That this minor figure nodded instead of detaining and questioning him was in itself a sign that the visitor had passed the first stage of introduction into those precincts and had won a certain right to enter there. The whole building shook faintly from the low-keyed, grinding noises of the rotary presses in the basement. He climbed into the oily vapors which were the characteristic smell of this domain. The air alone, with its machinelike, mineral quality, had the capacity to invalidate, to emasculate, any product of the intellect it touched. So, at any rate, it had often seemed to Kajetan. A massive current flowed here in which all form, all quality, were drowned: drowned in oily smells, and already evaporating in the editor's hand, if only by the way that hand leafed through a manuscript. Nothing was needed here. Every individual contribution, even if it had been an ode of Pindar, was expendable; only the total mixed quantum, taken all together, was essential.

And then the waiting. People on fixed salaries, and impressive ones at that, sat around discussing how the weekend could be spent most enjoyably. There was much talk on this subject;

and yet all that was said was superfluous since no one cared to learn anything from the various proposals. Rather, such conversation was designed to show that certain of the somewhat overweight men who happened to be gathered in that corner or standing together in that corridor were real men of the world who knew their way around, and who had already been everywhere. It was endless chitchat, blather of the utmost superfluity, friendliness of a minimal genuineness—so that smiles existed only as fixed grins upon the faces, or rather, only upon the veriest outer skin of those faces. No one was really needed here; each individual's accomplishments and abilities were dispensable and replaceable; only the whole mixed group was needed to keep the paper going.

It did not matter in the least whether you had certain intellectual equipment, but whether you happened to be in the good graces of, say, Fräulein Franziska Kienbauer, the secretary who also functioned as the mistress of Editor-in-Chief Cobler. What counted, secondly but most importantly, was who stood behind you. A Wangstein, for example, had no need to make himself excessively agreeable; he did not have to exert himself, for in actuality he supervised—with Prague at his back—Herr Cobler himself. In fact the editor-in-chief rather trembled before Wangstein. There were powers behind many of the apparent thrones here. Behind Holder, for example (as we may recall). Holder was the feature editor. Or behind Doktor Trembloner (business and finance): the almost legendary Oplatek stood behind him. Oplatek stood behind a number of people. Levielle stood behind him. It was a regular genealogy. Family trees could be drawn up, differing from real ones only in that all the generations existed simultaneously in the plane of the present.

But who really did the work? Although, as Doktor Trembloner once remarked, "a paper like this really writes itself," someone had to do something—sift through the material from the news agencies, say, and prepare it for the compositor; read an article that had been commissioned (or at least leaf through it quickly); slant an item to the right or left, or frontwards or backwards. Furthermore, someone had to make many telephone calls, and see to it that nothing was printed which might offend powers-behind-the-thrones (and that meant keeping a close watch on the critics, outside contributors, and feature writers—that fellow Holder, for example, kicked up a little dust now and then; besides, he associated with such a pack of idiots). Such duties as these constituted quite a bit of work, for which years of experience, practice, knowledge, and finesse were essential. Then the whole newspaper had to be properly laid out, so that each page was readable and decently arranged, with all its many headings; there must not be interlockings, interferences, or breaks. Here seventeen lines had to be added, there six taken away, to fit the lower margin! And all that had to be accomplished in a limited time, while fresh news dispatches were constantly coming in, from which someone with a sharp eye had to extract the most important items: thereupon the new material had to be fitted into the existing arrangement, so that the make-up was constantly being changed, right up to the last moment, to the final deadline—which occurred when the typesetters quit work and went home . . . At times the activity in the office could no longer be called work; it was the feverish rush of a slave-gang under the overseer's lash, with telephones bawling, with wild gesticulations, with violent sudden disputes and lightning ejection of associates who, having nothing to do, stood around offering unasked-for opinions and otherwise interfering . . .

Who, then, worked in the screeching, clanging, writhing

inferno into which certain portions of the editorial offices were transformed as the deadline neared?

The ones who worked were the "fathers." There were two of them, and their names were Glenzler and Reichel. They really worked; they slaved. Along with them Cobler, too, may have done his bit, but he went home early because he could depend upon the "fathers." In addition to the "fathers" there were possibly two or three other men known as "serfs" or "slaveys" who occasionally took care of local and police news, courtroom items, and the sports pages. Usually there was no one standing "behind" these second-degree fathers.

The ones who sat uneasily upon their thrones were the crowd who held protracted conversations in the corridors but whose genealogies did not extend very far back. They were scattered about here and there, so to speak, and tolerated. Their positions were built upon spider webs—that is to say, upon those fine threads extending from person to person which constitute the fabric of so-called "popularity." The prerequisite, of course, was unconditional docility or adaptability, which in the long run could be produced only by an honest natural kinship with the whole Alliance world. These people who lacked genealogy, or at any rate a truly noble line of descent, substituted for it by having an extremely refined sensitivity. Thus, they were constantly groping about with invisible antennae, smiling at one person, bounding forward at another with some small flattery, putting a brief factual question to still another; they were constantly probing to determine whether all was well, whether no intrigues were in progress against them. To be sure, they would gladly have done something useful. But they were not allowed to. For within the magic circle that enclosed the serfs and slaveys, action was high, hard, and fast, and everything had to roar along predetermined orbits; one hand had to work in close collaboration with the other. Here the bystanders could only be in the way. Now and then, however, there flew out of this seething volcano of current events a raw and unhewn block of lava in the shape of an emergency assignment. One of the low-born would snap it up like a fish rising for bait. Instantly, wrapped in a tremendous volcanic cloud of self-importance, he would rush upon the nearest unoccupied stenographer to flatten out his capture over the platen of a typewriter.

These men, most of them of less than normal height and more than normal girth, would display a particularly gracious amiability toward any stray René or Kajetan, at least until his utter insignificance in the genealogical sense had become apparent. But often their amiability would persist even beyond that point; for the most prudent among this crew would not discount even remote possibilities—such as, for example, that some perfectly ordinary Kajetan might someday turn into a "Cajétan." But they were never seriously afraid of direct competition from such characters, whose unfitness to play a part within this world seemed only too plain. Moreover, they themselves stood under the protection of Hector Zepler, who was of the very noblest genealogy and himself a kind of ancestor of a many-branched family tree. This protection was completely dependable against assaults from one side—against the Kajetans and the Renés, that is. However, it might not prove so stout in the case of real Cajétans.

It should be explained that Zepler was the founder and at that time the head of an organization which embraced everyone in the journalistic profession in our city, persons whose rights the organization was supposed to preserve and represent against the publishers and newspaper owners. There was an all-embracing general contract, and no one could be paid a fixed salary below a certain minimum. This contract was a boon to the employers, since they maintained (and every sensible person had to grant that they were right) that the burdens imposed by the contract (sizable severance pay in case of dismissal, for example) made it impossible for them to make any additions to the staff. That was unnecessary in any case. They kept on the people they had—in most cases without being under any genealogical compulsion—and had the greater part of the work, except for literary and artistic jobs, done by a curious type of person who might be considered the larval or preliminary form of all those people who chattered so blandly in the corridors. The larval forms also chattered, pried into things, and did their share of smiling. But there was in their manner a kind of covert and cringing aggressiveness, in contrast to the defensive, wide-awake blandness of their betters.

There was another essential difference: the larvae worked with a lust and madness which the developed forms no longer displayed. The mere fact of their fixed salaries relieved the latter of the need for such desperate activity; moreover, it lay beneath their dignity to snap up crumbs, however tasty. Among these crumbs the larvae crawled and squirmed (and bowed and scraped before Hector). They rushed about everywhere before they had been sent; in three hours they knocked out five articles on the typewriter, of which four vanished into the insatiable wastepaper baskets, while the fifth perhaps had the luck to be "Coblerized" and slugged into the light of day.

In general the larvae accomplished as much in a day—sometimes utterly in vain and without the slightest compensation—as an average editor (to say nothing of the serfs and slaveys) turned out in a month. Schlaggenberg told me of one such character—who to top it off wore a goatee—who after seven agonizing years of standing around, sitting by, waiting, chatting, prying, smiling, and questioning, at last succeeded in catching Hector's eye. Suddenly it seemed to occur to Hector that, damn it all, here was a man who should be able to put new life into his organization from the bottom up. But it is far more likely that after seven years the goatee succeeded in attaching himself somewhere as the farthest limb of a genealogical tree, and it was only then that Hector's previous blindness toward him yielded. The case of the goatee, by the way, is a completely isolated one. And by the time "Hector's organization" began taking an interest in him, his face was so distorted from ambition that he was considered an ugly specimen even among his companions in misery. Otherwise, there is scarcely a recorded case of a larva who succeeded in penetrating the charmed circle without genealogical aids. Common sense dictated that the larvae were far more useful as they were, and that far more profit could be extracted from them. Now it happened that one statute of "Hector's organization" held that anyone who repeatedly fulfilled assignments—in other words, collaborated for so and so many months—had a claim upon definite employment and the minimum wage. But there were ways for the editorial staff to evade this regulation. Many Alliance newspapers proceeded crudely and simply by having any larva who contrived to obtain too much work sign an agreement renouncing his rights. In the office to which Schlaggenberg took his stories, however, this procedure was not possible because Hector, the official guardian of the weak, was personally employed as an editor. Another way out was found. Let us suppose that someone (even some completely harmless learned idiot like, say, a René Stangeler) became a frequent contributor, succeeded in obtaining assignments fairly often through one or another of the editorial staff—sometimes, as a matter of fact, work was handed out quite freely and without much fuss to such a person, simply because there was a demand at the moment. In that

394

case, and assuming that the man was not entirely "reliable" (meaning a type who would make no demands), the "abortion" was performed long before the critical date. In other words, the larva was elbowed out; assignments ceased; manuscripts found their way only into the wastepaper basket; no editor would see him; and the vigils in the corridors assumed proportions that exceeded all endurable limits. After a few months, however, the "aborted" larva was welcomed to the fold again, for by that time the whole affair would have passed beyond the dangerous proximity to certain statutory rights. Since, however, the larva obtained his livelihood essentially from payment by the line, and was eternally anxious to sell as many lines as possible, he was always docile, and in time could be allowed a place at the feed-trough without there being any danger of his attempting to wedge himself in there permanently.

Thus these poor devils hovered eternally between a right which they could not assert—so that the theoretical right served only as a source of bitterness—and on the other hand a contempt for their accomplishments and an offhand treatment of their work which went to truly insufferable lengths, but which had to be suffered, even acceded to, with an amiable smile. For nothing was more easily replaceable than just such a larva. There would be more fuss over a broken doorknob or signal bell than over the departure or death of one of them. Any day some well-dressed young man with a somewhat impertinent air, whom people had scarcely seen before, would suddenly turn up as a new editor on salary—and the larvae had to stand by and watch this happen. *C'est la vie!* Pardon, in this case the phrase should be: *"C'est la genealogie."* The following week this youth would be complaining that the assignment for an article had been foisted upon him, how ridiculous, he would have to be getting to it today. Of course that sort of thing was not included in his regular duties; the article would be paid for separately, in addition to his salary, even if for lack of space or for whatever reason it never appeared.

Larvae, as we have mentioned, could hack out five such articles in three hours; but their average score was two hits out of ten random shots. So these pitiable creatures hovered and circled around Cobler and his office, never essential but always used; they clogged all the corridors, besieged every door, seized every pretext to be present at editorial meetings, followed like wisps of fog after Zepler. Altogether they resembled the souls of the unburied whom, according to the beliefs of antiquity, Cerberus freely allowed to enter through the gate of the underworld but whom Charon refused to ferry across the Styx; they could go no further and were compelled to haunt the antechamber. A larva naturally had to make every endeavor to belong to "Hector's organization." But the union dues of the organization were extremely high. If not paid on time, they exerted more psychological pressure and imperiled further an already precarious situation; if paid, they constituted one of the innumerable reasons for the existence of pawnshops.

Schlaggenberg's connection with this paper—and others more or less linked to Alliance—had always been of a somewhat tenuous and oblique character. This was true even in the physical sense: his field of operations had mostly been the corridors and waiting rooms. It vexed and disturbed him no end all through these years that he remained a stranger and outsider at the newspaper, and never seemed able to establish himself on a firm footing. Yet in this very circumstance, oddly enough, lay his only advantage. For persons like Doktor Trembloner could distinguish very clearly between him and the larvae, could perceive his utterly different aims, and thus could have no doubt of his innocuousness. The whole thing was as clear as day to

396

everyone but Herr von Schlaggenberg himself.

Schlaggenberg, fired by the desire to make progress some-how, was anxious to co-ordinate himself with the laws of this world, to take life by the forelock. This was his chief consid-eration; his empty wallet was only a secondary factor and did not always figure in his consciousness. Accordingly, he went to Cobler and asked for so-called *reportage.* His patron granted it without more ado, though looking up at him in some aston-ishment through a veil of nervousness—this veil being one of his permanent attributes, like the quivering air over a flame. And so Schlaggenberg set out on his mission, "representing the newspaper" here or there. Later, when he received his fees from the surly cashier, it always turned out that no notice had been taken of the number of lines in such items. Thus, whether he had written a filler of no more than a paragraph, or a min-iature essay, he found waiting for him exactly the same sum that he had always received for his minor prose pieces. In this curious manner Cobler kept Kajetan within bounds—bounds which the young man did not clearly comprehend, although for his own good he should have done so, for they held the secret of his whole position. And at the same time Cobler preserved the true and proper bounds of a newspaper, and of journalism in general. Schlaggenberg, however, fell into the trap of trying to increase the number of such assignments. Whereupon for two months not a single line of his was published. But when with great effort he swallowed his pride (it cost him dear precisely because he had not yet grasped the situation with sufficient clarity) and submitted one of his best essays to the newspaper, it was printed instantly, and the fee paid was the highest per-missible in such cases—though still a modest one.

That was Cobler from Czernowitz. There will be more to tell of him and his odd partiality for Kajetan—not Cajétan.

At that time, however—a number of years before the events to be related here—Schlaggenberg considered himself rejected, thrust back several steps, although he was also liberated from the psychological pressure of trying to adapt himself to a type of work which was basically alien to him. Quite incidentally the changed attitude of a number of the salaried editors and especially of the larvae showed him that he had been on the point of stepping out onto slippery ice over sloping ground. For to what had been mere physical proximity in the corridors and waiting rooms was added a disagreeable note of excessive fellowship just as soon as the counterpressure of forces which had maintained the invisible dividing line no longer held that line strong and rigid . . . Still and all, Cobler's grand "abortion" of Schlaggenberg put an end to the cause of the evil, although the effects were lasting and continued to rankle far longer than one would imagine.

Kajetan—at that time he was far from becoming a Cajétan—had in the course of years begun to see the light. The lamps of knowledge had been trimmed by such tribulations as the one we have just described, and shone a good deal more brightly. He realized that he was being thrown back on his natural, extremely "expensive" method of working. The curious aspect of this business was that the loud crude voice of social and economic pressure spoke exactly the same message as the low but penetrating whisper of his own conscience. And so once again, with the few sheets of a neatly typed manuscript in his breast pocket, a manuscript produced in sweat and tears, he climbed those stairs, passed the nodding Cerberus at the door, breathed in the oily vapors from the printing rooms. And now amid all this writhing and reeling, wheezing and seething, hobbling and Coblering atmosphere of self-importance, his task was to deposit his laid egg in the proper place, so that it would not be caught up in the torrential current and buried somewhere in the countless sands or washed to some stagnant spot where no current at all moved, there to be fallen upon by the larvae. He had to force his way through to the editor-in-chief's room and to Cobler's desk. Schlaggenberg resolutely avoided handing anything over to Glenzler, the all too hasty Father Time, although Glenzler always greeted him pleasantly and asked whether Kajetan had brought anything along—he would be glad to look at it right away. If Kajetan was foolish enough to commit it to his hands, the manuscript was lost. For once Father Glenzler had been grossly insulted by Editor-in-Chief Cobler on Kajetan's account. Glenzler (in all probability quite rightly from his point of view) had objected to Schlaggenberg's submissions as "too difficult and incomprehensible for a newspaper; I at least don't understand a line of what the man writes." "Because you're an old idiot and he has more sense in his a— than you in your head!" Cobler had bellowed at the retreating Glenzler with the door wide open. (That was the usual tone in the place anyhow.) At least a dozen persons with and without pedigree, smilers, questioners, probers, whisperers, and larvae, had overheard this little scene. The rest is obvious.

This story was told to Schlaggenberg much, much later, by which time he had already on his own come to avoid entrusting any manuscript to Glenzler. For five of his articles had vanished in this way, and with them the proper moment for their publication, in addition to all the fees, for payment was accorded only for items that appeared in print. In other words, Schlaggenberg belatedly obtained the deductive key to a situation which he had been forced to analyze purely empirically, a costly process, notwithstanding that it led him essentially to the correct explanation.

"But the devil take all this philosophizing," Kajetan

remarked when he told me about it. There were other shoals and sand bars to steer away from—for example, the feature editor at the time, Holder's predecessor. There was also Fräulein Kienbauer. On suitable occasions she too would jump at the chance to be unpleasant, since Schlaggenberg sometimes neglected to kiss her hand, an act of homage to Cobler's sex life which had become one of the established customs of the firm (only Wangstein was excused from it). In addition to Fräulein Kienbauer there were also certain unpedigreed persons whom Kajetan likewise recognized as unreliable. These fellows always volunteered in the most engaging manner to take care of an essay and deliver it to the editor-in-chief "later" or "when opportunity offers," so that Schlaggenberg would not have to wait; at the moment a "conference" was taking place "inside." There was always a conference; that was a permanent condition. The attendants here, a select group who quickly learned impertinence from the general mood prevailing in the firm, and passed their lesson along to visitors, were in the habit of dismissing any person who came to see one of the higher-ups with the word "conference." Translated, "conference" meant either "I don't know you," or "I have never received a tip or even a cigarette from you." If a "conference" was in progress, therefore—and sometimes there really was one—the manuscript had to remain in the breast pocket. For this egg had a relatively good chance of hatching only if it were laid at the very top of the swarming heap, where it would be stamped with the rubber stamp of supreme officialdom and roll safely to its proper department (though there, too, the poor thing might lie sterile). Most of the time, however, it would roll straight into the composing room. In connection with this, an odd point should be noted. Cobler was in the habit of taking Kajetan's essays, along with a daily package of other things, personally to the printers. He would burst like a missile out of his office with such an initial acceleration that it was far from easy for those waiting outside to brake him; if they tried, they had to be prepared for the consequences, which were a sudden translation of his high kinetic energy into warmth, in fact into heat . . .

Conference. And waiting. The manuscript had to reach Cobler's hands by evening, at the latest, if it were to appear on Sunday, so that by Tuesday Schlaggenberg could receive his fee, which alone made it possible for him to work the rest of the next week in peace. As for the intervening days—Thursday through Sunday to Tuesday—they depended upon whether Schlaggenberg was lucky enough to talk to Cobler quietly for two and one half minutes, to persuade him to commission a review of a lecture by a visiting philosopher from Germany which was scheduled for the next day, Friday. The philosopher might be as famous as you liked, yet here it was somehow necessary to prove that he was of some interest. But unfortunately this was the juncture at which every larval genealogist could strike a blow against Kajetan by coming forth, in all sincerity, with his own opinion. He could even invoke those higher sources over Cobler's head from which cautions were constantly emanating that the paper not be given too "heavy" or too "literary" a slant, lest the circulation should drop. (In their way these voices from Oplatek's heights were quite right.) Cobler was the only one in the whole place willing to sponsor Kajetan. The others knew that in opposing Kajetan they were moving along the line of least resistance, could never be accused of going counter to the spirit of the paper or operating against its natural center of gravity. To criticize Kajetan was to combat a foreign body; it was the eminently safe thing to do and could never cause a loss of ground or sympathies. Glenzler had sensed this well, and consequently had ascribed no practical

401

importance to the dressing-down he had received from Cobler. That is to say, at that particular moment he had refused to take his superior seriously—in any case, no one here took anyone else seriously; that was unheard of. Cobler, moreover, frequently committed infractions against the ultimate spirit of the newspaper.

Conference. And waiting.

Glenzler came by, paused for a moment, and said: "Better let me have the MS., Herr Doktor; they'll be a long time in there today."

At that moment a violent detonation took place.

The door to the chief editor's room was flung against the wall. Schlaggenberg was able to observe that the room was completely empty, and that no one had been in it except Cobler. This personage, the elements of whose orbit would have had to be calculated for an extremely high acceleration today, flew through the waiting-room in a flat ballistic curve—and braked abruptly.

We too come to a stop at an extremely significant point.

For Cobler said: "What's up, Herr Doktor?" He seized Kajetan by the coat sleeve and drew him into his office. The door slammed behind the two of them with a second detonation.

There stood Kajetan before the desk covered with innumerable heaps of confused papers, closeted with his strange patron. As at all such interviews, Schlaggenberg was invited to take a seat in one of the armchairs—an invitation which he rarely accepted, for he was painfully conscious of the editor's limited time. Cobler had seated himself behind the desk with a nimble, swift movement; he had a graceful figure—which seemed to have been emphasized by a tailor who must have been an aristocrat of his distinguished trade. Cobler was also extraordinarily ugly and at the same time (there is no other way to put it) actually handsome—an almost bald man of fifty with a vulture's profile. He was the arch-Journalist who did not give a damn for anything. Philosophies and ideologies, art, music, science, eternal life, death—none of these things meant a farthing to him in themselves. He gave not a damn for the devil himself—unless, for example, the devil had been seen in Paris, on the rue Vaugirard, say, and his newspaper could publish the first report of it. And now Kajetan stood before this remarkable man who spoke to him through a veil of nervousness that quivered almost visibly around him, like the air over a flame. What mysterious arc of sympathy was it that stretched from Czernowitz to southern Styria and back, that insured the Sunday article's acceptance the first minute, the German philosopher's admittance into the news columns the second minute, and Cobler's query the last half minute as to how Schlaggenberg was and how his major works were coming along? Nor were the questions casual; they were brief, nervous, and warm . . .

Immediately afterwards, Kajetan was striding out through the anteroom, nodding pleasantly to his colleagues on all sides, while behind him, violently detonating, Cobler started for the composing room, shooting into his predetermined orbit in a very shallow, extended ballistic curve and overtaking Kajetan about the middle of the room.

Then down the broad stairs—the building was already quivering slightly again from the low-keyed grinding noises of the rotary presses in the basement—past the nodding Cerberus, and so, by descending, Kajetan paradoxically reached the upper world. Always, at such times, he emerged a little astonished at what lay behind him, and a little relieved too. He went on through the brightening streets, for the lights were coming on, and paused at the curb, looking distractedly at the onrushing vehicles. Indeed he had something to muse about, for he was privy to a fact known only to the editor-in-chief and himself: Cobler, who would violently defend Schlaggenberg's work, especially when others attempted to slur it—who would hurl out phrases about Schlaggenberg's "extraordinary ability" and "eminent talent"—Cobler had never in his whole life read as much as a line of Kajetan's work. He had read none of his books, none of the smaller essays the young man had published, not even a single one of those manuscripts which he himself rushed to the composing room. He had once briefly confided this circumstance to Schlaggenberg during a tete-a-tete in his office, with this for an explanation: "Oh hell, no time, where would I find the time—nonsense, why read it, it's perfectly plain, perfectly plain." And this utterance was followed by a gesture which amounted to a caricature of Kajetan's physiognomy, bearing, and whole personality.

Such had been the situation for several years. And then Schlaggenberg had published the novel which, we may recall, Stangeler noticed in the window of a bookshop on the night of his violent quarrel with Grete Siebenschein. This book yielded Schlaggenberg a regular income for quite a while, and relieved him of the necessity of swimming so frequently in the Alliance stream. Henceforth Kajetan had passed Cerberus and climbed the stairs more rarely. On the other hand, he was enabled to analyze clearly in hindsight a law which he had always dimly apprehended: that writers of his sort had to remain outside the newspaper in order to make such progress that when they appeared within its precincts once again they would automatically stand in an unequivocal light and would be able to make their way directly to the proper place.

But at the time Kajetan withdrew, he did so without premeditation, simply because the pressure had abated. (To put the matter in less sparing terms: he withdrew out of laziness.) But it was well that he did so. For toward the end Cobler had been having a hard time maintaining Schlaggenberg against the current, against some palpable current which was growing stronger and was beginning to define itself more clearly. It was of mysterious origin, this current, but seemed to flow, as it were, out of the innermost bowels of Alliance. Some persons maintained that Kajetan had cooked his goose with a book that had appeared not long after the above-mentioned novel: the biography of his teacher, Kyrill Scolander. (Scolander was living in southern France at that time, as he did for some years to come.) Others said that no one had ever read this book anyhow; I happen to think likewise. Be that as it may, all that matters is that in time Kajetan became a rare guest in Cobler's domain, appearing only now and then. Indeed, his appearances were infrequent in a literary as well as personal sense. Ultimately he became a virtual stranger to Alliance.

Such had been the situation for several years . . . And while Kajetan (or was he by now Cajétan?) walked down the empty, smokily dim streets whose pavements were coated with the slipperiness of a misty, rainy evening, so that his own footsteps rang with an unpleasant loudness, all those details and many others purled and swirled through his mind like the eddies and whirlpools of a rather unattractive body of water. The years stood lined up as if on parade, and memory pranced up their length on the backs of a few living seconds full of density and vividness. But this initial clarity was soon succeeded by moments that were only a single, confused, clanging discord. And far down at the bottom sounded out-of-tune basses which simply would not blend with the brilliant upper voices. That is the menace that overtakes anyone who lets the reins hang loose while life stirs powerfully beneath him, tramping onward like a charger with a heavy gait.

At this hour, at this point in time, Schlaggenberg found himself weak.

He slowed his pace, and as he did so became aware incidentally that a fine sprinkle of rain was blowing in his face, as fine as the spray cast up by a glass of soda water. Knowledge of his own insecurity came upon him so suddenly, and with such devastating clarity—rolled out round and smooth, like a bead falling from a string—that he sought, startled and alarmed, to protect himself against it. In the effort to maintain the upper hand somehow he pitched on details (or, if we will, took flight in details), tried to think them through and arrange them in an orderly manner, hoping to get at the heart of the matter by starting at the wrong end. He would defend the step he was taking in terms of "common-sense thinking." But that kind of thinking (which he had to borrow from somewhere at the moment) could only play second fiddle. He felt that at once. Moreover, it played false, so that his shrinking from the whole business was intensified.

". . . Anybody can see that this is the opportunity of a lifetime. I mustn't let it slip . . ."

". . . Hang it, something shady has been going on ever since the old boy came to see me . . ."

". . . It's as though he put an idea into my head with his slimy insinuations that first evening . . ."

"In the first place, I have made him no promises."

"In the second place, why should I be drawn in the wrong direction—as I was that time I tried doing *reportages?*"

"In the third place, I would be free!"

So it went, approximately. In the end he succeeded in

"making order." The pros and cons all lay neatly piled one above another. He had paused in order to "sum up." Yet he could no longer repress a fearful, destructive melancholy which welled up from beneath the heap of good reasons. This whole business hung loosely from him, as though a portion of him had sheared off and rotted and was now infecting the whole body. His thinking stopped. A bead rolled. But it was a large one. Yet did it not show cracks, as if it had been scratched by a sharp object or corroded by some acid?

He closed his eyes. The rain sprayed in his face. Now there glowed again, far out on the horizon, on his horizon, on the edge of the space "not dominated" by him, that dim light. At first he only felt it, then he saw it far away, at the end of the long, long street, curtained behind the drizzling mist. It was nothing more than the glowing red letters of some neon sign.

"She's in England after all," he thought. His inward speech was dry and very feeble, as though his tongue were half paralyzed.

As he turned the last corner, the picture the street presented with its oblong building suddenly struck him as exceedingly familiar, "familiar in a repulsive, insipidly sweet manner," as he said. The past reached out for him with its sinuous tentacles, which he had tried here and there to fling off, but which were already entwining his whole body in a deadly grip. "Why have I separated from Camy?"—the thought swept through his mind, whispered from out of one of those dull, utterly formless intervals into whose vacuum he now stumbled for the fraction of a second. He reeled slightly with a feeling of giddiness, and his breath was almost choked off as he tottered above the abyss of the past. The future slipped away; a sweet odor of decay rose from his own body, while above him the last star went out. Streets, distant lights, the night sky, and somewhere out there the dark, domed treetops of the receding landscape of hills fled behind an invisible partition, behind a thick pane of glass. Suddenly all that mattered was to seize a few external supports in this mass of printed paper; those supports were now everything to him, and his standing or falling depended upon whether they held or gave way. At which point Schlaggenberg recalled again, this time almost with horror, Stangeler's account of his dream. But it had not been a dream, that part of it; Levielle had actually spoken those words to someone (ah yes! to Cornel Lasch!). That "Let him fall" and that "not good for anything any longer." And Stangeler, asleep, had referred it to himself: "Falling—bottomless." Then there had been a gigantic mill wheel, or something of the sort, that turned and carried him down into a dark pit filled with torrential, sweeping masses of water, and the turning, rumbling, dully grinding noises had swelled to a terrible roar at the dark moment of falling . . . Yes, that was how René had told it.

Now Schlaggenberg opened the heavy, brass-bound door of the main entrance, and in the course of this familiar movement—you always had to brace yourself somewhat, for the door did not open easily due to a defect in the lock—during this pressing and passing through, the weakened dike of the present collapsed completely, and two periods flowed together in a stream mingling murkily. Cerberus nodded. The whole building shook faintly from the low-keyed, grinding noises of the rotary presses in the basement.

CHAPTER 12

Our Crowd (II)

I WALKED down the Graben, that fine Viennese avenue in which the shop windows gabble to the street with their thousands of pretty objects. The air seemed to me mild and foaming, like a fresh solution of soap flakes, literally perfumed, and still containing huge solid blocks of coolness. The vast blue banner of the sky was not yet casting heat down upon the asphalt; only gentle streamers of mild warmth touched forehead, cheeks, and hands. I half-closed my eyes, and in a cloud of fragrance that now indubitably wafted across the sidewalk the ponderous pleated curtain concealing the past drew back and gave me, for the span of two breaths, a vivid deep view of that sunken world whose apparent pillars still stood so deceptively here, whose last years I had experienced.

In the old days, when all frontiers were open, Europe had poured through here, and just at this time of year the town had been at its liveliest. Even now the season's imperishable splendor played over the city whose innermost nature bore so close an affinity to the spring. But nowadays sunniness was alien to the city; rays of light broke against the jagged edges of consuming cares, against the fracture lines left over from onetime gaiety. When frontiers were open, Europe had poured through here, happily falling in with the polished local life-style, which maintained a pretty and inimitable mean between the great Empire outside and the here and now of hills, vineyards, old courtyards, and ancestral customs in the suburbs, as well as the modest gracefulness of the small townhouses of noblemen in a still and cool street in the heart of the Old City. Thus lay the here and now on the one side, which we might call the heart's side, the side of familial and social life, the little world of rounded forms; for outside lay the most variegated landscapes, climates, and costumes, lay the ice of glaciers and lowland plains, blue sea and southern vineyards, all the multilingual richness of a vast empire, full of pomp and rituals to which the individual owed certain duties inherited from fathers and forefathers. In balance between these two poles moved the nonchalance of the round-dance, the smiles of charming, worldly-wise women, the handsome men who succeeded, with an often astonishingly small application of intelligence, in being fully qualified representatives of one of the most charming cultures that ever was among the many that have vanished from our hasty continent . . .

I had come only thus far in my reverie, which could not have lasted more than a few seconds, when the fragrance surrounding me became too obtrusive, altogether too substantial. The fantasies that had only a moment before been haunting me inwardly now assailed me firmly and obviously from without. I turned around, and realized that I had come to a halt before the open door of one of our greatest perfumeries, the very shop in which I was wont to buy my lavender water. From the door came a veritable billow of super-refined coolness and fragrance. But in my maturer years I had already come to appreciate the value of illusions and to know very well that most thoughts are smoke whose fire we are denied. Thus this objective explanation of the magic by no means threw me off the track on which my emotions had started. On I strolled. To the left and right of me graceful outlines of women already dressed in fair, bright colors passed me by, going in the opposite direction. Blinking, I stepped out of the sun into the shade. My line of thought had been only briefly sidetracked, and here was where I came out.

The atmosphere of tiers of boxes and rows of orchestra seats in the great opera house wafted up inside me, an atmosphere of pure but lifeless velvet redolent of the lingering perfumes of fifty years . . . Every evening the house had been filled. The boxes and tiers in the wide semicircle rippled with restrained movements. A dress gleamed, a gem flashed in raven hair, and all the while a massive current flowed through the middle aisle down below, diverting to left and right into the rows of seats. People came to this place from surroundings which did not essentially differ from it, which represented merely another aspect of one and the same life with its fixed but easily practiced customs and its unspoken, scarcely conscious codes. This aspect of that life might, perhaps, be somewhat closer to the pomp of the grand old rituals—somewhat more remote, perhaps, from the familial and social circle, if only because of members of the Imperial House who were present within the community of listeners. And each individual had in turn been flanked by such a community; no individual had had any real awareness that life outside it could be possible.

I had a curious thought. As I walked with such a sense of ease and relaxation down the coolly sunny Graben, quite caught up in these surroundings which rang with a lightness no longer valid, and while the red-gold pomp and splendor of the image of the Imperial House grew increasingly vivid within me, and separated out into details, fitted into the fashionable atmosphere of tiers of boxes and rows of orchestra seats, so that I already began longing for, craving for, the glorious opening chorus in the golden belltones of the harp—in the midst of this vision the odd thought grazed my consciousness. It occurred

411

to me that the ones solely responsible for all the "devastation" were in the final analysis only people like Stangeler. It had all come, it seemed to me at this moment, only out of disloyalty, out of lack of discipline and moderation. And so once again I found myself baying at the heels of poor René.

As a pendant to that colorful picture there now came to my mind the variegated slow minuet that had taken place each time after the end of a performance on the broad staircases and in the round wide colonnade of smoothly vaulting pillars: from two sides the patrons of the boxes edged slowly down into the grand central staircase. The pastels and bright colors of the women's dresses descended like a beneficent cascade, intensified by the colored fire of brilliants in blonde or raven hair. Those flashing stones, to which the eye unconsciously clung, by concentrating all their force in a single point comprehended the constant sliding and glittering restlessness of the scene. The women descended the stairs as if plunging into a bath of noise and motion in the lower lobby. Here the din of the streets—the hoof beats of carriage horses and the snarling of automobile motors—was already pouring in through the swinging doors. The keener eye might detect in the women's movements a mood of submissiveness. They obeyed a compulsion, as though confined to certain paths which they must follow, although they were entirely unaware of this . . . They stepped forward into this surf, which was yet only a last lapping tongue of the larger sea, the whole nocturnal city, as into an infinitely ramified pit of voluptuousness. But they had only a narrow prescribed path before them; only a few steps separated them from the cars which would roll forward in a moment, enclose them, and shut them off from all that sparkling depth and variety . . .

In the course of this reverie I was seized by a veritable passion to visit once again our opera house, which, like all other survivals of the grand gestures of a vanished past, stands in this present time with a certain awkwardness, but all the same maintains its dignity. This desire to attend a performance again affected me like the discovery of something wholly new; for the longest time I had not had the slightest impulse in that direction. I suppose the reason was that I had been living more and more within the circle of "our crowd," absorbed in its affairs. (Moreover, even at that time I was increasingly occupied with arranging and writing these chronicles, with taking notes, asking questions, sounding people out, receiving reports; in fact I had become a regular everybody's aunt, a sponge absorbing the loves, tears, and sighs of others, even those of Fräulein Siebenschein.) Living out on the edge of the city, it never occurred to me to buy an orchestra seat, say. As I had indicated, I did not want for money.

So be it. I decided that this very day I would look up the program and procure a ticket—that is, do an errand for myself, for once. I always had two or three errands for Quapp and Kajetan, who were always asking me to do this or that when they heard that I intended to go into town of a morning.

With such pleasant plans in mind, I crossed the Graben, looking both ways to watch out for automobiles. To the left I glimpsed for a moment in the sky the fair slender hint of the tower of St. Stephan's thrusting upward into the sunny springtime air. Then I turned the corner at Stock im Eisen. A few steps farther on was one of the best-known pastry shops of our city, and just as I arrived in front of it, a big car drove up and Frau Friederike Ruthmayr got out.

I turned around at once and greeted her. This encounter gave me particular pleasure, for it followed the line of the day like an embellishment or variation in a melody, and came exactly at the proper place. Frau Ruthmayr seemed likewise delighted. "Come in and let's have a chat, Herr von Geyrenhoff; you have simply dropped out of sight and hearing. Gone to the artists, so to speak, eh? I mean, you're living in a kind of colony out there, in that kind of set, aren't you?"

I wondered at that. How quickly, and with what accuracy of anticipation, things acquire a final form on people's lips when they are only on the verge of happening. For a moment I had a vague insight: surely such terms and phrases, seized upon for the sake of abbreviation and simplification, and therefore usually falsifications, must have an important retroactive effect upon life in general. They exert a surely underestimated power of suggestion.

"Who told you that, *gnädige Frau*?" I asked.

"A young historian who belongs to your set—Neuberg is his name, he's engaged to the daughter of old Trapp."

The question of whether Neuberg belonged to our set would not have been so easy for me to settle as it was for Friederike. In any case, what was meant by "our set," and by "belonging to" it? Oh well, probably Neuberg, in his warm openhearted fashion, had spoken of "our crowd," perhaps talked rather lyrically about it . . .

Meanwhile we were enclosed in the fragrant and somewhat prissified atmosphere of the *Konditorei,* with its red and gold chairs and Maria Theresa chandeliers. There were the usual faces ("*les inevitables*"), and three or four people we had to greet on our way in. Finally we reached an out-of-the-way nook toward the back of the room. Only then was I overcome by admiration for this beautiful woman whom I now sat facing. I felt a strange compound of captivation by her charm, pity for her peculiar and obvious loneliness—which in some mysterious fashion emanated from her, was visible in her features, and present in the manner in which she had fastened her large dark

414

eyes upon the turmoil of the street as she stepped from her car outside—and nettlement with the whole manner of her life and its background. It is so easy to play the judge! We condemn ties, condemn conditions, in which we observe our fellow-creatures caught up. We think that this or that could be altered for the better with two or three reasonable decisions and actions. All very easy, from outside. The waker has no trouble rousing the sleeper; but the latter must face his nightmares alone, must suffer his own dreams.

"Well, what has you so preoccupied?" she said in a warm kindly way with an underlying maternal tone. And this maternal tone aroused my protest on two scores. In the first place I did not at all want her to assume this attitude of being an "elderly fat lady," as it were, toward me, for I was scarcely any younger than she. What I would really have liked to do was to tell her straight out that she was a splendid woman, for I felt that the very trouble with her lay precisely in this preconception about herself; there was the thorn she was pressing into her flesh. She was on the point of resigning herself finally to permanent membership in that class, to typing herself. The result would be premature burial of all the vitality she still possessed. As I sat with her, poking the tiny spoon vaguely into some pastry or other on the plate before me, I was intensely conscious of this misplaced resignation. Furthermore (and this was the second point), I felt an undefinable hatred for unnamed and unknown forces which must be at work somewhere in the background of her life, constantly nourishing this erroneous conception of herself. (This was where Levielle came to my mind.) I must admit, I really did toy with the naïve idea of "telling her straight out that she was a splendid woman"—really, the things we think of! At the back of our minds the most indescribable idiocies take shape all too often . . .

415

In order to have something to talk about, I spoke about the opera, and about the memories that had come to me while I was walking on the Graben. To which she replied with phrases such as "Ah yes, in my youth," and so on. Already beginning to frown at myself, I observed that in the face of her obstinate relegation of herself to a particular type, certain of Herr Schlaggenberg's notions began crawling around in my consciousness. "Ought to explain about that likewise," I thought, and then quickly: "Have you gone out of your mind, become rusticated, unhinged, out there in the suburbs, eh?"

"No, you will not buy a ticket," Frau Ruthmayr said. "You will give me the pleasure of joining me in my box, won't you?"

I hesitated. I really did not like the idea. At last I said: "My dear friend, please, please don't be offended—but when I listen to music I really would rather not be sitting with a whole party . . ."

While I was saying all this, I caught sight of the "misshapen Edam cheese," namely the wife of Trapp, the lawyer, at the entrance. Frau Ruthmayr had also spotted her. "What would you like to hear?" she said quickly to me. "*Rosenkavalier*? Of course! It is being given on Saturday, May 14, with an excellent cast. Make a note: first tier, left, Number 12. All right? And—we will be alone. So that you can listen."

Then the Trap or Trappist was upon us.

As she approached I had the opportunity to observe a bit of social by-play. She seemed to be uncertain whether or not to notice Frau Ruthmayr, and was possibly on the point of veering past our corner at a respectable distance, when someone came tripping from the other side of the shop, near the windows, straight across the room toward Frau Ruthmayr to greet her. This action on the part of Baron Frigori decided the situation for Frau Trapp; evidently it seemed to vouch for the

416

correctness of Frau Ruthmayr, or something of the sort—devil only knows what was going on in the Edam cheese's mind. Such brains are, as is only too well known, far more inscrutable and mysterious than the brains of the mightiest geniuses. It may be that old Trapp had once suggested to her a certain caution on account of Levielle, and so on.

Now, at any rate, reassured by Frigori (later I learned that he was one of her husband's best clients), she virtually fell upon Friederike: "Why, Friederl, Fritzi, well, well, how glad I am, may I join you here, good day, Herr von Geyrenhoff, so nice to see you in town for a change. How do you do, Baron—well, Fritzi, how are things going? Is that your nice car outside? Fine, fine, but you don't drive it yourself, do you? I learned last year, during the summer, because we have two cars now and my husband needs the chauffeur most of the day . . ."

"Salutations, eh what!" I thought, made a feint of rising to my feet, and gave my name; Herr von Frigori had at last condescended to introduce himself to me, since he had by this time joined us at our table.

Such people are common in Vienna. If you treat them badly—but really arrogantly—they for their part become quite decent. After I had twice deliberately ignored Frigori when he spoke, and not replied at all (in spite of my natural inclination, for after all Frigori's temples were already white; he was in his late fifties; but in our country you have to know how to deal with such arrogance), he turned to me in a most friendly manner and said: "Aren't you related to young Orkay recently with the Hungarian embassy here?"

"Cousin," I said, with a slight nod.

He straightened his monocle. "I suppose you see him now and then?"

"Often," I said.

"Well, very good, would you have the kindness to give him my very best regards? A few months back, when he was transferred here, I had a little dancing affair at my place on January 8th, nothing important, couldn't really say it was a ball, would have been most pleased to have him there, too bad, learned about it too late . . ."

"Géza did not come to Vienna until March," I said.

"Really? Well, then, of course—anyhow, Herr von Geyrenhoff, do tell your cousin to give me a ring sometime. You no longer go out, I take it?"

"No," I said.

"Well, well, why not, if I may ask?"

"I am occupied with some private scholarly work."

"Ah, very interesting—what did you say, *gnädige Frau?*" He turned to Frau Trapp. "The ball at my house? Yes? It was quite fun. Did you hear so too? Delighted to hear it. Oh well, a most modest affair, not at all what you would call a ball, but I did miss your youngster, yes . . ."

"The child has absolutely refused to go out this year; she sits at home all evening studying," Frau Trapp said. "For some examination. Good Lord, all this higher education is such a strain on the poor girls! But my husband is all for it."

"You know the two young Levielles, don't you, my dear friend?" Frigori said, turning now to Frau Ruthmayr. "They were there too, back in January. Capable young men. Excellent dancers too—though, well, with this modern prancing around, it's not so hard, the young folks learn it quickly. In the old days, now, a left-handed waltz, that was something else again, eh?"

Frau Ruthmayr smiled and nodded. I began to feel nettled again. In the Edam cheese some obscure, incomprehensible process had taken place; it could be observed in the passing change in the rind as Frigori mentioned Levielle's name.

Amid all these distractions, it only now occurred to me that on the very night of Frigori's ball which was not a ball, Frau Ruthmayr had come out on her garden terrace, taken the bottle gaily offered by Gyurkicz, to the accompaniment of a melting tango on Beppo Draxler's guitar! Unfortunately I thought of this too late. Otherwise it would have lent mirth to those last ten minutes, would have made me feel better over Frau Ruthmayr's submissiveness, would have made Frigori's dullness and social aspirations more endurable and allowed me to regard with far less grimness the processes within the cheese rind . . . I was vastly astonished that the lovely story of the bottle only now rose out of the depths of my consciousness, for it certainly merited emergence into the transfiguring light of recollection at the first sight of Frau Ruthmayr.

But by now I had had more than enough of it all. I took my leave of the three and set off.

I sauntered along Karntner Strasse. It was approaching noon, and the crowd of strollers grew heavy. Several times I had to greet someone, or return a greeting. The faces I encountered lay far apart in time: one I had known as a child, another I had met only in my last year in government service when its owner was transferred to my department. At last I became aware of how frequently I had to exchange greetings. Had my former life, to which I no longer belonged, been ground to powder here on Karntner Strasse and was it now hovering in scattered particles no longer connected to one another? What was happening to me outwardly also happened inside me. Both within and without I felt as if I were going through an incessantly falling rain of ashes, ashes of the past, with here and there in the shower a glowing ember. A few isolated points even held a flame. These burned on. Claire Neudegg, for example—Countess Charagiel—who had once dealt such an insult to

419

my schoolboy self. She abode with me, had done so ever since my walk on the Graben with Levielle. No, now I realized that she had been with me even longer than that, ever since I had begun living in Döbling. The multitude of villas with their gardens and garden hedges had summoned up Claire within me. Even though my parents' villa had not been out in Döbling . . .

Rapidly, the opposite stream of pedestrians flitted by me to the right and left. I felt as if I myself were walking very fast, just as one has the sensation of speed when one looks down from the bowsprit of a boat toiling slowly upstream into the swift-moving water of a river. In fact I was strolling at a very leisurely pace.

Out on the Ring I turned right and walked past the façade of the opera house, past the statues of Siegfried and Don Juan. The pair, engaged in their particular doings—one might almost say, discharging their particular offices—presented themselves on their pedestals: Siegfried busy with his dragon, Don Juan with his "stone guest." As I walked along the Burggarten I observed, just a few steps in front of me, Director Edouard Altschul. At the same time I realized that I had been following him all the way from the Opera without recognizing him. He was walking slowly, stooped, portfolio under his arm and cane hooked over his wrist.

We recognized and greeted each other almost at the same moment. He seemed to be having some difficulty tearing himself free from his thoughts, and even while we spoke, these were still with him. Altschul, good-looking and well groomed, whose intelligence and urbanity was as enjoyable to encounter as entering a cool quiet room after the noisy summer heat of streets—for some peculiar reason at this time and place, on the Ring in front of the spears of the Burggarten's wrought-iron fence, instantly produced a depressing effect upon me. It was as though I were now required to bear the burdens and small cares of my life without any kind of comfort, as though no garden suburb existed any longer and "our crowd" had vanished, as though the long stretches of sunlit streets with old trees dreaming against the sky, their tops at once light and heavy, were receding, fleeing from me: and as though the flashing spots of sunlight on distant roofs, windows, and vehicles were receding likewise—all of it escaping behind an invisible partition wall, a thick pane of glass. All that was left was the necessity for seizing upon a few supports in order to be able to live amid these jumbled cubes of stone . . .

With a sense of relief, I reminded myself of my own relatively favorable and secure position.

"The situation is extremely obscure at the moment," he said, continuing with what we had been talking about. "It is foolish to attempt to predict anything. You must not forget the purely human factor: everyone knows that the moral climate of the business world is no longer what it used to be, before the war. Nowadays, on the whole, England is the only place where things are as they used to be."

I could now actually see what before I had only sensed, that my old friend Altschul looked overstrained and worn. His face was lifeless, his complexion gray. It seemed to me that only his perfect grooming continued to hold him erect and served, like his judicious way of speaking, as his representative toward the outside world. I continued to listen to him, taking pleasure in his skillful and impersonal analyses, and feeling that vague respect for the complexities of the "general economic situation" into which anyone is apt to fall who is not one of the initiate, who cannot really envision such matters. Like most persons of his kind, Altschul spoke from an underlying assumption of the independent and governing character of economic affairs. Thus his earlier remark about business morality seemed to imply that the human element was only a key which might at times be used to unlock the treasure of economic knowledge. Yet on the whole I was deeply depressed by a kind of listlessness that I felt in the man. In a peculiar, almost inexpressible fashion, he seemed wholly confined within the sphere of our particular surroundings at the moment: the palatial banks and the neurotically crowded restaurants of the heart of the city.

"And how is your wife?" I asked in a pause in the conversation.

"Rosi is quite well, thank you," he said. The very tone in which he spoke this conventional and therefore relatively unstudied phrase betrayed his extraordinary exhaustion. He seemed to become conscious of this immediately, and quickly added something inconsequential—if I remember rightly, a remark that this year he and his wife intended to take a trip to Gastein.

Meanwhile we were passing the Burgtheater. From the terrace of one of the cafés behind it, three figures detached themselves—bobbed up, so to speak, out of a crowded pond—and stepped into the broad sunny square. I saw someone waving. Altschul waved back. The person waving was his wife. Her little group seemed to have been expecting Altschul to come this way, along Ring Strasse. I greeted Frau Altschul and Frau Martha Mährischl, and was introduced to the latter's husband, Herr Doktor Mährischl. A tall broad figure formed out of soft masses bowed slightly to me. In so doing he brought his puffy pale face closer to mine, and I was struck by the absence of any real eyes; instead, the predominant impression was of blue shadows and the veil of a melancholy acceptance of the circumstances of life. The veil could part just sufficiently to let pass a drooping smile, which in its turn expressed a faint mockery of his own docility. I noticed that the man wore a sort of bangle on his wrist consisting of a thin gold chain.

Rosi Altschul, amiably and attentively flanked by the two Mährischls, was extremely ebullient. Her glance darted in all directions. Meanwhile I was able to observe again in Edouard Altschul that curious exhaustion which seemed to be sapping his pleasant smile from below, so that he had constantly to shore it up . . . We stood around chatting a bit indecisively. I was already beginning to feel the noonday heat; it was late, I was hungry, and at the same time I distinctly felt myself superfluous here. It was apparent to me that these gentlemen had met for some specific purpose. I therefore bade them good-by, amid a flourish of friendly remarks on the part of all of them, and continued on my way down the Ring, making myself breathe deeply and squaring my shoulders under my light jacket. As I walked I tried to convince myself that my sense of depression came solely from an empty stomach.

In the restaurant it occurred to me that I was sitting in the selfsame room, perhaps at the same table, where not very long ago (though it seemed long to me) the first meeting between Quapp and Gyurkicz must have taken place—that meeting which the rest of us were to discuss eternally. In the meanwhile the couple in question had undergone certain changes. Quapp had recently moved. I believe I have already mentioned that fact. In general she seemed to have the faculty, or the inclination, to mark inner epochs by external changes. It was the usual thing with her. Possibly in this case her landlady objected to Gyurkicz's visits as too frequent and perhaps too prolonged. Whether this was or was not the precipitating factor, it was at any rate obvious to all of us that this latest move had something to do with Imre.

By having Quapp move, he succeeded in separating her from the rest of our crowd, in detaching her even more from our group. The two of them now lived "over the hill," as we called it—that is to say, in a lower section of the garden suburb which lay closer to the Danube River, and was separated from our much higher district by a hilly elevation, gardens, vineyards, a large park, and several sets of streets. For Gyurkicz had betaken himself away from our immediate vicinity a good deal earlier—if I remember rightly, around the time my nephew, Doktor Körger, took an apartment out there, shortly after his arrival in Vienna. Quapp and Imre were not living together, to be sure; that would not have done. They had found quarters in two houses on opposite sides of a street. It may be assumed that Imre, after having discovered a room suitable for Quapp in his immediate neighborhood, had not rested until she "moved after him over the hill" to quote Captain von Eulenfeld.

From this time on, at any rate, the rest of us accepted the relation between the two as an established thing. I would rather not go into the question of what effect this consensus may have had, in its turn, upon Quapp. We had come to accept the situation. If we decided on a visit, we would call on "the two over the hill."

To do so, we followed a gently sloping road through the vineyards which led up to the top of the hill, paralleled on the right by the jagged and jumbled masses of houses. Then along through several streets of villas, behind whose hedges the gardens lay at a surprising slope. And then we were at the top. Here there was a streetcar terminus, people were getting in and out, the red-and-yellow cars were being switched. And just beyond, the park dropped steeply away, the tops of the trees forming a high dome to which even the last and most oblique rays of the evening sun could lend a golden polish; while farther below, the playground rang with the sound of children's voices. As the days grew longer and hotter, it remained cool and shady in these streets. But you stepped out once again into the setting sun when you reached the square in front of the old parish church. All the houses around the square seem left over from an earlier century and display the firm, peasant chunkiness of that period. A wide courtyard reveals a window behind which, it is well known, Beethoven once sat bent over the "Eroica." Sometimes the window is open; flowers, laundry, and other signs of life can be seen behind it; but the room seems rather dark and not exactly pleasant. It is now the home of some most prosaic people.

And so on down the whole street. You look into open windows, into darkness wedged full of pieces of heavy furniture. Sometimes, through an open rear door, the greenery of adjoining gardens flashes momentarily. Now you can hear Quapp's bowing exercises, and you step under the smoothly plastered archway at the entrance to her house. She lives in a relatively new, a relatively modern house. When one hears her practicing, one feels reluctant to disturb her by ringing, for Quapp is usually alone in her apartment, her landlady being away most of the time. Moreover, it is necessary to ring very loudly so that she will hear the bell above her violin. But she is always overjoyed when one of our crowd appears, and always says that Gyurkicz too will be delighted, and that he is on the point of dropping over . . .

But no, that is not quite correct. I spoke with her alone there many a time. Her room was not especially attractive; actually it was pretty dark and on the same level as the narrow street, though buffered from the street by a small front garden. I have spoken with her there alone many times, and the same might be said by Schlaggenberg and others among us. But one did so with a hand on the gearshift, so to speak, and invariably shifted gears when Imre turned up; for in the end we all took the line of least resistance in regard to him and put up with him as best we could.

But once Quapp wanted to have a little gathering, to which she invited a number of our crowd. It developed, however, that we were not actually visiting her but attending an official if small reception in which Gyurkicz played the part of host and gallantly dominated the situation, while Quapp fretted and the rest of us sat around in some perplexity; nothing resembling a lively conversation managed to flow, which was a rare state of affairs among our crowd.

Absorbed in such recollections of the past few weeks, I ate absent-mindedly, and had barely finished the meal when a waiter approached me in that incredibly polished fashion of our countrymen, stood a bit to the rear of me, stooping slightly, and murmured: "You are wanted on the telephone, sir," and slipped away again. For the past half year I had been coming to this restaurant only on occasional visits to the city, which were rare enough, although before moving out to Döbling I had eaten here frequently. But a Viennese *"Ober"* will greet a former guest back from five years abroad with some such rhetorical question as: "We have not seen you here often of late, have we, Herr von Bamperl?" In this manner even total desertion is minimized into a series of trivial interruptions, and the fiction is upheld that the guest belongs heart and soul to the restaurant.

It was Schlaggenberg calling; he had correctly guessed that I might be here at noon. Would I be staying in the city? He wanted to come into town, had his work behind him for the day; if I liked we could do our errands together and stroll about a bit. "I have a craving for movement, color, a bit of urban romanticism, gossip—how about it? I can be with you in half

426

an hour; I've already eaten, by the way."

In fact he arrived on time, looking spruce and in good form. He wanted to go somewhere for coffee, so we set out without delay.

Kajetan gave me the impression of being in a highly agitated state. He was like a battery overcharged with nervous energy which might at any moment discharge explosively outward into the world—where it would probably be dissipated, no longer susceptible to any kind of useful concentration.

"Look over there," he said to me in a self-important tone just after we had entered a café. "I like that woman over there, the one in the brown dress. She's the type I go for now. Look at her carefully and you'll see what I mean, what I really like."

I followed his glance. "Listen here, Schlaggenberg," I said, "there seems to be something wrong with your eyes. Will you kindly look again, or find some reason for going across the room so that you can see her better. That woman is a fright."

"Yes, yes, of course, impossible!" he exclaimed when he came back to me, for he had followed my advice and gone over to examine the beauty at close quarters—a fat female around fifty with extremely ordinary features. "No, no, of course she wouldn't do, she exceeds the limits of my tolerance by far—all limits—really oughtn't to be allowed . . . Oh well, she just struck me that way from a distance."

As we looked about for a table, he began to tell his story: "You know, Herr von Geyrenhoff, I really must tell you the whole thing as precisely as possible . . ." But after only a few minutes, in which he had described very vividly his walk to the Alliance building, he interrupted himself: "See her over there? Yes—in the green dress—that's right, in the corner . . . There is the typical mature woman for you, undoubtedly horribly prudish, probably a housewife and faithful helpmeet and all that . . ."

427

"Schlaggenberg, I envy you your obvious bad eyesight—or do you see an Aphrodite in every woman who weighs over a hundred and sixty pounds and is past fifty . . . ?"

"All right, I'll go look at her too!" And he sallied off. He returned in short order. "Oh well, yes, of course, *c'est impossible,* altogether impossible; all I meant was the solid sedate look, you know—I was attracted for a moment by the breadth of her. But I grant you, she isn't my type. She isn't—*the* type."

"I wish I could see *the* type some time or other," I said.

"Well, you know, the best chance would be in that coffee-house on the waterfront . . ."

But I only laughed and waved his comments aside.

He continued his story: "The obdurate door closed heavily behind me. Cerberus nodded; the presses rumbled in the basement, conjuring up an image of gigantic mill wheels revolving in a deep walled shaft below the ground . . . I went up as far as the first stair landing. There I involuntarily paused; something extraordinarily important had come to my mind. Sitting here now, you may think it only natural, but there, and at the time, I felt as if a light were dawning. For I realized that I was completely alone! Do you understand what I mean? That in this Alliance world, on these stairs, surrounded by oily smells from the composing rooms and on the point of coming face to face with people on the upper floor, with whom I would have to speak, I was utterly alone. As alone as you may be in a jungle or in some other wild and deserted region. I was on my own, as the phrase goes. And I realized that in this solitude I must carry forward a part of my life, of my destiny. It scarcely mattered what my state of mind was in the process. It did not matter whether from now on I was going to dominate the—the area of my life wholly or partly or not at all. Every step taken would nevertheless have full and irrevocable validity . . .

"And you know, this sense of absolute loneliness in the wilderness suddenly gave me strength. Isn't that odd? I no longer felt scattered in all directions; I had come back to myself, collected myself, regained a measure of composure.

"At that very moment someone called my name down the stairwell. I looked up and saw Holder's black hair and glasses; he was leaning over the banister two floors up."

"I understand that very well, Kajetan," I said after a short pause. "That moment was undoubtedly of the greatest importance for you. I can only say that it was a lucky thing you hit upon that particular thought at the critical juncture . . . Otherwise you might not have behaved properly. Before you go on it would interest me greatly to hear, Kajetan—if you don't mind jumping ahead a bit—just what improvement you have made in your relationship with Alliance. I'd like to know how you stand with the people there, what they are offering you, and what prospects you have. You mentioned that there was a chance of a novel of yours appearing as a serial in their main paper. Has anything come of that?"

"Look at this," he said. Leaning forward, he raked a newspaper over to our table. I read: "New novel Thursday!" and so on. "Five hundred in advance, a thousand on publication of the last section of the serial. From the fifteenth of May on, I start as an outside associate of the feature section at a salary of four hundred, two hundred already received in advance."

"Hmm," I said. "Will you then be a member of the editorial staff?"

"Expressly not. And when I asked whether I had to take part in editorial conferences, I was told that this wouldn't be at all necessary. In fact they implied that my presence would not be desired."

"So far, then, you've received seven hundred in cold cash

from them. I should think that indicates serious intentions on the part of Alliance. Which seems to disprove my suspicions that the whole thing would turn out to be a matter of empty promises and that they would try to string you along. Now what about the book publishing end of it?"

"Just being organized. But my novel will have a high priority in their publishing program."

Both of us sat in silence for some time.

What I had just heard was certainly most gratifying, when looked at superficially, and Schlaggenberg certainly seemed in line for congratulations. Oddly enough, however, the whole story gave me a feeling of haste and high tension, of, perhaps, the short life span of these gains. And Kajetan himself did not by any means seem to be splashing about in a pool of delight or to have at last attained freedom from care. Granted, the whole affair had evidently unfettered, not to say aroused, his animal spirits. All very well, let him carry on as he pleased with his fat females! It was becoming more and more obvious to me that there was something else behind it all.

"You must have an importance to Levielle that I know nothing of, Kajetan," I said. "That is the only explanation I can see. If you know what it is all about, well and good. I have no right to ask you to tell me—although you know my keen and, I hope, objective interest in the whole situation. But of course you have already followed a policy of secretiveness even where there was no need of it . . ."

"I don't know what you mean," he said.

"Think of the visiting card."

His expression darkened and for the moment held a look of torment. "That is very simple, my dear von Geyrenhoff," he said. "I was ashamed to know this man—I did not want to be reminded of our acquaintanceship. Of course I knew perfectly

430

well that Eulenfeld and Stangeler had seen the card in the bowl
. . . Levielle is what you might call a piece of family inheritance.
But circumstances may arise in which such inheritances' pres-
ent unexpected complications. Moreover, I did tell you about
Levielle's call."

"Yes, what you did was more or less to use truth to put
across a falsehood. It was all so odd, the newspaper story and
the rest of it. At first I thought you had been lying outright—and
yet there was something else behind it, behind this patronage.
What did you really have in mind when you informed Grete
Siebenschein of Levielle's connection with your family? She
noted every word carefully, so that not long after our memorable outing she asked whether Levielle really had been your
father's financial adviser and no more. She said that you yourself had told her that Levielle arranged 'certain important
affairs' in your family."

"Fräulein Siebenschein has an excellent memory and has
quoted me quite accurately. However, the story is as follows: he
actually did arrange 'certain important affairs,' which in fact
had nothing to do with financial matters. In the course of so
doing Herr Levielle came into the possession of certain information which is known only to my mother and myself—not
even Quapp knows these things, now that my old man is dead.
Levielle promised my father, and repeated the pledge in his last
hour, to keep silent about it. At least until a certain time. To my
knowledge, that time has not yet been reached." (It sounded
somewhat preposterous to me that Levielle should have made
any pledges to old Schlaggenberg, but of course I kept this to
myself.) "You see, my dear Herr von Geyrenhoff, in this matter
I too am duty-bound to keep the secret. That is all I can say to
you about it."

Kajetan paused. Then he seemed to cast off the whole

subject as if it were a burden.

"It is still a piece of luck to be free and independent at last," he said, taking a deep breath and looking around the café.

"I should think, then, that you would be feeling very good," I remarked.

For the span of a thought he closed his eyes. "No, I am afraid that is not so. I have been—thrown out of balance. I feel unsure of myself. The matter has not created any essential order for me. And then, you must consider that we may possibly be on the verge of great changes, perhaps already in the midst of them, and one might well say"—again he lowered his eyelids as he spoke—"one might say that perhaps even now all this has already lost significance . . ."

"I seem to hear an echo of my esteemed nephew, Doktor Körger," I said. "I would wager you have been knocking around with him recently. Haven't you?"

"Yesterday."

"Well, then. Incidentally, what did he have to say about your teaming up with the Alliance people?

"He was most enthusiastic. 'Herr von Schlaggenberg,' he said, you must secure yourself a firm position there. That could be of the greatest importance for us.'"

"What ever did he mean by 'for us'?" I asked.

Schlaggenberg shrugged and passed over my question. "What disturbs me," he continued, "is that I cannot really cope with it all. I am not ready for the situation into which I have been steered. I felt that most clearly while Körger was talking with me. And later on, too, I could more or less estimate the distance that separates me from his kind of firmness and integration. You see, I feel rather as if right now something quite alien were on the point of intruding into my personality, destroying the growing oneness and tranquillity of this one

432

life I have, splitting it like a wedge, breaking it open, tearing its fibers apart. And possibly forever. Ultimately everything depends on how we see things when we are alone and close our eyes for a minute. And here the matter is plain enough. The whole business dangles from me like a broken wing from the body of a bird. In fact I feel as if part of me had sheared off and rotted, as if now it were infecting my whole body . . ."

"You exaggerate, Schlaggenberg. You're becoming obsessed with this. All these sensations will probably be incomprehensible to you by the day after tomorrow . . . Understand me: you simply must grow into this now established situation. You must prove yourself in it. Is it clear? You must! That is what living means. Holding contradictions in equilibrium. That's all. It's very simple. It doesn't take a Körger to do that. Think of those moments on the stairway in the Alliance building. I would say that what you arrived at then was exactly the right attitude toward the whole thing. There you were alone, really, yourself to the highest degree. In being that, it seems to me, you had already acquired the proper aloofness from it all."

"Yes," he exclaimed eagerly, "you're right about that! You're certainly right."

"All right, then. And now permit me, my dear Kajetan—still Kajetan and never Cajétan, not if there were ten Levielles!—permit me an apparent digression. I want to say something about an observation in connection with you that I made a short while ago, and that I keep making. Pay attention now. When I come to your place at six o'clock, I can see you just shutting up shop and—arranging your desk. You've prepared everything for the next morning; the manuscripts are gathered together and put away, the pipes cleaned; when you're finished, all your stuff lies in neat packets on the desk . . ."

What I went on to say about pedantry and the pedant as

a type went far beyond Schlaggenberg's particular case. But I was determined to say what I had to say, to present it in words and phrases, characterize it by the very sounds of the words, which are the real flesh of language; thoughts have to be clothed in that flesh to prove their viability. Not that I wanted to persuade myself of anything or prove anything to myself by my own words. I know for certain that I was entirely free of any such intention. But I was fighting against an intrusion from without, from Kajetan's mind; against something fundamentally alien which I felt as a threat to myself.

I will not set down everything I said on that occasion. But I do want to record just this: "Order is in itself praiseworthy and valuable; we agree on that! But I've noticed that you, for a long time now, forever and a day in fact, have been chiefly occupied with making order. In everything. A few minutes ago you were talking about order again, saying that the thing had not 'created any essential order' for you, or however you put it. There are pedants who turn into a strange type of domestic tyrant, not only in regard to pipes and pencils, but also in regard to their own biographies, so to speak. They insist that their life-stories fit into a predetermined orderly pattern, and eliminate anything for which there is no room in that pattern. They hope to construct a Tower of Babel to the God of Order out of the building-materials of life, which as always lie around in jumbled heaps. But in the end all that they create turns out to be no more than an extremely high hat which they must balance so carefully on their heads that they don't dare take a step forward. Of course they don't want anything new, any additions; the slightest disturbance and things will be dangling 'like a broken wing.' The smallest nothing upsets the 'growing oneness and tranquillity' of such a life. This oneness is nothing but the rigid pattern, the establishment of a second life, and anti-life."

434

"But suppose this inner and outer discipline has a purpose?" said Schlaggenberg, who in spite of himself had grown increasingly thoughtful during my discourse. "Suppose the purpose of it is to fend off that dull pressure or blunt impact which can so easily keep one from bringing one's work to completion?"

"Yet how easily such a disciplined person can dry up entirely, the water of life squeezed out of him," I said with an emphasis that seemed untoward even to myself.

"You are mixing everything up," he said suddenly, with a certain acridness. "First, to reply to what you said earlier: as far as I can see, everyone should do his best to become as pure a specimen of the particular type he happens to represent as he can; in other words, to become integral and integrated, and to do so before it is too late. The way he goes about it is his own affair. In any case he will constantly be faced with the necessity for negating and rejecting other possibilities. And with the necessity for cutting loose from old mistakes whose effects go on, and for breaking off false relationships. The weaker a person has been in the past, the more of this last he will have to do. When he is done, the sum total of the debts accumulated in his past life will be presented to him in one form or another. Everyone has to settle them for himself."

"My dear Kajetan," I said, "that may well be the way to justify oneself in hindsight, locking the stable door after the horse is stolen, as the proverb goes. But what has this to do with your present choice?"

"Quite so, logician!" he exclaimed. "That is precisely why I worry about it. Here's another example of something alien forcing itself into my life, leading my life far from its proper path. How is it going to end? Do you think I can keep faith, so to speak?"

"But Schlaggenberg, you are making far too much of the

whole thing. Keeping faith doesn't enter into it. That would be too fantastic! Don't forget that the matter is a purely practical relationship."

"You yourself can scarcely believe that, Herr von Geyrenhoff," he said bitterly. "Do you still refuse to see what my situation is, or are you deliberately trying to soothe me? Is that it? To comfort me? The whole thing touches an inflamed sore spot in me, a spot as red as a warning light. I can feel the ground of life caving in under me; everything is thrown open to question; the tautness of the bow slackens, the sinews of action are sliced through. And you seem to me to be working in the same direction, with your conciliatory talk! No—it's no pleasure to live when—when you feel yourself no longer capable of . . ."

"Of dominating the area of your life," I interpolated. "That is what you wanted to say, isn't it?"

"The devil take you!" he answered, laughing. His voice dropped abruptly and he whispered sharply: "Turn around! Turn around now!"

I did so rather halfheartedly, bored and amused in advance. But instead of one of those imposing female figures I had expected to see, my glance fell upon the exceedingly slender form of Fräulein Grete Siebenschein. She was coming from the other wing of the café, which lay at a right angle to our part; for that reason we had not seen her before. Winding her way among the tables toward the exit, she looked altogether charming. Behind her came Doktor Neuberg. They quickly reached the sidewalk, and we saw them crossing the street together.

"They did not notice us," I said.

"So much the better," Schlaggenberg observed.

"You were intending to tell me more about your recent first visit to Alliance."

436

"Right. There I was, standing on the landing with Holder looking down from above. He took possession of me at once, led me up to the features office, which is stowed away high up on the fifth floor, and promptly made himself ridiculous—for I saw that he knew nothing at all—by attempting to play his new role for all it was worth, and to patronize me besides. 'I assume you are bringing me a manuscript,' he said. 'I hope it is suitable so that I can publish it. Is it long?' Of course those few minutes had a certain value, for I recognized that the man is utterly innocent, really. 'No, it's not a manuscript. I was coming to call on Cobler in connection with another matter,' I said. 'Oh, then I'll send word down to him right away,' he said. 'I think it will be difficult, though—hardly possible that you'll reach him at all today.' He bobbed his head back and forth. 'There are so many people waiting down there today.' He picked up the telephone, obviously received a negative reply, and advised me to stick around in his room for a while; they would ring him as soon as Cobler was free. Incidentally, he had not mentioned my name on the telephone. I sat down but was not intending to stay more than five minutes . . . Meanwhile a woman I knew dropped in—the poetess Rosi Malik—she used to hang around at my publisher's. The two now launched out on a literary-soiree conversation with me. Malik was not exactly impudent; at least she's a good deal less brash than she looks, but she was obviously feeling her oats that afternoon. I soon saw why; it seemed that they were going to publish one of her silly pieces in the near future. At any rate I now knew why she thought it necessary to be there, aside from the fact that she really belonged there, generally speaking.

"I managed to get away and started down. On the stairs I ran into Doktor Trembloner, with whom I had a few friendly words in passing. It seemed to me that he regarded me with interest, but I could not determine whether he already knew something. In the case of Glenzler and Reichel, however, it was perfectly obvious, as quickly became apparent. The waiting-room was mobbed—there were eight or ten people there. I could have given the attendant my card or had myself announced, but out of curiosity I went on into the secretary's room next to Cobler's office, where the Kienbauer girl sits. She was alone—a rarity, because most of the time half of the staff is in there too, chiefly engaged in bothering the overworked girl. Impolite as ever—toward me, that is—she responded curtly to my greeting, said: 'Herr Cobler is busy,' and went on fussing with her papers. I was rather surprised at being treated this way, now that every-thing was supposed to be changed. But I had no time to think about it. Who should come in but Glenzler and Reichel, not to gossip, for once, but in a flurry of work; they had manuscripts and proofs in their hands. But still they found time to greet me like a long-lost friend. 'Have you already announced him?' old Glenzler asked the secretary. 'There's somebody in there!' she said. 'Oh, the devil . . .' Glenzler said, with a quick wave of his hand. He turned to me: 'I'll tell Herr Cobler pronto that you're here, Herr von Schlaggenberg.' There was no time for that. A moment before he could go into the office, the door burst open and there was Cobler himself. 'Aha!' he said, catching sight of me. 'Here already? Here already?' He turned to the secretary: 'Why didn't you say so, why didn't you say so?' And to me: 'Been waiting long? Come, come.' He shot another look at his mistress, shook his head, drew me along in his wake, said: 'Sit down,' took a chair opposite me. And now mark this well, Herr von Geyrenhoff! He did not squirm, did not gesticulate, did not say a word. Instead, he looked at me for a long, long time, with a steady searching look. Both of us remained silent. But I regarded him calmly and looked him straight in the eye.

The racket outside made the stillness in the room palpable. It so happened that the telephone on the desk did not ring once in all this time.

"Sitting thus, he seemed to me greatly aged. Not outwardly by any means. But his handsomely ugly, dry vulture's head seemed parched by the continual working of his nerves; his eyes were deep-set and I felt in them the kind of habitual torment you find in people who are troubled by violent headaches all the time.

"'Good,' he said suddenly. 'All in order. No need to talk much, Kajetan. Tomorrow morning at eleven o'clock you go up to Oplatek. About the contract.'

"Then we both sat in silence for a while longer—I felt no impulse to speak and stuck out the silence without any loss of dignity. Abruptly, he burst out: 'Tell me, Kajetan: why right now, all of a sudden? Now of all times? How come? Why not sooner, then? Well, I suppose you know!'

"Then I said—I stood up, went close to his desk and said—I spoke with great urgency and conviction, because it was after all the truth, I think—from which you ought to see that deep inside myself I did not think those stories about Stangeler and the music room a sufficient explanation—I said, bending down a bit toward him: 'Herr Cobler—I do *not* know.'

"'Go away,' he said, waving his hand as though trying to rid himself of an imposition, such as the imposition of being asked to believe anything so utterly crackbrained as the statement I had just made. But then he looked at me, stared penetratingly at me for the fraction of a second—crossly, I must say—as though a light were dawning and as though this imposition no longer seemed so monstrous under the glare of this new light. At the same time his look was still querying as he muttered, with his face almost touching mine: 'Go away—well!—can you

439

imagine—a fool!—you're capable of anything!' This last was roared out in his customary tone. 'The two of you are capable of anything!—fools—you're a fool too—see you soon, Herr Doktor!' And he snatched up proofs and several batches of manuscript, detonated, and the next moment I stood alone in his office, staring thunderstruck at this odd man's abandoned desk."

"If it were Levielle, he would certainly not have seen any light," I said under my breath, after a pause. "But—how is it that you yourself don't ask the same question: why at this particular time? Because that incident of René's picking up something not meant for a stranger's ears—that can't be the reason for this fat Alliance contract. Levielle might just as easily have done something for you one way or another in the past. But he never troubled about you at all, nor you about him. Or was there some contact I don't know about?"

"No, not since my father's death, so far as I recall. Incidentally—but no, that can scarcely be called a contact. He once called on Quapp at our place—we were sharing one room at the time, for financial reasons, but I happened to be away on a skiing trip. Anyway, he found Quapp at home and gave her several photographs of the old man, some of them pictures from 'way back,' which Levielle had somehow had in his keeping. He told Quapp that he had wanted to bring us these pictures for a long time since we had a better right to them than he, but had not known our address—we had moved shortly before. That's all. But enough of this idle talk. There's one thing I really want to talk to you about."

"Hm," I said, "fat females?"

"Fat females. Listen: as I left Cobler's suddenly vacated office—I had sat there stupefied for quite a while—and went out through the waiting-room, greeting the band of colleagues and larvae as chummily as you please, a woman came toward me from the stairway. As she passed me, she turned me with irresistible force upon my own axis. I simply *had to* look back at her. She disappeared into the secretary's office. I asked one of the attendants, Otto, who the lady was. He told me her name and a few things about her. Her name happens to be Tugendhat.[2] And she looks the name. It's very important how you say it. You mustn't say it like 'Turandot, Princess of China'—or 'Tugendhat, Princess of Alliance.' You have to say it, not like a title, but like a description—Tugendhat, she who has virtue. Understand?"

"You are talking like a blithering idiot," I said.

"No," he replied. "This is an important point. I mean, this virtue of hers is an important point. Because there's something enormously provocative about it. One aspect of it is irritating. Let's say it has something of the quality you feel in the Konterhonz girl. Only of course not so silly; this lady has far greater sensibility. But in the second place one feels that under this prim surface there may be an unspeakable conglomeration of traits. And there's no hint of that in Konterhonz or her kind. Not a particle. *Comprenez?* But you know—the reward of my attention was an annihilating look: the *personificatio* and *glorificatio* of unassailable virtue. *Capisci?*"

"You'll be running out of foreign languages in a moment."

"Look here," he said, ignoring my remark, "consider the symbol. Her name is Tugendhat. She knows that she has virtue and proclaims it in her name. Women like her all ought to have such a name! But she knows just as well, or even better, that there is another course, and that she has the physical prerequisites for it. And she lets this other possibility peep out like a hint

---

2. *Tugend* = virtue; *hat* = has

441

of her enviable *dessous* under the dress of virtue. As a result of knowing so much about this and that, about the concealment and the hint, about virtue and its tantalizing opposite—as a result of all this knowledge—there arises a high degree of dryness, a parched absorbent attraction, which in the nature of things shows through the windows of the soul. Which accounts for the mystery of such eyes."

As he spoke, my mind for a moment dwelt upon the person of Frau Lea Wolf.

"And this lady is the mother of a genealogist at Alliance," he added.

"And therefore a lady of mature years," I said.

"How banally you express yourself!"

"Does her weight come up to your standards?"

"Certainly over one sixty-five," he said in deadly earnest. His seriousness so stunned me that I thought the time had come to look a good deal more closely into this matter. Since the so-called "foundation festival" of our crowd, when Kajetan had come forth with an extempore oration on the whole delightful subject of fat females, the obsession seemed to have gained ground within his psyche. It seemed well on its way to descending from the heights of pure theory to the lower depths of succulent practice. Until this moment I had not considered any such possibility.

"I am going to go ahead with it," he said. "Which means that the matter now begins to concern you, and it will no longer do for you to wave your hands in horror and refuse to pay any attention to this side of my life. On the contrary. I demand that everything be included in your novelistic accounts—or whatever name you give your scribbling. For my part, I will undertake to supply the relevant chapters, gratis. These had better be grouped as a separate section of the complete manuscript, and given some such title as *'Chronique scandaleuse'*—a good title, I think, which occurred to me a while back.

"What!" I exclaimed, aghast. "All that trash is to go in?"

"It must," he said coldly. "You will find out eventually that it is absolutely essential to your tale, and so will your respected readers."

"But you'll ruin everything for me with your crazy nonsense," I said angrily. "The whole book will be spoiled."

"Aha!" he burst out, his voice at an unnaturally high pitch, by which he wished to imply that suddenly a "light was dawning." "So you want to write a book! You want to be a writer! A fine writer! Incidentally, my congratulations. How do you want me to address you henceforth? 'Dear colleague,' shall we say? Well, enjoy yourself. I'm delighted, anyhow, I'm delighted!"

"That's enough now, will you kindly quiet down, Kajetan?" I said, but could not go on, he made me laugh so. He was gesticulating furiously, making solemn gestures, bowing to me, but in the same breath inscribing in the air monstrous shapes of his new idols and repeating again and again: "It must go in. All of it. Must go in. Must. Every bit. Exactly. Exactly as it is. There's a job for you, my writing friend!" He laughed triumphantly.

"Schlaggenberg," I whispered at last, "behave yourself. You're making people look at us. No, don't think I intend to compete with you. I am not writing any books."

"Then who do you think is going to write it—the thing, the journal, the chronicle . . . ?"

"You."

"What in the world has put that into your head? Do you think I'm going to take on such a chore?"

"You're doing so as it is right now. No cause for excitement; I'm not asking more of you than you are doing. Stangeler and I together will handle the editorial and supplementary work."

443

"With the assistance of Frau Steuermann," he said a bit spitefully.

"Yes. And of others also. Incidentally—I hereby avow my willingness to include the *'Chronique scandaleuse'*—somewhat censored, of course. But Frau Selma Steuermann is under no circumstances to be delivered over to your tender mercies."

"Why not?"

"Official secret," I said.

He waved that away with both hands, imitating with considerable histrionic talent my own gestures, and we burst into laughter again. "It's going to be, going to be, going to be a book after all," he said. "He's going to write, write, write. It will come, I see it coming."

But I only shook my head.

"I have now firmly resolved," he continued his revelations, "I am absolutely determined to go ahead along this line, having recognized it as the right thing for me; to proceed according to plan, employing a clear logical strategy, as opportunity offers. I have made enormous sacrifices with the object of bringing order into my life and I shall cling to this order and strive to extend it."

What followed was in harmony with these sentiments and equally gruesome.

"I want mature women, big women, who know what they are after, just as I know what I am after. No romantic and melancholy mists. No 'duties' and 'responsibilities.' For the rest, I prefer to be alone. Or with friends. If a person cannot attain to any other plane above practical life except that plane of sentimental bosh—which I now find unspeakably disgusting, the private hunting-ground of every philistine with literary pretensions—why let him, let him make his sheep's eyes. But I'm through with it. The eighteenth century was still tolerably healthy in this respect, but since the romantic period it's been the very devil. And how serious they are about it all! And the scenes they make!"

He wound up with the following thunderclap: "Here, you see, I've had five more ads inserted in newspapers."

He pushed the clippings across the table to me.

"I scarcely think these ads of yours will bring in the desired results," I said. "I doubt whether you'll catch even a single woman with them."

"Why not?" he answered with great animation. "The point is to carve out as large an area as possible in which chance can operate in my favor. I am keeping my eyes open constantly, holding myself in readiness. I've also let some of my friends know of my new enthusiasm, and asked them to think of me if the occasion should arise. Of course I have not asked you, Herr von Geyrenhoff, because I fancy you would not breathe a word to me if you were to meet up with Juno in person—just to be spiteful." (He was not altogether wrong, although I did not care to be told that my reactions were dictated by spite.)

"What you say about carving out the largest area sounds sensible, Kajetan," I replied at last. "But I think your strategy is all wrong, because it is too mathematical. It smacks of the calculus of probability. It is one thing, in life, to be ready for an event which in the end you more or less bring about, conjure up, by your constant readiness. But what you are doing is virtually setting a trap for life—at least that is what your project sounds like. Like the people of Schilda who tried to gather the sunlight. You want to catch life in your nets, but I am afraid it is too tricky for that."

"Nevertheless! I mean to carry this thing to extremes. You are going to be shocked," he said, laughing. "Say what you will, I'm going systematically to open doors for lucky chances, as far as possible."

445

"But Kajetan," I exclaimed, "that's just it! Precisely because you are one of those people to whom the right thing happens at the right time, and in a far clearer form than to most people—(but I think it happens to everyone, more or less)—precisely for that reason your pedantic preparations and trap-setting seem to me so altogether misplaced, practically a violation of the basic rhythm of your nature, if you'll pardon the fancy language. Pedantry! That's it. You're trying to make order again!" I spoke with great energy and really thought at that moment that I was expressing a true divination. "Yes, that is the trouble. I think that at bottom you hate life. Or at any rate, you hate it right now. That's it, that's it. The pedant stands at the open window by his orderly desk. The landscape surges toward him, carrying gardens and streets and the multifold cubes of the houses on its flood . . ." ("You're becoming poetic," he interjected as I briefly paused.) "But the pedant neatly cuts off the little corner in which he stands—because he thinks he has the power to do so. This is where he is master. He turns back to his room and paces up and down, straightening out something here and there, feeling what a thoroughly righteous man he is. That's it. You'd like to arrange everything to the best practical advantage, Kajetan. 'Love' likewise, of course. But what is going to happen when the energy fails—let alone if it comes at you full force. Because then your anti-order would be crushed to dust like a glass bead. I am speaking of the energy you hope to catch in your cleverly constructed mills. What happens then? Ever since you broke up with Camy nothing really new has entered your life, no real joy. . . I seriously think you hate life!"

"Life! Life! How high and mighty you talk. It makes me want to puke," Kajetan said.

"Puke then," I said, undaunted by his rudeness. "But have you any idea, Kajetan, what may have passed you by during

446

this long interval you've spent in an attitude of stubborn resistance? Is this the way to keep your membranes, your receptive apparatus, in tiptop condition—for you need them to tell you what may be available to you, what may be right at hand, either here and now or in those apparently empty moments when, say, you jump upon the running-board of a streetcar, or by day or night, in some unknown garden perhaps . . ."

And here I broke off, in something like alarm, for a particular garden and a particular woman leaped into my mind. I sat mute, and Schlaggenberg spoke up: "My membranes or my receptive apparatus, or whatever other odd name you may find for the thing, tells me at this moment that you need only turn around if you want to see my type, the type I am really and truly seeking, in our immediate neighborhood. She is just sailing in from the open sea of this lovely café and will billow by our table in full magnificence in just a moment. Oh, those grand extrusions! They truly march in procession before and behind their owner, as Eulenfeld expresses it. In my mind's eye I see this woman parading stark naked through the café. And in reality that is what she is doing. Because, you see, she likewise has a great deal of virtue."

His dithyramb ceased, for the phenomenon had passed by and vanished.

When we stepped out onto the street again, we found that the thin warmth of the spring day had settled down into a kind of sultriness. The spacious squares, the pompous façades, the plushy green of the gardens and the domed greens of the treetops were laved by a surprising prodigality of sunlight which turned the lively traffic in the streets to sparkling splendor. Here and there slanting rays accumulated into massive bundles of light whose brilliance blotted out the more distant view. We walked toward the center of the city, and so for the second time that day I reached the crowded Graben, where we dropped into shops here and there. At one point I said to Kajetan: "There comes my cousin Géza." But he replied (perhaps alluding to my remark earlier): "Your eyesight does not seem to be very good." In fact, I had been misled by a certain resemblance at a distance of fifteen or twenty paces. Soon afterwards, however, as we left the perfumery whose unworldly fragrant coolness had aroused so many images of the past in my mind that morning, I exclaimed again: "But here he is, really coming along." Immediately I became aware of my error, though the similarity was truly astounding and had even deceived Schlaggenberg. However, when we turned into the Tuchlauben, I ran square into my cousin Géza von Orkay.

"Well, here you are at last!" I exclaimed, while Kajetan burst into laughter. "I've been expecting you for quite a while."

"How come?" he asked, completely taken aback, for we had made no appointment.

I explained the curious circumstances. "I am waiting for Kurt," he said—he meant my nephew Doktor Körger. "We arranged to meet here."

The two of them always seemed as thick as thieves. Before long, massive-headed Körger came sauntering along, looking off into space and not recognizing us until he was on top of us. He laughed with pleasure. "Why, folks, let's all get pickled," the bird Turul proposed. We decided, however, to fetch Eulenfeld and Höpfner, both of whom worked in this part of town. It was nearing six o'clock and they were probably finishing up at their offices.

In the course of fetching them our party unexpectedly acquired two automobiles—Höpfner's, a handsome car that stood in front of his firm's door, and Eulenfeld's notorious sports car, for as we arrived we found him on the point of taking it out of the garage to drive home.

"Quapp is sure to be alone this evening," Schlaggenberg said. "I know that Gyurkicz has made an appointment with the 'poetess' Rosi Malik and Holder; I happened to hear about it at Alliance. Gyurkicz is supposed to draw Rosi; the picture is going to be published in all the Alliance papers in connection with the impending performance of her play 'Captain Dash,' or 'Hyphen,' or whatever the miserable thing is called. But Quapp is home because the Wiesinger woman is coming out there at half-past six—you know, the one she plays sonatas with. Let's drive out to the country for some wine and pick up Quapp at her place."

Within a few minutes, we rumbled off. I sat next to Captain Eulenfeld. An old hat tipped against the back of his neck (he had his special name for it—his "mouse-gray headpiece"), black leather gloves open at the wrists, he guided the little car with casual skill through the rush-hour traffic. Höpfner, with the other three in his car, followed close behind. We drove rapidly, and while a cooling wind blew in my face and through my light summer suit, I gave thought to a remark of Géza's. A little while before, when I had transmitted to him Baron von Frigori's regards and invitation, he had dismissed the matter with a contemptuous gesture and the casual remark: "Impossible to go there." The bird Turul was no snob. On the other hand, people in the embassies were just the ones to know the lowdown on figures in social life. It dawned on me that Frigori probably stood badly in need of his obtrusive arrogance, in order to hold himself upright against an undercurrent which he obviously preferred to ignore.

Meanwhile we were speeding through the long suburban

streets, overtaking and passing crowded streetcars. The solid rows of houses opened out, dispersed themselves; the still feathery green leaped between them like flames. Now we were purring up the gentle incline, along a street lined with villas behind whose iron fences the gardens dropped away surprisingly. Glimpses of still denser greens, of branching shadowy paths, whirled into and out of our range of vision. Then we were on top of the rise, had passed the terminus of the streetcar line, where the red-and-yellow cars came home to rest. The road turned down again. We had come "over the hill."

There was an excellent tavern out here. We decided to go right in and left the cars. I went along with Doktor Körger and Schlaggenberg to fetch Quapp from her nearby dwelling, while the other three took seats at one of the plain deal tables under the trees at the back of the café garden.

From the playground came the echo of children's voices. The evening sun still licked the treetops against the blue sky, while in the streets lay the last and longest shadows, already on the verge of flowing into the dusk and uniting completely with it. Here a higher window still glowed, there again a patina of red-gold touched a sloping gable; but the colors were already fading. We crossed the square by the little old church. We also passed along the wide yard adjoining it, and by that window in whose dark rectangle, sure enough, a few pieces of laundry were as usual hung out to dry. They hung quite motionless, for there was scarcely any breeze. A small flower-bearing potted plant stood on the sill beneath them.

And then on down the street under overarching trees. As we approached the house we heard from Quapp's window not the endless bowing exercises which are the hallmark of the professional violinist, who "practices" but does not "play" as we laymen might term it. This evening it was the piano we heard.

It sounded for a few moments, and then the violin launched a savage, resolute assault. We stood under the archway in front of the entrance, and then we recognized what was being played. The hard, passionate, hammering passages of the "Kreutzer" Sonata were singing out to any waiting ears in this obscure, half-countrified street.

After the first movement there was silence. We waited in vain; the session seemed to be over.

The bell sounded in the empty cool hall and then we heard Quapp's rather heavy, trampling step. She grinned from ear to ear, so happy was she to see us. She threw her arms around her brother's neck. We told her what we were doing. She shouted: "Wonderful!" and of course wanted to come along. Once in her room, we found it lit only by the little lamps clipped onto the piano and the music stand; the lights were sharply outlined against the inflowing twilight. I greeted Fräulein Wiesinger, made introductions between her and my nephew, and invited her to join our little party. She said something about an engagement for the evening and having to go into town right away, but seemed pleased that I had asked her. Removing her horn-rimmed glasses, she looked at me amicably out of near-sighted eyes whose expression had remained about on the level of a fourteen-year-old girl's; like her turned-up nose her eyes seemed to be making an effort to withdraw more and more into her head, drawing the whole face with them. Everything was too small about that face, and surprisingly crowded together, when you looked at it from close up. Tall and tapering toward the top, she stood in front of Quapp's mirror, which obliged her to stoop slightly because it hung too low for her. She secured her hat with a hat pin and left.

After her departure we waited a few minutes while Quapp did a bit of primping in the hall bathroom. Then she rejoined

451

us, sat down between Körger and Schlaggenberg on the sofa, placed her arms around their shoulders, and said without transition: "When you are all here, and when I feel the connection with you, everything is different."

Back at the tavern Turul and Eulenfeld were still on the first bottle, but the level in it had dropped very low—all the more significant since Höpfner was scarcely drinking. A second bottle was brought in as we entered; it was well cooled, for the glass was heavily misted. Candles were being set up with glass globes about them to shelter them from the wind. Eulenfeld crossed the garden toward us and embraced Quapp in front of everyone. None of the guests thought anything of this; hardly anyone even looked up. All over the garden, at tables and under the arbors, couples were sitting.

It seemed to me that Géza greeted Quapp with distinct warmth and with more than his normal gallantry. He seemed to manifest a special respect for her, and perhaps something even more. But then I noticed these nuances whenever he met her. There had evidently been some joke on Höpfner, for suddenly Eulenfeld broke into laughter. Whereupon I made a point of listening. Pretty soon the name of Dulnik was mentioned. From what I could gather out of Höpfner's rather shamefaced whisperings—and to see a man so tall whispering through pursed-up bulky lips was in itself funny—it appeared that Director Dulnik wanted to cheat Höpfner out of the fruits of his advertising idea (which as Eulenfeld declared was a truly astonishing one), or at least cut back Höpfner's hoped-for profits.

The arrangement with Dulnik had been that the aforementioned newly discovered advertising surface was to be covered exclusively with verses of Höpfner's devising. And now, while we had been off fetching Quapp, and Höpfner had returned to the table after a brief absence (for he made a practice of checking the situation in each public place), inspection had revealed new grave violations of the agreement on the part of Dulnik. For what Höpfner had found in the little room proved to be the amateurish stammerings of some nobody, verses limping on every metric foot, the words themselves mutilated in an effort to fit the rhythm, and the sense of these jingles consequently quite lost. "You know my stuff!" he exclaimed in distress. "By now my work practically carries a trademark. In the beginning I was actually doing all the jingles. You remember, don't you, Herr von Schlaggenberg—it was during the winter, when you had that gathering at your place, we had just come out with this novelty. And now Dulnik is resorting more and more to other people's stuff—the clumsiest hack work—so as not to have to pay me at the stipulated rate."

"Yes, the whole business of advertising jingles ought to be controlled. What we need is a regular apprenticeship system, with people having to pass an examination and be given a certificate of competence. Otherwise we will be flooded with more and more of this botch work. The language is being murdered," said my nephew, who had an organizing streak. "That's so, unless the ads are authentic 'Höpfner.' What we need is a cartel, a union, a protected craft association . . ."

When we at last quieted down, after much merriment, we watched an extremely poetic moon rise beyond the grape arbors. The silver light penetrated gradually through the curvetting surfaces of the big leaves, came in penciled rays through the spaces between the rustic picket fence, and whitened the clipped grass around the flower beds, which seemed to be still warm from the sunlight of this fine day. Like squawking frogs the wine-drenched patrons greeted the orb of night; voices rose in song, with tenors piping and yodeling and humming in thirds below the melody and basses booming along; the harmony was fairly pure, and violins, accordions, and guitars quickly took the lead again. Moths lunged clumsily against the glass globes protecting the candles.

"I'm so happy," Quapp exclaimed, "that we're together again. And—all by ourselves."

"By ourselves—yes. Today I think we can say so," my nephew remarked in the peculiarly staccato manner of speech he sometimes had, and which might have been either an affectation or an affliction.

"Stangeler is missing," Quapp said.

"Yes," Schlaggenberg agreed loudly. "I have been thinking that all along."

I was on the point of saying: "I don't miss him." The impulse made me realize, beyond dissimulation, that all day long I had been carping in my mind at poor René. At what point I began to have these thoughts I could no longer remember. But he seemed to have become the very core of unpleasant involvements, or at least the center of a fabric which more and more distinctly revealed an ugly pattern. Today I saw him as far more troublesome a customer than Kajetan with all the latter's deliberate pranks and crazy whims.

We left the tavern in order to go for a drive: the warm night, with its moon which already belonged more to the coming summer than to spring, tempted us toward the high ridges of the hills, so easily accessible by car. At the last moment, however, we needed more wine, for Eulenfeld insisted, and so we had ourselves another glass with half of us already standing. Here and there a couple still whispered, heads close together, but most of the benches in the garden were already empty. "It's always the most fun when we fellows are by ourselves!" Körger said, drinking to Quapp, and thus including her.

It was true, we were by ourselves, and temporarily relieved of all the torment of sterile contradictions; we were free gentlemen among ourselves who could be gay with good conscience. I sensed what was going on behind Quapp's little forehead, which had such a tendency to wrinkle in well-defined furrows. "Why not always live this way?" she must have been asking herself.

We started off. Once again I sat beside the captain, who had not bothered to put on his hat, so that the wind of our motion ruffled his hair. As a kind of substitute for the hat, what with the hour's being late and the quantities imbibed considerable, he was wearing his monocle.

We roared up the incline. The motor hummed loudly. The great dark masses of heavily leaved trees overhanging the roadway swept rapidly back above our heads, almost alarmingly close. The street rose along the flank of the hill, turned in a single serpentine, and mounted to an open prospect. The eye plunged into a pit of darkness which upon closer inspection divided itself along a gently curving line into night sky and mountain. Far across the valley the lights of villas could still be seen, ranged one above another along the slopes. But now, after we had raced around the curve and proceeded on in the opposite direction, the appearance of the sky was troubled and inflamed by the reddish reflection of the city, whose sparkling lights, here dull and there trenchant, lay scattered below us to the margin of our range of vision, barred by the glowing gridiron of the streets. And this time too, under the dark night sky and with the wind dashing furiously into my face from the speed of the car's motion, I once again felt that the suburb and the people down below there, come what may, constituted my established native place to whose fateful movements I would remain closely bound.

CHAPTER 13

Pot-au-feu

IT IS scarcely surprising that to this day I have only a fragmentary knowledge of Levielle's earlier life. No one knew anything definite; no one could furnish a dossier. His origins, for example, remained altogether obscure, and in this there was a certain difference between him and Lasch, whose family were natives of Vienna. Levielle, we will remember, had a younger brother who allegedly resembled him very closely; this same younger brother had occupied a post on the surgeon-general's staff in the old Austrian army, and he was the man whose decision had become a turning-point in the life of Cornel Lasch: namely, his remarkable wartime diagnosis, of which Lasch himself had informed Stangeler and others with some satisfaction.

From that story it is abundantly clear that the two must have known each other even then. Moreover, they must have been very well acquainted indeed, for otherwise Levielle would not have procured such a favor for Lasch from his brother. The memorable diagnosis of "endocarditis obsoleta," a hidden and therefore undiscoverable cardiac defect, had freed Lasch from the army unit which was on the point of carrying him off perilously near to the front. Set free, Lasch fetched up, as we know, at that important post in one of the bureaus subordinate to the Ministry of War, which at that time was charged with the distribution of raw materials and with assignments to the most vital of the war industries. Here, having in the meanwhile acquired a lieutenant's gold stars, Cornel acquired a voice in affairs; he came to power, and he used his power. Lasch had at one time studied mining at a technical academy; he therefore possessed some specialized knowledge. The office for which he worked was known as the Metals Bureau. It was at the time the highest authority for all of heavy industry, which was then completely geared to military requirements. If a factory wanted a contract and the necessary raw materials, its bid went to the Metals Bureau to be examined. The bid would be submitted to, say, a lieutenant with some special knowledge of the subject who then drew up an opinion, reported to the general, and recommended rejection or acceptance and subsequent assignment of raw materials. It may well be said that everything industrialists needed flowed out of Lasch's hands—for example, the copper for the guide-rings of artillery pieces, and a host of other things. It flowed, and he recommended, he reported—but only under certain conditions. And so one day he was a rich man.

Herr Levielle must have been thoroughly pleased to have a man as obligated to him as Lasch come to such power. It may therefore be assumed that he continued to further Lasch's total career, once the famous medical diagnosis had cleared the way for the first upward step. Cornel's patron had no doubt recognized at once the young man's abilities. It is true that the financial counselor's business at the time had not the slightest metallic character, and consequently lay outside Lasch's sphere of influence. But to have a man on base in one of the numerous ministries, no matter which ministry, was never something to be despised. Levielle possessed many such men on base, especially where they could be instrumental in obtaining import and export licenses. This became Levielle's chief province in the postwar period. Various people in Vienna felt that they could not do without him where imports and exports were concerned, and would apply first to him and only later on to the proper bureau. Perhaps it really was disadvantageous to go over his head. At any rate, it became a settled conviction that he was essential.

During Lasch's metallurgical period, Levielle had begun to deal in another substance, namely wood.

Old Herr Eustach von Schlaggenberg, Kajetan's father, seems to have been one of the first whom Levielle helped onto the skids. At least it is my firm conviction that Levielle cheated von Schlaggenberg, although I have never been able to ascertain the precise details of the two men's complicated affairs. For Kajetan understood virtually nothing about such matters, and freely admitted as much. He could give only the vaguest answers to the few questions I posed, and could never be prevailed upon to stick to the subject; most of the time he quickly began talking of something else. As far as he was concerned, it was enough that he had suffered the consequences, as had the other members of his family. For significantly enough, the contraction of the Schlaggenberg fortunes, which had so cribbed and imperiled Quapp's and his own position in Vienna, dated from precisely that time.

Levielle's dealings in wood were largely a phenomenon of the postwar years. For instance, he frequently went to see the abbot of a monastery in Upper Austria which owned sizable woodlands, presumably to help him dispose of his lumber, but these kind offices, whatever they were, appear in the long run to have done the monastery no good, for in the end the abbot was called to book. One of the principal bases of Levielle's sylvan operations, however, was an institution whose history I cannot refrain from sketching. This was the Austrian Lumber Industry Bank.

What wood we have, here in Austria, is, generally speaking, not suitable for all purposes. There are no great forests of real maritime lumber, wood for masts and planking. In the main our wood is good for home construction and for firewood. During the first years after the war, there was an urgent need to revive our lumber industry, but for this capital was needed. For obviously the revival had to begin in the sawmills rather than in the forests themselves. Our saws were all outmoded; in Germany wood was cut with six, eight, and even ten blades operating simultaneously, while in our country three-blade sawmills were the rule.

The Lumber Industry Bank was organized to lend impetus to modernization and to start things moving. Had it been allowed to continue without interference, it might well have succeeded. The stock issue was well launched; a number of major financiers and banks participated. The name of the president of the Lumber Industry Bank alone was an indication that one of the leading firms in the lumber industry within the country was behind it.

Levielle, too, must have participated from the start; and from the start he must have angled in a particular direction, as was afterwards to become more and more evident.

We must consider that at the time he already enjoyed a great reputation. In addition to his own by then sizable fortune and his network of connections, the chief factor in his favor was, to my way of thinking, the persisting idea in people's minds that Levielle was an indispensable man, who had to have his hand in things, who must be consulted, who was needed. And this idea in turn sprang from the knowledge that ever since 1914 he had been the administrator of so tremendous a fortune as that of Captain Georg Ruthmayr. For Levielle had become executor of the estate immediately after the captain was killed in action. To my mind, this factor had a tremendous psychological effect. It gave him an extraordinary glitter, made him appear utterly trustworthy. And so before long a chair was reserved for him on every newly organized board of directors.

In practical life, it is well known, the unpleasant axiom that "everything comes out" really does apply in the long run. Keep them under wraps as we may, facts leak through like grease spots. But if someone does the opposite, and gives the already racing facts a kick in the behind to make them run faster, he can start a given piece of information coursing so rapidly through the public channels that in the end no one will not know of it. Even those who are not in the least interested will have to know. Thus I too knew, as may be recalled, all about Levielle's being executor of the Ruthmayr estate. I knew about it long before the conversation with Levielle on the Graben on Annunciation Day, which later was to prove so fraught with consequence for all of us. (But it was only then that I first began to take any serious interest in the fact.) Levielle readily took my knowledge for granted, and seized the occasion to remark that he had managed and was "still managing other affairs of this type." It is quite possible that other estates had been superimposed upon the first, that confidence in his trustworthiness had gathered like an avalanche.

At any rate, no sooner was the Lumber Industry Bank founded than the financial counselor had his seat on the board. He sat down in it and first of all proved bluntly to the others—most of whom listened readily enough to this particular tune—that revivifying the market in wood products was all very well and praiseworthy, but that a considerable part of the capital secured from the sale of stock ought to be employed in buying and selling foreign exchange, in order to compensate for possible eventual losses. He was in a position to justify his argument and to lend emphasis to his recommendations because the contracts already arranged by the president—including one

461

with the above-mentioned monastery—had undoubtedly been too expensive for the bank. Its operations had been conceived in a Great Power spirit, so to speak, with the aim of creating nothing less than a monopoly. The bank was actually forced to operate for a time in accordance with Levielle's suggestions. Surely it cannot be considered strange for a bank to engage in stock-market dealings. But when a bank which has been founded to give a lift to the lumber industry engages in little else but stock-market operations, it would seem to have drifted somewhat off course. By 1923 and 1924 only the smallest part of the bank's capital was employed in the field which was supposedly its proper one. However, as long as the president was living, all the investments of the Lumber Industry Bank were restricted to gilt-edged securities; he had always refused to have anything to do with "wildcat" stock.

At the beginning of September 1924, however, this man was killed, and killed by none other than his own cousin, who was reputed to have "something wrong" with him. Whether this was true or not I cannot say. I knew only the murdered man, not the murderer. I saw the bank director for the last time barely a week before the bullet struck him, on the occasion of a wedding which, incidentally, has remained in my memory as an extremely repulsive occasion. This wedding was connected with none other than René Stangeler, odd as that may seem. The bridegroom—a Herr Doktor Albert Lehnder—had once been Stangeler's tutor. At that ceremony, at which Stangeler was present as one of the witnesses, I saw the director of the Lumber Industry Bank for the last time. He too was acting as a witness; he was Lehnder's employer, incidentally, for Lehnder had been installed in the legal department of the bank. (I hereby reveal one of the sources of my knowledge of the bank's affairs.)

The annual statement for 1924, the year of the director's death, showed that the enterprise still had considerable assets. It is well known that in some circumstances this does not mean too much. Certainly the bank's affairs were heading down a steeply descending curve. The Leviellists won the upper hand under the new director—all the more so because the floating of new stock was a failure. The shares that were thrown on the market had to be quickly bought back with the bank's own money through the intervention of friendly brokers. The thing was nothing but a circular process.

The new president of the Lumber Industry Bank was in some respects a remarkable man: in the first place in regard to his appearance, which scarcely befitted a bank director; and in the second place in regard to the nickname bestowed on him by certain people. He was big and bluff, with hunched shoulders and black mustache—a great deal of mustache. Perhaps he did have extremely active relations with the opposite sex; at any rate, he had been given a title which actually existed among the sixteenth century mercenary troops, namely "Whore-sergeant." I do not know who thought up that nickname; very likely it was Lehnder, for he was a witty fellow. Our whore-sergeant had as corporal or subdirector (one of those, incidentally, who "drove down" the French franc) a man who was afraid of nothing, a real "hog" as such people are called on the stock exchange. He was in everything, no matter how wildcat it might be. The whore-sergeant had to endorse this kind of speculation because it offered perhaps the only possible way out. In these circumstances it was only natural that when the massive undermining of the French franc began, the Lumber Industry Bank plunged headlong into the wake of this movement. The patriotic conduct of the French government put an end to this business in December of 1925; the French franc, which the bearish speculators had sold for dollars, rose while the dollar fell. "Which meant that all the speculators were ruined, along with the Lumber Industry Bank," Lehnder commented in describing the catastrophe. Lehnder, incidentally, later became the head of a firm of lawyers—in Berlin, by the way, not here in Vienna.

Levielle, however, was not there among "all the speculators." *"Du reste–c'est etonnant."* After all, he was a Parisian, or at least half Parisian, and perhaps he really knew more than the others. Nor can it be said that he slipped out of the franc speculation at the last possible moment. He was out of it long before the debacle. He also slipped out of the Lumber Industry Bank. He resigned his office, he evaporated—one day he was no longer to be seen there. In all probability this evaporation was one of the fundamental causes for the astonishing fact that came to light two years later—and here for once I want to overlook the purely "psychological" and go considerably beyond it: the fact, namely, that the Ruthmayr fortune came through the crises unimpaired. I myself, on the basis of the little knowledge I already possessed in the spring of 1927, would never have foreseen such an outcome; I would have thought it entirely out of the question. Indeed, I harbored the blackest forebodings about matters that really lay quite outside my life, including the Ruthmayr money. But then again, such an interest in things that lay outside my life was characteristic of that whole personal era, and linked up with my scribbling here. And then suddenly these things began to affect me directly. And when that happened, the scribbling ceased. The chronicler tumbled off his hobbyhorse.

On the other hand, it is conceivable that the Ruthmayr fortune might have increased during the crises. But that too had not been the case.

The Lumber Industry Bank later arranged a quiet settlement in the course of which the family of the former president sacrificed their entire fortune. For years to come the widow of the man who had been shot portioned out her house in rented rooms. And Levielle? Here I can only reply that after abandoning this one track he continued to move simultaneously along the thirty-two or forty-five others (impossible to know the number precisely) which he had previously trod. The Lumber Industry Bank and everything connected with it had merely been one more of his numerous operations. Yet a side-effect ultimately developed which was significant for both Financial Counselor Levielle and our tale. For his involvement in the lumber industry appears to have led directly to his position in the Alliance General Newspaper Corporation—that position which empowered him to perform such little feats as finding a place on the newspaper for Schlaggenberg. This excursion into journalism was connected, of course, with paper production via the pulpwood industry. Long before "all the speculators" who had dabbled in the downfall of the franc went themselves to their downfall, Levielle must have entered the paper industry; and although he failed to win over such persons as Director Dulnik, for example, he was successful elsewhere. From paper it was but a step to newspapers. Incidentally, Angelika's father, old Doktor Trapp, always thought highly of Dulnik for having flatly refused from the start to become involved with Levielle in any way, and this at a time when "everybody" was running after the financial counselor. Levielle's thirty-two or forty-five other enterprises were merely an expression of his business-mindedness. For we may observe that, by and large, there appear to be two divergent ways to crass success in all business affairs: either the way of extraordinarily profound knowledge in some specific field—the expert's way, that is—or that innocent dreamlike

465

sureness of touch which characterizes the person who is completely alien to a field, has no frame of reference whatsoever, who with utter lack of prejudice or prerequisites will today deal in a hundred carloads of evaporated milk and tomorrow in the production and sale of operetta librettos. The exponents of these two antipodal approaches remain at the top; all hybrids are necessarily weaker. Levielle probably belonged to the second category. Nowadays the thing strikes us as fantastic, after what has happened; but the truth is that Levielle in person constituted a kind of holding company for a group of the most variegated enterprises, upon which he thrust good or bad deals according to the situation. At the beginning of the war the bankruptcy laws had been revised; the legislators had acted with the laudable purpose of protecting businessmen who through no fault of their own had run into difficulties. The idea was not to exclude from economic life those who had suffered from wartime dislocations. Later every loop and loophole of this commendable attempt to equalize burdens was utilized to achieve exactly the opposite effect. But there were few who were so skillful at turning the law topsy-turvy as our noble financial counselor. *C'etait etonnant!*

In a good many of Levielle's projects Lasch collaborated. Immediately after the upheavals of 1918 our Cornel immediately pitched like a tornado into the distribution of surplus goods—in other words, the liquidation of the vast stocks of everything imaginable and unimaginable which had been accumulated for military purposes. Like a tornado—there is scarcely another expression for it. For his purchases, made at utterly ridiculous prices—after all, he had so many connections through his post in the Ministry—sent flying through the air incredible quantities of the most variegated government surplus goods. Lasch's contracts covered a fantastic medley—three carloads of thread, say, along with 500 brand-new wheelbarrows. Or 3,000 infantry rifles. (These, too, were among his wares at one time, though they too were quickly disposed of— why should Lasch not have dealt in rifles? He was not afraid of pea-shooters; hadn't he been a soldier too?) Sometimes ersatz products found their way into the chaotic job lots he purchased—ersatz wartime goods which in better times became worthless. These stuck to his fingers like flypaper; and along with highly profitable trades he now and again had his troubles getting rid of, say, 200 carload lots of artificial soles made of a small fraction of refuse leather, a large percentage of sawdust, and paper scraps, all crushed together in a hydraulic press with tar as a binder. Lasch then had the 200 carloads insured against fire, and the buyer who was at last found acquired the insurance, paid a year in advance, along with the goods. Later, when the whole lot went up in flames, the insurance company lodged a criminal action, and pointed out that according to reliable witnesses Lasch had stated, in concluding the deal, that "the stuff will burn like tinder." Summoned to court, Lasch made no attempt to repudiate this statement. On the contrary, he confirmed it with the greatest savoir-faire, asserting that of course he had taken it for granted that the lot would be used as industrial fuel, for who would dream—now that leather could be imported again—of attempting to use such an inferior product for its nominal purpose? A number of such stories were told about Lasch. Perhaps none of them was strictly true, but taken all together they pretty much described him. He had the same talent for ambiguous and yet uncompromising statements as Levielle, who was in the habit of choosing his expressions with great care and with a general regard for future legal battles, exactly as if a stenographer were taking testimony on the other side of a wall. Perhaps there was an element of the disciple and

467

the handing on of the torch in Lasch's relationship to Levielle.

Director Edouard Altschul was first an acquaintance of Cornel Lasch. Levielle met him through the younger man at a particularly propitious time: namely, when Levielle had something to offer to a large bank. This something was a handful of newspapers. Cornel acted as intermediary, to the extent that once or twice he even graciously condescended to accompany his mother-in-law, Frau Irma Siebenschein, to the big café by the Danube Canal where the family conference on Grete's problems had been held. Naturally he drove Irma up to the café in his big car, which gave her great pleasure. Titi Lasch, née Siebenschein, was also drawn upon for such purposes, and so acquaintance was made with the Altschuls—first with Frau Rosi and then with her husband. Doktor Mährischl and his wife were introduced to the Altschuls on another occasion, at another café, and so there arose between the two ladies that friendship which soon disturbed Frau Lea Wolf, who may be regarded as a fairly attentive observer.

At that very juncture the director of a large bank must have been extremely pleased to meet such a man as Levielle, who could well pass for a newspaper magnate, at least by our modest local standards. Lasch, who had so effortlessly and naturally provided the contact with Levielle, must likewise have appeared to Altschul a valuable man. A special element entered in here. A rift had developed between the banks and the press due to a "scandal" which in the blowing off of steam had very nearly shattered "Hector's organization." In the end the head of that worthy body succeeded in "fixing" the matter only by enormous efforts, and had to resort, for lack of any other recourse, to a disciplinary investigation of almost all the members on the financial staff of one newspaper. In this connection Doktor Trembloner jestingly remarked that the editors had "accepted such insignificant sums that one might practically call them incorruptible." Nevertheless, something had to be done; and the "Bulletin" of Hector's organization came forth with a flaming editorial which spoke of the necessity for exterminating "degenerate journalistic vermin" (was this a reference to the larvae?). The whole story had "broken" when a rather small financial institution collapsed, with loss of the investors' capital. Moreover, a number of long since aborted larvae suddenly came rushing up with quantities of incriminating evidence which once upon a time—by chatting, prying, smiling, and questioning in editorial offices here and there, and above all keeping their ears open—they had managed to pick up with their antennae.

The affair soon blew over. Nevertheless, certain familiar ruts had had to be abandoned, and certain ties, for appearances' sake, broken.

In these circumstances the great banking institution of which Edouard Altschul was a director welcomed the opportunity to lay its hands on a large number of journals, especially such leading newspapers as were to be found united in the Alliance concern. Moreover, this concern embraced papers of extremely different and in part antipathetic political tendencies. Levielle made it plain at the beginning that, for his part, he desired only to interest a big financial institution in a number of sound growth industries. That seemed a not unreasonable compensation for his services.

The role of the Mährischls, husband and wife, belongs to this part of the story. Above all we must note that Doktor Mährischl had never been Levielle's lawyer. On the other hand, on Levielle's recommendation Edouard Altschul did draw upon his services for the bank, and from the start he took care of all contracts with various enterprises which resulted from the connection with Levielle.

As for Herr Mährischl's wife, Martha, I recall having learned at the time (from Frau Steuermann, who shortly after the spring fashion meeting began avoiding the café by the Danube Canal) that Frau Mährischl was literally "shadowing" Rosi Altschul. And chatterbox Rosi found in Martha a ready and patient listener.

Martha, then, knew about every step taken by Altschul, and about a good many he only intended to take. Had anyone in Vienna urgently wanted to find the director, she would have been the person to ask. Provided that she had been willing, Frau Mährischl could have given out such information as: Director Altschul arrived at his office at nine o'clock this morning; at ten o'clock he received my husband, at half-past ten Baron Frigori; at one o'clock he was at the stock exchange, arrived home late for a three-o'clock lunch, and returned to his office again at four.

The 14th of May was a day of dreary weather, with intermittent squalls of rain and wind. For that reason the windows in the office of the management were not opened, although the air was heavy with cigar and cigarette smoke. The conference had evidently been somewhat agitated, for all four participants were standing; no one had kept to his chair. They seemed to have forgotten to switch on the light, although it was already growing dark, earlier than usual. Before his visitors arrived, Altschul had spent a quarter hour on the interoffice telephone checking the status of several accounts from different departments.

"I must remind you again, Herr Levielle, that you yourself spoke of these people as possessing 'extraordinary assets,'" Altschul said, his voice weary but controlled.

"But my dear director," Doktor Mährischl interjected at this point, "I am afraid that I myself, as your representative, must remark that—that perhaps you took this phrase in too 'bookkeeping' a sense, if I may put it that way. Herr Levielle no doubt meant by 'extraordinary assets' energy, perspicacity, activity; I am sure he did not intend the words to be taken in a balance-sheet sense, if I may put it that way."

"I am certain, my dear director, that I used the words clearly in that way," Levielle replied amiably, indeed with the utmost good will. "If I rightly recall, I said that I admired the extraordinary assets these people possessed, and so I would say still. In any case I do not yet see any real grounds for discouragement."

"Good Lord, what business is ever really safe for widows and orphans?" Doktor Mährischl remarked (Lasch shook his head slightly at this). Mährischl waved his arm as he spoke, revealing a glint of the gold chain on his wrist. He gave a smile at once resigned and apologetic for his phrase "safe for widows and orphans," as if to suggest that he was aware that it belonged more properly to a lawyer's office than to the present scene.

At this point the door opened unexpectedly, and Frau Martha poked her head in. No one had heard a knock. "Oh—I beg your pardon," she said, with a gesture that seemed to indicate that she was on the point of withdrawing immediately.

"No need to go, madame," Altschul said politely but in a rather flat tone. "We are finished here." He had been standing in front of the desk, half turned toward the window. Now, with a little jerk, he seemed to tear himself away from the gathering twilight; he turned back into the room and pressed the light

471

switch. The callers shook hands and departed in a body.

"I only wanted to let my husband know I was here," Frau Martha remarked, apologizing again.

"Well, then, gentlemen, until the end of next week," Altschul called after them. He was left alone. The armchairs in the room had been pushed somewhat out of position, and a full ash tray stood on one of the mahogany side tables. Altschul returned to the window where he had been standing before.

The Mährischls preceded the others down the stairs. Levielle followed, with Lasch at some distance. Lights were burning only here and there down the broad stairwell, for the business hours of the bank were long since over. The gold-braided doorkeeper stepped out of his dimly illuminated cubicle on the ground floor and opened the glass door of the side-entrance for the Mährischls. He held the door open until Levielle and Lasch had also passed through.

Darkness. Some of the streets were already strident with light, through a wispy fog.

None of the four spoke. The Mährischls said good-by at once and walked off along the sidewalk. Levielle and Lasch went together to the massive open car which was standing a little way from the entrance. Lasch looked at his watch. He had to drive Levielle to the railroad station (the counselor was going to Paris for a few days), but he had promised his wife, Titi, that he would be at her parents' home by half-past six. Had Levielle been going to Prague today, as he did frequently, there would have been no reason to hurry, for trains to Czechoslovakia left from the station opposite the Siebenschein house. But as it was, Lasch would have to make speed; it was a considerable distance to the West Station. Levielle got into the back, where the bank's doorkeeper had already placed a shallow suitcase which had been deposited in his cubicle. Levielle let Lasch drive up front alone, as if he were a chauffeur; he did not sit beside him, although the windshield offered better protection against the wind and rain.

Lasch started the motor, snapped forward with a jerk, slewed the car around the corner of a narrow side street, horn bellowing, so that Levielle and his suitcase lurched from side to side in the back seat. With roaring motor the car hurtled out of the center of town and down the long, sparklingly lit suburban avenues.

Under the overhang of the old-fashioned West Station, Lasch remained seated in the car while Levielle beckoned a porter to take his bag. Cornel said good-by to Levielle without getting out. Before he threw in the clutch again, he caught a glimpse of Baron Frigori hastening up to Levielle and greeting him. Then Cornel turned around and roared off once again, leaving pedestrians still tingling with the shock of jumping aside and their ears still wincing from the low yodel of his horn. He drove very fast. The streets were crowded, partly with people who in spite of its being Saturday had been released late from the harness of their day's work and were hurriedly shopping—in some of the stores there were black swarms of buyers. In the lower-lying parts of the city the wispy fog was thickening. Here Lasch had to drive slowly, with the horn sounding its bass at every street corner. Big buses approached like illuminated rolling towers. Cornel stared with vexation over the hood of the car at the roadway. His jaws tightened, and he conferred upon the variegated swarms of citizenry going about their prosaic human ends and errands the cold glare of the driver. He ought to occupy himself with something sensible, he thought suddenly; with scientific work, for example. He made up his mind to buy a new microscope. Something different for a change. Not always and eternally the same thing: money. But he regarded his own desires just as coldly as he did the people at an intersection when a traffic policeman stopped him to let the pedestrians cross. Yes, Titi needed a great deal. The whole of today had been more than unpleasant, and tomorrow was Sunday, and the weather was going to be bad.

In fact this year spring did not come so manifestly; it did not tempt and prompt to the usual enterprises, could not be turned to use for outings and the like; nor did it always glorify the streets with transforming sunlight or vistas opening outward.

For the present it scarcely even warmed up.

The gray front of the snowless late winter of the city remained on the whole as it had been, though with a milder frown.

Then the rain sifted down, warm and thin. Mist hung between the greening leaves. The out-of-doors often felt like an enclosed space. It rained very evenly, very gently, like spray from a child's watering-can. The birds cried continually.

Quapp was hurrying "over the hill." This time she did not have to climb; her way descended, for she had hopped out of the streetcar at its last stop. Leaving the departing and boarding passengers, the arrivals and switchings of the red-and-yellow cars behind her, she dipped down into the park, choosing the shortest, steepest way, which consisted partly of steps. Shrubs were still swaying in the wind here and there, and moving against the gray clouds were the tops of those tall trees which on blue and sunny days seemed to stretch so incredibly high and far into the sky.

Quapp was not coming from the district where our crowd

lived. She had been in the city and had sat with Stangeler in a small café where he had recently established his headquarters. The sums he received from his improved relationship to Alliance (as if he had been taken in tow by Schlaggenberg) evidently sufficed for him to spend his working day in the café, and so he had taken his manuscripts and books from Grete's room and had them with him in a portfolio.

Quapp, then, was coming from the city, where she had been with Stangeler, and consequently she was arriving late. She no longer wanted to know precisely how late she was, and whenever she had passed a clock, as she did at various points in the city, she had each time turned her eyes away from the window of the streetcar and not looked out again until the clock was no longer visible.

Fifteen minutes more or less no longer mattered. Last Friday Imre and Quapp (incidentally, he always made a point of calling her Charlotte, giving it a French pronunciation, or else Lo, which we others thought ridiculous; in any case Herr von Gyurkicz carefully avoided using the nickname of Quapp which was usual with our crowd)—on Friday, then, Imre and Quapp had decided in a harmonious moment to have a cozy hour or two together the next day, Saturday—that being part of the weekend. Such notions as "weekend" had already penetrated far too deeply into Quapp's already somewhat deranged professional and inner life. She had long since come to regard it as something special if she practiced on a Sunday. Months ago, when she had been working with will and pleasure, Sunday practice had been superfluous. Now, however, it might have served her as the only chance to make up for the omissions of the rest of the week. But now the weekend and the Sunday were set aside—at least they were for Imre, who rejoiced in laying aside his crayons for a day and a half. In Quapp's case these "weekends" soon became the sole remnant of the order she had formerly maintained. For although she frequently did not adhere to her working schedule on weekdays, she was faithful to the custom of a Sunday respite. Or at any rate, that is how it almost always turned out, even if she did resolve to "catch up." Gyurkicz was free, wanted to see something of her after the week's labors; in winter the snow in the mountains was a temptation (soon she was going skiing only with Imre); and recently, when a prematurely warm spring day came along, sunlight and water could not be resisted: they lived so near the river, after all.

This weekend, then, when Imre would have finished all the drawings needed for the Monday comics, they had planned to have a pleasant couple of hours at least over a pot of Turkish mocha. For after five o'clock Quapp and Imre were invited to a rather large party, and they had long before said they would come. Still, there had been time enough. At one in the afternoon Quapp had had to dine with an old aunt in Vienna—an office she performed for her mother's sake once every two or three months (for Kajetan could not be persuaded to any such submissions). The affair was brief and by now relatively painless, since after an extremely lavish dinner there was nothing to do but say good-by, the old lady being in the habit of lying down and napping after eating. Consequently Gyurkicz had been expecting his "Lo" by half-past two.

And now it must be around half-past four. Besides, she would have to dress quickly.

For after her social call Quapp had found herself in the vicinity of Stangeler's new "headquarters," and had only thought to look in to see whether he was there. Of course he was there, and moreover in the best of spirits.

Now she hastened across the playground. Empty benches stood in a wide semicircle around its edges. The damp gravel, newly laid down and deeper than usual, sank down beneath the soles of Quapp's shoes, making rapid progress difficult. She walked stooped, her rounded back rather tensed, her handbag tucked under her arm and pressed tightly against her side. Once more, in the midst of her purposeful haste, the hours she had spent with Stangeler rose up in her mind, accompanied by flashes of recollection of similar times with "the Ensign": of their first meeting and of his peculiar description of a cavalry attack. René's oratory had stirred her up more, perhaps, than the slant-eyed scholar suspected. And as a woman she differed greatly from her brother, who—it had often happened—would shoot off like a rocket, simply forgetting all the other counterforces of his life since they happened not to be present at the moment and therefore did not hold him in their grip. Schlaggenberg could catch a glimpse of something and promptly decide that this was his goal. But nothing of the sort with Quapp. She was not inspired to break with Gyurkicz, thus very simply restoring "order" to her life. Her feeling for Imre and his power and importance in her life remained acute, did not suddenly evaporate or vanish in dense shadow because the cone of light happened to be turned in another direction. She was swept by no sudden blindness toward all that had been. Rather, she juggled all the contradictions to the best of her ability, and committed her self-betrayal with a clearer knowledge of what exactly she was doing than any man could have tolerated.

She stood still, having reached the end of the graveled square and the exit from the park. With an insight remarkably clear considering her haste and troubled state, she recognized the predicament into which she had fallen. For Quapp was by no means the victim of stubborn prejudices, and had a degree of perspective. It was clear to her, for example, that the next phase of her life would bring other difficult situations in its train, situations of quite another kind. She was, in fact, to the extent that it was possible for her to be so, at this time, in a fairly good state of mind. At least for a few moments. (Later she would actually use the expression: "I was happy.") She breathed deeply—and the bells of the church tower beyond the park, at her rear, began to rumble and clang very loudly. It occurred to her only after some minutes that this ringing meant that it was already a quarter to five. For she thought she was experiencing physically the tolling of her own distress; it hummed and clanged over the damp shining roofs, rippled off in widening circles, billowed down into the park, rose up like smoke to the gray clouds above the high tree-tops. She shook her head and went on, but at a slow pace. Crossing the square by the little old church, she passed by the window in which washing was usually hanging out. Today the window was closed and glistened black, silent, and meaningless. She turned the corner into her now deserted street, walked by closed doors and windows, and passed under the archway over the gate of her house.

The apartment was empty; as usual, the people with whom she lodged were all away from home.

Quapp wanted tea. That was what she wanted now; just to sit quietly over a cup of tea for a few minutes. This desire struck her with the force of an urgent craving, almost a compulsion; it was absolutely essential for her to gain a few minutes' time to compose herself. Everything else was of secondary importance, existed only in a vague veiled way: that, for example, she ought to hurry. And so she set the kettle on the gas. The room was silent around her in its predominantly brownish colors. The baby-grand piano by the window cast blurred reflections. The skinny collapsible music stand for the violin stood beside it, sticking into the air like a leafless seedling tree. Across the cool empty street she could see one corner of the house opposite, where Imre lived.

She might have changed her clothes while the water was coming to a boil. But she did not. Nevertheless, this omission was not an act of defiance.

Just as she had finished filling the teapot and was sitting down to it, the bell rang twice. That was Imre.

"Of course," she thought wearily. For a moment the idea of not opening the door occurred to her. For he could not have seen her coming down the street a little while before; his room lay at the rear of the house, overlooking the garden.

But then he would come to her ground-floor window.

"Of course," she thought again. Standing up, she walked with her rather heavy tread to the front hallway. Yet even now the nature of the crisis did not fully reach her consciousness; a dull soft layer of absorbent material lay between her and this crisis, lay there as a last remnant of that moment of relative lucidity she had enjoyed at the park exit, on the edge of the playground.

Imre's face, as Quapp beheld it when she opened the door, was gray, big, filled with a melancholy handsomeness, and at the same time arrogant. He entered without saying a word beyond his greeting, and followed Quapp into her room. She could see that he was fully dressed for the impending party, dressed in that manner so characteristic of him whenever he went out: neat, immaculate, determinedly conservative. Now, too, he was wearing a rather broad, very substantial four-in-hand, perfectly knotted.

Gyurkicz stood still and plucked at his overcoat buttons, but did not remove the coat.

Quapp straightaway returned to her teapot and poured herself a full cup. "Would you like some?" she asked casually.

"So you don't intend to come?" he said; this tea drinking appeared to be too great a trial of patience for him. "Then

I'll go back home; I certainly don't feel like turning up there alone."

"I'll come," she said. "Only I simply must have a cup of tea now."

"Better if you would hurry and change now. How long have you been home? I came over for the third time twenty minutes ago."

"I came back fifteen minutes ago."

"Yes, that's how it usually is when I'm looking forward to having some time with you for a change. May I ask where you were?" His face narrowed; the skin tightened over his cheekbones, and in spite of the heavy powder he patted on after shaving, it had a somewhat oily gleam at these spots. He looked as if he were suffering from a headache; possibly he actually was.

"I met Stangeler in town," Quapp said quietly. At such a juncture, with Imre out of temper and a social evening before them, a little fib would have been easy, obvious, and perhaps quite understandable. She might, for example, have said that her aunt had not been well and that she had had to stay on with her—which would have explained her fatigued and feckless state, and would even have excused her drinking tea. But she did not lie. There was no inner reason for her choosing not to; she was simply too sluggish; her rectitude was the result of her utter slackness and weakness of the moment. A dull soft absorbent layer still lay between herself and everything that was happening to her; she could not feel herself, and was still less conscious of her friend. So she drank tea and told the truth.

"Good-by!" Imre said, taking his hat. "I am going home." He was very pale. It was not only the powder.

"Don't be a fool!" she said, suddenly nasty and full of rage. But even as this outburst took place she was still watching

480

herself and knew with utter clarity that the only reason she was furious was that he was interfering with her drinking tea. If Imre had come only ten minutes later, she would not have told the truth; she would probably have apologized for her enforced absence. But now her brief spell of relaxation had been taken from her; she was filled with a stiff-necked determination to have her tea in peace, and consequently the whole situation had become stiff-necked.

"If anyone is being a fool it's you!" he said in a dangerously low voice. He lingered in the room.

"You gave me your word, once and for all"—she seemed to be speaking to herself, as if she were talking while climbing a hill and tossing the words from her like a pack of playing cards—"that you recognized and accepted as part of me my whole relationship to my friends, to our crowd, and especially to Stangeler, just as you did the relationship to my brother. And you also know that I feel no differently toward 'the Ensign' than I do toward Kajetan, so that nothing is withheld from you on that account; I am not taking anything away from you. I made this clear from the start and you accepted it. But with a logical inconsistency like a woman's, you are constantly demonstrating that you haven't accepted it."

"You always make intolerable demands upon others—intolerable in particular to a man. Note that, please! In any case, even if I do accept all that, you don't have to make me wait in this humiliating manner—aren't you ever going to start getting dressed?"

In reality Quapp was still possessed by an obstinate desire to drink her tea in tranquillity. Had she had five minutes in which to do so, she would immediately have realized that in any case her "tranquillity" had fled, that in fact she did not want to and could not sit still any longer. But as it was, she

481

insisted upon having, in addition to the major privilege which she firmly believed herself entitled to, this small privilege also.

"So you accept, you put up with me, you suffer," she said, remaining in her chair. "Of course. But at the start you were oh so manly: respect for the other's personality, of course, a clear resolve to take it as it is, and so on! You parrot sentences you've heard in our crowd, but when it comes to acting on them you show that you hardly even understand the words. Perhaps you don't understand German well enough."

"Kindly leave that for others to judge," he said. The increasing faultiness of his accent betrayed the degree of his agitation, which he could no longer conceal. "You have a fondness for speaking of things which you know little about. Stick to your music. If you care to know, an article of Stangeler's was turned down yesterday and they gave the subject to me to write about, which I did to satisfaction, even though I don't have a lease on literature and higher things. So my German is adequate. As far as manliness is concerned, I proved it sufficiently in the war, at any rate proved that I have more than is needed to bicker with you, which I consider beneath my dignity. You say I parrot things—but do you know that no one ever hears a single word from you that has not been said already by Kajetan or Stangeler? If you stuck to me, without all these unhealthy influences, you'd soon find yourself elsewhere and be more in happiness too. If I could, I would take you away somewhere, so that you wouldn't be seeing all those others any more . . ."

Quapp's posture had grown more and more hunched, until during the latter part of Gyurkicz's discourse it assumed the arched look of an angry cat. She was now sitting in that posture which, Stangeler had once said, one often sees in resting workmen, say construction workers during the noon recess: feet wide apart, her drooping body resting on her arms, hands dangling down between her knees. Her expression was hard and cruel. But the longer Gyurkicz spoke, the more the furrows smoothed on her little forehead, until at last her face was filled with an entirely self-contained, unmitigated contempt. She threw a look at Imre that for a few seconds lingered upon him with a cool, almost scientific interest; at the same time there appeared in her face an utterly monstrous presumption, an arrogance without limit or sense. She literally pushed Gyurkicz away with it. Simultaneously, a message of final farewell to tea and tranquillity seemed at last to have reached her limbs, for she stood up with a swift light movement, opened her armoire, removed various things, hurried into the bathroom, slipped out of her dress, returned to the room in her bathrobe, and now began scurrying back and forth while Imre went on without pause, sometimes addressing her directly, sometimes talking to her back (as she hurried out), sometimes calling to her in the bathroom.

"You say that nothing is withheld from me, nothing taken away from me. There you're dead wrong. You ought to be at home with me all the time and keep faith with me in every sense. It's easy to see that you women have never known the concept of honor. You think you can do it this way, have one man for intellectual stimulation, another for what you call love, which you know nothing about because you have no respect for the other person! As if I were your gigolo, existed solely for your pleasure . . ."

She had at that moment come scurrying like a mole out of the bathroom. Passing by him, she stood still for a moment and said quickly: "Please—little enough of that," and vanished again behind the open door of her armoire.

"That's a piece of low-down, lying insultingness and nothing else," Imre shouted after her. "What's behind it all is some

483

sort of stinking arrogance and I don't know what kind of justification by which you think you can treat a person . . ." Speech failed him along with syntax. He breathed deeply, and as if his chest hurt. Then he said in a broken voice: "There's only one way left to save you: to take you away from all that. You ought to live with me for a time, maybe seeing the few people I really like to be with . . ."

"What?" she cried. "That would be fine! Wouldn't that suit you! Rosi Malik, Hedwig Glöckner, Holder, maybe Höpfner too? To make an idiot out of me. Then I'd satisfy you. That's your respect for the other's personality—isn't it!"

And again she was out the door.

The dialogue went on in this eccentric fashion only a short while longer, for Quapp finished changing very quickly.

"I'd like to know what accomplishment you have that gives you the right to this damn contempt of yours!" Gyurkicz said when they had left her room and locked the house door and were hurrying down the deserted, rain-wet street. "You have pretensions like a genius."

It was as if she could no longer recognize the playground. The two of them strode side by side across the slippery gravel and through the park, and up the steepest, shortest path, where there were steps. They did not talk, saving their breath for the climb. But their hastening toward the streetcar terminus with its red-and-yellow cars was like a race to a goal: being the first to catch breath and so be able to speak again.

Laura Konterhonz's greatest difficulties began around the same time as Director Edouard Altschul's. But while in Altschul's case it was only one fat female, namely Frau Mährischl, who darkened the horizon, in Laura's case the entire range of vision was obscured and distorted by such figures.

Schlaggenberg continued to torment the hapless Laura

with his tales; but now he added the theoretical part as well. As a matter of fact, theory was his chief weapon, though he gave the air of plucking random examples from an already extensive practice. On one occasion—when I was by, moreover—he started on the very same lecture he had delivered at the "foundation festival": about the unfitness of the present generation of girls and the mission of mature women, and I would have had the pleasure of hearing all that amorphous rot once again had I not spoken up and stopped him. I really do not know what fat Laura made of these matters. Either she thought herself a "mature woman," or she pigeonholed all of these pranks of Kajetan's in the category of: "Such an interesting and original man." But it could not have been easy for her, since she suffered frightfully from jealousy, and there was no lack of vividness in Schlaggenberg's narratives. He was generous with that richness of detail which seems to us to confirm the truthfulness of a story.

It came to the point that in the street or in public conveyances Laura began behaving almost as strangely as Schlaggenberg himself had been doing of late: pursuing every fat woman. Laura too ran after them, as she later admitted to me. Could this one, say, be "his type"? Or that one, might she not really be one of his—after all, chance encounters like this are always possible? And so on. Now and again a woman would match Schlaggenberg's description so closely. After all, might she not be the very one? Such ghastly logic tormented poor Laura, and so she could never entirely escape her martyrdom. Wherever breadth swayed by, whenever processions marched, whether as vanguard or rear guard—Laura's head was bound to turn to look.

But then she would reassure herself again by deciding that these stories were only one more of Schlaggenberg's peculiarities—for to a mind such as hers virtually everything about Kajetan seemed peculiar, both his excellences and his absurdities. I did not take quite so light a view of the matter as Laura (who surely was entitled to what alleviation she could find for herself), but in a certain sense I regarded Schlaggenberg's "fat females" rather as she did. It became more and more evident to me that his love for grotesquerie was the dominant factor in this elaborate myth. In addition there was something that might be called a sublimated and innocuous form of malice. (His deliberate "theoretical" discourses to Laura, on the other hand, were far from innocuous.) His "I mean to carry this thing to extremes" and "You are going to be shocked" presumed a program of ever more dramatic "abominations" which he would collect in order, among other purposes, to flaunt them before me and our crowd. "Out of malice" (as he himself once said), and so that we would have something to be shocked about. It soon became clear to me that I was in some way necessary to his scheme. At every opportunity Schlaggenberg threatened me, with "diabolic" satisfaction, that hundreds of pages full of such material would have to be inserted in my chronicles, in keeping with our agreement, and that before long he would bestow on me more than a hundred finished pages. I laughed and did not believe he had written down a line.

Laura Konterhonz had a happy disposition, and managed to comfort herself fairly easily, as is the case with people who carry a childlike mentality into adult life. Most of the time she felt very good, and if Kajetan did not happen to be tormenting or twitting her, she was consistently cheerful. On some occasion or other I asked her whether she dreamed much. "I never dream, or hardly ever, and simply don't understand the dreams people are always making up and telling." Such a statement seemed just what she would say.

She was certainly cheerful on this rainy Saturday—if only because the weekend had come round at last. Moreover, a "social occasion" in her "new circle of acquaintance" was to take place. The house she was to visit was one she had never been to before, but a sure instinct told her to appear at least an hour later than the time for which she had been invited. This impulse, if traced by a professional head-shrinker to its ultimate root, would have turned up a fact I have quite forgotten to mention. In old Austria, when a man had honorably dined on army stews for more than thirty years, he was permitted to enter the hereditary nobility. Laura's father, the major-general, had eaten and entered. Consequently Laura's name was *von* Konterhonz. I never write it that way, because it sounds frightful.

She finished her toilette in a leisurely manner, and the sight of herself in all her substantiality in the mirror might well have made her feel more sure of herself in regard to Schlaggenberg. Dressed, she contemplated herself once more, and felt a pleasant glow: her appearance pleased her. It was a true Konterhonzian feat of tastelessness: wispy bangs over her forehead; her dress, buttoned high, had a wispy lace collar which lent an exceedingly ridiculous note to her whole impressive figure; and the tobacco-brown color of her dress quarreled with the brown of her hair. The dab of a hat, the cut of the coat, were of a piece with the rest of this unfortunate getup. Perhaps it should also be mentioned that she wore black stockings and black patent-leather pumps.

Since the weather was uncertain, she took an umbrella whose handle and fabric would have done well for a lady of seventy. Carefully locking the door of the apartment (her mother had also gone out), she went down the brown-linoleum-covered stairs. Outside, she decided to make herself still a little later by walking all the way. She liked to walk; we must not, however, consider this trait as part of her military heritage, for her father had been a cavalryman. That man in front of her was wearing a strikingly high hat, she thought. The ceilings in the Academy of Plastic Arts (she was just passing this building) were by Feuerbach, and famous. She resolved to see them someday, for she took the view that a person ought to know the sights of his own city—unlike the overwhelming majority of Viennese, who had no idea of the noteworthy things their city contained. Acting on her theory, Laura had recently climbed the tower of St. Stephan's.

She had had a guide point out all the features of the view, and had listened with deep interest to all the legends about the tower.

Schlaggenberg left her a good deal to herself, although their relationship had become somewhat more permanent.

Besides, he took no interest in cultural things.

Well, he had gone to the University and so knew everything. But a woman had to broaden her knowledge too.

The first twilight was already settling, and in the west, behind the monument to the high-seated Empress Maria Theresa (Laura could reel off the names of the mounted generals on the pedestal), the gray sky lifted above a watery yellow. Premature lights began to appear in the park. In this early dusk the lively streets took on more size and depth.

Twice Laura glanced sharply ahead and to the left, then immediately—in obedience to a compulsion—attached herself to the heels of a large, extremely sturdy woman who wore a brown jacket and a tiny hat of similar hue. That was all Laura could make of her. But it sufficed to draw her off her course. She had walked some distance down the Ring, but now she turned into a side street in pursuit of the fat female.

Along with the jealousy that possessed the unhappy woman, she was moved by a touching concern: she wanted to help Kajetan in his search! Since he seemed to be so obsessed by this thing, she thought she should be too. Perhaps she seriously imagined that sooner or later she would be able to cure him of his madness. But meanwhile Laura ate everything she could lay her hands on. She consumed whipped cream for breakfast (I have this on her personal confession to me), and on her way to the undemanding government job the old major-general had procured for his daughter she made it a daily habit to weigh herself on a drugstore scale. The results, unfortunately, might have pleased Frau Selma Steuermann, but did not suit Laura at all. She worried too much.

The banners nobly brandished down the side street proceeded ahead of Laura for only a short distance, then halted in front of a display of, of all things, bath articles: tubs sparkling with marble and nickel; soap dishes; shelves of glass and china. She too stared at all this civilized opulence, but also glanced searchingly sideways. And she observed at once that her neighbor at the window was anything but pretty, was in fact extremely common and utterly without attractiveness. Immediately Laura beat a retreat, and as she moved away she repeated to herself several times under her breath: "Of course, *c'est impossible,* altogether impossible." Things had come to such a pass that she had even adopted Schlaggenberg's expressions for her own. However, she was not aware of this.

The vacuum of disappointment left by this episode was soon filled by a sense of relief. She could look with less anxiety upon her surroundings, which only a moment before had been distorted and darkened. She continued on in her former direction. She had a way while walking of throwing her weight backwards, onto her heels, which together with her long stride gave her an extremely erect and self-assured carriage. Her gaze was now fixed more upon the distance than upon things close at hand. Noble banners, whole processions, passed her by without her noticing. She decided she must some day soon see the stage and stage machinery at the Opera and the Burgtheater; guided tours took place in both theaters once a week; it would surely be interesting. Kajetan would probably not want to go along.

The city was making a great din; now, after the close of the business day, it was still discharging a wild rout of people and vehicles into its outer districts. Crowds were gathered at the streetcar stops. It began growing somewhat darker; vibrant lights appeared on every hand.

Laura too turned toward the suburbs, and proceeded down a long, animated avenue which ended in a very broad square directly opposite one of the large railroad stations. On clear days you could see from here, beyond the towers that adorned the front of the terminal building, the blue border of the hills and mountains rising upstream along the Danube. Now, under the rapidly lowering darkness, the square lay outstretched in all its great width, with lights near and far, singly and in configuration. Several avenues terminated here; the red-and-yellow trams went through their exercises on intersecting lines of track, and from all directions automobiles approached in disorderly but swiftly flowing patterns.

Laura Konterhonz did not have to cross this square. Her destination was a large building on the side opposite the railroad station. It was one of those frightful bloated creations of the nineteenth-century real-estate boom, with a fancy entrance gate, candelabra, and a stairwell adorned with cords and tassels and idiotic mirrors. She started to look at the name plates in the hall to discover on what floor lay No. 14—the apartment belonging to the Siebenschein family. She was distracted by voices speaking quite loudly and rather violently above her in the narrow shaft of the stairwell, into which an elevator had been installed. She stepped back at once, because she realized that a quarrel was going on, which seemed to her a breach of propriety. At the same time she gave her ears free play. She had recognized Quapp and Gyurkicz, and knew that she herself had not been recognized. The fact that the two were quarreling instantly saddened her. She could not hear much more than: "If you want to come alone, although we were more or less invited together, if you don't want to appear at the same moment I do, that means you're ashamed, which I consider still another rejection . . ." Thus Gyurkicz. And Quapp seemed to be vehemently arguing back.

Laura waited until a door slammed upstairs. Then she gave up her intention of using the elevator and climbed—stirred by painful emotions!—very slowly up the stairs.

She rang the doorbell. A maid in a white cap appeared. The long hallway and the clothing rack in the vestibule were packed with coats and overcoats. The hum of a numerous company struck toward her, and along with it a multitude of odors. Individually such odors were all familiar to her—various perfumes and cigarettes, say—but to Laura they somehow conjured up an alien atmosphere. A girl ran by with a tray; a door opened in front of Laura, and she found herself looking through a spacious room full of noise and people into a second room where ladies and gentlemen—now she recognized Herr von Orkay—were jumping back and forth at big green tables, momentarily leaning far forward, then drawing back rapidly. They were playing table tennis—"ping-pong." The white balls bounded and clicked.

Frau Irma Siebenschein hurried up to Laura. "You're Fräulein von Konterhonz, aren't you? Everybody has been waiting for you . . ." With long strides, Höpfner came toward her. Laura, who towered over Frau Irma by a head, now saw Schlaggenberg in a far corner of the room, deep in conversation with a lady who was solidly, very solidly indeed, ensconced there. For the moment all other thoughts were driven from Laura's head. That one was really—she was absolutely . . .

It was Clarisse Markbreiter.

The table-tennis party which had been first planned on that outing of our crowd, in circumstances that will still be remembered, had thus really come into being. In fact, this was the second or third time such a meeting had taken place. It must be known that Frau Siebenschein was afflicted not only by frequent illnesses but also at times by sudden fits of hospitality and good will toward men (these seldom turned out well, but this evening, for example, she had already discovered that Schlaggenberg was undoubtedly a "superior person"). Frau Siebenschein, then, had suddenly decided to launch these table-tennis affairs on a grand scale. This combined ping-pong afternoon and five-o'clock tea on Saturday, May 14, was designed to show one or another of her relatives that she still had something of a flair in the social line.

In the adjoining room a fierce game was in progress at the moment: Orkay against Doktor Körger. There were numerous spectators. Among these was the captain, his arm in a black sling and his wrist, what of it could be seen, wrapped in bandages. To the questions which are inevitable in such circumstances he replied obligingly and glibly with something about a "mean fall." Frau Siebenschein had remarked—letting her gaze rise slowly upward as one might contemplate a tree—that "for a person your size" a fall must be very dangerous indeed. The captain's injury, incidentally, was not the only one in the company. Another member of our crowd had suffered some damage, it now appeared, though of the slightest sort. Still and all, her occupation being what it was, it behooved her to be careful. For it was Quapp, who kept one of her hands buttoned up in a white kid glove from the moment she entered. And although she had not flatly denied it, that time on the outing when her brother said: "You used to play table tennis pretty well," she did not now have to give proof of her skill. The little stratagem of the glove saved her. She had not needed to learn table tennis in a hurry during the past two weeks . . . Quapp also found precisely the correct and respectable thing to say to Frau Irma when she explained that her hand, after a minor operation on a fingernail, was virtually as good as ever, so that she could even practice, but that she felt it best to do no more. Especially since she would have to play for her teacher tomorrow . . . And so unfortunately she would have to give up the ping-pong, much as she regretted it.

"You're absolutely right there," Frau Irma said with a fine emphasis which sprang from her knowledge of an "artist's" responsibilities. "You're absolutely right. We must be able to sacrifice our pleasures, and for you art must come before everything else."

Who would wish to contradict that?

In the adjoining room, then, my nephew and my cousin were playing against each other. The postures they assumed during the game told the whole story of the differing natures of these unlike friends. Orkay played in the fashion that had become the prevailing style at that period—reheating before each ball, following through on each swing, and hitting the ball from relatively far out from the table. It was, on the other hand, fully in accord with the character and physique of Doktor Körger that he kept close to the table, bobbing around with short reach but extreme agility, reacting violently and rather jerkily, but rarely missing a ball. He gave his opponent a good fight; Géza could barely beat him by such scores as 21-18, 22-20, 21-19.

The hot contest attracted most of the spectators—some gathered around the small tea tables at a suitable distance from the players, while a few climbed on chairs. It seemed altogether natural that Körger and Orkay should form the center of attention here. For were they not, after all, the sponsors of this athletic gathering in the Siebenschein home? They felt themselves to be precisely that, and underlined it, although in a peculiar manner of their own. After the game, discovering Eulenfeld among the onlookers, they dragged him away to a corner of the next room where, on a small table surrounded by a number of miniature glasses, the only bottle of cognac in the house led a quiet existence. It was plain to see that in the Siebenschein family such a bottle was put to use at most every two or three years, when someone had an upset stomach perhaps.

"Please, Captain," Körger said, taking the part of host, "we spotted that at once and put it aside for you."

"Hmmm," our old hussar commented, "a welcome find for what it is. But in consideration of the microscopic proportions of those glasses I should like to take the liberty of looking around and . . ."

"Not at all necessary," Orkay said. Without more ado he opened a small cupboard with bull's-eye panes and took out a wineglass. "We are prepared for all contingencies."

The captain filled the glass and tipped it up.

"This supplement to our stocks must be regarded as welcome," he commented, and added in Latin: "*Ceterum habeo infantem obsoletum.*"

"*Mi az*—what's that?" Géza exclaimed, so astonished that he spoke in his native language. "You have a secret child?"

Laughing, Körger collapsed into a chair and explained what the captain meant by a child: namely, a bottle of schnapps. The captain had come to call it that because on outings, walking trips in the country, and so on, he usually carried it cradled in his arm like a child. (Körger did not mention Eulenfeld's elegant hip flask in its silver case. Why not? Perhaps out of discretion? It always formed the captain's iron ration, and he had it with him tonight too!) A distinction must be made, Körger continued, between large, middle-sized, and small children. This one, for example, was a large child, although its level had already dropped slightly. "Incidentally," Körger said, turning to the old hussar "what do you say to the soup we have cooked up?"

"Oh," Eulenfeld said, glancing into the adjoining room and at the large company in the rest of the apartment, "no imaginable spice has been omitted."

"But why did you say 'a hidden child'?" Orkay interjected.

"Because it's in my coat pocket outside," the captain replied deliberately. "Base depot behind the line of fire, so to speak. Incidentally, I must look to it—there are some folks here who know my habits—wouldn't want them to . . ." And off he went.

In fact some of the Düsseldorfers had come (so that no spice should be omitted), had in fact come in the train of Titi Lasch, who was present this evening. Her husband too was expected to arrive later on. Eulenfeld sauntered slowly across the large dining room and so passed by Laura Konterhonz. Sprinkled and spattered with chatter by a purse-lipped, eager Höpfner,

495

Laura's eyes and whole painfully racked soul were far across the room, where Schlaggenberg was evidently having the most amusing chat with Clarisse Markbreiter. (As for Laura, he had taken the time only to greet her curtly.) A most amusing chat, evidently, for the imposing upper stories of Clarisse's person were shaken by frequent gusts of laughter. Laura did not miss the opportunity to ask: "Why, Captain Eulenfeld, what happened to you? Did you hurt yourself?" But Eulenfeld scarcely had time to deliver his glib little speech about a "mean fall." Laura's eyes had been staring with fixed concern, in fact in sudden suspense, past him, to the other side of the room, and in the midst of his explanation she whispered under her breath, in a tone of unmistakable relief—which made it plain that she had paid not the slightest attention to the captain's obliging reply—she whispered: "Why, of course, *c'est impossible*. Absolutely out of the question."

Eulenfeld involuntarily followed the direction of her gaze. But all he saw was Frau Markbreiter rising gracefully to her feet and standing, small but surprisingly slender—at least surprisingly slender in comparison with the massive upper stories of her person and with the commanding impression she had made while seated.

But now it struck Eulenfeld, too, that Kajetan over there was staring at the woman for a few seconds with obvious astonishment, just as Laura Konterhonz was doing.

"Hmmm," an old hussar muttered to himself in the face of these incomprehensible parallels. He went out to look to his hidden child and exchange a word with it, and arrived just in time to find Titi Lasch engaged in a close inspection of his winter coat, while several of the Düsseldorfers looked on with interest. "Don't be angry, Otto," Titi said, quickly throwing her arms around him, and he really could not be angry with

496

her. In strange contrast to her sister, she had wheat-blonde hair (whether by nature or artifice I have never ventured to decide; probably both played their part) and a cheeky gamin's face. "You know," she went on, "it's simply dreadful, there's never a thing around at the old folks' place."

"Not quite accurate," Eulenfeld was about to reply, but he wisely swallowed these words before they were voiced. However, there was nothing for him to do but produce what was hidden in the depths of his coat pocket. By way of comfort, there promptly appeared a similar substantial contribution from a Düsseldorfer's winter coat and it was offered not without pride—the man in decency could not very well do otherwise. The captain lent the services of his corkscrew, and they drank a round straight from the bottles. Holder, who was standing by, smilingly expressed his appreciation. Wutschkowski—a dark young man with rodent-like teeth—proved to have a damnably good swig capacity; Beppo Draxler likewise; but the best performance was offered by a woman Eulenfeld did not know, whose hair displayed a yellow that could not possibly be a product of nature. (While everyone was showing what he could do, the captain skillfully hid his child somewhere, but not in his coat—next day the bottle was found empty in the umbrella stand). "It's nicest here in the vestibule," Titi said. "Cornel won't be along before half-past six." And she put the bottle to her lips again.

Just as she did so, the dining-room door opened. Frau Irma Siebenschein looked out for a moment but promptly closed the door again. Her state of mind must have been extraordinary this evening, and extraordinarily generous, for otherwise the little matter would have culminated differently.

Still, the captain felt it as somewhat embarrassing. It seemed however, to have made not the slightest impression upon the

Düsseldorfers; they sprawled about on the available chairs and benches, set down bottles under them (a third had just been produced), and began to smoke.

Eulenfeld slunk away, crossed through the dining room, and took up his post in the room where table tennis was being played. All around people were now eating and drinking; a large number of platters with sandwiches, confections, and ice cream in shallow bowls had been distributed everywhere in the rooms, and wherever you wanted to set down a plate, the space was already occupied by teacups or glasses of lemonade and almond milk. A continuous stream of refreshments and assorted delicacies has a remarkably stimulating effect upon any company, without the participants' being fully conscious of what is happening. Here too the whole turbulent crowd grew more fluid; people went back and forth, in and out, creating *in toto* a considerable din, with voices rising high and falling low, with cries of encouragement to the players, bursts of laughter at their sometimes vain efforts to get the ball back over the net. Eulenfeld looked on rather glumly at all this humming and cackling. Körger had just taken him by the arm and led him around as if the place were a curiosity shop or panopticon, calling attention to this or that "fine piece"—Uncle Siegfried Markbreiter, say—or indicating some striking successful mixture and juxtaposition, as for example Kajetan chatting away warmly and with outrageous loquaciousness with Frau Irma Siebenschein.

But on the whole it was pretty dreary for an old hussar (who moreover had moved away from his old crowd not too long before). Those two boys with their lying tongues, both of which had wagged so overeagerly that time on the walk, and solely by way of pretext—those boys had certainly cooked up a curious *pot-au-feu*. Hmmm.

Two new pairs had taken over the green boards: Grete Siebenschein against Stangeler, and at the other table Gyurkicz against Herr Egon Kries, Clarisse Markbreiter's son-in-law. The latter's spouse, the youthful wife Lily, had arrived somewhat later, and was soon afterwards discovered by the captain just as he was returning to the firing line from his first base depot (near the bull's- eye panes). Her husband, Egon, doggedly stayed at the table and lost one game after another to the invincible Gyurkicz. Meanwhile Lily Kries listened fondly to the rather old-fashioned pleasantries of Herr von Eulenfeld, all the more readily since Frau Irma had quickly briefed her niece concerning the gentleman's antecedents and station. A captain of the hussars was a bit of a change from Lily's usual acquaintances.

So for the present Herr von Eulenfeld consoled himself for time and change and for the setbacks within his life-story, out of whose remoter scenes and epochs a dense nebula was already rolling forward: soon it would be time to insert the monocle.

There was general pleasure and approval of Grete's and René's playing, and some of the spectators looked on with genuine emotion: Irma and even her sister Clarisse, with Schlaggenberg standing between them. (Doktor Körger took note of this triptych with particular pleasure.) It *was* so sweet to see the children playing.

That is to say, they were both quite inept and served the ball to each other without force, gently and as far as possible to the very spot from which it could be most easily returned. While they played they were in the best of spirits—as they had been constantly at the ping-pong table of late—and evidently their paddling gave them the greatest pleasure. At the adjoining table, however, the games between Gyurkicz and Kries were far more intense. The onlookers watched in some suspense, for Kries, who had at first been completely intimidated by our Arpad's sharp service—no doubt his usual opponent, Lily, served as placidly as Grete Siebenschein—Kries had gradually got on to Imre's dashing play. And while at first Imre had won every game by towering scores—say 21-6 or 21-8—the young husband now began creeping up. Finally he managed a 21-16, and everyone was eager to see whether in the end he would not be able to win at least one game. Egon Kries was working himself into top form; he was beginning to enjoy the sport. He was, moreover, naturally tall and agile, and incidentally quite good-looking. For Gyurkicz, however, the situation remained very pleasant; here he was in the part of acknowledged master, and was even asked whether this or that was the right way to take such and such a shot. He had become the center of attention, and was being looked up to like a champion by Höpfner, Laura Konterhonz, Holder, Titi Lasch, and all the Düsseldorfers—who in the course of events had turned up, much animated, in the inner rooms and distributed themselves about, talking loudly and continually. Gyurkicz threw out good-natured, obvious little jests while he played. That improbably blonde young lady from the vestibule was already lost in admiration for him.

Quapp had come to a halt behind the "triptych" earlier noted by Doktor Körger. Instead of drifting around with a forlorn look, as she had been doing, she now watched the table tennis. The character of Grete's and René's playing gradually entered her consciousness—though the game itself was a complete mystery to her—and as she watched, oddly enough, she increasingly felt this sort of playing to be something repulsive, almost indecent. Equally repulsive were the commonplace jokes that Gyurkicz brilliantly scattered around him with such facility, and in the best of humors.

The best of humors. Both René and Imre were feeling good. The former had no doubt left his "headquarters" in good time, without having to hurry, and had surely been looking forward to the ping-pong.

Quapp suddenly felt the weight of her body resting heavily upon the soles of her feet. Her legs were tired; she wanted to sit down. But she remained standing.

All the others were sensible and could enjoy themselves. She alone lived stupidly, foolishly.

To her left stood her brother.

She suddenly thought: "He takes charge of everyone's life, is all concerned about Stangeler—only where my life is concerned, he lets things go as they go."

She remembered that the day after tomorrow—or was it as soon as tomorrow?—he intended to leave Vienna. To see Mother; Mother had asked him to come. Quapp should have asked Kajetan for some money—nowadays he always had a lot more than he used to. It would have cost her no effort. But she had too little presence of mind; she had simply forgotten about it.

Tiny furrows crossed her low forehead. She wanted to come to some decision, perhaps to the decision to think of herself, of her own proper course; to find her way back to herself.

"Nice, isn't it, Fräulein—a pity you can't take a turn at it too," a friendly voice at her side said. It was Siegfried Markbreiter. "How well the two of them are doing!" He nodded in the direction of Grete and René.

Quapp suddenly realized that the words were directed at her. "Yes, charming," she replied, but her voice sounded utterly toneless, impossibly and ill-manneredly toneless. Markbreiter said no more.

There was a flurry in the group. Titi made her way

rapidly from the back of the room toward her mother. "Hofrat Tlopatsch has arrived!" she announced.

"Really!" Frau Irma exclaimed delightedly. She hurried away.

Herr Hofrat Tlopatsch was in fact an important person, and not only in the Siebenschein household, where he was usually called "Uncle Fritz"—for he was an old schoolmate of Ferry Siebenschein. All of Vienna knew the small, rotund, always exceedingly courteous Czech—all musical Vienna, at any rate. And musicality and music-making were then and are still in Vienna a habit left over from nobler days, especially among the middle class. In a sizable proportion of the populace music is taken very seriously indeed by people who think they are doing something with it—but who know, above all, that knowledge-able discussion of the tone of a violinist is an essential part of social *bon ton*.

Into such bourgeois musical circles Tlopatsch had introduced himself early in his career. His rank as a higher official served him well, for it insured his trustworthiness. Within a short time he had piped and fiddled and wheezed himself up, if not by his bootstraps, then by sitting on his broad behind (such as nature often confers upon the inhabitants of Bohemia) at the piano and pawing it rapidly, or curving the round fingers of his fat little hand in virtuoso style around the fingerboard of the violin. The conception began to form and fester in certain heads that he was indispensable, so that no sizable musical occasion in the home could be put across without his assistance. If a violinist, a cellist, a horn player, or a singer were required for some ensemble: Tlopatsch knew him, Tlopatsch brought him. Moreover, even before the war Tlopatsch had become secretary of an extremely important concert association; and after that he really held all the strings. He became an authority. His judgment was supreme—not only for the amateur, but also for the professional musician. He mediated, he "made accessible," he introduced, he recommended. For several years before the war a musical evening without Tlopatsch became by his very absence a thing beyond the precincts of good tone. Everyone thought him delightful; everyone was enraptured by his profound musicality, by his playing, by his winning amiability. For any person inside this world of music, or what was fondly called "Viennese musical culture," it was safest to think Tlopatsch charming. It was also advisable never to circumvent him, never to try anything without approaching him. For just as he could "make accessible," introduce, recommend, he could with equal facility do the opposite, quietly and without any fuss. Moreover, he was on an excellent footing with the newspapers; and the music critics of the Alliance papers, for example, often simply repeated what Tlopatsch had said at a concert. Whether they did so out of laziness, ignorance, or shrewdness is hard to say.

This, then, was the gentleman whom Frau Siebenschein hurried forward to meet, together with her husband, Ferry, of whom little had been seen until this point in the evening—probably he had been hiding out in his den at the back of the apartment. The children too, Grete and Titi, came forward. And as the news of Tlopatsch's appearance began to spread, this or that person who was associated with music or wanted something of the musical world likewise approached him. Even the Düsseldorfers had one such man; his name was Frühwald and he ran some kind of agency, but he was also an active pianist and specialist in light music. Holder, too, presented himself; to be sure he was a non-musician, but as a journalist it was best so.

Tlopatsch rolled toward his hostess, patted her hands, asked after her health, greeted Ferry, greeted the children, smiled without letup, expressed thanks for the tea, took a cigar, and accepted the formation of a circle around him.

Ferry Siebenschein also sat in this circle. And he sat there not only as a school friend of the avuncular pope of music but as a member of the musical community in his own right. For he was himself a thoroughly competent flutist and his services were often enlisted, for good flutists are not at all common in amateur musical circles.

This extraordinary fact of his playing the flute stuck up out of the man's prevailing viscous resignation, which formed the basic level of his life—stuck sharply up above the glutinous surface much as the instrument itself, with its high pitch, rises above the orchestra's massed resonance.

Fog was beginning to sift down in the streets and on the wide square. Soon all the lights were surrounded by a lusterless ring, as if viewed through thin panes of milk-glass. Every street lamp hovered in the air unattached. The pavement gleamed damply; it was darker everywhere, since the shops had long since switched off their bright window lights and the traffic was diminishing. Here and there the footsteps of pedestrians sounded as solitary and darkly echoing as in the dead of night.

Along the broad avenue which leads across the bridge of the Danube Canal to the railroad station came Angelika Trapp and the historian Neuberg, walking very slowly. Both seemed to have no business at all in the area from which they had just come: rather, they were only walking back and forth and had already twice circumnavigated the entire block of houses of which the Siebenschein apartment house was one. The couple were in no hurry. They had taken the precaution to inform Frau Irma a whole week before that they would be unable to arrive this Saturday before half-past six. "On account of a class"—a particularly apt excuse for a Saturday evening, by the way!

"I know you call on her and I'm not objecting to that, that would be silly," Angelika was saying. "Stangeler seems to have no objection. But there certainly is no need for you to sit around in coffeehouses with her. You have to remember that people take it for granted that you and I—Even if we ourselves aren't so sure. And then people come to me . . ."

"Who, for instance?" he asked.

"That is beside the point. Whoever it happens to be—it isn't exactly pleasant for me."

"Whenever it suits you, you fall back on that official or legal relationship that otherwise you pretend to despise."

"My father would also not be delighted if he heard that you were seen in a big café in the center of town with Grete Siebenschein."

"Seen by whom? Won't you tell me? No! All right, then I'll tell you myself later. Here you are suddenly bringing up your father—in fact, fathers in general, as such. Fathers are always on the side of the Dulniks. If you are of one mind with the fathers, you will soon be on the side of the Dulniks too. But that Schlaggenberg—I suppose he thought Grete and I didn't notice him—that he should have thought it necessary to come running to you with the news . . ."

"It was nothing of the sort. He ran into me by chance near the University and happened to mention in the course of conversation that he had seen you."

"In any case he was mighty ready to say so. I thought right off that it could have been he and only he, not Herr von Geyrenhoff, who was there with him and also must have seen us. But von Geyrenhoff never makes mischief, whereas Schlaggenberg is always putting his oar in. You're very much mistaken if you think his mentioning it to you was only by chance and in the course of conversation, as you put it. It had a meaning. He wants to 'intervene' here, too. I know the sort of thing; I'm not an idiot, and I've observed him closely. But he had better watch out; he's going to try his intervening on the wrong party one of these days. Other people can do it too, and perhaps in a more effective way."

"This is sheer paranoia," Angelika said.

"Oh no!" Neuberg replied heatedly. "I know perfectly well what's afoot. Grete Siebenschein could tell you a thing or two about that also."

"Schlaggenberg is perfectly harmless and not the least bit malicious, besides which he is a really important person."

"Do you know why you're defending him? Do you really know? Do I have to tell you? In the final analysis because that 'importance,' which happens to be so completely one-sided that it comes pretty close to being stupidity—that importance is by no means disagreeable or alien to you. That's the truth of the matter. And that is betrayal!"

"Why," she cried out, "you yourself said that you have a specially good understanding with Grete Siebenschein— in intellectual matters, I mean. I feel the same way about Schlaggenberg. He takes the words I cannot find out of my mouth and says them for me."

"And invariably makes them sound important! Oh, I know what's going on, I know perfectly well; I run into it more and more often. And you know what in the end will come out of your 'intellectual harmony'? A Dulnik. What a magnificent result . . ."

They had walked back again and come to a halt by the railing of the bridge. The fog here was denser than in the square. The water of the canal below them could be discerned only as a dull gleam. Here lay a bow-shaped valley between city and suburbs formed by a shallow broad turn in the bed of the river; but only a few strong lights traced the dim outline of this bow. The other lights were lost in the thickening grayish-white fog. The streetcar, its bell clanging loudly, loomed for a moment out of the veils of fog with bright imposing front and sailed up to and past them.

Only now did Neuberg realize that Angelika was keeping her head turned away from him. A light quivering of her shoulders revealed to him that she was crying.

"Why, Angi . . ." he said in utter perplexity.

"I just don't know where I am or what I am to do," she burst out, her sobbing now quite audible.

He wanted to say: "Does that mean that you yourself have become doubtful of . . . ?" But he did not finish the sentence, in fact scarcely began it; the phrases died on his lips.

She pulled herself together. "Let us go, come," she said. "Give me your little handkerchief, the one you have in your breast pocket."

Only now did they become aware that a policeman was observing them from the other side of the street.

They walked on, stopped again. Angelika took out her compact. They crossed the square and were about to cross one more narrow street which ended at the Siebenschein house when for a moment two headlights close by them cut into the fog, flattening everything in their path. A deep horn bellowed, and the heavy car lurched around the corner and stopped just short of the front door. A short thickset figure emerged from it, slamming the car door behind him.

"Lasch," Neuberg said. "Let's wait until he's upstairs."

He kissed Angelika. "I didn't want to hurt you. I love you. That's the only reason." For a few seconds she reposed in his arms, eyes closed. Then they entered the building and climbed the stairs together. They heard the door close up above them, and the elevator returned empty. Neuberg and Angelika paused on the stairs. They kissed again.

Fräulein Wiesinger, the pianist, nearsighted and snub-nosed, trailed modestly along in Tlopatsch's retinue. In spite of her tallness she had scarcely been noticed. She was narrow at the shoulders, broad below, shaped somewhat like a hay-stack with the pole through the center, on top of which children had spitted a green apple. However, she was not stupid, only completely twisted and eccentric. She had become wholly incurable through having once fallen into the hands of a psy-choanalyst—worse still, while she was still an adolescent. The man's theories had been only too efficacious and had been her undoing. For she had obtained a neat skeleton key for every-thing in the world, for whatever oddities she encountered in her fellow-men. She used this key to open them up, and sure enough always found inside a neat label or category. Content in her enjoyment of this magical terminology, she seriously believed herself in possession of profound insights. That was too much for her fairly adequate but still limited intelligence. She went overboard; that is to say, she lost her balance and became conceited and arrogant, precisely as true fools by birth generally are. In place of her assortment of ills she had finally and forever acquired psychoanalysis itself as an illness. Quite an achievement for a medical science. She also continued per-manently under "treatment," year after year, sacrificing a large part of her hard-earned money for it. She is an old lady now and is still undergoing therapy, or so I have heard.

Now, at any rate, this psychoanalytic clavicembalist sat in Tlopatsch's magic circle; that is to say, she sat around the Hofrat as respectfully as Frau Irma and the others. Yet, respect-ful or not, she did not shrink from identifying the good man's

508

"repressions," which seemed to have entirely emasculated him, for in fact he looked exactly like a capon. His voice, too, was high and sweet. Simultaneously, however, Fräulein Wiesinger was wondering why Charlotte von Schlaggenberg—of whose presence here this evening she was well aware—had not joined the circle. That was clearly imprudent; it was almost incomprehensible. Fräulein Wiesinger thought very highly of Quapp in every respect, and moreover took an interest in her as an ambivalent type. But as far as prudence and practicality were concerned, she thought Quapp capable of any degree of ignorance and folly. She might for example, never have met Herr Tlopatsch, through sheer neglect. It was even faintly conceivable that Quapp did not know who Herr Tlopatsch was—and such a state of innocence might in some circumstances be extremely dangerous.

A new chamber music group, the Kolischer Quartet, was being discussed.

At this point Tlopatsch's views diverged from the rhapsodic notices of the Alliance music reviewers. Tlopatsch preferred to be cautious, to wait and see, to take shelter behind reservations. He alluded to Beethoven, who had obviously never been in favor of playing from memory, had always kept the score in front of him, even when he was playing his own works. Of course Tlopatsch admitted the "possibility of development" on the part of these "four young artists." But he regarded the principle which they carried out so rigorously—namely, to play even the longest and most difficult compositions solely from memory—as a step in the direction of acrobatics rather than artistry.

Herr Frühwald spoke up, though he was only a specialist in lighter music: "I should imagine that playing by heart might very well permit a deepening and concentration of the conception of the music, and thus an improvement in the shaping of the whole, since the distraction produced by reading notes is eliminated."

"Do not be so sure of that, my dear Herr Frühwald," Tlopatsch genially took issue. "No matter how solidly entrenched in the memory the pieces may be—and incidentally, between ourselves, that is not so impressive an achievement as it may seem—a great deal of strength is nevertheless lost in the mere effort of playing by heart, wasted in the subconscious straining of the memory, if you understand what I mean. On the other hand, if I have my score in front of me, I can really throw myself into the music." (His face actually became transfigured; Fräulein Wiesinger noted this, for she was watching him closely.) "In such a case I may very well play from memory without having specially set out to do so. But the public would not be aware of that."

"What fun!" Ferry Siebenschein commented. "A fine thing for the nervous system: Will I get stuck, won't I get stuck, will I get stuck, won't I get stuck? Enough to make a man end up in the loony-bin."

"Since we happen to be talking about the unusual," Tlopatsch said, "I'm involved at the moment in a rather difficult project—organizing a group to play some seventeenth-century music with the original instruments. So far I've rounded up the viola da gamba and viola d'amore, but I still need three first-rate guitars. Not easy to find, you know, a guitarist who can play something more than accompaniments, something that calls for virtuosity. I'll probably have the two from the academy, those being the only ones who are working with that instrument at the moment. All right, fine, but where is the third to come from?"

At this point Frau Irma looked radiantly happy. Tlopatsch's

remarks about Kolischer and company had been quite painful for her, since she was one of the most enthusiastic admirers of this quartet. But here was a breach into which she could leap.

"I can help you there, Uncle Fritz," she said triumphantly. "I know the very man. In fact, he's here tonight." She rose quickly and marched off toward the ping-pong room, leaving the circle of music-lovers slightly floored.

At the green boards, meanwhile, there had been no slackening. The situation had changed. Things had become more difficult for Gyurkicz. He was now playing against Doktor Körger, whom he had repeatedly challenged, for he thought himself at least the match of Herr von Orkay and had carefully observed the faults in Körger's attitude and technique. But now our Arpad had to exert himself. My stocky nephew with his jerky returns did not look very elegant, and no doubt consumed a disproportionate amount of energy, but all the same Imre could barely eke out a victory every second or third game, by a score of, say, 21-19. The rest of the time the score was reversed in favor of Doktor Körger. It was a regular battle. The other table offered a more amiable sight. Here mother and daughter were playing against each other—Clarisse Markbreiter against Lily Kries—while the young husband and the captain (Eulenfeld already wearing his monocle) looked on. Clarisse moved very swiftly and skillfully, which, considering her extraordinary corseting (may we refer the reader back to the chapter entitled "Cheese Pastry," written indelicately but with strict adherence to the truth by Schlaggenberg)—considering this circumstance, was quite an achievement. In her manner of handling the paddle there was something reminiscent of the way many ladies in that big coffeehouse by the Danube Canal held their spoon, especially when eating whipped cream (Frau Mährischl, for example)—namely, with the little finger slightly extended.

Schlaggenberg, who kept drifting back and forth between the ping-pong room and the adjoining room where the captain's first base depot was located, now and then glanced with almost unconcealed disapproval at Frau Markbreiter's graceful lower stories. Once, in fact, he shook his head, whereupon he retreated again to the bull's-eyes. The captain's first depot had long since been discovered by others; in fact, a certain static quality had developed in this area, although the bottle of brandy was not surrounded in quite the same manner as Herr Tlopatsch. Rather, this space, which happened to be Titi's former room, offered certain advantages in itself, being off the main line of traffic—people did not want to disturb the ping-pong players by passing to and fro too much. And so little knots formed here, where there were opportunities for more serious and substantial conversations.

Nearly all evening Herr Jan Herzka had been sitting in a corner of this room, legs outstretched, a cigar in his mouth, body substantial and well formed, face handsome. The handsomeness, however, seemed only a kind of base upon which something quite different had been added layer by layer. At first sight you might think this was an important face, next moment that it was exotic; next you would be struck by a certain unctuousness, and then conclude that in any case it was extremely attractive. At the same time he emanated a certain well-ordered satiety which no doubt was related to his business. This was an old Viennese firm inherited from his father and continued in the old tradition with extraordinary exactitude and circumspection. Herzka was regarded generally as a model businessman. On his mother's side, incidentally, he was of aristocratic origins: his mother had been a Baroness Neudegg.

Among the others loitering near the bull's-eye-paned cupboard was—in addition to Schlaggenberg, who came in now and then, only to return to the ping-pong room for another disapproving glance at Frau Markbreiter—René Stangeler. Herzka was plaguing Stangeler with all sorts of questions about cultural history, which for some incomprehensible reason seemed to be a matter of deep concern for him. As usual when he had once been pried open, "the Ensign" poured forth a cornucopia of knowledge. Géza von Orkay drank cognac (when challenged to a game by Gyurkicz he had begged off on the ground that he was all tired out) and listened with great attention. The captain, too, drifted in later on and refreshed himself; evidently the conversation with Frau Kries had been somewhat of a strain on him.

At the green tables, meanwhile, fresh changes had taken place. First of all, Quapp had at last settled down in a chair. She felt altogether weary and dull. Secondly, disaster had at last descended upon Imre in the shape of Herr Beppo Draxler. Until now Draxler had been a mere onlooker, but Imre had challenged him several times during the games with Doktor Körger. And now Imre was being soundly thrashed. (Later it turned out that the sly Draxler had won several championships.) The scores speak for themselves: 21-11, 21-9, 21-14—that was what Gyurkicz was up against. Quapp watched and felt enormous disgust at the possibility that she might now be feeling something akin to gratification, for Gyurkicz was no longer in good humor and had entirely lost that knack for making many little jokes which earlier had produced such good rapport between himself and his audience. The latter had gathered in increased numbers around the tables again, drawn by the fury of the contest. In spite of his opponent's obvious superiority, Gyurkicz soon began to move up; he reached 21-17.

Nevertheless, Quapp might well have had to pay in some fashion for having witnessed this defeat if Frau Irma—fresh from the musical circle—had not come in and fluttered straight up to Beppo Draxler. Apologizing profusely for interrupting the game ("If it were not a really important matter, I certainly would not disturb you, my dear Herr Doktor"), she took him with her. At the same time she also kidnaped Quapp, amid a flurry of emotional, murmured exclamations ("Why, Fräulein von Schlaggenberg, don't you know that Hofrat Tlopatsch is here? You don't know him? Then I absolutely must introduce you; this could be so terribly important for you!").

Thus the coming musicale acquired an excellent guitarist, and Quapp found her way into the circle of music-lovers where, at least in Frau Irma's opinion of the moment, she properly belonged. At the green tables, meanwhile, an inferior species of play had taken over, a harmless paddling of balls back and forth, to the accompaniment of innumerable witticisms. The participants in this lackadaisical sport were a number of jolly Düsseldorfers under the leadership of Titi Lasch.

"Under whom are you studying, my child?" Tlopatsch said, turning to Quapp, after having arranged matters with Beppo Draxler—in the course of which negotiations it was necessary to make such lengthy courteous speeches that it was some time before the new member of the ensemble could return to the green boards and resume serious play alongside the silly dalliance.

Quapp gave her teacher's name.

It was remarkable to see the effect this name had upon the circle.

Everyone acted as though he had just caught sight of something very remote, which was nevertheless familiar enough. No one pretended not to have ever heard the name. All manifested aloof respect, as if for some foreign, some wholly exotic sovereign, who still and all was a sovereign although here, in one's own country, he would naturally possess far less importance or authority than the magistrate or constable of the nearest village.

Quapp sat rather helplessly, holding the name in both hands as if it were some heavy object while the whole circle looked on coldly.

"Hm—ah yes," Tlopatsch commented. "That is very interesting indeed."

"Do you think his method has real value, Uncle Fritz?" Grete Siebenschein petitioned the authority, speaking right past Quapp herself. "If so, why has it not become more widespread? . . . You have never studied under another teacher?" she asked Quapp directly at last.

"No," Quapp replied, turning away. Wherewith a hostility was proclaimed which had been long foredoomed to come into the open.

"Is this method really based on psychological foundations?" Fräulein Wiesinger asked, though she really knew better, since she had been working with Quapp for a long time. But here, in Tlopatsch's presence, she posed her question.

"Hm—I can scarcely say precisely as to that," Tlopatsch declared. He laid his cigar on the ash tray and turned with great friendliness to Quapp. "Here, I imagine, is the person competent to speak."

"Well?" Fräulein Wiesinger now asked; here in this place she had become a stranger to Quapp. "Is this type of instruction really founded on psychology?"

"I really don't know what you mean by that," Quapp said in a little outburst of despair, still firmly and loyally holding the heavy object in both hands. Her tone was somewhat curt, and lightly shaded by anger, for she was just beginning to detect the treason that was being committed here (sometimes her stupidity was enormous). Her anger mounted rapidly, for the recollection of the many hours she had spent with the pianist, during which Quapp had been led to speak of her teacher—this recollection suddenly burst through her state of dull resignation and she now saw herself transformed into a traitor as the result of the many confidential remarks she had made to this Wiesinger woman.

With Quapp's last words the common membrane, which for a while had enclosed her and the entire circle, snapped.

That could be read in Frau Irma's disappointed face.

Quapp sagged, collapsed into a state of utter exhaustion. She already felt as if she had been poisoned, as though in some mysterious fashion the last remnant of her strength had been taken from her during the few minutes this conversation had lasted. Here she sat. A "chance" had been offered (that was how Frau Siebenschein had meant it). But Quapp had been unable to take advantage of the opportunity. She had not been prepared. Preparedness was always and everywhere being demanded of her; but all evening a soft, toughly resilient partition had separated her from it. Here was the real, the essential betrayal of her teacher; it consisted precisely in this state in which she found herself. Now she again saw Imre entering her door, saw his big, gray, melancholically handsome face in front of the door as she opened it. From then on it had all been over. The rest of the evening lay like a tumor inside her, with everything swelling under its pressure. This was the way she lived. Only others were sensible, had their "headquarters," found work and livelihood, took advantage of opportunities, in the end enjoyed themselves.

At the moment she despised everything, including herself. And meanwhile she sat captive and crushed within this company and its musical chitchat.

She was relieved of her painful predicament by the arrival of Cornel Lasch. For in the burst of greetings which ensued, the circle temporarily broke up. It became apparent that Frau Irma Siebenschein had other centers of gravity in addition to the Muses—her son-in-law, for example. Now she bustled around him. The greetings exchanged between Lasch and Hofrat Tlopatsch were replete with unusually ceremonious expressions of mutual delight. Tlopatsch in fact thought highly of Lasch as truly "a man of intelligence and culture," as he had once remarked to Frau Irma.

This evening son-in-law Cornel seemed somewhat restrained, his mood a bit clouded, not to say blackened, by gravity. It became obvious at once that he was disinclined to form the life of the party, which normally he was only too glad to do, especially in the home of his parents-in-law. With undisguised haste he beat a retreat, greeted his wife in the ping-pong room—where the Düsseldorfers formed a reception line and even the resumed duel between Draxler and Gyurkicz was interrupted. At last Lasch arrived at the bull's-eyes and joined Jan Herzka, whom he greeted with special cordiality, and Stangeler and the others who were still holding forth on cultural history. Lasch seemed very pleased that this was so. Outside of business and family circles he liked to talk of nothing but scientific, philosophical, or artistic questions; in social life he always modestly avoided subjects which might seem more in his line, or gave vague answers, as if he were completely igno-rant in such matters. In the "higher" realms, however, he was capable of stubbornly, and even passionately, defending this or that point of view.

Lasch, then, settled down here with visible relief, took a glass of cognac, and with silent attention followed the course of the conversation, which went its way undisturbed, since Neuberg and Angelika Trapp, who had come shortly after Lasch, likewise joined the group of listeners in silence. So also did Quapp, who had escaped during the temporary dissolution of the musical circle, and Grete Siebenschein, who in the end had found the Tlopatsch worshipers too boring.

Schlaggenberg, however, continued to hang around the green tables, although the in-spite-of-all attractive object of his disappointment was no longer playing. Instead, the company of music-lovers entered the room for a few minutes before being resoldered into a technical musical conglomerate. Herr Tlopatsch wanted to have a look at the "sporting event" of the evening. He stood looking on, with Fräulein Wiesinger gaping through her glasses over his head, at a game between Draxler and Gyurkicz which the latter barely won by a tremendous outpouring of fighting spirit. The victory improved his mood considerably, for the straw-blonde of the vestibule was now one of the audience. Draxler's game had fallen off greatly since the interruption, either because he was then, distracted, or by now indifferent.

Shortly afterwards Schlaggenberg escaped back to the bull's-eyes; but he had occasion to overhear a memorable little conversation, a supplementary chat, between Tlopatsch and Draxler; Uncle Fritz took Draxler aside as he stepped away from the green tables. The conversation was conducted in low tones, but Kajetan pricked up his ears and played the eavesdropper. ("I really did so for your sake, Herr von Geyrenhoff," he said later, "I thought this might be something of interest to you.") The conversation ran as follows.

"May I ask you, Herr Doktor, what your present professional work is? In banking, ah yes, ah yes. But no doubt you would prefer to enter some important law office before too long and begin writing briefs . . . ? Quite true, it is not always easy to find the post that is both suitable and promising. You've already had your year in the courts, I take it? Put that behind you anyhow? Well, my dear friend, I can only say that you will find your best opportunity right here, at our little musicale in which you will be taking part. It really falls out splendidly for you. The host is, as you no doubt know, head of one of the most important law offices in Vienna, a good friend of mine. What's that? Why, of course, of course, I certainly could, I shall gladly put out a little feeler . . . Incidentally, the young lady who just arrived, a Fräulein Trapp, will be coming with her mother . . . I don't know where she is right now"—he looked around—"well then, I'll introduce you at the musicale; her father is a highly respected attorney, also an old friend of mine. Naturally there are always several gentlemen of the legal profession present on such occasions . . ."

From time to time during these expositings by Hofrat Tlopatsch, Herr Doktor Draxler bowed slightly, smiling appreciatively, as it were expressing his gratitude in advance. As a marginal comment I should like to add that all this ultimately proved the first step in a highly successful career—which had thus, with "typical Viennese graciousness," been born by way of music.

So much for the report from Schlaggenberg, who then made his way to the bull's-eyes.

Here the conversation was curious indeed—there was, incidentally, some cognac left.

Out of what corner of his life or personality this Herr Jan Herzka could have drawn so profound an interest in the witch trials of the sixteenth and seventeenth centuries seemed for the present inexplicable. The conversation had enlarged itself beyond all bounds and had indeed come to comprise all of "general culture," a subject on which everybody today may have his say—is, in fact, required to. For if a man spoke only of the things he took seriously—what would there be left to talk about? In good society you tactfully avoided exposing anyone to the danger of revealing the narrowness of his true concerns.

Accordingly, everyone was far too well bred to inquire what cause Herr Herzka had to take such a lively interest in witch trials.

Stangeler, meanwhile, had succeeded in clearing away the crudest misconceptions—among others, that the witch trials had been a characteristic phenomenon of the "Middle Ages." Specialists, it is well known, have the ever enviable possibility of being able to "document" their utterances or arguments (and by the aid of such "documentation" often slaughter the truth, although that did not happen to be the case right here). Our ex-ensign of the dragoons, then, cited the papal bull *Summis desiderantes* of the 1580's, which first opened the way for the whole system of witch trials.

"In this field, then, modern times brought no progress as against the Middle Ages, but rather retrogression, wouldn't you say?" Grete Siebenschein put in. She was in raptures that René knew so much and that therefore everyone was listening to him.

"That cannot really be said," Lasch objected. "For as we have just heard, the field itself did not yet exist in the actual Middle Ages, certainly not in any such developed and systematic form."

"Yet it did emerge from the Middle Ages," Grete said.

"Perhaps this concept, too, is not entirely correct." The second "specialist," Neuberg, turned to Grete with great courtesy. "You might say that the witch trials were not in harmony with the Middle Ages, but were rather a sign of the collapse and downfall of the medieval world."

"To return to what we were discussing earlier"—Herzka took the floor—"you were telling us, Herr von Stangeler, that the generally accepted view that it was only old and ugly women who were persecuted as witches is entirely false, and that rather many young girls and beautiful women were among the victims. Did I understand you aright?"

"Yes," the specialist replied. "So it appears from the sources. The records, for example, of Wurzburg for the years 1627 to 1629, which list the people who were burned alive, are full of items which bear out that fact. These particular records are paralleled by many others. In the beginning the accusations may have been launched against old and malignant-looking women; medieval men seemed to have had a peculiar dislike for such unfortunates. In this early stage of the witch trials, I should say, certain ancient Teutonic conceptions of the nature and appearance of witches were operative. Later that element vanished."

"Then it cannot properly be said that only senile or half-idiotic old women were involved," the captain commented.

"What do you know about the procedures used against those women in Wurzburg?" Herzka asked.

"Not very much," Stangeler replied.

"Would there be any way of finding out?"

"It would depend on whether, in addition to the lists I mentioned, the records of the trials have been preserved, and where these records are kept. Since the trials were held by an episcopal inquisitional court, the records might very well have been preserved, since such episcopal offices have an unbroken continuity."

"Then the most likely place would be Wurzburg itself," Herzka said.

"Yes. At any rate one would have to start the search from there."

"And—do you think this is really possible? I mean, that these documents would be accessible if they exist?"

"They no doubt would be, for anyone with some scholarly qualifications. If you have some such brandname hung around your neck, things of that sort are usually easy. You prove that you are doing research for a paper, and so on. Of course a so-called private person might find it more difficult."

"Unfortunately that applies to me," Herzka said.

This interest of his, which plainly went so far beyond the pale of ordinary intellectual curiosity, was beginning to disturb the others, but without their being totally conscious of that effect. The general feeling seemed to be that here was a person with a vital concern which they did not happen to share.

"Even if they were not old and half-idiotic women," Angelika Trapp put in a word, "they were still and all subject to pure hallucinations."

"I don't think that was quite so," Neuberg said, to Grete Siebenschein's astonishment; she threw him a look of surprise. "What is your opinion, Herr von Stangeler?"

"There can be no question of 'hallucinations' in the present-day sense of the word. But that's a subject which we cannot really go into here," René said with a sudden look of sulky obstinacy. He stared down at the floor.

"Why can't we go into it?" Grete objected. "When you say something so surprising, you must be able to prove it too."

"There are cheap proofs which can be offered to anyone and which call for no prerequisites. I can prove to anyone that two and two is four, or that it is socially advisable to build orphanages. These are matters anyone can understand. But there are other, deeper proofs which can be given only to people who bring something to the subject."

"And you mean that we bring nothing to it." The corners

of Grete's mouth twitched; the discord and tension that had suddenly sprung up between her and Stangeler must have been plain to all.

"I am not saying that," René replied. "But a thing can only be understood from within, from the core of its own being, and not by lightly touching it as a stranger from outside. Anyone who is not in tune with—perhaps I should say 'in love with,' since we understand only what we love!—the world of the Middle Ages, has an altogether different vocabulary, to mention only one point of difference. The very language he uses does not have the same meaning. If I use the word 'hallucinations,' I mean a more or less neurotic or hysterical phenomenon. But it is a complete misunderstanding to apply the same word to a time . . ."

"Now you are speaking of the Middle Ages again," Grete interrupted him. "And just before you were saying that these trials had nothing to do with that period." Her pleasure in René's knowledge seemed to have evaporated. Neuberg regarded her with mingled astonishment and admiration.

"Yes, now I am speaking of the Middle Ages," Stangeler said with an unshakable calm that seemed quite suddenly to have come over him. "For if any age is to be understood in its forms and manifestations, we must go far back into the past beyond this age and fix our regard upon the given period by looking forward rather than backward. A really intimate knowledge of what was considered 'old-fashioned' by any given generation, but a knowledge which looks forward from this particular state of old-fashionedness rather than backward as if we were studying the window of an antique shop—such knowledge makes it easy to work ourselves into the new period that follows. By the time we get there, the subject strikes us as entirely familiar. History is not at all knowledge of the past, but in actuality the science of the future—of, that is, whatever in the given segment we are studying was to be the future, or hoped to be. There we find what really happened; there lies the center of the stream, where the current runs strongest."

Grete remained silent. She had evidently given up trying to oppose him. Perhaps she was influenced by Neuberg's frequent nods of assent. (At least that is how Doktor Körger later explained it.)

René turned suddenly to Quapp: "If history is the science of the future, then you understand that its task is to find the corresponding spring-house, the corresponding frog of the bow, for everything that afterwards acquired a name. Do you see?"

"Yes," Quapp cried in an abnormally loud voice. "It is perfectly clear."

"I imagine you have your perfect clarity all to yourself," Grete said. But Quapp completely disregarded her.

Neuberg, who at first had been utterly nonplussed, suddenly burst into laughter, though he himself probably did not know why. Schlaggenberg nodded to Stangeler, and Körger protested, as he had done once before on our outing, near the rickety bench, under the thin spring sunlight: "You're already turning every conversation into nonsense with your crazy jargon!"

"Never mind," Stangeler said easily. "I said that by way of shorthand. You would understand it too if you had happened to be by when the code phrase was first coined. . . Lots of people have their private languages. I could explain it all—but it would bore everyone. Besides, it's in the nature of such symbols or expressions that they lose their force if they are said too often. They should be utilized as seldom as possible."

"I would wholeheartedly recommend that," Grete said.

Stangeler turned upon her a look of great patience ("which sprang from the clear and inescapable realization that Grete

Siebenschein did not even know what was under discussion"—thus Schlaggenberg commented in his description of this scene).

"But look here," Angelika Trapp spoke up once again. "You were saying, Herr von Stangeler, that hallucination was not a word that could be applied to the witches, not in the present sense of the word anyhow. You began to explain that, and I think I followed you as far as you went. Won't you say more about that?"

"All right," René said, "I'll try. It's this way: that our age has almost entirely lost the knowledge mankind once had of the power of imagination with which 'blessed and possessed spirits peopled heaven and hell, which otherwise were empty though nonetheless real'—as Scolander once put it. Consequently, what we do is to classify that particular power as a malady, although it is fundamentally nothing of the sort. Rather, it has its place within the picture of the whole man just as much as other powers of the body and the psyche. We, however, are familiar with such phenomena only in madmen; in our times the mysterious course of disease can split the psyche of some poor chap so wide open that we see down to the traditional, inherited materials which lie at the bottom, under deep layers of slag. But when, nowadays, this inheritance wells up, it can only form strange bubbles that soon burst. In a state of vigorous health—and that is the only valid criterion—no one possesses that imaginative capacity any longer. In our civilization, its very appearance deforms the personality, makes its possessor a kind of freak. Or else it is found in conjunction with schizoid mental disease. In our times, a person who could command such an imagination while remaining in healthy balance would be a monster. But in those days such a person was entirely 'normal.'"

"A concrete example would be useful here," Lasch remarked

behind his cigar, which he drew out of his mouth only by a fraction of an inch in order to speak.

"I have one ready to hand," Stangeler said. This evening he himself seemed to be in a state of happy balance which not even his Grete's little side-blows had been able to upset. "I happen to have one ready to hand," he repeated, "and a very clear one at that."

What had made Stangeler feel light and happy all during the previous conversation had been the deftness with which words had come to him, so that he was able to say what he meant and uphold his argument even before a group of people who had no background other than their intelligence. For it was only too usual in such situations for his own impatience to throw his words into disarray, so that he seemed not even able to make orderly statements, far less to back up his point of view.

There were in fact two languages that Stangeler spoke. The one could scarcely be called language; it was not expression and not communication, but only a verbal means for engendering a particular impression in the listener. On the other hand, when René wanted nothing for himself but was wholly taken up in saying something which urgently needed to be said about the subject at hand, he could sometimes hit on the most felicitous phraseology and find the perfect temperate tone.

("Even though I had just been raising those stupid carping points, I loved him, while he was speaking, beyond anything"— thus Grete Siebenschein in her later description of this evening.)

Stangeler suddenly turned half around and addressed Géza von Orkay, thus focusing the attention of the group upon my Magyar cousin, who had hitherto merely stood by listening, with his rather gloomy, impassive face.

"Do you remember, Géza," René said, "the time we talked about that curious episode involving the sacred Hungarian royal crown?" Orkay nodded. "The crown was stolen—stolen by a Viennese woman of the burgher class on the night of February 20, 1440; she was acting on behalf of the widow of Albrecht II, the German Emperor. Albrecht's widow was expecting a child, hoped for a son, and intended to have the infant crowned without delay as the legitimate King of Hungary. This in fact was done. We happen to be precisely informed about the hair-raising adventure of the Viennese woman, for the story was later written down from her dictation and can be found in the archives of the National Library. The manuscript runs to seventeen closely written pages—in other words, is a fairly detailed account, dealing with events both before and after, with regard to the coronation of the little king, the whole related in the form of a very lively first-person story—a rarity in the Middle Ages. From the tale, one thing is perfectly plain: that Frau Kotanner—that was her name—was a sober, sturdy person with a pronounced sense of reality, a matter-of-fact temperament, and—this again may be concluded from certain details—physically robust. She was also quite young. During the excitement of that night at Castle Visegrad on the Danube—where the crown was kept under strong guard—this woman was twice tempted by the devil. What happened was this. She was creeping down the dark corridor which led to the chamber containing the crown, when she heard the guards approaching with a great noise of tramping and clanking of armor so that she thought herself and the cause lost. And then nothing appeared. She crept forward once again and convinced herself that the passage was empty. The second time, however, the din was so great that the possibility of her being mistaken did not even occur to her, as it had the first time. Instead, she was far more frightened—'so that for fear I was all atremble and a-sweat,' as she put it. The first time she thought a ghost must have made the noise; the second time she realized at last, and almost with relief, that it was the devil trying to ruin her undertaking. Since it was the devil, she resorted to prayer. The devil was put to flight. Our explanation would be that she had had an auditory hallucination. But basically it is only a question of names. In any case she had experienced something which for a few moments had an enormous effect upon her nerves, her heartbeat, and her breathing, and directly influenced her actions. For she crept forward and looked around. And then she realized that it had been the devil. Can anyone deny the reality of this experience? In a woman today no creative strength would flow from such an experience; rather, it would end in a 'nervous breakdown' or a 'hysterical crying fit.' Which last would have turned out damnably ill for Frau Kotanner. But there you have it. Immediately afterwards Frau Kotanner proved herself to be a sober, sensible, efficient person. In those days any healthy and fully effective person included in the gamut of his emotional experiences what we today call 'hallucination,' something that for us smells of pathology and hospitals. In those days, however, hallucination lay within the range of normality, thus had validity. Against this background, then, we must consider the witch trials we were discussing; otherwise we remain lost in empty platitudes like 'superstition' and 'hysteria,' which may mean something in reference to our own times but do not mean a thing in reference to those days."

"Very good," Lasch said under his breath, as though he had been enjoying an artistic performance.

"But still there are facts," Grete commented, but now without that earlier militant tone. She spoke plaintively and looked up at Stangeler with a melting, loving, almost worshipful awe.

"Certainly there are facts," he said, returning her conciliatory look, "yet even facts are open to serious question—moreover, by the English, who surely cannot be denied a strong feeling for facts. In the eighteenth century a number of their philosophers attempted to construct a view of the world entirely on an empirical basis, without any premises or prejudices. They went about it with the utmost logic and consistency, and in the end there emerged the dubiousness of all 'facts' in general. I think we can trust them; they thought the thing through absolutely to the end. Personally I have no opinion on that. But there are enough evidences of the questionableness of every so-called perception, and recently a whole new mess of such evidence has been brought in by a semi-medical or semi-scientific discipline—namely, psychology."

"That is highly interesting," Lasch said. "Please explain." He looked over toward Quapp (Schlaggenberg observed this odd glance) with a certain pride, probably because the girl plainly revealed that she could no longer follow. Rather, as she listened she had to ponder, with a kind of four-footed thoroughness, everything that Stangeler had said before. And now he was going on to something new!

"These psychologists have shown," Stangeler continued, "that in every perception, even in the simplest, there lies hidden a creative, a productive, a contributory element. They found this out by experiment. In such experiments life is simplified to the point of being unrecognizable; everything is reduced to bare essentials; certain conditions are established, as far as possible universal conditions which will apply in all circumstances. These experiments are as boring as they are unappealing. But the results were highly significant. A number of healthy and reliable experimental subjects were shown a rapid succession of quadrilateral figures, each one being 'exposed' for a precisely determined span of time and then vanishing. The experimental subjects stated what they had seen. They one and all attested that they had been shown so and so many closed quadrilateral geometric figures. In fact, however, a considerable number of these figures had been unfinished open on one side, with only three corners or three sides, the fourth not even drawn. Nevertheless, in every case the complete figure was seen. The concept already lodged in the minds of the subjects proved stronger than the actual perception. The figures were all seen as quadrilaterals—really seen so. Now reality is what really seems real in life. Those figures were 'in reality' all quadrilateral; but inside the apparatus that projected them they were not quadrilateral. The missing parts were added by the observers. Now the relationship of such an experiment to life is about that of a single isolated atom of protein to a whole man . . . I mean, when more complicated conditions begin to enter, when innumerable perceptions and the additions our minds make to them begin to intersect . . . But enough of this. Naturally the psychologists carried the whole thing to extremes, set the results down in tables, with duration of exposure, permutations of succession, percentages, and so on."

He fell silent.

"Yes, but—where does such a view bring us?" Angelika said. "We simply have no ground to stand on."

"For man's tasks in practical life such ideas cannot be fruitful," Lasch commented.

"It strikes me that the sacred cow of objectivity is beginning to stagger on all four feet!" Schlaggenberg threw in, and Körger began to laugh loudly.

Perhaps it was this laughter, with its coarsely mocking note, that once again aroused militant impulses in Grete Siebenschein.

"I beg your pardon, Herr Doktor"—she turned directly to Körger rather than to Schlaggenberg, who had actually

530

spoken; Körger's laughter sounded so strongly affirmative, was so crude a form of agreement, that it evoked her opposition far more than everything that had been said—"I beg your pardon," Grete said. "We may admire the times of which René has spoken as much as we like—but what in the end did they lead to? Such terrible things as these witch trials, for example, such vast cruelty! And what was at the bottom of it all? Delusions upon delusions! Why do you laugh at objectivity? It will do far less harm to people, perhaps it represents our greatest, our most decisive form of progress."

"I see that you believe in progress," Körger said, still half laughing, although Grete had fallen into a sharp, or at least somewhat captious tone.

"Yes, why not? Why, that's ridiculous. Life today differs in essential points from life in earlier times!"

"Would you mind citing just one of those essential points?" Körger requested.

"Well, to take the first example that comes to mind," Grete replied, looking feverishly around the circle, "the altogether different kind of security people enjoy today. In that respect no earlier period can compare with ours."

"Ah, if only you don't suffer quite a jolt to your security one of these days," Doktor countered. "If I were you, I would not place such great reliance on it."

However, scarcely anyone heard his words, for something happened which startled everyone, and which was destined not be forgotten among our crowd.

No sooner had Grete Siebenschein spoken the word "security" than a sudden loud sound was heard, uncommonly like the grunting of a large pig. This noise, quite plainly an expression of disapproval, issued from Captain Eulenfeld.

It was promptly followed by something equally startling

because so out of character: Herr von Orkay began to laugh uproariously, uncontrollably, a regular horselaugh. It took him some time to subside.

The word "security" must have made an uncommonly deep impression upon the captain in his drowsy and somewhat befogged state. It must have pierced through the alcoholic mists and pricked him like a thorn, leaving behind some sort of scar or mark. For months later, whenever he was drunk and out of sorts with something, he was in the habit of burbling: "Y'know what, that's another of their damned securities . . . all we needed, by God, all we needed."

The seriousness of the conversation was soon restored, however.

"Yes, but then what meaning can life have at all?" Angelika Trapp was heard to exclaim. Swiftly, galloping over the dubiousness of the factual world, they came to a halt at no lesser a point than this. So they behaved like the archer who puts an end to his misses by laying aside the bow, going straight up to the target, and placing his arrow plumb in the center of it by hand.

The party up to this point was described to me in detail and, as may be imagined, from many different angles. I must, however, account for my own failure to be present.

I spent that rainy Saturday at home, not leaving the house at all until evening. Frau Siebenschein's invitation had arrived more than a week before, and I had already replied with thanks, that unfortunately on the afternoon of May 14 I had to attend a conference concerning a matter which had been in my charge while I was still in government employ, had been tabled for a time, and had not been taken up again (after all, an official file has a stubborn life). Now, I informed her, I had to come to the aid of the former colleague who was at that time established in my office; he had asked me to help him untangle this case.

The whole story was a lie, of course; and in saying this I am admitting that I purposely absented myself from that table-tennis five-o'clock tea at the Siebenscheins'. However, I had promised Frau Irma that if there were enough time before the opera I would at least drop in for a few minutes—having also told her (this time truthfully) that I had an invitation to the opera for Saturday night.

And so I spent the whole of this cool rainy Saturday at home, not leaving the house until evening. Distant sounds of cars or the bells of streetcars seemed to demarcate the silence like frontier posts set far apart. This silence was emphasized, given an inner stress, by the humming of a water pipe or foot-steps on the floor above; and that day I bored into the silence like a tunnel-digger into the rock of a mountain-side. I was tense and irritable. I had realized that at this particular time it would do no good for me to be present at a "plenum" of our crowd—as this table-tennis tea had promised from the start to become. In spite of all, I was still fighting against my state of mind, although I had long known that it had nothing to do with "mania for gossip" or "too extended sympathies." Rather, it had to do with the by now inescapable realization that I had not fallen in with a group of eccentrics or what Nietzsche called "backwoodsmen," or into any other unusual company. Rather, that this group of mine was a pretty good cross section of what I might expect to find anywhere in this city.

While I paced back and forth in the room with my doubts— they followed me like a pack of silent hounds—the sun broke through the rain clouds. This was about noon. For a moment the sunlight struck the meadows which I could see from my window, then aimed higher and laid a pallid path across the room. Far beyond the trees in front of my house a red-and-yellow streetcar backed up the wide avenue. For a brief moment I saw this spot through the green of a treetop, and then it seemed to be sitting upon it. "Like one of those painted eggs we have at Eastertime," I thought.

The noiseless dogs abandoned their pursuit. For a few seconds I felt an impending clarity; I literally sensed it hanging above my head, a nameless prescience of the future.

The ray of sunlight faded away. Today I firmly believe that it was an anticipatory ray of that same light which shines for me now, as I look through or set down all these little tales, in Schlaggenberg's "last studio," under the slanting rafters and the bright skylight. In which the empty sky is framed.

Many are dead now, and many no longer in the country.

With the fading of the sunlight, the dogs began their silent pursuit once again. In self-defense I took a bottle of gin from behind the bookcase. Besides which my landlady appeared—I had informed her that I wished to eat at home—and with her came lunch.

Toward half-past five I began to change, since I would need to be in evening dress for the opera. The idea of having to present myself at the Siebenscheins' in such stiff-shirted formal attire was distasteful to me, since a man in full dress in a company of people in everyday clothes always stands out, or looks like a waiter. But I had no choice.

A glance out the window showed me that the lower-lying parts of the city, especially those toward the Danube, were concealed by a steadily thickening fog. However, the rain had stopped.

I went to the bathroom and began the usual proceedings with shaving soap, brush, and comb.

The unearthly, excessively fragrant coolness of the lavender water opened a door into the past. As if at the end, or rather the beginning, of a long succession of rooms there appeared a large nursery with white-enameled furniture in which I could just make out the nurse's outline in the glow of the table lamp. I also saw a house on one of the lakes in Salzkammergut, and that cook—a woman with very light curly hair—who always turned her face away when she was slaughtering poultry, and so ultimately cut her hand badly . . . For a few seconds all that came far closer to me, was far more tangible to my senses, than the porcelain, china, the faucets of the hot-water heater, or the glass shelf in front of me on which soap and shaving brush stood. In that straight succession of rooms—it ran perfectly straight along an axis, with nowhere a bend or turn—the midway point was oddly enough occupied by trenches and barracks. In fact there was a whole battle squadron parading by, still proudly mounted. And there also was that excellent cavalry sergeant Alois Gach. I was a young reserve officer at the time and liked to stay near Gach; he radiated bravery. Not a mere spit-and-polish bravery intended for military purposes but a firm calm fortitude which he must have possessed toward life in general. It was all one and the same, and the whole could be grasped all at once. Only now, nine years after the Great War, would I be able to step around a corner, truly and inwardly, and throw off this vision and acquire a new prospect. I felt, with a clarity I had never had before, that that campaign had not succeeded in marking a new epoch in my life. Nor had the collapse of the old Austrian Empire.

But now, without the roar of artillery, without the revolutionary shouts in the streets—only now a door closed within me, and another opened. Quietly, quietly.

A small pearl rolled across the glass shelf. It had fallen from my shirt; I had been trying to fasten it to my white shirt-front. Now it lay on the glass, gleaming with a subdued light. I had stood unmoving for a long time. And I had looked into my life as into the palm of a hand. Now for the first time I bade farewell to the small pleasant nursery at the beginning of that string of rooms. It had all been so perfectly proper: obedience at home, obedience in the office, or obedience as a soldier; I had been obeying laws which I myself had not created, and to which I had added nothing. The intact fragrance of a wholesomer world, which had remained whole within me, which still lived in me along with cool deep chambers of the little palace in the aristocratic quarter in the heart of the city—a fragrance which persisted in many things that I possessed, clung to leather suitcases, lingered in a saddle, almost imperceptibly inhabited a piece of furniture—the fragrance of that world rose up once again and moved away from me, behind a parting gulf. The straightness of the succession of rooms ceased, broke off abruptly.

I took the pearl and pressed its pin through the starched linen.

I knew that I had been on the point of becoming an elderly gentleman. But that danger was past now. A new past was growing up within me and around me, though as yet it was scarcely six months old.

Dusk had barely begun to fall when I stepped out onto the street. I had plenty of time to "drop in" at the party. That today of all days I would later be going to the opera struck me with a strangely melancholy force. Here in the streets of our suburb the easygoing animation of a Saturday evening prevailed; everyone still had a few purchases to make. Customers were jamming the food stores, which were still open and already illuminated; most of them were women with strained expressions, inasmuch as they had just begun considering their needs here in the store and were holding up the salespeople and the other buyers with their choosing and hesitating. In this respect they were a veritable horror to the bachelor, who knows what he wants before he enters and promptly produces from his pocket the slip of paper on which it is all noted down, so that no time will be wasted. For now in spite of all his own efficiency he must wait, while the woman before him engages in a protracted act of choice between radishes and carrots.

I let myself drift with the crowd, did not take the streetcar, but continued on foot. The fog was already beginning to be noticeable; darkness would be coming earlier than usual tonight.

When I finally did board the streetcar and we headed toward the parts of the city lower down toward the Danube, we rode deeper into the fog with every turn of the wheels. In the big square in front of the railroad station it was so thick that the illuminated spheres above the roadway or in front of a café seemed to be floating freely in the air.

Nevertheless, I instantly recognized the tall man crossing the square directly in front of me. It was undoubtedly Public Health Officer Dr. Schedik, Kajetan's father-in-law. I was on the point of catching up with him when he turned at the Siebenschein doorway and disappeared inside.

We met in front of the elevator. His destination was, in fact, the same as mine.

"Cheers!" I thought. How could this have happened?

We got out together and closed the elevator grille behind us.

The maid opened the door. Ferry and his wife both happened to be in the vestibule. The greetings were hearty, but when Frau Irma caught sight of old Schedik her cordiality became so excessive that it struck me as altogether vulgar. I understood at once that she had not expected him among her guests and was embarrassed at his running into Kajetan. Old Schedik went on into the apartment visibly pleased, but I hung back, since I had to stow a big white silk scarf—whose function was to protect my full-dress splendor—into the sleeve of my overcoat. And thus I overheard—Frau Irma seemed so beside herself that she simply forgot my presence—I overheard the following connubial dialogue at the front door.

"You invited him! You do have cuckoo ideas sometimes . . . What's got into you?"

"Why not? He makes things jollier . . . He's such a nice person."

"Sure, I know that. But are you such an idiot? With Schlaggenberg here . . .

"Oh well—they won't eat each other up."

I entered and greeted Frau Markbreiter, Hofrat Tlopatsch, Höpfner, Siegfried Markbreiter, Gyurkicz, Beppo Draxler, and all the others—all in a wild confusion. For I did have the impression of wild confusion as I entered, at least for the first moment. Fräulein Wiesinger smiled pleasantly, her whole turned-up little face lighting up behind her glasses. I went on through the room to where the big green tables stood abandoned, and came to the bull's-eyes. Here I paused in the open double door.

For something remarkable was going on. In the middle of a circle of people Stangeler was now standing bolt upright, gesticulating, and loudly speaking the following little piece: "All right, if life has to have a 'meaning' which is not simply taken for granted, then this meaning certainly will not be found in the facts which you are so concerned with—outside, in other words; it will certainly be found inside (he struck his chest lightly), and will consist in the fulfillment of one's proper destiny, as it was meant to be fulfilled from the beginning, but which takes years to catch up to . . . It will consist in filling out the lineaments of the shape that was imposed upon one, so that one does not lose oneself, drift, stumble sideways into realms of indifference, where the guiding words are: 'Let him fall!' and 'Worthless now!' and 'Ruin him!' . . . Yes, let him fall—into the bottomless pit . . . !"

Stangeler uttered these last words in a strikingly high voice with a falsetto intonation, which plainly indicated that wittingly or unwittingly he was imitating someone.

Schlaggenberg, who was seated directly opposite the doorway in which I stood, smiled and threw me an expressive look. Lasch, whose back was to me, observed this ocular interchange and whirled around swiftly. He looked at me and I at him, and this mutual staring lasted a long few seconds, during which we gnawed at one another with our eyes.

From then on I knew that I would have him as my adversary in a battle whose positions he knew exactly, and I altogether inadequately.

I had floundered my way into this struggle like that Roman Pontius into the Credo.

Enough—from now on I was an actual participant. I knew this quite clearly, even while Cornel and I were still crossing glances.

Meanwhile the others had noticed me, and the subsequent flurry of greetings temporarily effaced the crucial event of the evening. Lasch and I were the first to greet each other; he stood up, bowed slightly, and we shook hands. Quapp, whose gloved and bandaged hand I noticed, received an especially vigorous handshake, the sort I reserve for those in the best of health.

And when the captain, with his arm in the sling, extended his left hand to me, I did not trouble to ask what had happened to him. I no longer remember whether I had been privy to these little tricks beforehand. If not, I was easily able to guess. It would not have taken much intelligence. All one needed to know was that this whole affair had arisen out of an embarrassment, out of cowardice, out of a white lie; the whole party had sprung from a fraud.

I was still thinking this when Schlaggenberg pulled me aside, brought me a cognac, and began: "It is astonishing the way Stangeler has helped me to consolidate my own and thus also his position at Alliance."

"Yes," I said, "a seeing hen could not have found the corn with greater certainty."

"And yet he is not really blind. It's only that he has a technique of seeing indirectly, just as artillery men fired indirectly during the war. He sees around corners, as it were—but sees very well. However, my dear Herr von Geyrenhoff, leaving this aside, I want to inquire a little into your affairs, to push a little inquisition, to send a maelstrom or whirlwind of doubts around your esteemed person, to let the angelic voices sing a choir of inquiries . . ."

"I'm waiting!" I said, draining my glass. While he was speaking I had fallen into sudden and rather fundamental reflections, was brooding over my nephew, Doktor Körger, who stood fairly close to us.

For the circle around the bull's-eyes had more or less dispersed at my appearance, which had evidently interrupted a conversation past its climax and already exhausted. They were now all standing around in groups of two or three, chatting as Schlaggenberg and I were doing. Herzka alone resumed his place in the leather armchair with his legs outstretched before him. Some of the group trickled through the room with the green tables into the other room. Lasch had led that movement; probably he was going to see after his wife, for I had noticed immediately after my arrival that she was thoroughly drunk.

I was still looking at Doktor Körger, staring at the back of his fat bull neck and his bald pate. And so I saw, paradoxically and perhaps for the first time, his real and true face. Thus I also recognized that people can have their faces in various parts of the body, not necessarily only at the front of the head. Körger, for example—you simply had to see him walking away from you, betaking himself off; only then did you really see him as he was (he was at this moment just going out through the double door). His reverse was in essence the front of his personality, with those ramming rounded shoulders, sausage-shaped dangling limbs, bull neck in which future folds were already apparent as preliminary wrinkles . . . Yes, there was a man who certainly knew everything from the start. Who possessed a round sum of knowledge the way he possessed a round sum in the checkbook which at night he habitually drew from the rear pocket of his trousers and tossed onto the night table beside his bed; his key ring sailed clanking after it, and then he would kick off his shoes. What a humorous advantage over others such a man enjoyed, since no new acquaintance and no one he dealt with could possibly see him as he was until the last word was spoken and he had turned to go and was walking away . . .

My thoughts swung suddenly to Herr Trapp, whom I had never looked at quite so closely—but he came to mind just now for a reason. I already felt that at the point where that inner row of rooms broke off, many things must change, a whole perspective must be transformed. And in the new perspective the Körger sort of self-assurance no longer seemed desirable, nor even refreshing. My eyes flickered around the room.

They fell upon Stangeler. He was leaning against the opposite wall, hands in his trousers pockets.

Meanwhile Schlaggenberg was gabbling at me: "So you were tricking me after all, in a certain respect . . . That time in the autumn when we met again for the first time . . . you kept referring to that café where you also played bridge with the husbands, with the husbands of those maturer women, that is . . . And so you knew these Altwolfs and Starkbreiters . . . And now it comes out, now were looking straight into the horse's mouth . . . This Starkbreiter broad is out of the question, though, absolutely the wrong number. Can't really call her a broad at all . . ."

"But she could be called by her right name," I suggested.

"All right, all right—but now I beg you, I plead with you to tell me this: does Frau Steuermann also come here sometimes? There isn't one in your café who looks like her! I kept thinking all evening she'd turn up after all, because Starkbreiter herself appeared all of a sudden. And I'll bet you know all those women from here, don't you? And don't you know other circles where more of the same can be found? Tell me: is Frau Steuermann a visitor to this house? I don't want to ask Starkbreiter herself about her, not so directly. . . And tell me honestly, won't this Steuermann broad turn out to be a wrong number too? Won't she?"

"In your sense, Kajetan, she is certainly not a wrong number," I said wearily. "You are constantly accusing me of untruthfulness. But don't you understand yet that there are no 'other circles,' that I haven't tricked you—because the whole circle is one and the same? You ought to have found that out long ago, but you pretend to be stupider than you are. Or perhaps your horrible mania really has made an utter idiot out of you."

"That may be," he said quite calmly. "Nevertheless, everything is still going to be carried to extremes . . . if only for the sake of our book. But tell me again: doesn't Frau Steuermann ever come here?"

"No, so far as I know she does not. It's different with Frau Markbreiter, since she is her sister."

"I know that, I already know that."

"Incidentally, Kajetan, you ought to know that your father-in-law arrived at the same time I did."

"Really?" he said, but this information seemed not to disturb him in the least. "A great old fellow in his way . . ."

Doktor Körger came back from the games room and headed toward us. "Well, what do you say?" he appealed to me. "Haven't we served up a wonderful *pot-au-feu?*"

"Certainly," I replied. But suddenly bitterness rose up in me. "Incidentally, a great deal more is going to be served still. Much more important than *pot-au-feu*," I added with a malicious equivocation that made me astonished at myself. I suddenly realized that I had come much closer to the limit of my good temper than I had imagined. I left Doktor Körger abruptly and went through the double door into the room where the green tables stood. Schlaggenberg followed me.

The tables were by now no longer abandoned. At one of them our host stood, laughing, and with him Dr. Schedik. Ferry Siebenschein had obviously been trying to explain table tennis to his guest. But without waiting for the full explanation, the doctor promptly hit one of the balls, striking it with the paddle sideways and upward, either because he wished to joke or because he really thought that was the way to go about it.

"Why, doctor," Ferry exclaimed, spluttering with laughter, "it isn't a billiard ball! Besides which masse shots are forbidden even in the coffeehouses!" he added as the doctor held the paddle in a perfectly horizontal position.

Now they both noticed Kajetan and me.

The salutations between the old gentleman and Schlaggenberg were most easy and friendly. "How are you doing?" Dr. Schedik asked.

Siebenschein promptly gathered us together in a cordial unit: "Gentlemen, let's all four of us retreat to my den and have a glass of some marvelous old port a client presented me with yesterday," he said. He patted me lightly on the back: "I'm delighted that you found time to run up, Herr von Geyrenhoff. Come along, Doktor, and you, Herr von Schlaggenberg—we'll slip out without attracting attention . . ."

So we did. Our oddly assorted quartet moved with conspiratorial smoothness and swiftness through the large front room and through the vestibule to an extremely comfortable little room beyond, whose bookcases contained a huge collection of law books and decisions of the Supreme Court reaching back to the last century. From behind the books Herr Siebenschein produced a bottle, and then he took four small glasses from a wall cupboard with bull's-eye glass panes similar to the one in the other room.

Cigars were lit; we clinked glasses. "Pleasant place you have here," Dr. Schedik said to Ferry, and our host replied: "*Ad vestram!*" and raised his glass.

I must confess I felt very much at ease. The wine was of extraordinary quality.

"Is your work going well now?" old Schedik asked his ex-son-in-law. And Kajetan replied, as he always did to such questions, very modestly: "Oh, so-so."

Suddenly the door was opened and Frau Irma peered in through the crack for just a moment. But this time she did not remain mute (as she had earlier when she looked in on the

544

assemblage of Düsseldorfers in the vestibule). This cordial stag session pried her lips apart, though she said little. In fact only: "Well—I'll be!"

And she closed the door again. We smiled, finished our glasses, and returned to the rest of the company.

In any case it was time for me to be going.

Music was heard.

The green tables had been removed; a phonograph was playing against the back wall; and several couples were dancing.

I noticed that several new guests had meanwhile arrived. Among them was Frau Irma's second sister, slender Minna Glaser, the hotel "directress." In the doorway between the front room and the former ping-pong room two members of the Austrian aristocracy stood, each leaning against a doorpost. I knew both of them from my days in government service. They belonged, as I later discovered, to Titi Lasch and Eulenfeld's *troupeau*.

Schlaggenberg strode up to Frau Glaser, bowed, invited her to dance, and swung off with her.

This somewhat puzzling incident was the last I saw of the party. In the meanwhile I had quietly bidden good-by only to host and hostess, in order not to interfere with the fun. Outside, I concealed my stiff-shirted splendor under silk scarf and overcoat, deposited a silver coin for the maid in the visiting-card bowl, and descended the stairs.

Outside the front door, I stepped into the fog as into a wall.

My emotions were churning.

I thought of Kajetan's wife and that description of her inner life which she had once given to Schlaggenberg. In truth, I certainly did not, like Camy, feel my own inner self to be a tight

545

familiar room, closed on all sides, out of which nothing incomprehensible to myself, nothing altogether new to me, could ever possibly emerge and bear down upon me. If that were really the case with those people, then someday there would have to be a parting, and one without understanding. And without virtues and good qualities and without . . .

I strode rapidly along into the white cotton that completely surrounded me, and I imagined that I would have to continue walking in this utter isolation until I understood the world and all complex relations as clearly as I had understood my own affairs this evening back home—like the palm of a hand. Then these white walls around me would dissolve of their own accord.

However, the fog did diminish, since I was soon walking uphill, toward the center of the city, farther from the Danube Canal.

A taxi came slowly by. My time was growing short. I signaled to the driver.

No sooner had I stepped through the swinging doors into the lower lobby of the opera house than someone greeted me. I did not really recognize Herr von Frigori until he spoke my name. "My respects, Herr von Geyrenhoff—odd coincidence—your name has already come up this evening . . ."

"Really, how so?" I asked, altogether out of touch with the situation. I felt clumsy and heavy.

"Yes," he said, laughing, "Herr Levielle happened to mention your name and the fact that he knows you. That was at the West Station—I met him there. He's off to Paris again today."

"Is he?" I said in a friendly tone. Then I added: "I think we had better take our seats, Baron." I glanced at the people streaming into the lobby from all sides and now beginning to move more hastily. "Good evening, enjoy yourself . . ."

On the central staircase the last groups of box holders were already streaming upward, dividing at the top to left and right. The soft green runner on the steps completely absorbed the tramp of feet. Here you suddenly stepped into silence after the surge and haste of the lobby below, where even the whine of automobile motors in front of the opera house had been distinctly audible through the swinging doors, which were almost constantly aflutter. Amidst this silence I was once more swept by the annoyance I had felt before, only in an even stronger form. When Frau Ruthmayr invited me for the evening, she had mentioned that we would be alone. That meant that she had already been informed that Levielle, who usually was in her box on Saturdays, would be out of reach today. She had been informed like—like a wife to whom her husband has said: "I'll be coming at half-past six" or "I'll be going to Paris on May 14." That is, she was privy to Levielle's casual plans. As if she were his wife! For a few seconds my mind circled obsessively about this idea, and I clung to my annoyance—although the occurrence itself was really perfectly natural.

First tier, left, Number 12 . . . The attendant greeted me with considerable ceremony; he was an old man, a lackey of imperial days, well shaven and unimpeachably polite. I even imagine he may still have recognized me. Oddly enough his first name was Achilles . . .

I knocked and heard her voice within.

"Well, Herr von Geyrenhoff, high time," she said, laughing, as I entered. But the wide red-gold ring of the orchestra was still illuminated. I kissed her hand and slipped out of my coat. We sat right up against the railing. The choice atmosphere of the boxes and the rows of orchestra seats surrounded us, an atmosphere compounded of fifty years of velvet and lingering perfumes. The house filled; a temperate current down below flowed through the middle aisle and divided among the rows of seats . . .

Then the lights went out.

Abruptly, the prelude dominated the house.

I felt exposed, high up there, sheer against that railing. I was very far indeed from that state of mind requisite for attentive listening.

Then the curtain rose upon the golden room of Belvedere Palace, for that room had undoubtedly been the model for the decor then used in the first act of *Rosenkavalier*. With complicated tonal hues the instruments of the orchestra underpainted the voices of the singers, which at first sounded isolated, ringing out in sheer vacuum.

The crowded orchestra pit below us respired darkly, charged with restrained movement.

I heard virtually nothing. I sat looking above the stage, above the upper part of the curtain. I felt—with Frau Ruthmayr right beside me, no less—like an exposed figurehead installed on the prow of a ship that now began to sail forward slowly, with a heaving motion, rising and slanting away and above all this carrying both of us on ahead, over all this historic magnificence which we, so wrongly and so ridiculously, arrogated to ourselves, over this golden room regarded as pure artistic pleasure . . . No . . .

I breathed deeply. My chest expanded; the stiff linen crackled, arched; there was a barely perceptible little snap.

A small pearl rolled down in front of me upon the red velvet of the railing.

I stared obliquely across the orchestra pit.

"Stangeler," I whispered under my breath, half consciously.

"What is that?" Frau Ruthmayr asked softly.

I turned to her, looked full at her, and did not reply. Could I explain that, or anything else, at that moment?

PART TWO

CHAPTER 1

On the Open Road

I AWOKE next morning feeling as if I had been inwardly uncoupled, like a passenger who by some fantastic mischance has been forgotten in the compartment of a sleeping car; he awakens to find himself far out of town, alone in a wilderness of sidings, instead of at the railroad station. A summer day brightens the sky; through the window of the compartment he can look out upon underbrush and a gentle slope beyond the maze of tracks. He sees a sand pile and children playing, and beyond these the deceptive reverse side of a large strange city—the suburban avenues which disappear eventually into green countryside. In the distance he discerns many intelligible projections, such as factory chimneys, and another which seems unintelligible (later, when he knows the city, he passes it daily; it is an excessively rambling and dreary public building wearing a roof like a helmet). Our traveler, who is off the beaten track in every sense, feels tempted to linger for a while in the obtrusive silence that surrounds him here, for such a holiday is certainly not usual, to say the least; but there is something about such situations that prevents him from experiencing them in depth. He embellishes the silence only by washing his hands in the sink, wondering a bit at how the water continues to run properly from the taps. Then he prosaically prepares for departure and leaves this ponderous, now stationary place which already seems as familiar to him as his own house—descending with some difficulty because of the high step and his suitcase. And finally, standing beside his bag upon the cinders between the rails and ties, noting the sprouts of green coming up through the roadbed and considering his next steps, he begins to come to grips with the whole situation.

I, for my part, continued to lie in bed, but simultaneously I attempted to look out and up that gentle slope, the green meadow which then rose outside my windows (today it is partly built up, as I recently observed), and which had already become for me the accustomed foil to what I charitably called my thoughts. Today, however, my view was blocked, though not by any solid opaque object intruding crassly into empty space. Rather, there was a kind of jelly or gelatin that prevented the harmonious functioning of both eyes, which is essential to seeing. No doubt I myself was producing it, but it seemed to come from outside me. In a moment I became aware of it as the clearest and most comprehensible of leftovers, the essential symbol of the night before: the back of Körger's neck.

Only then did Lasch appear. What did I care about him? I looked sluggishly at the vision. It was quickly and easily driven out of the field of consciousness by the recollection of my supper after the opera with Frau Friederike Ruthmayr.

Still the back of my nephew's neck remained. It danced away from me, with sausage-shaped limbs dangling from it, and moved through all the scenes of a table-tennis five-o'clock tea at the Siebenscheins' which he himself had arranged for comic effect. Now the neck floated jellylike toward me again. I could not simply chase it away, blow it away, wave it away with a gesture. I had somehow something to do with it. It had already become a kind of authority which I myself had virtually recognized during my walk through the fog—overwhelmed and wearied as I had been by the whole stage-setting. That was the neck's power. I became conscious this morning, with gloomy uneasiness, of the dangers and personal afflictions of a new life—which I had entered not yesterday but months before.

And now I wanted to walk out on it again, although in the next moment I recognized that the impulse was a desire to make order, like my friend Schlaggenberg; that I was on the point of making such order and badly needed it . . . I promptly became absorbed in details. Those that thrust themselves most insistently into the foreground concerned Lasch. Lasch emerged into prominence. He took his place beside the neck. I had never yet seen him in such a position, but now I saw that he belonged there.

I had entered this particular blind alley voluntarily, and on a purely rational basis (so at least I thought), and now there was closing around me, above my head, the domed foliage of a new jungle. The thing had begun that day last year, at the beginning of winter, when I met Schlaggenberg on the path between the leafless vineyards. And now—now they were right, the whole thing was already a tasty, piquant *pot-au-feu;* not an ingredient was missing; in the person of Stangeler two altogether disparate threads crossed; I had acquired Lasch as an adversary; and in addition was racking my brains to determine what could really lie behind the patronage which Levielle extended to Kajetan (Cajétan) and René . . .

Up to a certain point, which at the moment I could not determine, this fundamental knowledge had still been with me. That is to say, at the very bottom I had known the origin of all these already existing facts, how they had been built up into facts and observed as such. Thus I had personally possessed the facts, had been able to see in every wisp the mass of thread-like roots which connected it to an unchanging central origin. For some time, however, this had no longer been the case. The process of growth seemed over, and the finished organism confronted me, whole and incomprehensible, at the same time wonderful, certainly something whose existence could not be controverted. There were a few protrusions upon this solid wall of facts, this shield that had come into being, within whose concavity there rested a deception that I could still faintly remember, as one remembers some almost forgotten origin of one's own—very vaguely. Today, however, it could no longer be denied that, say, Frau Ruthmayr's fortune might possibly be really in danger. Nor could the grotesqueness of last night's stew be denied. In short, here began the neck's altogether justified and legitimate power, not to say authority. Yesterday he had surrounded us with a collection of such facts, and we had been forced to recognize their existence. In fact, we had been driven so far that our original knowledge of the actual source of all these phenomena (as manufactures of the neck himself that is) had become much too dim to be used against him.

Having arrived at this point, however, I was able once more to get air under my wings, which had already become stuck to the viscous, gluey ground on which I had lighted. And strangely enough, it was a lane of sunlight pointing across the meadow outside my windows which roused within me the urge for independence, for withdrawal, for achieving a station several removes from all these details which were distorting my life. I wanted to go back to the time before all these complications, not in any sentimental sense, but the way an archer draws back his bowstring in order to give his arrow enough impetus to hit the mark.

I had to go back. I had again to find a point at which I could see straight down the succession of rooms that had opened before my mind's eye the day before. All of a sudden I was struggling to find that point, as if my life were at stake.

There was a knock at the door.

With many apologies the maid held out to me a polished tray on which there lay a letter. "You di'n't want to be 'sturbed yisterdy, sir, and then you wint out an' I di'n't have a chance to give you the ledder."

"It's all right, Maruschka," I said, speaking with the tip of my tongue, with pursed lips, "bring my breakfast, please." The envelope was of grayish-violet paper and its shape was longer and narrower than most of ours. It is inexplicable why I should have thought at this moment with perfect clarity: "Of course it's from Edouard Altschul, whom they want to kick out. 'Worthless now, let him fall!' Who else could it be?" The thought lay right beside the violet envelope on the silver tray. The stamp, I noted, was English. Whereupon I realized that the letter must be from Camy Schlaggenberg.

Here was a lifeline back, a rope that life was throwing to me in the nick of time. Far from being alarmed or fearing complications on Kajetan's account, or anything of the sort—I did not even think about the possible contents of the letter. Rather, as it lay there, violet-gray on silver, intrusion from another world—any other, but at least another—that very fact sufficed, that helped me. It was enough that I had known Camy longer than Kajetan, could glance back in memory to her girlhood out in Hietzing, could see the sun of earlier years shining as if through an opened aperture. My sense of well-being even struck me as disproportionate and unfounded. My morning tea arrived, and I began to read:

> *"Dear, kind Herr von Geyrenhoff,*
>
> You must forgive me for not having written to you before. But during the first weeks and months, after all that had happened, it was truly difficult for me to turn my thoughts back home, even so much as to write

an address like 'Vienna' and 'Austria.' I could not, and really did not dare, and just barely managed to summon up the courage to write to Papa once a week. The only purpose of this letter is to tell you that I shall probably come home for three weeks in the middle of July. Yes, that is how firm and cured I feel. I want to ask you expressly not to say anything to Kajetan. I must trust you in this respect, and I feel sure that I can. I am announcing my visit to you this early because I so very much want to see and talk to you, and am afraid you might take a trip to Italy or somewhere for the summer—all the more since you are no longer in the Ministry and therefore are free to do so. I shall surely not stay the entire three weeks in Vienna; you can understand that I would not want to do that. The most sensible course would be to go out to the country somewhere with Papa. I have a terrible longing to see him! The family I am staying with here—a middle-aged lady and her two married daughters, who happen to be here at the moment, although their homes are in America, very pretty and sweet, the elder is really indescribably beautiful to my eyes, at any rate—all of them want to go to some French seaside resort during the summer, after a trip to Paris with their husbands and the husbands' relatives from America. All this was settled by letter just a few days ago. Naturally I am supposed to go along, but can take a vacation for three weeks. It is even possible that the whole party will come with me to Munich, Salzburg, and Vienna—that depends on the Americans. In any case, I am coming . . . Now I ought to tell you about myself, how I am, and so on. I must say, I could scarcely have made a better choice. I am teaching the two little girls of the family piano, theory, music history, French, and a little German on the side. But I quickly obtained quite a few outside pupils; I am really completely independent, or could be any time I chose. Here I am simply treated as a member of the family, probably because of the almost instantaneous sympathy and intimacy that sprang up between myself and Mme Libesny. Such, then, are the outer circumstances of my present life. I have already indicated what my inner circumstances are. But I am not always so 'firm and cured.' Nowadays everything connected with Kajetan seems to me indescribably frightful, altogether incomprehensible, and—like something not pertaining to me at all. I really don't know whether I am expressing myself quite rightly. But my life has really been lost these last ten years; and now I've left all that behind me again . . . Do you ever think of Hietzing? You know, I did have a pleasant childhood and girlhood—and then that darkness! Here I have none but kind people around me, and the most delightful milieu; amusingly enough, there is even a Viennese chambermaid working for Mme Libesny, with the comical Bohemian name of Kakabsa. She looks after me with such sweet considerateness. I am writing this sitting at a darling little Empire desk and looking out between gauze curtains into the park by Albert Bridge where a few tiny birds are fluttering in the tops of the trees. I have this charming room to myself; it is square and very bright and still, everything green and white; I am very fond of it. In the corner is a lovely old chest with inlay work, comical pictures out of English history—Henry VIII looking like a village idiot, surrounded by all his murdered wives, each in a medallion. I have no cares and am all right. But often I feel such a fearful emptiness and weakness inside, as if I were made of thin glass. And you know, especially when everyone is so kind and good to me, or when I am alone—precisely when I am all right—which I usually am—I feel such a frightful pain. Because so late and so pallidly and as though I already belonged to the past I am finding myself again, becoming the way I should have been all along, the way my whole life was aimed, even as a child, and certainly as a girl. That was the way dear good Papa brought me up. And now—it is as if I were only a guest in the native land of my own personality, a belated guest who is allowed to sit for a while on the margin, on the margin of everything that is good and peaceful which I always loved so keenly. And you see, dear good Herr von Geyrenhoff, now I am really going off the deep end like a tearful old aunt . . . But oh, you will understand me. Everything is so terribly final, and I feel so glassy and cool, and sometimes it really seems to me that I hear something like an Aeolian harp singing . . ."

There it was, that was the breath of outside air that I needed. With an altogether naïve egotism, without any real sympathy for Camy, without spending a thought on her fate and Camy herself and her future and her unhappy love—I absorbed this letter with passionate greed, taking in the new and different background of a life that emerged from it. And if Kajetan's unhappy wife was contained at all in this inner activity of mine, it was only as a faded picture attached to my thoughts because she had provoked them. I promptly leaped over her and away from her. In the near future I was to have tea with Frau Ruthmayr; she would let me know when. That would take me far away from "our crowd." And I had also promised old Schedik yesterday to call on him soon. And what about the Stangelers? That fellow René was still contriving by a mute and stubborn magic to block me from seeing his family; as soon as he came on the scene they faded somehow into nonexistence. This now seemed to me very odd indeed. Yet it was so. And now as I rummaged around among the stocks of my imagination, seeking additional bases, I suddenly remembered my former department head of the days when I was a raw beginner in the civil service: Hofrat von Gürtzner-Gontard. But then, of course, the name had come up only the day before. At supper Frau Ruthmayr had mentioned the family. Perhaps I was even going to be meeting him at her house for tea; that was possible; I could no longer recall what she had said in regard to that. My supper with her the previous night had struck me as somehow incomprehensible. Where in the world did this tranquillity, this utter calm of hers, come from? Could she possibly be very stupid? I wondered, as if anxious not to fall under her influence—for she seemed to me in fact grand and wise! Possibly her eyes were a little oblique and slanting, the outer corners just a hint higher than the inner. That gave her beautiful, gentle face something—fishlike—yes, that was it. The way we will sometimes see, behind the glass wall of an aquarium, the head of a rare ornamental fish, mute, noble, sad, really profoundly benign. Old Schedik kept tropical fish. Yes, I would call on him. And telephone Gürtzner-Gontard . . . I suddenly realized my imperative need to talk, to talk myself out, and to be contradicted by someone who mattered, who could apply an impartial standard to my confusion. Perhaps I would be able to see Gürtzner-Gontard this very afternoon. But everything was receding now. As though the missing tone of a triad were completing the chord, the pointing path of light across the meadow outside the window penetrated deeply into me as I stood at the window looking long and quietly at it. Now the golden rod silently entered the room, rested upon the floor, and illuminated the brown and red weave of the rug.

The house in which the Gürtzner-Gontards lived was situated on the very square where "our crowd" had met before the outing to the country, the square dignified by the Palace of Justice. The latter building had not shown the slightest reaction to Grete Siebenschein's scornful criticism of it, nor to the somewhat vehement rebuttal by Herr Körger; it was quite unchanged and just as beautiful or ugly as it had been. At any rate it was indubitably huge.

The sun had not succeeded in consolidating its morning breakthrough. When I left home out in Döbling I had found the daylight once more dimmed. Spring hung with bated breath around the crisp red and white triangles in the tops of the chestnuts, hung in the moist silence which was animated and cut only now and then by a long bird-cry from the gardens. Ordinarily there would be many walkers at this time on a Sunday, but today, it was apparent, people were in fear of the impending rain, for the air was warm. By now I was extremely fond of my neighborhood out there in the suburb, in spite of the longer rides into the heart of the city which it involved. And today in particular there spoke from within me a mute appeal to all mute things, to the moist leaves behind the garden fences, to the bare asphalt, the entrance gates, the paths and corners: an appeal to them to open up, to tell me something, to confide some secret to me. For the messages borne by the silent world around us—by rooms, streets, smells, lights—are the most concentrated expression of the temper of life at any given time. Is it for or against us?

The entrance and the house stairs had remained familiar; I noted this with pleased surprise. (So much, I must add today, was I already unhinged, under the pressure of "our crowd," that with my sharpened instinct for self-preservation I seized upon the smallest, most insignificant factor that seemed to partake of stability.) Leaving my coat with the girl in the vestibule, I went on in and saw the old gentleman approaching me with slow but long strides. Behind him, outside, beyond the long windows, was suspended a view, complete to all its numberless details, like an antique tapestry: the background rendered in a muted dove-gray into which had been marshaled parts of the city, with their excess of precise and simultaneous statements about the form and outline of houses against the horizon. These suburbs which one saw from here—the Gontard apartment was on the top floor of the house—rose steeply uphill in their farther reaches, toward what is called "Mariahilf," and there they seemed to be piled in layers vertically atop one another.

Old Gürtzner-Gontard genially took me to task for not having called on him for so long, and likewise chided me quite bluntly for having retired prematurely on a pension. "You might have stuck it out until you were a ministerial councilor." When two persons say the same thing it is not the same, I thought, for Levielle had expressed himself in precisely the same terms when we met on the Graben on Annunciation Day. Moreover, Gürtzner-Gontard himself was one of those who ceased to take any pleasure in their desks at the Ministry very shortly after the introduction of republican institutions . . .

"Out in Döbling," I replied when he asked where I lived now.

"Oh yes, I did know that," he said. "You have a great many acquaintances out there too, haven't you? I heard that from your cousin Orkay; he came to see me only a few days ago." ("What is going on here behind my back?" I promptly thought suspiciously, and "At exactly how many weddings has Géza been dancing all at once?")

A minute later we were deep in talk about "our crowd."

What happened in this connection was very curious. In order to explain clearly what it was that disturbed me about this group of people, I had no choice—or could think of no better alternative—than to stress that ever-present conflict which has been more than sufficiently described. To stress it and perhaps to exaggerate it, if only because I thought that this sort of thing must be rather remote from Gürtzner-Gontard's sphere, so that I must first bring him somewhat closer to it and represent to him its importance—for what I wanted of him was precisely an opinion spoken from the perspective which he fortunately had.

But even as I spoke I realized that I lacked any real point of view. And at the same time I wanted to draw back as far as possible from the subject itself, back "to the time before all these complications." In my imagination that time took the form of a slanting lane of sunlight that dropped like a pointing finger out of the clouds and down to the meadow outside my windows. It dwelt within me in the form of a high entrance gate flanked by lilac bushes and a garden path beyond the gate winding off to one side. It fell away behind me like the bare, damply reflecting pavement of the streets; it accompanied this flight from behind a garden fence, with the leaves of shrubs glistening from rain. As I hied past, it opened as does a side street when we pass it by on the avenue, and then again as a straight row of rooms, toward the rear of which the light I sought shone only for a brief moment. It blew against my dark inner vision and brought the intact fragrance of a wholesomer world, cool deep chambers of little palaces in the aristocratic quarter in the heart of the city—a fragrance which still persisted in many things that I possessed, clung to leather suitcases, lingered in a saddle, almost imperceptibly inhabited a piece of furniture.

And while all this was going on in my mind, I talked—as though I were Eulenfeld or Schlaggenberg or even Körger himself. Not that I spoke so wildly and excitedly as those gentlemen, nor took such an intransigent position. But I tried in vain to turn my rudder against their current; I said things I did not want to say, with words which trapped me like thrown switches. I rode within the confinement of those rails, for all that I struggled to escape at every bend; I could not get off the tracks. Since at the moment I had no words of my own, and yet was under a compulsion to speak out, the words of others seized control of me. And so I nailed myself down upon one single point which was precisely the point I was trying to get past and beyond, in order to be able to examine it more closely, to determine its true nature. Every additional word I said only established more firmly a fundamental misunderstanding. This became all the worse when I virtually quoted thoughts I had had and spoke of the "parting" which would have to take place sooner or later, and "one without understanding . . . without virtues and good qualities . . ." That last was one of the products of the day before, and truly conditioned by the fog. "It cannot go on this way," I concluded, by that meaning nothing more nor less than my own oration. That was the last straw. I fell silent in astonishment, feeling as if I had fallen out of a window: on the first floor a moment before, and now lying flat on my face on the ground. I looked at the pattern of a very beautiful Turkish tapestry on the wall, and completely forgot the tea tray which the girl had put down at my side.

"You have become a revolutionary, my dear von Geyrenhoff," Gontard said, laughing. "Incidentally, a few days ago little Orkay said in substance about what you have said. But he is no revolutionary, only a *basci* as we in Vienna often call the Hungarians . . ." (So Géza had been making a track here before me and I had only traveled in his rut.)

"Why do you say that I am a revolutionary?" I protested.

"Come now, don't take it amiss, Geyrenhoff, but you evidently want to change the world some, if I understand you rightly. 'It cannot go on this way,' you say, referring to the circumstances you have described. That is what all revolutionaries say."

I took upon myself the yoke of the misunderstanding I had created. At the moment, in fact, I felt better about it, easier at heart. I even smiled, and held my peace. That I completely refrained from trying to set another person right about myself and my attitudes—this was, for me, something completely unusual. For a few moments this abnegation revealed to me, like something seen through a tiny slit, a new way to live, a new magic. Letting everything lie unchanged, just as it was, just as it happened to have fallen—and I had good reasons, no doubt!— enabled me to see everything much more distinctly. I struggled to find a way to generalize that attitude and knowledge, which seemed so illuminating and vital as well as an altogether new discovery for me.

"Don't you think so, Herr von Geyrenhoff?" Gontard asked, laughing and holding out his opened cigarette case to me.

"I suppose I must," I said. "And that naturally makes me thoughtful. Then you would say that anyone who wants to change anything about the world is a revolutionary?"

"I gather that this definition does not satisfy you. And you are right, it is somewhat faulty. If, for example, a farmer cuts down every second tree in a growing stand, so that the rest can develop better, he is not a revolutionary, although he does want to change an aspect of his environment and actually does so by physical intervention. Or a miller who displaces and regulates the flow of a stream in order to have a better supply of water for his 'race.' Such men are working, under the conditions set by nature, toward a specific end, and are reshaping those conditions only to reach that end in their particular case. Their actions do not signify a protest against the crowding growth of trees due to nature's overgenerous distribution of seed, or against the ways of unregulated streams. Neither the farmer nor the miller has the slightest desire to alter the course of nature itself; any such attitude would strike them as altogether abstract and ridiculous."

I studied him as he spoke, and thought, as I had done in the past, that there was something theological about him; he was a sacerdotal type. His tall slender frame, the gliding motions of his hands, the high eyebrows like the pointed arches of church windows, and the long nose between like a pillar on which these arches rested—the whole physique fitted the simple and rather preacher-like parables he had chosen. Rather less suitable to the sacerdotal type was a Turkish fez with a tassel which he wore on his close-cropped head, on which natural loss of hair had produced a small tonsure. Wearing this fez at home was, no doubt, in part a coquetting with old-fashioned, vulgar philistine habits; in part the old fellow may really have felt that his head was cold (the heat had been turned off, and winter lingered in these big high rooms; even outside the new season had not entirely won the day, and would be slow to penetrate such walls as these). But in the third place the fez actually commemorated the link with Turkey; his father had there attained the rank of bey or pasha, without having to renounce Christianity—a rare case, and all the more amazing because old Hamdi-Bey—that had been his Turkish name—represented the Porte as an envoy at foreign courts for many years. A good many precious Turkish objects hung in the room; they had been brought back by this old diplomat, who incidentally had not lived to be old in years—I mean only that he had belonged to the old school. Hamdi-Bey himself surveyed the room with the pale and strangely handsome face of a bold adventurer from the gold frame of a large portrait which hung above the desk.

As an extremely young officer he had deserted the Austrian army because he had been detailed to command an execution squad. The future Hamdi-Bey had taken the men he was supposed to shoot across the Turkish border. Many years later, if I remember rightly, an Imperial pardon brought an end to this ancient affair; an elderly relation of mine once told me about it. I believe the condemned men had been innocent, or at any rate not guilty of a capital crime. At any rate, Hamdi-Bey was once more free to set foot on Austrian soil, and had died in Vienna.

"Accordingly, it is generalization which makes the revolutionary, and you become one when you depart from the tangible and concrete," I said, replying to his rustic similes. I said this quite casually; the words seemed to remain right in the center of me, as in a monologue. I had acquired perspective through my contact with him, as though permeated by a dye in which he was steeped. And not he alone, but the whole environment here. I had been thinking of my psychological situation as extremely complicated and novel. Now I found myself unexpectedly confronted with a simplifying standard. For a moment I rebelled against it, demanding to be understood in all my complexity and asserting that such a standard would not do.

But on the whole I felt this simplification as good. Oddly, too, I was pleased by the fact that we seemed to have abandoned my original subject, on account of which I had come to him. In leaving it behind, we had left its narrow scope. While my gaze rested upon the portrait of the "old Turk," as the grandfather was called in the family, the wisdom of simple and unvarying standards began to dawn on me.

"My father, for example," Gontard remarked, as if his thoughts had been directed that way by my glance, for he too now looked up at the portrait, "was not a revolutionary but a mutineer and adventurer. He was certainly a person who remained within the sphere of the immediate and the concrete. He'd simply been unable to shoot those boys, and so he escaped with them. But in his later life he was by no means a notable opponent of militarism, or an enemy of the court-martial. He never wrote anything at all on the subject, and as you know he wrote and published quite a bit in his lifetime. At the Burgtheater, they still recall his dramas of Turkish history with more or less pleasure."

"Then you would define a revolutionary as someone who wants to change the general situation because of the impossibility or untenability of his own position," I said.

"Rather say: the fundaments of life in general. If enough people find themselves in the same impossible and untenable situation, the one who shows them a tempting way out—that is, a way to slip by the law of circumstances, and to do so moreover with moral exaltation—that person becomes a revolutionary leader. A person who has been unable to endure himself becomes a revolutionary; then it is others who have to endure him. The abandoned, highly concrete task of his own life, with which he has been unable to cope in a personal and individual fashion, has of course to be consigned to oblivion, and along with it the capacity for remembering in general, memory as the foundation of the personality. When that happens, the slogan is born; and that same hour marks the burial of immediacy, of concreteness, of quick measures, of direct relationship to inimical or friendly persons. Henceforth such relationships depend less upon physiognomical affinities and far more upon the involutions of a doctrine which has been installed more or less as a regulator of relationships among all human beings. That is why it so often happens that the revolutionary finds himself in a group of persons essentially hostile to him, who likewise have somewhere and at some time run away, after their own fashions, from their concrete immediacies. Perhaps that is the explanation of why in such groups murder goes the rounds like a bean-bag."

I regarded him with astonishment. He seemed to guess my thoughts.

"You are wondering," he went on, laughing, "where I could have learned all these things. Well, I'll give you the key shortly, the key to old Gürtzner's theories. But first you must listen to a bit more. I say further: in times of panic and of upheaval, standards are smashed. If someone does not bring his standard with him to a given situation into which he has fallen—his standard in regard to what is human and what is permissible within the limits of humanity and human dignity; if instead he leaves his standard lying somewhere behind him and merely borrows a standard from the given circumstances—this is, to say the least, the most terrible of betrayals, pretend all you like that this is an evidence of vitality and nimbleness of mind, of 'being close to real life,' or whatever else you may choose to call it. Once a man has left the most primitive stage of human life behind him, he does not like to perform this maneuver without some rationalization; both in individual and in collective life he will want to call in the aid of some sort of theory. That is the beginning of that 'revaluation of all values' which we underwent after 1918. The man who acts under the stress of circumstances, and in addition by the new standard which he has derived from those very circumstances, feels himself absolutely in the right, and so enjoys an exalted self-assurance. One might call this the euphoric stage of every revolution. Certainly it was present in all the revolutions of the past."

It seemed to me that meanwhile the intonation of his voice and the rhythm of his sentences had changed. The preachiness, the sacerdotal unctuousness, had almost entirely disappeared, been rubbed off, and a more granular layer was coming to the surface.

"That man becomes a revolutionary," he continued, "who from the beginning perceives realities too vaguely because of his own poor eyesight. For that reason realities lead in his mind the wretched, degenerate, unsubstantial existence of trivial facts. Thus none of them are for him definitive, none are unchangeable, none cannot be removed from their place, none are the expression of permanent laws which life always spontaneously follows. Rather, all realities seem to him in some way subject to improvement. Seen from such an angle, this life necessarily becomes only a question of arrangement, of proper rearrangement, rather, of rational classification, of will power, order (as he sees it), and efficiency. All revolutionary programs and persons necessarily have this rationalistic trait—which is one of their attractions—and suffer from the same ignorance of the stubbornness, the weight, the coercion of life's normal relationships, intellectual relationships included. Such persons have never felt the importance of these because all such normalities are parched and dead within them. Thus you might say that a priori abstraction is the mother of all revolutionaries. The

571

revolutionary flees from what is hardest for him to bear, the aimless variety of life; he seeks perfection, which in the world of his trivialities can at best mean completeness. The people as such may well rebel or revolt momentarily against unbearable oppression on the part of its rulers; but a people never becomes revolutionary precisely because it is too familiar with the stubbornness, the weight, the coercion of life's organic relationships. For that reason, when a people is incited to revolution, something else soon comes to the fore: its natural skepticism. With that, the euphoric stage of every revolution ends."

I took a cigarette, with an apology for having to smoke, and paced twice back and forth across the room. He merely nodded—the tassel of the fez swinging forward. I came to a stop at the window, and soon resumed. Outside, the spacious prospect was dissolving into the lavender-blue of beginning dusk. From the edge of the sidewalk down below, a street lamp arched its gray swan's neck as high as the second floor. And now suddenly the glass balloon flamed; but the light remained crushed inside it and seemed spindly, because it was still daylight. Everywhere I saw strings of street lights that had been switched on early. It was curious how, at an already vague point in the distance, there could be distinguished a green tree sticking up between gray houses like a brush or broom. But my gaze did not stay with the wider prospect; it dropped to the neck of the street lamp and lingered there. Listening, then, I returned to my armchair.

"The special relationship of youth to the revolutionary temper, its leaning toward that temper, also stems from vital weakness, at least within the comprehensive scheme I am outlining. Incidentally, this scheme did not originate with me. A young person simply refuses to enter life under the conditions offered to him. He does not even want to dirty his hands by

572

touching these conditions; he prefers to shut his eyes and hold his hands in front of his face, which oddly enough is the position of the child in the womb . . ."

He made a number of other remarks. Among them, the following: "Anyone who is somehow or somewhere too weak to live in the world as it happens to be will tend to 'idealize,' to absolutize a condition which ought to be as opposed to what actually is. No matter what political direction such an 'idealist' chooses, the longed-for condition will always have the same fundamental characteristic: that weakness, which is what it is all about, will be able to appear as strength. In a 'racially pure' society every blockhead and brute who has been unable to get anywhere will at least be able to achieve the rank of 'Aryan.' Take an 'idealist' headed in another direction: the proletarian. He too can distinguish himself by his very lowliness. In the one case you have an assumed community of race, in the other of class—it's the same difference. Classes can become races, and vice versa. That has already happened here. Here in Vienna a kind of race has developed out of a pure occupational class: that of concierge. Every Viennese knows that. It is the same in Paris. Enough. In both cases the self-assurance necessary to support weakness is drawn from a common fund, whether race-consciousness or class-consciousness. Both produce the same amount of animal warmth. But in the long run true community cannot rest upon a base that is held in common; it must rest upon what is not common, upon the singular, the personal, the noncommunicable qualities that each possesses; upon what makes him irreplaceable. Otherwise the community has no lasting quality and degenerates into commonness, crudeness, baseness. We are already on that path."

Toward the end I had been listening to him with my guard up, not to be too much swayed by his point of view. I tried reminding myself of his age, his origins, his past life within the ceremonious Hispanic-Burgundian hierarchy, and the similar spirit of a high ministerial post. Nevertheless there was much in his argument which I found piercing.

"And now, von Geyrenhoff," he added after a few moments of silence, "I must at last expose myself as a plagiarist. I am not the one who concocted all this. All these ideas came to me from a remarkable young historian."

"A book . . . ?" I asked hesitantly.

"No," he said, "a person. In this very room. You even know him. Young Stangeler."

"What!" I exclaimed, and my mouth literally, not figuratively, remained open in sheer astonishment for a moment.

"Yes, René Stangeler," he repeated. "A character in some work of Oscar Wilde's—Lord Henry Wotton in *Dorian Gray,* I think—remarks that he makes it a principle to learn only from young people. I have followed that policy in this case, for what this young man had to say impressed me, impressed me deeply, or I would scarcely have been able to repeat his line of reasoning. Of course I have not done so completely, for there was a good deal more to it, but the rest was too complicated for me."

It may seem laughable today when I set down what thought flashed to my mind after I received this more than surprising information. I thought of my hobby, which had developed a serious flaw only that morning and was now threatening to fall completely to pieces on me. Quite literally my thought was: "Now the whole chronicle is ruined. I've drawn him all wrong and completely missed the point." I do not want to suppress this detail—or any other, for that matter; for now, collating and working over these accounts, scenes, entrances, and exits extracted from such a variety of sources, I cannot help being deeply concerned about my own biographical veracity, and

574

feeling that I have no right to conceal, but rather must note precisely, what ideas I was plagued with at any given time. Incidentally, I make it a strict rule to quote precisely what was said of me or to me when one of my informants or collaborators refers directly to me by name—although sometimes this accuracy comes hard, especially in the case of Schlaggenberg, whose impudence sometimes knew no bounds (as we shall see).

"Do you know the Stangeler family?" Gontard asked.

"Yes," I replied. "Quite well, in fact. But I have not visited there for a long time."

"For my part," Gontard said while I was still hopping through various chapters of my chronicle as frantically as a frightened hen fluttering and cackling across the hen yard, "for my part I have been playing tarok with old Stangeler and a few other gentlemen every second or third Sunday for fifteen years. The others have been members of this group for even longer. I joined in 1912 or 1913, although I did not stay with it regularly. Our little gatherings were suspended during the war and the period immediately afterwards, of course."

"You old fool!" I suddenly said roughly to myself. "Do you by any chance think you can portray this slant-eyed individual through his opinions? A sackful of fleas! This must have been simply one of his extravagances, like so many of his other remarks for example, his Bolshevist interjections, or the comment he made to Neuberg in front of the library or somewhere: 'To be a professor and married strikes me as the height of gruesomeness.' He must have been improvising on this subject, and poor old Gürtzner-Gontard was simply taken in."

"As a result I've known the young man since he was seventeen or eighteen," he added.

"So have I. Perhaps longer. I used to go to dances at the Stangelers', and now and then went on picnics with the daughters. The parents rarely came along. Frau von Stangeler always made a point of not bothering the young people. Probably she was bothered a great deal during her own youth and missed the freedom which young people enjoy nowadays. I think she grew up at some petty court—the Duke of C.'s in Gmunden, if I remember rightly . . ."

"Aha—that is something I did not know!" he said, raising his index finger like a schoolmaster. Now that the conversation had taken this turn, he seemed exceedingly stimulated; I could feel that he was intimately concerned with all this social chat, had summoned up his forces; that in this realm he allowed himself a wee bit of self-importance (which I had altogether shed of late). Still it seemed that the old fellow also had a strong need to play down this trait, so that he rather went out of his way to treat all such subjects as trivial. He was more than casual when he mentioned some name or other—and he of course mixed with almost the entire aristocracy and former leaders of Austrian society and government. He was, and always had been, extremely careful about such name-dropping. But what remained in spite of the studied casualness was this always visible vivacity when such themes were struck.

"That must account for the relationship to the *primarius,* Dr. Hartknoch—he is one of our tarok partners, and the only one, incidentally, who is at all remarkable, aside from our host himself. There is also a second Doktor Hartknoch, a professor; he is the *primarius's* brother; the first Hartknoch was personal physician to the Duke of C. in Gmunden. I have an idea that the father of the two Hartknochs also held the same position. Mucki Langingen mentioned that to me not too long ago, and the Langingens used to see a good deal of the Duke there in Gmunden."

There came back to me the scene I had witnessed the night

before when I was on the point of leaving the Siebenschein apartment to go to the opera: the front room, and Schlaggenberg
going up to Frau Glaser and bowing slightly; back of that the
open double door filled with the flitting forms of dancing couples, and leaning against the doorjambs those two men, one
of whom old Gürtzner-Gontard had just mentioned. I saw it
all now, but from a great distance, and recalled with dim wonderment that I had somehow bridled at the presence of Count
Langingen and his companion in coat-of-arms at this party. As
if these gentlemen had been entrusted with property of mine
and were now handling it frivolously before my very eyes. Or
something of the sort. Recalling it, I felt mildly disturbed—and
yet at the same time I was relieved, as though a new but widening space were separating me from an entanglement from
which I was anxious to escape, as though an evil were passing
and my spirits were rising. Groping around among such emotions, I put forward a question as a mere screen: "You mean the
Count Langingen whose father was once Minister of Finance?"

"Yes, yes," Gürtzner-Gontard answered lightly. "But Mucki
won't climb to any such heights; he's not exactly a shining light.
On the other hand he collects antiques, and has a good nose
for them, so I've heard. He pokes around in the flea market. So
then you probably know our René Stangeler's sister, and the
whole family, I suppose? Frau Grauermann also? The consul's
wife?"

"Yes," I said, "Etelka, who was so much older than René—
she was married to Pista Grauermann, of course."

"Odd that she should have been given a Hungarian name
as a child," he remarked, "and later married a Hungarian
and lived in Budapest and even died there. Took her own life,
they say—right? Orkay used to visit the Grauermanns back in
Budapest, now and then. Or so he said."

Géza had never said a word to me about knowing the Grauermanns. But I was scarcely surprised. Our "bird Turul" was scarcely communicative; he listened, observed, and kept things to himself, just as he had kept to himself the fact that he knew Gürtzner-Gontard, called on him, and even discussed "our crowd" with him. In which conversations my name had no doubt come up and he would probably have learned that the old man had known me since my youth . . . Whereas I lived with our crowd; I had, as Frau Ruthmayr had chosen to phrase it, "gone to the artists, so to speak"; I was "living in a kind of colony out there, in that kind of set." But now that seemed on the point of coming to an end. I had wrapped around myself a shell of involvement, jokingly at first, but then in the further course of events I had unexpectedly come to regard it as the interior of the universe. Now this shell had to crack.

"Utterly outrageous!" I said to myself. "Deaf, dumb, and blind—living in a capsule. Our crowd! Sheer nonsense. And all that sort of thing!" But not only Frau Irma Siebenschein with her standing phrase entered my inner sermon, but I also heard a voice saying in a faintly impertinent tone: "If you please, Herr von Geyrenhoff, kindly dismount from your horse, your hobby-horse, for a change . . ." "Be still, Kajetan, and behave yourself. People are already looking at us . . ."

Aloud, I said: "If I may venture a guess in regard to the Stangelers, I might say that the father's strong choleric nature did not in itself have to operate oppressively, or let us say 'deformingly,' upon the individual development of his children . . . Rather, I would say that the mother's guidance may well have been the decisive factor. Her chief concern—I am trying to wrest something definite from my vague recollections—was to get on well with her husband. That sometimes meant an effort beyond her strength. But since this was her chief endeavor, everything else in the family had to fit in with it, as far as she was concerned. She loved and admired her husband boundlessly, and that was what mattered to her. She herself, the family, even a card party, absolutely everything, had to be arranged as far as lay within her power according to his principles—and you know how Herr von Stangeler spouts principles! Everything had to be organized so that nothing vexed him, so that he remained in good humor—for only then could she breathe easily and happily."

"Which, incidentally, seems to me quite as it should be," Gürtzner-Gontard replied quite emphatically. "You speak of an oppressive or 'deforming' influence that a father's strong nature might have upon the individual development of the children. Believe me, there isn't much to that. Of course as a bachelor without a family you cannot know. Besides you are really a revolutionary and will find your revolutionary motif in everything. But as a father, all one can do is to fill one's place decently in life and so provide a good example to one's children of all the principles one wants to transmit to them. It seems to me, von Geyrenhoff, that you don't like principles—that, by the way and confidentially speaking, is an unrevolutionary trait! But still and all, we can't do without principles entirely, especially when we have children. A decent upbringing does rest upon a few such principles, which to my mind are immutable and cannot be reformed or improved. They will always remain the same and have always been the same. There must be respect for parents, and a certain distance between parents and children is part of that. If that distance is too large—which is, however, better than its being too small—it attracts attention, of course . . . I noticed it in the case of the Stangelers too; I admit that; I'm not trying to make any great point of it. But in the nature of things the father is the natural center of the household, the paterfamilias . . ."

I was struck by the force with which he spoke, no longer with his normal easy urbanity, but as though he had to hold down a counterweight, as though his words were throwing up a wall around some blind spot within himself, which he was determined to keep blind; an area of unconditional resistance within him seemed to have been touched.

I spoke placatingly therefore: "Of course—there is no question about that."

We were silent for a little while. Equilibrium seemed to have been restored, the surface smoothed.

Gürtzner-Gontard took up his earlier theme: "Now as for Herr von Stangeler: anyone who has had one of these 'strong characters,' as they are called, in his family, whether as father, brother, son, or close friend, cannot simply get away—as strangers sooner or later will do. Neither will he ever succeed in assuming the clinical detachment necessary for dealing with such personalities. Try though he will, he will never be able to effect a reconquest of the territory lost through weakness of the nerves and constant retreats. In fact, he will in the end have to answer for this weakness of the nerves as his share in the crime; life's slow machinery of justice will never forgive him for his tendency to truckle under.

"The solitude of a man of stature is centripetal; the drive inward takes place too rapidly for friends—let alone the outside world—to follow. On the other hand, the loneliness of one of your powerful personalities is centrifugal; as it expands outward and others retreat before it, such a character is assailed by hapless longing, longing for a final struggle, a craving for someone to stand and fight without fearing the choler of a thwarted sovereign will. But there is longing also for love. This struggling soul thrusting ever outward toward the mirage of an exterior life craves a love that will take it as it is, not treat it with clinical detachment; a love that can reach over the parched, wasted, abandoned stretches of his nature and with gentle hand bring them to life again, turn over their soil, create a blooming garden. Nor would it be so untoward, what such a love would accomplish. Because love can transform rabid dogs into lambs and dragons into ducklings . . ."

There was considerable emotion in his voice. For the first time during the evening I felt that the old man was glad to be having this talk with me. The fact that I had taken note of certain psychological processes in him seemed to me almost embarrassing and indiscreet. The next moment, however, I changed my mind and decided that this keen-eyed attitude on my part was more dignified, compared to the large-pored sentimentality of a merely absorbent sponge—which, after all, promptly releases all the water it has taken in just as soon as it is squeezed.

But if I had been reassured for the moment in my stupidity, my memory, up to now completely absent, suddenly drew back like a hammer above an important point and smashed my new-found complacency. Why, of course—the old man was speaking of himself. Realization of this threw a new light upon all his attitudes; like a sharp beam striking the scene from the side, this light suddenly brought out the three-dimensional qualities of the situation. Gone was the shallow, superficial relief of academic discussion; instead I saw the deep somber crevices and the highlighted ridges of a vital, extremely personal affair. He had had two sons; he no longer had them; they were alive and well, but had fled the parental household, gone off on their own without a penny to their names. They were in the New World now, and life had proved them right; one of them had become a distinguished medical man, discoverer of an astonishing technique in cardiac surgery; the younger was instructor of political economy at Columbia University. The grandfather's blood in the boys had rebelled and proved its worth. Here was an abandoned old man. (In the heat of this discovery it did not occur to me that he still had his wife and daughters.) This, of course, was what he had been telling me—though he had sought to make distinctions by way of depersonalizing the story. Still he had clearly marked the positions of the conflict with spaces left blank here and there, or outlines boldly drawn in with sharp brush strokes. The resulting picture was a twilight genre-painting, misty and smoky in part, but still and all effectively composed with orderly rows of cirrus clouds converging upon the gleaming portal of insight that still stood wide open on the horizon.

Of course I said nothing. I tried quickly to reshuffle my ideas. But I failed. Random echoes drifted through my mind ("Living in a kind of colony out there, in that kind of set"—well, she was certainly right!). And then an impertinent voice said: "Losing your view of the whole, forgetting the most important things, already in difficulties after these few months! Well, forgive me for saying so, Herr von Geyrenhoff, but that's just the sort of thing that happens to the dilettante." Ah, I was tempted to make the familiar gesture of drawing my forefinger in a loop around the neck, with a slight upward extension, meaning plainly and bluntly: "Hang yourself, Schlaggenberg!" But what would the old gentleman, my former department head, have thought of such a performance on my part? Would he think I was answering his little speech that way?

He was already continuing: "Well, I was not the only one who quietly observed the Stangelers . . . I used sometimes to discuss the matter with mutual friends, and our notes more or less agreed. I found such discussions highly fruitful, inasmuch as they yielded certain insights . . ." He hesitated, but then added, half involuntarily and speaking more to himself than to me, but with the thought close enough to the surface to make his vocal cords throb slightly and produce the words: "Although too late."

That was the first small rift in his self-control this evening. For a single moment the sharp gusts of grief had blown aside the puffy smoke of speech, and I saw distinctly the repudiated fire, small, dim, red, painful.

That ideas grow from an emotional and all too personal starting point does not invalidate the results of a man's thinking—as many persons triumphantly imagine when they have discovered that emotional source. The ideas are not thereby discredited. Rather they take on the greater reality as a form of self-conquest; the private and specific cause has all the potentiality of a bursting seed-pod. Thinking pure and simple exists no more than does "absolute music," which cultivated people may like to talk about but composers never. Now I knew what Gürtzner-Gontard saw in those card parties, why he kept on with them, and above all, what his new association with René Stangeler basically signified. All these activities were nothing but a secret, incessant dialogue with errors which (he was convinced) he had committed and could no longer make good.

Perceiving this, I could not any longer beat a retreat from the whole question and leave him alone with his anguish. No, that would have been impossible. I no longer hunted for the proper approach, though I was lucky to hit on a half-casual tone when I asked, after an appropriate pause: "Do you hear from your sons, sir?"

"Yes," he said. "The boys are good about writing. Not to me, to Mama." His shoulders twitched almost imperceptibly. "Franz—he is the the older one, the doctor—is married now.

Quite well, it seems. Pris is her name. The family name always escapes me. But it isn't English. Bohemian or Moravian or Viennese. Nice of you to ask me about the boys, von Geyrenhoff. *Je vous en remercie.*"

He spoke these last, French words softly, and yet they held more stress than everything that had come before. He was a master of manner as well as manners. And I suppose I had lost some of both; among "our crowd"—"living in a kind of colony out there, in that kind of set . . ." Still and all, I had struck the right note this time, perhaps from the pressure of having to sympathize. Possibly in the past I had not yielded to such pressures. Now, however, after my habituation to our crowd—that clique certainly talked freely enough about everything. Was I then already deriving my standards from them? My God! . . . All this went on in my mind within a few short moments, even while he was still murmuring, "*Je vous en remercie.*" He patted me twice, very lightly, on the back of my hand. It was as though this tapping were a form of praise.

Twenty minutes later I stood on the street. It seemed like an open road, a line of gleaming asphalt that appeared to be running past me. Some settled moisture made it as shiny as fish skin.

In the vestibule of the apartment, as he was bidding me good-by—Gürtzner-Gontard had insisted on showing me out himself—a door had opened and a girl had emerged from her room. My host introduced her as Renata. She was about sixteen.

It was the selfsame person who had seemed to be standing beside Schlaggenberg on the ridge of the hill and who had, in descending, split our whole party in two by passing through the middle of us.

She was the same person who had again passed by us later

on the same outing, after Stangeler's "inspired" description of the conversation between Levielle and Lasch whose climax had entered his consciousness between dream and sleep. She was the same—I knew it now, in spite of Gyurkicz's having maintained the opposite at the time.

By now a third point established the triangle firmly on its base: she was the same girl also who had crossed our trail that time we went skiing, that girl who came by on her skis, with her jacket off and wearing a blue, short-sleeved blouse. It was she. My eye had somehow lingered on her that time during our spring outing, below the ridge of the hill, as well as later beside the gray rickety benches under the still mild sun, when Stangeler was telling his dream.

Compared to all of this, it seemed only the last straw that as I descended the stairs I caught sight of Dr. Schedik's name on a doorbell. Kajetan's father-in-law lived in this house. At the moment I could not recall whether I had known this previously and forgotten it or was just discovering the fact. Enough. Seeking to escape from our crowd and its complications, I had come to call on Gürtzner-Gontard, only to land in the midst of the hornets' nest. So, at any rate, it struck me, quite aside from the revelation of the intimacy between René and my former department head. For this last seemed to be altogether accidental and therefore unimportant. The girl on the ridge, on the other hand, I took to be a far more central and meaningful discovery. (For I completely forgot what the basis for René's association with my former superior was.) With all this in mind I still stood under the gateway of the building as if it were a marquee—as if this big gateway had a projecting roof composed of all my contradictory thoughts. For some moments the visit appeared to me an outright mistake. I wanted to go, but stood where I was. Floating in my mind was the figure of speech the old gentleman had used: of the embryo pressing its hands over its eyes. I saw this fetus before me, about its natural size; it hovered back of my thoughts like a rising and falling spot of color on the inner eyelid when our eyes are closed.

CHAPTER 2

On the Other Shore

IN THE house where the Siebenscheins lived, the apartment opposite theirs was occupied by Professor of Anatomy Storch and his family. Storch was the head of one of the University's institutes. A middle-sized man with dark hair and a brown complexion, he was one of the liveliest persons in Vienna: handsome, cosmopolitan, a tremendous worker, a career man. He was of the type who have a kind of moat between themselves and their many good qualities—the moat consisting of their knowledge of those qualities. But this moat did not go so deep that it separated and isolated the core of the personality. There was a thoroughly solid foundation down below. Further up, within the moat, there was a lively display of versatile talent: Storch at the microscope, in the lecture room, during consultations, in all his many departments, and above all Storch playing up to women. Where women were concerned, the qualities danced about like the sparkling sections of a suit of armor, united by smoothly functioning joints.

His wife, Kathe, was just a wife, but in the best sense of the word; by no means unattractive. She was tall, slender, good-looking, and looked amazingly young, so that wandering-witted René Stangeler had once addressed her as "Fräulein"—he often failed to recognize people he had met, or assigned them to the wrong category. Besides which, Frau Professor Storch was seldom seen. She was an invalid. In the end she died young, probably of cancer.

587

In the dim vestibule of the Siebenschein apartment, however, René had mistaken Frau Storch for her younger daughter, whose name was Felicitas but who was commonly called Fella. Fella was seventeen at the time and was ever so much smaller than her mother. She was an insect-sized little article, extraordinarily pert.

Professor Storch was highly amused by the mistake when he heard of it, and did not fail to congratulate his wife.

Fella's older sister was called Dolly. She was a little sultaness, a dark oriental beauty. A sweet small head, and a somewhat too developed body for a young girl.

Fella, however, was slender and blonde like her mother.

There was a certain amount of social intercourse between the Storchs and the Siebenscheins.

Stangeler had something of a shock once when he came upon the professor in the midst of a lively conversation with Grete in her room. "*Servus*," Oskar Storch said to René. He shook hands with him and went on with what he was saying. He had the habit of pacing back and forth as he talked. "Fifty per cent of your mother's problems have nothing to do with her character. It's all a result of the menopause. You must keep that in mind."

"All?" Grete asked.

"I said '50 per cent.' Of course not all," the professor answered easily. "Incidentally, she oughtn't to take too many drugs. But of course old Schedik only gives her harmless stuff. He understands perfectly. Delightful man. I saw him yesterday. So long, Gretel, I must be going. *Servus*." And he vanished.

Stangeler felt an astonishment that bordered on envy. "How you two talk with each other!" he said under his breath.

"Well, why not, my sweet?" she replied, laughing.

"He more or less belongs to—you might call it our fathers'

generation. And he talks with you absolutely . . . *d'egal a egal*. I must say, I find that wonderful. To me that sort of thing opens up an entirely new prospect somehow."

"Magnificent," she said. "My sweet is simply a Stone Age man." She put her arms around his neck.

"His wife is very beautiful," René said. "She has something in common with you. Purity, austerity."

"I hope I will not be as unhappy as she."

"Unhappy?"

"He has so many other women. He very rarely goes to her. She told me so once."

"Goes to her," Stangeler said under his breath. "Odd . . ."

"What is odd now?" she exclaimed, laughing again.

"Well . . . goes to her, goes to her. What does he go to her for . . . ?"

"What would he be going to her for!"

René had fallen into one of those states of idiocy peculiar to him; they usually came over him when he was mulling over the meaning of some word. Oddly enough, Grete Siebenschein never seemed to be annoyed with him when he became like this.

"You're staying to dinner," she said.

"I would like to go to you," he said abruptly.

"After dinner," she replied smoothly. "The folks are going out." He was stunned. It was a sweet poison that pierced its way deep into him: her awareness and her willingness.

Trix K. and Fella Storch had become more closely acquainted only after Trix's mother had her accident and was away in Munich at Professor Habermann's institute. Throughout that period the Storch daughters and Grete Siebenschein often went upstairs together to visit Trix.

It is only by exception that they can be thus grouped together as the Storch daughters. For otherwise the girls never went anywhere together. Yet they slept in the same room and attended the same Gymnasium, though in different classes. Their lives, however, ran along altogether separate tracks, among quite different circles. Fella's accorded perfectly with the company that Professor and Frau Storch would have wished for her from the educational and social points of view. Moreover, such genteel companionship suited Fella's frigidity. For her mother's coolness had degenerated into frigidity in her. The elder sister, Dolly, went other ways entirely.

But during this summer and autumn of 1926 it turned out that they appeared together, and perhaps this was the doing of Trix K., who always made a point of inviting Fella's sister. It is questionable whether she did so only out of politeness. Possibly Trix wanted Dolly for protection against Fella, toward whom she felt a nervous affection mingled with anxiety: an emotion quite new to her.

A very small, extremely low-slung sports car stopped in front of the house. Two long impudent blasts of the horn drew Dolly's dark head to the window. With some difficulty her friend Oki Leucht clambered out of the low vehicle, a hulking young fellow, six feet two, with puffy Negroid lips. Then he entered the house.

The small car stood alone at the curb.

It was late afternoon on a day in the latter part of summer.

The crowded streets were weightlessly floating away in the flood of sunlight. Almost a shame in such weather to stay in a room if it were not absolutely necessary.

The bell rang in the apartment. Trix had to go to the door. The maid was out.

Trix had to go to the door. With an effort, she tore herself away from Fella, with whom she had been sitting where her mother used to like to take her breakfast—by the fireplace, although there was no longer any fire there this late in the year. Suddenly Trix saw her mother sitting there. With two legs, very lovely legs, uncovered because she was wearing a skirt much too short for a mature woman. She saw her mother sitting there just as one sees a deceased person in one's mind.

Trix felt grief. Plainly she could not explain to Fella what her mother's accident meant to her. She felt grief now not because of the accident but because of Fella's wholly different nature.

After the bell had rung, Trix stood motionless for a few moments.

There sat Fella like a strange butterfly that had fluttered to rest.

From the side street, which ran down to the Danube Canal came the shouts of boys at play: a noise appropriate to the season.

The bell had rung.

A year before everything had been different.

Now Fella sat there.

There are times that form circles, just as in a mass of cigarette smoke an unexpected ring will suddenly float through the air.

Trix went to the door.

Fella never worried about her mother's illness. That was Papa's affair, she asserted, "especially since he's a doctor."

"Yes, of course," Trix could only reply.

Now Dolly and Oki Leucht had joined them, and somewhat later Hubert arrived. However, he did not ring; he opened the door with his own key.

Trix's brother Hubert was an extremely handsome boy. He had his mother's face. In fact his whole personality seemed to be a contraction of Frau Mary's into the leanness and firmness of a slim youth. Some sepia brown appeared to have found its way into the picture, although this particular tone was absent from the white-skinned, dark Titian-red mother. At twelve or thirteen, perhaps, before Mary became a woman, she may well have been inwardly constituted as her son now outwardly and actually appeared. He was evidently one of Mary's possibilities: her potentiality, say, for becoming a slender Arab girl, a daughter of the desert, instead of the womanly Rachel, the fruit bursting with sweetness, which she had actually become.

Now there were five of them in the living room, sitting or standing. Oki had brought a bottle of curaçao with him.

Whenever she had Fella with her, Trix found that the arrival of her brother created an entirely new situation. One important factor was that Fella was "older" than Hubert—by all of three months. Did Trix fleetingly imagine that she had to protect her brother? But no, her intelligence was much too clear to condone such rapid little falsehoods. Rather, she felt penetrated down to the soft parts of the soul by the taproot of jealousy. This was unsparingly brought out every time Fella addressed Hubert, which she did with an affectionate overtone that was otherwise never present in her voice.

Actually, Fella had no feelings for Hubert at all. Once, for a whim, she had decided to turn the boy's head, and so she kept at it. Trix knew that too. But what she did not know was that no one could turn Hubert's head. For he had none, in any real sense; he possessed only a very handsome façade which concealed a correctly functioning apparatus. There was no back to the head, so to speak.

Trix could not imagine such a state of affairs. She only believed her brother to be extremely serious—because he seldom laughed and avoided all exaggeration. Of Fella it may be said that although she had hit upon the wrong person altogether for her experiment in head-turning, this was probably happening to her for the first time, and it might well be for the last time as well. She was not a girl to ignore or misunderstand her experiences.

Now, however, she smiled at Hubert, looking exceedingly droll, pert, elfin, blonde; she was wearing a short, lavender-blue dress.

Dolly and Leucht were drinking seriously. The matter already had some importance for the two of them; they were more or less tanking up. Leucht even ran down to a tavern and came back with soda water. He also brought straws which he had managed to pick up somewhere in spite of his hurry. The drinks tasted better that way. Aside from Dolly and Leucht, however, no one was very fond of the strong orange-flavored gin (Captain Eulenfeld thought this beverage altogether preposterous and called it an "outrageous prettifying of honest hooch").

Oki Leucht and Dolly in themselves constituted a bridge between this newly forming circle of young people around Trix and the captain's gang, the *troupeau*—also known as "the Düsseldorfers." Oki and Dolly both belonged to it. And the captain himself was destined to appear on the horizon in this new group, though much later on . . . Trix knew virtually nothing about the *troupeau;* at most she had heard a few stray hints from Grete Siebenschein, since Grete's sister, Titi, had stuck with her old crowd even after her marriage to Cornel Lasch. Cornel made no objections. He had too much familiarity with his wife's character and was far too prudent to commit any such folly; he preferred to guide Titi by the long reins of his bank account.

Fella had no connection at all with the *troupeau*. Not so much because she was so very young; Dolly would have been glad to take her sister along on one of their frolics. When the professor was away at some congress in Munich or Paris and Frau Kathe was in the country—for the girls' mother was fond of withdrawing to the country, and of late had taken to doing so more and more—Fella would sometimes encounter members of the *troupeau* at the apartment. All the "*troupistes*" thought very highly of her. But she completely lacked an affinity for the group. With unsparing clarity she saw the parched and sterile nature of this particular pasture; nothing would ever grow in it for her. She also saw her older sister pursuing paths that were in her opinion altogether false. But she did not care.

Trix would not have understood this indifference. But she did understand Fella's lack of affinity for the *troupeau*; and the fact aroused warm feelings of happiness within her. That lack of affinity, in fact, was for Trix one of Fella's attractions—although Trix was by no means conscious of this.

Trix had gone into the kitchen to make the coffee, since Marie had not yet returned. The successive arrivals of Dolly and Leucht, and especially of Hubert, had made it possible for her to tear herself away from Fella. Alone with her friend, she would promptly have sunk into lethargy and dazed absorption in contemplation of her.

On the gas stove the sugar water began to boil in an over-sized Turkish coffeepot with curved spout. This method of preparing coffee had been adopted during the First World War, as a result of much contact with Austria's allies of the Ottoman Empire. Along with it, however, people had not adopted the

594

Turks' extreme moderation in the enjoyment of coffee; they take the beverage only in tiny quantities, and prepare it separately for each person.

Trix stirred in the ground coffee and let the brown foam boil up three times, between times tapping the pot gently against the stove to make the liquid fall again. Then she set the pot aside and covered it with a copper lid surmounted by a wooden knob. She stood by the stove, rubbing the finger tips of her right hand against one another until she realized that her fingers were sticky and adhered slightly to one another.

This was one of the things Trix could not endure. She was never able to go on with her work if her fingers became the least bit gluey; if, for example, they stuck to her fountain pen just a little, for whatever reason. Trix had to go wash her hands at once.

The stickiness probably came from the sugar water; she must somehow have touched it.

She went into the bathroom. Fella came in immediately after her.

They washed their hands together in the washbowl, and Trix saw Fella's thin forearms and hands moving rapidly alongside her own over the white porcelain, like wriggling animals. Trix dried herself, and since Fella lingered in front of the mirror, Trix sat down on a small low white chair which stood next to the washbowl—it dated back to her mother's childhood. Fella fixed her hair; she had brought her bag in with her and taken out her own small comb and the other apparatus necessary for the refurbishment of females . . . She stepped to one side, looked at her profile in the mirror, and in so doing came close to Trix's head. Trix had all her toilette things laid out here in the bathroom, and it would have been natural for Fella to have used these rather than to take hers from her own bag.

Trix thought this with an altogether disproportionate intensity; it was too much, added to an existing overbalance in her; it was too much; she bowed her head slightly under this burden. Fractions of an inch still intervened between her and Fella's hip in the lavender-blue dress. But then Trix's red-blonde head lay against it. Fella quietly turned a little toward Trix, her hand already in the reddish hair; and suddenly the face underneath that hair pressed hard against Fella, burrowed in. Fella held her ground with a kind of circumspection, as though she were determined not to disturb what was happening within Trix. Even the gentle movement with which she gradually hitched up the lavender-blue dress and pulled and pushed away something underneath, had an altogether circumspect quality Trix felt something that was absolutely new to her: as though she were entering behind Fella's exterior, before Fella's face, as if she were entering into Fella herself. But the fragrance into which she pressed deeply now suddenly released so enormous a process that she melted and dissolved away from the belt down, it was as though an overpowering hand completely enclosed her small belly, her small innards, turning all to a liquid flow. She sagged, collapsed. Fella remained almost immobile. Cautiously some garment was drawn back and the skirt fell.

The doorbell rang. Immediately afterwards they heard footsteps—Dolly going to the door. A male voice could be heard. Fella, leaning backwards, looked at the bolt once more. She had closed it earlier.

The ringing of the doorbell alarmed the girls in the bathroom only a little. Trix stood up, calmly embraced Fella, and kissed her on the mouth. Now it was plain what stuff Trix was made of! No silly flutteriness in the face of the completely incomprehensible thing that had happened to her. She accepted it; it had happened to her; something had come as close to her as Fella's lavender-blue hip. It had come to that. This was "the seriousness of life."

They straightened themselves out in front of the mirror. They left the bathroom. From the living room came sounds of English dance music. That meant it must have been Bill Frühwald who had rung while Fella and Trix were in the bathroom. Sure enough, he was seated in front of the baby grand with his back to the door, so that he did not at once notice Trix and Fella. Then he broke off, turned around, stood up, and went toward them: a tall young man in wide trousers and thick-soled shoes, with an overhanging thick brush mustache, but the beginning of receding hair above his forehead. There was something relaxed in his manner; he seemed to feel at home inside his skin. His face was roundish and rather puffy, with protrusions here and there—on the whole too large. It was rather like Oki Leucht's, but lacked the pronounced Negroid lips and the rough-and-tough quality altogether. Bill had no such tendencies. He came from a good family, was the son of a well-known Viennese architect. Bill, too, was a *"troupiste."*

Something entirely unforeseen was taking place one floor below in the apartment house. There René Stangeler sat in Grete Siebenschein's room weaving sentences for an Alliance newspaper. This time, however, he had an ear cocked for the doorbell. He was alone in the apartment. Everyone had gone out, including Grete. Irma, however, who always took delight in assigning complicated commissions, had this time succeeded in placing one with René. It was this way: she really ought to stay home, since Frau Storch would be dropping by, though only to bring her two boxes of a special kind of cake from town, which she had promised to leave for her; you could get this cake only at a single baker in town, and Frau Storch happened to be going downtown to shop that afternoon and would be in that very neighborhood and on that very street because of some errands of her own. And all that sort of thing. Now if Frau Storch had purchased and brought back with her the brand of cake which had a blue wrapper, she, Frau Siebenschein, wanted René to ask Frau Storch to please let her have three packages this time. But if the wrappers were red, then only two as usual. "Do you understand me, René? Yes! I'll settle up later with Frau Storch. And I promised her some homemade bake stuffs—she'll have them by tomorrow noon at the latest. And kindly listen to me when I tell you something. I can talk my head off—and all that sort of thing." She had already explained everything to Frau Storch and told her that she had to go out to Mödling with her husband that afternoon to call on an old lady who had suddenly fallen seriously ill. Frau Storch, if she came at all, would not expect her to be there. Though she, Frau Siebenschein, might drop back home again with a bag of pistachio nuts for her baking.

Very well. But now Frau Irma was happily gone and it was quiet, had been for some time. Stangeler was writing the following interesting sentences:

> "Joan's life provides one of those rare examples of clairvoyance which can be checked and verified by internal evidence. Thus, for example, at one o'clock in the afternoon of May 7, 1429, during the battle of Orleans, Joan was wounded by an arrow between her throat and shoulder. Now a letter of April 22 of that year has come down to us, written by a Fleming named Rotselaer to Duke Philip of Brabant; in it Rotselaer reports that he had heard of a remark by *la Pucelle* that she would be

598

wounded by an arrow at Orleans but not fatally. When this event which she had foretold did indeed take place, the scribe in the audit office in Brussels took out the letter and made a marginal note next to this passage. Thus the matter has come down to us."

Whereupon the doorbell rang.

Frau Storch, however, did not merely hand the expected package in at the door, but began some explanation and allowed herself to be bowed into the vestibule by René. She was loaded down with all her purchases and had apparently not yet gone to her own apartment. It seemed the blue cakes were there, but only two boxes, there had not been any more, and in the shop everything had been packed together, her own orders and the blue cakes for Frau Irma, and some other things that she had bought elsewhere, including a bag of pistachio nuts that Frau Irma would need for the baking she was so obligingly going to undertake for her . . . All that would have to be sorted out now . . . Stangeler bowed her on, and Frau Storch preceded him, and at last they stood in Grete's room.

"Do you work here?" Kathe Storch asked.

"Yes," René replied. "Grete won't be coming until after eight. It's so very nice and quiet here, no one home, even the maid is gone; she had to go out to Mödling with them to carry a basket of things. At home, where I have my room, there's a baby in the adjoining room right now . . . It disturbs me . . . So that Grete sometimes lets me have her room when she's going to be away for any length of time . . ."

He had simply invented that item about the baby on the spur of the moment, to save complicated explanations. (We know the true situation from his conversation on this point with Captain Eulenfeld—though that took place much later, in the early spring of 1927.) He went on to say that the second floor of his parents' house, where his room was situated, had formerly been inhabited by his favorite sister, Asta, and her husband, the architect Haupt. They had moved out not long before, he said, and now distant relatives of his mother had taken over this apartment. They had agreed that René would be able to keep his room; but unfortunately they were now trying to make it as unpleasant for him as possible, to induce him to leave . . . This was approximately the truth, as we know; those disagreements which he related later to Eulenfeld were already beginning. Stangeler, too, now observed that he had come out with the truth—rather like a swimmer who is approaching the shore and suddenly strikes bottom with one of his strokes. Whereupon he wondered at his fictitious baby; it had been altogether unnecessary.

But beneath all this talk, René was conscious of an increasing delight in this Frau Kathe Storch, with whom he had been thrown together for the first time, practically speaking. And while he was attempting to explain his presence so that it seemed both sensible and decorous, his effort was really directed (by a curious process comparable to mimicry in animals) and intensified by the desire not to offend this Frau Storch, whom he was much taken with. He did not want to appear incomprehensible or alien to her.

He was not. She did not even listen closely to what he was saying with such modesty and fluency. She simply felt that she had no particular desire to leave at once with her mission accomplished. She had laid aside her bundles and parcels. But instead of opening the bakery package, she stepped up to Grete's desk and looked at Stangeler's manuscript. She read without more ado the sentences he had just written—René's handwriting was neat, and people without literary habits are not the least shy about reading a manuscript lying open on a table.

"How curious," she said.

"Do you find it interesting, Frau Storch?"

"Oh yes. And your style is so flowing."

This last remark struck him as something dating back to 1880. But at the same time this old-fashioned and long since empty phrase contained curious charm for René. There was a ladylike allure about it. The two held each other's eyes.

"Thank you, ma'am," he said, taking her hand and kissing it.

But it was not this look they were exchanging now which settled the matter; the first one had already done it, while she was still in the doorway. Her hand was long and slim and warm. Whereas before René's eyes had taken in Frau Kathe's appearance in a single comprehensive sweep, they now discovered details. The ash-blonde hair. The dry pure complexion. Now he noticed—only now, and with a start of alarm—her very high breasts.

Strength sprang from its cage.

She had turned to Grete's beautiful Biedermeier chest, on which she had placed the packages. Now she attended to them, and at last unpacked the two boxes of cake and the bag of pistachio nuts. She held them in her hands.

René had stepped up beside her. He bent over the chest and kissed her hands several times in rapid succession. She let him have them, but without letting go of the packages.

Outside, unseen by both of them, the sunset spread itself across the sky as though some highly inflammable liquid had caught fire. Within doors the cloud that had picked up the two of them carried them safely and surely over still possible and embarrassing intermediary stages. Already Frau Kathe was seated upon the chaise longue, and now she placed the two blue boxes of cake on the floor beside it and dropped the bag of pistachios on top of them. Then she simply clapped her eyes shut. The now rapidly accelerating express train of lust needed no more than this signal of a clear track. She sank back. Stangeler's hands flew. He plucked off her clothes as one peels petals from the calyx of a flower; some of the clothes were petal-white. They lay scattered about; he had almost entirely depetaled Frau Kathe. She sank smoothly into his arms; she seemed without consciousness. The energy on both sides was tremendous, an outpouring accompanied by a torrent of kisses; finally both together raced through the goal. René imagined his ears were filled with thunder.

Stangeler continued to behave correctly—that is, very tenderly. That was easy for him; he inclined that way anyhow.

He had just got back into his clothes, straightened his hair and tie, and at her request brought Frau Kathe a glass of water (meanwhile she too rearranged herself, but was still half undressed)—when the doorbell rang.

"Who can it be?" she asked quickly but calmly.

"It might be Grete. She didn't take her key. Perhaps she is coming home sooner than I expected."

"René," Frau Storch said, composed and controlled, "go and open the door at once. I'll lock this door behind you. Tell Grete I brought the things for her mother, felt ill here, had you bring me a glass of water, and closed myself in this room to lie down on the sofa for a bit. Clear?"

"Yes, ma'am," he replied. She made a horizontal movement with her hand, as if completing their interview. René bowed very low and left the room.

It was Grete. "Frau Storch is in your room," he said easily but with somewhat gritty overtones, as if he were annoyed at having been interrupted at work. "She's locked herself in, I think. She felt ill. She'd just unpacked the things for Mama."

"And you just left her there and ignored her?" Grete said, horrified and reproachful.

"She only wanted a glass of water," René replied.

Goodhearted Grete was already hurrying with long strides through the apartment and to the door of her room. "Kathe!" she called in a low voice and knocked gently. "Are you ill?" There was a reply from inside the room. Then the key turned. René saw Grete slip through the partly opened door.

It was some time before the door opened again and Grete's arm held the empty glass out through the crack. "More water, René," she said softly, "to take a pill." René went and filled the glass.

He then remained in the dining room.

It was quiet here. From the floor above he could hear a piano; its notes sounded glassy and solitary.

Here lay a newly forged link in a chain of lies, here it lay bright and shining. Grete's concern about Frau Storch, this fuss . . .

The ladies emerged.

Again René bowed very low.

"That woman may be sicker than she suspects," Grete said upon returning from accompanying Frau Storch to her apartment.

René said nothing. He went into Grete's room as if to set things to rights, as though he might have forgotten something. Perhaps it was his interrupted work that drew him there. On the floor beside the chaise longue stood the two blue cake boxes. "Like mushrooms that have grown up here in the meantime,"

Stangeler thought. He picked them up, together with the bag of pistachio nuts that lay on top of them, and carried them into the kitchen to Grete.

Thus on both floors and on different planes displays of feminine wisdom had been enacted. Afterwards, Grete and René also prepared to go up to Trix's apartment. First they ate something, and "my sweet" was given a great deal of tea, dark, as he preferred it. Grete was very pleased with René's essay on Joan of Arc; she bent her classical nose over it once again when Stangeler left the room for a moment, and was much impressed. But she did not say so.

This is the appropriate place to mention that René scarcely ever saw Frau Storch again. A year after the events described the lady died. Much, much later, René told Grete about the whole incident. It is characteristic that she said with genuine emotion: "That was very good of you, René. Really, very good of you." And after a few moments: "Of course I caught on to it at the time." But that was a lie.

Upstairs, in Trix's apartment, a little dance was in progress when Grete and René entered. For this, thanks were due to Bill Frühwald, who still sat at the piano. At the moment only Fella and Hubert were dancing. They danced very well, but altogether lifelessly, like moving waxworks. Hubert, lean and small-boned, was always impeccably dressed (Mary never economized on clothes); and Fella's lavender-blue dress was pretty too. These two light slim creatures moved with perfect self-assurance over the parquet floor of the big room, which gleamed under the chandelier. The rug had been rolled up, the tall drapes, ripples of blue and green, had been drawn. Outside it was growing dark.

This self-assurance of theirs was a curious thing. It was the kind of assurance we find at the nadir, the ultimate bottom of weakness; assurance that simply cannot be endangered by any tension arising out of the blood and the soul. It is the assurance of the overleaped generations after great and long wars. These generations missed those wars because they were not yet there, and in the future they will never be anywhere, never be in on anything—until the next catastrophe. Members of such generations are embodied intervals. They impress real life with the stamp of sheer vapid folly or indecency. Yet objectively speaking, this is in itself an accomplishment of no small magnitude, and bespeaks a kind of bravura. So that in the strict sense there really are no overleaped generations. Every generation, always, has it within its power to do some extraordinary things in a new manner. The gate is always open.

Had René Stangeler been able to share in these thoughts, he would have been easier in his mind.

He sat beside Trix. A pure cloud rested beside him, a cloud of straw and lilies of the valley. That was his sensation of her. And he sank into this delicate matter of no density like a stone. It was like a cry for help when he asked her what news she had of her mother.

"Good," she said. "Whatever Mama undertakes, she carries out with all her might. And so she'll succeed with this business of the artificial leg. You don't actually know my mother personally, do you, Herr von Stangeler?"

"No," he replied. "After all, I only started coming up to see you this summer—when Grete brought me."

Only now did he observe something going on in her that apparently had no connection with him. For the fraction of a second a little fold appeared between her eyebrows, as if there had been a flash of lightning in her face. The finger tips of her left hand rubbed against one another; she seemed considerably upset.

René, being the kind of person he was, promptly assumed that it had to do with him after all, that he must have said something wrong.

The chair beside him was empty. Trix had risen lightly and swiftly to her feet and left the room.

The so-called Danube Canal—in reality an ancient and very deep, rapidly flowing arm of the divided main stream—separates two parts of the city. From the house where the Siebenscheins lived it is only some 350 paces to the bridge and across it to the other bank of the river. Rut the change in atmosphere is profound. Both parts of the city are old—Alsergrund probably even older than Brigittenau, but the latter quarter, too, is by no means modern. It had already won some note in dark (though sometimes very jocund) medieval times, so that the Brigittenauers have even come to take an interest in their history and origins—especially since the days of that excellent historian Heinrich Jasomirgott Zwicker, who conducted researches and founded a local museum.

Yet things took a very different turn in the two districts. Not in the days of the Turks, who wreaked equal havoc on everything that lay outside the heart of the city and the defending walls. But in the 1800's, when a different brand of Turk and heathen came along—the kind called entrepeneurs. Factories were built whose machines, oddly, produced far more people than goods; people to whom no one paid attention at first, as if they did not exist at all. But by and by these people made a number of justified demands, which at first only had the effect of calling unpleasant attention to them. Later on, however, they started to become really and truly disagreeable about it all. But nowadays one can only look back upon that era with nostalgia, for these people have long since outgrown earlier restraints, have gone far beyond their betters, have been caressed and coddled at the expense of these betters. Socialism has already begun to reach a dead end.

Well, then, Brigittenau had become a working-class district.

Here the flourishes and ornamentation soon ceased, as did the winding narrow lanes and the bulging oriels with likewise curving windowpanes and perhaps geraniums upon the window sills, and the "sweet little baroque houses" (Grete Siebenschein), and all the other stuff which so delights the philistine devotee of "art history." In general all special nooks and crannies ceased here. For the man who believes that his social class will inevitably rise, as the result of the standardization and regularization of life and history, joins certain special attitudes to these beliefs. Such a man's street has no little gateways ("sweet little baroque portals") always sealed, but one day here and there surprisingly standing open, so that one can slip through them and come upon an altogether unsuspected turning of the road. The possibilities for a personal turning of the road, for deliverance, for an altogether indirect approach to a goal which it seems far too perilous even to envision—such possibilities do not exist for the person who expects everything to come from a change of circumstances, and from a tremendous massed advance in which 10,000 men will simultaneously set one foot over the threshold of the earthly paradise.

For that reason all little baroque portals, even the sweetest, eventually end up in the museum as objects of cultural value. There in the museum, everyone presumably has some

607

benefit from them. Of course no one can walk through them any longer.

For that reason everything in the working-class quarter is on a big scale, no matter how temporary or shabby, dreary or austere, how much of naked truth, it may be. The streets are broad and march straight ahead, as if determined to reach a still empty future. The walls surrounding the factories extend for great distances; behind them, gloomy but within their own context handsome, rise all sorts of structures—water-towers, cranes, catwalks. The men pour in each morning, during the winter in thick darkness, and at evening come out again likewise in darkness. Here sheer necessity is plain to see; everyone sees it in everyone else. No one here struts or drives about in a manner calculated to raise his credit, or at least not to endanger it. No one is furiously intent upon building a reputation. A man who can work well, who for the most part is not a mean son-of-a-bitch, who sticks by the others, does not have to try to distinguish himself, by fair means or foul. On the way home from work men walk in groups, or in twos like Zilcher and Zdarsa, or even alone, as did Leonhard Kakabsa, and no one holds it against him. Here a man, naked and unadorned, is still worth something; here the heart is still weighed.

Once a week, on Thursday, Fella Storch walked the 350 paces from the door of her house across the bridge to the other shore, and then on into the working-class district. But not deep into it. Only as far as the square which is still named after the seventeenth-century imperial generalissimo, Wallenstein. For on the first floor of the corner house on Jäger Strasse lived her schoolmate Lilly Catona, the daughter of a physician.

The building (which still stands) is a fright. Every corner bulges and goiters into oriels, as if made for spiteful inquisitive glances at the street—of which practice, however, the Catonas were not guilty. Of course they did look down at the street, but not spitefully, and only once a week, at precisely 6:15 p.m. every Thursday.

From three to six Fella and Lilly studied together. The strengths and weaknesses of the two girls neatly complemented one another; moreover, this weekly discussion of scholastic strategy and tactics had been going on for many a month. Each of the girls was now well adjusted to the other's methods of work. Slim Fella had the better head for mathematics, geometry, and scientific subjects. She also made strikingly neat drawings. Plump Lilly, on the other hand—a very pretty reddish-blonde who laughed a great deal and exuded a pure healthy odor halfway between the light perspiration vapor of blondes and the milky smell of calves—plump Lilly was good in Latin, Greek, and composition. Other subjects, in which a great deal had to be memorized, such as history or classical civilization, were crammed and recrammed jointly; the two rushed repeatedly from Marathon to Leuctra. Before more important operations, class papers and suchlike, they carefully prepared any frauds that might be needed, following tried-and-true methods and making sure that they were ready in good time. However, these frauds became more and more dispensable as a result of the regular, the rhythmic plowing through their subjects on Thursdays. During these hours together the girls also checked on what each was learning by herself. After some months, the whole apparatus of fraud was held in readiness only as a safety valve, for extreme emergencies, really rather out of a sense of duty and for the sake of order. In practice scarcely any cheating was done. Latin ablative constructions and Greek aorists were firmly established even in Fella's mind, and Lilly not only calculated the way a well-trained parrot talks, but now also knew all the formulae by heart; whereas formerly she had not even been very certain about the binomial theorem or the law of cosines. Now, thanks to Fella and Thursdays, she could even independently derive every required mathematical formula—a procedure which normally takes mathematical understanding that Lilly did not possess. In composition however, she always had to help Fella out a little, whether in class or in home preparation of interesting themes. That came easy to Lilly. She had the gift of swiftly flowing, agreeable chatter—her talks in speech class were famous. When she was writing a composition for Fella, all she had to do was to roughen up the smoothness slightly, and to stumble left-footedly now and then, in order to avert suspicion. She knew Fella's style, insofar as it can be called a style, precisely. She herself wrote a so-called "fluent" style—probably the worst there is. But people liked to read it, or rather see it, for such styles can be read with the eyes alone, without hearing a single word inwardly. Apparently Lilly's teachers liked that.

What with their Thursdays, the girls soon no longer had any worries about school. Such cares sank below the horizon, no longer rose threateningly above it, as had been the case with Fella's elder sister, Dolly, who could not stand the strain and in the end was to drop out of Gymnasium. This being free of cares was the sole purpose of all of Fella Storch's and Lilly Catona's busy cramming. Their fathers wanted them to attend the Gymnasium. Very well. They would go. But with an amazing grasp of the total situation, the daughters refused to have their lives made wretched by this fact.

Neither of the two had the slightest interest in the subjects they studied. Nor was any one preferable to any other because it fell more into line with their own gifts. Rather, every subject without exception was a matter of complete indifference to them, as was school and the whole process of learning. They moved about in the material and in this area with the aloofness and security of tourists. They thought it would be silly to have bad marks; but they were also not at all concerned about unusually good marks. It would not do to raise their parents' sights, they felt; they wanted to enjoy themselves and not be bothered. Fella laughed when Dolly worried about her schoolwork. She already knew more than her sister, although Dolly was in a higher class.

Lilly and Fella were also indifferent to each other. Outside of school and their Thursday afternoons, they scarcely ever saw each other. Dr. Catona, as it happened, was also the Storchs' family doctor. Professor Storch was a theoretician who specialized in pathological anatomy; understandably enough, he refused to practice medicine, particularly in his family. He thought very well of Lilly's father's professional abilities, and would remark now and then that medicine would be done for if the time ever came when there were no longer real general practitioners like Dr. Catona, who could handle a sprained ankle as competently as an obstetrical case.

By six-fifteen, in the warmer seasons, Lilly Catona and Fella Storch would have finished their studying and would be leaning out the window, looking down at the street.

There was no window opposite, such as schoolgirls love. The square was too wide.

Soon the streetcar would come howling up, emerging from the depths of the working-class quarter, and would stop on the opposite side of the street—in those days in Vienna the trams still traveled on the left track. As soon as the two red-and-yellow cars had gone, Fella and Lilly would usually see Trix standing across the street, waving up at them.

She was coming from her place of work.

Trix had never cared to go to a Gymnasium, with the

prospect of going on to the University. Intent upon early independence, she chose a solid commercial education. Foreign languages were needed for that, of course, and she proved as gifted in learning them as her brother Hubert. Sensibly, a good deal of stress was laid upon this point in the K. household; but no one attempted to force Trix to studies which did not attract her. Herr Oskar K., her deceased father, had always believed in freedom for his children. In this he resembled Ferry Siebenschein and differed greatly from the rather autocratic Professor Storch. Mary K. had always upheld her husband's views. Trix passed successfully through all the requisite courses, and at the age of fifteen could write a decent business letter in French or English. And then she went to work, at first as a volunteer.

The organization in which the girl now sought to find her place was a large and remarkable company; moreover, before her period of probation and apprenticeship was over, she was assured an excellent permanent job in it. And it may be taken for granted that Trix, with her calm dependable nature, would make out well on the job.

The company was the leader in a highly important field, although to the outsider this field might at first glance seem humble, not to say a little repulsive. For the company dealt in old clothes, in rags and tatters of every type. The collection, sorting, and preparation of such rags for the paper industry forms a very necessary link in the industrial process. Not for newsprint, to be sure, but for the better types of paper. If that essential link were missing, the reader of this text would scarcely have a pure white background for the black print.

Thus the firm, like others of its type, extended its operations into the humanistic realm, although one of its employees, our pretty Trix K., wished to have nothing to do with humanism.

But we never operate directly, and we do not always accomplish what we intend.

The plant and the offices, housed in a large modern factory building, were located far out on the outskirts of the city, upon the banks of the Danube.

The management of the company—perhaps out of emotional, perhaps rational considerations—had so equipped the plant that the employees could regard it almost as their home. There were pleasant dining rooms for the noonday meal; in summer there were roof gardens with facilities for sunbathing and showering. Whoever worked there belonged to the company, enjoyed its advantages, had his convenient locker and his own key to it. There were a good many small perquisites for the workers beyond those the law required the employer to provide.

Trix's deceased father had known someone in the management. That was how Trix had first come to work there.

Every day just after six o'clock she left the building along with the rest of the shift, walked a short way toward the big bridge over the Danube, and entered the streetcar. A few minutes later she could change cars at the Praterstern. From this point Trix could ride directly to the square in front of the railroad station and get out near her house.

On Thursdays, however, she got off three stops before her usual destination. Fella and Lilly Catona would be lolling at the window sill. They waved. Trix waved. Fella came down. That was the usual procedure. Only on rare occasions did Trix go upstairs.

The two girls would then stroll together through the now crowded streets, heading generally homeward but detouring along the Danube embankment or lingering on broad Wallenstein Strasse. Here there was a tea room named

Freudenschuss's. The surging noises of the street, the warning bells of the trams, receded as they went down the steps which led from the bridge to the river. The embankment was green, the trees along the riverside avenues above were also green, and this color of nature seemed to blanket all the distracting artificial din, to act as a sort of buffer which absorbed the multitude of battering sounds. The bridge was so high, however, that from the top of the stairs you could look upstream to the triple windings of the nearby mountains.

When they leaned out the open window, waiting for Trix, the noise of the streets filtered into the room. It was a pretty room of no great depth, with furniture of the then modern type. Lilly had it to herself. She was the only child. Books and notebooks would still be lying on the big folding desk at which the girls had worked, their pages fluttering slightly in the draft. But these articles belonged to Lilly; after the study session Fella had immediately packed her books into a handsome leather bag which now stood ready so that she could run down at once as soon as Trix appeared across the street.

To have waited down in the street, at the streetcar stop, would have deprived Fella and Lilly Catona of an amusement which they greatly enjoyed and to which they always devoted the last minutes before Trix's arrival.

For down in the street they could recognize various persons who turned up every Thursday at the same time on their way home from work. Some such recurrent figures got out of the streetcar along with Trix, and others came by on foot. The girls had already assigned nicknames to some of these persons. A young man in workman's clothes was called "the Sailor" because of his slow and somewhat rocking gait. He sometimes passed by shortly before Trix's arrival, but quite often came by at the same time as Trix's streetcar; once, in fact, he had been seen to pass right by Trix while she was standing and waving.

The girls could pick him out, along with other well-known figures, from a considerable distance; then the streetcar would overtake and pass these pedestrians. Trix appeared. This time she was slightly ahead of "the Sailor." Lilly and Fella would have laid a bet on who would come by first—such bets would always be paid at the Freudenschuss tea room.

One day, however, when Fella and Trix had reached Wallenstein Strasse, out of sight of Lilly's apartment, Fella simply stopped "the Sailor" by dropping her schoolbag in front of his feet when she was certain that he was behind her and on the point of catching up to them. Leonhard stumbled and almost fell. Nevertheless, he picked up the bag and handed it to Fella, who promptly apologized in a high voice, with a look of alarm and frailty, but also a certain pertness.

"I hope nothing is broken," Kakabsa said good-naturedly, indicating the bag.

"Nothing to break in it," Fella said. "There are only books."

"Books!" Leonhard exclaimed—they were now walking on side by side, all three. "What kind of books?"

"Textbooks," Fella replied. Instinct as well as Leonhard's appearance, for he was easily recognizable as a worker by his dress, suggested to her that she should not conceal the fact that she was being exposed to higher education. A certain small superiority might always be won from that.

They had reached the vicinity of the bridge. Here, with the view opening out, the liquid golds of twilight began to flow everywhere.

Trix had been struck by the intonation Leonhard gave to the word "books." In it was something which did not bode well for any forthcoming skirmish with Fella, which in fact ignored her whole person. Trix now looked closely at Leonhard, who was walking to the left of Fella. Her eyes darkened, as was her way when something stirred within her. The wind and sun caught in the red-gold of her hair as the trio stepped up onto the bridge. Leonhard saw it now. Before, he had scarcely noticed Trix.

"You are a student?" he asked Fella.

"Yes," she said. "I go to the Gymnasium."

From his right, from Trix's direction, a roseate glow wafted toward Leonhard. A roseate glow in every sense; he was conscious of it now. But he went on speaking to Fella: "If that is so, Fräulein, I'd like to ask you a favor. Would you let me see the books you have in your briefcase. Please—it would mean a good deal to me. We might just go down on the embankment for a few minutes."

They were standing close to the stairway leading down from the bridge. Fella did not feel that she had been thrust aside, although that was actually the case. She regarded herself as identical with her books; or rather, she thought that Leonhard's interest in her books was really only a pretext. Trix already knew better.

"All right," Fella said, "let's go down."

Trix walked behind Leonhard. She saw his brown, very slender neck above the blue workman's blouse, and the thick hair, a mass of small curls (he seldom wore a hat).

As they began to descend the steps, the sun was just setting behind the higher portions of the city across the canal. The evening blaze attained its greatest radiance; it lay like an outpouring of white-hot metal upon the windows of the houses above the Brigittenau embankment. The green of the water turned deeper and harsher, almost artificial, like colored paper.

616

"We might sit here," Leonhard said. Without more ado he slid out of his smock, revealing a rough checked shirt underneath, the sleeves rolled up to the elbows. He spread the smock out on the grass and with a wave of his hand invited the girls to sit down on it. They did so without constraint. Leonhard sat down next to them—on the right, this time, beside Trix.

The historical atlas fascinated him at once. A picture of the ancient world (after Niebuhr). He looked at it for a long while. In silence.

Herodotus. The Greek text. Leonhard looked at the Greek print. For a long, a very long time, although he could not read it. He said nothing.

There! Scheindler's Latin grammar. Yes, that was his. Edition? Date? He leafed rapidly through the front matter. Yes, it was his. Exactly. He had the right book.

And Trix observed him carefully while all this went on.

It went on for a very long time. Leonhard was entirely engrossed in the books. Others were produced from the bag. He looked up, into the luminous concert of the sunset, and then back down at the books on his knees. By now Trix knew exactly how Leonhard looked: eyebrows grown together over the short straight nose; head round, compact. His chest and shoulders seemed enormously broad, since he was of only average height; they made him look very strong. But perhaps that illusion came about because Leonhard several times took long deep breaths. Still, his brown, moderately hairy forearms were beyond a doubt unusually powerful. Then, almost at the same time as Fella, Trix noticed a tattoo on his left arm: an anchor and twist of rope. Fella began to laugh, high and clear. Leonhard raised his head. His expression was somewhat absent, but friendly.

Fella explained that she and a certain schoolmate of hers named Lilly had long been calling him "the Sailor," and she also explained why.

"But I've never been on the ocean," Leonhard said. "I only worked on a Danube scow."

"*Naus mélaina*," Fella said.

"What's that?"

"It means 'the black ship,'" Fella replied. "It's Greek. The poet Homer always refers to ships that way."

"Again, please," Leonhard said.

"*Naus mélaina.* And the plural—black ships—is *nees mélainai.*"

"*Naus mélaina—nees mélainai,*" Leonhard repeated. He seemed to have a keen ear.

"Bravo," Fella said, but her tone was indifferent. She had really had enough of school subjects for the day.

"Do you go to the Gymnasium too?" Leonhard asked, turning now to Trix.

"No, I work in an office," Trix replied.

Her eyes must have been exceedingly dark as she spoke. Leonhard looked squarely into them. Now Trix became aware of the firmness and hardness which showed in his eyes side by side with amiability.

"Have you been through the Gymnasium?" he asked.

"No," she replied, meeting his look, which suddenly seemed to her quite inquisitorial. "I'm not even sixteen yet. I'm a probationer, a volunteer helper." She mentioned the name of her firm.

"Why didn't you want to go on with your education?" Kakabsa asked. "Or was it a question of money?"

"Not really," Trix answered. "I was never interested." As she spoke, with Leonhard's eyes resting upon her, she had the feeling that never before in her life had she spoken so candidly. That was nonsense, of course—she thought at once—for she had always spoken most candidly with her mother, far more

618

candidly than she was doing now.

Fella wanted to go home.

They went their separate ways, up at the bridge.

"A highly intelligent man," Fella said as they entered the lobby of the house on Althanplatz.

The circle around Trix, or more properly speaking, the circle in Mary K.'s apartment, had widened with the onset of autumn. Widened or been enriched, if you will.

Hubert brought two girls, likewise students at the Gymnasium. Frühwald came with a *"troupiste,"* Dolly with a schoolmate. Moreover, Lilly Catona was also welcomed into the company (warmly welcomed). Her bright laughter rang out, her fluent chatter spilled over. Trix went to wash her hands.

At that time, luckily, the captain was still far off. The chinking was extremely moderate and of a "prettified" character.

Altogether, there was nothing *"troupistic,"* nothing wild, about these gatherings. Hubert saw to orderly discussions. Although he had at first considered Leonhard Kakabsa's appearance in the group as unsuitable ("unsuitable, to put it mildly," he had said to his sister), he soon began to esteem him. Leonhard's solid, taciturn, listening manner, the skillful impulse he gave to the talk by interposing little questions, contributed something essential to conversation. He prevented dispersion. He rested heavily on all the talk like a paperweight. Everyone had to keep a closer grip on himself. Leonhard acted as a check and balance.

He had been brought there by Trix. Amazingly enough.

At first Fella maliciously agreed with Hubert. She would even stay away whenever she heard that Leonhard was coming.

The unhumanistic Trix, however, who actually had a certain natural alliance with Leonhard—both of them were "working people," after all—would lose him each time to the humanists who drifted in and out of the place. (The captain, with his continual spouting of Latin, would have been all Leonhard needed!)

In the long run, however, Leonhard was only a passing member of the group.

Around this time another shift in his working hours made it possible for him to wait for Trix at six o'clock now and then (he had already taken to avoiding the Thursday encounter), not at the company gate, but near where she boarded the streetcar each evening. When he stood there for the first time and she came along with her light step and her gleaming red-gold hair, the same roseate glow wafted toward him that he had experienced on the bridge the first time he had seen her. Now, however, Trix seemed not especially surprised but rather pleased.

She did not take the streetcar. They stayed in the neighborhood, strolled slowly back in the direction from which Trix had come, turned toward the river, and went down to the shore at a spot where a stone staircase descended to the water. The water stood still, scarcely splashing against the steps. Somewhat farther out in the river, however, the water moved more swiftly. The river washed the city. It came. It left. Incessantly. A youth, to use Holderlin's phrase. The autumn was still mild and warm. Haze blurred the other shore—you could not quite make out details on the other side.

They sat down, once more with Leonhard's smock under them for a rug. Perhaps that was an element in common, a shared past: to sit on the smock by the water. It was more than that: it was intimacy. They were sitting together after work. Trix liked sitting there. After half an hour they went back to the streetcar line and Trix boarded her car. Leonhard looked after her. She waved back.

They frequently sat on the steps this way.

Without talking.

It was true peace.

It was more: bliss. Only they did not really know it.

One time she had hard candy with her. Another time he brought some—exactly the same kind.

But there were also the Thursday evenings, and usually Leonhard arrived before Trix. Then the girls would wave briefly to him from the window, whereupon he would walk on slowly. Fella began to lose—doughnuts at Freudenschuss's—because she always stubbornly bet on Trix. Of course, before the shift in his working hours—which was only temporary—Leonhard often was not the first to arrive. Sometimes, in fact, he missed the girls completely; they would already have gone on toward the river. Fella strong-mindedly advised against any waiting or lingering, even for a few seconds. Trix, too, was not especially eager for anything of the sort; and later, after all, she had the steps by the river. She said nothing about that. Leonhard, when he knew that he was too late, no longer expected to see the girls at the window. The window would then be deserted or closed.

Lilly Catona occasionally came along, when she had a bet to recover at Freudenschuss's; and now and then the girls came to the tea room with Leonhard. Which made the proprietress rather lift her eyebrows. It was not usual for girls of good family to go to tea rooms with young workmen. They would then continue on, all four, to the embankment. Lilly Catona thought "the Sailor" very nice; he had to show the anchor on his arm and tell about his voyages on the Danube scows.

In those days Leonhard always carried a little pad with him, and a pencil.

He would carefully go through the contents of Fella's schoolbag. He would make notes of titles, dates, and editions.

He already owned the historical atlas.

The picture of the ancient world.

After Niebuhr.

Our Leonhard, our dear and excellent young man, had not only spent many months poring over the Latin grammar of evenings. He had crammed and practiced so—somewhat in the way he might have learned to handle a complicated machine—that he developed an astounding fluency in the forms, in declensions and conjugations. It gave the two schoolgirls quite a shock one day when the whole apparatus of Scheindler was stirred in him to precise, rattling, clanking movement; it was as though the Roman legions were on the march. The only comfort Fella and Lilly could take was in the discovery that although Leonhard had all the grammatical rules of construction—ablative absolute, and so on—faultlessly in mind, he was slow and clumsy at handling these constructions. They had simply not had time to settle into his blood. Fella thought it extremely tasteless to discuss school subjects while they were having refreshments. However, it all came out now, all about Leonhard's home studies, about Scheindler and even the newly acquired historical atlas. It had been bound to come out, since whenever Leonhard was with the girls, he was always fishing for information and hints. And so the Scheindler machinery had suddenly been jarred into motion, to Leonhard's great alarm—for he had only wished to ask for an explanation of something and had wanted to show exactly where the trouble lay . . .

Trix was thunderstruck.

Three days later on the steps by the water she asked him about it.

That was a curious moment, not without pain. It was as though they first began to look upon each other. It was the expulsion from a paradise of innocent understanding. They were being expelled from it before they fully realized that they had been in it.

"Do you mean to look for a different type of work?" Trix asked.

"Why?"

"Because you are continuing your schooling, I've noticed," she said.

"Continuing my schooling . . ." Leonhard repeated. "I don't want at all to continue my schooling. Or change my type of work. I want to stay as I am. I like things the way they are. I want to stay where I am."

"Then what are you learning all that for . . . Latin . . . and the historical atlas? Are you also taking courses?"

"No," he said. The gap of incomprehension began to open between him and Trix; he could almost see the crack forming. Nor could he fasten upon the right words to bridge this gulf before it became too wide. He could not express himself. He was hampered by a certain clumsiness, as in the use of the ablative constructions. Except that in this case Leonhard did not even know the rules. Not a one. It had never even occurred to him to attend adult-education courses. Now he was suddenly reminded of the smell of the school in one such extension division in Ottakring; he had once gone there with someone and had never gone again. Such schools, such smells, had nothing to do with his Scheindler, nothing to do with the picture of the ancient world, despite the fact that there were courses offered in such matters.

"Here comes a tug pulling some scows!" Trix exclaimed, pointing to the middle of the river.

Leonhard was scarcely able to grasp the sense of her words. Only now was he becoming fully conscious of the welter of confusion into which her casual question had plunged him—while she, for her part, could lightly skip to something else entirely.

Slowly, with grinding machinery and belching smoke-stacks, the tug came up the river; seen from up front it looked broader than long, but gradually stretching out, while the four black scows, big as ocean-going vessels, one behind the other, gradually hove into view, each one creating its own massive billows. Upstream the voyage is long, is slow, is endless. Leonhard thought of its stages from Budapest up to Szob, to Komorn. The last, already cold sun-glow upon the woods along the banks. Sitting in the wheelhouse on one of the scows, or in the cabin. The sense of being locked up, crammed together, to the point of terror. The impossibility of moving away. And the smell came back.

Slowly the past drew up the river. Now, at last the tug and its scows were halfway by; animated waves interrupted the static picture. Water splashed high on the stone steps, threw spume almost to where he and Trix were sitting.

Leonhard said nothing.

He had nothing that he could have said to Trix. He had nothing at all. Something had him, to the point of inexpressibility.

They lingered there for a while on the steps.

Without talking.

Trix turned to him; her eyes grew extremely dark; for a second she laid her hand on his. "Have I offended you, Leonhard?"

Now, on top of it all, he was utterly defeated.

But at night, for all that he ordinarily slept so soundly, something new happened to him.

He dreamt that he was reading the following sentence in Scheindler's Latin grammar (only the book looked very different; it was very thick): "The optative (form expressing a wish) throws every clause into the subjunctive mood, and the fundamental meaning is thereby lost."

This ridiculous gibberish echoed in Leonhard's ears when he awoke and turned on the light.

He was even able to repeat the sentence to himself.

It was very uncomfortable.

He repeated it again.

And in so doing he discovered that he was beginning to think in an entirely new language. Not Latin. But he was thinking differently now in his mother tongue. Suddenly Leonhard recalled speeches he had heard, at celebrations in the factory, in union meetings; speeches on an elevated plane. Right. The written language had to be spoken that way; you pulled yourself up, as you did on the parallel bars, above the level of everyday language.

But: "The optative (form expressing a wish) throws every clause into the subjunctive mood . . ."

That flowed smoothly; there was no pomposity about it. It was like everyday language, only rather more tempered. It was not Latin. But it was not actually his mother tongue, not the language he had learned from his mother's lips. With profound astonishment Leonhard realized that he had for some time been reading to himself in that new language (sometimes moving his lips). It had become his customary inner speech. Now he was even dreaming it. Now he was whispering it to himself after awakening. His inner language already hovered on the threshold of his outer speech.

Immediately after this, Malva, the bookseller's daughter, swam into view. Leonhard had not gone to her father's shop for the historical atlas, but elsewhere.

He knew why now.

He had not consciously been avoiding Malva.

But he had not seen her for a long time.

Here she was now.

With swelling breast and sweetly prominent belly of Venus, feline eyes peering slantwise, a light veil of smoke over the face from the cigarette in the corner of the mouth.

He knocked against her now, like knocking against the wall.

Just the same sort of collision had taken place with Trix, there on the stairs by the water.

The light switch clicked. Now he lay between the two in the darkness, as though between boards, his arms stretched straight along his sides.

While our dear and excellent young man performed a decisive act at night, nothing less than crossing the dialect frontier, which in Central Europe, at least, marks the beginning of the true life of the mind—at this same time Trix (later, on the steps by the water, the two spoke of this night!) lay boarded, almost coffined, between Fella and Leonhard. She lay on her back in the darkness and wept. Beside her the other twin bed, her mother's, stood empty.

It was Fella who arranged a rendezvous with Hubert. The boy had scarcely asked for it. But now it had come about, and she made her preparations.

Midnight-blue, this time, with a touch of red; not lavender-blue. Add to that her dark gold hair. Objectively, we must remark that she looked *extrêmement* sweet, thoroughly huggable, a pert little, thin little gnat! Transparent, though. A clearwing (*Sesia myopaeformis* L., Dwight Williams would probably have identified the specimen).

It fluttered away, of course, with such deliberation that it arrived on the scene very late.

The rendezvous was set for Nussdorf, the square in front of the brewery and the big family-run coffeehouse. The very place where, a good long while before, Frau Mary K. had stood up an admirer of hers—Doktor Boris Nikolaus Negria, the Rumanian, whom destiny had nevertheless decreed to pass by her like a phantom a few minutes before her terrible accident . . .

Fella, of course, knew nothing about all this.

She got off the streetcar. The passengers scattered. Fella prepared to stroll quite casually toward a certain person. But there was no certain person there; the traffic island under the clock was deserted.

Swiftly considering the situation, she felt extremely exposed, as if she were the target of innumerable arrows flying at her from all sides. Late though she was, Hubert may not have left yet. He would be standing or sitting somewhere, watching her, enjoying her perplexity, and would put in an appearance in a moment . . . For she simply assumed that he had her personality. But that standard did not suffice, not for this particular passionless shepherd.

The big front garden of the family coffeehouse was almost empty. It was bathed in autumnal sunlight, gaily spotted with fallen leaves. But there was another café, a small one, directly opposite the brewery. A pleasant red-and-white marquee with scalloped edge fluttered in the breeze. Only now did Fella become aware of this smaller café. She turned around, and then back again. She ought to go away. She realized that already. She still stood.

"Fella!" someone called across the square.

Shouts and laughter, many voices, came from the little garden under the red-and-white marquee.

She knew at once that her defeat would be enormous if she went away now. The group swarmed out of the café, a half-dozen boys and girls, among them Hubert. She was surrounded, her hand shaken.

"We've been watching you all the while!"

They liked Fella, were glad that she had come, had no intention of hurting her. The party was an innocent affair. Only the person who had assembled the group here and made them apparently chance spectators of Fella's appearance was not so entirely innocent.

He greeted Fella, however, with conspicuous cordiality, and then, when everyone went back to the café, promptly took his seat beside another girl, with whom he had been sitting before.

The whole business struck Trix as more than a little cruel. Fella need not have told her about it, save that she wanted to make trouble for Hubert. It was necessary to reveal that she had been counting on meeting Hubert alone. Here was an altogether needless candor, almost incomprehensible; certainly there was an element of shamelessness in it. Was there not? Did she tell it in order to strike at Trix too? And that she brought up the matter when the two of them were in the bathroom, where a certain procedure again took place of which we have had an inkling—that was when she told her whole story to Trix!

628

Trix took up the matter with her brother.

"Did she come complaining to you?" he said, laughing.

"No . . ."

"Then how do you know?"

"She told me . . ."

"And . . . ?"

"How could you treat her that way!"

"I didn't do her any harm."

"I thought . . . that you liked her a little, anyway."

"Like her? Oh, well. I don't care about her one way or another. She can like me, if she wants to. I don't like anyone."

"Not me either?" Trix asked.

"No," he said. "You're all ridiculous."

Yet Hubert was not a bit unfriendly to Trix as he said these things. He even patted her hand. Then he gave one more short laugh, shrugged his shoulders, and left.

Up to now Trix had always rather idolized her brother. He was always so clever. He spoke well and concisely. He never exaggerated. Without half trying, he was first in his class.

But that night she lay confined within three boards, so to speak: Leonhard, Fella, and Hubert. The last was a kind of cold underlayer from which there came a permanent icy draft.

She was longing for her mother. At last, when the autumn was almost over, news came that her mother was ready to return. Marie was to go to Munich to accompany Mary K. back to Vienna.

Trix asked for a few days' leave from the office and simply went along.

The express train glided out of the station early in the morning, though not quite on time.

The Vienna Woods were still swathed in smoky mists, out of

629

which here and there mountaintops arched their backs. Close by, the woods ran like a picket fence past the train.

That Mother had sent for Marie to be her traveling companion was, of course, almost a good sign. After all, on the trip to Munich she had needed to have a nurse. And of course it was understandable that Mother could not have made the journey by herself. But still, the fact jolted Trix into a realization of her mother's helplessness, and made her fear that her mother's general state might be far worse than she had indicated in her letters to Trix and Grete Siebenschein lately. Perhaps what she had said in her letters had only been intended as reassurance . . . After all, it was odd that Mama had flatly forbidden them to visit her in Munich during her entire stay there; she had something very difficult to accomplish, she had maintained, and she did not want anyone to see her engaged in it. She had said this in advance, before her departure, and had afterwards repeatedly laid stress upon it in letters.

And now she had sent for Marie, so it was all right for them to see her again.

Trix fought in vain against her anxiety. Rumbling, the train slid into a tunnel. By the time it emerged, the sun had broken through; banners and slopes of glowing autumnal golds poured toward the moving train. Now another tunnel. Shortly afterwards they were riding high up onto a viaduct; it was like rising in an elevator. The trees accompanying the roadbed dropped away; distances opened out: brown hills, spacious sky, a *tutti* of blue.

Trix felt in a better frame of mind now.

Prefigured in Vienna, the journey had seemed a whole, a solid block of time to be got through. But it was not that; it dissolved into its parts, melted away, and fell to pieces. In fact it proved to be quite short, really. Wels, Salzburg, Rosenheim.

Before long they were riding between solid streets of houses, around Munich, through the East Station without stopping, over radiating tracks in the yards, rattling past rows of standing cars. Here was the station. Movement hissed out in a last gasp of brakes. The train stood still. It seemed at last to have regained its full heaviness.

They made their way along the platform.

Mother stood at the barrier.

Mother stood at the barrier, leaning lightly on her black ebony cane; the hotel porter was with her.

Trix felt acute shame, real grief, at the way her own glance slid rapidly downward along her mother's body.

Mother stood at the barrier, on two slender legs, laughing.

Now they were in each other's arms.

Trix thought she could feel that her mother had grown somewhat frailer and thinner. Nevertheless, she looked lovely and in the best of health.

The hotel porter had taken their two bags. Mary led the way. Her walk was a masterpiece: tilted just slightly to the right, just slightly depending on the cane, only incidentally hampered, and reducing this hindrance to play and parody by a certain irony in her movements.

Back in her hotel room, Mary gave them a formal demonstration of her skill in walking back and forth, and faithful Marie, losing all reserve, began to kiss her mistress effusively.

Trix remained quiet, though her eye darkened. Her mother's feat filled her with profoundest admiration. And to think that someone had lain in her bed as in a coffin, but recently in Vienna, and had wept.

Mary told them that she still encountered occasional difficulties; there were pressure sores, and so on. Professor Habermann was entrusting her case to a medical colleague of his at Vienna University, and he had also given Mary the name of a firm which could be consulted in case anything went wrong with the artificial limb. But she anticipated no trouble. She could already wear the prosthesis uninterruptedly for an entire day without pain, she said.

And so it was. That evening she went out with Trix. To the theater, the small Riemerschmid Theater on Maximilian Strasse, and then to supper at the Neue Börse.

At table Trix told her about the circle that had sprung up in Vienna during the past few months, about Fella and Lilly Catona, Frühwald and Hubert's friends. Leonhard, too, was mentioned. Trix described the whole thing in the spirit of its all belonging to the past, being over and done with, simply because it had to cease now. But her mother seemed not at all disposed to take this view.

"That's exactly what I need. I'm looking forward to meeting all these friends of yours," she said. "It has worked out very nicely, it seems to me."

Then Trix spoke in more detail of Leonhard.

"Are you in love with him?" Mary asked.

"Almost," Trix said. "Yes, I think I am. But there's no getting over the strangeness, the utter difference between us."

"From what you say, I have the impression that that isn't only because of his class."

"No, it isn't only because of his class," Trix agreed, looking down at the tablecloth. Mary placed her warm hand on Trix's delicate white paw, and they went on talking of other intimate matters.

Among other things, the matter of Fella was brought up.

"Don't take that too seriously," Mary commented. "It really is completely incidental. So many young people together—you know, it's almost like kittens in a basket crawling all over one another. In the circumstances such things can become almost inevitable."

Next day Trix went sightseeing in Munich, where she had never been before. She didn't pay much attention to what it offered in the way of art, but was all the more intrigued by the aura of a city which in comparison to the one she came from seemed younger, clearer, more highly polished. It struck her this way altogether without reference to historical data, of which she knew none. All in all it seemed to her that it would be an easier city to live in than her native one—an illusion that overcomes us more or less forcefully in every foreign city, if it should chance to be beautiful and lively.

She stood on the Stachus, watching the unending stream of cars that turned into Lenbachplatz, an incessant rumble of motors and stench of exhausts and general noise and flow. Yet Trix had been in Berlin and Paris, where all these phenomena were multiplied tenfold, especially in comparison to her far quieter native city. Or was the din actually no less in Vienna? Did her own city swallow up the roar of traffic and people simply because—because she did not like noise and would not recognize its presence at home? Or was it that her city was a quiet one because of an altogether different reality which existed, still wholly uncontaminated and immaculate, amid the blue shadows of the suburban streets and reached from them, though with the beginnings of contamination, into the heart of the city? Something of the same sort existed here, although the underlying soil was newer, shallower, built over so much later, for the ground here was not a kind of morass with the deposited debris of two millennia. The dialect spoken here— as a Viennese, Trix could easily understand it!—had nothing to do with the clatter of motors, did not mingle with them in a barking roar. Rather, it set itself apart, self-assertively and with a tranquil power, from all the bustle. In this the language was like the people here. Trix was much taken with them; they had a distinctive manner. Through the windows of the characteristic "Bräu" she saw them sitting in silence, firm on their foundations, over their beer. In Vienna they sat in silence over their wine. In both cities they sat, offering the enormous counterweight of their posteriors, the squat resistance of a not always wholly savory body politic—to the age's efforts to drive with roaring motors straight into the abyss, that being the age's burning desire.

To be sure, such thoughts did not come consciously to our Trix. They were present more as a premonition, as a sensation in her innards, in her little belly. Yet she had them; she had made contact and established rapport with this city of Munich—more so than a good many of those who trotted from the Schack Gallery to the German Museum, or from the Propyläen to the Glyptothek. Not that she entirely neglected the established sights. Trix looked at the Frauenkirche, stood for a long time before this enormous broody hen. She contemplated the rococo dream on Sendlinger Strasse (it was very close to her, like something from home), and walked a little through the old Rathaus arch down into the "Valley," and along the food market.

The return journey to Vienna passed smoothly and pleasantly.

Perhaps Mary had been a little worried beforehand. The trip involved wearing the artificial limb for ten or eleven hours, without any opportunity to take it off. But she walked down the platform on her own two legs and not in a wheelchair; she was able to get into the railway car like any other traveler, although

Trix and Marie gave her a hand.

Somewhat more than eight hours later the train glided with a rumble through two tunnels, and there they were: the Vienna Woods. There, in fact, began the sense of being home, with those rising and falling mountains, like a succession of curtains constantly being raised and lowered before the eyes: mountains with the polychrome depth of woods through which the slanting sunlight shot glitters and glazes, throwing the shadows of the trees into the compartment like a quivering, moving picket fence. Here were the glimpses into valleys, the misty dips, the ancient woods, and the ancient city.

Back at the apartment in Vienna, the tumult of greetings soon subsided. Hubert had come to the station to meet them, of course and Grete Siebenschein, who had commanded René Stangeler to be present, in case physical help was needed. At home the parent Siebenscheins and Storchs emerged from their apartments. (This was one of the very few occasions on which René saw Frau Storch again, and he bowed very low.) Dolly was likewise there, and behind her appeared a specimen of *Sesia myopaeformis* L., delicate of limb and translucent.

Mary walked slowly through the apartment. Already the smell of the coffee could be detected; Marie was in the kitchen preparing the *Jause*. Trix set the table. And Hubert repeatedly tried to offer his mother his arm, but to no avail. Preceding him, she strode quite rapidly through the rooms.

No smoke of the hearth surrounds the penates in a city apartment. Rather, they look mutely on from everywhere, out of every piece of furniture, every picture. They are no longer present in any fixed place, no longer established in niches around the chimney-piece; they have been sublimated, are distributed as a fine powder or emulsion throughout a home.

At the coffee table Mary became aware that it had taken

more than a year to make up for a few thoughtless, impatient, awkward seconds on September 21, 1925, a year of suffering and striving and resolution.

But it had been done, as well as it was possible to do it. She smiled at her children (Trix looked sweet) and remained seated at the table. Only an hour later did it occur to her that she had not even thought of unstrapping her artificial leg and lying down to rest. She felt no need to do so even then, and so she let be.

CHAPTER 3

In the East

ONE OF Leonhard's fellow-workers in the webbing factory, Nikolaus Zdarsa, who was unmarried, had a new acquisition. This time he had brought home not a girl but a motorcycle, which he was paying for by installments. The machine, an Indian, was long and had a low center of gravity, so that it would ride well even on bad roads. This was a prime consideration for Zdarsa, since he was thinking of the roads of the Burgenland, which were at that time in as wretched shape as the highways of Hungary; the area had been part of Austria only since 1919. Nikolaus had rather prosperous relatives down there, in Stinkenbrunn. Since these relatives were vintners, the attraction was obvious. The back seat of this remarkable machine cried out for occupancy, and so he generally took Leonhard along with him, since no female companion happened to be available at the moment. It is worth noting, incidentally, that Leonhard made himself useful in the home of the Zdarsas of Stinkenbrunn much as he had done in the beautiful Palais Ruthmayr in Vienna: that is, by quietly and effectively taking care of domestic repairs which would otherwise have been long neglected. Leonhard even did this unasked, as soon as he became aware of malfunctions: and a doorbell that he temporarily repaired went on working perfectly for five or ten years at least. Perhaps Leonhard was bored at the Zdarsa house in Stinkenbrunn. At any rate, he sought occupation. Niki Zdarsa, once he had dismounted from his motorcycle, did just the opposite; that is to say, he did nothing at all, and no power on earth could have made him bestir himself. He devoted himself to "Stinkenbrunner." This, along with such well-known names as Rust or Oggau, constitutes one of the few vintages noted beyond the limits of the Burgenland, whose Hungarian-type wines are for the most part used to blend with and sharpen the ordinary wines of Lower Austria. The connoisseur, of course, prizes the somewhat rarer wines of this district, which well deserve to be drunk by themselves. Among such connoisseurs, incidentally, was Bismarck, who used to import his red wine from the Burgenland.

Niki Zdarsa, then, would make a trip to the southeast every Sunday that was at all pleasant, on into the late fall. Leonhard would be planted on the back seat. During those years, 1926 and 1927, the motorization of wider classes of the populace was already beginning to be noticeable. Every Sunday when the weather was reasonably good, the large cities would expel a ring-shaped cloud of vehicles into the countryside. That expulsion had certain orbital elements, exactly like analogous processes in the cosmos, and a predictable initial velocity.

As a result of the compulsion to drive, the compulsion to pass, the compulsion to listen to thudding pistons, a ring-shaped band of emptiness forms around the metropolis, beyond which the swarm distributes itself in diminishing density over the open countryside. Thus, too, the Vienna Woods closer to the city have become an excellent place for solitary Sunday walks. All one need do is to lag behind, as the woods more and more lie untrodden behind the highways filled with motor vehicles. Pedestrians no longer trouble the quiet of the woods, for all the pedestrians are now on the highways, borne along by the rushing stream of traffic. The woods are returning to themselves, and wild creatures are already growing more trustful. We are once more able to learn from the woods this tranquil and temperate laggardness, to enjoy a bit of quiet nature without the exaggeration and the special emphasis which makes for eccentricity. Linger a little behind progress, keep your hand from the knob of the radio and your eye from the newspaper and screen, stay behind on Sunday in that no man's land around the city, whose peace is blemished only mornings and evenings by the din of departing and returning vehicles—lag a little behind progress, and in a trice you will be as solitary as Herr Walter von Stolzing when he was snowed in on his estate, or as you may be at your own fireside in wintertime. Prometheus, the solitary bearer of fire, no longer creates progress today. Progress has become a centipede. It proliferates. It dwells in every one of the multitudinous houses that line the street; there are many of them, for the sheet is long if not infinite. Solitude is for the tranquil and isolated man who is content to lag behind progress. In this, our time, he can be far more solitary and set apart than any snowbound lord of a medieval castle. And perhaps Prometheus has meanwhile changed his quarters once more, unnoticed; perhaps, in a silent, empty ring around the great cities a new and progressive race devoted to culture in the best sense is out taking strolls. For the present there may be only a few specimens, but someday they may rule over us; perhaps they may survive all the gasoline vapors of the present and hold the future in fee.

Niki Zdarsa and Leonhard Kakabsa, for their part, traveled far beyond that empty zone around the city—which in any case was not yet so clearly defined in those days as it now is. Their initial velocity usually carried them in a single spurt as far as Stinkenbrunn, or somewhere thereabouts—say Hirm, where at that time the sugar industry flourished. Sometimes they went much farther, around the Neusiedler Lake, say, to Illmitz and

Apetlon. Or if they were not in the mood for a long trip, they liked going to Wulka-Prodersdorf, Drassburg, or Klingenbach.

The Zdarsa house in Stinkenbrunn was shady.

That did not matter so much then, when the heat of mid-summer was over; in summertime the hot days weigh fearfully on the Burgenland, which partakes of the fiery climate of the Hungarian plain. In the autumn no one wanted the shade, rather sought out the mild sun; and the coolness no longer affected you when you came in from the sun as a blessing at last attained. Nevertheless, the shadiness of that house remained palpable even in winter. For Leonhard that circumstance led to one of those questions which are never asked because they are too silly. Such questions really cannot be put to any other person, yet nevertheless loom darkly in the mind, possess a kind of blurred distinctness, we might say. And only because we feel as though the eyes of others have rested upon us even as we thought, and because we apply others' standards to our thoughts, do some of the smallest and yet most essential phenomena of our lives remain unexamined to the very end. In all likelihood others would not have interfered with these thoughts of ours; but we do the interfering for them, as their deputies.

The Zdarsa house, then, was shady. We will venture to explain that on entirely physical grounds: the house had many corners and corridors, an arched windowless vestibule, no verandas, all sorts of cubbyholes, and few real rooms. It was not a country house. Rather, it was the dwelling place of half-rural people, semi-peasants; one of those numerous houses into whose windows we have glanced when passing through middle-sized towns: low rooms, city furniture. There will always be an accumulation of things, usually of rural origin, piled on the polished chests; there will be tables under hanging lamps, armchairs around the tables, quilts. Outwardly such houses are neatly painted, have two stone steps before the door, and to the right of the lower step a footscraper is sure to be installed: a dull blade of metal set vertically above two rods.

Rustics who no longer till the fields, and who live in a street of solid houses amid urban household gear, easily take on a slight but perceptible degree of repulsiveness. That is also true of rustics whom the winds of destiny have cast into the city. They will, for example, in their city apartments keep large vessels of lard and bowls of eggs on top of the polished wardrobe in an icy bedroom. The bedroom will be austerity itself, except for the white pillows displayed upon the beds as if on parade. If the peasant is separated from the soil, his juices turn sour. He becomes susceptible to every ailment, from tuberculosis to regional poetry; the latter is not always confined to the sacred stillness of the mountains.

There are Boeotians even in the midst of literary life in Athens or Vienna.

Now Stinkenbrunn was not, of course, a town, and the Zdarsas still tilled the soil. The vineyards belonging to Father Zdarsa and his son-in-law lay behind the house, behind the solid row of houses which formed the village. The son-in-law, Alois Pinter, was a man of considerable property in his own right. His land lay toward the woods known as the Hartlwald. The vicinity of this village is hilly; there are elevations rising as high as 900 feet above sea level.

Father Zdarsa was also one of those who had motorized himself. Here was one more piece of evidence for the observation of Johannes V. Jensen, the Danish writer, that low-grade minds are always most susceptible to progress and its technical toys. In the barn behind the house there stood a motorcycle which quietly scented the air with the smell of oil, and at times with gasoline fumes. For at the right and proper intervals it was thoroughly cleaned and tended.

Careful upkeep was essential, if only because it was used so hard. When he roared through the village astride his wheeled horse, old Zdarsa looked like the keeper of a tobacco shop gone mad. The procedure had something of a witch's ride about it. Zdarsa was a wizened little fellow—moreover afflicted with a gray goatee. He rode too fast. There was something quite uncanny about it, and an involuntary reminder of the portentous proverb: "The Evil One rides fast and never rests." Yet Franz Zdarsa was in no way evil. He was nothing at all, not even, strictly speaking, a vintner, although he possessed the manifold techniques and knowledge that such an ancient and involved occupation requires. But the occupation had only come his way through circumstances—inheritance, it was said. Perhaps that accounted for the fact that his vineyards were widely scattered, and by no means located only in Stinkenbrunn, where Pinter had contributed most of the property to the joint enterprise.

This Pinter was a dark, handsome, stocky man with black eyebrows grown together over the bridge of his nose. Pinter came from a family of vintners; in his case wine growing was virtually a trait of character which drew all other traits along with it, so that these followed in the track of viticulture. People generally called him "Pinta," thus ignoring the German or Germanized ending of his name. He was said to be a Croat, a "Crovot." In the Burgenland, the south of which is Croat, that was no derogatory term any more than it is elsewhere in Austria. Quite the contrary. The Croats are held in high esteem, and rightly so. It was ever the prudent policy of the Austrian government to protect this charming national group as well as their language, whose works have long belonged to world literature.

Pinta would occasionally mount the motorcycle behind his father-in-law, when he had occasion to work in distant vineyards. But he seemed to take little pleasure in committing himself to this vehicle. By preference he would pick up a ride on a passing horse-drawn wagon. Once he arrived at his destination, Pinta would frequently occupy himself there for some time. It often happened that he would be quite far from Stinkenbrunn. Old Zdarsa owned large vineyards at Mörbisch, which lies between the hilly country of Rust and the belt of reeds around the Neusiedler Lake, close to the Hungarian border. All that might be needed at these vineyards in the way of tools and materials were kept there, in a well-locked shed. There was also a hut on the property, where the proprietor could spend the night.

Pinta reached his land by turning to the right off the road to Fertörákos (which in German is called Kroisbach) in Hungary. On foot, he would climb along the upward-sloping edge of the woods to a deep bend in the straight line of trees. Here lay the hut, far back in a corner of the bend, half among the deciduous trees. The hut was in fact directly below the highway from Hausberg to Kinzingriegel, which highway forms the border with Hungary at this point.

There was a stove and a bed in the hut and Pinta continued to come there even after his grapes had been picked. He would come tramping up the slope along the woods with a heavy pack on his shoulders. The burden was liquid. It consisted chiefly of a monster, wicker-covered bottle full of wine.

Arriving at the hut on one such autumn day, Pinta lit a lamp and opened one of the window shutters on the side toward the woods. Not long afterwards steps were heard, and the visitors announced themselves at the window with a greeting in Hungarian. The first to enter the cluttered room—at least a

643

third of which was filled with tools and tin canisters of that lizard-green spray-material used against the grape louse—the first to enter bore upon his face like an exposed underlayer the bold and curious marks of his nation. And yet it was a face that also revealed much more than nationality. Ancient and deep layers seemed in it to be refined, without transition or diversion, to an extreme cultivation; the refinement cut through the uppermost strata of later times, the mound of disparate shards, the physiognomical rubble heap which the faces of every European people offer to the eye nowadays. So it was that in the face of this Hungarian count the lowest levels had come to the top again, the source had become terminus. His delicate body weighed perhaps no more than 110 pounds. In every step and every gesture of the hand he far surpassed any of the requirements of elegance which might have been posed by a club in Piccadilly or the race courses of Paris and Vienna, with which indeed he was very familiar. This would have been so, that is, even when he was on foot, which is to say only half present. For his full personality to assert itself, he had to be mounted. Indeed, he had four times won one of the most difficult of European hurdle races: the Austrian Imperial Army Steeplechase.

The bird Turul—we mean Herr Géza von Orkay—would have looked, beside this fellow-countryman, like a gingerbread dove beside a living falcon.

Pinta bowed to the count and was greeted. Several more men entered. One was new. "*Szefcsik sásados-ur*," the count said gracefully ("Captain Szefcsik"), indicating this gentleman. Pinta stepped back with a formal bow that incidentally suggested the Slavic element in his nature. To Pinta, of course, the name meant a great deal, little as it awakens any echoes today.

The face of this Captain Szefcsik presented an entirely

different, and undoubtedly later development, of the Hungarian countenance than that refinement drawn from the primeval stratum which was so apparent in the count's face. Here a different type of compromise with Western features had been achieved. In this face, various further mixtures, probably certain Slavic elements came to the fore. (The Magyar spelling of the name was of no consequence.) Such Hungarian faces are broad and not slant-eyed. The Mongolian fold, the so-called epicanthus, is lacking. Nevertheless, the face has a distinct Mongol cast, such as can also be frequently observed in Far Eastern faces: there is less sculpturing in depth to such faces; the cheekbone is less developed; the eye is seated shallowly. The facial expression is on the whole more amiable, though we also sense that this amiability is perhaps founded in an amazing lack of sensitivity, toughness, and durability of the nerves . . . Such countenances are most common in western Upper Hungary, around the region of Neutra, where Magyar elements have penetrated deeply into Slovakia.

Szefcsik was a benign-looking executioner. He belonged, like the no less notorious Lieutenant Pronay, to the party of the regent-to-be, Miklós Horthy de Nagybánya, who came out of Rumanian exile and with Rumanian assistance liquidated the dictatorship of Béla Kun. The post-liquidations were then carried out in the cellars of the Hotel Britannia in Budapest, under the aegis of both these gentlemen, and went on for some time.

These representatives of "Awakening Hungary" seemed to have so thorough and sound a sleep behind them that they sat gaily over their wine until long past midnight. To Pinta these men were fundamentally as mysterious as they are to us. This may account for part of the powerful attraction they exerted upon him. Equally unclear to him were the contradictory elements in his own conduct. As long as this country had been

Hungarian he had, as a Croat, experienced the constant pressure of Magyarization which oppressed all members of foreign nationalities living under the Hungarian crown. Of course Pinta had been young at that time. Nevertheless, his parents' determined adherence to their mother tongue, and a good many frictions and thrashings in his Hungarian school, formed the basic fabric of his early memories. Yet here he was associating with these people, felt himself to be on their side, and on the side of those unwilling citizens of Austria who cherished similar if not purely Hungarian aspirations. Vaguely, Pinta shared their ideas. Pinta, and others like him, had forgotten that as late as 1920 Austrian troops had fought hard against strong Hungarian bands who opposed the incorporation of the Burgenland into Austria—for all that the region was mostly German-speaking. Pinta, and others like him, seemed to lose sight of the fact that those who now came across the border as allies might ultimately have something else in mind besides the struggle against the "Austro-Bolsheviks," as they were prone to call the Austrian Social Democrats. For the Social Democrats had a strong local organization in the Burgenland.

Not that any political conferences, any plans, plots, or conspiracies took place in Pinta's hut. That is not how Hungarians do things. They gathered there primarily to drink wine, laugh, sing a little, and express regret that there was no gypsy present to play for them. Whereas in the West the dense ideological cloud in any given group covers the underlying emotions with views, interests, objects, and all the things that "are needed," so that the ideological cloud truly becomes smoke which denies the presence of its fire—here the core of the matter frequently shone through, like the intestines in young amphibians.

"What is Preschitz doing?" the count asked in high good humor. "Has your old man been to see him again, Pinta?"

"Who is Preschitz?" Szefcsik spoke up amiably, his tongue already thickening from the wine.

"Why, he was *in illo tempore* the deputy for the president of the Sopron court, didn't you know?"

"*Bószama!*" Szefcsik swore. "*That* swine! He's the one who killed Pastor Nikitsch."

"But he says it isn't true," Pinta replied.

"To whom did he tell that story?"

"My old man, Zdarsa."

"And what is he up to these days?"

"He is leading the Drassburgers," Pinta replied.

"There's a fellow I'd like to have inside the royal Hungarian boundary posts," the count said under his breath. It was by no means a passionate exclamation—his voice remained at its customary even pitch, and he spoke slowly, as always. Only his face darkened somewhat; a Hungarian countenance like his can darken swiftly and profoundly, and when it does, the incomprehensible elements in it emerge, come suddenly to the surface. The little English mustache which this gentleman jockey wore was of the bushy type which falls somewhat over the upper lip. The count's eyes, unlike Szefcsik's, were deep in their sockets. His aquiline nose seemed to thrust forward. His similarity to long-dead ancestors, to those, say, who had participated in King Andrew's crusade or other such ill-organized but stubbornly pursued adventures, was perhaps far greater than any that his cronies in the hut could remotely imagine.

There was a silence. The candle flickered. Its broken and dispersed light made the farther reaches of the room, with the clutter of tools and canisters, resemble a confused heap of ruins.

"Bastards like that ought to be cut up for pig-feed," Szefcsik said at last.

"But only to teach the pigs a lesson!"

This made them laugh. The count's laughter was not exactly amiable. His face retained that incomprehensible underlying note. By comparison Szefcsik looked harmless, or at any rate understandable.

"Two weeks ago in Vienna I was sitting with Lieutenant-colonel Hiltl at the 'trough,' as they call the bar there, of the Hotel Imperial," the count said casually. "He brought a German cavalry captain with him. Eulenfeld, Otto, Baron. Excellent chap. Hiltl knows more of the sort there. Eulenfeld has a friend, Schlaggenberg, Kajetan, who is a writer, naturally has plenty of connections. But I don't place so much value on such people, literati and that ilk. Anyway, the two of them, the captain and this Herr von Schlaggenberg, know Gyurkicz, Imre. Naturally, I told the captain what I knew about the ambiguous role the fellow has played."

Szefcsik listened with interest. He was far from underestimating the importance of this group in Vienna that was in process of formation. Incidentally, all people with ideologies tend to be exporters. At that time Austria was a country importing from three sides: East, North, and South.

"Next year, I hear, Géza Orkay is supposed to be transferred to Vienna, to Bank Gasse." (That was where the Hungarian embassy and consulate general were located.) "He's taking the place of Pista Grauermann, who's gone into industry. Well, you know, Orkay is one of us. Grauermann has been a regular consular bureaucrat. But then, he's a Kraxelhuber."

Hungarians used this word to characterize their fellow-countrymen from Pressburg (Bratislava) who were of German origin and had German names. Pista Grauermann, René Stangeler's widowed brother-in-law, was one of these. Hungarians have a good many odd, and often highly trenchant expressions. For this and other reasons one is seduced into liking them.

The conversation left the realm of politics as easily as it had entered it. What remained was the semi-darkness of the hut, filled with drifting cigarette smoke. What remained was a song, sung in four parts by Szefcsik's and the count's cronies, who had for the most part held their peace but who now contributed to the evening with their masterly singing. It was as if the song drew into the room the land to the south and east; as if the country beyond the Neusiedler Lake floated on the music, with its swamps and its many smaller lakes and ponds, suffused with sun down to their clean sandy bottoms—lakes in which Hungarian peasant women bathe by going in with all their clothes on. But the Neusiedler region and the misty skies and wet meadows of Hansag form only the threshold and antechamber of the East; the antechamber continues beyond, lost within itself, as far as the Flatten Lake, as far as the Bakonyer Forest; and only there does the mighty Hungarian plain, the Hungarian fatherland really begin. Where the gypsies in their haunting melodies proclaim what Franz Schubert is credited with saying: "There is no such thing as merry music."

When making his small repairs in the Zdarsas' house, Leonhard sometimes had the assistance of Elly Zdarsa, Pinta's wife's sister. She was five years younger than her married sister. Elly held a candle for Leonhard in the dark hall of the house when he was changing fuses, or she stood on the ladder a few rungs below him, holding the light up toward him, or she handed him a tool. It had become a habit. The occasions were fairly frequent; for many years all sorts of things had been neglected in the house. Here a washer had worn off a bolt, there a faucet leaked. Leonhard brought the odds and ends that he needed for these repairs with him from Vienna.

While Elly held the light as high as possible, the sleeve slid down her outstretched arm, and Leonhard, turning to take a tool from her free hand, would see into the darkness of her armpit. A true blackness, it was. It struck him as extraordinarily large. He would turn back to the loose wire or the box which held the porcelain knobs of the fuses.

In the living room with the tablecloth and hanging lamp— the time in question was two o'clock in the afternoon, so that the lamp was not lit; it only flashed on once when Elly, after Leonhard had again replaced all the fuses, reached through the half-opened door to test the switch—in this living room Father Zdarsa, Pinta, and Niki Zdarsa sat at table. They were drinking Stinkenbrunner: Niki in quantity, Pinta with moderation, the father only for form's sake. He took no pleasure in wine at all, preferring beer or hard liquor. But he went along with the others—he was tolerant and did not like to be a spoil-sport. He did not really take pleasure in beer or hard liquor either. In fact he liked nothing, was nothing; or at any rate, people never found out what he was, which amounts to much the same thing. Why he planned to go to a workers' meeting in Hirm that afternoon likewise could not be determined. For old Zdarsa was obviously very far from being a socialist. How little he knew in this year of 1926 about the aims of the movement struck those who knew him as utterly ridiculous; such ignorance would have been reprehensible even in a completely nonpolitical person. It is likely that he was absolutely unaware of the prominent figures of the socialist movement, even in Austria. If anyone had asked him who, say, Viktor Adler was, his reply would have been astonishing, to put it mildly. Yet he went to meetings now and then—when, for example, Thomas Preschitz was to be the speaker. Pinta, who sometimes accompanied the old fellow, had long since discovered that his father-in-law did not listen at

650

all and would have been incapable of giving the most general summary of any one of the speeches.

The blackness he had looked into lingered stubbornly in Leonhard's mind, a center of disturbance, a humming bumble-bee, even while with Elly's help he carried the ladder out of the hallway and restored it to its place in the shed. Now that her mission for Leonhard was accomplished, Elly probably should have returned to the kitchen to help her sister, Rosalia Pinta, with the dishwashing, or at least with the drying. But she and Leonhard took their time about handling the ladder, and only after some effort did they succeed in putting the long clumsy thing back in its right place and in its right position.

The excessive blackness Leonhard had glimpsed did not at all fit in with Elly Zdarsa's weak, waxenly pale arms, nor with the rest of her person. There was much about her which was like her sister. Both had sensitive skins, prone to blotches and small pimples, and the very whiteness of their complexions—as opposed to the healthy leathery tan of Alois Pinta's skin—stressed these impurities. Both, the married woman and the girl, were soft in their movements. And although they were slender—Frau Pinta was a bit fuller of figure—there was something languid about the very shape of their bodies. They were the exact opposite of buxom; the exact opposite, that is, of Malva Fiedler. Neither of the sisters seemed overfond of hard work; perhaps they were physically not up to it. Nor was it expected of them since there were no children in the house, two pairs of women's hands were sufficient to keep this orphaned household (Mother Zdarsa had died before the war) in order, or at least in the condition that was regarded as order there. Leonhard, however kept making new discoveries of general neglect, and more and more extended the range of his efforts.

In these chronicles we have already pointed out—on

the occasion of Herr von Geyrenhoff's encounter with Frau Trapp when he was sitting with Frau Ruthmayr in Gerstner's *Konditorei* in Vienna, which scene has already been described by Geyrenhoff in his sensitive if all too prolix fashion—we have already pointed out, on that occasion, that bottled-up members of the bourgeoisie and petty bourgeoisie of both sexes are far more difficult to grasp and seem far more obscure and mysterious than even the strangest and profoundest of geniuses. Could it be that biographers prefer to deal with such figures not only for their greater eminence but also for the lesser difficulty? Would not many a writer who sets out to describe and explain a Juarez or Cromwell an Alexander the Great or Franz Schubert, fail utterly in dealing with an Edam cheese, which is to say Frau Trapp, or with a motorized goatee, which is to say the tenuous Zdarsa? Would he not prove powerless to poke even a little under the rind of said Edam cheese, or to lift just a little the beard of said motorcyclist to reveal an abnormally feeble chin formation and thus expose the reason for the wearing of such a goatbeard? We, too, lift inadequately, but only in the case of a Zdarsa. It is, for example, difficult to say what the latter thought, wished, undertook in connection with Leonhard and Elly. It may even be that he was afraid of something, and would be brooding over the fact that this Kakabsa fellow was after all nothing but an ordinary worker.

At any rate Leonhard was disturbed in the shed at this point—though by now the ladder at least rested in its proper place, and the slight suction-cup-like contacts with Elly, which had occurred while it was being pushed, had been broken off again. Still they had lingered for a few moments. Leonhard, then, was disturbed in the shed; old Zdarsa and Niki came to get their motorcycles. It was time for the meeting in Hirm.

Not long after this incident Leonhard met Mathias Csmarits. The occasion was a visit to that tavern where once upon a time his contentment with his lot in life had caused a wall of misunderstanding to build up rapidly around him. Csmarits was a disabled war veteran: he had had one eye shot out, for such are the quaint things that happen to people in wars and armies. Csmarits did not wear a glass eye; he kept his reddish lids pinched shut over the empty socket. This, together with his oversized parrotlike nose, gave his face a not exactly pleasant appearance. Moreover, his skull seemed quite square. The one-eyed man usually had a bright-eyed small boy with him, Pepi by name. This was not his son, however, for he called Csmarits "Uncle."

A group of men were sitting together. Among them was that elderly worker who had once taken Leonhard under his wing, supported him against the growing opposition, and at last broken through the solid front with his gentle forcefulness. The disabled veteran had just come from Schattendorf, which lies close by the Hungarian border. Asked about "conditions down there," he made a few remarks which suggested casual sympathy with the socialists, attenuated, however, by a general skepticism which probably sat rather deep in a person whom the so-called course of history had already cost an eye. A man of this sort is not prepared to tear out the other one voluntarily for the sake of any cause whatsoever. Deep within him is an inexpungeable suspicion that all the people who shout slogans are really aiming at our eyes, whether they are socialists or the onetime authorized representatives of His Majesty's government (six of one and half a dozen of the other). Still and all, Csmarits was a member of the "Republican Protective Association" in Klingenbach. It may be that down there in the Burgenland membership in this private army of the socialists was unavoidable.

At the narrow end of the table little Josef Grössing—that was the small boy's full name—was zestfully drinking a raspberry soda. Leonhard sat opposite the one-eyed veteran. But he was not paying attention to the conversation, although it somehow concerned him and he might even have been able to contribute something to it (for had he not ridden to the meeting in Hirm, though not very willingly, on the back seat of Niki Zdarsa's motorcycle?). But he could not concentrate. There was a pressure upon him, like the light touch of a hand: a point which he had not been distinctly conscious of by itself but which he now felt as the third point in a triangle which was palpably growing and enlarging within him, and at the same time caging him within its sides. This triangle, to establish its co-ordinates quite precisely as Leonhard conceived them, rested upon Malva Fiedler's belly, upon Trix K.'s red-gold hair, and upon the blacknesses seen and postulated in Elly Zdarsa. The trouble was that the vertices of the triangle did not lie all in one plane. Elly especially; her position with regard to the geometrical figure was only adjacent, and yet the triangle did extend one apex toward her to form a long, highly acute angle; the lopsided figure stretched all the way to Stinkenbrunn, into the shady house, into the dark hallway where the shadow condensed into a deep, deep blackness.

At such moments as this, Leonhard seemed to see the whole situation from outside; he saw himself confined within this imaginary geometrical figure, and felt a wholly cool but real grief at the loss of his freedom. Here at the tavern table Leonhard now took the second decisive step in his intellectual history—he had already crossed the dialect frontier and now he made his first creative formation in the language whose realm he had newly entered through the good offices of Scheindler, author of his Latin grammar. Surely we may speak of intellectual history in connection with a single individual, no matter how modest he may be. Any absolute scale of magnitude in such matters is utter nonsense. And even though we may be dealing with someone who functions in profound darkness, unimaginably remote from that absolute scale, we never know but that he may sometime suddenly appear publicly right in the midst of it. That depends only upon the degree of his genuineness. And in Leonhard the degree of genuineness was high indeed, almost a maximum. He hit on the phrase "adjacent entanglement" for the third and dark point of the triangle, and thereby felt a sense of release. He could go home feeling that he was to some extent in control of the situation. Come what come might, the meaning had been grasped and formulated.

We can report no political tensions in the Zdarsa-Pinter household, although it would seem logical to expect them. The "Old Goatbeard" utterly lacked any real political ideology—another word for seeing the world through a slit cut askew, hating what one does not see and does not want to see, from which it is evident that one nevertheless has really seen these things. Zdarsa's politics might all stem from certain strong impressions made upon him during the time when the Burgenland was still Hungarian and Preschitz, during the dictatorship of the soviets, had been deputy president of the court at Odenburg (which the count would have called "Sopron," for that is its Magyar name). Zdarsa was afraid of Preschitz, although there was no longer the slightest reason for it. But somehow Preschitz had put the fear of God into our landowner. By now things had stabilized and the Burgenland was under the Austrian flag. Law and order had been restored, and Preschitz no longer had the power to conduct a reign of terror. But perhaps Zdarsa was too profoundly convinced of the mutability of all things to alter his fixed attitudes, even though the pressure and coercion would seem to have passed and there was no longer any reason to stay on the right side of the Bolsheviks.

This being the psychological situation, the goatee was not particularly avid for political discussions and debates. And Pinta, for his part, lacked all desire to express his opinions. He was not talkative and never spoke of politics. He had already found his escape-valve in political matters at Mörbisch, as we have seen.

And so whatever demonstration he made against Zdarsa was by manner, but never by words. He even rode to meetings on the back seat of his father-in-law's motorcycle; but maintained a stubborn silence behind the heavy eyebrows that grew together over his nose.

Thus there were no political bumblebees humming in Leonhard's head in the Zdarsa house in Stinkenbrunn; they were quite different bees, dark, black, furry. His "political" act in going along on the trip to Hirm without trying to get out of it—he had gone along without demur—nevertheless indicates that in this realm he was following in a deeply worn mental track which he no longer recognized as such.

There is no escaping certain paths—that is it. And Leonhard had only recently realized this in the tavern while Csmarits was talking about "conditions down there." He had realized that he was only nominally free, in reality under the triple constraint of a lopsided figure whose apex stretched all the way to Stinkenbrunn. Yet as the bumblebee humming increased, as the center of disturbance swelled, he was in a certain sense already beyond it, past it and matured, through having formulated such a phrase as "adjacent entanglement." But of course he could not hold such a head start without being challenged.

An onslaught was made against him; indeed, it was as if he had vexed and provoked the center of disturbance by the very aloofness of his phrase for it.

The onslaught came suddenly, interrupting a renunciation which, deep within himself, was already in progress. For once, when Elly Zdarsa and Leonhard were briefly alone in the house, there had taken place on the sagging red sofa at the back of the living room approaches of an unprecedented intensity. These, to be sure, had been initiated by Elly, but she had no sooner begun things than she promptly drew back, so that a kind of empty space was created across which he had to leap; which he did to a large extent out of timidity before the very emptiness of it. What followed became rather passionate, although Leonhard by no means proceeded to widen the revealed crack immediately into a breach, for someone might come in at any moment. And in fact someone did. Since it had begun to rain and shoes were rather muddy, Niki Zdarsa somewhat circumstantially cleaned off his motorcyclist's boots on the scraper provided for that purpose outside the door. Perhaps he even had Leonhard's interest at heart, for he attended to his boots with what seemed unnecessary noise, clearing his throat, muttering low curses and bumping against the front door. By then Leonhard had long since reached an armchair by the table. Toward the last he had buried his face completely in Elly's armpit.

When Pinta awoke in the hut at Mörbisch, threw off the horse blankets under which he slept, brought a pail of water from the clear forest pond close by the frontier, made coffee and washed—it was usually very early, almost dark still (unless he had had guests the night before; guests, incidentally who left

657

so many Hungarian banknotes lying on the table that four big bottles of Mörbisch or Rust wine could easily have been bought for the sum).

He left the hut and the edge of the woods. Traversing the slope horizontally for a short distance brought him into the vineyards. He could see the day dawning clear, without fog. It was as though the rosy morning emerged out of the lake's farther, eastern rim. The water lay like a delicate membrane stretched over the land behind the gray-blue belt of reeds which bridged the boundary between the two. The morning, not yet born as the first narrow segment of sun glowed above the margin of the sky, nevertheless had the crystal and fragrant aura of fall: the air pure as clear varnish, and none of that vast rent in the sky which precedes a summer's day.

Pinta stood there for a long time, gazing toward the east. Behind the heavy eyebrows his whole nature lay compressed like the kernel of a hazelnut in its hard shell.

That autumn was a prolonged one. The house continued to seem shady. Above the wooden stairs hovered the ingrained smell of the banister's rough paint, of floor wax, and of many other things which would baffle the scientific chemist. For there was more to it than chemistry. One would have to resort to alchemy to analyze these smells, since they were not chemical but chimerical. Chemists, were they asked by Herr von Geyrenhoff—who at times thinks himself a writer and accordingly asks self-important questions—could not inform him precisely why a sandwich tastes better out of doors than in.

As far as Niki Zdarsa was concerned, he obtained at least one benefit from these trips to Stinkenbrunn: they cost him very little and yet brightened his Sundays. Father Zdarsa did not charge for the Stinkenbrunner. Niki—laying his ears back, so to speak—had become aware that Old Goatbeard was in some ways currying favor with Leonhard and himself. In political discussions he would produce the kinds of remarks he thought ought to please a worker who belonged to the Social Democratic party organization. He seemed to have quickly found out that much about Leonhard and Niki. The latter, however, had the wisdom to remark to his back-seat companion—they were having a bit of a rest by the roadside one Sunday—that it would be just as well to leave old Zdarsa with his beliefs and never so much as hint to him that they too were by no means adepts at politics or experts in political questions (though in comparison to Old Goatbeard they were virtually trained socialists!). It was perfectly clear, Niki commented, that Father Zdarsa would never have the guts to join a political party. But on the other hand, his Stinkenbrunner was first class; and since the old man was scared stiff of Preschitz, they might as well let him transfer some of his fear to them. At least they could get a few bottles of good wine out of it.

In the course of this conversation it became apparent that Niki despised the old man. Every real proletarian tends to have such feelings toward the petty bourgeois whose fears for his livelihood are clamped like a clothespin on his skinny neck and who guards his whole nature as if it were a jug of vinegar.

About Pinta, their opinions were divided. Between Leonhard and Pinta there existed an uncertain bond of sympathy. Uncertain, but enough to keep Pinta's reticence from being quite as intact as it normally was. Niki declared flatly that Pinta was a fascist, but added that he personally didn't give a damn and there was no reason for them to put a flea in the ear of Pinta's father-in-law.

Privately, Leonhard admired Niki's intelligence, not without twinges of conscience. For as far as he himself was concerned, he had grown extremely remiss in every respect. The bumble-bees hummed, and paradoxically enough more than ever now that winter was approaching. They buzzed again in Wallenstein Strasse, and just when he called on old Fiedler for books to be used as an antidote; perhaps that had been only a pretext. For the antidote he really sought was, probably, Malva. He met her in the bookshop, or rather in front of it—it was long after business hours and she was arranging the show window. The glass pane stood diagonally across the sidewalk, supported by a small stand that looked like an automobile jack. This time, too, the apprentice was on guard to see that no one blundered into the glass. Old Fiedler was not present. Leonhard helped Malva. When she was finished, they carefully locked up and he accompanied her home, across the bridge and along the Danube Canal. Darkness had long since fallen.

But in the meanwhile something had happened. It had happened imperceptibly—only the result became palpable all at once. But there could be no doubt about it: the preponderance had shifted to that vertex of the triangle where Trix was located. Her golden hair with glints of red now dominated Leonhard as he walked along beside Malva, leaving behind, segment by segment, a route evenly marked out by street lights. Down below and to the left was the embankment, was the water in which the fights stood on their heads. Almost at the very moment that Leonhard recognized the shift in the center of gravity within himself he became aware that beside him walked a devouring maw—that rapid, icy tornadoes awaited only his signal to spring up with unimaginable force. He realized clearly that he could plunge in without more ado—in fact there was almost an obligation to do so. Only then—then everything would be over. What would be over? Everything. Innumerable joints and hinges stood ready to clap shut; and if previously he had only been under constraint here he would be finally and completely surrounded, would be nothing less than separated from his own life. Nothing less than that. He would have a life consisting of nothing but circumstances. The idea sent a tingle of both anxiety and voluptuous pleasure through Leonhard. His feelings were somewhat like those of a person who toys with the thought of suicide.

Later when he returned alone along the canal and back toward the bridge, for the briefest moment the notion grazed his mind that everywhere around him many people were living exactly as he would be doing after such a self-annihilation. Not that he framed the thought so drastically, nor even flashed the dark lantern of conscious thought upon the notion that had so rapidly slipped past him. So far, friend Leonhard, we had not yet come; far from it! He thought of Trix. Two weeks before he had visited at her home. Her mother, he had heard, would be returning soon. Undoubtedly that meant the end of those little parties, talks, dances. From the very start, he had accepted the surroundings there with composure, although this was actually the first time in Leonhard's life that he had gone in and out of such an apartment (it reminded him of the movies). He had simply sat there with his fishing-rod out, waiting to catch instruction. And was interested to note that many of these young people had put on socialistic airs—perhaps for reasons remotely resembling old Zdarsa's.

Leonhard came to the bridge.

The expression he had just used in his thoughts—"for reasons remotely resembling"—came from the other side of the dialect frontier. Those four words could scarcely have been pronounced in the dialect; they would never have occurred in it. Leonhard was quite clearly conscious of that as he crossed the middle of the bridge. The sidewalk and roadway for the cars drew him along of their own accord. He looked neither to the left, out over the river, nor to the right, down into the darkness that plunged on into water, a darkness decimated and almost dissolved in the distance by a multitude of lights. For the first time in his life Leonhard felt his situation in life to be one that had been arbitrarily thrown his way by external circumstance; he felt it as temporary, and was half conscious of a new situation that he was just entering as if it were a railroad station. He walked on, passed by his own street, Treu Strasse, continued down Wallenstein Strasse, also passed by the corner of Jäger Strasse, and the famous window through which Lilly Catona and her friend had kept him under surveillance. The thought of dropping into a tavern somewhere around there, between the Danube Canal and Wallenstein Platz, was quickly banished by a vision of the familiar faces he would encounter. On the threshold of each tavern or café he could have said which of these faces he would meet. It was all utterly hopeless, led to nothing, would come to nothing, just like the cases of Malva, Trix, and Elly.

It is difficult to define precisely the line at which a human being's personal environment ceases and the atmosphere of his age begins. Nevertheless, Leonhard had left his own immediate district by now. He strolled on past the former Northwest Railroad Station, with its blinded look now that no trains entered or left it. It was a long distance that Leonhard traveled on foot this Saturday night (no trip to Stinkenbrunn was planned for the morrow). He was on his way to Anny Gräven.

He spent part of the night with her in her room in the big, ancient, rambling house. He had not seen her for a long time

662

and she told him all sorts of trivia in gay confusion, with a childish pleasure that was extremely attractive and almost reconciled one to the ordinary background of her life. Meisgeier had been in the bar that night (the bar where Leonhard had met her; this was not Anny's regular hangout, for she kept Leonhard away from that one)—Meisgeier had been in the bar, and of course there had been a row, but the boss had stood up to "the Claw" and so he had had to retreat—"you don't need to call in the police so long as you keep your nerve."

Who was Meisgeier, otherwise known as "the Claw," Leonhard wanted to know.

"I kind of think the boss must have something on him," Anny said, already diverted from Leonhard's question. "Otherwise why would he have cleared out without saying boo?"

"That sort of thing might lead to trouble for the boss," Leonhard remarked. "Especially if he knows too much."

"You think so?" Anny exclaimed, alarmed.

Next day Leonhard rose early, although he had not got back to his own place until the wee hours—he had gone out with Anny Gräven for sausages and beer. Curiously enough, Leonhard invariably made a point of taking Anny Gräven out to some small eating place "afterwards." By means of this Leonhard was able to give a more innocent cast to their evening together. For Anny sat at the table as if before a heavy curtain which concealed the other aspects of her life. Unfortunately, the whole business was rather boring, since on the whole he knew precisely what lay behind the curtain: almost nothing. There was only a barren empty stage on which stood a bed, or a mere sofa. On these occasions, when they sat together afterwards, Leonhard always made a point of behaving with particular courtesy, even tenderness, toward Anny. He exaggerated a little, and in doing so felt a slight unhappiness, a sense of hollowness—but no feeling of "adjacent entanglement." Anny appreciated his manner and responded with cordiality and confidences. Of course it must be said that she was used to a somewhat better tone than was usually accorded to women of her sort. She had her steady group of men friends, some of whom were quite well off and by no means stingy. But Anny was frivolous; though Leonhard was always telling her she ought to save, she put nothing by. When he reproached her, she only laughed at herself, at her own frivolity.

Now, back in his room early on a gray Sunday morning, Leonhard was forced to recognize that the lever arm which he had employed, whose outer extreme was Anny Gräven, was nevertheless far shorter than that apex of the triangle which extended out to Stinkenbrunn. It was cold in the room, the first cold day of the year; it felt almost like November. Leonhard put on a warmer jacket and picked up a scarf. He was holding it in his hand when there came a knock at the door: his landlady, the widow of the warehouse attendant. She had noticed that he was already up, and since it was so cold she wanted to heat his room. In fact Leonhard, who had risen early with the wish to study, had been standing around in some perplexity in the uncomfortably icy room. Soon a fire was crackling in the Dutch stove. The old woman attended to the bedding and briefly opened the window. She also brought him hot black coffee, so that he would have something to warm him; there was no milk in the house yet, she said, she would be going out to get it in a little while. But now, she commented, it was at least nice and warm for shaving. She had also brought hot water.

And then the usual dialogue:

"Goin' to church, Herr Kakabsa?"

"You know I never go to church."

"Oh, well, no matter, I'll do your prayin' for you."

The room had in fact warmed quickly. Leonhard shaved and washed. He had set the pot of coffee on the stove, where it stayed hot. On the night table lay cigarettes, which Leonhard did not usually have; he had bought some the night before for Anny, who was a chain smoker. One of the packs had remained in his pocket. Carefully, he brought the bedside lamp over to the table; the cord was just long enough. Now he could read near the stove, for there was still not enough daylight. While he drank his coffee he tried one of the cigarettes. The smell and taste of the tobacco early in the morning gave him quite a new sensation. The fragrance seemed to have a penetrating deliciousness, although different from the smell in the taproom the night before when Anny Gräven had been lighting one cigarette after another and he had sat continually in her clouds of smoke. This was a solitary cigarette. And the smell of coffee mingled with it. Leonhard looked at the clock. His attention was drawn to the almost complete silence. It was only six-fifteen. On a Sunday morning at this hour everyone was asleep. He could not hear his landlady either. Perhaps she had gone out for the milk.

It was astonishing, Leonhard thought, how pleasantly everything had worked out this morning, how every little thing he needed had walked in at the door, so to speak. Here he sat now in warmth, in good light, his nose over the cup, drinking in the fragrance of the coffee. The first puff of the cigarette produced a gentle intoxication. Here in the stillness, far ahead of the bustle which on Sunday would begin later than on a weekday, he felt as if he were sitting upon the roof of life, felt himself master of all his decisions, as if they were all capable of recall, as if he still held them all in his hand, like unplayed cards. But the premonition that there might be a way to a state of being in which such fortunate coincidences were the rule, an open switch through which one slid along a smooth track again and again—this premonition filled him with a deep and stimulating unrest. For he had drawn this conclusion unconsciously from multiple small signs, not by clear and rational reflection—of which Leonhard was incapable in this connection. He was, however, capable of feeling within his own breast the possibility of expanded freedom. And thus at the same time he was aware of his present limited freedom as of a small stabbing pain.

The pain was quite different from the one Trix had administered to him on the stone steps by the water when she had asked him whether he wished to change his line of work, since he was "furthering his education," and so on . . .

It was a more intelligent pain.

That other pain had been stupid.

Leonhard formulated this thought exactly as it is set down here.

In so doing, he was approaching closer to the center of the triangle which had been constraining him for weeks. And he moved further away from at least one vertex, the one named Trix. Stinkenbrunn, to be sure, was held down only by a thin layer of narcosis. Malva, on the other hand, had been effectively annulled the day before by Trix. And Leonhard already had inklings of more intelligent pains. The small stabbing sensation he had just experienced left him with a craving to condense his premonition, to get a firmer grip on it. For several seconds he seriously pondered means of doing this. But he could think of none. Again he saw himself sitting on the stone steps by the water, with Trix. The vision came to him more vividly than ever now. Leonhard looked inside himself as if into a hollow space. Inside that space he could easily locate the "stupid pain." He was pushing against a wall that separated him from Trix. By doing this he conferred upon Trix the right to judge this pain, to acknowledge or deny its reason for being. And in his assiduous studying, too, Leonhard depended upon Trix and her judgment. The separating wall, then, did not really and effectively separate. He had to push himself away from it.

Leonhard made a little gesture in the air.

It suddenly occurred to him how lightly she had digressed, had turned her back on his whole problem, passing to something else that had attracted her attention: "Here comes a tug . . . !"

Slowly, with grinding machinery and belching smokestacks, the tug came up the river. That did it. Leonhard retreated from the crystalline wall that had grown up between himself and Trix. And at once Trix lost all trace of a right to give value to his studying, or to take it away.

She had been annulled.

But in a manner quite different from the annulment of Malva the day before.

At this point Leonhard had come to the end of his own resources, and so he reached for the *Introduction to Classical Antiquity.*

He had never let up on his studies, even during that spell when he and Niki had driven out to Stinkenbrunn nearly every Sunday. Invariably he went at his Scheindler every weekday evening, and for some time he had been working over the exercise book, devoting at least an hour to each lesson. Otherwise he would no longer have been able to sleep. There was never a threshold of laziness to cross, nor was there any longer any sense of merit to be won; that already lay behind him. Leonhard had changed. That is the most significant of accomplishments: to change inwardly. Having arrived at the plateau of new habits, he could only now see the heights still to be climbed.

Having already plowed through two-thirds of the exercise book Leonhard was close to having a fairly good knowledge of Latin. This success in so short a time can only be explained by his method of studying: the machine-like drill he underwent, as if learning to run a new piece of apparatus or a complex tool. There is only one kind of drill that may be compared with Leonhard's: the rehearsal of musicians in a military band. The piece must be note-perfect. No one gives a thought to the music. Leonhard, too, did not spend a moment thinking about the beauties of the Latin language, the mother of all grammar. He was completely untouched by such considerations. What he demanded of himself was an ever-ready knowledge of every single detail of all that he had previously learned. Flawless execution of all prescribed motions, manipulation of the apparatus with the gearshifts in every possible position. Knowledge of why a form was thus and not different. (Each time old Fiedler corrected Leonhard's notebooks, he would shake his head again and again in astonishment.) Since, then, Leonhard had proceeded with unceasing vigor and purposiveness, the rewards accumulated above his crammed head, so to speak, and exerted an increasing pressure. Possibilities accumulated. As yet he had never read a Latin author, although Fiedler had recommended Cornelius Nepos and even Caesar. It is hard to say why Leonhard refrained from taking them up, for he had already bought the books. Perhaps he set them aside for the same reason that he had set the exercise book aside for so long. It may be that he feared any jolt to his technological drilling, any complication which might hamper the smoothly running mechanism which he had, so to speak, devised himself. His instinct commanded him to use it for the journey into the unknown because it was familiar and reliable. However, in the meanwhile Leonhard was already reading Greek authors in German translations—following Fiedler's suggestions and availing himself of the paperbound *Universal-Bibliothek*. He already knew large parts of Herodotus, and Xenophon's *Anabasis*. But these books were only presents to himself after his grammatical studies. The same could be said of the textbooks on Greek and Roman history which he was reading.

For the present he was far from conscious of how much Latin he already knew. He was equally unconscious of the increasing precision of his language, or of the capacity of his intellect, which could already grasp and hold an idea in all its ramifications like a pair of tongs. He was, we might phrase it, becoming ever more distinct and accurate in his intercourse with himself. It is quite possible that even in this early stage of his studies Leonhard, when he was alone, had already developed an incomparably greater skill in the manipulation and separation of his ideas than many an intelligent and so-called cultivated person.

Leonhard spent the Sunday at home, looking into one textbook and then into another. This practice of his of shifting from subject to subject proved, perhaps more than anything else, his happy instinct. Meanwhile, a mental floor or two below his cramming—cramming because he was so set on making everything "stick"—a kind of package was being shifted in incessant alternation from one vertex of the triangle to another. The package had diminished in size; it weighed very little, seemed scarcely tangible. Yet it was there, or rather here and there. It did not occur to Leonhard to boldly divide it up. Other men would have long since made three packages of it, and converted the three sides of the triangle into three parallel lines: tracks with switches in between, to provide easy alternations. But in this matter Leonhard could not behave as he did with his books. Again and again three cards were being played against one another; they fluttered down like leaves, but none conclusively took the trick. Anny Gräven, however, remained outside the competition, *hors concours*.

The leaves were already fluttering down everywhere. The next Sunday would be the last autumnally pleasant one of the year. Niki proposed a trip around the lake. Leonhard was glad to go along. He left Stinkenbrunn behind as though what might have happened there was over and done with, by virtue of comparisons consciously made. He might as well allow that vertex of the triangle to dwindle, as had happened with Trix. The dark bumblebee buzzing, to be sure, went on exerting a powerful attraction upon his ear. We may almost think that this was so simple because—viewed from outside and without benefit of any fascination—it was altogether the most unreasonable of the three possible ties. Moreover, he did not care for Elly's complexion. Her skin, as we have mentioned, was prone to blemishes, and even at times looked oily. So that he was tempted in spite of himself.

Everything remained undone. They flew along on Zdarsa's "Indian" steed. The wind of their motion was already rather chilly, but they had special warm jackets on for these motorcycle trips and hoods and goggles which protected the upper parts of their faces. The stable cycle sped along low above the road, which steadily ran past their alert eyes, while everything to the left and right of it streamed by as a vague gray-green veil, with here and there long white streaks—for everywhere in the Burgenland are those friendly processions of geese. The pleasure that one takes in them has always a culinary quality; from the point of view of the geese, such smiles as one gives them cannot be described as benevolent. The sight of the birds is enough to stimulate the gastric juices, not to speak of those other glandular activities which "make the mouth water." The goose—or rather the *levée en masse* of geese—is one of the invariable features of the Burgenland, as well as of Hungary and Slovakia. Its simple needs, its intelligence, so markedly at variance with its reputation for stupidity—when they come in from grazing in the meadows, each goose will part from the flock and go correctly to its own little stall, while in groups the geese turn squads right or squads left as if at command, with never a one missing from its place unless it has been stolen—its simple needs and its intelligence, then, make it one of the favorite animals of the above-mentioned beautiful and gastronomically advanced lands. As for its reputation, the geese have had no part in it; that reputation has arisen only because every human being knows far too many persons whose look and bearing extraordinarily resemble that of geese; hence the false conclusion by analogy that geese are just as stupid as human beings. Incidentally, there are ganders too.

Fraunkirchen lies to the east of the lake, and some five miles away from it.

In the tavern called "The Stork's Nest," opposite the massive old pilgrimage church, there now sat—it was after Sunday Mass—many peasants, most of them German-speaking. All the rooms were crowded. Niki and Leonhard found a seat only after a prolonged search; two young men seated opposite each other at the end of a long table took their leave, and Leonhard and Niki promptly installed themselves in their places. At the narrow end of the table, in front of the wine-tap, sat a vigorous white-haired man who had just been brought his meal—a quarter of a goose. It looked so appetizing that our two young men promptly ordered the same. The rooms at the inn, buzzing with conversation and bustling with men going back and forth, were in any case emptying rapidly. Everybody was going

671

home to what surely would be an ample Sunday dinner.

Leonhard's and Niki's meals were served shortly. The vast portion of goose lay brown and succulent on the plate; the dumplings looked marvelous; the Oggau wine sparkled in the big glass.

"Are you from these parts?" Niki asked the old man.

"No, from Eisenstadt," was the reply. "I am the weighmaster." He employed this rather old-fashioned expression for his office as commissioner of markets. "Alois Gach is my name. Did you two gentlemen come on the train that arrived here three quarters of an hour ago?"

"No," Niki said, "on an Indian." And seeing that the other did not understand, he added: "Motorcycle."

"So did I," Gach said.

"What type of machine?" Niki asked promptly.

"Why, I really don't know what the wheel is called," Gach said, smiling. "It belongs to an acquaintance of mine who wanted to visit someone here, and I came along for a little country air. Now he's off to see them, and I suppose they've invited him to dinner. I'm just waiting here."

The look that Niki gave Gach showed that he had rather taken a liking to the man but was put off by his antiquated phraseology and his deliberate aloofness from the sport of motoring: that he chose to say "wheel" instead of "machine," and could ride along on a motorcycle without even knowing the make.

"Are you from Vienna?" Alois Gach asked.

"Yes. We work at the Rolletschek webbing factory in Brigittenau," Niki said. He and Leonhard then introduced themselves, rather belatedly, but Gach did not appear to take it amiss.

They had dined splendidly, and with some good food in the

stomach the fine flavor and beneficent effects of wine are most satisfactorily felt. For the first time in his life Leonhard really enjoyed wine. But they drank moderately.

Leonhard too had been rather taken aback by Gach; but what struck him was some special quality in the man's language. To have once crossed such borders himself, to have traveled from the language of his birthright into another which was nevertheless not foreign, from a linguistic here into a kind of linguistic hereafter, is an act not easily forgotten. And from then on a man remains sensitive: frontiers of being make themselves felt each time that frontiers of language are touched. That straddling step over the dialect frontier which Leonhard had performed one night—by day always readjusting to the dialect again, so that he came to approach it more and more from outside—that straddling step did not straddle the linguistic personality of Alois Gach; it did not pass over his manner of speech as a stage overcome and left behind. Rather, Gach's speech lay to one side. The whole man seemed to be leaning to one side; but there was considerable latent strength there. You felt it; you felt a kind of blockade exerted by it. Oddly enough, it acted as a check.

It was precisely the same kind of check that Leonhard had exerted, some time before, upon the educated young people in Mary K.'s apartment.

Though, to be sure, without his suspecting it.

Gach, too, did not suspect.

Meanwhile Leonhard was already beginning to suspect something; but it was nothing more precise than that. He had an inkling, but of what he did not know.

At any rate, both young men took a liking to the old fellow, and it was not only the wine that made them speak freely. Alois Gach turned out to be a little timid and embarrassed in his manner, and perhaps he felt at a bit of a disadvantage because he had known nothing about the motorcycle. At any rate, his kindness and friendliness were unmistakable, and in addition his appearance directly bespoke a man worthy of respect. He was unquestionably stiff and upright, and his manner contained a potential sternness, but never unpleasantness.

The conversation turned to politics. That was a subject ready to hand in the Burgenland in those days, though not precisely in this region to the east of the Neusiedler Lake; but after all none of the three was from the region. Nowadays we can scarcely imagine how, given the tremendous political tensions prevailing in Austria at that time, such questions could have been discussed in so relaxed a manner between persons of such differing views—and this only nine years after 1918, when the dominant brand of socialism was still a young and struggling faith. In 1926 so-called "ideologies" were still real opinions and convictions far more than they are today, when these hollow forms must serve not only as instruments for personal advancement (which is not so bad) but also as screens for not quite normal emotions.

"I suppose I may assume," Gach said, puffing out the smoke of his Sunday cigar, "that you gentlemen are Social Democratic party members." (Leonhard and Niki allowed that they were.)

"That can be taken pretty much for granted nowadays. And when I look at the great achievements of socialism, I must in all justice admire it. The municipal government of Vienna has some notable accomplishments to its credit; enough to make a man a Social Democrat in his old age."

But Niki could be a rebel upon occasion. "All very true, Herr Gach," he said, "and all very well if a man joins voluntarily. But we are forced to join the union."

"Not officially," Gach said.

674

"That's neither here nor there—we have to," Niki replied. "Nobody could keep his job at Rolletschek's if he weren't in the Social Democratic party, although the boss makes a point of not trying to influence the men and is glad if he doesn't hear anything about the whole matter. That isn't freedom, it's compulsion. And we have always said we are for freedom."

"Without compulsion there could be no freedom," Gach said.

"Yes, that's what they tell us."

"It's the truth, too," Gach went on, undeterred. "Only a man must make the compulsion himself; then he is free. If, for example, you realized deeply enough that the strength of the working class rests upon the unions, you would be in the union of your own free will. I must say that, even though I am not a socialist."

Niki, somewhat cowed at first, proved by his reply that he possessed no mean intelligence. For a reply was required. Gach fell silent and waited. And Leonhard, behind his meeting eyebrows, seemed to have made up his mind to avoid every superfluous word. Gach's quiet waiting pushed, Leonhard's silence pulled; between these dual forces, Niki had to speak. And he did so, not at all stupidly, after taking a swallow of wine.

"I grant what you say, Herr Gach," he declared at last. "But if it is necessary for a person to realize something so that he does, the right thing of his own free will—then I ask you, isn't it true that he has to be a real person in himself, to stand alone for himself, or however you want to put it? But in our party newspaper all I ever read is 'the people,' 'the masses,' and always 'the masses.' It's the masses that matter, the masses that count. But I'm not the masses, I'm a human being by myself. And that don't mean a thing to them."

Gach only nodded. There was a silence. But it was a

comfortable silence, with an undertone of deep, shared emotion. At one point during this pause they raised their glasses and drank to one another. Objectively speaking, this conversation was taking a course that in the light of present-day conditions seems almost incredible—in the first place because of its lack of inhibitions, and in the second place because of its orderliness. No one interrupted. We need only think of the muddled mutterings of the populace in taverns as we know them today. Even in those days something of the sort must have been the rule. Let us not consider the question of whether such an exception to the rule would be possible at all nowadays.

A crucial circumstance, in comparison, is the freedom with which the three men talked here, at a table in a tavern which stood quite precisely on the border between Central and Eastern Europe. Such freedom was by no means newborn; it was far older than the republic which had come into being in 1918. But at that time this freedom was little appreciated. And not a year was to pass from the day in the fall of 1926 that Gach and the young men drank and talked so easily at Fraunkirchen to the time when freedom was denied for the first time in Vienna, when its very existence was no longer recognized.

If only for that reason we have set down the innocuous conversation (basing it on Leonhard's account, for the one who keeps his mouth shut always in the end knows most about what has gone on).

"You put that well, Herr Zdarsa," Gach replied after reflecting for some time on Niki's last remark. "In fact you have made it clear to me why I cannot be a Social Democrat. The class in which a person is born, his station in life, cannot possibly be the most important thing about him. That is something he has in common with hundreds of thousands of others who represent it just as well as he does. But it seems to me that the most important thing about a man is what he has in common with no one else, the thing in which he stands alone for himself, as you put it. If he is merely a man of his class, he can be replaced, and anyone can replace anyone else. That is the real weakness of the proletarian, and that is why he has to join together with others. So that if you want to be socialists, you cannot get around the trade union; and to have them you probably have to exercise a certain amount of compulsion. There must not be any comrades outside the union, or more than one union in a single field; in short, it won't do to have 'scabs,' as you say. For then the class can never reach its goal. I'm sure the thing is basically just. Before the war I often thought that at bottom every decent person ought to be a socialist in some way, whether organized or not. Nowadays, though, things look rather different. I couldn't exactly say how—but things are different. Perhaps because a good deal has been achieved already. In hindsight everything looks different from the way it does beforehand."

"Right," Niki said.

They fell silent again. Then Niki asked: "Then why didn't you become a Social Democrat before the war, Herr Gach?"

"Because that did not go along with my station in life. A station is something stationary—it doesn't wriggle all over the place. You pretty much have to wear the suit that life drapes on you. There's mighty little proof for the belief that everything has to be changed or can be changed. Most things stick good and firm where they are, like a well-driven rivet. Where a man stands is probably where he belongs. And in the end it doesn't matter much where that is, so long as he does his job decently. I was finished with my apprenticeship as a blacksmith and wheelwright when I met my future employer. He was a big landowner—Captain of the Reserve Georg Ruthmayr, may he rest in peace. He hired me to work on his estate, but didn't leave it at that, had me taught all sorts of things. I became a trainer, learned the whole veterinary part of the business too. Later I was in charge of the whole stable, and finally the stud; we had twelve stallions in the string, later a good many more. Herr Ruthmayr rode, I rode, three boys rode under our supervision. We also sold quite a few animals, and at good prices too; but everything was on a quality basis, we wouldn't have anything to do with dealers, only private buyers, and more and more of them kept coming to us. Captain Seunig-Strobelhof—in those days his riding school was already famous—used to visit the place every summer and look over our horses. Then we would be given precise instructions on what each of them needed in the way of special help and additional training—I mean the colts, of course, but also the ones that were well along and almost trained mounts. We had to work them on the track and later over the hurdles. Wonderful life I had, though it meant work from morning to night; we used to be up at four, Herr Ruthmayr too. He was a good man to work for, Herr Ruthmayr. Once he said to me: 'Lois, you're a cavalry genius; what would the stud be without you!' I was so proud I went around for days with a swelled head. But of course that really put the ambition into me. Natural enough—young fellow that I was."

He fell silent and shrugged.

Leonhard was engaged in a fierce struggle with Gach's language. Like a ship pitching against the waves, with bow dipping low and then being flung high again—so he advanced into this language. But he did not succeed in holding himself on course, straight against the swell. The push came from the side, so that he began to roll. That step he had once taken at night—and then repeated innumerable times by day, in brief seconds, when he recalled the nocturnal experience—that step was insufficient for him to step over Gach and his way of putting words together (and to Leonhard the weighmaster existed only as language, not as interlocutor, which was his function for Niki). That language of Gach's came from a territory different from the one Leonhard had abandoned. And it was going nowhere! That was the most astonishing thing about it to Leonhard. It remained in repose. Whereas our dear and excellent young man had ceased to think of language as anything but motion, as an incessant struggle. At the same time the weighmaster's tone engendered in Leonhard a kind of longing not unlike that which a young boy may feel for a girl; it attracted him powerfully, and seemed to come from some remote space, from somewhere down below or across, out of an utterly unknown depth of time which, nevertheless, Leonhard could possibly conquer.

Strangely enough, the mention of Captain Ruthmayr made scarcely any impression upon Leonhard, although the name did not escape him.

Neither Niki nor Leonhard said a word while Gach paused and drew on his cigar. Gach's story had a novel attraction for Zdarsa, too; it was as if he were leaning over a high railing looking out into a distant view which he had never seen before.

"Then it was suddenly all over, because I had to do my stint in the army. That was in '96. I was sent to Wels, to the dragoons. Among other things they asked every new man whether he'd had anything to do with horses, or whether perhaps he could even ride. Well, of course the men from the country, and most of them were that, had to admit that they'd led or hitched up or driven a horse. I said the same; the captain'd warned me not to say any more. But he didn't belong to the Wels dragoons; he was with the Brandeis dragoons. And when I was asked to write down my occupation in civil life, I didn't put down 'trainer' or 'chief trainer,' but just 'agricultural employee.' That might mean just a better-paid farmhand. The thing was not to let them get the idea that you could ride. If they did, they would set you right off on a regular tiger and give it a whack behind so that you'd be sure to cut a fine figure. Well and good. But pretty soon we did mount the hams—or so some called the horses—to be lunged. One man stands in the middle; he gives the individual instruction—a corporal or other noncom. He has a dragoon stand beside him to help with a long whip, but it's only used to tickle so that the horse stays in the same gait. The horse is on a long line, the allonge, as they call it. It is attached to a cavesson, as that metal noseband is called; the horse is hitched with side reins fastened to the saddle so that the horse will round its neck and have proper support, because the recruit still has to learn the right way to handle the reins. All well and good. Well, when I mounted they couldn't help seeing that I knew how to seat it. So one day the ham got a neat little smack on the crupper, so it hopped with all fours, and then hopped again, and then reared up, and then the allonge-corporal gave a nice little pull. Of course I knew that nothing could happen to me because no horse can fall over backwards when someone is holding it in front with the allonge. So I just stayed in the saddle. They didn't say a word. Afterwards, when the first stage of training was over, the lunging, and it sure went on long enough, we got around to the outdoor riding school, a little square. Naturally only with the simplest bit, the ordinary snaffle. Well, after that there wasn't much use pretending any longer, because our squadron commander, the captain, was there; he always conducted the recruit training himself. Our captain was a Highness, a Prince Croix. The fifth or sixth time that we were in the outdoor riding school there was a short gallop after the trot, and then the captain orders: 'At a walk, down

680

the center.' So we all passed close to him, one after another, and just as I was riding by, he orders: 'Halt!' And then to me: 'What is your name?' 'Beg to report, sir, Dragoon Alois Gach.' 'Write the man down for report,' he said to the sergeant who was standing behind him, to his left. 'Aha,' I thought to myself. When I come to report, the captain says to me: 'Well, Gach, d'ya know why you're here?' 'No, sir.' 'Because you can ride, you faker, why didn't you speak up? Think you can string us along?' 'Beg to report, sir, a recruit can never ride.' He laughs and says: 'You're right there, you're right; you're a sly dog.' And he reaches behind him into the pocket of his red riding breeches, English cut they were and right smart-looking, Captain Ruthmayr had some like that too, and he takes out a long silver cigarette case, snaps it open, it was full, and clears out one side of it. I can still see the cigarettes, imported Turkish they were, in the white leather of his glove. I hold open my hand, he gives me the cigarettes, placing them in carefully, and says: 'As you were, Gach,' and tells the sergeant: 'Dismiss the man. Overtime till reveille and give him tomorrow off.'"

Gach fell silent. He shrugged again, as he had before. His tone did not suggest that he particularly reveled in such army anecdotes; rather, he seemed to be getting at something else. And his two listeners—eager listeners they were—seem to have sensed that. At any rate they made no interjection; they waited.

Any such behavior would be altogether extraordinary today.

"Well then, all very well and good," the weighmaster continued. "I was only trying to show you that I wasn't given too bad a time of it in the army. The food was first-rate in those days; a good many of the men had never had such meals outside. I was one of the first to be 'bridled,' that is, allowed to ride in the corral with curb and snaffle, and soon they had me riding in the ranks with the full tack, as the complete bridle and reins is called . . . So as I say, I did all right; later I got the riding and shooting medals, and in my third year they made me corporal. But to tell the truth, I was miserable in the army. Aside from the riding, of course—and even that was something entirely different from the work in the stud—riding in the cavalry on that deep army saddle—the one just can't be compared to the other. Besides, I felt that if I went on that way I'd soon loose the little I'd learned about dressage. Natural enough—riding in the cavalry isn't a sport; a low firm seat is what you need: you have to learn to swing the heavy saber from the horse and to stay in your right place in the line. All that makes it different, of course. But that was not why I was so miserable, even more miserable later on, and not only during my time as a recruit, which was naturally easier for me than for lots of the others. But rather, the fact that you were constantly being driven from one thing to the next—starting with washing and brushing your teeth, because they even supervised that, and pretty well had to in the case of some—it went on that way all day long, every minute of the time there was an order to do this or do that, and then you'd find your name on the blackboard again for stable duty, and then there was medical inspection, then instruction, then drill on foot. And always being ordered around, this command and that command. And yet they were all friendly enough, even the officers: I never really heard an angry word, aside from the training, where I admit it was sometimes like a circus full of monkeys. But taken all in all they were after you all the time, from reveille to retreat. At the stud farm I did ten times more than I had to do in the cavalry, but I knew what I had to do, there wasn't any need for anybody to keep after me. Once, that was after my recruit days, I left the squadron for a while, went to help in the smithies because on my papers it read under 'previous training': smith and wheelwright. I had it easier there, without that everlasting ordering around, because as a craftsman a man knows what he's got to do. And I wanted to stay there. But the captain fussed and fussed, and went to the colonel about it—the company sergeant told me at the time—until they had me back riding in the squadron. He's supposed to have said: 'I won't have my best riders taken away; I must have that man as wing man in the first row of the first platoon; at parades none of the others stands as quietly for the line of hams as he does; the others can really fine up decently by him.' But you can believe it or not as you choose, I never had any ambitions in the army. I would soonest have stayed in the smithy. At the stud farm I did have ambitions, I'll tell you. But not in the cavalry. And now I'm coming back to what you said, Herr Zdarsa, to what you said about the union. I guess I've gone rather a long way around. As I say, I was miserable at that time—really didn't like it in the army. There I stood one day in the squadron yard, between the two stables, from where you could see out over the paddock, and behind was the hurdle course. It was evening, summer, the sky was still red. I could have left—I even think I had a pass good until midnight. Suddenly it hit me: 'This is a prison,' in spite of all the room there was behind the buildings and all around the place. At the smithies they were still working; the singed smell that comes when horses are being shod came drifting over to me. I thought to myself: 'Go away.' Then I thought: 'If you can go away, you can just as well stay.' I plunked myself down on the bench in front of the barracks. And I thought to myself: 'If a man is locked up in a little room, and he doesn't pace back and forth the whole length of the wall, but only uses half the space, then he's already free, he's made himself a certain amount of freedom.' So I stayed and sat on the bench in front of the barracks. And gradually, that same evening, the thing turned over inside me . . ."

Leonhard was literally suffering. Sweet anguish. Like the pangs one feels for a girl who is far away. It was impossible to penetrate this linguistic wall. The substance was solid; it only looked loose.

". . . The thing turned over in me," the weighmaster was saying, "and it suddenly seemed to me that I'd sooner free myself of all the ordering around if I ran away from it by seeing to it that everything was done before they ordered it, so that I was ahead of the game all the time. That's the attitude you have to take about the union, Herr Zdarsa; in fact, as a man with socialist principles you'd have to be in that sort of thing even if there weren't any yet. Because that is your standpoint. Because then the clock tells the right time. For my part, I became a kind of model soldier, although I didn't like the army one bit. But then it was only a beginning; I didn't stay with the army forever, and afterwards I kept myself 'way ahead of all ordering around. You know you can work things so that there's nobody to keep nudging you in the back because you're so far ahead; you turn around and there's nobody behind you any longer. You've become a free man."

At this point he finally ceased. Niki was rebelling a little inwardly (obstinate rebellion), but he said no more. Scarcely anything need be said about Leonhard. He went on listening to the weighmaster long after Gach had finished. The reader is by now surely aware of the fondness the author has for Leonhard; but at this point it must be remarked that Niki was also a good breath of fresh air. Alois Gach was plainly enjoying the company of the two young workmen from Vienna, and their deliberate and moderate drinking also helped to arouse his confidence. The absence, or sublimated absence of Leonhard, did not strike him, or make itself felt in any unpleasant way; he simply accepted Leonhard as a quieter type.

684

Niki went off on another topic. Perhaps the conclusions to be drawn from what Gach had said made him uncomfortable.

"Were you also in the war with the cav'ry, Herr Gach?" he asked curiously.

"Yes, of course," Alois Gach replied. "I was a reservist, a sergeant by then, although I hadn't many years of service and wasn't a 'regular.' Later they stopped having cavalry, naturally enough in a modern war, but at the start it was pretty flashy."

"Then I suppose you fought against Cossacks too, with the saber, on horseback?"

"More than once when we first went into action in 1914, and once or twice later on too."

What remained most vividly in Leonhard's memory of these moments, while the above exchange was going on, was not the thought on which he was concentrating with considerable effort. Rather, the sunlight on the broad square outside filled his spirit, and the wide high façade of the pilgrimage church opposite, the separate green strips of grass, the white files of waddling geese. Yet he could not see all this, for the windows of the room in which they sat did not look out on the square. Hence Leonhard was beholding what he could not see—and that very fact bred in him an intense sense of well-being, as if his entire inner self were becoming lighter and more relaxed. Thus stimulated, he only now began to grasp what the weighmaster had really said in that curious flowing language of his—for hitherto Leonhard had listened to the manner of speech alone. Now he grasped it, carried the thought on—and remained caught as in a noose. A question thrust his mouth open and he spoke, posed this question. As happens when a person has remained silent for a long time and at last takes the floor, at once the others' full attention turned toward him.

"Sergeant . . ." he said (and oddly enough, this military title

remained attached to old Gach for the rest of the conversation),
"couldn't a person run ahead of something that another person
hasn't ordered him to do; I mean, couldn't a person also run
ahead of something inward . . . ?"

He broke off. Not because he was ashamed of the inade-
quacy of his manner of expression—of which Leonhard was
well aware—but because he had found himself using a word
belonging to Gach's language. He had no doubt that the word
belonged to it although the sergeant had not once used it in
his story. It was the word "inward." Leonhard gave a start of
alarm. And fell silent.

As for Gach—a person can very well grasp the tangible
beginning of something and yet become suddenly blind if someone points out further implications. There is a kind of intention
behind such behavior, intentional not-seeing.

"Oh well," he said, "that may be."

But our Niki did not wish to be sidetracked by Leonhard's
"highfalutin' ideas" (as he called them) from a subject which
aroused his curiosity and gave him again that feeling of leaning
over a high rampart and looking out toward a distant view he
had never seen before.

"Please, Sergeant Gach," he said, "would you mind telling
us what one of those cavalry battles was like?"

Suddenly Leonhard thought of the talk he'd had with the
bookseller Fiedler. In the spring, that was, on the embankment
above the Danube Canal landing-place. Things had long since
been green. There was also a wrong kind of running ahead,
he thought—and precisely that was what old Fiedler had been
asking of him. "Change your occupation." He relived once
again his struggle with the language that time with a speech
still three-fourths enmeshed in the nets of dialect: "It remains
to be proved, remains to be proved . . ." Now that sort of speech

came forth effortlessly: "The genuineness of a movement of the intellect is best tested by a material counterpoise." At that moment he recognized the tremendous span of time, and the enormous tension of that span, which he had since passed over, which there and then in his own person he was gathering together, summing up. Simultaneously the segment of time proved to be severed from everything preceding by the slash that had occurred in a few nocturnal minutes. ("The optative . . . throws every clause into the subjunctive mood, and the fundamental meaning is thereby lost.") Behind the bookseller, Malva stepped forth. Then Trix, a rosy glow, saying: "Continuing your schooling . . ." She was pale—not her face, but the whole image of her. Now she merged with the bookseller Fiedler. Malva, however, was like dammed-up water behind a dike. With her, you could commit suicide, open the dike. Her rich bosom sprang toward him in one glassy-smooth tremendous billow. But it fell away, ebbed, was already past. Yet something still remained of the rosy glow. "Continuing your education," she said. That glow was more dangerous than anything that emanated from the bookseller, or even from Malva herself. Only the third vertex of the triangle was far away now, beyond the lake, in Stinkenbrunn, where she had been left behind; she lay muted, lay dead, like a bell circuit whose current has been switched off.

The sergeant demurred a bit. "These old-fashioned things couldn't possibly interest you gentlemen. A cavalry attack. That sort of thing has gone out completely."

"That's just why it interests us," Niki exclaimed. "That's just why." He continued to insist, his eyes flashing. Gach gave him a friendly look. He leaned somewhat out of the window of his advanced age. It may be—were it not that his whole personality was a little too stiff and stern, at any rate in its façade—that some trace of deeper emotion could be detected.

"There isn't very much to tell," Gach said. "The Cossacks sit their beasts differently from the way we do, though they rode in an even deeper saddle than we—the saddles were often padded with red plush. They sat like buck-jumpers, leaning forward, with knee-contact short stirrups; imagine the posture as looking something like a clothespin, though that's an exaggeration. They held lances too, but not firmly in the crook of the arm like the German uhlans; rather, they stood up slightly in the stirrups and held the lance high and rammed with it over the horse's head. Of course, with that kind of riding, when the crash came they flew off their mounts by the row; because you couldn't have got our men out of the saddle at all; you would have had to pry them loose. As for the lances, it was easy to turn them aside if you just sat quiet. After the fifth or sixth time, we had the feel of it. Some of our men stopped holding the saber in the regulation position, straight out over the horse's head with the blade up" (he indicated the saber position for "attack" by holding his hand across the table). "They held the saber upward to the right above the reins hand. That way they caught the pole of the lances right off and could follow through by striking. Captain Ruthmayr did it that way; I saw that more than once. Besides, the Cossacks rode on only a snaffle, and their beasts were a lot smaller than ours, and agile, let me tell you, even though they weren't ridden with the curb."

"But what about the first time, the first time you met the Cossacks in battle?" Niki asked excitedly.

"The Cossacks were good," Gach added, deliberately continuing his earlier remarks. "Very brave; they really had guts. But the Cossack troops weren't meant to be pitted against proper battle cavalry attacking in a body, but were chiefly for reconnaissance. And at that they were grand. Like Indians.

Rode through thick and thin and mud and water over stock and stone with those little cats they called horses. With my own eyes I've seen Cossacks galloping downhill on glare-ice roads with loose reins, buck-jumper seat and all, where the weight comes more on the forefeet, you know, and some of them turned right around while riding and called back to the others. Let me tell you, our pampered hams would have landed on their noses in such a deal. In some respects the Cossack horse was the best mount there was. Those fellows would dismount, leave the cat standing, and she wouldn't move from the spot. We once watched some of them through Captain Ruthmayr's field glasses; they were climbing up a steep hill, every one of them on foot behind his horse, and they were hanging on to the tails and letting themselves be pulled. I'd like to know what our curried and polished army mounts would have said to that! Incidentally, I didn't go out with the regiment I'd served with, in '14, but the Captain Ruthmayr; that is, with the Brandeis dragoons and in his squadron. The captain fixed up my transfer. But after the captain was killed, they sent me back to the replacement squadron at Wels when I asked, and so I went out to the field again with them. At that time Prince Hubertus Croix, who'd been my captain while I was on active service, he's the one I was telling you about, Prince Croix was already a lieutenant-colonel. In the cavalry they lost more than half the officers during 1914 and 1915."

Gach took up his glass and raised it, but instead of drinking set it down again. For the moment he looked old, a weary old man. "They were good chiefs, nice men, both of them, the prince and the captain," he said under his breath, and fell silent.

Our young men also remained silent. Perhaps that cost Niki some effort. But youth is fairly sensitive, and the temporary sagging of the sergeant's face had much the same connotation as a collapsing fire which suddenly becomes feeble embers lying on its grating.

"Well, Herr Zdarsa, you wanted to hear about the first time we tangled with the Cossacks," the sergeant resumed at last. "At that time Captain Ruthmayr's squadron had been detached from the regiment. We'd been sent out on a reconnaissance, a distant reconnaissance. We rode through a flat valley with a road in the center, the hills on our right and left covered with forest. Of course we had our side patrols out to secure the line of march; they rode on a level with us, up on the hills, in the shelter of the trees. They could see all the same because the woods were thin, sometimes thinned away to nothing, and now and then we'd see them riding up there too. Not a sign of any enemy far and wide. We rode along pretty cheerful, mostly at a walk, because our side patrols in the woods couldn't move very fast. Most of the regiment were boys from Bohemia, and there were some of them in the squadron; they were splendid at singing in harmony, singing those pretty Czech songs of theirs. Usually on the march when we were riding at a walk, the captain had them sing; he liked to hear them, and afterwards they'd all get a gulden apiece from him, which they liked pretty well too. But now of course we had to keep good and still, because we'd heard the place was full of Cossacks. All the same we didn't see hide nor hair of them for days. The weather was clear, a bit windy, not a bit hot. I can still see that road in front of my nose, with feathery trees on the hills to both sides. The captain rode alongside the first platoon, where I was, and he says to me the valley will be coming to an end soon, according to the map, and then we'd come to flat open terrain without any trees, meadows. He was in good humor, and I thought to myself: 'How young he looks.' The captain, he had an odd sort of face, eyes very wide apart, cheeks round and plump, rather

690

like a child's, but still he was tall and lean. While we were talking a man came back at full gallop from the advance patrol to report enemy cavalry beyond the meadowland, where the valley ended; strength about one or one and a half squadrons, partly drawn up in formation. The captain immediately sent out a rider apiece to the side patrols and the rear guard, and galloped up ahead. When he came back, he called the officers to him; they spoke only briefly, then went to their platoons, and in a moment we broke up the long marching column of fours and deployed in platoons, so that every platoon was developed with its two ranks; 'in column' the formation was called. It was an easy maneuver; the road had no ditch, and we were able to ride in good close order 'in column.' Then we came to the end of the valley. It was clear that the enemy didn't expect us— otherwise they wouldn't have been standing around there so without cover. The van and the advance patrol closed in with us; the rear patrol had to stay with the field kitchens and the rest of our gear, to cover our rear. The captain had us deploy at once from column to developed line, then stop, straighten our line, and then came the 'Attack! At a walk!' At that the men gripped their sabers and fastened the hand-strap. I was, as I've told you, in the first platoon. While the other two platoons— the fourth was guarding the flanks to the left and right—rolled forward, so that they'd reach the front line, one after anoth- er—'left, forward!' which means that the line starts forward from the left man on—while we in the first platoon were taking short paces, I caught sight of the enemy. But they caught sight of us at the same time. Must have been 800 yards or so away. Then we saw them carry out a movement also. Our captain galloped along our front—we were all in good close order—and called out to the men in Czech and German: 'Hit them hard, fellows!' He waved to the officers who were riding in front of their platoons and went back to his place at the head of us all, with the bugler right beside him."

Niki's right fist lay tense and tightly clenched on the table, almost as if he were holding the hilt of a saber. His head was propped in his left hand, and he sat looking fixedly at Sergeant Gach.

"It seemed to me," Gach continued after a brief pause for reflection, "as though a big gray-green mass were rolling toward us from across the meadow. I thought: 'There must be more than one and a half squadrons, and if they spread out they'll have us on the flanks too.' But that's just what they didn't do. The captain gave the saber signal for trot, and the bugler blew it—a strapping young corporal he was, a Viennese. Soon after that: gallop. I look to the left; the squadron is keeping a straight line even at the gallop, and the men are calm, only they're staring for all they're worth at the others. So am I, and now I can see only single riders, the mass has disappeared, and then they came closer fast, tightly packed bands of them. And at that moment I see clearly that they outnumber us. Now the bugler blows again, and clear as a bell, let me tell you, not a waver in a single note. I think to myself: 'Has that boy nerves,' and then, just as we shout 'Hurrah!' Lieutenant des Grieux, the baron, jumps in front of our platoon, saber swinging, jabs the spurs into his horse a bit, and whoop! he's right in the middle of the Cossacks and slashing away at them. He carried his whole platoon with him. The crash was something to see, let me tell you. Three or four times I make the same stroke against the lances, turning them off to the right every time, but I can't follow through, they're already past me. We're still galloping. But then we come to a halt, there was such a mass of them. For a second I think to myself: 'This is dragging out, we haven't been able to ride them down.' Still and all enough of them flew clean off when we crashed. But, I wouldn't believe it if I hadn't seen the thing with my own eyes, the way those Cossacks went right back up on their little cats again. And at our men, saber to saber, as soon as they lost their lances. I had to fight too, but there weren't really any single combats; one swing and we'd be separated, there was such a whirl, I tell you. 'This is dragging out too long,' I says to myself. Then I see that the squadron has gone right through, the enemy's been split. All of a sudden, in the middle of that infernal din, I hear shouts of 'Hurrah!' and I wonder what's coming, from left and right. And just at that moment like on orders, the Cossacks spurt apart in all directions, like they'd practiced it—and they were gone. We see them riding away in a wide semicircle, pretty near 400 separate mounted men. Pursuit's impossible. And we didn't feel much like it either. What happened? You see, we had those two flank patrols out here, like I told you; they rode further on in the woods, to where the ground leveled off and widened out, with big open meadows on both sides. That way they covered our flanks, just as they'd been ordered, and so they could see what was going on. While we deployed for our attack those two patrols hurried on ahead, so when the fight started they were level with us. Then, when we got stuck because there were too many against us, they came riding out of the woods almost at the same time, shouting 'Hurrah!' and charging into the Cossacks from the side and almost from the rear. But the main thing is they made a shout like a whole squadron. So the thing didn't turn out too bad. The Cossacks didn't leave a single empty horse and not a single man behind; it's hard to believe, but just like us they must have had only a few light casualties. All our booty consisted of a few lances, and they were broken in several pieces. It was just like a lieutenant of the hussars, a Hungarian count he was, I can't remember the name right now but he was a famous gentleman jockey, won the army stee-plechase in Pardubitz four times—it was just like this lieutenant told me about the Kalmucks: a single hussar squadron rode down three squadrons of those Kalmucks one after the other without being stopped, just like we were; and at first, when the collision came, there were dozens of empty saddles among the Kalmucks and afterwards not a horse unmounted and not a single Kalmuck was left on the field; they must have bounced right up on their cats again and made off."

With that the sergeant's story ended. Niki's fervor was such that he was literally panting; he was like a child listening to a Redskin story. But Leonhard, too, had finally been somewhat carried away by the account and only belatedly taken in the content of Gach's remarks.

"Leo!" Niki exclaimed, bringing the palm of his hand down hard on the table. "That would have been something for us! Believe me, Sergeant, we would have put on a good show. We would have slashed away pretty well, I tell you."

"No doubt about it," Gach said, laughing. "The Viennese were always plucky, and fellows like you boys were always the best. But I ask you in all sincerity, don't imagine the war was anything like that one episode. That was just at the very begin-ning. What came afterwards, all those long years, that was just one dreadful, really horrible misery; and there mustn't ever be anything like that again, under no circumstances, never again, and if your party can really stop war, then it has a reason to exist, but only then. That's my opinion. Of course it's nice to think back, now and then, on all the old forms and ceremonies; but that was the first thing that went out, with modern war; that was only stuff left over from Grandpa's times. Well, your health!"

They drank cordially to one another. A small boy came

running into the tavern and called out: "Is Herr Gach, the weighmaster from Eisenstadt, here?" When Gach answered, the child said his piece: "Mama sends her regards and wants to ask if Herr Gach won't at least drop in for dessert and coffee since he wouldn't come to dinner with us and I'm to show Herr Gach the way."

"Not a bad idea," the weighmaster said, laughing, and called the waiter to pay his check. The two young men rose and shook hands heartily with Alois Gach. Preceded by the boy, the sergeant left the tavern.

Roaring, the motorcycle went its way, stable and hugging the road, like a keel plowing through the waves. Zdarsa rode fast, perhaps too fast; the *élan* of the cavalry attack still inflamed him, and he seemed to be giving his Indian steed the spurs. The flat landscape, too, was an invitation to fast motoring.

They flew along the highway which shortly after Fraunkirchen turns from its southeasterly direction to go almost due south and passes through St. Andrä to the railroad station of Wallern, paralleling the tracks in the latter stretch. Beyond the station they could take a side road to Apetlon, reaching the town after riding in a shallow arc south of the Lange Lacke pond.

All the while Leonhard on the rear saddle had the feeling of flying up a long, straight, gently rising ramp, which was not at all actually the case. St. Andrä, in fact, lies at a slightly lower elevation than Fraunkirchen, and Wallern lower than St. Andrä. But Leonhard rose, was drawn upward. Like a big white sheet of paper the triangle fell behind him and below him, that triangle of Malva, Elly, and Trix among whose points he had been circulating. It was not a matter of one's replacing another, of one's gathering force at the expense of the others. Now all three flashed one last time, like white wings, and vanished in the darkness in the manner of a flock of pigeons disappearing into the canyon of a street.

That was the last ride that Niki and Leonhard took together to the Burgenland. Zdarsa economized by returning the license plates of his Indian steed and garaging the vehicle over the winter.

Scheindler benefited by the cessation of these trips. Although Leonhard had not, as we have said, ever seriously slackened off in his studies, he now regularly devoted his Sundays entirely to that purpose. "Goin' to church, Herr Kakabsa? Well, no matter, I'll do your prayin' for you." The landlady poked up the stove and made coffee.

Here is the place to pay tribute to District School Inspector Scheindler. He was one of the most frightening personages who ever lived. When he descended upon a class for one of his regular inspections, he shot questions at the pupils in a foghorn voice, especially when pronouncing the name of one of those excessively troublesome tribes who figure in the reports of Julius Caesar: namely, the Trevans. (Leonhard of course already knew all these tribes, without having read Caesar in Latin: the Ubians, Allobrogians, Tencterans; the last, for some reason, always named in more dulcet tones by the district school inspector.) Yet Scheindler's *Latin Grammar for Schools* is an illustrious work of art. It is pervaded through and through not only by the deeply serious love of a great grammarian for the language of languages, but also by love for the pupil who is to be transformed step by step from a crude and lawless barbarian into the equivalent of a rational and logical citizen of the Roman world.

Leonhard had the right book. That much he had determined while sitting alongside of Trix and Fella Storch—not between Trix and Fella—on the embankment which dropped down to the water. But it was not that Leonhard had come to the right man in finding the district school inspector; rather the reverse. That immediately becomes evident when we think of the generations of lazy and lumpy schoolboys who have passed through the hands of the district school inspector. For many a year, for many a decade, Herr Scheindler's love had been unrequited. Now the old eagle (eagle of the legions) glimpsed his late but proper prey; he plummeted sharply from the grammarian's heaven and caught Leonhard in his talons.

Happily, our old teachers can still occasionally descend upon us in this way. They were all too good for us; we only catch up with them later on, and in most cases never. How full of knowledge and competence they were! And they poured it all over us like precious essences, far too generously; it hardly made sense, considering how little was retained. We had a Greek who even read the *Gorgias* with us: that colossal struggle of the ethical genius of a Socrates against a Greek sophism gone mad. How masterfully he guided us through that dialogue, employing even Socratic techniques to reach our immature minds. We had a mathematics teacher, a Czech. (In Austria most of the mathematics teachers were Czechs—how is it that this significant fact has gone unnoticed?) He was a terror, but a superb teacher and at bottom lovable too, for he made everything so crystal-clear that in the end it all seemed easy even to dunces like us. We ought to keep their names written down in a little book and piously make a cross for those who, alas, have passed away. Annually, on All Souls' Day, we should light a candle alone in our rooms: *pro defunctis omnibus nostris magistris, doctoribus et praeceptoribus.*

Old Scheindler, then, had his day at last, and adopted Leonhard.

The warehouse attendant's widow had already taken to poking up the stove a little about the time that Leonhard returned home from work.

Then she brought coffee. He became accustomed to that.

Nowadays he liked to have his supper an hour later.

His daily sessions had long since been taking place by electric light. The autumn fell away into grayness. Occasionally the summer would appear momentarily in the background, like a wing beating from the sunlight into darkness. The bridge, the steps down to the green embankment, Trix, Fella, the books, the leaves of the trees still green across the water, stiff as colored paper. But that had all been toward the end of September; Fella had just begun a new school year at the Gymnasium. That was a fact she had mentioned. For the first time in a long while Fella came to his mind. He had long ceased to see the girls leaning out the window; the weather was too cold. And on his visits to Trix, Leonhard had not encountered Fella among the group of young people.

Now, however, she returned, and for a surprising though sufficient reason. The vanishing of his conflict about Trix, Malva, and Elly, the three vertices of the triangle which had governed the summer and fall, which had formed the basic configuration of those two seasons, in a sense converted this geometric figure into an indifferent straight line. Fella had been so aligned from the start; now all four were strung out in the same row.

It may be noted that Leonhard understood perfectly well why he thought of Fella without any outward prompting. He was growing more familiar with his own psychic apparatus. For quite some time now he had been placing his hands more knowingly upon the governing rods of the intellect's machinery.

That had already been evident in the way he alternated among his studies.

"What're you studyin'?" the old landlady inquired one day.

At once Leonhard felt embarrassment at possible conversations about "continuing schooling" and questions of what he needed Latin for. Nevertheless he said: "Latin."

The old woman went out of the room without a word. Two minutes later she was back with a scrap of paper in her hand.

"A student who used to have this room—this was years ago—once wrote this thing down for me. I've forgot what it means; he told me what it was but di'n't write it down. Would bring me luck, he said."

The handwriting was small and neat. Leonhard read: "*Eripe me, Domine, e necessitatibus meis.*"

Leonhard understood this as easily as if it had been written in his mother tongue.

His translation was odd, neither literal nor really free. He said: "'Lord, pull me out of the things that compel me.'"

"Does that make sense to you?" the widow asked, looking at him out of her watery eyes.

"Yes," Leonhard replied, and not another word. He shut his mouth so decisively that there was an audible click; in this way he bit the thread of a conversation that might have spun on. The old woman stared at him for a few moments—perhaps in astonishment—and then shuffled out.

He already knew, then, that often everything depends upon not getting involved with people. He had already garnered some experience in the technology of the intellectual life, and these discoveries were beginning to become part of his flesh and blood; that is, they were becoming peculiar to him, were well on their way to becoming traits of Leonhard.

"Old crone," Leonhard thought, sitting by the stove and

looking toward the door which had just closed behind the warehouse attendant's widow, "always toddling off to church happily enough, but when someone tries to show her something for a change—she doesn't want to understand. Of course she doesn't want to. What is there to understand?—it's obvious." He now spoke the Latin sentence precisely, slowly, like a formula. His eyelids lowered, his eyes closed to a slit; and already he was flying along on the rear saddle of the machine, sitting behind Niki, over the highway between St. Andrä and Wallern. Already he was rising, being drawn upward. Like a big white sheet of paper the triangle fell behind him and below him, that triangle of Malva, Elly, and Trix among whose points he had been circulating. And then all three flashed one last time and vanished into darkness like a flock of pigeons disappearing into the canyon of a street. At the very end the big white surface behind him had broken into many individual pieces, as if a huge piece of crockery had been smashed.

"I can't do it myself either," Leonhard said aloud to himself.

Immediately afterwards the splendor of summer was present again; it raised and lowered its wing twice in the broad airy spaces above the valley. Leonhard had left the park on the uphill side through a gate that led out into the woods. A path cut at a level across the steep slope. In the distance and higher up, a haze hung over a rocky cliff. A bird that had sounded its song in the depths of the woods fell silent now. It was perfectly still.

Like a boat coming at night across smooth dark waters, stirring them but slightly so that they make the faintest of splashes and then lying in perfect stillness against the pier—so Anny Gräven now touched once again upon Leonhard's life. Certainly without creating an adjacent entanglement for him!

700

But what did he know about her? The idea that there was nothing to know became so obstinately established in his mind that we might almost call it ossified. It was an idea which he never doubted, for it was altogether in harmony with his observations. When they went out afterwards and had a bit of supper together—Leonhard clung to this practice as to a ritual—he saw Anny invariably as sitting before a closed curtain, a shabby piece of cloth which screened the rest of her life without Leonhard's being in the slightest curious about it. He knew that there was a bare and barren stage behind, the only prop being a bed or sofa. Period.

We do not wish to deny that such was actually the true state of affairs. Yet at the same time Anny's lively chatter could hide a profound secretiveness. It is an established fact that real interest sharpens the ears of the hard-of-hearing, rouses the somnolent, makes the man distracted by a hundred tasks instantly composed and attentive. So, too, a serious danger seals the lips of the most careless chatterbox.

It had been happening ever since Anny entered into a closer relationship with her fellow-professional Hertha Plankl. Hertha was a blonde, stoutish girl of incredibly minute intelligence—from the Burgenland, incidentally. She maintained certain connections with "the gallery," as professional petty criminals are called in Vienna. The upper crust of "the gallery" consists of crooked gamblers, pickpockets, document forgers, distributors (not makers) of counterfeit money, swindlers of every kind, ordinary fences, and receivers of stolen goods difficult to turn into cash. "The gallery" also branches off into recognized occupations; drivers at the trotting races in the Prater might belong to it, bookmakers, café owners, and some vaudeville acrobats whose extraordinary abilities were sometimes much in demand.

Hertha, because of her stupidity, was entrusted with the keeping of certain packages. She was not paid for this, though occasionally she was treated to wine.

The "gallery punks" are despised by the serious major criminals, and do not sit down at the latter's tables. But now and then they are called in on a special job. Cases of low-value loot occur. Thus, a burgled jewelry shop might have yielded fifty gold watches which were not gold at all; which, in the normal course of affairs, would have been sold as honest "imitations." Here is an opportunity for the gallery punk, who buys these watches for a song—and buys along with them one genuine gold watch from the same haul, which looks exactly like the imitations, and by means of which he will be able to turn his bargain watches over at a tidy profit. Or there may be a small lot of scrap gold left over from a slightly equivocal division of the spoils after a successful coup. Things like that could cause ill-feeling, not on account of the paltry few ounces of gold but on account of the mean dishonesty involved. That, at any rate, was how Meisgeier "the Claw," as he was generally called because of his vulture-like appearance, felt about it. But they had pulled that kind of low-down trick on him for the last time. For quite a while now, the Claw had had his eye on stupid Hertha. He knew that she was in on all these deals. And when Hertha, sitting in the taproom, flipped her feather boa over the small parcel lying on the bench beside her, it was already too late. Being stupid, she thought she was perfectly safe, for Meisgeier had just that moment entered. The gallery punks had given her the thing twenty minutes before, and now sat there in all innocence, without any sort of briefcases or packages, not even with their coats. It was still warm weather. Anny Gräven sat at a different table from Hertha's, likewise alone, for the women were waiting for their customers. Hertha was in the fortunate position of being able to attend to these customers in the house right next door. However, she did not always make use of this convenience. It wouldn't do to take everyone to her apartment—Anny Gräven had impressed this precaution upon her. It was not that Hertha's room was not comfortably furnished—she even had a small kitchen, like Anny: only the window did not offer an open view out toward the Prater, as was the case with Anny's quarters; it gave on a narrow courtyard through which the racket from the taproom often traveled disturbingly—funneled, in fact, by the air shaft. And in addition to noise came this and that: the room was afflicted by bad ventilation. To air the place somewhat, a draft had to be created by opening a kitchen window. Thus Hertha's place had some distinct drawbacks in this and other points, especially at that time, when a summery warmth still prevailed. But on the other hand she was in good with the police there; they did not bother her at all, any more than they did Anny over near the Praterstern, within her thick old walls.

The Claw came into the taproom and, ignoring everyone, sat down by himself at a back table. The gallery punks did not venture to greet him. That he sat with his back to the others in the room, and therefore to Hertha also, did not reassure Anny. At this moment she literally hated Hertha for her stupidity and the little parcel under her feather boa. Not being stupid, Anny did not comfort herself with the platitude that Meisgeier had no eyes in the back of his head. Still, there was no deciding for certain from the position of two mirrors there at the back what he could and could not see. Anny Gräven sensed the danger, though not by the slightest outward sign did she show it. Fear crawled under her skirt and underwear, crawled over her rounded thighs like an army of ants, while waves of cold invaded the region around her heart. Her concern for Hertha suddenly proved to be deeper than she had known. At last the stupid cow looked over toward her. With her right hand held close to her body, our Anny gave Hertha a sign which could mean nothing else but "Beat it!" She unmistakably pointed toward the door of the taproom. What was more, our Anny's eyes flashed the same signal. They flashed furiously, in fact; Anny was capable of that, although rarely; perhaps only toward her stupid friend was she capable of such vehemence . . . Hardly toward anyone else. If Leonhard had ever seen her that way . . . !

Still and all, Hertha made use of her feather boa very skillfully as she departed. And although it was too late—had been too late for a long time, ever since the cow had gotten mixed up with the gallery punks—for the time being, at any rate, nothing happened, nothing could very well happen. Meisgeier did not stir, took no notice whatsoever of anything . . . There. Anny had crunched these few minutes between her teeth now, and that cretin of a Hertha with her little parcel was no doubt up in her room by now, behind a locked door.

Anny glanced at her wrist watch. It was half-past eleven.

Around nine o'clock in the morning she was due to call for Hertha. They were going out together to Loipersbach, in the Burgenland, to visit an aunt of Hertha's. The kindly woman had promised the girls a capon, which was certainly worth the trip. They were planning to roast the bird in Anny's kitchen. Anny had the key to Hertha's apartment in her bag. For when Hertha slept—and like Anny, she was accustomed to sleeping late into the day—you could hold your thumb on the doorbell for hours and nothing would stir. Hertha would have to be routed out of bed early for the impending expedition. Anny, who was in any case more wide-awake by nature, owned an alarm clock.

Hertha had been gone a little while when Anny experienced

the reaction. The excitement of fear had affected her bladder; she had to go. To do so it was not necessary to pass the Claw's table. She had just closed the door of the cubicle behind her and was groping for the light when she heard footsteps. She hesitated, did not switch on the light, and peered through the narrow crack of the door. To her terror, Meisgeier passed close by her and went into the *pissoir,* which together with the men's toilets lay on the other side of the narrow corridor, with no door between. Anny saw Meisgeier's back. She was about to close the door tight and bolt it, but the Claw's strange behavior restrained her. Instead of going up to the wall, as might be expected, he remained in the middle of the room and peered upward several times, as though taking the measure of a height. Then he drew from a pocket in his wide flannel trousers a pair of heavy leather gloves and put them on. He seemed to gather his strength, he crouched, jumped up, and for a moment his legs dangled down into the middle of the room. The next moment they were drawn up and vanished

Noiselessly, Anny Gräven closed the crack of the door and quietly pushed the bolt.

At first she did not understand. Then she heard a low sound above her, to one side, obviously on the glass skylight of the *pissoir,* which could be opened, in warm weather, to catch a little ventilation from the air shaft.

The last and essential conclusion still escaped Anny Gräven.

Nevertheless, she looked up at the open window of the cubicle and then without a sound climbed up on the seat. At that moment Meisgeier's legs passed close by her nose; he seemed to be walking on the window cornice outside. Only a light scraping sound could be heard. He was making his way along the outside wall. Then she could see his whole body. He was outstretched along the opposite side of the air shaft, at about the height of the first story. And now he began moving silently upward between the dark windows. His long arms reached over his head; his slight body was drawn up with light and almost graceful movements. It all looked sure and effortless. The spectacle took Anny's breath away. It was an altogether incredible demonstration of strength, skill, and courage, made possible at all only by the old-fashioned construction of the houses in this neighborhood with their wide cornices and projections.

But as she looked on up ahead of the breathtaking path he was taking, there sprang into view on the fifth floor, like a bright block of solid light in the prevailing darkness, the illuminated open window of Hertha Plankl's room.

Anny did not scream.

In no time at all Meisgeier had worked his way up to the fourth story.

Something incomprehensible was going on inside Anny Gräven, something that would not allow her to disturb the magnificent performance going on before her eyes, or to place any check upon this as yet uncompleted task. She waited in suspense for the moment that Meisgeier would appear in that bright rectangle and climb over the window sill. She waited with her eyes popping out—and oddly enough, without any fear for Hertha. Her friend had probably fallen asleep already, with the light on, as she so often did. She would notice nothing—except the disappearance of that parcel the punks had planted on her. Serve her right, too. Anny, so violently was her heart pounding, almost missed the brief darkening of the bright rectangle as Meisgeier climbed in. She saw only a shadow gliding across the window sill. But now her hearing extended itself like a stretched fireman's net to catch the slightest sound that might descend from above. But none came. Rather, the Claw appeared again—she might barely have counted to fifteen between his climbing in and climbing out. And he was empty-handed. Had he stowed the parcel in his flannel trousers? He was already descending, clinging like a twitching spider to the wall.

Scarcely any time passed, and again his legs were for a moment close to her face. She crouched. Now she heard a slight scraping noise against the steel frame of the skylight. For a while there was complete silence; no doubt Meisgeier had to make sure that no one was in the *pissoir* or the men's toilet. Then Anny could hear sounds again, and immediately afterwards a light slap of foot soles against the floor. He must have lowered himself already. Then the Claw suddenly became very loud; a toilet was flushed, and simultaneously Anny heard him brushing his clothes with his hand. Then water splashed into the wash basin. During this activity, which took some time, Meisgeier cleared his throat loudly. Then he went slowly back into the taproom, while another guest entered the *pissoir.*

All this time Anny had been taking comfort in the knowledge that she was behind a bolted door. Now at last she turned on the light and took care of her business. When she returned to the taproom, Meisgeier was sitting over a fresh mug of beer, reading the newspaper.

But not for long. He called the proprietor, who brought the drinks around himself, and asked politely how late it was.

"Ten to twelve, Herr Meisgeier," the proprietor replied, fawning a bit.

"Why, how's that?" the Claw said, apparently somewhat distracted. "How the devil long have I been sitting here?"

"Not very long," the proprietor answered, too obliging for words, leaning forward somewhat across the table. "You only came shortly after eleven; I happen to notice because Frau Hertha left just after, without an escort. She usually stays longer."

"You mean the plump blonde?"

"That's right, that's right," the proprietor said.

"Too bad," Meisgeier remarked. "I would just as soon have drunk a glass or so with her."

"Oh well, there'll be occasion for that some other time," the bartender replied, smirking, "she's a good kid."

"Yes, a nice doll," Meisgeier said. He paid for his beers and remarked: "I'm going straight to the Alhambra from here, if anybody asks for me."

"Very well, Herr Meisgeier," the proprietor replied. The Claw left.

Anny Gräven had heard most of this conversation, and grasped the general drift, if not every single word. She instantly and irritably thrust away the preposterous temptation to be lulled by Meisgeier's friendly remark concerning Hertha, for she was perfectly well aware of the meaning of this little chat. She knew, too, that the Claw would now actually go directly to the Alhambra Café and strike up a similar conversation with the proprietor, the waiter, or the cashier; and just as he had done here, would find some pretext for establishing the exact time. Whereupon, after Anny had clearly recognized these preparations for an alibi, she was suddenly overcome by fear again. But it was much worse than before; the wave of coldness in the region of her heart now filled the greater part of her chest.

A man entered and sat down at the table which Hertha had occupied previously, and which had remained empty up to this point. The man, now that Anny looked at him more carefully, was a gentleman, and obviously did not belong here. That sort of thing could happen. There was nothing sinister-looking about the tavern; rather, it gave the impression of being neat

708

and well-tended. In its modest fashion it even looked inviting, and the goulash and beer were good. The late guest applied himself with relish to both. The proprietor served him personally with marked courtesy. He liked to have strangers of this sort in the place, not only because they did no harm and paid well, but also because their occasional presence acted as a restraint upon the shrewd and perceptive police detectives when, as they occasionally saw fit to do, they conducted one of their raids, checkups, or shakedowns.

Anny considered the strange gentleman a possible and highly acceptable customer; she also suddenly felt an overpowering craving for wine, which she did not like to pay for out of her own pocket. But her business competence was certainly not at its height at the moment. There was something like a lump of lead inside her. Moreover, she suddenly realized that she did not know what she really looked like at the moment; perhaps she was extremely pale, upset-looking; perhaps the dark rings under her eyes showed up too plainly; perhaps her nose was shiny . . . She had not checked her appearance for a good hour or more. Though there had probably been a mirror in the washroom; she did not recall . . . Now, at any rate, she took out her compact and inspected herself in that covert but unambiguous manner which was intended to indicate to the newly arrived guest that she wished to pass muster in his eyes, that she wished to please. Her condition was better than she had expected. Her eyes were shining; her complexion had the proper softness; her lipstick was still sufficient. Only a minor rearrangement of her hair was necessary. Anny had come to herself again; the tools of her trade were all in order. The guest had meanwhile finished his late supper, had pushed the plate aside—the proprietor promptly hurried forward and removed it—and had taken a vigorous swallow of beer before setting down the mug. Now he smiled with friendly unconstraint at Anny, who at the moment was looking down into her mirror—which she discreetly held below the edge of the table. Nevertheless, she took note of the glance which concerned her directly. And so she returned the smile. Her moment of paralysis had passed. Soon the new guest sat at her table, and a half liter of wine appeared. The proprietor served diligently.

It was pleasant here; the tavern had almost emptied by this time. Anny was glad of her present company. She had a few friends of this type. That the stranger belonged to the same sort, Anny determined at once by her sense of smell. Only then did she take notice of everything else: hands, language, and so on. At the very end, manners, for hers were not bad. In a way this type all had something in common with Leonhard. But she liked Leonhard better. Perhaps she loved Leonhard. At times she really believed that. She thought of him often, even now while the gentleman was pouring wine for her. All these gentlemen behaved, at bottom, like a person who does not immediately drink from a full glass that is standing ready for him, and who when it is empty sets it down even more carefully than when it was full. Actually they were all very nice. But Leonhard did these things best of all, when "afterwards" she went somewhere with him to eat sausages or drink wine.

Anny laughed, raised the glass to her new acquaintance, and drank it to the bottom. The wine slid like a last missing consolation down her throat, and washed away all fear. "What kind is this?" she asked the proprietor, who was just passing their table.

"From Neusiedler Lake, ma'am," he replied. "Ruster."

"Have I chosen one you like?" the gentleman asked her; he had selected this wine from the wine-card.

"Yes, this is good," Anny said. "Usually I drink

Heiligen-steiner here." Tomorrow she would be going to the Burgenland with Hertha . . . (By now Anny had actually forgotten what had happened, what she had witnessed.)

She now began to see her new acquaintance more distinctly, and in somewhat more detail, and as she looked him over she thought: "A nifty feller, but he looks mis'rable; worried about something, prob'ly a woman." She guessed him to be around forty. What she liked was the energy of his face, the broad shoulders and the broad chest, although he was otherwise lean—she'd liked the look of him even as he strode over to her table. What alienated her were the finely etched features that stood forth sharply, as though they had been darkened with a drawing-pen. Anny began to chatter. She knew it suited her; she had charm when she talked. Of course she told nothing but lies, whatever came into her head, but in a good-natured way that had no deeper purpose, rather tended to win the listener's forbearance for what she said, for her whole personality. This listener, however, really knew how to listen; he seemed to like her babble, and even when he spoke made no remarks on his own account but only posed questions which helped Anny to gabble on. As she talked she had a feeling as though a shining concave mirror were moving back and forth in front of her, and she saw in it, amusingly distorted, her cheerful prattle, which had already become slightly inflated from the wine; one moment the image was magnified, then it suddenly diminished. She realized that he probably did not believe most of what she was saying; but his questions indicated that he was observing and absorbing her merry pack of lies, which consisted of broken and jumbled fragments of life and reality. Where he seemed to feel a lack of invention or verisimilitude, he wanted supplementary material, so that Anny had to keep repairing "afterwards" the flaws in her windy improvisation.

711

Like a riding instructor who insists that a corner in the paddock be taken properly, not cut short. If lies were going to be told, it had to be done artistically.

Herr von Geyrenhoff would simply have said that Schlaggenberg was "ebbing" this evening.

He was, at that time, at his lowest point. He was still far from that—in his opinion—ultimate decision on the traffic island which took place, we will recall, in November of the year 1926, when he stepped with one foot off the island, so that a car had to swerve sharply to avoid him.

Gradually Anny recounted the whole prehistory and history of her marriage—her husband, the dental technician's, drug addiction, and how things went from bad to worse for him. And quite casually there flowed into the story, in between, the frank confession that she for her part had also been a sinner, for during a short stay in Berlin, where she was visiting relatives of her husband, she had gone and sold an expensive fur coat they had given her, only to drink and gamble the money away. But she had run into some jolly company in the course of this junket. Anny still seemed quite pleased with herself for her devil-may-care conduct at the time.

Kajetan obviously thought it quite extraordinary that she herself had in the end been able to kick the morphine habit. He actually seemed to believe her proud boasts to that effect, and observed Anny attentively while probing a bit around this point.

It was here, however, that the reflections in the concave mirror began to make Anny uncomfortable—here, at the point in her narrative at which she had to step into the terrain of truth. She then and there became more conscious of a desire that had been pressing upon her all the while: to leave this place, to remove herself from the proximity of an overpowering experience which was still there, within her, a solid unbroken block, though she had momentarily forgotten it. Also she disliked sitting with such a nice gentleman in this low dive, whose essential character he might not know. In fact, Anny felt it would be a piece of downright trickery to stay on here. It simply wasn't being fair to her new acquaintance from another world.

For in such cases Anny was always quite conscious of the difference of worlds.

And so they left, at her request, much bowed out by the proprietor.

They stepped out into the street. The night was still warm.

They drifted around a great deal that night—oddly enough, without Schlaggenberg's spending any sizable amount of money (he wondered about this himself the next day); for Anny Gräven was not the type of girl who likes to see a man throw his money around—in fact, she occasionally restrained her men friends from unnecessary expenditures, which did not exactly please the café owners, who expected a girl to put some "life" into the party. Moreover, Anny on principle kept away from expensive night spots. The idea was, of course, that if the man spent less money elsewhere, there would be a bit more for herself. Kajetan, too, was not stingy when at last they arrived in Anny's apartment. He liked it there. He thought it impersonal, clean, and even smart-looking in a simple way. They had brought a bottle of wine with them; wineglasses stood on a small table, and Anny reclined on the sofa. She had made them coffee from her own stores. The whole evening was turning out nicely. In particular she liked the look of Kajetan; then also he let her chatter and bought her as much wine as she wanted—and she could take a great deal; wine was after all a harmless substitute for the stimulants she had formerly used.

Furthermore his lively and sensitive manner pleased her. She watched him as he paced the room, hands in his pockets. A curtain half drawn back permitted a distant view of solitary lights on the edge of the Prater, where a railroad that girdles the city crossed the broad boulevard on its viaduct.

"I have a sister," Kajetan said, "who many people think looks like me. But I know that she is not my sister, not even my half sister. She has a different father and a different mother. I know who these people were—in fact the mother is still living—but I have never seen either of them."

"Are your parents living?" Anny asked.

"Yes, my mother," he said.

"Does she know—that you know?"

"Yes, of course. I've often spoken with her about it."

"And your sister doesn't know?"

"No."

"Then somebody ought to tell her sometime. How old is she?"

"Well past twenty."

"And how do you get on with her?"

"Very well!"

"No more to it than that?"

"Maybe more—but not what you think."

"I don't think anything. Do you like her?"

"No, not that way. She isn't really feminine, to my way of thinking."

"Student?"

"Musician."

"How did the whole thing come about?"

"Well . . . it was a case of a foundling, so to speak. It happened to a young girl my parents knew—the daughter of good friends. She was very close to my parents, closer, perhaps, than

to her own. The girl was twenty at the time. She went abroad for
a year, and my parents went away for just as long a time—officially somewhere else entirely, of course . . . and before the end
of that year my parents sent out announcements—from some
little town in southern France, I think it was, where nobody
ever came—announcements of the birth of a baby daughter . .
. It was easy enough to do. They traveled in North Africa and
Spain at the time too. They left me at home—I was still a small
boy."

"That was long before the war, then?"

"Oh yes. In 1901."

Only now did Kajetan understand why he was saying these
things to a strange streetwalker, things which he himself was
surprised to be revealing to anybody, here in this unpredictably
smart little flat on the Prater . . . It was the need to cast some
illumination from outside upon an absurd situation which he
was obligated by a deathbed promise to his father to keep secret
as long as Quapp's real mother lived. To tell the story to a perfect stranger was to test it by the standards of "common sense."
If the whole thing could be summed up for the benefit of a
person who had no background and no relationship whatsoever to this group of facts, it meant that the facts did not fall
wholly outside the sphere of rationality. If the story could be
told, and briefly too, even more briefly than Schlaggenberg
had imagined, then it could not be utterly preposterous. Every
secret that has been forcibly repressed for a long time starts
to grow rampantly in all directions. One has only to air the
matter a little and the thicket starts to retreat; the core of the
matter emerges and may suddenly appear rather trivial compared with many other matters of the same sort. Kajetan did
not regret that he had told the story to this stranger. Telling the
story had helped him to achieve an altogether different feeling

about this whole family situation, about all such familial affairs. Now he was illuminating them from the side, and seeing them from a superior perspective, like those isolated bluish lights out there on the edge of the Prater where the railroad that girdles the city crosses the broad boulevard on its viaduct.

"Your father must have been a very good man," Anny said. "Come, sit down beside me."

"Yes, he was," Kajetan said, going over to the sofa.

"Does anybody else know the thing besides you and your mother?"

"Yes," he replied. "A man who was a sort of . . . adviser to my father. He helped my parents at the time, arranged the whole thing. This man knows that my sister is not really my sister."

"And has he kept his mouth shut?"

"Yes. My father made him promise to, on his deathbed."

Anny looked into the air, poured herself some wine, and considered.

"There's one thing about the whole story I don't get," she said at last. "If he—I mean the man, whoever he was—got a girl of good family, as they say, into trouble, why didn't he marry her? A man doesn't run out on a girl, at least that's what we hear—not in those upper-class circles."

"Yes, that is the oddest part of the whole story; you're quite right about that," Kajetan answered and laughed. "But it's very simple: she didn't want to."

"Why not? Was he so awful?"

"Not at all. He was a handsome boy. Dead now—he was killed in Galicia in 1914. But he was middle-class. And she was a baroness."

"And yet she liked him well enough for . . . well . . ."

"It's part of the story that she was an unusually disgusting

716

idiot of a female, and probably still is . . . And yet he would have made an enormously rich son-in-law, and the old baron was very fond of him personally. Just imagine that! The father wouldn't have given a damn that he was middle-class. But the girl wouldn't have him, and so they figured out this excursion of theirs, with my parents' help."

"Well, did the bitch catch herself a nobleman later on?"

"You'll laugh—yes. A French count, no less. An old dodderer. He left her a lot of money. That's how it's done."

"Yes, that's how it's done," Anny said, stretching out comfortably. "There's one thing I wonder about, though. If the real father had, as you say, a lot of dough—he must have left something, eh? And wouldn't he have left it to her—your 'sister'? Or to your parents—for her, I mean, for the girl. After all, it was his kid. And then what about the mother—didn't she ever do anything for her kid?"

"No, certainly not. That I know for certain."

"Nice people. So there's nothing for your sister, from any of them?"

"No."

"Somebody's doing some cheating there," Anny said, and no more.

But in asking these last questions and in dropping this remark, Anny had stepped upon a terrain below whose ground-level there had long lain for Schlaggenberg the oppressive knowledge of scarcely tangible and yet weighty omissions. That he had never pursued this matter suddenly struck him as a kind of snobbery, an absolute pose. For it was a pose for a person to occupy himself with intellectual undertakings, and pretend to be absent-minded and disinterested in the serious material fundamentals of life. He had allowed himself this intellectual luxury in the face of his mother and sister's financial

717

predicament, while at the same time being a financial burden upon them. And all the time he knew quite well that they—as a consequence of Levielle's lumber dealings with his poor father—scarcely had enough for their bare needs.

A dull pressure upon the conscience speaks more clearly than any thought, and throws open to question attitudes which but a short time before appeared nobly emancipated and sublimely unbourgeois. As for Anny's final remark, that applied, Kajetan saw, directly to the person of Levielle—who had, after all, been the executor of Ruthmayr's testament. But how to prove anything, how to do anything about that?

Thus Kajetan was undergoing an experience similar to Anny's. For she, a while before, unburdening herself to him, had also come to the point at which she must step forth onto the terrain of truth—namely, to the subject of her "habit" and the truly bestial sufferings she had endured in kicking it. That cure, forced upon her in part by necessity, stood as the unique symbol for all the self-conquests which were otherwise entirely lacking in her life. Nevertheless, Anny Gräven could not bring herself to recollect that period—it was unendurable.

They left Anny's flat.

They drifted around a good deal longer together that night, companions of a sort, although in this connection it must be said that Anny had done all that could be expected of her to speed things to their conclusion, whereas Schlaggenberg had done nothing of the sort, in no respect. He became well aware of that in the course of the night—a night in which sleepiness refused to come and the thought of bed was instantly associated with a picture of tormented tossing. So they continued to drink black coffee, although they had already had enough of it; but Anny no longer wanted anything alcoholic.

Still, one gain from this night had already been chalked up; perspective had been achieved, and something heavy and oppressive, heretofore shoved contemptuously aside, had now been placed like a package on the table. There it lay, tied and knotted. It would have to be laid aside again, for it would not be right to open it. But at least it had been properly viewed for the first time, its rather considerable size seen, its weight weighed in the hand.

Secondly: for the first time in a long while Kajetan had spent a few hours without thinking of his wife, Camy, née Schedik, of the conflict with her, of the last scenes, of his father-in-law, of the painfulness of the whole situation. It was incomprehensible, almost a gracious inner miracle, but still the fact: all that had been momentarily forgotten. And when he left Anny's room, casting a last look through the window of the already darkened chamber out at the distant margin of the Prater, where the bluish lights stood, these lights too seemed to illuminate from the side the things that had filled and consumed Kajetan's days: to illuminate or to take them into their wider perspective.

Anny and Schlaggenberg even drifted around to the Café Kaunitz just about the time "Noise Phase III" began. The lungworm was wheezing, the proprietress was singing—but immediately afterwards she stared down at the playing cards again, her nostrils twitching. Tailor Jirasek was threatening to have everyone taken forthwith to the "police presunk," which meant that he would very soon begin singing. But he was dragged out to the washroom in time, and there given a beating for the so-and-so-manyth time. Hirschkron, the bookbinder, wandered like a hapless soul through hell; he had happened in here on this particular night but now stood around in helpless perplexity, the half-full, long since warm glass of wine in his hand—a *pro forma* drinker who could no longer find a decent card game to survey in his capacity of kibitzer, now that Ederl, the painting contractor, had finished with his last victim ("it was a slaughter, you couldn't call it a fight"). The proprietress's eyes, too, were now staring discontentedly into space, while a cold puddle trickled from their pretty blue-grayness. However, Hirschkron was recognized, called out to, and greeted by Schlaggenberg, who knew him and appreciated him doubly, both as a person and as a master of his trade. With Anny's permission the bookbinder was invited to take a seat at the table. "If you don't mind Herr Doktor," he said, sitting down. Thus Anny was made cognizant of Kajetan's academic dignities—which, however, seemed to make little impression upon her. It is remarkable, incidentally, that when Schlaggenberg excused himself for a few minutes, she didn't take advantage of this opportunity to ask the bookbinder who the gentleman really was. Nothing of the sort. But she ordered three glasses of plum brandy, insisted on paying for them at once, drank to the bookbinder's health, and laughed childishly when Kajetan returned. "I've stood you both to a round of slivovitz," she said.

As it happened, Herr Hirschkron instantly recognized Anny Gräven's type and occupation; and if she had tried to pump him about Schlaggenberg, would have been careful to tell her nothing. But she had not pumped, it did not even occur to her to pump, and this struck Herr Hirschkron, so that some time later, when Herr Doktor von Schlaggenberg came with some musty old books he wanted bound, Hirschkron saw fit to refer to the incident. Which is how we know about it.

Kajetan and Anny left the Café Kaunitz before the "expulsion," that is, before the revolving door began to turn faster and faster, until in the end it was whirling deliriously when the owner, her colorless sister, and the concierge who was paid specially for such bouncing activities began to clear the place with ruthless brutality. Kajetan and Anny realized that they were hungry. Anny knew a good cheap place. They went to the "Goulash Hut" on Rotenturm Strasse. After all the various beverages they had downed in the course of the night, the hot delicious stew, seasoned with paprika, was like good medicine, and the substantial restfulness of the beer drew a line under the night, a line of clear separation from the wine, the brandy, and from such nervous follies as too much black coffee. The beer refreshed. They stayed, lingering over it. The effect of the beer was to place them upon another foundation, a more massive base; the hollow exhaustion of late hours vanished; but for the time being sleepiness also remained at a distance. And so Anny and Kajetan sat over their thoroughly plebeian pleasures, which one always comes down to in the end because they are the oldest and the most salutary. When at last they climbed the steps from the basement restaurant to the street, they found themselves entering broad daylight, which shone strangely down upon them as if it were itself surprised by this pair of night owls. It did not throw itself at them with morning sunlight and a high blue sky. It remained gray. Kajetan put Anny Gräven solicitously into a cab, thanked her, patted her hand, and pressed upon her a small banknote for the ride. A few moments later he stood alone in the street. It was as though a taut wire had snapped and now dangled limply.

But in that region in the high mountains where Leonhard had spent his summer vacation—in the factory's rest home, which had formerly been a large private estate—the day dawned less cloudily. We will recall that behind the neglected gardens with the empty stone basin of the pond the hill rises steeply and soon disappears into the darkness of mountain forest. The garden fence has a small gate opening on the side toward the hill. The effect is more of stepping into woods than stepping out of a garden. Not far above the little gate—there is only a slight embankment to be climbed—a path runs athwart the steep slope. If you follow this path for a few paces, the woods cease entirely on the right and between the big stout trees on the edge of the woods you see across the wide airy space of the valley, and if you raise your eyes somewhat you look upon the gray garment of the bare rocky slopes that rise above the woods.

Now it was still dark here. But the eastern sky, partly concealed by trees, was already weakening the night here among the trees. Out of the darkness of the forest sounded delicate chirpings, slitting the silence at perfectly regular intervals. As more and more details emerged out of the slashed velvet of the night, the chirping swelled rapidly; more complicated cadences became audible. Then, just before the moment that the glowing edge of the sun appeared over the dome of foliage in the east, there was observance of a general intermission, for as the majestic sphere rose into the lacquer-clear sky, the forest remained for a few seconds perfectly still.

Seated in the cab, Anny Gräven passed across the bridge. The gray-green water of the Danube Canal lazed along far below her. As the cab entered Prater Strasse, she caught a glimpse of a clock. It read eight minutes after six. To be coming home at such an hour was nothing unusual for Anny.

Suddenly the early part of the night—that dark courtyard with the Claw climbing like a spider—crashed into her mind in the midst of the broad daylight and streets already coming to life.

At six o'clock concierges unlocked front doors.

She leaned forward and gave the driver Hertha's address. He was to take her there, not to the address she had given him before.

Frau Pawliček, the concierge, was sweeping the sidewalk in front of her house when the cab rolled up. She greeted Anny without any contempt or condescension, for more such "girls" tolerated by the police lived in the house; they could not very well be stingy about tips, and their visitors were even less so. "Why, Frau Anny, so early?" she said.

"Yes," Anny laughed (she laughed easily, and in an altogether natural manner; it went swimmingly), "I have to get Hertha out of bed. We're taking a little trip to the Burgenland today, to Loipersbach. Her aunt there has got a capon for us."

"Aha," the concierge said. "That's a thing you don't wanna miss. You got the key, Frau Anny? So that's why Fräul'n Hertha came in so early las' night. Me, I was still on the stairs. But y' know what, Frau Anny, it's a sin and shame the way that girl wastes light. She must've gone to sleep again without puttin' off her light last night. It was burnin' this mornin' at a quarter to six, I see it from the court. It's a waste of good money, you ought tell that to Fräul'n Hertha, I've told her so more'n once."

Anny went up the stairs.

She inserted the latchkey and went through the well-kept vestibule. To the left was the kitchen, which Hertha Plankl had modernized at considerable expense. Anny opened the door of the large living room. The three-armed chandelier in the center was switched on, but the glow remained in the bulbs themselves, concentrated there by the daylight all around. At the table in the center of the room sat Hertha—sleeping. In front of her lay letter paper, along with the small stained writing-case which Anny knew well. Anny was heartily annoyed at this stupid girl who could go to sleep wherever she happened to be; and perhaps also there was a small dose of envy in this annoyance, envy of such basic rustic health, envy mixed with affection, and perhaps also with dislike, for Hertha's healthy vigor also bordered on outright sluttishness.

"Hertha!" Anny called. But what good was her loud voice against the solidity of this sleep. Now she shook her friend's shoulder. In its sluggishness the girl's body remained rigid. But almost at once Anny noticed that Hertha Plankl's eyes were not fully closed. She immediately reached out for the right hand, which lay on the table. It was cold; so were cheek and forehead. There was no sign of breathing. On the table lay Hertha's diamond ring, which the girl had probably removed because it impeded her when she wrote. But the ring was not the only valuable around. On a chair close by the window lay the telltale package. Anny sprang toward the chair, lifted the package by the string, and weighed it in her gloved hand. As she did so, her glance fell upon a little wall cupboard where Hertha usually hid her money in a small drawer that could be kept under lock and key. This drawer now stood pulled out, with the key in it. Hertha sometimes kept sizable sums there; the day before, Anny knew, there had been 3,000 schillings, for Hertha had decided to pay a long outstanding bill she owed her dressmaker . . . This money was missing then, must be missing! Anny sprang to the drawer, took out the wallet. It contained 3,500 schillings and a bill from the dressmaker. She tossed the wallet with the banknotes back into the open drawer and stepped back. Now she looked down at the dead girl and at last observed a tiny tear in the blouse under Hertha's left breast—Hertha lay leaning backward in the chair. Around this spot the blouse showed a brownish-red discoloration.

Only now did Anny realize what had taken place here. Had the ring been gone, or the package of scrap gold, or at least the money lying in the open drawer, the murder would have seemed far less terrible. As it was, the act was one of naked terror; it was terror of a higher type, of pure revenge. An example had been made. Here was threat, power, intimidation.

Anny quivered; her whole body shook. We prefer not to examine the question of whether her distraught state prevented her from a quick act of fishing in troubled waters. It would have been simple at least to take the money in the drawer before calling the concierge, when the police would be sent for and all this would be lost. We prefer to say that Anny simply no longer had the strength to place this little court-plaster upon the gaping and bleeding wound of terror. A gust of wind burst into the courtyard roared and raged down it, threw a feeble puff into the room itself. In front of the dead woman the letter paper lifted for a moment, a staring page of paper, an envelope with a stamp on it but no address, a page with a few lines; the pen leaning against the ink bottle was blown down, a pencil rolled. Anny went up to the table. There was the beginning of a letter, the date on the right, a few lines. Hertha had probably been on the point of answering a promising advertisement, for the letter began: "Dear Sir, by chance I came across your interesting advertisement in today's newspaper." No more had been written. Below, in pencil, and in much larger letters, were the words:

It was Meisgeier   heart   through the window   dying
I swear   Hertha Plankl
                                     Prostitute

Had anyone called her that, our Hertha Plankl would have been affronted to the point of slapping that person's face or flinging an entire chamber pot of insults at him. That she herself, in her last breath, applied that word to herself represented an ultimate attempt, on the threshold of eternity, to discharge in a single word something resembling a universal confession.

At the sight of that, Anny's shudders overwhelmed her. While the scene she had witnessed, of Meisgeier climbing from story to story, appeared again before her eyes, her hands performed the following acts. She gently took the once-folded sheet of letter paper and wrote on the back of the second fold:

Take good care of this, Didi. Tell you more when I see you. Anny Gr.

She immediately put the sheet into the stamped envelope, sealed the envelope, and addressed it:

Frau Anna Diwald
Freud's brandy shop
Liechtenstein Strasse . . .

She even knew the number of the building. She put the letter into her bag, took the key, and rushed downstairs. Now her last crumb of self-control had been consumed. She screamed and became hysterical; it was as if she were flinging a veil of agitation around her which did not allow anyone else to say a word, so thick and fast came her cries, exclamations, interjections. "Here, take the key. I'll run to the police." And she was off. That moment of freeing herself was one of liberation: for she had to get that letter into the mailbox. It might have occurred to the concierge to get in touch with police headquarters by telephone. Then she would have had to wait here, with that letter in her bag and the possibility of being held by the police for a while, having no chance to drop the letter into a box—and in the end it would be found on her.

Now she was free.

Panting, Frau Pawliček climbed the stairs.

Anny ran out of the house.

On her way her eyes sought and sought for nothing but the yellow surface of a letter box, and when she found it at last, it seemed like a shining pearl to her.

At the police station Anny learned that the concierge had already telephoned in the meanwhile. Anny was kept and questioned, while the proper officials appeared at the scene of the crime.

When in the following weeks and months Anny again lay on her back beside a half-slumbering Leonhard, staring up at the white ceiling of the room, she realized each time something that she already knew: that he did not love her. But at such moments the fact came to her more tangibly, more imperatively than usual. It grew into a self-evident fact. If he loved her at all, he would not be able to let her lie by his side, let her lie aside, like a carefully sealed, in fact airtight jar. He would have had to try to open it, to release the contents under constant pressure, to try to get to know what was bottled up in her. But Leonhard showed not the slightest sign of doing so.

We by no means wish to say that he was entirely unaware of a hereafter in the here which encompassed his own "hereness" that he was not conscious of its presence. But his picture of Anny Gräven's life had already petrified, as we have suggested earlier; it coincided with popular notions and with Anny's frivolity and lighthearted chatter, for Leonhard had soon become aware of the innocent falsehoods of which her prattle was composed. The result was that in time he completely ignored the essential contents sealed and screwed down tightly within the person who lay at his side. The ritual "afterwards," of beer and sausages, more and more stood substitute for a true relationship of person to person. What relationship there had been grew more and more shadowy.

Insofar as that content under pressure is concerned, it soon settled down, and the pressure abated (although the murder did not thereby become any more comprehensible or digestible, as far as Anny was concerned). Anny Gräven avoided Didi, as a matter of caution, for much more than two weeks after the death of Hertha Plankl. When she did finally meet and talk to Didi, she learned that the letter had arrived and was being most carefully preserved (in that well-nigh bursting leather briefcase which Editor Holder had once told "our crowd" about during that noted walk). Didi commended Anny's conduct as sensible and right (she had been wise, too, not to take anything). It was better to have Meisgeier in your hand than to turn him over to the police. That was clear. Such was Didi's opinion. Incidentally, she knew a couple of other things about him, she said.

Anny Gräven was questioned several times, but the concierge's statements cleared her completely; moreover, the police were well aware of her harmlessness. She was unable to contribute any information that helped to clarify the case. The statements of the taproom-keeper agreed with those of Frau Pawliček: Hertha Plankl had come home alone shortly after eleven o'clock, had had the front door unlocked for her by the concierge, and the door had been closed behind her. None of the other girls living in the house was allowed to have a key. Of course skeleton keys were always a possibility. But everyone knew that the concierge was as sharp as a lynx; it was hardly possible for anyone to come into the house without her knowing it, for she always crawled out of her nether regions at the slightest noise and peered up the stairs—these being the hours when she cashed in on visits from various gentlemen. These paid twice, coming and going. Consequently Frau Pawliček was usually out of bed and up and about most of the night; she read newspaper serials and worked out crossword puzzles, and was always asking coming or departing visitors the name of an Egyptian ruler in six letters, or the French word for lighthouse, for which, however, only five letters were allotted. At police headquarters the concierge reconstructed the whole of that critical night quite correctly. She was able to state precisely which of the girls had come home with an escort, at what approximate times, and what the escorts had looked like. She even knew one or two of them. Here was evidence.

But the police had scarcely got this far in their investigations when—as soon as the afternoon newspapers had published an account of the murder—all those gentlemen came trotting to police headquarters. Every single one of them came; not a single precious head was missing; the number corresponded exactly to that sworn to by Frau Pawliček. And very wise of them to have done this. The tactful authorities repaid them for their cooperation by discretion toward the newspapers. Only, unfortunately, none of these gentlemen could throw the faintest light on the murder. It may be taken for granted that all the girls were sharply interrogated. And a number of other things may be taken for granted, though the laymen inexperienced in criminological procedures may not do so. It must not be thought that Meisgeier went entirely unmolested. The possibility of a climb through the open skylight of the *pissoir* did not escape the sharp-eyed police. Meisgeier was arrested in the taproom of the selfsame restaurant as he was sitting there placidly eating a bowl of goulash. Brought at last before the chief of the detective squad, he merely remarked: "Cap'n, if I could do all the stunts you fellers think I c'n, I would've gone straight long ago and earned me a good living as a highflyer in the circus." An act of God prevented the police from being able to prove that the Claw had in fact engaged in acrobatics. For his hands and feet must have left traces in the soot and dust on the cornices and projections in the courtyard. But a wind which soon mounted to an absolute gale raged through all the streets and courtyards on the morning after the crime, Frau Pawliček, incidentally, who had omitted to close one of the doors to her nether regions, found herself at noon assailed by a whistling current of air that almost knocked her over. And while the shaking, rattling, banging, and clanging host of all things not firmly nailed down humbly and obediently responded to the force of the storm, the possible traces of Meisgeier's climb were wiped out. Instead, false clues turned up. For example, a key to the front door was found in one girl's apartment; it had, moreover, been greased—perhaps it had fallen into her butter—and this merely unappetizing fact acquired some importance because doors can be opened more silently with greased keys. Nevertheless, the lady in question had rung for the concierge to open the door when she came home that night with a gentleman friend. And what is more, the gentleman friend—he was the one, by the way, who happened to know the French word for lighthouse—had been one of the first of those who came to the police station the next day. A further hitch was that Meisgeier had never worked as a "second-story man," or cat burglar, and the police did not have him down on their blotter as an expert in such stunts. Moreover, stabbing the heart with a file was not typical of him. He had applied neither technique before, and never made any other ventures in that direction. The file in question must have found its way to the bottom of the Danube Canal long before the discovery of the murder. One single but vague circumstance incriminated the Claw. That was the sheer killing, the act of revenge (but for

730

what?), the crime of terror, with no valuables taken. Meisgeier was noted for an odd kind of negligence where money was concerned. Finally, the packet of scrap gold also pointed in his direction; it might possibly have come from a burglary which the police had attempted—though without success—to "pin on" Meisgeier the year before. All these factors, however, were not enough to keep him under arrest for more than twenty-four hours. The constitution and the law stand guard over everyone, including the criminal. The Viennese police, who have a high international reputation, applied their considerable ability, their deep experience, perspicacity, diligence, and devotion to duty wholeheartedly to the solving of the crime. And their vain efforts—quite exceptionally vain—aroused the sympathy of the general public, which was well aware that the officials of this branch of the government did not shrink from risking their lives in the performance of their hard duties. In spite of their failure the Viennese police won widespread approval from public and press for their conduct in the case of Hertha Plankl. Meisgeier, meanwhile, continued to sit in the selfsame restaurant over goulash and beer.

Gradually, as the autumn advanced, all the pressures and impressions produced in Anny Gräven by Hertha's fate began to slumber. They continued to hold a place within her mind, but the first cataract of forgetfulness was beginning to veil her view of it, perhaps all the more easily because everything remained sealed and screwed down tightly within her—Didi being the only human being with whom she had shared her knowledge. Consequently, in contrast to her daily life the affair began taking on almost the lesser reality of pure fantasy; it grew stranger and odder, like every secret forcibly repressed for a long time so that it can no longer be matched against the outer world.

Nevertheless it remained within her; it had pierced her and it stayed inside, even though she might possess a feeble

731

memory, even feebler than the memories of women leading a more normal life. And so these vague landscapes of swiftly coming, going, and dissolving ideas in Anny's mind were sometimes adjacent to Leonhard too—a frontier hereafter right in the here.

It may be that he sensed them; but as we have said, he remained enslaved to the petrified commonplace image that he had formed of Anny.

A good deal of hereafter surrounds all of us. We are, in the here surrounded by never grasped and imagined, perhaps really unimaginable borderings, adjacent entanglements, descending pressure areas, suctioning vacuums. That was the case with Leonhard, certainly, and not only in reference to Anny Gräven and the background of her life which he thought hardly worth asking about those days. Had he not traveled up and down the Burgenland with Niki, drunk Stinkenbrunner at old Zdarsa's and Ruster in Fraunkirchen with old Gach, attended meetings in Hirm exchanged views—sometimes rather tensely—with Pinta—without acquiring any halfway clear picture of what was really going on in this region and what might be ahead? Bumblebee humming—that had been the main thing! And in the end, perhaps, the main thing had been even more that strange sensation of rising and leaving the past behind when he rode on the back of Niki's motorcycle between Fraunkirchen and Wallern.

They had, to be sure, discontinued their trips by the late fall, and the things that were going on beyond the Leitha River did not enter an acute stage until the end of the year, did not develop to the point of visibility at which the avalanche of tangibles and intangibles begins to roll. At which point the whole affair might well cease to have any interest for us if only we had taken sufficient interest in it earlier. For had we only done so, we might by proper conduct have escaped all liability. The sometimes surpassing stupidity of happening, descending, and precipitating facts would no longer be able to affect us. In the Burgenland, then—flat country and therefore not good for our avalanche metaphor—these facts began to precipitate around the turn of the year—in fact, exactly on New Year's Eve. The events in question happened, in fact, at a New Year celebration; just at that time in the middle of winter, the "avalanche" began to roll.

The time had come. The time had in fact come long before, although Niki and Leonhard had noticed nothing, or nothing definite. Perhaps they rushed by everything too swiftly on their motorcycle. At any rate, the area had long been swarming with adjacent entanglements. The New Year celebration was altogether private, a gathering of party friends, far more of a clubby than a political affair. It had not been intended as provocation, was in no way directed against any other group. Nevertheless a certain group—those who identified Orkay's, Körger's, Eulenfeld's, Schlaggenberg's political views with their own—burst into the party, attempted to break it up. Blows were exchanged, and they were thrown out. It would have been interesting to introduce the above-mentioned gentlemen, members of "our crowd," to these disturbers of the peace; our friends would immediately have seen that so-called "ideologies" can lead men into far worse company than vice. Ideologies can be shared with stupid louts, and vices—drinking, for example—with excellent men.

In the course of the brawl on New Year's Eve—it took place in Moser's Tavern in Schattendorf—no shots were fired. The "Republican Protective Association" at that time did not yet carry weapons. The "Veterans of the Front," however, seem to have considered themselves justified, by virtue of preparedness

733

and manliness and because, as the poet said, the "God of Battles who made iron grow" wanted "no serfs" (a misstatement, by the way, for the iron grew precisely for serfs, if for anyone at all). At any rate, the serfs had unfortunately taken to firing their guns upon occasion.

They did so on Sunday afternoon, January 30, 1927, at Schattendorf, which lies close to the Hungarian frontier. The shooting took place not out of preparedness or manliness, nor because iron had grown, but essentially out of fear. People, by the way, who commit crimes justifiable by "ideologies" present a shabby picture compared to professional hardened criminals, whose lives at heart exemplify the qualities of solitude, resolution, and courage. The others hide their actions behind numbers, are carried along by the crowd, and their deeds are in large part not their own—in contrast to those of the professional criminal—but mere reflections of the doings of others. The Red fighting force had marched out from its base—the Moser Tavern—that afternoon to the railroad station in order to give a suitable reception to a group of "Veterans" who were due to arrive on the train. How is it that they knew this, so that they mustered in force in Schattendorf? Their information came from a "painter and graduate of the Academy from Vienna." Or so it was said later; truth and falsehood always form an inseparable compound in the train of misinformation that trails behind sensational events like the tail of a comet. The nonsensical tale persisted, although no such informant was necessary: the Red assemblage in Schattendorf had simply been waiting there from the beginning in the knowledge that their opponents would appear. As the Reds marched past Tscharmann's Tavern (a well-known "Veterans" base) in rank and file and uniform, several shots were fired at them. Nevertheless, the march to the railroad station continued. There the responsible leaders on both sides agreed that the Veterans should withdraw, in view of the superior forces confronting them. This they did; that is, they rode back in the same train; the stationmaster had taken the precaution to stop said train outside the Schattendorf-Loipersbach station. The Protective Association then marched in closed ranks the long way back from the railroad station to the village, and then down the single village street and past the Tscharmann Tavern again. Both times some members of the Protective Association entered the bar "to buy refreshments," as the party press later put it. It is not quite clear why, coming from Moser's Tavern or on their way back to it, they should have stepped out of their line to give business to a tavernkeeper whose hostile sentiments were obvious enough. Everyone in Schattendorf, Klingenbach, Drallburg, Baumgarten, and the other villages in the vicinity knew that Tscharmann and his two sons, Josef and Hieronymus, had "different ideas"—insofar as ideas played any part in the matter. In point of fact the contingent had not stepped out of line "to buy refreshments." They were temporarily occupying the tavern—a reasonable enough procedure after the firing of the shots—and the Tscharmanns had been forced to retreat into their house in the rear, which was separate from the tavern. There they may well have felt considerably frightened. But then they fired a second time—from a room in the upper story of the house, a room with barred windows. They fired, moreover, after the tail of the procession of Social Democratic party soldiers had passed them by. Such an act can be regarded as a sign of panic, or of rage resulting from their fear, or as sheer outright murder. The last rows of marchers consisted of twenty-eight men of the Klingenbach local group, the "Klingenbachers." Among these was a one-eyed war veteran named Mathias Csmarits, who worked in the Neufeld lignite storage depot. He was struck twice, just as he was seeking cover behind a tree, was peppered with twenty-three pieces of the heaviest grade of hunting shot, and died instantly. Every single piece of shot struck him in the back. The other casualty was a small boy. He was Pepi Grössing and he had only come along on the march because an uncle of his—this same one-eyed man—was marching. Csmarits had often taken the boy with him. This time another uncle of Pepi's, Binder by name, was also there and likewise watching the march-past of the private army; it was he who picked up the dead boy. At the autopsy seven pieces of heavy shot were found lodged in the child's body.

Such incidents are harrowing to relate, even when they are only touched upon, as we are doing. We mention them because several persons (for whom we need to feel less pity than for poor Pepi) were affected by the further consequences: namely Meisgeier, Didi, and Anny Gräven, not to speak of Leonhard. Oddly enough, these happenings led, by strange detours, to the clearing-up of the murder of Hertha Plankl—on July 18, 1927, to be exact. At that time Anny Gräven was arrested.

The poor victims of that year 1927, including little Pepi, were the first to die in a forest so enormous that nowadays we can no longer see it for all the trees. It has long since grown over our heads. There we have the secret of callousness.

The Schattendorf case was tried in Vienna more than five months after the event, on July 5, 1927. In the course of the interrogation it turned out that one witness, whose ear—long since healed—had been grazed by a piece of shot, was no longer able to state whether it had been the left or the right ear. The testimony of the other witnesses was equally unsatisfactory. The whole business took place within that by now extremely pallid comet tail which trailed after the events, and in which truth and falsehood were mingled in the finest particles. Public interest was small. There was no trouble obtaining a seat in the big courtroom; no need to apply beforehand, as is the case with sensational trials. The whole affair was pretty dim; it had taken place five months before. At the beginning of February, to be sure, the noise in the press had been tremendous: the Left threatening, the Right embarrassed. The conservative wing of the Alliance newspapers in particular had had a hard time of it. It had, on the one hand, to condemn the act itself, but it had at the same time to reprove the chorus of voices crying for revenge. The demonstrations and protest strikes had to be deprecated. They were unnecessary and merely added fuel to the fire. At the same time the Alliance newspapers had to be careful not to become identified with the "Veterans," and this whole diplomatic enterprise had to be shrouded in a complicated superstructure of arguments and ideas. However, the excitement in the press subsided relatively soon. When the trial finally began in July, many people in Vienna had not the slightest idea what it was all about. Among these was Charlotte Schlaggenberg, Kajetan's sister, who later had to have the whole thing explained to her from the beginning by Géza von Orkay—to which account she listened with open-mouthed astonishment. Gyurkicz was, after all, connected with Alliance and wrapped himself in silence. Körger grinned. Even in working-class circles there were people who knew almost nothing of and took little interest in the trial. Niki and Leonhard, too, were hardly well informed.

The prosecuting attorney, it must be said, knew what was at stake. In situations such as these, objective and modest jurists acquire an almost supernatural dignity. The attorney for the defense, Doktor Walter Riehl, filed a complaint against the prosecutor because he made use "in an unprecedented manner" of his right to reject jurymen. It seemed that he had vetoed anyone who might be suspected for any reason whatsoever of having political sympathy with the defendants. It took a long while before the prosecutor had a jury that suited him; he declared flatly that he did not wish to see members of political parties in the jury box.

This jury, then, voted nine to three in favor of the defendants. The president of the court announced the acquittal. On the following day, July 15, 1927, a spontaneous demonstration—the Social Democratic leadership really had no hand in it—brought the workers marching into the heart of the city. They did not march because the murderers of a child and a war veteran were getting off scot-free, but because the child had been a worker's child and the veteran a worker. The "masses" were demanding class justice, against which their leaders had so often cried out. The people stormed against the verdict of a people's court, against their own verdict. That broke the backbone of freedom; from that point it was maintained in Austria for only a short time, and artificially. The so-called masses have always been fond of settling in a compact group upon the branches of the tree of liberty which tower into infinity. But they must saw off these branches; they cannot help themselves; and then the whole crown of the tree collapses. Sit where he will, the man who listens to the "masses" has already lost his freedom. The police unfortunately attempted to break up the demonstration: they routed the marchers from the broad Ring Strasse. That same afternoon the Palace of Justice went up in flames. In the struggle with the police, who were chiefly trying to clear a way for the fire department, a frightful number of people were killed. Among them were Meisgeier and Anna Diwald, known as Didi. Neither of them had anything to do with the purpose of the demonstration: Meisgeier's sympathies, in fact, were with the fellows who had been acquitted.

But that burning July was still a long way off in the wintry gray days of the year 1925. On Sunday afternoons, between about two and four o'clock, an almost perfect silence reigned. Even before the first snow the light in the room seemed pale and whitish. Such light was now falling upon the page that Leonhard had just turned. He wondered at the complete subsidence of the attraction that had streamed from each of the three girls during the fall; there was no reviving it. Once he had wanted to do so. But the impulse failed; his thoughts slid away. Yet the most important factor of all was something he did not even notice. It was a tremendous thing, a confirmation of the great step he had taken, already taken for granted now and therefore no longer noticeable: that he had ceased to know boredom and therefore no longer attempted to escape from it into something else. Leonhard was spending less money than ever before, although he had not set himself to save.

Once, after work, he found a letter on the table in his room. That was an altogether unusual phenomenon. It was from Trix. Very briefly: would he like to come to a little gathering the following Saturday night? Her mother was already back and would be very glad to meet him. The handwriting was, to Leonhard's mind, too energetic and resolute for a girl of barely sixteen; the few lines ran smoothly across the page. Written without effort, he thought—and did not reply in writing. He was moved to visit a small café in the neighborhood, from which he could telephone his reply to Trix.

First Leonhard sat and read newspapers. What stirred him at the moment was not the possibility that he would soon be talking to Trix, but rather that this possibility left him unmoved: that was the novelty in his feeling about his life. He sat comfortably, lowered the newspaper, and looked around the café.

Suddenly Leonhard realized that he already had a past. That thought provided the spark; he suddenly wanted to converse with his past, and went to the telephone booth.

Trix herself answered.

She thanked him pleasantly.

Her voice on the telephone was as smooth and sure of itself as her letter.

In the late summer of 1926, at various points in the Burgenland, on Sundays and occasionally even on weekdays, a gentleman from Vienna might be seen out of doors, sitting in front of a small easel and painting, or bent over a sketchbook engaged in drawing or water-coloring. He was also seen here and there during the winter, and more frequently the following spring. Alois Gach noticed him several times, not only in Eisenstadt, but once in an altogether different area, to the north of Deutsch-Altenburg, which lies on the Danube and is not part of the Burgenland. Mostly, however, this painter—rumor had it that he was a well-known artist from Vienna—was seen in places close to the Hungarian border. He spoke Hungarian fluently; perhaps it was even his mother tongue.

He was good-looking and kept his well-groomed, big face carefully shaved. His eyes were blue and easily took on a rather childlike, pining expression. His rather broad necktie fell precisely down the center of his flawlessly cut colored shirt; his suit and shoes were those of a sportsman and tourist, the shoes of a solid, wide, rather triangular shape with sharply defined corners, rather uncommon at that period. Heavy, light-colored leather gloves were an inevitable part of his outfit, and occasionally he wore a similarly light-colored belted fall coat. He wore his summer hat square on his head, without tilting it toward the right or left ear.

As for the drawings or small paintings on which the artist worked—often applying himself with patience and diligence to a single one which, moreover, he would do over and over again—people noticed them and called them excellent. By that the layman always means a successful imitation of nature, illusion, *trompe-l'oeil*—which, of course, can always be surpassed by photography, particularly color photography. But by chance the water colors and drawings were also spied by members of the Eisenstadt Art League, which was not quite its usual self at the time. Two or three of its painter members had drifted to Vienna and Paris, where they had stayed for years; and just at this juncture, in the late summer of 1926, they had reverted to their native town—whose provincial ways, however, they could not stand for long. These young artists were so much taken with the work of their Viennese colleague that they pressed him to exhibit at the Art League. Some forty of the little works were accordingly shown, and more than a dozen sold—quite a success for a Viennese artist in the provinces, which are usually unreceptive to the urbanite. Moreover, what won the local people to these little paintings and sketches was not the use of regional motifs, landscapes, or familiar old buildings. True, the artist seemed concerned with the light and atmosphere of this eastern province, but not really with the region itself, with any specific portrayal of it. The things represented—a curving fence in tricky perspective, a fisherman's net stretched on its rack by the lake, or a picture of one of those reed-thatched barn roofs that slope almost to the ground—such features were not really typical of the Burgenland. They could have been found elsewhere, aside from the strange barns whose construction stems from prehistoric times and whose roofs offer the most incredible plays of color, from violet to deep moss-brown. It must be said, however, that in catching these tints the artist had really wrung the most out of his paint box. Yet he stressed that by profession his specialty was drawing, drawing for the press. In fact, his name was familiar to a few of the visitors to the exhibition. At any rate, the show was a success.

The artist came to Stinkenbrunn once, and even had a chat with old Zdarsa. In the course of this conversation the name of Preschitz was dropped, quite casually, in a tone implying that the artist was rather well acquainted with the commander of the Protective Association and leader of the "Drassburgers." It can easily be imagined that this fact made some impression upon Old Goatbeard. Even more of an impression was made— in fact, it gave him quite a turn—when the artist advised him incidentally and confidentially to keep an eye on his son-in-law, Herr Pinter or Pinta, who was undoubtedly a fine fellow, no two ways about it, but perhaps inclined to be a bit foolish in political matters. Nothing serious, of course. But still it would be better for Herr Zdarsa to know, though he need not mention the matter to Herr Pinta right off.

Old Zdarsa was in fact far from inclined to bring the matter up with Pinta. He asked no questions, did not press the gentleman from Vienna to say anything more, or to be more precise. He would rather know nothing at all. What he had just learned was already too much for him. It certainly would never have occurred to him to speak with Pinta about such things, or even to ask him a single question about them; and he was relieved that the painter's advice actually discharged him of any obligation to do so. In general, if you observed the life of Old Goatbeard for any length of time—insofar as the word "life" applies at all—you could not avoid the impression that he was in constant fear of a beating; that, in fact, the only reason he rushed about at such a rate on his motorcycle was that he thereby lessened the danger of being stopped and given a beating. At least the danger was less than if he had gone about on foot. Perhaps old Zdarsa harbored the fear that Pinta would give him a thrashing someday. And so he said nothing. He asked no questions even when his son-in-law, a few days after the chat with the painter, returned from Mörbisch to Stinkenbrunn with a huge, skill-fully wrapped bandage around his head. He made the whole place smell like a hospital. Pinta reported that in the forest hut at Mörbisch he had stumbled on the tools and had had such a bad fall that he had had to go to the doctor and have himself bandaged up. "Well, well, a nice how-do-you-do, hard luck," Old Goatbeard said, and nothing more. It must be granted that for a husky fellow like Pinta it would have been no trouble at all, even with a bandaged head, to thrash the little old man. But old Zdarsa was the only one who thought of such dire pos-sibilities; his mind was filled with Preschitz and beatings and suchlike menaces, among which he dodged on his two-wheeled steed like a witch astride her broom, wearing an eternally anx-ious expression.

The painter had also come to Mörbisch.

He sat for a short time in the tavern with a small group of uniformed members of the Protective Association—who were a rare sight in this region, near the belt of reeds that runs around the Neusiedler Lake. There was no space for frictions here, no dance floor for opposing forces. The socialists behaved quite peacefully; they only ate and drank. That afternoon the painter worked close to the lake, on the other side of the belt of reeds. When dusk was already gathering, he crossed the reeds on a firm, well-tracked path, his equipment tucked away in a hand-some leather bag. He reached the road to Fertbrakos (which we Austrians call Kroisbach) in Hungary to the south of Mörbisch. By that time it was beginning to grow quite dark. The painter

743

left the road and made his way along the sloping edge of the woods on the other side of it. Where the woods receded, far to the back of a clearing and already half in among the deciduous trees, he could see the lighted window of Pinta's hut.

Although he had all along moved without any unnecessary noise, he now trod the last few steps more ponderously and slowly, though very calmly. He knocked gently on the door and called out in a friendly tone, in Hungarian: "Good evening, Herr Pinta."

"Come in!" a voice from the hut called, likewise in Hungarian.

Pinta rose from the table, on which lay an illustrated newspaper beneath a hanging lamp.

"My name is Imre Gyurkicz of Faddy and Hátfaludy," the man said smilingly as he entered. "Please excuse my disturbing you; I won't keep you long. But I felt it my duty to come by this evening to give you a hint that might prove useful to you."

Pinta recalled the name at once (lest anyone think him stupid or dull). It had been mentioned by the count just two weeks before, when they had sat here drinking with Captain Szefcsik.

"Please take a seat," he said.

"The thing is simple and harmless if you are prepared for it," Gyurkicz remarked by way of introduction, fixing his blue eyes upon Pinta's face. He proceeded to inform him that "Protective Association" soldiers were in Mörbisch and that they seemed to have got wind that he, Pinta, sometimes received visitors from across the border in his hut—"visits from our friends," Imre put it. They intended to surprise him here in the course of the night. "I heard about the thing in the tavern; the Reds were discussing it. It would be best, Herr Pinta, if you were to give our friends a signal that the coast isn't clear and that they should stay away. Can you do that? If those other fellows come, pretend to be utterly innocent, and if they tell you why they have come, then request them to stay here to protect you. And of course address them as 'comrades' all the time. They won't do you any harm. Have you wine?"

"Yes," Pinta said, "may I offer you . . . ?"

"No thanks," Imre said, laughing. "I don't drink. But you will need wine for the Reds, understand?"

This last remark won the Croat's confidence. Up to then he had construed it that Gyurkicz wanted to keep the Hungarians away in order to put him at the mercy of the Reds. Now he began to take a different view of the situation. The Reds were not going to harm a single man who sat here in an unlocked hut, welcomed them in, and behaved hospitably. No, they would not—he knew them well enough for that, from seeing them around Hirm, and from the meetings. Everyone is ready enough, incidentally, to see the virtues of his enemies if these virtues happen to benefit him. Moreover, the members of the Protective Association never carried weapons.

The childlike look in Imre's blue eyes might also have led Pinta to believe him.

"Thank you very much, Herr von Gyurkicz," he said. "I'll stay alone, then, leave the door open, let them come, ask them to stay, and when occasion offers, come out with the wine."

"That will be best," Gyurkicz said. But he for his part could not be persuaded to stay or to take wine, and vanished.

Pinta decided to follow his second hunch. Consequently he closed the shutter in front of the window on the side toward the woods. If this shutter were open, and the lighted window could be seen by persons coming from the border, it meant that the coast was clear. Now his friends would stay away.

He sat down at the table, drank four glasses of wine, and read an installment of a novel in the *Illustrierte Zeitung*.

Two hours later they arrived. He heard them outside. The knocking at the door was vigorous. "Come in!" Pinta called out in German. The men came in without a greeting and looked around carefully.

"Good evening, comrades," Pinta said.

They said good evening. Suddenly one of them exclaimed: "Why, it's you, Comrade Pinta? I've seen you at our meetings in Hirm."

"Yes, of course," Pinta said. "I've often gone to your meetings, with my father-in-law and two comrades from Vienna. Won't you sit down? What brings you here? Night exercises?" (In those days such exercises took place among the paramilitary formations.)

The men sat down, one after another. Then the leader of the small group—there were only five men—said that they had come more or less for his protection, to make sure that he was all right, since there had been illegal border-crossings by the "Magyarones," the Hungarian fascists, in this vicinity.

"Damn it to hell!" Pinta exclaimed. "And you think they might be by tonight?"

"They might," the leader said.

"Then I'd appreciate it if you comrades would stick around for a while. How would a glass of wine be?"

He had luck. The men were not teetotalers—though many of the socialists were. The leader of the group looked around at the rest of his men. Pinta's suggestion seemed to meet with their approval. Pinta produced a bottle and glasses. He had plenty of glasses; larger companies than six had drunk in this hut.

The present assemblage, however, differed radically from any Hungarian conclave. Whereas the Hungarians touched only casually upon the subjects they wished to discuss, these

746

men maintained a certain solemnity; they tried to express themselves in cultivated and well-schooled terms. In this respect the leader of the group stood out. The men themselves were fresh and vigorous, and not at all rough young fellows; but they were all suspended from some kind of wire which was not common hatred or common love, but rather a common cable of assured knowledge in which each had his certificated share, which answered every question for him, even the question of the meaning of life (which always ought to remain open), or of humanity, not to speak of humanity's history and development. For all these matters there were a few set expressions of a sociological character. As a matter of fact, Pinta liked these men very well; they were fine sturdy fellows. He could not have said, basically, why he could not warm up to them while he was with them. Pinta seriously believed in political antagonism, and so he explained the matter to himself merely on that ground.

This evening there was no singing, no Hungarian melodies sounded. To be sure, the wine was good. A more animated glow rose to the young men's faces, as though red blood were flowing under a pallid chitin armor. They touched glasses with Pinta, who was beginning to feel the wine, for he had had four glasses before they came; now he was annoyed with himself, for this was the wrong time to get drunk. This was, in fact, the critical hour. Pinta wore a wrist watch and so was able to note the time without attracting attention. It was nearing eleven. For the past half hour at least his friends in the woods must have been waiting for the sign that the coast was clear. Well and good, they would have to wait in vain. He was sitting here virtually a prisoner. What troubled him painfully was something else: his own state. The manner in which these men talked as they sat on the benches around the table seemed to squeeze Pinta tightly, or dry him out; it was like the rustling of a great deal of printed paper. It even seemed that they had brought a smell of that sort with them, the dead smell of schoolrooms . . . It must be something of the sort, and he became aware of it again and again, for brief moments, in spite of the cigarette smoke which gradually thickened in the small room. Pinta felt numbed, stiff, clumsy. The only unhampered action open to him was to pour the wine, but there was not much opportunity; the Reds drank very moderately. After a while Pinta began to feel that he was somehow separated from his own personality, as though half of him were made of wood, or as though he were entirely enclosed in glass. The smoke had already become unbearably heavy. Pinta rose and opened the door, for ventilation; he thought of placing a wooden block in front of the door to hold it open. But then it became too cold; the late fall night was brisk. The only window was the one on the side toward the woods; opposite this, by this door, was a tiny hatch with a piece of glass crudely held over it by means of bent nails (through this Gyurkicz had seen the gleam of light as he approached). Just as Pinta closed the door again the young man sitting closest to the window opened it and threw open the outside shutter. Pinta, feeling ultimately overcome by a leaden helplessness, simply sat down at the table again, drank half a glass of wine, and remained where he was. Not long. Perhaps ten minutes passed—during which Pinta subsided more and more into a doze. Then the lamp suddenly flickered wildly: a stone the size of a fist came flying through the window, grazed the Croat's head, and thudded into the wall. Pinta sagged against his neighbor on the left and then fell like a sack under the table.

"Light out!" the leader of the socialists called in a quiet tone of command, since he sat too far from the lamp to put it out himself. One of the young men—the one who had seen Pinta at Hirm—rose, without casting a single glance at the window, calmly screwed down the wick, and blew out the light. "Out! Follow me!" the leader said. They had to leave Pinta lying where he was. In the darkness they were given a warm reception by superior forces pouring from both sides, from the woods and around the house. A shove, a blow in the darkness, a leap aside. "Follow me," the leader called out again, in a remarkably calm, strong voice. He was honestly sorry that they had to leave Pinta behind; the man might well be seriously wounded; he said so repeatedly later on, but always added that for five men—against a dozen or more "Magyarones"—there had been nothing to do but beat a hasty retreat.

With fists and good luck they fought clear of their opponents and fled along the edge of the woods; the others could not follow them too far into Austrian territory.

Inside the hut, the light had been turned on again. The table had been cleared of glasses and Pinta placed on it. As he came to, the count was bending over him, and also a trained medical aid, who had just opened his kit, cleaned Pinta's face, and placed a dressing on the sizable cut and bruise on the right side of his head. The man who had thrown the stone—one of the roughest and simplest boys in the count's following—spying the uniformed socialists in the hut, had decided that the Croat was a traitor who wanted to lure the Hungarians into a trap. "You can stick a horse's tail up . . ." the count had sworn at him.

Pinta was soon able to talk and the matter was cleared up. Imre von Gyurkicz's name was mentioned also. Out in the woods the count's men were standing guard. "We'll take you across the border now," the count said to Pinta. "I have a car waiting on the road to Fertőrákos; I'll drive you to the hospital in Sopron. You have to be examined at once, *lege artis*. I hope you haven't got a *commotio*. But you Croats have thick heads. If it isn't anything serious, I'll drive you back to Stinkenbrunn tomorrow or the day after."

By then order had been restored in the hut. Pinta's things were packed into his knapsack, the light was carefully put out, and the house locked up. Then the party set out, penetrating deeper into the woods. Pinta was carried by two men who were relieved every hundred paces; the count did not want him walking until he had been seen by a doctor. They proceeded in a southeasterly direction and finally moved downhill, coming out of the woods near to the waiting car on the highway to Fertőrákos.